I0747971

First paperback edition: October 2022
Second paperback edition: November 2022
Third paperback edition: October 2023
Fourth paperback edition: December, 2023

Cover text by Brock Mays
Cover illustration by Jessica Nielsen:
Illustrations by:
@yessidraws on Instagram
@creators_hideout on Twitter
@Astraelogical (Twitter/Instagram)
@skr3m_art (Twitter/Instagram)
Maps by Brock Mays

ISBN: 9781733816588
Website: bit.ly/theascensionsaga
Instagram: @BrockMaysAuthor

СЛАВА УКРАЇНІ

ACKNOWLEDGEMENTS AND CONTENT WARNING

I wrote the first draft of *Spring Always Comes* based on my studies and knowledge of the history of the Baltic States and the Soviet Union, as well as relations between NATO and the Russian Federation, which were the focus of my undergraduate and graduate studies.

I completed the first (and most of the second) draft before the events of the war of Russian aggression against Ukraine. Like others, I am horrified by the violence Russia has and currently still is (at the time of writing this page) perpetrating there. I have spent several years of my life living in Lithuania and spent a week in Kyiv, Ukraine that left a lasting impact on me, and those areas of the world are beyond dear to me.

If you are reading this, I assume you've at least read *Embers*. In that book, it is revealed that the world of the Ascension Saga is actually set in a post-apocalyptic Earth in the years 2549–2555. I have always been inspired by the strength and courage of the people living in the former Soviet-occupied space. That is partially why in my books out of all the world, this side of Europe is one of the few places on the planet that wasn't destroyed and turned into 'The Deadlands.'

If you compare the world map to one of modern-day Europe, you will see that most of Sangora lies within the current borders of Ukraine, Moldova, and Romania. This was not intentional based on the events perpetrated by Russia. You will even see many cities named after our modern equivalents spelled in the Sangoran manner.

I was horrified to see that in the first draft of *Spring Always Comes,* I had written certain events that mirrored those happening in Kharkiv, Mariupol, and Bucha (among others) a little *too* closely, and I removed them. However, I left in certain aspects and storylines that now pay tribute to the hardships experienced and bravery shown by the noble people of Ukraine.

There are a few instances, however, where I intentionally inserted commentary on the war in Ukraine or pay reference to the wonderful people there, such as one line referencing President Volodymyr Zelenskyy's words, when he said:

"'Was' - a simple verb. Merely a part of speech used in everyday life. But it's not that simple for us. Because now the everyday Ukrainian simply cannot say "was" without bursting into tears. This was my home. This was my friend. This was my dog. This was my car. This was my job. And this was my father. And this was my daughter. The millions and millions of Russian wounds are bleeding. Russia has drowned Ukraine in tears and blood and children's corpses. But there is one thing Russia doesn't get. 'Was' is the sword that describes its life. And we Ukrainians already know what will come next. We will win. And there will be new houses. There will be new cities. There will be new dreams. There will be a new story. Those we've lost will be remembered. And we will sing again, and we will celebrate anew. Ukraine was beautiful but now it will become great."

This is the indomitable spirit of the people of that region, rather than actual events, that I've tried to capture in my books ever since my first draft of *Embers*. Perhaps, that is an impossible feat. But I've tried to emulate it here – just as perhaps, in my outsider's opinion, President Zelenskyy currently represents all of Ukraine and all people who love and unselfishly appreciate their freedom worldwide, I wrote Mara Bartunek not only to represent the fictional people of Sangora, but also anyone who has gone through grief, trauma, or pain of any kind, including you. That is why *Ashes* was dedicated to *you*, and why *Spring Always Comes* is dedicated to the people of Ukraine and anyone else who suffered due to Soviet oppression, including those exiled to the Gulags.

Spring Always Comes is, in my opinion, darker than both *Embers* and *Ashes*. That being said, **<u>I would like to include a content warning:</u>** This book includes not only fantasy violence, but also depictions of war, murder, genocide, death, mental health issues such as trauma, grief, panic attacks, and PTSD, as well as commentaries on prejudice, racism, homophobia, and brief mentions of sexual assault and rape.

Beyond these borders lie
The Deadlands
Thanatanos
Melnik
Krakov
German
Mytborth
Narkiv
Bruntal
Terna
Adess
Born
Zubatas
Voznesensk
Dashga
Laniras
Zvolen
The Plains
of
Adess
Gulf of
Dasgha
Sitonik
Nitra
Lusinec
Kbishinau
Zersbaan
Pata
Here there
be
Monsters
Turnava
Sangora
Vudapas
Dakthaan
Zinok
Adess
City
Krim
Cineca
Arad
Vaslui
Zalain
Siofak
Timishuara
Doftaan
Sevastaan
Datova
The Shadow
of
Doftaan
Feren
Bukaral
Doftaan
City
The Black
Sea
Balgorod
Parzbani
Petr
Safija
Manzhala
The
Gban
Sea
Novamoskva
Codruta
Ripan
Sapez
Varna
Kjustendil
Talohira
Tal-Abosh
Alboras
Naskova
Gehir
Town
Likio
Kurash
City
Sanzhanski
Mia Port
The Great
Wall of
Kadir
Sangotan State
Country Capital
Sangotan State Capital
Tesalonikos
Khavala
Country Border
State Border
The Olum Desert

Doftaan
Akademrajon
The University of Doftaan
Talohiran Embassy
Vydraka
Čahmadoška
Palace of the Empress of Blood
Thannish Embassy
Ceveržapath
The Wingling House
Eastern Prison
Naraka
Jempratanrajon
Zvužajecy
Kurashian Embassy
Shrine to the Goddesses
The Boulevards
The Church of Elafris
Malakurash
The Spires of Doftaan
Maranparkh
Paudzuhoth
Paudbramah
Kaljacjana
Dubovparkh
Doftaan Hospital
Southern Prison

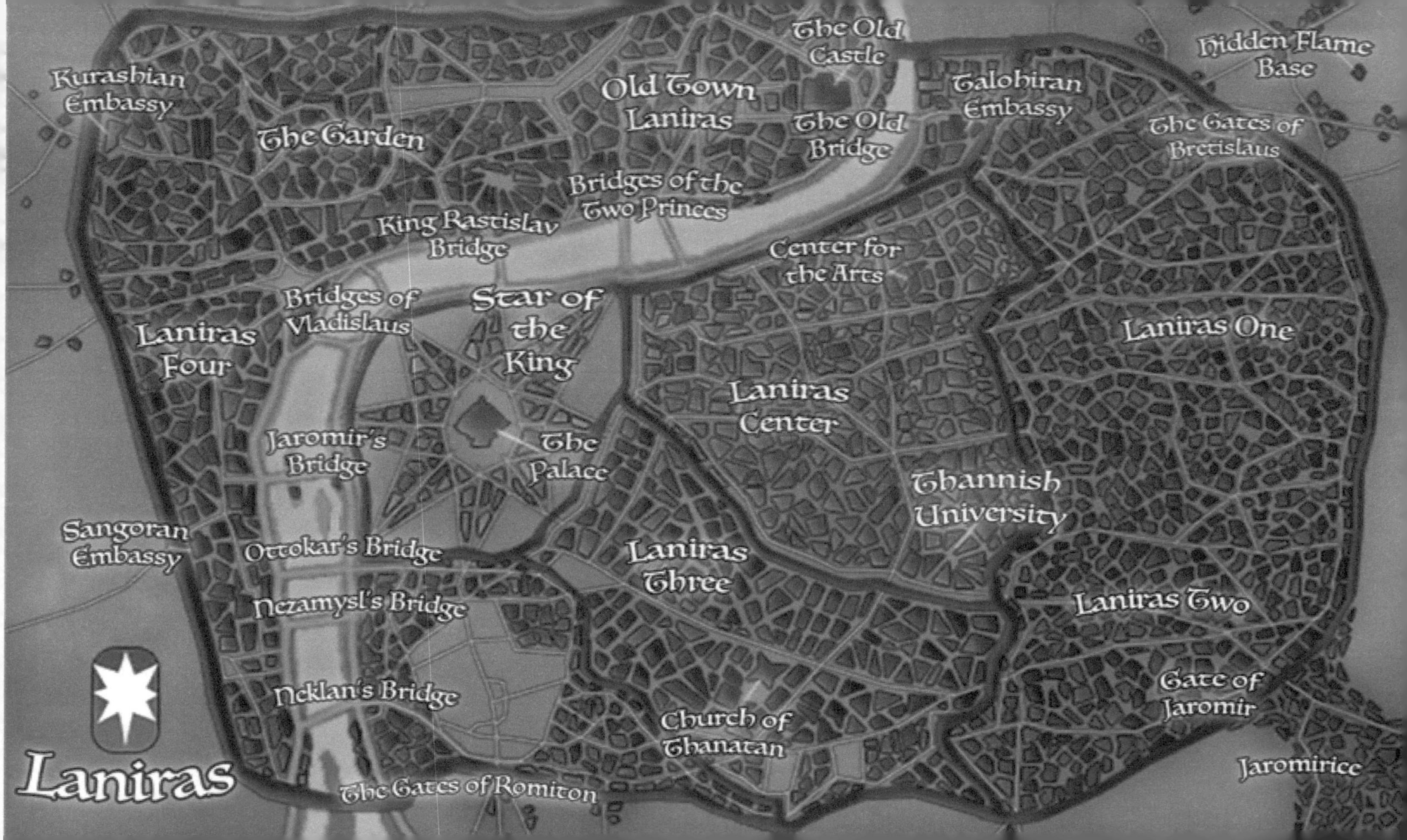
Kurashian Embassy
The Garden
Old Town Laniras
The Old Castle
The Old Bridge
Talohiran Embassy
Hidden Flame Base
The Gates of Bretislaus
Bridges of the Two Princes
King Rastislav Bridge
Center for the Arts
Bridges of Vladislaus
Star of the King
Laniras Four
Laniras One
Laniras Center
Jaromir's Bridge
The Palace
Thannish University
Sangoran Embassy
Ottokar's Bridge
Laniras Three
Nezamysl's Bridge
Laniras Two
Necklan's Bridge
Gate of Jaromir
Church of Thanatan
Laniras
Jaromirice
The Gates of Romiton

The Plains
of
Balgorod
The Balgorod Academy
of the
Hidden Flame
The River Vah
Port
District
Balgorod
Industrial
District
Residential
District
Eastern
Slums
Ża Drogasteju
i ż'Alboru
Western
Balgorod
Festival
Grounds
Prison
Complex
Kurashian
Embassy
Thannish
Embassy
The
Prickly Rose
Sangoran
Embassy
Talohiran
Embassy
Southern
Slums
The Dor
River

TABLE OF CONTENTS

SPRING ALWAYS COMES

BOOK THREE OF THE ASCENSION SAGA

Brock Mays

CHAPTER ONE

THE LEGEND OF MARA BARTUNEK

She could still see the masks whenever she shut her eyes. That image of crimson paint splashed like blood across a soulless steel face would forever haunt her dreams, but she knew it wouldn't be the only thing keeping her from sleep.

Footsteps. She tried to make herself as small as possible, pressing herself into the snow behind the crumbling wall. Where was Karel? Had they already found him?

As the footsteps and voices moved on, Nadezhda lifted her head and pushed herself up as she tried to stifle the cough that threatened to betray her to the cultists. There, in the shadows of the alleyway, she realized the snow where she had been lying was now dyed dark red with blood.

Her own.

She must have ripped the stitches out when she threw herself to the ground, and she swore under her breath. She knew it wasn't a fatal wound by any means, but a girl covered in blood was hardly conspicuous when on the run from monsters.

She lifted the corner of a soggy wanted poster on the wall to reveal a sketch of a woman with dark hair and piercing eyes staring back at her. Her heart leapt, and she gasped, clasping her hand over her mouth. Her heart thundered in her chest, and she gazed with joy at the portrait.

She didn't have this one.

There was no name scrawled beneath the image, but her heart thudded in her chest all the same. It had to be *her*. The Empress of Blood was *real*. She read the name and long list of crimes beneath the portrait.

WANTED: BY ORDER OF HIS MAJESTY, KING VERAHIM ROMUS:

Deicide.

Regicide.

Desolation of the city of Nitra

High Treason against king and crown.

Murder.

Sedition.

Considered highly dangerous - Do not approach.

She took care not to make any noise as she removed the poster and rolled it up, sliding it into the waistband of her trousers before covering it with the hem of her tunic. She couldn't wait to add it to her collection—if she ever got home.

They'd stopped hanging the wanted posters of Empress Bartunek around Laniras, knowing that she'd never appear there. That's what made the poster so valuable—not to anyone but Nadezhda, of course.

Despite her best efforts, another cough forced its way out of her throat, and she heard a shout from nearby, bringing her back to reality. She shut her eyes and hugged her knees as if it would make the monsters go away. Or rather, the men who *served* the monsters, but the dark truth was that there wasn't a difference anymore.

"Nadezhda!" hissed a voice from above.

She looked up and let out a sigh of relief to see her brother, Karel, reaching down for her with a kind smile from atop the abandoned bakery. She reached for his hand and tried to use her feet to climb, but a thick sheet of ice coated the wall, rendering her unable to gain the proper traction to climb.

"I can't get up!" she said in a frantic voice that she tried to keep as low as possible. As a naturally loud person, her brother had always told her she was horrible at whispering. She hoped now wasn't one of those times.

Karel groaned as he pulled on Nadezhda's arm. Tears filled her eyes as the stress on her shoulder felt as if he were going to tear her arm off. At last, she was able to grab hold of the drainpipe with her other hand and scramble up the rest of the way on her own. As she stepped on the pipe, it lurched and broke away from the dilapidated building with a resounding clang.

"Well, damn."

They both winced.

"Did they see you?" Karel asked as he pulled her to safety. His breathing was heavy, and Nadezhda could see his fear in a dark cloud around his head.

"No, but is there any chance at all they didn't hear that?"

"Absolutely not."

"I killed us!" She gesticulated wildly at the broken drainpipe, an exaggerated look of horror on her face.

Karel swore. "It's not your fault. Let's get out of here."

"I beg to differ, but okay." She grabbed his arm. "I found a new wanted poster—"

"You're still collecting those as we're running from these *things?*"

"No, listen. It's of *her.* I've been looking for this one for ages," Nadezhda said. Karel nodded, understanding his sister's excitement, but more worried about their safety.

"Yeah, well, they've been looking for *us* for a long time, too, you know."

Crouching as he went, Karel led Nadezhda across the roof of the bakery and leapt over the gaping hole in the ceiling. Nadezhda took a deep breath and followed, landing hard on her ankle, which twisted beneath her. She tried to catch herself and felt tiny bits of roofing shingles dig into her palms.

"I've got you," Karel said, taking her hand.

As he helped her up, she tried to put weight on her foot and groaned. Panic began to set in, and she glanced around for a way off the building without jumping. The voices were louder and nearer.

They weren't getting away—not this time.

"Go," she said as she brushed her blonde hair matted with blood and sweat from her eyes. "You know I'm just gonna slow you down."

Karel shook his head.

"No way," he said. "I've got you."

"I taste way better than you. Those monsters will like me more, and besides, it'll take them a while to finish the meal, so—"

"Stop it," Karel said.

"You never wanted a sister anyway."

"Stop."

"Nadezhda chops with blood sauce? Maybe with a little cheese?"

"Gross. Would you stop making jokes?" Karel asked. "We're getting out of here together. We'll head south toward the border."

"No way I'm going near Nitra," Nadezhda said, shaking her head. "That place is cursed. And for my jokes? No, I need them to mask the existential dread inside."

He ignored the second comment. "No, not Nitra. We can head to Pata or Cineca or some other town, come on, let's—"

"You think I'm going to limp out of Laniras all the way to *Cineca*? They're bound to see us."

"If they even can see without faces..." Karel replied. "Come on, I'll carry you."

"Again, all the way to the border?!"

Karel was stocky and strong, but she would weigh him down, and they both knew it.

Nadezhda shuddered. King Verahim had said that the creatures were supposed to work for the people of Thanatanos to lighten their burden, and there was some truth to the statement. Laniras and Thanatanos had prospered in the two years since they had arrived, but she had seen them mutilate people trying to leave the city without a pass to leave.

Because of that, while the more affluent neighborhoods prospered, the outskirts of Laniras were now suffocated with despair, since the people there were far too poor to move to nicer areas. People like Nadezhda and Karel.

Karel pressed himself to the floor and motioned for Nadezhda to get down; she dropped into the snow as flakes drifted down onto her hair. The side of her face stung against the snow, and she shut her eyes once more, praying to the old gods that it would all be over soon—not that she knew how praying worked, but she tried it all the same.

"Blood! They were here!" The voice came from below, right where she had been lying mere moments before. They heard someone fumbling with the broken drainpipe, and Nadezhda gripped Karel's hand.

"It's okay," he mouthed silently.

She knew he was lying. She always did.

He smiled at her, but fear snaked itself around her mind and would not let go. She let out one long breath and then yelped with fright as Karel shot up and leapt over the gap, swinging his rusted, bent dagger as he landed. Just as one of the men in the masks appeared over the precipice, Karel thrust the weapon downward.

The blade tore through the flesh on the masked man's neck, and he fell from the wall with a scream and a muffled crunch in the snow. Nadezhda covered her mouth with her hands.

"You just killed one of them!" she exclaimed. "You just killed a *Purist!* You know what they'll do to you!"

"Nothing they weren't going to do before, Nadya."

She'd seen the public executions for people who wronged the cultists that worshipped and served the faceless creatures and their masters. Images of Karel being strung up filled her mind—images that she couldn't banish once they were there.

Without warning, there was a loud boom, the building began to shake, and the wall beneath Nadezhda crumbled. With a scream, she managed to grab hold of a broken beam, which she used to drop down to the building's lower level, careful not to land on her injured ankle.

As she crawled to a stable part of the building, the rest of the wall collapsed in a shower of debris; several more explosions sounded below, shaking the world.

"Nadya!" Karel cried as she stumbled toward him.

"Go, Karel!" she said, pushing him. "There's a way across. They've got someone with powers down there, I think!"

Karel hesitated before grabbing Nadezhda's hand. He pulled her to the precipice between the two buildings.

"We can make it," he said.

"It's too far, even for you," she said. "Stop it!"

"We'll be okay."

Nadezhda shook her head in disbelief.

"You know you can't lie around me, right?" Nadezhda said, gripping his hand tightly. "It's literally impossible."

"I love you kid, you know that?"

And *that* wasn't a lie.

The words spilled out suddenly as if he knew he wouldn't have another chance to say them. At that moment, the corrugated tin roof gave way beneath their feet, and he shoved her hard so that she wouldn't fall. She reached for his hand as he fell, screaming, to the ground.

Nadezhda scrambled forward but couldn't see him amidst the rubble of splintered wood and shattered stone. She couldn't even scream, as much as she wanted to, as she collapsed, hyperventilating in the corner.

She glanced down to see a man light a string trailing from a round, metal object. He ran away, and a few moments later, there was another explosion. Fear and unsurety crippled Nadezhda, and she froze, hugging her knees. He had to have magical powers—how else were they creating explosions? She knew there was nothing she could do to stop them.

There weren't many powered people left here—not after the war with Talohira and Sangora that had ended five years ago. She'd been barely thirteen years old back then, but like many in Thanatanos, the impact of those horrible years still haunted her and her brother.

Ever since, they'd called her a witch. She knew they were chasing her because of her powers, but she wondered if they also knew her other secret—the one she kept in the pocket. The one Karel was ready to die to—no, that thought was too terrible to entertain.

She'd turned her trousers inside out so that the pocket's opening was inside, rather outside her pants. That way, she reasoned, they'd have less of a chance of losing that shard of a gem they'd stolen.

Karel had told her she was crazy, and she had told *him* that it was the newest fashion in Vudapas. He'd laughed at her joke. He *usually* did.

Now, she just felt empty.

Five more of the masked Purists appeared from a door on the building across from her. They each wore the smooth silver masks painted with red over their dark robes and matching armor.

"I love you too," she whispered, knowing Karel could not hear her. She could still feel his fear, but then it was gone. He'd never hear her say it again.

She shut her eyes and tried to block out reality.

Their horrible cheers let her know they'd found her. The pounding below had stopped, and instead, the men on the other building were readying themselves to jump over to her. She could feel their excitement, their ecstatic hatred, pride and… what was that? Desire? Disgusting.

She curled into a ball and pressed her forehead against her knees. Nothing mattered. Not her throbbing ankle. Not the fact that she had found a poster of Empress Mara Bartunek. Not even Karel's death. She was numb, and now they were going to find her.

Screams and shouts broke through the frigid darkness, and Nadezhda looked up, expecting the men to have reached her by now. As one of the Purists leapt over the gap between the buildings, a dark shape shot up from the alleyway and intercepted him. The man cried out in surprise and then screamed as he plummeted to the ground below.

Nadezhda lost sight of whatever had killed the man in the darkness, and she crawled to the space between the buildings to see two shadowy figures dueling with the Purists. She crawled forward and peered down over the ledge.

The men below were fleeing, and she screamed in defiance as she saw the Purists carrying Karel's body away. They tossed him atop a cart with other bodies with as much indifference as if they were loading hay onto a wagon.

Would they dispose of him in a mass grave, or give his body to the men without faces? Would he become one of them? She tried to shut the thought out, but it lingered there, haunting her as it likely would forever.

She glanced back to the men on the other building just in time to see a Sangoran woman twirl between the men in a dance of blades and blood.

"She's here!" called a woman behind her cultist's mask, but the Sangoran severed her throat and pushed her to the ground as more masked figures dared venture closer. The

Sangoran's companion got a running start and threw herself from the building. Nadezhda gasped, knowing the petite woman couldn't possibly make the jump.

Her savior, or perhaps someone else bent on capturing her, levitated across the chasm and landed with grace on the ledge before stepping down. She removed a dark hood, letting dark auburn hair free into the wind with a kind smile. She said nothing but reached out a gloved hand.

"Who are you?" Nadezhda asked.

The auburn-haired woman shook her head and tapped her right ear with an apologetic, but urgent expression. She wiggled her fingers to urge Nadezhda to take her hand.

She took the deaf woman's hand as the Sangoran across the gap drew her bladed wings from the last attacker's chest; the dead man fell from the building in a ruined heap below. Why was a Night Witch helping her? Or was she just picking off the competition?

She'd heard stories that Night Witches ate babies. She told herself that she was safe—she wasn't a baby, of course. She hadn't been one for a long time, but—

A horn sounded in the distance, and the Sangoran shot into the dark sky. The auburn-haired woman grasped Nadezhda's hand, and they floated after her companion in silence. It was a gentle sensation, not like when Karel had nearly ripped her arm out of its socket trying to pull her up. They were weightless; Nadezhda could feel the woman's emotions: compassion and exhilaration, a cloak that hid a hint of fear...

A horrendous groaning filled Nadezhda's head. The collective hunger, agony, and despair of a thousand minds seemed to envelop her entire soul more than any emotion she'd ever experienced or sensed from another. She looked back for Karel's body but knew the monsters without faces were coming, and it would be impossible to get to him.

Despite the overwhelming emotions of fear and despair assaulting her mind, her own soul felt cold and dark. No tears trailed down her face. Not yet. She knew they would when reality finally set in, but for now, the only thing Nadezhda could feel was emptiness as she floated, weightless, behind the deaf woman and her Sangoran ally.

It had to be a dream. Karel wasn't dead. She wasn't flying.

The lights of Laniras below almost looked like misplaced stars as the trio soared over the king's palace. The Sangoran woman led the way as they passed over the wall surrounding Laniras and away from the living barricade of Faceless protecting the city.

They landed amongst the rolling hills blanketed with snow several miles away from the city, and Nadezhda collapsed as she put weight on her injured ankle.

"I know you're not alright, but can you stand?" the Sangoran woman asked as she offered her hand. Nadezhda took it and used her one good foot to step up. She tested her ankle and immediately collapsed again. The Night Witch caught her and supported her until she was able to balance on her one good foot.

"Stand or walk?" Nadezhda asked, stumbling yet again. "Well, apparently no to both questions."

She gasped as she stared into the face that adorned her newest wanted poster in the flesh.

Mara Bartunek, the Empress of Blood.

She fell over again.

She didn't know how to react, so she stumbled up into an awkward bow and stepped with her bad ankle for a third time.

"Come on, they'll be close behind," Mara said, pulling Nadezhda's arm over her shoulder to support her. "It's nice to meet you…"

She trailed off, and Nadezhda said, "Nadezhda, or Nadya, if you prefer it." She winced. Why would the Empress of Blood herself want to call her by the familiar version of her name? Only Karel ever called her that anymore. She hated when anyone else did, anyway.

"It's nice to meet you, Nadya. I'm Mara, and this is my friend, Hanna."

She wanted to say she already knew who the empress was, but no words came to her mouth. Mara gestured to a cart led by four large horses. Nadezhda could see the urgency in her expression, and the Empress helped her step up into the vehicle. Hanna followed close behind and shut the carriage door.

The inside of the cart had two benches facing one another, each wide enough for three people. A dark-haired young woman around her age with pale skin sat in the furthest corner from the door, seemingly looking at her own reflection in the frosty glass, or perhaps off into the snowy distance. Maybe both. Nadezhda sat opposite the silent girl and looked to Hanna as if expecting an introduction.

Mara stayed outside, speaking with the driver just quiet enough that Nadezhda couldn't make out what she was saying.

"I'm sorry about your brother," Hanna said as she sat opposite Nadezhda and next to the other woman. Nadezhda jumped with a start, for Hanna had spoken at a much higher volume than she had expected. "Are you doing okay?"

"Oh, I don't know yet, probably not," Nadezhda replied, glancing at the floor. She looked up to meet Hanna's concerned gaze. As she started talking again, Hanna broke eye contact, instead staring at her mouth. "It hasn't set in yet. Ask again later."

"What will you do?"

"What do you mean?" Nadezhda asked. "I can sneak and hide, I don't know, I'm not really a fighter, but—"

Hanna shook both hands in front of her to prompt her to stop talking.

"What can you *do?*" Hanna asked as she removed an intricate, silver ring set with a pearl from her left hand and made it dance around her palm before slipping back onto her slender finger, all with her mind.

"Oh," Nadezhda replied. She scratched her face and began picking at a scab on her lip. "I can feel and see others' emotions. It started when—"

Hanna reached out and grasped Nadezhda's wrist and lowered her hand away from her mouth then tapped her ear again with a wink.

"I'm so sorry!" Nadezhda exclaimed, having forgotten about Hanna's deafness; she must have been trying to read her lips this whole time. Guilt crept into her mind as Hanna smiled back at her. The woman's kindness, hope, and concern wafted around her in a slow cloud of drifting white and yellow.

"So? And enunciate, I'm not a very good lip reader."

"I can feel peoples' emotions," Nadezhda said, careful to exaggerate her lip movements. She wondered if it was offensive to speak slower and louder so that Hanna could read her lips, but she said nothing of it. "I can see them too, kind of like an aura or weird fire of different wavy colors."

"Sounds exhausting," Hanna said. She pointed to the other girl in the carriage. "Valeniya can find anyone and sense people with powers. It's how we found you."

"Oh, well, thanks, Valeniya," Nadezhda said. Valeniya did not reply but traced the design of ice forming in the corner of the window with her finger. "And Mara? What can she do?"

"Mara?" Hanna asked. Nadezhda wondered if she had mumbled the question, making it hard for Hanna to read her lips. She felt guilty again, but Hanna chuckled. "What *can't* Mara do?"

As if on cue, Mara stepped into the cart, shut the door, and it lurched forward to traverse the rolling hills. She took her seat next to Hanna and shivered, wrapping herself in her great black wings like a blanket. She signed something to Hanna, who replied in kind with a shake of the head. Mara nodded with a slow sigh.

"Hanna tells me the boy was your brother," Mara said with concern in her eyes. Before she could stop herself, the words slipped out in a somber voice. "I'm so sorry. I had a brother once too."

"What happened to him?" Nadezhda asked.

"I don't know."

Nadezhda didn't push the issue. Mara stared out the window until her head began to bob as she fought sleep. Nadezhda didn't need to use her powers to be able to tell how drained Mara was. Dark circles shadowed her crystal blue eyes, and her eyelids drifted downward, and then a few moments later, she was asleep.

Hanna grasped Nadezhda's hands as they began to tremble.

"You should sleep too," Hanna said, again in a loud voice. She let go and pulled Mara's shoulder toward her so that her friend's head rested on her shoulder. Mara's dark eyelashes flittered as if she had awoken, but she was soon still again.

Hanna laid her cheek against the top of Mara's head and set her feet on Nadezhda's bench. Soon, she too drifted off to sleep. Valeniya looked over at her for the first time, and Nadezhda let out a small gasp upon seeing her white irises. A glassy sheen swirled like mist across them in the torchlight. She said nothing and turned back to watch the ice forming in the corner of the window.

Nadezhda sighed as she followed Valeniya's gaze to watch the snow drifting down outside. She gripped her inside-out pocket to make sure the jagged piece of crystal was still there. She let out a breath of relief, feeling the sharp edges through the fabric.

Her thoughts turned to Karel again. Would the snow cover his body and give him the funeral Nadezhda could not? She buried her head in her hands and began to cry.

Sometime later, the cart came to a stop, and Mara awoke with a start. Nadezhda must have dozed off as well, because as she looked out the window, there was a massive creature outside that wasn't there before, its gargantuan snout sniffing the carriage.

"What is that?!" Nadezhda exclaimed.

"That's Hippo," Mara said. "He's excited to meet you."

Nadezhda couldn't feel the creature's emotions, but it bounded up and down like a happy puppy, shaking the earth.

The shaking woke Hanna, who took a groggy step to stumble out of the cart. She helped Valeniya down as Mara gestured with a smile for Nadezhda to climb down before her.

"Don't worry, he's completely harmless," Mara said as Hippo began gnawing on a felled tree. Immense warmth radiated from between his rocky scales, and Nadezhda closed her eyes, basking in the warmth. She hadn't been warm in…well, since they'd stolen the broken gem. As Mara touched Hippo's side, he unfurled massive wings that resembled her own. "Alright, climb on."

Nadezhda's eyes widened, and she hesitantly followed Mara up Hippo's snout, over his head, down his neck, and onto a huge saddle strapped to his back that could carry dozens of people. Mara helped strap her in as Hanna did the same for Valeniya.

Without much warning, Hippo shot into the sky; Mara curled up in the hollow at the base of the beast's neck and smiled back at Nadezhda.

She'd never known a Night Witch to be so welcoming and kind before. Everything she knew of them came from Nitra, which had been destroyed by the Sangorans, and Laniras, which had almost been so.

She looked down over Hippo's side to see the lights of camps housing thousands of Thannish troops amassing at the Sangoran border. She had heard whispers that King Verahim's armies were gathering near Sangora, but she thought they were only rumors.

The wondrous feeling of flight was powerless compared to the draw of sleep, and it soon overtook her just as they soared over a winding river.

Hours later, Hippo landed just outside a set of massive gates. Nadezhda awoke just in time to see a group of human and Sangoran soldiers open the way, and the beast tromped forward, waking Mara, who sat up and looked around in a groggy haze; she set her elbows on her knees and rubbed her eyes before glancing back up at Nadezhda.

"Welcome home," Mara said while signing for Hanna. Her cloud of emotions pricked at Nadezhda's mind; there was sadness there, loss, but also empathy and hope. "I know it won't feel that way for a while, not without your brother. Karel, you said? But I hope, well… I hope it'll do."

Nadezhda nodded and faked a smile, but she knew it was too much and that it must look forced.

She glanced out the window to see crimson banners of Sangora lining the street. "Thank you, Empress." She realized she had no idea how to address the ruler of Sangora. "Where are we? Is this Doftaan?"

Anxiety twisted in her stomach as she saw Night Witches in flight and walking around town. The city was much smaller than Laniras, but everything seemed taller—fitting for a race of people that could fly.

"No," Mara said with a laugh. Nadezhda felt an amused mirth twisted around dismay and, what was that? Definitely not regret, but some kind of nostalgic disappointment and longing, perhaps?

"My Sangoran geography isn't very good," Nadezhda said, embarrassed. "The old stereotype of ignorant Thans not knowing anything outside their country is true, I guess."

The self-deprecating comment resulted in a puff of magenta amusement from Mara's soul, visible only to Nadezhda.

"I'm sorry, I didn't mean to laugh. Doftaan isn't safe right now. Not for us. Maybe sometime soon," Mara said. "No, welcome to Balgorod."

The name of the city conjured images of a poor, desolate town, but the city was in good repair and people seemed free, safe, and happy. The opposite of everything she'd ever heard or imagined about Sangora.

"I've heard about Balgorod, but I always thought it was a little more… I don't know, destitute? Is that the right word?" Nadezhda cringed, hoping Mara didn't catch on to her attempt to impress her with a more sophisticated vocabulary than she actually possessed. She was answered with a cloud of fond affection and pride.

"It used to be, but Master Shanthah, Lord of Balgorod has really turned things around here," Mara said. "The slums don't seem to want to change, but he's made progress."

"Shanthah Kalen?" Nadezhda asked. She turned to her pack and after a few moments, drew out a folded sheet of faded parchment and handed it to Mara.

The empress took the parchment and unfolded it. Her laugh of pure elation filled the air, and she hurried to show Hanna.

"*Why* do you have this?" Mara asked, still chuckling. "He looks horrible."

Hanna sat up as Mara handed her the wanted poster. Hanna let out a laugh even louder than Mara's and clutched it to her heart. She signed something, a motion from her chin.

"She says thank you," Mara said. "I think she needed the laugh. I did too."

"What's so funny?" Nadezhda asked as Hanna handed her the parchment back.

"Shanthah's a friend of mine. Hanna's fiancé, actually," Mara said. "You'll meet him soon, I hope, and you'll see that they definitely got his face, and, well, everything else wrong."

Hanna signed something to Mara, and they both laughed.

Nadezhda couldn't help but close her eyes in contentment as she breathed in Mara and Hanna's elation.

"Well, they did a better job on you," Nadezhda said. Mara's eyes went wide, and she held out her hand. Nadezhda lifted her tunic and drew the other wanted poster from her waistband. She handed it over, and Mara's eyes lit up. She nudged Hanna, who smiled in silent joy.

"Deicide. Hm," Mara said, nodding.

"What is that, even?" Nadezhda asked. She had been wondering what several of Mara's supposed crimes meant, and she hoped for the stories behind them.

"Long story," Mara said.

"Is it true, whatever it is?" Nadezhda asked.

"Oh, yeah, very much so," Mara said, but she did not elaborate. Nadezhda didn't press the matter, but Mara didn't *seem* dangerous.

Other than the blood-stained knives on the ends of her wings, of course.

Mara and Hanna led Nadezhda through town across a bridge to a fortress surrounded on all sides by a river that ran through the city. She followed them to the gates where they met a couple guards.

"This is Nadya," Mara said. "Can I call you that?" Too anxious to correct her, Nadezhda gave a thumbs up, but she thought she sensed Mara's apprehension to use the name. "Please take her to the dormitories and make sure she's comfortable. Bring her some dinner too, please. The good stuff. Ambassador Kraev can do without a fancy dinner for one night, yes?"

"It will be done, Empress."

Nadezhda thanked Mara and Hanna for their help again, and she followed the soldiers away down the corridor lit with welcoming flame.

Hanna turned to Mara.

"*You're not staying, are you?*" she signed.

"Hanna, I have to do this," Mara said and signed, to which Hanna shook her head in an angry flurry of auburn hair.

"*You can't do this alone. Please, please don't,*" Hana signed back, her gestures much more emphasized while begging *please*. "*You are tired, girl. You're totally exhausted. If you go, you're going to die, and I won't let that happen. No more strokes. No more seizures. What's life without my favorite Mara in it?*"

Mara chuckled, but her eyebrows turned sad, and Hippo gave an anxious groan audible from outside. She knew her friend wasn't speaking in hyperbole, especially as Hanna brushed her thumb over the scar on the shaved side of Mara's head.

"I don't know what to do," Mara said. "My people are dying. Even if I can't save them, I have to know what's happening. I'll be safe, I promise."

"*I never told you not to do it, just don't go alone. Just wait until morning, please. I'll go with you. It's dangerous with the Thans all over the border.*"

Mara smiled. "Of course."

"*Get some rest. Go tomorrow. We'll both go—we'll bring Shanthah or Alia or Kamil or someone to come with us too. We can bring a picnic or something. We'll make a day of it.*"

Mara hugged Hanna, said her goodbyes, and turned away as Hanna climbed the stairs to her own quarters. However, she glanced out the window to see Mara leave the fortress to guide Hippo back to his enclosure. As she did so, Hanna let out a deep sigh, knowing her friend had already made up her mind.

CHAPTER TWO

THE PAST NEVER DIES

The torches lining the corridor flickered as Mara strode past. A pair of guards sitting on the steps leading up into the tower stumbled to their feet at the sight of their empress and raised their fists to their forehead in a hasty salute.

"At ease, ladies," Mara muttered with a nod to the two guards. They dropped the salute and assumed their positions once more.

As she began to climb the spiral staircase, she smiled to herself when one of the guards whispered to the other, "Of course the one time the empress comes by, we're sitting on our butts…"

"Yeah, of all people. You're the one who suggested it!"

She followed the staircase to the tower's fifth landing. She leaned against the colorful stained-glass window that ran the entire length of the corridor to catch her breath. Even in the darkness of night, the moonlight cast a spray of beautiful colors through the glass into the dim corridor. It reminded her of the windows back home in Doftaan, and her heart dropped. She was running out of options of how to get back there and retake her beloved city, and doubt crept into her heart about if it were even possible.

She continued down the hallway and rapped on a door there twice. At first, there was no answer until she was welcomed with a soft, "Come in."

Mara twisted the doorknob to let herself into the dark room, shutting the door behind her with a soft click. A cool breeze drifted in through the open window, playing with the satin curtains. The ethereal, silver light of the moon silhouetted a figure sitting with her back to Mara, facing the window.

"I'm sorry, Leniya, did I wake you?"

"No."

"Good, I'm glad," Mara said.

She approached the bed, and Valeniya Talohir glanced over her shoulder then back at the moon through the open window. At that moment, Mara realized Valeniya was sitting there completely naked.

"Oh, by the goddesses, why are you naked?" Mara asked, pulling a thin blanket from a round table in the corner of the room. "You're going to freeze, girl."

She draped the blanket around Valeniya's shoulders and sat beside her.

"Everyone is naked to me," Valeniya said in a dreamy tone. "Why should it be strange that I am?"

"Wait what? Always?" Mara exclaimed, bunching the neckline of her tunic into her fist to cover more of her chest. She had never thought of just what Valeniya saw when she used her powers, but she dismissed the thought with a shake of her head.

"How are you, sweetheart?"

"I am fine. How are you, Mara?"

Mara smiled. It wasn't like the girl to ask such a question or make small talk in any way.

"I'm worried," Mara replied. Thoughts of the Thannish armies near the borders of Sangora ready to strike at any moment filled her heart with dread, but she wouldn't bother Valeniya with that detail. "I came to ask you for a favor."

"You want me to find someone," Valeniya said.

Mara nodded. "I do. I hope that's okay."

"Of course. I like to help my friends," Valeniya said. Mara's heart swelled, for she had always felt completely unsure of Valeniya's feelings toward her, or anyone, for that matter.

"I know this is a lot to ask of you, but I need you to find someone that I thought was dead."

"I can't see dead people."

"No, I know. It's complicated. I thought he was dead, but it turns out he might not be," Mara replied. "I'm scared he's going to hurt Hanna."

"Hanna is kind, and I don't want anything to happen to her," Valeniya said.

"I think so too," Mara said. Valeniya said nothing, lost in her own world as she stared at the silver moon. "I need you to find Thanatan."

Valeniya's head snapped toward Mara, eyes wide.

"Father wanted me to find him once, and when I looked for him, he looked back," Valeniya said, her voice trembling. "No one has ever seen *me*."

Guilt filled Mara's heart as Valeniya's breath quickened.

"Can I touch?" she asked. Valeniya nodded, and Mara wrapped her arms around the young woman's bare shoulders. "You don't have to do anything you don't want to." She waved her hands as if wiping away the request. "I'm sorry, Leniya. Will you forgive me?"

Valeniya said nothing in reply, but her eyes clouded over with a silvery sheen. Mara waited for a long while, holding Valeniya's hands in her own.

At last, Valeniya snapped back to reality with a deep breath. Her eyes returned to normal—as normal as white irises could be—and Mara put a concerned hand on her back.

"What is it?" she asked. "Did he see you?"

"No," Valeniya said before looking Mara in the eye. "Don't go to him. It's too dangerous, even for you."

"Why not?" Mara asked. "So, he's alive, then?"

"No, he just isn't dead."

Mara cocked her head. "Is that not the same thing?"

Valeniya replied with a slow shake of her head. Her eyes had once been a deep brown, the same color as her father's. Mara wondered if the constant use of her powers had turned them pale.

"Where is your father?" Mara asked, although she hadn't planned to ask about Valistaran.

"In Bukaral. My brother Valis is with him."

"How are they doing?" Mara asked.

During the two years since she had been ousted from power, Valistaran and his son, Valis—Valeniya's half-brother—had been hard at work ending Talohira's civil war; it had been hard work, but they had managed to form a government of sorts, with Valis crowned as the youngest king in the country's history.

They had asked for Mara's blessing, of course, as Talohira was still under her rule. She had responded that it was about time it became an independent nation again, free from her rule forever. The situation there was still unstable, but King Valis was doing a good job maintaining order through respect.

"If they're both together and home, don't you want to go home too?" Mara asked.

"I am home," Valeniya said, a confused look crossing her face. "Home is where I am."

"That's…actually very insightful," Mara said. "Thank you, Leniya."

They sat together in silence looking up at the moon for a long while, and a thin smile appeared across Valeniya's lips. At last, Mara patted Valeniya on the knee and stood up.

"Thank you for spending time with me."

"Of course," Mara said. "I enjoy spending time with you. You're my friend, Leniya."

"You are my friend too, Mara."

Mara stepped toward the window, looking down with a happy expression to see Hippo, her winged behemoth companion, stomping in a patch of pumpkins far below. She chuckled as he made cheerful grunts every time he found and burst one of the pumpkins under the snow.

"I like watching him," Valeniya said.

"Me too. He's silly, isn't he?" Valeniya nodded. "I know it will be dangerous, but Hippo and I need to go to that scary place you saw. I promise we'll both be safe, though," Mara said. She felt silly asking it, but the words slipped out. "Would you watch out for me?"

Valeniya's face lit up at the question. Her eyes clouded over once more, and she turned her sight back to the silver light of the moon. Mara shut the window so Valeniya wouldn't freeze but left the curtains open. She left the room, peering over her shoulder at the curious young woman inside before pulling the door shut.

Mara made her way downstairs past the guards, who were now standing at attention. She strode all the way to the front gates of Shanthah's fortress where another pair of guards were waiting. They heaved open the heavy doors for her, and she walked out into the crisp night air.

She made her way around the fortress, following Hippo's happy grunts. The earth shook, and Mara smiled as he came bounding around the corner as he sensed her coming. He lowered his big rocky, reptilian face to Mara's level, and she placed a hand on his snout with a loving pat.

"Hello, you big silly boy," she said. He snorted, and hot, sulfurous air engulfed her. "That warm air feels nice, buddy, but it sure stinks! Ready to go?"

Hippo squealed happily and lowered his head for Mara to climb on. She unfolded her wings and flapped into the air above him, stepping down on his back lined with craggy stone scales. Mara settled between his wings, and he shot into the sky.

Winter's chill bit the exposed flesh on Mara's face, causing tears to form in her eyes as her nose ran into her scarf. Hippo shot through the sky toward Terman, the northernmost Sangoran state. She had long ago passed over Timishuara, the state governed by Lavinia Daktha, and now flew over the plains of Adess, the largest and most sparsely populated state in her realm.

She squinted to make out the line of torches that extended all the way to the horizon and out of sight; had Florenta's forces built a wall in the expanse between Adess and Doftaan? If so, was it to protect her capital from an invasion, or to keep the people of Terman and Adess captive? She screwed up her eyebrows out of curious suspicion and turned her head to watch it disappear into the distance.

Nearly another hour died away as they passed over a dozen or so tiny villages far below. And then, she saw it.

In the distance, the light of thousands of torches and campfires glowed amongst the dark hills, and her heart sank in her chest. There shouldn't be a city there, so the rumors had to be true, but she told herself that couldn't be so.

With every moment the encampment grew closer, her heart shattered into even smaller shards. She wanted to deny the reports that Florenta's government and the Thannish crown had set up slave camps in her own country, but the evidence was there before her eyes.

Hanna had told her this wasn't her fault.

That was exactly why Mara hadn't brought her along.

She blinked away tears as she willed Hippo to land, knowing the warm orange glow emanating from beneath his rocky armor would act as a beacon to whomever awaited her at the Thannish slave camp. Stealth was definitely not one of his strengths.

After everything that had happened between Talohira and Thanatanos and the camps, King Verahim had done the exact same thing. Worse, by the sound of the rumors.

Hippo let out a low whine as he plopped down to the frozen ground and let his beloved master climb off. Mara scrambled down her companion's forehead. His eyes followed her as she took a step off his snout, extended her wings, and glided to the rest of the way to the ground.

Despite being so far north, no snow had yet accumulated, but the morning dew had frozen on each blade of grass, painting the earth white.

The grass cracked with each step, and Hippo whined again, unwilling to take his eyes off Mara.

"It's okay, buddy. It's okay," she said, patting his massive snout. He let out a puff of hot, sulfurous air, and Mara laughed, breaking the complete stillness of a night that promised to be unforgiving.

"Stay here, okay?" Mara said. She knew that through their mental connection, she could communicate directly to his mind, but it was nice to have someone to talk to. "I'll be safe. Stay here, and I'll see if I can get the woodsmen to chop you down a nice oak tree when we get back to Balgorod. Does that sound good?"

Hippo stood up on his hind legs and slammed down again, his jaws wide open in what Mara recognized as a smile. She had forbidden him from eating any living trees that grew in the forest outside of Balgorod, but he had carried her all this way and deserved a tasty snack upon their return.

"Oh, you are so cute," she said.

Hippo lay on his stomach, extending his massive, but stubby legs behind him. He nestled his snout against a rocky outcrop, and his breath thawed the grass around him.

"Love you buddy. Stay hidden…as much as someone like you can."

She felt him acknowledge her command and began to dig a pit to lie in. She extended her wings once more and shot into the sky toward the camp, memories of her own enslavement amplified by the silent darkness. No matter what she did, she couldn't get the images of the horrors she had seen during her time as a slave out of her head.

She felt Hippo's mental link fade as she glided toward the looming light. The warm glow should have felt welcoming in the cold, but instead, all it did was break Mara's heart.

Guard towers were set at the top of hills surrounding the camp. She landed on one of their roofs far enough away that she wouldn't be seen, and she began to spy on the camp. It seemed that no one was on duty in the tower beneath her.

A high fence connected each tower, and a dome of jagged, metal wire extended over the entire compound, obviously to keep the Sangoran prisoners inside, but it did nothing to prevent the cold or the elements from creeping in. Several dozen buildings stood in rows beneath the cruel dome.

She glided to the frozen earth and crawled closer, using her wings to blend in with the shadows. A horn sounded, and the grinding of the buildings' metal doors opening filled the night. She pressed herself to the ground as a glowing flame amplified by a collection of mirrors upon the guard tower cast a light, scanning over her position. When it had passed on, she crawled ever nearer to the fence, peering through the chain links at the horror she never hoped to see again.

She pressed her hands over her mouth in shock. Hundreds of people, more than should fit inside, began to file out of the barracks; she expected the flow of bodies to end, but they kept coming until thousands of people stood in the freezing open air.

A couple snowflakes landed on the back of her neck, and she adjusted the hood on her fur coat as the spotlight on the guard tower moved again. She took her chance and shot into the sky, landing silently atop another structure.

Guilt and pity stabbed her heart as she beheld the gaunt faces and emaciated bodies of the prisoners, human and Sangoran alike. She had never, not even during her time as a slave on the Arcship or in the Talohiran slave camps, seen people as famished and broken as those she now looked upon.

She watched a skeleton of a man collapse moments after emerging from his barracks, but the guards did nothing to help him, forcing those behind to continue their march into the open area. She shut her eyes and shook back tears, knowing the man would be trampled under his fellow slaves' feet.

She'd seen it before. People had chosen death in the Talohiran camp rather than endure the suffering inflicted on them by the cruel slavers, and others had thrown themselves overboard to escape the hell on the Arcship.

She crawled over the guard shack's roof and for the first time caught a glimpse of one of the banners hanging on the nearest guard tower: a viridian background with a white star hung beside a fist on a field of crimson.

That confirmed her fears—Florenta's forces were in league with Thanatanos. How could this be…? She thought back to the day her throne and people had been taken from her. The day Rehor and so many more good people had been murdered at the very event meant to bring peace—the day her world was shattered.

Her mind raced. With Florenta dead, perhaps the people of Thanatanos had taken the Queen's Control… No… It had been destroyed. It didn't make sense. Perhaps, sadly, the most valid theory was that Verahim had sold out to Florenta's government after her death.

These people weren't slaves being forced to work. They served no purpose to build Florenta's empire or Verahim's kingdom, yet here they were, forced to endure the punishing cold of steel and nature. And for what?

She wiped a tear and some running snot from her face as the cold bit her exposed cheekbones and nose. She could only imagine how horrible the freezing cold felt to those in the camp below, for it chilled her to the bone atop the guard tower even wrapped in a heavy fur coat. She wished with all her heart that she could give it to just one person below.

She still didn't know if using her powers would cause another stroke, so she couldn't risk it. Even if she did break in and fight off the guards and save the prisoners, the guards would kill hundreds before she was able to save them.

And even if Hippo breathed lava through the camp and tore the horrible men limb from limb, the people inside would have no way to escape this frozen stretch of the plains of Adess and make the trek home. She could take around fifty people on Hippo's back, but there were thousands down there, and they'd all die before she could make it back for another trip.

Was there anything she could do?

She turned her back on the camp. It was too horrible to behold, and although guilt tore through her very soul, she extended her wings and shot into the night. She reached out with her mind, and a dull ache began to throb on the side of her head. She groaned, but sensed Hippo's consciousness, called to him, and then closed off the connection. She redirected her flight path in his direction.

Although the dull pain was beginning to subside, and she had stopped using her telepathy to sense Hippo, she felt something lingering in her skull, as if someone were mindspeaking to her. She shook her head to banish the feeling, but a low laugh filled her consciousness.

"I can save them."

The words came into her head like a chisel into her skull, and she fell from the sky with a scream. Hippo's orange glow filled her eyes as she caught herself before hitting the ground. She landed at the base of his neck and sprawled out against his stony flesh, tears streaming down her frostbitten face.

"Get the hell out of my head. You're dead."

"There is nothing more you can do, and this is all your doing. You know both of these things to be true."

Mara let out a deep breath.

"Congratulations, you can read my mind," she thought back to the disembodied voice in her head.

"Come to me in Nitra. I can save them."

And then the connection melted away, leaving her alone with her own thoughts. She covered her eyes with the palms of her hands and wept bitter tears as she pulled her knees close to her chest. There was nothing she wanted to do less, but she was running out of options.

Hippo groaned as he carried her through the sky, turning west at the command of his empress.

West.

Toward Nitra.

CHAPTER THREE
OF BACON AND WHISPERS

Nadezhda's dormitory room in the academy was much more comfortable than she had expected it to be. For whatever reason, images of prison cells and dark dungeons had flitted through her mind until the guards showed her new residence with a smile and departed; when she entered, she was pleasantly greeted by a warm bed with an *actual* pillow, several blankets, a desk, a bookshelf with a few books, and a wardrobe of her very own.

There was even a key so that she could lock the door for privacy, although she'd quite have liked to have been assigned a roommate at the academy so that it wasn't so lonely. But perhaps, it wasn't that kind of school.

The short time she'd spent in Balgorod had been a blur of too many introductions and an avalanche of new information. Much to her surprise, she'd been informed that all Thannish refugees, including herself, were granted admission, room, and board.

The day after she arrived, a Sangoran woman of some important status called a Mistress of Dusk (which she thought was a rather silly title) named Ruta had given her a warm welcome and showed her around the fortress.

She'd explained to Nadezhda during the tour that the space served not only as Master Shanthah Kalen's administrative building, but as an academy for young people where she could learn history, mathematics, languages, and what she was most excited for, courses on how to control her abilities in productive ways.

Nadezhda had emptied her scant belongings, including a sharpened kitchen knife with a broken handle, a second pair of socks, and a small, torn, portrait of her brother and parents into the drawers. And lastly, she placed her stack of wanted posters on the desk with Mara's face at the top.

She could still sense the hatred seething from the mirror-like surface of the gem. It was the only non-human thing she'd ever sensed emotion from with her powers, and it terrified her, but she couldn't bring herself to get rid of the accursed thing.

It wouldn't let her.

The jagged, broken gem was about as long as her hand from fingertips to wrist; it looked as if it had been cracked in two, judging by the break. She stared at it for a long moment more until she shoved it into the back of the drawer within the threadbare pair of socks. A fitting place for such a horrible thing.

That had been two days ago. Although Nadezhda had kept to herself in her room, it wasn't a jail at all, and the Sangorans were all friendly and welcoming, contrary to everything she had ever heard of the country.

She sat up in her bed the third morning in Balgorod to the routine knock on the door: breakfast. She hurried to the door, unlocked it, and a young woman held out a tray of food. Eggs, biscuits, a tomato, even a few strips of bacon that smelled unbelievable.

"Thank you," Nadezhda tried to say, though her mouth was watering in anticipation of the meal.

"Of course," said the Sangoran woman. "Remember, this is the last welcome meal before you'll eat in the common eating area with the rest of the students."

"I know, thank you," Nadezhda replied.

The woman smiled and turned away as Nadezhda hurried to her bed, door still ajar, as she placed the tray on her pillow. She stuffed a forkful of eggs into her mouth with a contented sigh.

And then, she carefully picked up the first crisp, aromatic piece of meat and took a bite. She closed her eyes, the heavenly taste filling her mouth and soul.

"I. LOVE. BACON."

She heard a chuckle from outside the door, but she didn't care as she held the second strip of meat under her nose and took a whiff.

She finished her breakfast and grabbed the sheet of parchment from the floor where it had fallen the night before. She smoothed it out against the edge of the desk and reviewed the schedule written there.

The letter explained her schedule for each day. At the end of the week, it explained that she'd be informed of what to expect moving forward, should she wish to remain at the academy.

The Balgorod Academy of the Hidden Flame. A bit pretentious, she thought, but who was she to judge?

She'd have her introduction to the class on abilities later that day—an orientation of sorts. She scrunched the schedule into an unceremonious ball before shoving it under her waistband and into her baggy trousers' inside-out pocket.

And then the voices began.

They crept from within her drawer, whispers in the shadows too faint to understand and too evil to want to. She felt herself drawn to the drawer, and despite her reluctance to open it, she did so and retrieved the jagged piece of crystal.

"Nadezhda."

She dropped the crystal, and it skittered across the floor under her desk. Her heart thundered in her chest as she cautiously crouched to look under the low table as if the hunk of mirrored glass would jump out and attack her.

It had never said anything in Thannish before. The voices had always been like soft wind over the sea, words in an odd language that were *almost* distinguishable but became inaudible the harder she tried to listen.

It was not so anymore.

The mirror had said her name.

"Hello?" she whispered, crawling on all fours beneath the desk. No answer, apart from the shadowy whispers that usually accompanied the crystal.

She crawled beneath the table and folded her legs beneath her. She gingerly picked the crystal up with thumb and forefinger. Nothing. She let out a sigh of relief. Had she imagined the voice? Perhaps, the woman outside had—

And then, "*Nadezhda.*"

The glassy surface swirled with dark shadow.

"Not my imagination," she whispered.

"*No. Not your imagination.*"

"Damn it."

The voice snaked through her mind, and not her ears, but she spoke aloud to reply all the same.

"Who—what—are you?" she whispered. "What do you want?"

She glanced over her shoulder and crawled over to the door, pushing it shut, before hiding under the desk once again.

"*I want to be your friend,*" said the voice.

Nadezhda squirmed under the desk, peeking out to make sure no one was listening in.

"Why, exactly?" Nadezhda asked. "I don't have many of those, so I'm pretty cautious who I let—"

"*Because I believe we can help one another.*"

"How so?" Nadezhda whispered into the crystal. "I might be wrong, but I'm pretty sure hearing voices is generally not regarded as a good thing."

"You long for your brother to come back to you. I can feel it in your soul. If you do something for me, I'll bring him back," the Voice replied.

"Back from the dead?" Nadezhda asked, brushing her bright blonde hair from her eyes to tuck it behind her ear. She caught a glimpse of her reflection glaring back at her from the shadows within the gem. "That's impossible. Tell me the truth, or you're going back in my socks."

"Your brother is one of the Pure, now."

"Wait, so he's not dead?" Her heart pounded in her chest.

"Not alive, but not quite dead. Just as I am."

"Okay, weird. But then, who are you?"

"You wouldn't believe me even if I told you."

"Well, what do you want?" Nadezhda asked, turning the crystal over in her hand. To her surprise, her reflection no longer followed her actions, and it remained on the surface of the jagged gem as she turned it over in her hand; she looked back into her own face reflected back at her. The 'other' Nadezhda smiled, her hair dark and face pale, but with a strange expression of victory etched on her face. "What is this? That is *not* me!"

"In due time, dear Nadezhda."

"No, not good enough," Nadezhda replied. "Answers, you disembodied voice. Now."

"You are bold, aren't you?" asked the voice. *"Very well. Let's get started, then."*

The Voice's words froze Nadezhda in fear, and indecision tore at her soul as the gem pulsated in her hand like a heartbeat—a dark imitation of life.

"Okay, well, if we're going out of here, you have to stay quiet," Nadezhda said. "I feel like I'm smuggling an animal into—"

"*I am no animal.*"

"Didn't say you were, guy. But what should I call you if you won't tell me your name?"

"*Don't.*"

Nadezhda rolled her eyes and slipped the crystal into her pocket as the Voice's mental instructions guided her through the corridor and out the door. She followed the Voice down the stairs into a cellar she had never noticed before.

"*There aren't many who will be able to hear me, and you are the only one who can truly understand me.*"

"Okay, vague and scary. Now what?"

Why was she doing this? Her mind screamed and ordered herself to stop, but she did not.

"*Go through the door.*"

Nadezhda turned the knob with a trembling hand and pulled the door open. She flinched, expecting some kind of arcane monster to match the voice to jump out at her. Instead, all that she saw were a few rats scurrying about amidst dozens of barrels of food supplies, each labeled with their contents.

"Hungry, voice?" Nadezhda asked. She felt a wave of amusement wash over the foreign consciousness. "Oh, so you do feel humor."

"*Perceptive,*" said the Voice.

"Yeah, well, you kind of have to be when you're on the run from those monsters," Nadezhda said. The Voice did not respond. "Okay, now what?"

"*The rats.*"

"You don't have a mouth. If you expect me to eat those things *for* you—"

"*Lay my heart on the ground. I will do the rest. Do so, or I will find someone else who will.*"

"Your *heart?*" Nadezhda asked. No answer.

She decided to comply, laying the shard of the mirror-like fragment on the ground. Several curious rats scurried over to peer into the glassy surface, drawn there as if called by their master, and as soon as they peered into the gem's face, they collapsed, let out one last breath, and were still. This continued until five rats had done the same, their bodies shriveled and drained of life.

"What are you doing?" Nadezhda asked. "Balgorod's got a rat problem, yeah, but I didn't think they'd hire someone like you as their magical exterminator."

"*Funny. No. I require life-force to bring your brother back from what he has become,*" the voice said. Nadezhda nodded.

"Got it. More rats, then?" she asked.

"*Yes. Later,*" it answered.

"I assume you want life force for your own dastardly deeds too, right?"

"*I wouldn't call surviving dastardly, but yes.*"

Nadezhda stooped down to pick up the gem, and as she did so, it burned the fleshy part of her palm, and she dropped it onto the ground where it bounced out of sight.

She had no problem locating the crystal gem under the shelf of barrels, but she had to stretch her fingers in order to reach it.

"Almost lost you there," Nadezhda said.

The gem was now ice cold rather than burning hot, and she stowed it in her pocket. The Voice ignored her comment, but it filled her mind all the same.

"Go about your day. I will not intrude further, but I will let you know when I require your services again."

"Okay," Nadezhda said. "But you better keep quiet."

She felt the Voice's amusement.

"I like you, Nadezhda."

And then the Voice and its dark whispers were gone, leaving her alone in the cellar.

The hours passed, and Nadezhda sat in the ledge below a tall window watching the sun dip below the western mountains; the pinkish glow on the clouds painted the hallway in its warm color, although she could still feel the chill from outside with her arm pressed against the window.

She had lost track of time, and the excitement of attending her first classes at the Balgorod Academy had been replaced by obsessive thoughts about the Voice—could it really bring Karel back from whatever he had become?

She patted her hip to make sure the hunk of glassy crystal was still in the pocket of her inside-out pants, and then she followed the flow of students toward a classroom at the end of the corridor.

As she bumped shoulders with the other students, her good mood returned, especially as the palpable cloud of excitement emanating from the others filled her soul.

She breathed it in, and a smile crossed her face. She was surprised to see that not every student was young like her; many elderly people hobbled along, and children even younger than herself hurried into classrooms. It seemed to be an academy for all ages.

The classroom's high vaulted ceilings and elegant windows seemed to Nadezhda more suitable for kings and their audience of diplomats; indeed, perhaps that was once its purpose, now that she thought of it. She selected a desk near the front row of desks beneath the light of a flickering torch. Not the front row. The teachers would see her there. But not the back, of course. Her mother had always taught her not to sit at the back of a room you were happy to be in.

The professor, whoever they were, had not yet arrived, and the rest of the class was talking amongst themselves, so she decided to join in.

"Hi," she said, tapping the Sangoran girl sitting in front of her on the shoulder. She seemed to be about her own age. "Nadezhda."

"No, I'm Ana. Ana Sala," said the girl.

Nadezhda laughed. "No, *I'm* Nadezhda. Nice to meet you, Ana Sala. Bacon?"

"What?"

Nadezhda reached under her waistband and pulled a wad of napkins from her inside-out pocket. She unfolded it and handed a strip of cold, but crispy bacon to her new friend, who accepted it with a laugh.

"Pocket bacon," Nadezhda repeated. "I think I've found the key to making friends, and this is it."

"Were you keeping that in your…pants…?"

"Inside-out pockets mean no one can pickpocket me."

Ana glanced under Nadezhda's desk and saw her pockets dangling on the outside of her trousers.

"That's a good test to see if someone will be a true friend. If they think you're too odd for them, they're not worthy of being your friend," Ana said. "And I, for one, appreciate the pocket bacon, and for the recommendation for more secure pockets."

Nadezhda offered a small bow.

"Thanks for saying hello, by the way. I've been too frazzled by all of this—" she gestured to everything, but nothing in particular, "—to make friends, so, you know, thanks—again, I mean."

Nadezhda chuckled. Ana threw her dark hair over her shoulder, revealing a tattoo of a scarlet rose emblazoned on her light brown skin just behind her ear. The flower's stem disappeared beneath the girl's high collar.

She raised her slice of bacon, and Nadezhda tapped her own against it as if they were toasting in a pub.

Ana let out a bright laugh; Nadezhda smiled, and her heart leapt.

"Yeah, well, I've been alone with myself for too long, and she's pretty poor company. So, you're my friend now,"

Nadezhda said, cramming the rest of the bacon into her mouth. As she chewed, she asked, "When'd you get here?"

"A week ago," Ana replied.

"I'm so sorry, I haven't talked to another human being in like four days, so if I'm a bit—Oh, by Elafris, I'm an idiot. I didn't mean to call you human, I—"

"Yikes, friendship over, right?" Ana asked with a laugh, wiggling her wings. Nadezhda replied with an exaggerated frown.

"No, I get it. You're fine. Don't worry about it," Ana said. "I'm from here—Balgorod—I thought it'd be a good idea to come here. You know, learn to protect the new country and all that, but it's been pretty lonely. I'm sure that'll change now that the term has started, though, now that I have your 'pretty poor company' to keep me entertained."

"Oh, for sure. I'll make sure of that. And new country?" Nadezhda asked. She hadn't had time in Laniras to keep up on international events. "Sorry, I'm uncultured Thannish trash. Don't mind me."

Ana laughed again. "Yeah, Alboras. The old Sangoran state of Karpaska is a free country now. The old Empress got overthrown, and that horrible Florenta lady became queen. She was horrible, so Alboras decided to leave, or something."

Even with her scant knowledge of international politics, Nadezhda knew that Ana's explanation of events had to be a gross oversimplification, but she said nothing of it.

"I met that overthrown empress," Nadezhda said.

Ana's eyes grew wide. "You met Empress Bartunek?"

"Yeah, she rescued me from Laniras," Nadezhda replied. She could feel exuberant joy and a bit of curious jealousy coming from Ana's heart. "I always thought she was like a dictator or something, though."

"A dictator?!" Ana exclaimed. "If you hadn't just given me a piece of bacon, I'd have to give you a piece of my mind and probably a slap."

Nadezhda chuckled. "I guess she's not as popular in Thanatanos as she is here. Sorry, uncultured Than, remember?"

"You just don't know her like we do," Ana said, shaking her head. "You'll see. She lives in Balgorod now, and I've heard she visits the academy sometimes!"

But before Nadezhda could share her reaction with Ana, the entire classroom reacted at once to a man materializing from thin air atop the desk, his arms outstretched.

"Welcome, one and all to the first ever term of the Balgorod Academy!" exclaimed the man theatrically, as if welcoming them all to the Vudapas Circus. His long cloak swept papers and quills from atop the desk as he surveyed the room. Nadezhda recognized the man, more or less, from one of her wanted posters. Although now, she could understand why Mara and Hanna had laughed when they saw it. "My name is Shanthah Kalen, Master of Balgorod, founder and leader of this academy, yada, yada, yada. You don't care about that, I know, I know."

Ana turned around to whisper to Nadezhda.

"He led the Alboran revolution. He even fought in the Battle of Balgorod, you know?" she whispered in an excited, but low tone. Nadezhda did not know what that meant, but she smiled, nonetheless, happy to see Ana's puff of golden joy floating around her head like a cloud.

Master Shanthah dropped into a seated position on the desk, his legs dangling so that his feet nearly touched the floor.

"I'd like to address a few things before I introduce the curriculum and teachers that will lead your classes. Goals, what this academy is for, what it's not for, and the like. There are rumors I'd like to dispel."

"There are those who will claim I'm forming an army. That's simply, utterly not untrue," Shanthah said. A confused whisper filled the class. "But at the same time, it *is* untrue. We're making an army of thinkers. Of good, compassionate, intelligent people. You see, in the past few years, without going into complicated politics and a long, boring history lesson, Thanatanos has, shall we say, become broken. It has gone from being a keeper of the peace in our world to the main instigator of death, intolerance, and war in the region."

Shanthah's jolly expression turned sad as he gripped the edge of the table, looking over the faces of each pupil before continuing.

"There will be no room for intolerance here. Which is kind of an oxymoron, I know." He laughed to himself. "I am training defenders. I do not expect any of you to fight on the front lines. I'm not sending any of you to war. I will never make you do anything you don't want to do. But I must let you know that our diplomats have met with King Verahim's councils, generals, and leaders, and they have no intention of ending the war with Sangora, and by extension, with us here in Alboras. I'm sure you've heard news that their army is gathering at our border. I'm sorry to have to tell you that. I'm sorry to have to know it myself. But—" he gave an exasperated gesture, "that's the world we're living in, right? It's the world we need to change and defend, and that's not going to happen with swords and blood."

"Then why are you training defenders?" asked a man at the front of the class.

"Good question. When the war comes, I want you to be able to defend *yourselves* first, and Alboras if you're able and willing," Shanthah said. "We're not a war academy. While there are elective courses on fighting and the politics of war, we are training you with education. The only way to end this war is to eliminate ignorance. Swords and blood will always remain, I know that. You know that." He screwed up his face, and Nadezhda could see tears form in the corners of his eyes. "But I also know that we can win this war in a way that doesn't end with so much death. And that's why a focus of this academy is to help you learn to think, not just how to fight. You will be the army of Alboras and Sangora that will save the world without causing bloodshed.

"For that reason, it is the express interest and command of the leadership of this school that you do not attack Thanatanos. We will defend our homes from them, if need be, but we will not draw first blood. Anyone who goes against that rule will be removed from the academy, and we will work with Thannish diplomats to ensure that you are brought to justice. Is that clear?"

The classroom nodded in a jumble of yeses.

"Now!" Shanthah exclaimed, hopping back onto the desk as his jolly demeaner returned. "I'd like for you to meet some of your teachers here at the academy. Please, come forward!"

With a sweeping gesture, he invited some people standing at the back of the classroom to come forward. They filed to the front and stood at either side of Shanthah's desk.

"You'll be assigned to classes, workshops, and other similar activities based on your abilities or lack thereof. Those with similar powers as you will be able to help you progress and use your powers correctly and productively. Bullying and harmful competition won't be tolerated, of course, especially against those without powers. And, of course, you'll have classes other than learning to use your powers. Now. Will any healers in the room please stand, raise your hand, hoot or holler, scream, or make yourselves known in any way you see fit?"

About a dozen students, including Ana, stood around the room; some called out, while others simply raised their hands in silence. Ana let out an awkward, "Woo!"

As she sat down, Nadezhda leaned forward.

"*So* embarrassing," she whispered.

"Let me introduce Ms. Alia Shadid," Shanthah said, and a petite, brown skinned Kurashian woman stepped forward to offer a wave and a smile. "Or rather, would you like to introduce yourself?"

"Sure, thank you, Shanthah," Alia said. "My name is Alia Shadid, like he said. I am originally from Kurash, but I live here in Alboras now. I have family in Talohira, so I guess you can say I've been all over the world, which is fun. I will lead courses on beginner and advanced healing techniques both with and without powers. I'll also be teaching Kurashic language classes, and I oversee the main healing center in Balgorod. If any of the healers here would like to volunteer there, please let me know, and I'll arrange it. Thank you!"

She stepped back, and a burly man with dark skin and a thick black beard stepped forward with a wave of a large hand.

"Josman Faros, everyone," Shanthah said to introduce the man. "Watch this!"

Shanthah drew a hidden dagger, and to everyone's surprise, he thrust it into Josman's chest, but the blade bent and then shattered as it struck his sternum. Josman grabbed the blade and tossed it in the trash can next to Shanthah's desk.

"Thank you for that," Josman said with a booming laugh. "We didn't plan that, by the way."

"What in the world?" Nadezhda whispered to Ana.

"He's a Steelskin," Ana replied. "Armored skin."

Nadezhda gave a thumbs up as Shanthah continued.

"Mr. Faros, our illustrious own captain of the guard, will be teaching Thannish language courses to those of you who need it, some military tactic courses, as well as some art courses"

Nadezhda smiled to herself and kicked her feet in joy; she'd always wanted to try art classes. She'd drawn silly figures as a child, but perhaps, this would be a good time to develop her skills. Suddenly, her heart dropped—Karel had loved to paint. She hadn't thought of him since leaving her room.

She looked over the rest of the teachers as Shanthah introduced a professor of geography from Doftaan named Ivona Reitera and then a man named Daniel Elafris—an odd coincidence, that the man had such the same surname as the devil himself—he would teach philosophy, history, and science courses.

Nadezhda jumped as she met the eyes of a Kurashian man standing next to Alia; she averted her gaze, but she could still feel his lingering on her. She felt a strange tingling coming from the gem in her pocket, and then an odd sensation as if the Voice were tunneling into her mind. Was it hiding from the Kurashian man? She placed a hand over the gem, which thrummed with life.

She didn't pay attention as Shanthah introduced Francesca Serbana, professor of Mathematics, or two Generals, Anca Zamfir and Rayna Cotula who would co-teach military strategy, and she didn't even care when Ruta Vaal was introduced as the teacher of politics, international relations, and the Sangoran language.

Why didn't she care? She was so excited about all those things. It didn't make sense. Was the Voice draining her of her excitement somehow? It wasn't until the Kurashian man stepped forward that her attention turned away from thoughts of the Voice.

"Kamil Ramzi, our resident master Mindspeaker," Shanthah said. Kamil waved, and then his voice filled the minds of everyone in the room.

"Hello, everyone. Like Alia, I hail from Kurash, and I am excited to meet each of our ten Mindspeakers in the room. Can I have each of you stand?"

Nine Mindspeakers-to-be stood, and people began to mutter as they noticed that there was one missing. Kamil turned his gaze back to Nadezhda before he motioned for her.

"Me?" Nadezhda asked. Kamil nodded with a welcoming smile. "Oh, no, I can just see people's emotions. I'm not a Mindspeaker. Sorry!"

She shifted uncomfortably in her seat, and the gem in her pocket seemed to do the same.

"Sometimes powers of the mind overlap. Your own powers as a Soulreader may have manifested this way, but I can sense in you the ability to Mindspeak," Kamil said telepathically. Ana turned to her with an excited expression as Kamil addressed the class. *"Soulreaders have an ability called empathetic synesthesia where they can actually see and feel your emotions, even if you don't know they're there! They can possess many of the same abilities as Mindspeakers, but not the other way around. What a pleasure to have you here!"*

"Oh, okay then. Nadezhda. Yes, hi, Nadezhda. I'm Nadezhda," she said, knowing she had said her name far, far, too many times, especially since no one else had said theirs. "Oh dear," she muttered to Ana as she sat.

"So embarrassing," Ana repeated with a quick wink.

She could feel the Voice's disappointment about her actions, for whatever reason. She'd have to ask later, but it troubled her. Had Kamil been looking at her because he sensed the Voice's gem in her pocket, or did he truly believe she was a Mindspeaker? Or perhaps as—what had Kamil called it? A Soulreader? Perhaps because she was a Soulreader, that's what the Voice had meant when it said she was the only one that could understand it.

"Kamil will be co-leading the class on mental abilities with my hilarious, lovely, drop-dead gorgeous, genius of a fiancé, Hanna Samsa," Shanthah said, leaping down from the desk to greet her as she stepped forward with a wave. "Mindspeakers and Telekinetiks will meet together."

He interpreted for the auburn-haired woman as she signed to the class.

"Thank you for the warm welcome, everyone," Shanthah interpreted. "I am—she is, rather—excited to get to know each of you, and I promise you won't all have to learn to sign to come to my classes, but you will if you want to come to my bar in town."

A laugh went up across the room as Shanthah added his own words, "But you'll be her favorite if you do."

He smiled and gestured for a well-dressed Sangoran woman in a dark suit to step forward. They spoke in a hushed tone for a moment; Shanthah nodded and gestured for her to step forward.

"My name is Raluca, sister of the former queen of Sangora, Codruta," she said. "I'll be co-teaching a course on non-mental abilities with Empress Bartunek, who apologizes that she couldn't be here today."

Ana turned around with an excited expression, and Nadezhda grabbed her shoulder with a wide smile to acknowledge her new friend's excitement. Across the chamber, others did the same until Shanthah silenced them.

She didn't hear what Shanthah said next as the Voice filled her mind for a brief moment.

"Stay away from Kamil Ramzi. He is a dangerous man."

Laughter filled the room, and Nadezhda joined in, although she had not heard Shanthah's joke.

"He's so funny, right?" Ana whispered to Nadezhda.

"What? Oh, yeah."

She offered a smile, but knew it wasn't convincing. Ana cocked her head and looked into Nadezhda's eyes for a long moment until Shanthah spoke again.

"And now that you've met most of your professors, I want to address one last thing. Several years ago, before King Valistaran the second took power, of course, Talohira set up slave camps to enslave people with abilities. Many of you may have been a prisoner there. I was. Hana, Kamil and Josman were. So was Empress Mara if you can believe it.

"But I want to assure you that that is not our intention here. You are *safe* here. You can come and go as you please. We will feed you and take care of you, but if you choose to live outside the fortress or leave altogether, there is nothing stopping you.

"But once again, I am thrilled to welcome you to the Balgorod Academy of the Hidden Flame, and I'll be even happier to talk to any of you if you see me around the fortress or at Hanna's Bar—for those of you who are old enough to get in, of course."

Another laugh filled the chamber, but Nadezhda felt the gem's whispers crawling up her spine to her mind. As Shanthah dismissed the class, Nadezhda said a hurried goodbye to Ana and then was the first out of the door.

CHAPTER FOUR
THE GOD MIRROR

Mara pulled her cloak around her body while Hippo let out anxious grunts as he stomped across the frozen earth through the blizzard. For whatever reason, the storm around the ruins of the once great city had not stopped for two years.

Everything before her was obscured in a blanket of white. She considered turning back, but she could sense a presence within the storm. One that she feared above all else, but the very one she sought.

Mara drew the fur collar of her cloak closer to her neck as the icy chill bit into her skin. The howling winds and driving snow obscured their path forward and hid the way back, but Hippo pressed onward. Every time she tried to convince herself to turn away, she felt an eerie prickling on the back of her neck and the irresistible pull to find the god she prayed was dead.

Soon enough, Hippo broke through the wall of swirling snow, and Mara let out a deep breath as she beheld the destruction she had caused two years prior when she unleashed the Weapons of Ages Past.

Most of the city had been reduced to charred rubble, and at its center was a deep, circular of blackened earth. They'd thought Thanatan was dead that day.

Recent events suggested they were wrong.

"Well, we're back, Hipp," Mara said.

He bowed, and she climbed off his back before gliding to the ground on her dark wings. She marveled at the curious storm but couldn't help but look in horror at the destruction around her.

Nitra: The city she had destroyed twice—or what was left of it.

"You coming with me?" Mara asked. Hippo shook his massive head and backed away from the crater. "Understandable…Don't want to see your old master, huh? Neither do I, buddy…Neither do I."

She raised her hand to pat the front of his snout, resulting in another puff of foul air. She turned away and delved straight into the storm.

The ground cracked under her feet as she stood upon the precipice of the vast pit. It should have been pitch dark at the center of the storm, but the crater was illuminated by a pale, green glow.

She glided down into the pit toward the light.

The far side of the crater was obscured in darkness, but she guessed it had to be at least a hundred meters to where her keen Sangoran vision and the dim glow failed. She glanced over her shoulder as she felt something akin to a breath on the back of her neck. She placed a cautious hand there as a chill crawled down her spine.

She whirled around, but no one was there. She sighed in relief and reached out to touch the walls of the crater. At first, she thought they were coated in ice, but as she brushed the snow off the jagged surface with her fingertips, she found it oddly warm.

Intrigued, she tried to snap off one of the seemingly random geometric patterns of crystal jutting out of the cliff face, but to no avail.

The Empress of Blood took a deep breath and ventured into light. Whispers and disembodied voices followed her with every uneasy step over the crystals lining the pit. Once again, she glanced over her shoulder to find no one there.

She pressed on.

"I know you're there," she called into the darkness.

For a moment, relief flowed through her in the silence. However, she found a small part of herself disappointed that no one answered.

Until someone did.

"I knew you would come."

Mara stopped in her tracks and extended her bladed wings high over her head. She sensed a presence circling her, and from the corner of her eye, a darkness taunted her, reflected in the pillars of diamond around her. She turned to face it and only saw her own image in the crude mirror looking back at her, and she leapt in surprise.

The source of the eerie light was a towering outcrop of diamond spikes protruding from the darkness at the center of the crater. She approached with caution and curiosity, and the incessant darkness lurked at the edge of her vision.

Mara turned her head, and the shadows vanished, reappearing on her other side, just out of sight. She shut her eyes and let out one long, deep breath.

"Why are you haunting us?"

"*Why do you seek out a dead god?*"

"Answer the damn question."

"*How else would I get you here? I thought you would both come.*"

Mara opened her eyes expecting to see someone standing there, only to see the crystal mass looming before her.

"What do you want?" she asked.

"*The same thing as you.*"

Mara hesitated for a moment, fearing the answer. "And what is that?"

"*Revenge. Justice,*" the voice in her mind said as the presence lurked just out of sight. "*Call it whatever you want. It's all the same.*"

"Well, I'm here. Come out and face me," Mara said, her arms outstretched. A dark feeling of emptiness filled the pit in her stomach as deep laughter echoed around the crater.

"*No, you misunderstand. I wanted you to come to enact my justice.*"

"And why would I do that?"

"*I have many things that you want. Knowledge. Healing. A path to regain your power…Just to name a few.*"

The scar on the scar on the shaved side of her head. It prickled as if the dark presence had brushed a cold finger along her skin.

"Why me?"

"*Why? Perhaps, I want to watch you fail. Or maybe, I just want to reward the women who truly made me a god.*"

"What are you talking about?" Mara asked. "We *killed* you. We burned you and this horrible city to the ground."

"*Yet here I am speaking to you. I was bound to a physical form, just as you are now. But now? You've bonded me to all of creation. I am the eternal abyss, the voice in the night, the nightmare that will haunt you until your death.*"

The pit in Mara's stomach lurched, and she leaned against the mass of jagged crystal obelisks. And then, she felt it again. The breath on the back of her neck. She lashed out with her bladed wings, and once again, the darkness shifted just out of sight, but she knew it was there, reflected on the diamonds. But no matter where she looked, it evaded her gaze.

"If not revenge on me or Hanna…Who else?" Mara asked, beginning to examine the mass of crystal.

"*On whom else, indeed.*"

"You tell me," Mara said, exasperated.

"*My Pure haven't turned wild, and they still serve Thanatanos, as was my plan. Why do you think that is?*"

"Someone else is controlling them," Mara said.

Her mind turned to Drahomir, but she knew that he had led his people, a faction of the Faceless, thousands of miles east of their world.

"*A keen observation. Who?*"

And then it all made sense. The cult of the Purists. The secret for which they were killing people with powers. The reason Thanatan had been pulling Hanna towards Nitra. The very reason Mara was standing in the crater now.

"Your Magistrate is still alive," Mara said, "and you want me to kill her."

"*Smart girl.*"

"Do it yourself. Why would I help you?" Mara asked as she made her way around the mass of crystals. "Or better yet why not have those cultists of yours do it?"

As she waited for a response, she realized the mass of jagged protruding diamond wasn't random at all; it was an interlocking pattern of crystal that formed a seat in the very center of the crater.

A throne. Mara scoffed.

"You think I'm going to help you for *this?* What, you want me to rule this dead city?" She shook her head and turned away from the crystal throne.

"*Is there anyone more fitting to rule this place? Mara Bartunek, destroyer of Nitra: Queen of the Damned.*"

Mara paused and turned in her anger back to the throne as if Thanatan himself were seated upon it. Instead, she once again saw her own face staring back at her from the mirrored surface. She pointed one accusatory finger at the throne.

"I'm leaving."

"*I know that you are dying, Mara, and I know what has become of your brother.*"

"Seriously? To what desperate depths has the dead god of Thanatanos fallen that he is resorting to whatever *this* is."

"To the same depths that brought you here. We're both desperate. Don't try to convince me otherwise."

Mara massaged the bridge of her nose and let out a dark chuckle. She took a few steps toward the crystal throne.

"So, what? You fix my broken brain and tell me where my brother is, and I kill the woman who stole your glory from you? This does not seem like a fair trade. She has everything you ever wanted while you are stuck here, and I bet that just kills you, doesn't it? I could leave right now, and you'd be stuck in your personal hell."

"Again, you misunderstand. I do not want you to kill the Magistrate. I want to kill her."

"Grow some hands and do it yourself, then!"

"No, the Magistrate will die by your hand," Thanatan's voice echoed in her mind. *"But I shall be your blade."*

Mara went silent, waiting for Thanatan to continue. She watched her own reflection in the throne staring back at her. She jumped, startled when it reached out its hand toward her. The empress took a curious step toward the throne, gripping the jagged, diamond armrest to pull herself up.

Her reflection held something in its right hand; it reached out of the glass of the throne with its left, diamonds twisting from the surface to form a hand. Mara extended her own hand but hesitated for a moment. And then, with trembling intrepidity, she gazed into the soulless face of her diamond reflection and took her hand.

The diamond Mara helped her step up to the throne and melted back into the mirror as she sat upon the crystal seat.

A million questions thundered in Mara's mind, but one most of all.

What was she doing?

Mara twisted around as the diamond hand of her reflection brushed her neck, and then the other hand appeared, shattering it at the elbow. Mara screamed and leapt up from the chair as the crystal arm tumbled to her feet.

"No! I'm done! What the fresh hell is this?!"

"*As I said.*"

Mara raised her hands in defiance as she stepped down the crystal steps leading to the throne, but she turned around to face the seat again.

"What do you want from me?" Mara asked in exasperation. "Enough of this, demon."

"*Take what I've given you. Take it to Kurash; I know you intend to return there soon. There is a device there called the Forge of Ohun, deep in the desert. Forge this crystal into whatever weapon you see fit. I shall guide you.*"

"Again, why?!"

"*The Magistrate's telepathic abilities dwarf even my own, and they have only grown since my defeat. I once had hold over her, but now my grip is broken. Without me, even you stand no chance. She has caused more suffering than perhaps anyone else in your time.*"

"You will be my blade," Mara said in a soft voice, echoing Thanatan's earlier words. "More than a metaphor."

"*Quite.*"

"And my brother?" Mara asked.

"*You will find out soon enough, I do not believe you are ready to know the truth.*"

Mara's heart pounded. What had become of her brother?

"Ready, or worthy?"

"Ready. The truth would drive you mad."

She stepped back toward the throne and with disgust and hesitation, took the severed arm of her glassy reflection, all the while thinking of the horrible things she'd seen in the slave camp in Adess. *That* was the reason she was doing this.

As she lifted the chunk of crystal, the sky above parted, and a gleaming beam of sunlight broke through the storm, illuminating the crystal throne. It glittered with the light of infinite stars, entrancing Mara in its beauty.

"It can all be yours. Doftaan awaits, Godslayer."

Mara took a deep breath and shot into the sky through the break in the clouds. Hippo soared up to meet her, and as she landed on his back, the storm swirled beneath her, and the throne and Thanatan's domain were lost to view.

CHAPTER FIVE
HANNA'S

A weathered sign with bright orange lettering swayed back and forth above the door to an old, but newly refurbished, pub. Mara smiled as she looked at it, remembering the day that she, Aleksander, Hanna, and Shanthah had carved and painted it. It had taken all afternoon down by the river, and Shanthah had sliced his fingers so many times that he'd given up trying to carve it. Hanna took over, finishing the sign without cutting herself even once.

Mara looked at the letters and smiled: *Hanna's.*

She pulled the fur hood from her head and pressed the door open. The warmth of the homey bar welcomed her as she shook the snow from her raven feather hair. She glanced toward the bar to see Hanna with her back turned to her while serving a group of young Sangoran men at the end of the bar.

Mara smiled again and hung her fur coat on a hook near the door before stowing her thick woolen gloves in the coat's pocket. Before the Battle of Ages Past, Mara would have called out to her friend, but Hanna had been rendered deaf by the hellish explosion they had caused to destroy Thanatan's physical body.

The Sangoran men caught sight of Mara and did a double take; a few women called out to her in greeting, and she offered a friendly wave in return. The men at the bar carried their drinks to a booth in the corner, watching Mara as she approached Hanna. Their stares were not conspicuous.

Hanna turned, brushing her long hair from her eyes, and then her face broke out into a glowing smile.

She leapt onto the bar and pulled Mara into a tight hug, wrapping her arms and legs around her while still sitting atop the bar. Mara laughed and pulled Hanna close before backing up to sign to her friend.

"*You're back!*" Hanna signed, her hands trembling with excitement. To Mara's relief, she said nothing about leaving her behind. "*Before you get started, I have to show you something.*"

"What is it?" Mara asked and signed.

Hanna said nothing but pointed over her shoulder. Mara followed her gaze and then broke out into bright laughter that filled the bar.

There, on the menu board above Hanna's head was the name of a new drink: The Empress of Blood.

"*I've never felt more honored,*" Mara signed with a wide smile, pulling her friend into another hug. "*What's in it?*"

Hanna scooted back on the bar and used her telekinesis to pull a bottle of alcohol from one shelf and some other ingredients from under the counter, mixed the drink, poured it into a hardy mug, and passed it over to Mara.

"This is the cup you put it in? *So* elegant," Mara said and signed. Hanna nodded as Mara took a sip of the 'Empress of Blood.' Her eyes widened. "I think I'll need two of these bad boys."

"*Two Empresses of Blood? Sounds like my kind of party,*" Hanna signed with an exaggerated wink.

Mara buried her face in her hands and shook her head. After mixing two more drinks, the two women settled into an empty booth on the far side of the bar with their drinks. Hanna levitated a wooden spoon to poke her employee at the other side of the bar to take her place.

"*Lucky is a good worker. She likes bartending way more than being a prison guard,*" Hanna signed.

Liliana, or Lucky, as Hanna referred to her, had been a prison guard in Doftaan until the prison was destroyed; she had helped Hanna escape, and she now lived and worked in Balgorod.

Hanna set down Mara's second 'Empress of Blood' and lifted her own drink to her lips.

"*You know, Shanthah says his drink, 'The Phantom' isn't as good as yours, and he needs another,*" Hanna signed with one hand as she took a sip. "*Also, I can talk and drink at the same time now. Silver lining, I guess?*"

"*Good to know I'm more appetizing than your fiancé,*" Mara signed back. "*I'm sure he'd like one called Mistress of Dusk.*"

Hanna snorted with laughter.

"*Given up trying to make him use 'Master of Dusk'?*" Hanna replied before taking her warm mug in both hands.

"No, you know I don't care," Mara replied. She smiled and downed the rest of the first 'Empress of Blood.' "I'm trying to think of a new title anyway. That one's outdated and reeks of my predecessors and a dark time in Sangora's history."

She took a sip.

"*So, I assume you found something in Adess you didn't like if you're that keen to down two 'Empresses of Blood',*" Hanna signed, a look of concern etched on her face.

Mara just nodded. She knew Hanna knew exactly where she'd been. Hanna took a deep breath but said nothing, taking a long swig from her mug.

"It was horrible," Mara said at long last. Her fingers trembled as she signed, "*Like nothing I've ever seen.*"

"*And Elafris knows we've both seen some horrible things,*" Hanna signed back.

Mara debated telling her about Thanatan's offer, mission, and the chunk of crystal in her satchel, but she decided to keep it to herself.

"*You can tell me about it, you know,*" Hanna signed. "*But it might need to wait. The others are coming soon for Josman's birthday. You remembered that was today, right?*"

Mara's head slumped and she let her forehead strike the table. With her head still pressed against the oak table, she signed with a huge frown, "*I'm a horrible friend.*"

"*You're just a stressed friend. You've been very distracted from 'real life' lately,*" Hanna corrected, emphasizing the word 'stressed' with a flourish of her fingers. *"With good reason, so I think you get a pass. You're here—he won't know, you know. Unless, you know, you didn't bring him a present."*

Mara smiled and shook her head. She got up and hurried to the bar, and with a flap of her wings, stood upon the counter. Hanna waited as Mara wrote something in chalk on the blackboard. She climbed down and plopped back down next to Hanna, taking another sip of her drink.

"What did you do?"

"If he asks, I convinced you to name a drink after him too," Mara signed.

"Done and done, although that does seem more like a gift from me. What's it called?"

"An 'unbreakable'."

"Love it. Consider it done," Hanna signed. For a few moments, they discussed what should go into the drink before Hanna said, *"Now, about your recent, and, I assume, very troubling adventure…"*

Mara scooted her mug closer, staring at the crimson liquid. She pursed her lips tightly and shook her head, trying to keep the tears from welling up in the corner of her eyes. She took a deep breath and glanced up at the ceiling for a few seconds. Hanna had not taken her eyes off the empress for a moment. At last, Mara met her gaze.

"Thanatanos has set up some prison camps," Mara said and signed, her hands trembling. "Together with Florenta's government, I think."

"You're serious?"

"Yes. As much as a nightmare as ours was, I can't even describe how horrible what I saw was." Her voice and fingers both shook now. "There are thousands of soldiers packing people into tiny barracks and forced them to stand in the cold for no reason other than to torture them. We were slaves used to build Talohira—not to justify what they did, but…this camp was just to torture—Oh, gods, Hanna— It's another Sangoran genocide, and I can't stop it. They're just sick dogs in a kennel, waiting to be killed."

Hanna scrunched her eyebrows together and screwed up her mouth, deep in thought. She stared into one of the bar's two fireplaces for a moment, watching the crackling flame.

"*Are they those Purist cultists, or actual Thannish soldiers?*"

"Both," Mara replied. "It seems the Thannish army is supporting the camps and what Verahim is doing. Even if they're just following orders, they're guilty of perpetrating the king's crimes."

"*What do we do?*" Hanna signed.

"I don't know," Mara replied, anxiously picking at a hangnail on her thumb as her knee began to bounce beneath the table. "What *can* we do? It's in a really, really, remote part of Sangora called the plains of Adess."

Hanna sighed and grasped Mara's hand and gave it a squeeze. As she looked out the window, her face lit up, although she was unable to mask the thinly veiled worry that managed to peek through.

Mara followed her gaze to see Josman, Shanthah, and Kamil peeking through the window of Hanna's bar at them. Shanthah and Josman had their faces pressed against the glass, distorting them into horrendous shapes as Kamil held his arms across his chest, doubled over in laughter. Fresh snow began to flutter down around them.

As Josman and Kamil pulled their faces away from the window and made their way to the door, Shanthah fogged up the glass with his breath and drew a large heart and then tried to write 'HANNA' and 'MARA' backwards within it but failed to correctly form the R in Mara's name. Mara let out a cheery laugh, and Hanna blew him a kiss through the window as Kamil, Alia, and Aleksander grouped together to try to see through as well, pushing Shanthah out of the way.

Mara's heart leapt as she caught sight of Aleksander, who had been undercover gathering intelligence in Thanatanos and therefore gone from Balgorod for several months. She smiled and waved, and Aleksander leapt up and down like a happy puppy.

Shanthah pushed open the door with a friendly, "Hello, there!" Josman followed close behind, leading the rest of their friends into the bar.

"Happy birthday, Josman!" Mara exclaimed.

Hanna swung her legs out from beneath the table and stood to her their massive friend, planting a friendly kiss on his cheek.

"Ah, Mara!" Josman boomed. "Welcome home, little miss Empress!"

Mara stood and wrapped her arms around Josman's torso; his mighty arms engulfed her in a friendly embrace, and he clapped her on the back.

"Lookin' good for twenty-nine," Mara said with a smile. At that, Josman broke out into a fit of raucous laughter.

"Yeah, I've had quite a few twenty-nineth birthdays at this point. Let's not say how many," Josman said.

"Well, I just used up my one and only 'twenty-nine', and now I'm an old maid, just like you," Mara replied. Josman jostled her hair with a meaty hand, and she chuckled as she brushed it back into place with her fingers.

"Yeah, well, this *old maid* needs a drink," he replied.

"On it!" Shanthah exclaimed, signing with Hanna to arrange a round of drinks. Hanna winked and squeezed Josman's arm before leading him to the bar.

Mara watched with joy as Josman saw the new drink that she had invented for him.

"Happy birthday, Jos!" Mara exclaimed, gesturing to herself.

"I've been trying to get a drink named after me for months! Did you do this?" Josman asked. Mara nodded with enthusiasm, and Josman gave a joyous shout, trying to sign to Hanna for the drink.

"Mara, how do you sign unbreakable?" Josman asked.

Mara demonstrated the sign then said, "but don't worry about it, buddy, I think Hanna already knows what you want to order." She gestured to Hanna, who was now preparing several drinks.

Alia stepped around Josman and stood up on her tippy toes to kiss him softly on the cheek.

Aleksander skipped the bar and greeted Mara with a warm hug; she pressed her face into his shoulder and let out a silent sigh, trying to let the embrace replace the horrors she had seen over the last few days. She knew nothing would, but it was comforting, nonetheless.

"Welcome home, you," Mara said.

For a moment, she felt the pull to kiss him, but after a moment of hesitation, she led him by the hand to their booth. She took her place across from him and scooted her last 'Empress of Blood' toward her.

"Yeah, you too. How have you been? I've heard you've been away?" Aleksander asked, stuttering slightly through the sentence. With a soft expression, Mara's memory turned to the awkward boy Aleksander had been when they first met. After all these years, that's who he truly still was. And that was why she felt the way she did.

"You know we're both horrible at small-talk," Mara said with a wink. "Let's go ahead and skip that."

"That we are," Aleksander said with a nod. "So, where'd you go? Hanna seemed very worried. Everything okay?"

Mara's feigned smile in response was anything but convincing, and Aleksander raised an accusatory eyebrow.

"I think you can read me well enough to know the answer there," Mara said with a dark chuckle. She took a sip from the mug and turned in the booth, pulling her knees up to her chest and resting her feet on the cushion.

"I do, yeah," Aleksander said. "But I've also been gone for a few months. A lot can happen in that time."

"I took Hippo and went to Terman," Mara said.

"Oh," Aleksander said, staring at the drink in Mara's hand. "I assume that's the reason you've had two of those already."

"Yeah," Mara said, glancing at the second, empty mug. "So, you know…" She trailed off. Aleksander waited for her to speak, but she never did.

"Yeah," was Aleksander's only response.

"What do you think I should do?" she asked.

"What do you want to do?"

She shrugged. "I feel like I'm out of options."

She considered bringing up her visit to Nitra, but Aleksander replied before she could.

"I was going to bring this up later in an official meeting or something, but if you've seen what I think you've seen, I don't think you can wait," He stared into Mara's crystal blue eyes reflecting the light of the warm hearth. "The Thannish army and navy are almost entirely supportive of what Verahim is doing with the camps and how he's administering things in Thanatanos. The people less so, but many do. Most of them do support that alliance with the Faceless—they feel safe with that blasted wall those things have constructed along the border, and most people don't need to work if they don't want to…They don't know the evil that's given them their prosperity. I'm not sure they'd care if they did."

"It was horrible."

"I know," Aleksander said. "I know you're probably beating yourself up in your mind right now about it."

"Gonna tell me to stop?"

"No, of course not," Aleksander said. Mara scooted her mug back and forth across the table from hand to hand as Aleksander cocked his head.

"Oh," Mara said, taken aback. "I guess I'm just used to people doing that. Can I be completely candid?"

"I'd be disappointed if you were anything but," Aleksander replied.

"Here, try this first." Mara handed her mug to Aleksander, who took a long sip. "It kills me, completely kills me, that I can't help them. If I was in Doftaan, I could give one order and have a battalion sent to Terman to liberate the people in the camps and bring them home. I could set them all free. But instead—"

"You're blaming yourself," Aleksander said. "And before you ask, I'm not telling you not to. I know you, and I know that won't do any good."

"Hanna says it isn't my fault," Mara said. "I like to believe her, but…" She trailed off with a shrug before trying to take another sip of her drink only to find it empty. "You drank the rest of my drink?!"

"Hanna's a smart lady," Aleksander said. "And my opinion is probably the same as hers. The only way this would really be your fault is if you were the one who ordered that the camps be set up and to start the famine, and—"

"The famine?" Mara asked. Concern washed over her face in the dim torchlight splashing over her face from outside the frosted glass window. "What famine?"

Aleksander seemed taken aback. "You don't know?"

"I know about the camps, but only that they're there. Nothing else."

"Oh, gods, Mara," Aleksander said, letting out a slow breath. She waited, scooting her empty mug back and forth between her hands. "Whoever is in charge in Doftaan—they're saying it's you, as you know, probably—whoever's in charge in Doftaan is in league with my brother, and, oh, Mara…" Mara took his hand. He smiled as he tried to regain his composure and formulate his words properly.

Hanna had finished pouring everyone's drinks, and they were now coming over. Josman pushed a second, long table next to the small booth, and Kamil and Shanthah were busy scooting wooden chairs next to it for everyone.

When Aleksander spoke again, he did so in a hushed tone so the others wouldn't overhear.

"At Doftaan's request, Verahim sent peace-keeping troops to stop another revolution like the one here in Alboras," he said quickly as the others sat down, still chatting and laughing amongst themselves. "They've created a wall to prevent food or outside forces from getting in. They're starving everyone to quell any further insurrections, and it's not just those involved in the revolution that are suffering. They are justifying it by saying they're getting rid of Florenta's people here."

"Oh my goodness," Mara whispered, a tear rolling down her cheek. "How many are dead?"

Aleksander shrugged. "Around ten thousand so far. More every day."

"And the camps—the people involved in the revolution?"

"That's what I thought at first, but after doing more research, it's not quite the case," Aleksander responded. "Once most of those involved in the revolution were out of the question, Doftaan and my brother's forces began rounding up any and all Termani people, even ones who were no threat to them. They're trying to—and these aren't my words—cleanse the state of their race and make it safe for Thans."

Mara's stomach dropped. The Termani were a minority ethnic group in their own northern Sangoran state of Terman, and she feared that it was a result of the Alborans' revolution in Balgorod and what had used to be called Karpaska.

"We'll talk later," Mara said, squeezing his hand.

"Yeah. I promise. The last few months have been pretty heavy finding all this out. I'm sorry you had to see it too," Aleksander said. "I know the feeling, although maybe not quite like you do...But at least, well, at least we can go through it together."

Mara squeezed his hand, but before she could respond, Shanthah sat down in the booth next to Aleksander and clapped him on the back.

"You forgot this, but don't worry, I'll cover you," Shanthah said, scooting a drink in front of Aleksander.

"I can always depend on you," Aleksander responded with a laugh. "What is it?"

"Hanna's new drink, the 'Empress of Blood' Shanthah said. "It's so much better than the drink named after me. You should try Josman's new drink too; it tastes just like you'd expect."

"Strong?" Aleksander asked. "Or smelly?"

Josman let out a raucous guffaw, spilling some of his drink. "Both, I hope!"

"Hey, I invented that drink!" Mara exclaimed.

"Exactly right!" Shanthah said. "You're many things, miss Empress of Blood, but you're a lousy barmaid."

An hour of merry friendship passed with no talk of the war. Eventually, Mara's smile lit up between rosy cheeks as the alcohol convinced her to begin singing.

"Šaaaaslyv rotheeeendan!" Mara exclaimed, the first two words of the traditional Sangoran song for celebrating birthdays. After that, the song broke down into whatever melody and tempo the singers wanted to use to regale their victim, repeating the words "šaslyv rothendan" over and over in different ways.

Shanthah sang it as operatic as possible, and Mara stood to join him atop the table, sharing the same dramatic tune as the others began their own melodies. When the song was over, Josman cheered, and Shanthah and Mara bowed.

"A wonderful concert fit for the courts of Doftaan!" Aleksander exclaimed, helping Mara down from the table. They sat back behind the booth.

Aleksander strained his arm to reach his mug and smiled as he took a sip from the mug of 'Empress of Blood.'

"Not the first time you've had the Empress of Blood on your lips, is it?" Mara asked just loud enough for him to hear. He coughed and spat up the drink, hacking through an awkward chuckle, and Mara roared with laughter at her own joke.

"You are definitely drunk, Mar."

Mara's mischievous smirk caused the bridge of her nose to wrinkle. "Yup."

They spent several more hours enjoying one another's company, sharing funny stories and memories, laughing, and playing some games with a pile of cards Hanna had produced from behind the bar. At last, when Shanthah stood upon the table again, Josman deemed it time to call it a night, pulling his friend from the table before he could remove his shirt.

"Booo, no!" Hanna shouted at Josman, and then to Shanthah, 'Take it ooooff!'

Shanthah reached for his fourth drink on the table, but Aleksander extended his hand before he could reach it. He snapped his thumb and forefinger to let a spark of flame fly, setting the alcohol inside ablaze.

Shanthah howled in despair and defeat as Josman carried Shanthah outside and dropped him into the snow. Kamil and Aleksander hurried to the door; Aleksander turned to Mara, who winked and gestured in Shanthah's direction.

"What are you waiting for? Go get him!"

Aleksander and Kamil rushed outside like little children excited to play with their friends. Shanthah had vanished long enough to evade Josman, but his drunken stumbling gave away his position as he ran into the low fence outside the bar.

The snow fell from it as he struck it and rematerialized on the ground.

As Josman hurried toward him calling his name, Shanthah reached up and grabbed a low branch laden with snow, causing it to fall on Josman, Aleksander, and himself. Aleksander tossed up a curtain of flame to melt the cascade of white just before it buried him.

Josman caught Shanthah in a bear hug and tossed him into the snow again. As he raised his fists in victory, Aleksander dumped a handful of snow down the back of his shirt. Josman yelped, and then the snowballs began to fly.

Their voices and laughter filled the night air.

CHAPTER SIX

THE SILVER KEY

As the men frolicked and played in the snow like happy children, Hanna scooted closer to Mara, and Alia took Aleksander's spot.

"Why hello, you two lovely humans," Mara said with a smile.

"How are you, lady?" Alia asked as Hanna cuddled next to Mara, taking her hand. Hanna shut her eyes, and Mara signed in her hand while she simultaneously spoke to Alia in Kurashic. The form of physical contact signing was a useful characteristic of Sangoran sign language, one that Thannish sign lacked.

"Exhausted," Mara answered.

"When did you get back? We missed you at the academy's beginning of semester feast and ball," Alia said. She then added, "And, you know, everything else."

Mara shook her head and pressed her fingers to her eyes. "I am so sorry about being so absent."

"Oh, no, honey, no, I'm not trying to guilt you. I know what you were doing was more important than a school ball. Hanna told me where you went. We just miss you when you're gone, is all."

Hanna signed in Mara's hand, "*I know, I know. She asked where you were, and I blabbed.*"

Mara just signed back, "*I love you anyway, traitor.*"

"I just got back today, and thank you," Mara said with an appreciative smile. "I think I'm too drained emotionally and physically to talk about it, but I'll update you all in the next council meeting, or when you finally have me over to teach me to make that *kibbi.*"

Mara's mouth began to water thinking of the Kurashian dish Alia had prepared for her several weeks prior.

"Sounds like a deal," Alia said with a kind turn of the head. Her dark eyes always radiated a warm kindness, and they made Mara feel safe. A mother's eyes.

Mara drew a silver key from her pocket and set it down on the table. Nearly two years ago, she had risked her life to save Kadir, the Supreme One of Kurash, who had in turn, in a frustratingly selfless act, in Mara's opinion, given his life to save *her* before naming her the new Supreme One. She'd since visited Kurash, and the people were not receptive of the news. Many had accused her of murdering Kadir and called for her capture.

The other leaders of Kurash had not welcomed her and cast her out, rejecting her as the Supreme One's heir despite Kadir's last wishes. It had created a deep, lasting sense of guilt within her.

The silver metal seemed to glow without reflecting the light from the torches, and it was ever-so-slightly warm to the touch.

"What is that?" Alia asked with a particularly cautious edge to her words, as if she already knew the answer.

"I meant to show you this two years ago when the Supreme One made me his heir," Mara said. "I didn't know what it did, so I kept it secret."

She continued to tactilely sign in Hanna's hand to translate the conversation, and Hanna signed back, *"except from me."*

Mara chuckled as Hanna nestled in closer.

"I wanted to ask you and Kamil the same thing. If I had access to my library in Doftaan, I might be able to find the answer, but as I don't..." She trailed off. "There's nothing about it in Valistaran's library in Bukaral. I meant to ask you about this earlier, but with what happened in Kurash, it became less of a priority than helping my people *here*."

Alia looped the key's thin chain around her finger to pull it toward her. She examined the diamond set in its end, holding in her palm. Her eyes scanned over the elegant calligraphy scrawled on the side.

"I assume you understand what this says, right?" Alia asked. "It's in Old Kurashic, but you probably know that."

Mara nodded and recited the text without looking. "With the blinking of an eye, the stars are reunited."

"Kamil might have his own opinion, but we have an old legend in Kurash about a winking statue in the heart of the Ohun desert. A children's fable. Have you heard it?"

As Mara translated for her, Hanna slammed her fist on the table, her eyes wide and frantically signed, *"Like from the play?!"*

Alia cocked her head and tried to reply but didn't understand the final sign in the sentence and instead looked to Mara for a translation.

"Is there a play of some kind?" Mara asked.

"Yeah, a play?" Hanna also asked aloud, quite loudly.

"A play? What do you mean?"

Mara translated for Hanna as she signed.

"I'm from Vudapas in Thanatanos. A group of Kurashian performers came one summer and held a festival. They sold food and there were performers, but I remember watching a play called the Legend of the Star of Ohun," Mara translated Hanna's words.

"Oh, amazing! I never knew it was adapted into a play, let alone one that traveled to Thanatanos," Alia replied. She turned to Mara again to respond. "Hanna is right. In this story, there are two lovers, and each one holds half of a diamond that fit together."

Mara gestured to the Supreme One's key, and Alia shrugged.

"The legend is thought to be only a myth, but if the Supreme One gave this to you when he died…Well, it does make me wonder about that. He was not a sentimental man."

"Why is that?" Mara asked. "About the key, not his lack of sentimentality."

"Well, as you know, when the Supreme One chooses a new heir, it must be someone who has risked their life for the other, and the reverse. In our culture, it is the only thing that is seen as a way to be worthy of taking someone's rule. As a second choice, two people who have devoted their life to one another, like spouses or the best of friends. We think bloodline rule is ridiculous."

"What if that never happens?" Mara translated as Hanna signed into her hand. Alia shrugged.

"Then we just elect a new leader. But the longer the Chain of Sacrifice, as we call it, continues, the more beloved the new leader becomes. Anyway, in the story, the Star of Ohun, the man, obviously named Ohun, risks his life for his love, Handan. It turns out, the woman he loved was actually a moon goddess named Mehtap. So, long story short, in return, she granted him a kingdom, which is, of course, the origins of Kurash."

"The first Supreme One," Mara said. Pulling the key toward her. She felt its warmth in her hand, and Alia nodded.

"So the story goes," Alia said. "Back to that winking statue. There's a statue of her in the Ohun Desert that just before sunset on the day of the Festival for Mehtap, the longest day of the year, the light shines in such a way that only one eye is lit up, so it looks like it's winking. I've never seen it, but people often take pilgrimages there to see it."

"*Well, we have to go,*" Hanna signed. "*It has to be where this key leads. Maybe Mara would have better luck this time.*"

Mara bit her lip, Alia let out a deep breath as she contemplated how to answer Hanna's comment.

"Perhaps. The pilgrimages are very, very dangerous," Alia said. "Many people never make it back. There are guides who claim to know the way, but most of them are just scammers who guide their victims into the mouths of the snakes and monsters or murder them in their sleep."

"Those people don't have a friend named Hippo," Mara said with a wink.

"That they don't," Alia said with a smile. "We are lucky to know just such an individual."

Mara could sense Hippo rolling in the hills and playing somewhere to the north.

"So, what if we just flew there on his back?" Mara asked. "He can carry as much water and food as we need, and we could even set up a tent on his back to shield us from the sun."

"I don't see why not," Alia said with a shrug. "I have no idea where it is; like I said, I've never made the journey."

"Do you know anyone who has?" Mara asked, a sneaking suspicion nagging at her brain. "Maybe someone we both know…"

Alia chuckled. "Oh, yes, my dear ex-husband—your current one—tried once," Alia said with a smirk. Mara buried her face in her hands. "I know, I know, you hate when we mention that. But hey, the prince in the story found love with the diamond, maybe it'll give you some luck to get *out* of your marriage."

Hanna burst into laughter at that, but Mara just shook her head.

"One can only hope. Would he help us?" she asked.

"I don't see why not," Alia said. "We're all on relatively good terms, right?"

"You said he *tried.* I assume you mean that he wasn't successful."

"You're right about that. He thought that if he could find it, it'd make him the Supreme One of Kurash—the aspirations of a foolish young man who had just fallen in love, wanting to give a woman a kingdom. This is *way* before he was king of Talohira. Back when we, well…You know."

"But he did get a kingdom, and he didn't give it to you," Hanna signed.

"Not for lack of trying," Alia said. "Valistaran never found it, but his companion did."

"Who?" Mara asked.

"Kadir," Alia responded. Mara recoiled in shock.

"But I thought you implied that Kadir had risked his life for someone else," Mara asked.

"He did," Alia replied. "Not many people know this story. I honestly don't know the entire truth, but Valistaran told me what happened once…Again, before I tell you, I don't know how much of this is true. You know how much of history he has tried to rewrite in his path to power."

"I do, yes," Mara replied.

"He had a group that accompanied him into the Ohun. His best friends and companions that all wanted to seek treasure and adventure."

"Would those people have happened to refer to themselves as the Immortals?" Mara asked, remembering that Valistaran and Kadir had seemed to be friends of some kind at one point in time, and therefore why he had come to their defense in Zinok.

"Yup," Alia replied with a nod of her head. "They did. I always told them it was a stupid name. Look where it got them all…"

"So, a young Valistaran Talohir and his friends, Kadir of Kurash, and…" Mara trailed off, waiting for Alia to finish the list.

"Crown Prince of Thanatanos, Romiton Romus, a Sangoran—"

"Ronin Jakoni," Mara said. Alia shook her head. "It had to be. He was one of the Immortals that came to help us two years ago. Valistaran is the only one of those people still alive."

"No, he was only a little boy at the time. He joined them later—there was with a Sangoran woman whose name I honestly can't remember now. But Valistaran ended up falling behind and had to go back to Tal-Ahosh. He met with his friends after their victory, but I don't think he actually knows the way."

"Despite what he says," Mara said, thinking. Alia nodded.

Kadir had died to save her, and Ronin had been killed by Lavinia Daktha two years ago, preventing him from killing hundreds of thousands of people in Thanatanos. Meanwhile, King Romiton Romus had been killed in Kurash when Valistaran had sought the power of the Secret Keepers of Kurash, and—

"That's it!" Mara exclaimed. "Even though Kadir and Ronin are dead, and Valistaran never found the statue in the Ohun, I know someone else who can!"

Alia cocked her head. "Who?"

Mara glanced out the window just as Aleksander got a snowball right in the face, courtesy of Josman. Hanna clapped her hand repeatedly on the table as she too realized Mara's point. She made a joyful sound and shot to her feet, clearly too excited to sit.

"He's right outside," Mara said. "I think it's about time the Secret Keeper of Kurash returned there, don't you?"

"Perhaps a good thing," Alia said with a nod. "And I'm kind of embarrassed none of us thought of this until now."

"One more thing," Mara said. "Do you know anything about a Kurashian legend about a magical forge, or I don't know…" She trailed off with a sweeping gesture.

"Well, the story of the Star of Ohun mentions that they forged their love into diamonds, but I don't think it meant a literal forge."

Mara thought for a moment, wondering if these threads of fate had combined for her to create the weapon Thanatan had promised her *and* gain legitimacy as the Supreme One of Kurash. Maybe, just maybe, those two things could help her free her people in Terman and across Sangora.

"Well, what do you say? Want to go see if the story is true?" Mara asked. Alia and Hanna both nodded. "Great, it's decided. But before we go, there's a battle we need to win."

"What?" Alia asked.

Mara pointed out the window at the men's snowball fight. The bell over the door chimed as they rushed outside.

As Aleksander wiped the remains of a snowball from his face, he let out a surprised cry as Mara tackled him into the snow with a bright laugh.

At the same time, Hanna used her powers to knock all the snow from a tall pine onto Shanthah and Josman, nearly burying them in a cascade of white.

They retreated, brushing the snow from their hair and trying to get it out from beneath their collars.

"Victory!" Alia shouted, completely untouched by snow.

Meanwhile, Mara had managed to pin Aleksander down in the snow and was now sitting on top of him. He glanced up with a hopeful look, but whether it was for a kiss or mercy from the snowball in her hand, she didn't know.

She opted for the snowball.

CHAPTER SEVEN

THE TWO KARELS

A persistent knock on the door roused Ana Sala from what had been a restless sleep. She swung her feet out of bed, brushing her dark hair from her face to tuck it behind her ear. Her wings dragged along the floor as she opened the door. She peeked out to see Nadezhda's face beaming back at her from the darkness of early morning. She was holding a large, empty crate in her arms.

"Hi!" Nadezhda said as she set the crate down and slid it into Ana's room with her foot. "Get your stuff!"

"My stuff? Like, all of it?"

Ana yawned and stretched her arms above her head as she struggled to wake up; to her surprise, Nadezhda patted her open mouth with her hand, interrupting the yawn.

"What was that for?" Ana asked with a confused giggle.

"Wake up. Get your stuff," Nadezhda repeated. "You said you were lonely, so I pulled some strings and talked to Master Shanthah to get you reassigned to a new room."

"You what?" Ana asked. She laughed again and motioned for Nadezhda to enter. "Thank you, I think."

"To my room, I mean," Nadezhda said. "I don't think I explained that. You, me—roommates."

"I assumed as much," Ana said, opening her wardrobe.

Nadezhda peeked over her shoulder to see that she had only three shirts and a single nice, pink dress hanging inside over a pile of socks, undergarments, two pairs of shoes, and a crumpled pair of trousers. It was still more than Nadezhda had. After a moment, she realized the intrusiveness of her stares, so she turned away.

It only took Ana a few seconds to fold her clothes. She piled them into the crate before crossing the room to pull open her drawer. She retrieved a few more belongings: a couple tattered books, a leatherbound diary, a small painting of her family, some quills and parchment, and a bag full of coins.

"You sure this is okay?" Ana asked as she hefted the crate of her scant belongings. "I don't want to impose."

Nadezhda grunted as she pulled Ana's mattress off the bedframe and dragged it across the room, bumping her back into the doorknob with a yelp.

"What? Oh, yeah. Impose away. Didn't I force this on you? Shouldn't I ask *you* if it's okay to impose on you to come with *me*?"

"Why are you stealing the bed?"

"There's only one in there. Figured you might need one," Nadezhda said. "Unleeess…"

"Starting to wonder if you really did talk to Master Shanthah about this."

Nadezhda poked Ana's nose and said, "Okay fine, of course I didn't. I talked to Mistress Ruta, and she said it'd *probably* be okay. I took that ambiguity as, 'go for it, Nadezhda', and now, well, here I am, stealing you and your bed."

"And when they notice a girl and her mattress have been stolen?" Ana asked, watching Nadezhda grunt as she pulled the bed out the door.

"That's why my 'steal-Ana-and-her-bed' heist has to happen in the early morning, so they won't see. Let's worry about repercussions later," Nadezhda said.

"Want some help, or would that bring less glory to your heist?"

"Less glory," Nadezhda grunted, stumbling backward into the hallway while dragging the bed. The sound of footsteps down the hall made Nadezhda look at Ana in mock horror. "Go, go, go!"

Ana sprinted, laughing, down the hall as Nadezhda awkwardly stumbled backward dragging the mattress. They rounded the corner, giggling, toward Nadezhda's bedroom.

"Left it unlocked for a quick getaway," Nadezhda said, and Ana opened the door to her new room; she disappeared inside, and Nadezhda groaned as she lifted the side of the floppy mattress, tripped, and fell beneath it.

Ana stepped out of the room and onto one side of the mattress to see Nadezhda lying defeated and out of breath beneath it. She crawled over the mattress to see Nadezhda's face poking out from beneath, her bright hair splayed across the cold stone tile.

"How's it going?" Ana asked, resting her chin on her hands, lying on top of the mattress with Nadezhda crushed underneath. She smiled down at Nadezhda. "Need some help yet?"

"Heist…failure…death…imminent…" Nadezhda said. "Go on without me. Take my stuff. But not my bacon… bury me…with my bacon…"

Ana looked up to see Master Shanthah walking toward them with a raised eyebrow. All he said was, "Suspicious."

He put a finger to his lips with a wink as if to say that he'd tell no one what he'd seen and continued down the hall.

Ana looked back at Nadezhda from atop the mattress and reached down and touched a strand of dark hair amidst the mess of blonde.

"What?" Nadezhda asked, turning her head to try to see what Ana was doing. "A bug? Did you find a bug in there? Oh no, not again. They're back, aren't they? Not again!"

"What? No," Ana said. "I like the dark streak in your hair. Bold choice. Looks good."

"Dark streak?"

"Didn't you do it on purpose?"

"What? No," Nadezhda said, pulling the hair behind her ear in front of her face so that she could see, scrunching the skin on her neck into an unflattering double-chin. "Hmm. You're right though. Looks good. Maybe I'm just getting old."

"That'd be gray, not black."

"Oh, right. Now, off."

Ana laughed and pulled the edge of the mattress up for Nadezhda to squirm out.

"It looks like you'll get to live to eat more bacon," Ana said. "And I'll be there with you."

Nadezhda stood, dusted herself off, and Ana helped her pull the bed into their shared bedroom.

"Love what you've done with the place," Ana said, gesturing to the room, which was bare of any decorations except a pair of crumpled pants in the very middle of the room.

"Oh, dear, such a mess," Nadezhda said, kicking it under her bed. "Not much room to hide the spoils of my heist."

"Those spoils include me, right?" Ana asked, setting the crate of her few belongings on the desk. "You're not just stealing my mattress to form a mega-bed?"

"Alas, my evil plans are laid bare," said Nadezhda dramatically. "No, just kidding. Of course you are. May no one ever steal my spoils." She thought for a moment before dragging the mattress next to hers, but about a foot lower. "I'll go steal your chair… Maybe the desk…"

"I never used it anyway, I just wrote using the back of a book on my bed," Ana said with a shrug. "More comfortable. Leave the rest of the furniture to whoever inherits the room."

She plopped down cross-legged on the mattress on the floor.

"Well, here at the Nadezhda Babkova Inn, your comfort is our priority. That's our motto. Oh, and that's my bed. The one we just stole, I mean. Yours is that one next to it,"

Nadezhda said. She pointed to the bed that had been hers only moments before.

"Nadezhda," Ana said with a disapproving look.

"Ana," Nadezhda replied, mirroring the expression.

They stayed that way, disapproving of one another until Ana finally reacted first, bursting out into laughter.

"I knew I'd break you," Nadezhda said.

"Thank you for doing so," Ana replied. "I was nervous to come to the academy. Thought I'd be bad at making friends, so, you know, thank you."

"I forced you to be my friend, so you still might be bad at making more," Nadezhda replied, tossing Ana a cold strip of crispy bacon and an apple from her desk drawer. Ana smiled. "Only joking."

"You're probably right, though."

"Hey, how I see it, one amazing friend is better than fifty you can only sort of stand. So that means you're in the running for 'Nadezhda's best friend'."

"Do I have a shot at winning the position?"

"You're literally the only contender," Nadezhda replied, and Ana gave a lighthearted chuckle and let out a contented sigh. She stepped over the mattress on the floor and sat with her legs under her bottom on her new bed.

"What time is it anyway?" Ana asked.

"I don't know, five something."

"Five?!" Ana exclaimed. "Well, back to bed for me. I need my ten hours."

"Ten?!" Nadezhda replied, mimicking Ana's voice tone. "I only need four."

"Whatever do you do with all that extra time?" Ana asked.

"Make plots to steal you and your bed. Is that not obvious?" Nadezhda replied. "But now that that's done, I'll need to find something else to steal."

"Are you going to invite me into your life of crime, or what?" Ana asked. "I'm an accomplice now, so I'm not letting you go down alone."

Ana plopped down on her pillow, and Nadezhda pulled the blankets up over her chin before tucking them tightly under her shoulders.

"Comfy?"

"You literally just swaddled me, so yes." Ana laughed, squirming so that her face was free of the blankets. "You going back to sleep?"

"And let you hear my screaming?" Nadezhda asked.

"Snoring, you mean?"

"No, screaming. The nightmares, you know," Nadezhda said. After an awkward pause, "Please don't leave me."

Ana giggled. "Never. Even if you take away my ten hours with your screaming."

Nadezhda gave a thumbs up, and Ana turned over to get comfortable. Nadezhda lingered with a smile in the doorway for a moment before shutting it softly.

The Voice's dark whispers didn't crawl into her mind until she made it to the end of the corridor.

"What the *hell* do you want?" Nadezhda asked before the whispers even became actual words. "I'm happy right now. Can you not show up when I'm actually in a good mood?"

"I have left you alone while you went about your business, and now I expect you to go about mine."

"Oh, you do, do you?" Nadezhda muttered as she walked aimlessly down the hallway.

"What else do you have to do?"

Nadezhda sighed, and images of Karel filled her mind. Not as they usually did—not images of their time playing in the orchards back home. Not as her brother.

Images of his reanimated corpse clad in the robes of a purist, his face—she waved her hands and shook her head to clear the images the Voice had forced into her head.

"No, fine. Fine!" Nadezhda said. Her heart thundered in her chest, and she choked back tears. "What do you want?"

"What do we want, Nadezhda," the Voice corrected. *"Do not forget that in helping me, you get a step closer to your brother."*

"I know," Nadezhda said. "Last time I ask before I lock you in my sock drawer. What do you want?"

"Ah, yes. The sock drawer. Right next to Ana, with all that vibrant, delicious life left in her."

Nadezhda's thoughts turned to the lifeless rat in the cellar that they had drained of life force.

"No. She's off limits, you hear me?" Nadezhda asked.

"Then head to the prison," the Voice said.

"I don't even know where that is," Nadezhda replied. She felt a sense of direction fill her mind as if the Voice were pointing her in the right way.

"You do now."

The Voice did not speak again as Nadezhda ventured out the front gates of the Hidden Flame Academy. They were unlocked, true to Shanthah's word, and the guards on the steps outside nodded to her as she stepped into the cold.

"Miss?" asked one of the guards, a Sangoran woman.

Nadezhda smiled in response. "Oh, just going for a walk."

"You're going to freeze out there," said the guard. "Where is your coat?"

"Oh, I won't be long," Nadezhda said with a dismissive gesture. She was, however, already, shivering.

The guard gave her a disapproving look and unfastened her cloak before wrapping it around Nadezhda's shoulders.

"Bring it back before the captain notices I'm out of uniform, yeah?" the woman asked with a wink. Nadezhda gave a thumbs up.

"Deal," she said with a nod of her head. She began to go down the steps, but the guard called out again.

"Stay safe!"

Nadezhda hurried down the steps. The ice had been chipped away from the steps, but a thin layer of new snow crunched under her feet as she headed toward the bridge leading from the fortress island to Eastern Balgorod.

"How am I even going to get in?" Nadezhda asked.

"The guards will not be a problem," the Voice replied.

"What did you do to them?"

"Nothing. They're off duty. But they won't be for long."

"How do you even know that?" Nadezhda asked. "You know what, don't answer that. You're a disembodied voice that talks to me through a glass rock. You're weird, I get it. Never mind."

She looked up to see a Sangoran man looking at her with a raised eyebrow.

"Practicing for a play at the school!" Nadezhda called and gave an awkward double thumbs up before the man continued about his business. "He totally bought it."

"He did not."

Nadezhda crossed the bridge, careful not to slip on the layer of ice that had coated Balgorod since the previous night's storm.

Her breath floated up before her as she pulled the guard's cloak tighter and took the steps at the bottom of the bridge two at a time. She cried out as she slipped on a patch of ice covered in snow and tumbled to the ground, dropping the Voice's crystal into the snow.

She lay there, dazed, for a long moment, contemplating letting the gem be buried in the next snowfall. But then someone else would find it, and—

She scrambled in the blanket of white to find it, her hands red, cold and wet when she finally did so. She put the Voice back into her pocket and continued into the Industrial District.

"That wasn't very smart."

"At least I *have* feet to trip with."

The Voice seemed to appreciate the quip but said nothing.

Even in the early morning, smoke billowed from the factories around the industrial district, and the sound of people hard at work already filled the frosty morning air. She wondered if they had just started work or if they had labored through the night.

She made her way through the winding streets. High buildings designed to house as many workers for the nearby factories as possible loomed over her; more than one on the street seemed to be burned out, their windows smashed and the brick on the exterior burned and broken.

She hurried through the area, and eventually she emerged from a narrow alleyway onto a thoroughfare that connected the various eastern neighborhoods.

She wondered why so many people were already awake as she crossed the wide street, careful to avoid being trampled by steady traffic of horse-drawn carriages. As she stepped onto the path toward the prison complex, a portly woman gave her an angry look before gesturing to the place where she was *supposed* to cross the street.

"Sorry!" Nadezhda called.

"*You are not,*" the voice retorted.

"She doesn't need to know that," Nadezhda replied, not trying to hide her words from the woman, who scoffed and crossed into the industrial district, disappearing into the same alleyway Nadezhda had just exited.

Sangoran soldiers wearing blue and white, the colors of the independent Alboras, paced along the high walls of the prison complex. One called out to the other, who laughed, and Nadezhda wondered what they were saying.

"Won't be a problem? Off duty?" she asked, sarcastically imitating the Voice's dark tone. "Yeah, right."

The Voice did not respond.

She took a deep, frosty breath as she started toward the gates of the prison complex. She had no plan, but for whatever reason, she trusted the Voice despite her brain screaming at herself not to.

She tried to convince herself to walk away as a guard gave a wave and approached her. She still had time to run before he saw her face. She hadn't done anything wrong, and—

"Hi," she said.

Why did she do that?

"Hello," said the guard, a tall human man clad in a warm fur cloak. The flag of Alboras, a white stripe above a blue one, was emblazoned on his armor beneath. "Can I help you? It's a bit cold to be out this early, don't you think?"

"I'm here to visit my uncle," Nadezhda said. She hadn't planned to say it, and the words just tumbled out. She didn't even have an uncle, let alone one locked up in a Sangoran prison.

"Visiting hours aren't until later," the guard said, but Nadezhda felt the gem in her pocket grow warm. She slid her hand into her pocket and clutched it, and at that moment, she could sense the man's thoughts.

The confusion of finding her out in the cold so early.

His concern that she would freeze.

"*Tell him again.*"

"I—I want to visit my uncle, though," Nadezhda said. The guard shifted and shook his head.

"No, I'm sorry. It isn't the time for that."

"*Again. With feeling.*"

"Let me inside."

The foreign sensation inside her mind made her want to scream, but she held it in; the man nodded his head and blinked his eyes. Disoriented. Submissive.

"Yes, of course," said the man, leading the way toward the gates.

He led her through a small door into a chamber that circumnavigated the main gates, and he led her down the hallway. None of the other guards or soldiers inside seemed to care, although some did greet him with a friendly wave.

"Who is your uncle?" asked the man.

"Uh, Tomas," said Nadezhda, thinking of the most common Thannish name possible.

"Tomas…" the guard asked, gesturing for more.

"Tomas Babkova?" Perhaps using her own last name wasn't wise, and of course, that person almost certainly didn't exist.

"Hmm," the guard said, flipping through pages of a thick book of names and other information on the prisoners. The man's aura flickered from the pale blue of a calm helpfulness to a suspicious confusion of cloudy red that waved like a flag over his head.

"A little help?" Nadezhda asked under her breath.

"Sorry, what was that?" the large guard asked, stroking his beard as he tried to find the name Babkova where it should be between the surnames *Babak* and *Bahatec*.

"Ask for Karel Hajek."

The name Karel pierced her heart, but she blurted out, "Sorry, wrong uncle! It's early… Sorry! His name's Karel Hajek. Hajek, with an H… I'm his niece, Violeta Hajek."

"Charmed. Private Tihomir Chirilov," the guard said as he set down the book. "Didn't know Hajek had a niece."

Nadezhda squeezed the gem in her pocket, her heart pounding.

"Take me to see Karel Hajek."

Private Chirilov responded with another slow nod, as if his brain were fighting against the actions his body was performing.

"Right this way, miss Hajek."

Her heart ached as she, or rather, the Voice, commanded the man against his will, but she followed him down the staircase, nonetheless.

"Karel? Really? Couldn't've chosen any other name?" Nadezhda whispered, and she felt the Voice's dark amusement.

"I had to remind you why you're doing this."

They entered a series of tunnels below the main prison building. They twisted into a maze that Nadezhda was sure she would get lost in forever if she didn't remember the way out. No barred cells were visible, but she assumed each thick iron door contained a dangerous prisoner.

"Here it is," Private Chirilov said. "Enter the second door behind this one, and knock twice when you're ready for me to seal you in. Knock four times when you're ready to leave."

"Seal me in?!" Nadezhda asked in terror. For whatever reason, she wondered what Ana was doing at that exact moment. Probably sleeping peacefully in her room…while she used a dark spirit to mind control guards to show her to a dangerous criminal, apparently.

"Yes," said the guard. "Your uncle is a dangerous man, as I'm sure you know. Ready?"

Nadezhda gulped and nodded. Chirilov opened the door, and she stepped into a pitch-dark antechamber. The guard locked the door behind them, then let Nadezhda into the second chamber before locking her in.

"Uncle Karel?" Nadezhda asked for the guard's benefit.

"Who's there?"

The voice came from the shadowy wall out of reach of the flickering torches behind thick iron.

"It's me, your niece Violeta," Nadezhda said, unsure of why she said the words. There was no Violeta Hajek.

"Who?"

Nadezhda crept forward as 'Uncle Karel' peeked out of the darkness. She hated that the man shared her brother's name, so she was determined to call him by his surname.

"Listen, Hajek," she said. "I honestly don't know why I'm here."

"I don't have a niece," said Hajek.

"I don't have an uncle," Nadezhda said, sitting cross-legged across from him a meter or so away. His arms were chained to the wall behind him, but she still didn't feel safe. His gray hair and beard were long and unkempt, and a wildness lingered behind his eyes.

She could see the man's emotions, a mixture of boredom, loathing, and hatred with a distinct lack of guilt.

"*Place my heart on his.*"

"Your heart?" Nadezhda muttered.

"What?"

"Not you," Nadezhda replied. The gem in her pocket thrummed to life like an animal kept in a crate. She pulled it out and held it in her hand, hesitant to do the Voice's bidding.

"Who are you?" Nadezhda asked.

"Shouldn't I ask the same thing?" Hajek asked. His hair hung to his shoulders, and his beard was thick and hung to his collarbones. Nadezhda could see tattoos on both of his arms; on his left was a Purist symbol, a star overlaid with a sword. And on his right, the Star of Thanatanos.

"You know who I am. Shouldn't I be the one asking?"

"*Do it,*" the Voice urged.

"I just want to know who you are. I see your tattoos," Nadezhda said. "I wanted to know who you are before I do what I'm about to."

"What is this, an interview?"

"Why are you here, Mr. Hajek?" Nadezhda asked.

"You see my tattoos. That's why," Hajek replied. "These people here are monsters and hate me just because I'm Thannish."

"I'm Thannish," said Nadezhda. "They've treated me with nothing but love."

"They just want to control you. They want something."

"Don't we all?" Nadezhda asked. "What do *you* want?"

"To get out of this damn place," replied Hajek. "Want to help me, 'niece'? What'd you say your name was? Violeta?"

"*You know how you can help him.*"

"Where are you from?" Nadezhda asked.

"Krakov," the man replied.

"You're a long way from home," Nadezhda said. "I bet that's scary."

She didn't know why she said it.

"Krakov is infested with Night Witches these days. I don't miss a thing," said the man. His emotional aura was dark with hatred.

"Who hurt you?" Nadezhda asked.

"Getting to know this man won't make this any easier."

"Are you serious? I served in the Thannish army. I fought in the battles of Nitra and Laniras. I've seen what they can do," Hajek said. "You're Thannish. Where are *you* from? Wherever it is, I'm sure you can say the same."

Nadezhda nodded. "If I got you out of here, what would you do? Would you visit your family?"

"I don't have a family. No, I'd kill that traitor Shanthah Kalen for joining these dirty people here. We served together in the King's Guard, the Kraluv Mek. Can you believe he's set up a school for other traitors? He's making an army to kill Thans!"

"Shanthah's not a traitor."

"Oh?" Hajek asked. "I knew that man for many years, and then one day he deserted his post and turned up a couple years later as the king of his own country of Night Witches."

Nadezhda didn't know the story, but she shook her head. She pointed to Hajek's Purist tattoo.

"Do you think Purists can change?" she asked.

"We can, but why should we?" asked Hajek. "Lord Thanatan gave his life so that we can live forever. He died so that the Pure can serve us and bring us joy. Why throw that away?"

"Have you ever seen those things?" Nadezhda asked.

"Of course I have," said Hajek. "Laniras is prospering."

"While the rest of Thanatanos fights for scraps," said Nadezhda.

"They should believe in Thanatan, then." The Voice hadn't spoken in some time, but she wished it would give her some guidance. "Look, why *are* you here?"

Nadezhda lowered her gaze. "I think I'm here to kill you."

"What?" asked Hajek. "You think?"

"I just wanted to make sure I was doing the right thing before I did," Nadezhda said, pulling the Voice's crystal heart from her pocket. She set it on the ground between them. It hummed to life, and Hajek tried to kick it away, but it was just out of his reach. "I wanted to know you were a bad person."

"Well, that makes you no better than those Night Witches out there. The only good Night Witch is a dead one, and you're as good as one of them."

The man fought against his chains as the Heart began to drain his energy, even from afar. He coughed and tried in vain one more time to break free from his shackles as Nadezhda got to her knees. She scooped up the Heart and placed it on his chest, and he let out one final, pained groan.

"I am so sorry," she whispered, a tear trailing down her cheek. She sensed his fear, anger, and loathing; she felt his hatred, but also his sadness. His loneliness.

The man's chin slumped to his chest, and he collapsed against the wall, his chains still. The man's terror dissipated, and Nadezhda slumped to the ground as several strands of her messy, blonde hair faded to black.

Karel Hajek's emotional aura was gone.

"*Ah. Good.*"

And then the Voice was silent, although she could still feel its satisfaction.

She lifted her sleeve and the wrappings underneath to reveal her own tattoo; the Purist sword stared back at her. And then, she hurled the Voice's Heart against the wall; it clattered to the ground and rolled, silently, toward the door undamaged.

She scratched at the Purist tattoo on her forearm as if she could peel it off, and she cursed the day she and Karel had gone to them with nowhere else to go. They'd been on their own since their parents' death, and they were out of options…

"*I won't bother you again for some time. Go about your day.*"

"Go about my day?!" Nadezhda shouted, picking up the Heart. It did not answer, and she stowed it in her pocket. "How do you expect me to just go about my day after this?"

Private Chirilov opened the door in alarm.

"Miss Hajek, are you—"

She pushed past him without a word.

She attended her classes that day. An art class with Josman Faros. The introductory course on the general use of and history of powers. Even Ana by her side in her Mathematics class didn't raise her spirits.

She could tell that Ana knew something was wrong, but she said nothing; Ana's emotional aura was a flurry with dark worry that spiraled around her head.

But all Nadezhda could think about were the two Karels—and that they were both dead because of her.

CHAPTER EIGHT

THE SUPREME ONE AND THE BUTCHER KING

Mara found herself yearning for the bitter Sangoran winter as the immense heat of the desert surrounding Tal-Ahosh, capital of Kurash, scorched her face. She'd waited two long weeks to set out from Balgorod. She tried not to think how many of her people had died in the Thannish prison camps during that time, but horrible thoughts plagued her mind.

Aleksander, Hanna, and Alia were there with her, and Kamil and Josman planned to join them in Kurash as soon as they finished with some important duties at the Academy.

Mara knew they had to hurry with their plan to find the forge in the Desert of Ohun, for a massive fleet of Thannish ships was sailing directly for the coast of Tal Ahosh.

"*Should we be doing this?*" Hanna signed, her hands trembling. "*What if they kill Aleksander or keep him here forever?*"

Mara chuckled; she didn't expect the people of Kurash to try to kill Aleksander. Several years ago, the memories of the history of Kurash and the rest of the world had been forced into Aleksander's mind against his will. While she was in power, diplomats from Kurash had often met with her to help facilitate the safe return of the secrets stashed away in Aleksander's mind.

"Well, if he's dead, then he won't have to worry about helping us," Mara said and signed with a shrug.

"You aren't wrong," Aleksander agreed. "Is it weird that that makes this a little easier?"

"A little." Mara chuckled and looked out over the city. From their vantage point, most of the beautiful, golden city was visible.

Alia led them up a steep, narrow street in the heart of Tal-Ahosh. Aleksander wiped the sweat from his forehead and let out a deep breath. The rims of his sunburned eyelids hurt, and he adjusted his hood to shadow more of his face.

"You know, it wasn't always this hot here," Alia said. "A long time ago, this place actually had a really nice climate. And then, I guess our ancestors did something to ruin it, and it got infinitely hotter here."

"Well, thank the ancestors for me," Mara said, taking off her sunhat to fan herself with it. "Sorry, did I say thank you?

I meant dig them up and kill them again. No place should ever be this hot."

She slumped against the doorframe as Alia slid a wrought iron key into the lock, twisted it, then pushed the door open.

"It's good to be home, even if only for a little while," Alia said, immediately heading into the small kitchen. "Please, get comfortable!"

"As comfortable as we can in pools of our own sweat," Aleksander said.

Alia smiled. "If you all don't stop, when we're back in Sangora, I'm never going to shut up about how cold it is there all—the—time."

It was considerably cooler within her home, much to their relief. Even Alia seemed more content.

Mara settled down in the corner of the old, yet extraordinarily comfortable sofa. She held one of the small rectangular pillows covered in complex Kurashian designs of interlacing, geometric shapes on her lap and absentmindedly played with the fringe dangling from the corners. Aleksander sat next to her, while Hanna settled into a deep, high-backed chair across from them.

Mara turned to see Hanna staring right at her.

"Hi, Hanna," she said with a laugh.

"I know you're dying to get home. But Alia told me she really appreciates us being here for her people. I hope we'll be able to find some way to help Sangora while we're here too," Hanna signed.

"Thank you."

"I love your place, Al," Aleksander called, picking up an album of portraits on the sitting room table. He brushed away the thin layer of dust that had accumulated since the last time Alia had been home and flipped it open.

"Oh, thank you!" Alia said amidst the clank of teacups in the other room.

Aleksander flipped through illustrations of Alia, Valis, some people he assumed were Alia's relatives, and sketches of various scenic locations in Kurash. He paused as he came across a faded painting of a young couple in traditional Kurashian wedding attire. He lifted it up to show the picture of a young Valistaran and Alia to show Mara.

"Ah, yeah. My loving husband. Aren't I lucky?"

Aleksander chuckled, staring down at the former king of Talohira's young and handsome face.

"We don't have much time until the Thannish navy gets here, and if we're right about what they want, we'll need to be quick. But that doesn't mean we can't relax and catch our breath for a moment," Alia said, placing several teacups in front of the others. She rolled a massive samovar on a rolling cart into the room.

"Hot tea on a hot day?" Aleksander asked with a pained expression. He quickly added, "Not to be ungrateful, of course!"

"I know it sounds counterintuitive, but it'll cool you down, I swear!" Alia said, handing Aleksander a cup. Mara accepted one as well with a gracious smile.

"You're right," Mara replied, flipping the pillow on her lap. "There's nothing we can do about the ships, but Kurash has already seen them coming."

"Can't take too long, though. If we're right about this, the light will only shine on the statue for a few days, and who knows how long it'll take to find it," Alia said.

"Convenient for us that it's open right as we needed it to be," Aleksander said, turning his head to look at Mara with a raised eyebrow.

"Yeah, lucky us," Mara said.

Aleksander didn't look away, and Mara averted her gaze. It was no coincidence that Thanatan had influenced her to go to Kurash at this exact point in time, and she knew it.

Mara took an apprehensive sip of the hot tea.

"I have another theory about that key of yours," Alia said. Mara looked up as she swallowed. "Valistaran once told me that every Supreme One has crafted their own crown."

"Cute," Mara said. "Anyone up for craft night?"

Alia looked at her with a raised brow like an amused mother who had to act disapproving of her child's actions.

"Sorry," Mara said.

"They're not considered legitimate rulers until they do so," Alia said. "I think I'm right about this—I'm pretty sure Kadir gave you the key so that you could craft yours."

"That's not the only thing you're going to forge," said Thanatan's voice in her mind. *"Don't forget."*

Mara shut out his voice, but she knew the dead god was correct. She'd have to tell them eventually, but as she tried, her words failed her.

"I hope you're right," said Mara. Her mouth opened in a wide yawn, and she nestled against the sofa's armrest while hugging the pillow. She gulped down the rest of the tea, set down the cup, and drifted off as her friends continued their conversation, albeit at lower tones so that she wouldn't wake.

At Alia's request, they spent the rest of the afternoon waiting for the sun to die down before they ventured into the desert. As mentioned, the window for them to find the statue in the Ohun desert was still open for several more days, and they had all decided it would be best to recover and begin their quest during the relative cool of night.

Several hours later, Hippo had carried them far out of Tal-Ahosh. He descended near a rocky outcrop jutting out of the sandy dunes and plopped down, pulling Aleksander from sleep.

He looked around, disoriented for a moment, as he awoke with his head still in Mara's lap where he had fallen asleep. Mara looked down at him and stroked his hair.

"Good morning," she said with a gentle smile.

"Did I miss anything?" Aleksander asked.

"Yeah, I made the crown and we're headed back."

"Ha, ha." Aleksander crawled to Hippo's side to look over the desert. "Any sign of pilgrims to lead us to the statue?

"No. I don't think anyone is making the pilgrimage this year," Mara said, shaking her head. "Did *you* see anything?"

Before he had fallen asleep, Mara had told him to try to tap into his Secret Keeper memories, something that generally only happened at inopportune moments.

"No," Aleksander said. "Not unless the Secret Keepers of Kurash wanted me to know there was a stockpile of fried cheese somewhere in the Ohun."

"*That's* what you dreamed about?" Mara asked with a laugh. She knew of Aleksander's fondness for the Thannish pub food of breaded cheese fried in oil. "Hardly helpful. Dream of food often?"

"More often than you'd think," Aleksander said, glancing over Hippo's side to see the sands of the Ohun Desert drifting by in the wind. "It was a nice dream until Shanthah went to war with me over it."

"Hanna, control your man," Mara called, but Hanna was still asleep next to Alia. Aleksander and Mara shared a laugh and a lingering moment of eye contact.

"I was really hoping some of those Secret Keeper memories would come in handy," Mara said, averting her gaze.

"It has in the past. It was worth a try," Aleksander responded. "Maybe we will see something that'll spark one. Let's not worry—everything will work out."

"And what if it doesn't?" Mara asked, a look of concern on her face. Aleksander cocked his head.

"There's something you're not telling me."

Mara bit her lip and looked over Hippo's side, hoping she'd be able to spot the Forge of Ohun nearby before having to admit the truth to Aleksander.

"There is," she replied.

"What is it?"

"Please don't be mad," Mara said. "I did what I had to. There's no other way, and—"

"Mara, there is no one in the world I trust more than you. If there is something you had to do, I think I'll understand.

And even if I don't, I'll support you in your decision. You're smart, and—"

"Not about this."

She was silent for a long moment, her raven's feather hair billowing in the sandy wind. She covered her eyes with her hands and pulled her knees close to her chest with a low groan.

"I think I know someone that can help," Mara said.

Aleksander racked his brain to think of someone Mara would be ashamed to ask for help.

"Valistaran?" Aleksander asked, watching Mara gaze at the dim glow of the sun rising over the rolling dunes at the horizon. "Alia already told us he never found the forge."

"No, not Valistaran," Mara said. Her heart thundered in her chest, and her voice failed her as she began to speak.

"Mara," Aleksander said with a reassuring look to urge her to speak.

She pushed her eyebrows together and rubbed her temples with her thumb and forefinger.

"You have to understand that this was the last thing I wanted. I've been fighting it. I wanted to find another way, I really did," Mara said.

She could feel Thanatan's approval in her heart. She hated him, and at that moment, she hated herself.

"What have you done?" Aleksander asked.

"I went back to Nitra."

"What? Why?

He could tell Mara was fighting back tears of shame. He touched her hand, but she pulled it away and began to pace along Hippo's back, looking out into the dark desert. Aleksander followed after her.

"Hanna and I hoped to figure this out before we told the rest of you, but we've been hearing his voice. And for Hanna, that's the only thing she *can* hear. He's been haunting us, Aleks."

"Who?"

"*Say my name.*"

"Don't make me say it, Aleks. You know who I mean," Mara said. She tried to hush Thanatan's voice in her head.

"So, what? He's alive?" Aleksander asked. "Is he back? Are we in danger?"

"No. The world is safe," Mara said. "But I'm not so sure I am." Aleksander said nothing, waiting for Mara to continue. "Yes, I went back to confront him. Hanna knows—she was going to come with me, but I left in the middle of the night while she was asleep in Balgorod. I went on the way back from spying on the slave camp in Terman. I didn't want her to come, and I'm glad she didn't see what I did."

"Okay," Aleksander said in a skeptical voice.

"When Hanna and I set off the Weapon of Ages Past, we killed Thanatan…kind of."

"Kind of?"

"I don't think he can come back. He doesn't know how, if he can," Mara said. She sensed Thanatan confirm her words. "But he can't die either. We immortalized him somehow."

"What do you mean?"

"When the weapon went off, it crystalized the earth at the blast site. I guess it's grown or spread somehow, influenced by his soul or mind, or whatever you want to call it," Mara said. "I don't know. Something to do with his crystal armor, too. I don't get it, and I won't let him explain."

"You mean you *didn't* let him explain?" Aleksander asked, stepping so that he could look into Mara's face. Mara was silent. "Mara?"

"I told you, I did what I had to," Mara said, tears rolling down her cheeks. "He's here, with us."

"What?!"

Hippo flapped his massive wings, climbing back into the sky after resting for a moment. They had to steady themselves to keep from falling. Nearby, Alia and Hanna stirred.

"I spoke to him in the crater the weapon left in the center of the city. He's somehow influenced the crystals to form a mirror around the edges of the crater. He showed me things. Oh, and he fashioned a throne, too, somehow."

"A throne?" Aleksander asked. "But you said he can't return. Mara, why didn't you tell us about this earlier?"

"It's not for *him*," Mara said. She shook her head and set down her satchel and sat on the ground. She lifted the hand-shaped hunk of crystal from the bag and held it up.

"This look familiar?" Mara asked. She held up her own hand next to it for comparison. It was a perfect likeness, save one was flesh and one fashioned from crystal.

"I don't understand."

"I knew you wouldn't. I don't even understand," Mara said. "Thanatan was the first one to tell me about the Forge of Ohun. He gave me this to bring there to forge."

"So, he's made you a throne and given you this… hand…?"

"The hand is a metaphor. He wants me to kill the Magistrate for him." She winced at the revelation.

"The Magistrate is alive too?!"

"I'm sorry. I meant to tell you earlier. All of you," Mara said. She felt a weight lift from her shoulders, but the shame remained. "She's alive, and Thanatan wants me to change that."

"Okay," Aleksander said. Mara covered her face with her hands. "Mara, it really is okay. We had our suspicions while I was undercover in Laniras. It all makes sense now, though. Verahim's not in charge anymore—the Magistrate is."

"He said that the Magistrate would die by my hand, and that he would be my blade," Mara explained. "In return, he's going to help me take back Sangora. I don't know if Valistaran and his son will be able to keep Talohira stable *and* help me, and if I can't convince the Kurashians to trust me— Aleks, I don't know what to do."

"*I can show him where to find the forge.*"

"So how is he going to help?"

"As you probably expect, he's not the most open of companions," Mara said. "But he says he can help you see the location of the forge."

"He knows where it is?" Aleksander asked. Mara shook her head. "And do you mean *us*? Or he'll help me specifically?"

"No, but he can help *you* see it. If you can't access the Secret Keepers' memories on your own, but he can help."

Aleksander hesitated.

"We're playing with fire here, but if you trust him, so do I," Aleksander said at last.

"Just like that?" Mara asked. Aleksander nodded.

"You've learned from past mistakes. We both have," Aleksander said. "I trust you with everything I am."

"You know how desperate I am to help my people," Mara said, her eyes red and full of tears. "What if I'm doing the wrong thing?"

"Then I'll be doing the wrong thing right there right beside you."

A thin smile crossed Mara's face, and Aleksander took Mara's hand, and she wrapped her fingers around his. As soon as he did so, a crack of thunder that was very out of place in the desert, echoed overhead.

"*You need only ask.*"

"Thanatan," Aleksander whispered. "Please, help me see."

Thanatan's approval filled each of their minds, as his soul snaked into his consciousness.

"*Ah, so this is what the soul of a prince looks like.*"

They both heard his voice this time, and Aleksander looked at Mara in shock and fear, feeling Thanatan's influence creep through his mind. He gripped her hand, and she squeezed it back, holding him close.

"Ah, yes. There it is. Interesting."

Aleksander slumped against Mara, glassy eyed and incoherent. Alia and Hanna ran to his side, and Mara held his head in her lap. She hastily stowed the crystal hand back into her pouch as Hanna crouched next to her.

"Hey, you two," Mara whispered, wiping tears from her eyes. "There's something I need to tell you."

ONE HUNDRED AND EIGHTY YEARS AGO

Blinding light filled Aleksander's eyes, replacing the dark gloom of morning in the Ohun desert. He beheld a massive, domed temple with hundreds of spires sticking up out of the dunes, which seemed to be swallowing it up; the dome was tipped with a massive statue of a beautiful woman with gleaming diamond eyes.

And then, the side of the temple exploded. His head turned on its own, for he was seeing out of the eyes of another; a horde of men in shining armor swarmed toward the temple, and what looked like thousands of Kurashian men and women stood between them and the temple.

The temple was sinking before his eyes, being pulled beneath the sand, and it seemed that the Kurashians were allowing it to happen. The two sides of the conflict clashed one against the other in a terrible spray of blood and screams; the man through which Aleksander watched the battle rushed forward, drawing a short, curved sword.

He called something in Kurashic, and the men around him clad in elegant gold and scarlet armor more opulent than that of the other soldiers readied their weapons as they followed him. Through the memories of the Secret Keepers, he understood that they were the royal guard of the Supreme One of Kurash—and that he was seeing through the eyes of Murtaza, a Supreme One of Kurash from long ago.

The Supreme One and his entourage headed straight for the leader of the attacking Thans, a man dressed in a helm with a high plume and dark green coat covered in medals.

Aleksander recognized the man not from the Secret Keepers' memories, but from a painting in Laniras as his own four-times great grandfather: Ottokar the Butcher, third king of Thanatanos, a man universally despised by modern Thanatanos due to a genocide of certain religious and ethnic groups.

And then The Supreme One Murtaza's blade clashed with Ottokar's, and their men began to slaughter one another in a deafening clash of metal and screams.

Murtaza himself screamed as one of Ottokar's guards severed his wrist, and his blade dropped to the ground. Several of his guards jumped in between them. One of them, a woman holding a shining spear, took a savage blow to the chest with a war hammer; a blow that was meant for Murtaza's head.

Murtaza stumbled over the woman as his guards helped him to his feet. As Aleksander, through Murtaza's eyes looked at the man, he recognized her through his implanted memories as Yadira, Murtaza's successor as Supreme One.

And then, Murtaza raised his blade against Ottokar, hacking at him with all the fury left in his body and soul. His blade severed the Thannish butcher king's muscle and sinew in a spray of blood. He struck with such ferocity that blade meant bone, and soon, Ottokar fell to his knees just as he thrust his blade into Murtaza's stomach. As he stumbled, Murtaza lashed out one last time, removing the king's head with a sickening squelch. His head struck the sand.

The Supreme One who was called Murtaza fell onto his back, and his vision blurred; before it went completely dark, he drew a silver key on a chain from his neck and handed it to Yadira. And then all was black.

Aleksander wheezed as new air filled his lungs, and he bolted upright; Mara steadied him, and he shook his head and adjusted his seating against Hippo's wing. Mara sensed Hippo's concern for their friend.

"I know where the statue is. Hippo, turn around, head north-east," Aleksander ordered. Hippo groaned in understanding, looping around in the sky. Mara grasped at Hippo's rocky hide to avoid falling, and held Aleksander close, making sure he didn't either as he steadied himself.

"Are you sure?" Alia asked.

"I saw it in excruciatingly gory detail," Aleksander replied. "I'm sure."

He excitedly rummaged through his pouch for his map of the Ohun. Still breathing heavily, he spread it against Hippo's back and pointed to one location in particular, placing his finger right in the center of the desert sketched upon the parchment.

Mara mentally showed Hippo the exact location on the map, and he bellowed again in understanding.

"As fast as you can, Hipp!" Mara exclaimed.

Hippo shot higher into the sky with a bellow that echoed across the Ohun; his shadow darkened the dunes below as the sun creeped over the horizon behind them.

"The sun's getting higher. We won't have long to act before we have to wait for tomorrow," Mara said as Hippo barreled toward their destination.

"It's going to be dangerous," Alia said. Hanna hooked her arm underneath Mara's and smiled.

"Whatever it takes," Aleksander said.

Mara nodded, resolve in her eyes.

"Whatever it takes."

CHAPTER NINE

THE SUNFORGE

Hippo carried them for another hour before they reached the location Aleksander had seen in his vision. Mara, who had been unable to fall asleep, scrambled to Hippo's side to get a better look as the behemoth began his descent.

"He says we're here," Mara said, gesturing for Aleksander to come to her side. "See anything?"

A flash of the implanted memory sparked in Aleksander's mind, and he saw the tip of the buried temple from the flashback sticking up out of a dune.

"There!" Aleksander shouted. "But it's buried, just like I saw!"

Mara's heart dropped.

"Then how do we get in?" Mara shouted over the wind as Hippo soared toward the sand.

"There should be a gate at the base of that tower, underneath the sand. But I don't know how we're going to reach—"

The sound of thunder erupted from Hippo's throat as a stream of molten lava erupted from his gaping maw, carving a deep pit through the desert dunes. With several flaps of his great wings, much of the remaining sand covering the entrance blew away. The thick lava formed a relatively solid barrier, preventing the sand from cascading back down against the gates.

"Well, that worked," Mara said.

She leapt from Hippo's back and before sliding down the dune until she reached the gate. Hippo lowered his head to let Aleksander, Hanna, and Alia to climb down as they coughed through the sand still drifting down around them.

"No monsters yet," Aleksander said as he hurried to Mara's side.

Mara placed her palms against the metal doors trying to find a keyhole. "Maybe the sun will reflect on the spot where to put the key? There was a tale about some dwarves from the Deadlands that your brother told me where they needed to wait for the moon to shine—"

"Nope! Here it is!" Mara exclaimed, shoving the crystal key into a slot between a group of dusty diamonds protruding from the door.

Aleksander glanced over his shoulder; from his vantage point, the sun looked as high in the sky as it could possibly be. Mara twisted the key, and a deep, resonating voice filled the desert.

"Kiman ifadi anta hurana?" the voice asked in Kurashic. *Who sent you here?*

"Al'Asimas, yadeni Kadir!" Mara shouted in reply. *The Supreme one who is called Kadir.*

Something within the door shifted followed by the grinding of gears and other ancient, forgotten mechanisms.

"We kiman omakun ant?" *And who are you?*

It was warm, deep and strong, as if the very desert itself were speaking to them. The opposite of Thanatan's cold, dead voice.

"Mara Bartunek!" Nothing happened. She turned to Aleksander, a look of worry on her face. A little less sure this time, she repeated, "Mara Bartunek!"

Aleksander stepped forward.

"You address The Supreme One of Kurash who is called Mara Bartunek, Empress of Blood and rightful ruler of Sangora and Queen of Talohira, and you will open!" Aleksander shouted, but nothing happened.

"Ben al'Asimas, vadeni Mara!" she shouted. The gateway opened, and the sound of stone and metal scraping against one another filled the morning.

"Biklini, Asimas, vadeni Mara. Li'atsi. Antik khaamitir omakiz biklinir." *Welcome, Supreme One. Enter. Your servants are welcome.*

Mara and Alia both burst into a fit of laughter.

"What?" Aleksander asked.

"It said my servants are welcome," Mara said. "Come, my servants."

"After you, master," Aleksander said with a chuckle, but Hanna just responded with a rude gesture as they delved into the darkness.

Aleksander ignited two balls of flame in either palm as the door shut behind them with a crunch, making him wonder if there was something wrong with the door.

For the briefest of moments, Mara worried that they'd sealed themselves in their own tomb. She shook her head, told herself it was just her anxiety getting the best of her, let out a deep breath, and set out down the hallway. If all else failed, Hanna would probably be able to break them out.

Hanna clung to Mara's arm with an encouraging squeeze. Alia stepped ahead with Aleksander. As they delved deeper, Mara sensed Hippo's worry outside, and she sent him a mental image of a pile of oak trees—his favorite treat—to appease and assure him he would be rewarded for waiting.

His joy filled her heart, and she smiled.

The four friends descended into the temple, taking the wide, spiral staircase down into the inky darkness below. Alia ducked under a broken archway and called to the others.

"Uh, guys," she said. "You might want to see this."

Before following Alia into the next room, Mara traced her finger along a damaged mosaic, appreciating the beautiful, intricate artwork.

The next staircase through the archway lay in ruin, and they stood upon a balcony that overlooked a massive chamber. Aleksander let out a burst of flame that was swallowed up in the shadows. He let out a slow whistle.

"Your entire palace could fit down here," he said. "And, of course, no way to get down. You know, for those of us that can't fly."

"Okay," Mara said in the silence. "Now what?"

As if awaiting her command, a thin shaft of light poured from the ceiling like a glowing waterfall, widening into a beam that illuminated a massive forge in the shape of a dragon's head.

"Right on time," Alia muttered.

"Or we're late. We still need to light the forge," Mara said. "I won't get much forging done without fire."

"Too bad Hippo couldn't fit down here," Aleksander said. "But fortunately for us, he's not the only one who can make fire." He turned to Hanna.

"Can you get us down there?" he asked and tried to sign.

Hanna nodded and levitated over the precipice.

"Are you serious?!" Alia exclaimed, gripping the railing tightly. "I'm sure we can find stairs!"

Hanna floated next to her and patted her on the head before telekinetically lifting her and Aleksander over the railing.

Mara climbed up and squatted on the railing, lifting her powerful wings. She shook them out, took a deep breath, and leapt from the safety of the balcony.

Hanna set Alia and Aleksander down; Alia cried out in Kurashic and kissed the ground as Aleksander hurried off to examine the machine.

"Can we not do that again?" Alia asked.

"Well, you're going to need to get out of here too," Mara replied with a wry grin. "Don't worry, flying gets more fun the more you do it."

"I don't *want* to do it enough for it to become fun," Alia said. "No, no, no."

"Hey, can someone who speaks Kurashic help me out?" Aleksander's voice echoed across the chamber.

"That's my cue," Alia said, hurrying off toward Aleksander behind the forge. Hanna stayed behind.

"Tell that good for nothing god we killed to tell us what to do with the light," Hanna signed. Mara chuckled and connected with Thanatan's consciousness in the hunk of crystal in her pouch.

"Well?" Mara thought. *"Are you gonna be useful or not?"*

"You need only ask."

Thanatan's voice seemed to permeate the entire chasm; Hanna gasped, for she had heard it as well.

"Help us."

Mara felt her mind connect to the world around her, as if the very forge itself was an extension of her own body and soul. She could sense the inner workings and mechanisms of the forge.

She met Hanna's gaze, and based on her friend's expression, she knew that she had felt the Connection to Creation as well—Thanatan's power that had haunted and served her two years prior.

They both set out at once; Hanna floated next to Mara as she took flight, landing on a high platform hidden in the shadows. Upon the deck behind the forge high above Aleksander and Alia was a massive trough with pipes that led down into the neck of the statue.

Hanna groaned and looked at her hand in the dim light; it was stained with dark liquid. She wiped it on the sandy wall with a sneer before admitting defeat and wiping it on her trousers.

"Oil," Mara whispered.

Hanna tapped her ear and then signed, "*What?*"

"Oh, right. Sorry," Mara said before signing, "*There was a substance in the civilization of the Deadlands. A type of oil that burned very, very hot.*"

"*And it's what will power the forge?*" Hanna signed back.

Mara shrugged. "I assume so… Aleks, we need you up here!"

"And I need you down here!" Aleksander called back.

"Aww, you two!" Alia shouted. They both ignored her.

"*Hanna, please go get him?*" Mara asked.

Hanna nodded and levitated to the ground floor, reappearing a moment later with Aleksander.

"I think I know how to light the forge," Mara said.

"Yeah, I beat you to it," Aleksander said. "Or rather, the Secret Keepers did."

He tapped the side of his head with a smile.

"Oh, well, good," Mara said. "I need you to light the forge, then, and I'll go follow the light."

"Alia found it. There was a Kurashic inscription where the light was shining, and she thinks as soon as it illuminates a gem, it'll open a vault," Aleksander said. "Better get down there. Hanna and I will handle this up here."

Mara nodded. She unfurled her wings and glided to the ground, skipping a little as she landed next to Alia.

"It's starting!" Alia exclaimed as the light of the sun illuminated the gem, but nothing happened.

"Nothing's happening," Mara whispered. Then, frantically, "Why isn't anything happening?"

And then, they heard Aleksander call out in joy, and then the edges of the chamber were engulfed with flame. Trails of fire burst from the sides of the Sunforge's maw and traveled in trenches that led toward the walls, then climbed up toward the ceiling.

Soon, the entire chasm was aglow with hellish flame.

"Was that good?!" Aleksander shouted. "Tell me I didn't just kill us! Mara?!"

"We're fine, Aleks! Thanks!"

Just as the light moved off the gem, something within sparked to life, and a panel in the back of the forge's massive head slid open.

Mara and Alia both rushed toward the vault; Mara reached inside and retrieved a perfect cube made of cold metal. Next to it lay a mold with a round indentation set within.

"What is this?" Mara asked. Alia picked up the mold with a confused look.

"Not sure," she muttered. And then, with an excited smile exclaimed, "It's your crown! To become the legitimate Supreme One, you need to forge your crown!"

She handed the crown mold to Mara just as something else clattered to the floor.

"What was that?" Mara asked, alarmed they had lost something important. Alia bent down and scooped up a shining ruby.

Aleksander and Hanna levitated to the ground next to them, and Hanna wiped her brow of the sweat that was beginning to drip down.

"That thing is huge!" Aleksander exclaimed. "You could buy an entire army or kingdom by selling that thing."

"Or I could earn the respect of Kurash by *not* selling it," Mara replied. "Come on, let's go."

As they walked away from the vault, a cloud passed over the open roof of the tower buried in the sand, and the light from the beast's eyes faded away. The vault sealed itself shut.

"Just in time," Aleksander said. Mara nodded as they took the steps down to approach the front of the flaming forge.

The Empress of Blood approached the roaring inferno, the heat nearly searing her skin. She gripped the edges of a long trough that led to some kind of drain.

"There's a slot here, Aleks," Mara said. After setting the ruby back into a slot in the mold. She felt Thanatan's influence guiding her as she said, "Put this in there."

She handed the mold to Aleksander, who obeyed, sliding it into the slot with a click. He looked up expectantly, but nothing else happened.

Mara placed the cube of shining metal into the trough and looked up to see Aleksander leaning on a massive lever wrapped in warn and blackened leather.

"Step back, you two," Mara said, and Alia and Hanna backed up. She looked to Aleksander, then gestured to the lever with her head, and then they grabbed it together. At first, it didn't budge. Mara groaned as she planted her feet and wrapped her wings around a pillar for more leverage.

With a shared cry, they managed to slam the lever into a downward position, and the jaws of the forge snapped shut. Smoke billowed from the creature's nostrils.

Aleksander fell onto his backside, and Mara laughed, helping him back up.

"Look!" Mara exclaimed, holding out a hand. "I think it's working!"

Slowly, the jaws opened, and the inferno inside once again lit the room, bathing their faces with raw heat. The metal cube had disappeared, and the molten metal was nowhere to be seen.

"Now what?" Aleksander asked, echoing Mara's earlier question.

"*Now, you wait,*" came Thanatan's voice into their minds. She could feel his mind pulling her toward a set of six anvils that lined the bottom jaw of the furnace between the fangs.

"What was that?!" Alia exclaimed; at that moment, Mara realized Alia was the only one there who didn't know the truth about Thanatan.

"Aleks, would you mind explaining..."

She gestured to her pouch. Aleksander nodded.

"She's not going to like this conversation," Aleksander said. "You know that, right?"

Mara winced. "Yeah."

"Don't worry," Aleksander said, gripping her hand. "You've got this. Go. I'll explain everything to Alia."

Mara squeezed his hand, and he walked away. Hanna waved to Mara, brushing a layer of dust from one of the anvils.

"*Is there a hammer?*" Hanna signed. "*I'm assuming you're not going to make this work with good looks alone, right?*"

Mara chuckled and gazed up at the furnace as Hanna rummaged in a compartment beneath the anvils. A moment later, she emerged with an armful of tools.

"I'm not sure if any of these will help, but here you go."

She dumped the tools on top of the massive anvil's face, and Mara approached to examine them.

"I've done some research in my libraries in Doftaan and my Dreamstate on forging, but not extensively," Mara said and signed, picking up a heavy mallet and patting it against her palm. She nodded. "Yeah, these'll do."

"Will we have any help from beyond the grave?" Hanna asked. Mara chuckled.

"Yes," was Thanatan's simple response to both of their minds.

As Mara selected a hammer, she and Hanna both jumped back to avoid a face full of steam as the mold popped out of the side of the forge. Mara attempted to slide it out with her hands but yelped as the heated mold burned her fingertips.

"Smart," Hanna signed, and Mara responded with an exaggerated frown.

Mara peeked over to see Aleksander and Alia finishing their conversation; Alia looked simultaneously understanding and terrified. Hanna handed Mara a pair of smith's gloves.

She slid the mold out and set it on the anvil, opening it up with an expectant expression.

"What is it?" Aleksander asked as Mara opened it up. "A weapon?"

"No…" Mara said, cautiously poking the metal circle within. "Alia was right. It's a crown."

The metal was already cold to the touch. Mara turned it over in her hands, marveling at the elegant simplicity of the silver ring with a ruby set in its face. Somehow, the forge had evidently crafted the entire crown within itself.

"Kamil would love to take this machine apart and look inside," she said, marveling at the crown. She stowed it in her pouch.

"Kadir must have set the machine up for his successor before he died. I knew it!" Alia exclaimed and raised her fist. "Go Alia!"

"I'll need to remember to do the same," Mara said. "But we have more pressing issues to attend to."

"If that thing made the entire crown inside itself, what's the point of all of this?" Aleksander asked as he gestured to the anvils lining the Sun Forge's maw.

Mara shared a glance with Hanna as she emptied her satchel on one of the anvils. She handed the empty bag to Hanna, and Aleksander and Alia stepped forward in anticipation.

"*Ready?*" Hanna signed. Mara responded with an apprehensive smile, but then she nodded. She turned the crystal hand on the anvil; the flames from within the Sun Forge made the crystal glow brightly as if it contained a small sun inside.

"*Help,*" Mara thought in her mind, and she felt Thanatan acknowledge her request, guiding her hand as she looked into the flames.

"How can we help?" Aleksander asked.

"Get ready to pull the lever when I say to," Mara said.

Aleksander readied himself near the forge's lever, awaiting his next orders. Mara gazed up at the massive jaws of the forge; flames licked at its teeth, and heat seared her face.

Mara wiped sweat from her brow, rolled up her sleeves past the elbow, and set the crystal hand into the trough where she had melted the metal for the crown.

"Now!"

Aleksander pulled the lever with all his might, and the jaws snapped shut. Although they knew the jaws would slam shut, all four companions jumped in surprise. After a few moments, Aleksander pushed the lever back up, but the crystal hand had not changed.

"*It needs to be hotter,*" Thanatan informed them all. Each of Mara's friends squirmed uncomfortably as his message filled their minds.

"How?" Mara asked, but she could already feel his consciousness connecting to all of creation to explore the room and discover its secrets.

"Should we close it again?" Alia called.

"Yeah, try it," Mara responded.

Aleksander pulled the lever, and the jaws snapped shut once again. This time, they heard a loud crunch from within. The forge had smashed the crystal arm.

Mara followed Thanatan's influence to the other side of the forge. There, she discovered another handle; she gave it a pull and extended a rolling mechanism that drew a massive bellows from a hidden slot in the wall.

"I found the bellows!" Mara shouted.

"Good! Let me know when to shut the forge again! The glass shattered, but it's not melting!"

Mara called for Alia, who appeared a moment later, her bronze skin moist with sweat.

"I need your help over here," Mara said, and Alia nodded.

"I don't think it's any secret that I've never worked one of these before, but I'll do whatever you and the god in your head tell me to," Alia said. "As much as we don't trust him."

"That's fine. All I need is for you to keep pumping the air."

Alia hoisted the lever at the base of the bellows as Mara hurried back to the anvil. It worked much more efficiently than the one to close the forge, and Alia was able to pull it up and with ease to pump air into the forge. It glowed ever brighter and hotter, filling the room with hellishly warm air.

"Aleks, give it another go!"

Aleksander shut the forge, and when it reopened, the crystal hands shards had begun to melt.

"Again!" Mara shouted, rushing back to the bellows. Alia pumped the bellows several more times, heating the Sun Forge as much as possible.

The jaws snapped back open, but Aleksander had not released the lever. He swore loudly and looked at Mara in panic.

"It's broken!" he shouted.

This time, it was Mara's turn to swear. She did so under her breath then turned to Hanna, signing, "*Can you get the forge shut again?*"

Hanna nodded, stood with a wide stance, and groaned as she gripped the top jaw of the forge with her mind. She brought her hands down, and the forge slammed shut with a resounding clang.

"Okay, bring it back up!" Mara called.

Hanna released her hold upon it, and it smashed upward, the mechanism within unable to slow it down.

"Sorry!" Hanna called aloud.

Mara braved a peek into the trough and cheered as the crystal fragments bubbled together and began to flow down the groove toward a drain.

"*Divert the flow,*" Thanatan's voice echoed. He guided her to a switch that changed the flow of molten crystal from where the mold for the crown had been to a second mold.

The sound of crunching mechanisms from within the ancient forge escaped the hellish inferno within, and Mara cursed again.

"What's going on?!" Alia shouted.

"*The machine is broken. There is too much heat in the system, and it's beginning to melt down. It's going to explode if you don't fix it,*" Thanatan informed them.

"No more air, Alia!" Mara called.

"Got it!"

"Well how the hell do we do that?!" Mara asked Thanatan. No answer, until Aleksander and Hanna hurried past her from behind.

"He showed me how to fix it!" Aleksander called as Hanna used her powers to lift him on top of the forge. "It's gonna get hot in there, but unfortunately, I'm the only one who can take it."

Mara knew Aleksander wasn't being overly tough to impress them; as a Dragonsoul, one who could summon fire, his body was resistant to heat and healed from burns quickly.

Mara withdrew the mold from below the trough, and inside was a long, crystal ingot. She drew a simple ribbon from her satchel and used it to tie her long, black hair matted to her face back into a ponytail to keep it from getting in the way.

She pulled on the smith's gloves and steeled herself for the work she was about to perform. She dumped the rectangular chunk of crystal onto the anvil, brushing away ash and dust onto the floor as she did so. It was already cool to the touch, although the anvil was nearly too hot to touch.

"Hammer."

She grabbed the handle of the mallet inlaid with gold and gems from the anvil and twirled it in her hand.

She felt a flow of instructions fill her mind as she heard Aleksander's pained cries from above as he worked to repair the mechanism. She hoped for his safety, but she knew she wouldn't be able to help now.

Mara raised the hammer, bringing it down again and again, pounding the bar into a long, thin rod.

Sweat dripped into her eyes as she hurried the blade back to the forge; she placed the rough blade into the flames then placed the white-hot crystal back onto the anvil. Thanatan continued to guide her in shaping it.

The clanging mechanisms above stopped, and Hanna and Aleksander's cheers echoed down. A moment later, Hanna levitated down with Aleksander in her arms. They stumbled to the ground, and Alia hurried to Aleksander's side.

Mara gasped; Aleksander's body was covered in intense burns, his skin blackened and charred. She set down the hammer and set toward him, but Thanatan's voice filled her mind.

"No! The crystal works differently from other metals, and if you quit now, all will be lost."

"Listen to him!" Aleksander called, wheezing as Hanna put Mara's satchel under his head for a pillow. Alia tended to his wounds as his own powers began to ease the pain.

After a moment of reluctant hesitation, Mara returned to work, hammering away at the blade, which was now beginning to take shape.

She could hardly breathe due to the immense heat, and she placed the hammer and gloves on the anvil next to the glowing blade, her heart beating so fast in her chest she thought it would explode.

She wiped the sweat from her brow, nearly collapsing from the heat.

"What are you doing?" Thanatan's voice echoed through their minds from the glowing crystal blade that contained his soul.

"Dying of heat—now back off, before I throw you in the forge and leave you there."

Mara pulled her charred and filthy tunic over her head and used it to wipe away the sweat, ash, and grime.

She dropped it to the floor and
hoisted the hammer high above her
head, her undergarment wrappings
sticking uncomfortably to her
chest, wings, and armpits. The
toned muscles around her
many scars glistened with
hard-earned sweat
as she struck the
bar again and
again.

The sounds of her hammer echoed through the room like a heart made of metal. She heard Hanna whistle at her as she worked, and she shook her head with an amused expression.

Thanatan guided her in shaping the guard and pommel of the weapon until it was finished. The crystal was more workable than regular metal, and she realized that Thanatan was helping her shape it with what control he maintained over the substance.

She plunged the blade into a vat of liquid and withdrew the steaming weapon, holding it aloft. She fastened the guard to the blade, and the crystal fused with itself; intricate, beautiful designs sprawled over the blade and handle at Thanatan's whim.

And then, it was finished. She gripped the handle of the blade and held it over her head; it shined in the light of the Sun Forge, reflecting cyan light across the chamber.

There she stood, coated in grime, sweat, and ash, but with all the air and nobility of an empress, herself forged in fire. There was no mistake. Mara Bartunek was a warrior. A queen. An empress. The Supreme One of Kurash.

From her position kneeling on the ground, head bowed, Alia handed Mara's crown up to her in her palms. Mara placed the blade on the anvil then set the ringlet upon her head. The silver metal glittered like the moon and stars against her dark hair.

"Supreme One," Aleksander said with a smile. Between his and Alia's powers, most of his burns had healed, although his clothes were now tattered and charred. The bare flesh peeking through the fabric was still pink and tender, but it would be healed in a matter of hours.

Both Aleksander and Hanna knelt upon one knee next to Alia. All three of Mara's companions had wide grins plastered on their faces.

"Oh, get up," Mara said, rolling her eyes.

"Would calling you 'hot' be too on-the-nose of a joke?" Hanna signed, and Mara burst out into laughter.

"I'd say it's appropriate," Aleksander said, handing Mara her satchel and grimy tunic.

"Oh, is that so?" Mara asked with a wink.

She pulled the garment on and pulled it down over her chest and stomach, and Aleksander glanced away, unsure of what to do. She smiled. *There* was that boy she had met and fallen in love with in Cineca. She placed a hand on his cheek and turned his head to face her before planting a kiss on his lips. The first one in over two years.

When she pulled away, his eyes were wide, and his smile even wider. She patted his ash covered cheek and walked away with a wink.

She set the blade on the anvil, and the others hurried forward to look at it. A design of intricate vines, roses, and thorns extended up the blade.

"What are you going to call it?" Alia asked. "All good swords have a name. Everyone knows that."

"The Godblade," Mara said, picking it up to look up and down the blade. "Fitting, right? I mean, a sword with the soul of a dead god inside..."

The others nodded.

"Looks like we've got a chance now," Aleksander said.

"Now, back to Kurash to meet up with Kamil?" Mara asked.

She gasped as the sword shattered into a million pieces that levitated around her wrist for a moment before seeping into the pores of her arm.

"What the hell?!" she shouted.

"I will be here when you need me."

Mara shook her arm until the tingling sensation went away. She held out her hand, and the blade's crystals materialized in her palm and the weapon appeared in a flash of light.

"We can figure out what that thing can do later. We've got no time to waste," Alia said. Mara nodded, and the blade shattered and disappeared into her arm again. "Even with this new weapon, there's no telling what's happening back in Tal-Ahosh."

Mara wrapped her arms around Aleksander, unfurled her wings, and shot into the air as Hanna levitated with a screaming Alia behind her.

When they emerged from the buried tower into the bright desert sun, they were met with a multitude of Kurashian citizens that had been drawn by the thick plume of dark smoke that rose high into the sky.

To Mara's surprise, the entire multitude bowed before her. Many carried gifts, and Hippo was decorated with fine Kurashian silks that he seemed to enjoy very much.

"I don't think I'm ready for this," Mara muttered as she and her companions headed toward the crowd. Aleksander squeezed her hand, and Hanna led the way, making the sand around them dance around Mara as if to present her to the people.

Alia stepped forward and called out in Kurashic, "Hamak Al'asimaskiz vadeni Mara!" *Behold the Supreme One who is called Mara Bartunek!*

Mara walked through the crowd, greeting the people. *Her* people, now, as odd as it was.

"You know you can't guide them and your people in Sangora at the same time," Thanatan's words filled her mind.

She knew he was right. It was another title and throne she never asked for. She couldn't lead these people forever, especially if she wanted to save Sangora, but for now, she would love and protect them, however briefly her time as Supreme One would last.

Kurash had a new ruler.

CHAPTER TEN
NONSENSE AWAITS!

The dark feeling of guilt that had been gnawing at Nadezhda's heart had faded somewhat after a couple weeks of classes. She was enjoying them more now that the Voice wasn't harassing her every day. Since that dismal morning in the dark basement of the Balgorod prison, the Voice had been silent as if respecting Nadezhda's new life in Sangora.

She looked at the aged grandfather clock in the corner of the classroom counting down the minutes until she'd be free from Kamil's mindspeaking class so that she could run to meet Ana to prepare for the Alboran Independence Day festival. Evening classes had been canceled for the festivities, but all morning courses were still being held, much to everyone's chagrin.

Ana had developed a cough over the last couple days, but she had insisted it wouldn't get in the way of their plans to celebrate and spend time together.

Kamil's voice filled the minds of everyone in the classroom.

"I know, I know. You're all watching that infernal clock in the corner. I'll let you go early because I want to get out there with my friends as much as you all do, but I have one last exercise I'd like to do with you."

Nadezhda raised her hand, and Kamil gestured to her, indicating that it was her turn to speak.

"How about we do the exercise as we walk to the festival?" Nadezhda asked, turning to the rest of the class before beginning to chant, "Fes—ti—val! Fes—ti—val!"

A few people in the class joined the short-lived chant, but it quickly died out as Kamil laughed and shook his head.

"Sorry, but no." He looked around the class, counting each student. *"We've got an odd number of students today. Looks like some of your classmates have the same idea as Nadezhda."*

A chuckle floated around the room, and Nadezhda could see a cloud of mirth and bolts of excitement around her classmates. She felt something else too, but she couldn't quite make it out… Was it coming from the gem in her pocket?

"Today we'll be practicing projecting images to someone else's mind. It can be trickier than speaking telepathically, so listen carefully, and then we'll practice. Seriously, listen carefully. It can get very embarrassing if you get it wrong," Kamil said. *"But don't worry. It'll be fine. But, perhaps, knowing what I know about some of you… I'll choose the pairings."*

Laughter rippled through the class again, and Nadezhda reached down to pat her inside-out pocket. She squeezed the gem inside. Making sure it was still there had become an obsession over the last few weeks but touching it this time was to see if it was active and warm to the touch in her pocket. However, to her relief, it was dormant and cold. The odd emotion she could sense was not emanating from the Voice's gem.

"Now, as I said, we have an odd number of students today, so I'll be with Nadezhda," Kamil said as the other students paired off, dragging their small, wooden desks from their usual spots to face their partners.

Kamil explained the process of how to focus on an image and project it into the mind of another before dragging a chair next to Nadezhda's desk. He sat on it sideways, facing her with a welcoming smile.

"Okay, let's do this, boss," Nadezhda said, breaking the silence. "I guess I'm the only one talking in a silent room, so this just got awkward."

"But you're not the only one communicating. Don't worry, they should be too busy mindspeaking to care," Kamil said, waving off her vocal outburst.

Nadezhda focused with all her might, trying to reach into Kamil's mind, but she couldn't sense a single thought. She screwed up her eyebrows and averted her gaze.

"You can do this, Nadezhda."

She let out a slow breath, shut her eyes, and tried to focus again. She reached down and grabbed the crystal again; at once, whispers began to flit into her mind, but not from the Voice. The eerie emotion she couldn't place returned as she concentrated on Kamil's mind.

And there it was, now, a wavy ripple around his head. Curiosity, perhaps?

Her heart began to race, and she tried to resist thinking of the Voice, or anything embarrassing, for that matter, while Kamil sat so close to her. For whatever reason, she tried to banish all thoughts of Ana.

"*Try again,*" Kamil repeated in an encouraging tone.

She was worried he would find out about her secret if she participated in the exercise, but she made the attempt anyway to not raise suspicion. Suspicion—that's what it was, not curiosity.

"Sorry, sometimes my anxiety gets in the way of mindspeaking," Nadezhda said. "I'm trying. Sorry, really, it's bad right now."

Kamil gave an encouraging smile.

And then, the Voice spoke to her mind. "*He will hear what we want him to hear.*"

She nodded and opened her mind once more. This time, she felt her mental presence merge with Kamil's, establishing their mental connection.

"*Hello there!*" she said to his mind.

"*You made contact! Good work!*" Kamil's mental voice sounded happy and proud. The suspicion was overclouded with a wave of genuine pride and elation. "*Now, try to make me picture what you want me to see. Let's go with something like a childhood home, a favorite book. Something so familiar that you love more than anything so that you can picture it perfectly.*"

Nadezhda thought for a moment then laughed, thinking of something she loved more than almost anything else: she pictured a plate of greasy, crunchy bacon.

But the image Kamil received was one of a short, dark-haired and brown skinned Sangoran girl with a wide smile and a scarlet rose tattoo behind her ear.

"*Wait, no!*" Nadezhda thought, clapping a hand over her mouth as if she had let out a vile belch. "*You weren't meant to see that—see her. I wanted to show you—*"

"*The thing you love most in this world,*" Kamil replied. "*I know. I could sense your intention before you sent me the image. I guess you can see how tricky it is to project an image—*"

"*I'm sorry, this is so embarrassing, I… Yikes. I am mortified. I can't show my face around here anymore, can I?*"

She sensed his amusement, but then a wave of compassion wafted over her skin like warm air.

"*Never be embarrassed or ashamed of love, Nadezhda,*" Kamil said with a kind smile. An image of a Kurashian man with kind eyes filled her mind and then faded away.

"*You, too?*" she asked. Kamil nodded with a smile that did not reach his eyes. Nadezhda knew there was so much hurt and so much love behind the expression, but she said nothing. She felt a wave of sadness that seemed to weigh her down from above. Before she could stop herself, she thought, "*What happened to him? Oh, gods. I'm sorry. Again. I didn't mean to ask that, I was just wondering, and I forgot we were mindspeaking. You don't have to answer that.*"

She covered her face with her hands, but Kamil pried one finger away from her green eye and she looked into it with a dark brown one. The sensation of suspicion seemed to fade, but it was still there, hidden beneath waves of compassion and kindness—and some kind of warm, tingly sensation that Nadezhda interpreted as…what was that…? Solidarity? No, genuine empathy.

"He was killed about seven years ago, and then I had to run away from Kurash," Kamil said. The heavy emotion settled on Nadezhda's shoulders again. *"But you don't need to hear about that. I think it's time for you to go to the festival and meet your… I'm sorry, what was her name?"*

"You know her name," Nadezhda mindspoke. *"You're just being polite with the mindspeaking."*

Kamil smiled. *"You're very perceptive. Enjoy your time with Ana, Nadezhda."*

He stood and clapped his hands, breaking the silence and the concentration of a dozen Mindspeakers learning a new skill.

"Okay, enough learning for today. You're free to go. You still have a few hours until the festivities begin, but go, be free!" He smiled and gestured to the door, before quickly adding, *"Ah, actually, one last thing—sorry! This will be our final class for a few weeks. Empress Bartunek is sending me on an assignment to Kurash, so I won't be back for a while. I'll be leaving immediately. But don't forget to practice, the term isn't over!"*

He waved, and everyone filed out of the room except for himself and Nadezhda.

She hesitated for a moment, wanting to tell Kamil about the crystal gem in her pocket, but then the Voice's influence filled her mind, and she decided not to tell him.

"Did you need something else?" Kamil asked with a pleasant smile as he dusted chalk from the old chalkboard.

"No," Nadezhda said aloud. "No, I just wanted to thank you for the lesson. Uh, I haven't been able to, you know—"

She pointed to her forehead, and then to Kamil's.

"Well, then I'm proud of you. You did very well," Kamil said. *"Most of the people here today didn't manage to project an image to their partners. You projected the wrong one, but you did it. A strong one, too. Very clear. And we had an entire mental conversation, so great job."*

"I wanted to tell you that I can feel and see emotions," Nadezhda said. "I think the mindspeaking just…I don't know, comes from that, I guess?"

"You're a Soulreader," Kamil said with a nod. *"I know. Whenever someone feels a strong emotion, I can see it on your face and hear it in your mind, even when I'm not listening. It's very…loud. That's a rare gift for Mindspeakers."*

A Soulreader. That's what Thanatan had called her, too.

"Well, I'm a rubbish Mindspeaker," said Nadezhda. "But I'm glad at least there's a name for what I'm good at."

"Is that name 'bacon-eater'?"

"A bacon-eater," Nadezhda said with a laugh. "Yes, that's right."

She must have successfully projected that image before accidentally revealing her secret about Ana.

"Well, enjoy the festivities. I'll be there myself with my own friends. And hey, don't only work on your mindspeaking. Make sure you listen to your Soulreading, but don't use it against anyone. Especially, when you're with… Well, you know."

"I do," Nadezhda said with a nod. "Thank you."

Kamil smiled, and Nadezhda returned the gesture before abruptly leaving the room. She could feel friendly emotions emanating from all around the academy, but the prickling feeling of suspicion, like fingers on the back of her neck, also returned. It wasn't quite distrust anymore, but close.

She skidded around the corner leading to her bedroom and tripped, dropping her copy of *Mindspeaking for Beginners by Kamil Ramzi* just as Ana emerged from within the room. Nadezhda tripped over her own feet as she tried to pick it up and sprawled across the floor.

"Falling for me, I see?" Ana asked with a twinkle in her eye as she stepped out of their room. She extended her hand to Nadezhda up. She dusted herself off, and Ana scooped up her textbook, hugging it against her chest.

"I can't believe Kamil insisted on having class today," said Ana. "Miss Alia knew no one would show up, so she canceled everything for the weekend."

"Well, I don't know about you, but I'm ready to go eat some festival food," said Nadezhda. "I'm so excited!"

Indeed, it was the first time she'd been excited about anything since she had killed a man.

"Oh, that reminds me, I have a surprise for you when we get out there," Ana said. "Two, actually, and I know you'll love them."

"Well, then let's go!"

Ana handed her the mindspeaking textbook, and she grabbed it, tossed it unceremoniously on the floor of their room, and pulled the door shut. Ana grabbed her hand and together, they ran down the hall.

They passed other students and teachers on their way out of the fortress, and as they made their way to the open front gates toward the bridge, Ana slammed head-long into Josman trying to go against the flow of festival goers.

"Ay!"

"Oh!" Josman exclaimed in response, helping Ana to her feet. Then with a glint in his eye, he smiled and said, "Keep an eye on this one."

Nadezhda nodded. "She'll behave, Mr. Faros. No more nonsense from her."

Josman chuckled. "No, I think there's always room for more nonsense."

Ana and Nadezhda shared a laugh of their own as the large man waved them on, a head taller than most of the rest of the crowd.

They made it across the bridge without running into anyone else they knew. Nothing but joy floated around Ana's head, her mental aura white and yellow.

"This way for nonsense!" called Ana as she leapt from the top of the three steps leading up to the bridge. Her wings carried her to the bottom as Nadezhda giggled and hit the ground a bit harder.

And to the amusement of the onlookers and fellow festival goers, Nadezhda shouted a resounding, "Nonsense awaits!"

CHAPTER ELEVEN

THE OVERWHELMING BEAUTY OF THE SOUL

The festival was to be held in New Balgorod, the more opulent and wealthy section of the city. During Florenta's rule, it had been partitioned for the wealthy and privileged: aristocrats and oligarchs that had hoarded the region's wealth and oppressed those in the slums in and around Eastern Balgorod.

As Master of Balgorod and newly elected leader of the independent Alboras, Shanthah had quickly torn down the walls around that part of the city. Next, he had led a successful, but ongoing, investigation into corruption in the wealthy class, outing many of the Karpaskan oligarchs, trying and imprisoning those who did not flee. He'd managed to seize much of their wealth and used it for the betterment of Alboras, giving it back to the people in the form of improved infrastructure, education, and more.

Finally, he had opened New Balgorod to anyone at the lowest possible prices just for the sole reason of annoying the pretentious, corrupt former residents enough to make them relocate. Many went to Doftaan, others to other cities near the capital like Vaslui or Zalam, but none were welcome anywhere in Alboras or Timishuara. If they stayed there, no one knew it.

And so, this day was the second anniversary of independence from those horrid people, from Florenta Karpaska, Talohira, and everything—even Sangora itself. Although the people in Alboras had a deep love for Mara, she had insisted that they become independent with their own new country, although when she regained the throne, she would see to it that they were protected and guided by her government.

And despite the looming invasion by Thanatanos with its troops amassing near their newly constructed border wall, today, there would be joy and celebration.

Candles suspended in glass bubbles were draped from wires over the streets, which themselves were lined with little booths and shops selling linens, food, and other goods. The delicious aroma of food of all kinds mingled with the fresh scents of various oils and soaps in a festively nostalgic air.

Ana pulled Nadezhda toward the first booth, letting go of her hand so that they could both get a view of what the vendors were selling. Nadezhda looked over the selection of carved wooden spoons, bowls, and plates. Many were plain, but most were decorated with wood-burnt, traditional, Alboran designs.

Other spoons and spatulas were carved with the silly faces of witches and gnomes from traditional Sangoran folklore. Nadezhda stepped up to a booth full of ceramic bowls and cups. She admired them from afar, knowing that if she stumbled any closer, she'd knock everything off their shelves. Many of the bowls bore the vague likeness of the Empress of Blood, her waist length, black hair flowing in the wind and a crimson banner of Sangora in her painted hand.

Nadezhda looked over to see Ana peering over shoulders and heads and pushed her way through the crowd after her. The cloud of joy, excitement, and other positive emotions wafted around Nadezhda, tickling her skin and lifting her spirits up; the sensation of everyone's joy at once was exhilarating and, at least for the moment, it patched the holes where loss and mistakes were buried. Those pains would return, but for now, the collective joy of thousands drowned out anything negative.

The feeling was overwhelming, but not debilitating. Wonderfully, all-encompassing light and movement made of pure joy visible only to Nadezhda—clouds of pink and yellow, shining white and fluttering auras of yellow and white floated and whipped like ribbons and glittering powder in the wind around the people enjoying the festival. She had never been around so many happy people at once.

She let the wide smile stay on her face, following after Ana, who stopped at one particular stall. As Ana tried to get through the line, Nadezhda twirled in the street, arms outstretched as far as she could without touching anyone. She took a deep breath to take in the joyous emotions radiating off the festival goers.

She knew she probably looked crazy, but she didn't care what other people thought. She never had and hoped she never would.

"Nadya! Over here!" called Ana, using the diminutive form of her friend's name.

Nadezhda stopped spinning to see Ana grinning ear to ear as she poked her head up above the crowd; a heavenly aroma *almost* as beautiful as the palpable emotion around her wafted from the stand behind Ana.

She half walked, half skipped in time to the live folk music playing nearby over to Ana. She was now next in line; others called out as she cut to the front, but Ana replied with a single curt word in Sangoran, and they seemed pacified.

"They think you were just cutting," Ana explained.

"I am just cutting," Nadezhda replied. "What'd you say to them?"

Ana shrugged. "Told them to stop it."

"I learned the word for 'stop' in my Sangoran class, and it isn't that," Nadezhda said.

"Okay, what I said was a bit stronger than 'stop', but it worked didn't it?" Ana asked with a laugh, grabbing Nadezhda's hand. Her heart leapt.

"You know, people don't usually call me Nadya," she said. She meant to say, *"not since my parents died,"* but she didn't want to ruin the mood, because she liked how Ana's fingers felt between her own.

As she thought the words, she felt the Voice's gem grow warm as if thriving off the negative thought. Whispers trickled up her spine and into her ears, but she focused on the beauty of the colorful emotion tickling her skin and mind, and the whispers and the sensation in her pocket melted away.

"That's okay, people don't usually call me by my full name, but you can if I can call you Nadya," said Ana. "Only my very favorite people get to call me that."

"Okay, An-ezhda," Nadezhda said.

"No, Tatiana, silly," Ana said, pulling on Nadezhda's hand as they moved up in line. A Sangoran man stood inside the stall, his face obscured by a low-hanging awning. He called to Ana in Sangoran that it was her turn.

"Stay here," Nadezhda said. "Don't ruin the surprise!"

She ducked beneath the awning. Nadezhda offered an awkward wave to the woman behind her.

"Hateri behončiljev, halaška," Ana said in Sangoran. *Four bacon-chilis, please.*

Nadezhda smiled and apologized to a passerby who bumped her shoulder as she waited for Ana to reappear. She zoned out for a moment, brought back to reality as Ana's bright, smiling face appeared right in front of her from beneath the awning holding four—

"What are those?" Nadezhda asked as Ana handed two of the snacks to her. "Are these bacon?!"

Ana took Nadezhda's hand and led her from the stall.

"Yup. Bacon. Wrapped around a Kurashian pepper, filled with cheese, and fried. They're called behončili. Be-hon-chi-lee."

"It's pronounced—marry me," Nadezhda said. Ana laughed as Nadezhda's eyes grew wide. They stepped away from the crowd between two tents.

"Okay—ready? Take a bite on three. One, two—"

Nadezhda took a bite right before Ana exclaimed, "Three!"

Not only did the beautiful aroma and even more incredible taste fill her mouth, but she felt Ana's joy at seeing Nadezhda enjoy herself sweep like a feather up her arm, shoulder, and neck before tickling her under the nose. Ana giggled and wiped some of the creamy cheese off her lip before taking another bite.

"Good, huh?!"

"I will hoard these creations and live in a cave in the mountains, eating them and only them until the end of my days, growing fat and happy with my one true love," Nadezhda said, finishing off the first behončili. She slid the bare stick into a stranger's purse to dispose of it.

"One true love?" Ana asked with a wink. Nadezhda raised the second behončili with her mouth still. "Ah, yes.

You and behončili number two will live happily ever after, I foresee it."

Nadezhda closed her eyes. She could still feel the emotions from the crowd, but she focused on Ana's as they bathed her face and body, just as Kamil had suggested she do. Contentment. That one was like a soft blanket that settled around her shoulders. Peace. That one was obvious: it was the weightlessness and wispy white clouds like steam. Joy: the pink ribbons of light that snaked across her vision. But one more… a unique one she hadn't felt before. A warm feeling that glowed near Ana's heart, rather than her head—

"Come on!" Ana said, grabbing her hand again to guide her through the crowd.

Together, they ran from stall to stall, examining the wares and food within. Ana pulled out two small sacks and handed one to Nadezhda.

"What's this?" she asked.

"For our spoils, duh!" Ana replied in her warm Sangoran accent. Then, with a smirk, she added, "What, do you plan on keeping all your snacks in your inside-out-pockets?"

"I was planning on it, yeah."

Ana handed a few coins to a woman at a stand who handed her two soft, round buns. She handed one to Nadezhda and slid the other into her bag.

"At these festivals, it's tradition to put all the food you don't need to eat warm into your bag and eat it later. It makes the holiday last longer," Ana said as Nadezhda took a whiff of the bun. "Mostly children do it, but I'm pretty sure you didn't have a childhood, so I'm giving you one now."

Nadezhda couldn't stop the laughter from bursting from her soul.

"Have I ever told you how much I love your accent?" Nadezhda asked. Ana beamed.

"Your Thannish one is boring. But in Sangoran, you sounded so cute the few times I've heard you speak," Ana replied. "Say behončili."

Nadezhda did so, and Ana smiled with a tilt of her head. She squeezed Nadezhda's hand and tossed her black hair over her shoulder.

"So, uh, what is this one?" Nadezhda asked, holding up the bun Ana had purchased.

"It's filled with grated carrots, and vanilla. You'll love it! Come on!"

"Carrots?! Are you trying to poison me?! The only thing worse is celery!"

"Oh stop," Ana said, cramming one in Nadezhda's mouth. Her eyes lit up, and she gave an enthusiastic nod of approval.

She looked out at the crowd; Ana was correct. It seemed only the young children carried the little bags, but most of the festival goers were now wearing colorful masks with high plumes and beautiful designs shaped like animals.

They darted off to another stall where they purchased a small paper dish of breaded, fried cheese, which they munched as they hurried to the next stand. There, they found an array of masks.

"Hyello, gorls," said the Sangoran woman in shaky Thannish behind the stand. "You want? You buy? Mask, yes?"

"Jo, maskuv nam kupiti trembama," she replied. *Yes, we need to buy masks.* She handed the old woman a few coins. Then, with a toothy grin, she moved aside so Nadezhda and Ana could each pick one out.

"Pick one out!" Ana said with a smile. "My treat."

"Wasn't everything else your treat so far?" Nadezhda asked.

Ana shrugged. "Well, I like treating!"

"And good thing I like treats!"

"Good thing we *are* treats," Ana replied.

Nadezhda beamed as they perused the masks. There were masks that bore the faces of animals: birds, oxen, horses, and dogs, and then some that bore the likeness of mythical creatures, like crocodiles, dragons, and elephants.

"Look at this!" Ana said with a laugh, pulling a mask down off a hook to try it on. The mask had faux dark hair that trailed off with a high silver crown with a comically large, fake ruby set in the front. The mask covered the top half of Ana's face, and around her eyes were large, fake, blue ones.

"What is that? Are you just a girl?" Nadezhda asked.

"No, I'm Empress Mara!" Ana said in a jolly tone. "I'm getting this one!"

"Why do you want to be her?" Nadezhda asked, picking up a monkey mask. She knew the mythical, humanlike creatures from some old stories of worlds beyond Thanatanos, and its large nostrils and big ears made her smile.

"You can be anything, and you choose to be another person?"

"Oh, don't worry, I'll be me again later tonight," Ana said, the warmth of her Sangoran accent emphasizing each syllable as she spoke over the crowd. "When it matters."

Nadezhda put the monkey mask back on the rack and pulled another off. She recognized it as Mara's terrifying but gentle beast.

She held up the mask to show the vender, who nodded and said something in quiet Sangoran with her toothless mouth.

"Let's go!" Ana said. "I think they'll start fireworks soon!"

Nadezhda's eyes lit up. Thanatanos had fireworks, and they were fine, but she had heard tales of the Sangoran ones that exploded in different colors; the Thannish ones were just blasts of gold and white. Of course, they were dull compared to the emotions she could currently see and feel, but she was excited, nonetheless.

They stopped at a few more stalls, gathering some wafers flavored with vanilla and cardamom, some others sandwiched around a hazelnut filling, and finally, a bowl of milky cinnamon pudding dusted in flakes of dark brown.

"It's svjathova haša! Celebration porridge!"

"What's on top of it? That brown stuff?" Nadezhda asked. "I have never once celebrated by the means of *porridge* before."

"Chocolate!"

"What is chocolate?" Nadezhda asked.

"Oh, Nadya," said Ana. "If you think you like bacon…
just wait until you try chocolate."

Nadezhda dug out one of the wooden spoons they
bought at a previous stall and took a spoonful of the
porridge. She expected breakfast porridge, but to her surprise,
a sweet, milky flavor filled her mouth, and the chocolate…
oh, the chocolate.

Her eyes went large, and she gave an exaggerated nod.

"Like it?" Ana asked through bouts of bright laughter.

"Do they make bacon covered in chocolate?"

"No, that's so weird," Ana replied.

At the next stall, they found something called vutopentsi,
sausages in jars stuffed with small, pickled cucumbers and
spices. Ana purchased a circular, fried bread of some kind
covered in sugar and cardamom, and finally, she introduced
Nadezhda to her favorite treat of all at a stall near the end of
the boulevard.

"These are dumplings full of fruit," Ana explained. "You
never know what flavor you'll get, so they're called packi
buloši—trap bread—but don't get scared off by the name!
They're either apricot, strawberry, blueberry, or plum!"

Ana handed her a small bag filled with the dumplings.
Some were dusted with sugars, and others covered with a
syrupy glaze. A few of them had leaves poking out of the top,
making them look like little doughy fruits.

"Well, I'm allergic to plums, so let's hope it isn't that!"
Nadezhda exclaimed in a brave voice, taking a bite out of the
first one.

"Wait, no!"

"Plum! Plum!" Nadezhda exclaimed, collapsing to her knees holding her throat.

"What?! No!" Ana shouted. "Nadya, oh no! I killed you! Are you—"

Nadezhda could feel panic replace Ana's joy; it was a shaking feeling that squeezed Nadezhda's arms from the wrists to elbows, but it was invisible to her, one of the few emotions she couldn't actually see.

"No, I'm only joking," Nadezhda said with a laugh as she stood up. "I'm so sorry."

After slugging her on the shoulder, Ana stuck her arm into Nadezhda's sack of dumplings and pulled one out.

"Hey!"

"It's a 'being mean to me' tax," Ana said. "Any time you're mean to me, you give me a pacak buloš, okay?"

"Deal," Nadezhda said with a laugh as she finished her own plum dumpling. "But I like these, so that puts me in a weird situation."

"You don't *have* to be mean to me to earn dumplings, Nadya," Ana said.

"Ah. That makes sense. Anyway," Nadezhda said, taking Ana's hand. She slung her small pouch of treats over her shoulder and led her friend to the edge of the crowd.

As they passed a happy gaggle of children all roped together on a long line, the pure, innocent, childlike joy that swept over Nadezhda nearly overtook her, and she stopped and soaked it in, unable to see through the overwhelming silver sheen in her vision.

"You okay?" Ana asked.

"Soulreader stuff," Nadezhda replied, swaying with the flow of light in her vision.

"Are you okay? Do you need to sit down? Or leave? Oh my goodness, I hadn't even thought of your powers. Are you overwhelmed? We can leave!"

"No, it's beautiful, stop worrying. I'm more than okay," Nadezhda said, grabbing Ana's hand. "I wish you could see it."

And then it hit her: she *could* show Ana what she saw. Kamil had taught her how.

She focused on the feelings in her mind as Ana led her blindly up a hill outside the crowd. They made it to the top, and Ana said, "We can watch the fireworks up here. My family always found a tree on a hill to sit by every year. That's the best way to watch—"

She stopped and slumped to her knees as Nadezhda shared what she could see, hear, feel, and otherwise sense with Ana's mind; the gem in her pocket did not heat up. She was tapping into the mindspeaking powers without it.

"Oh, wow…"

Nadezhda knelt next to Ana in the dirt next to the tree upon the hill as they experienced the emotions surrounding them: childlike joy and wonder. The deep love of an elderly Sangoran couple sitting on a bench watching their grandchildren play. A reunion between friends who had not seen one another in months. The constant joy from the festival goers. And then, from Ana's own chest, something bright and warm. That unknown feeling Nadezhda had felt earlier…

Nadezhda took Ana's hands in her own, and the warmth flowed from her chest, down her shoulders, elbows, and wrists toward Nadezhda's own heart.

A brilliant aurora of bright pink and silver cascaded over them both, invisible to everyone else at the festival; it pulsed with light that illuminated their faces with its warm glow. A tickling sensation started at the base of each of their necks and went down their backs like rain dripping down them, and an overwhelming sense of joy filled their souls.

Nadezhda felt something new; it felt nervous, but not the scratching up the forearms that nervousness usually was. A good nervousness, perhaps? It rose up her arms like the pleasant sensation of fingernails brushing over skin.

New love. That's what it was.

And then, Ana, still overwhelmed by the intense beauty of the joy in the crowd, placed her hand on Nadezhda's cheek and leaned forward, kissing her on the lips.

Nadezhda's eyes shot open, and she smiled from ear to ear as Anna pulled away.

"No, come back!" Nadezhda exclaimed, wrapping her arms around Ana. "More!"

Nadezhda and Ana each smiled, their foreheads pressed together.

"I think we're missing the fireworks," Nadezhda said.

"I don't know, I think I felt some," Ana replied with a wink, and Nadezhda let out a shaky chuckle, for once at a loss for words. "Is this how you see the world every day, Nadya?"

"It is," Nadezhda said as Ana lay next to her, watching the fireworks in the sky exploding in various shades of glowing red, green, and yellow. "The festival is full of happy, excited people, though. So, it's better tonight than usual."

"And do you know what everything means?" Ana asked. "Like, can you differentiate between the different colors and patterns?"

The 'good nervousness' crept up Nadezhda's arms again.

"Mostly," Nadezhda said as a flurry of golden fireworks sparkled overhead. "Sometimes I feel something..."

She trailed off.

"Something you've never felt before?"

Nadezhda smiled, then softly said, "Exactly."

Ana's dark eyes lingered on Nadezhda's green ones as more explosions rocked the sky. Nadezhda lay on her back and pulled Ana to the ground next to her. She took her hand, and they stared up at the sky.

"You know, fireworks are kind of lame after seeing that," Ana said, gesturing to the air around them. "I still like them though, of course."

"Sometimes I wonder if a Soulreader invented fireworks so they could show the world what we see," Nadezhda said.

"And the bad emotions?" Ana asked.

"They can be just as vivid as that," Nadezhda said.

"So, at like at a funeral, or…" Ana said. "Sorry, morbid."

"Hey, I like morbid," Nadezhda said. "Dark sense of humor. You'll come to understand that."

Ana laughed. "Yeah. Me too. What's life without a little of that?"

"Not as good…as…" Nadezhda said. "Without…it…"

"You didn't have a joke ready when you started talking, did you?"

"No, no I did not."

They lay there watching the fireworks for a while, the sound of the Sangoran folk band playing near the hill. After a while, Ana turned her head to look at Nadezhda.

She reached out and twirled the dark streak in Nadezhda's bright hair around her forefinger. Nadezhda turned her head with a smile.

"Like my mutation?"

"Your what?" Ana asked with a giggle.

"That's what I call it. I don't know what it is, I didn't color it, so logic says that it has to be a mutation," Nadezhda said.

"Makes sense."

"Yeah."

"Oh, and yes."

"Yes what?"

"Yes, I like it, you mutant."

"Yeah, well, you kissed a mutant. Gross."

They both laughed.

"I have a gift for you," Ana said, and Nadezhda shifted to her side, propping her head up on her elbows in order to look her in the eyes.

"Go for it."

"Close those big green eyes," Ana said with a wry smile. Nadezhda shut them, expecting a kiss. "And open your mouth."

"Wait, what?" Nadezhda asked, and as she did, Ana shoved a behončili into her mouth.

"You thought I was going to kiss you."

"I think I won either way?" Nadezhda asked, chewing the behončili, finishing it in two huge bites.

"That was my last one," Ana said.

"True love," Nadezhda said. "I mean, true—"

"It's okay, I think that works," Ana said. "I think…"

"Yes?"

"I think I'm falling in love with you."

Just then, a dark strand of shadow whipped across Nadezhda's vision, sending a cold feeling down her throat.

"I—did you—" Nadezhda began. She cut herself off and said, "I *know* I'm falling for you."

Ana kissed her again.

"Did I what?"

"Did you see that?"

"What?!"

The dark shadow whipped across Nadezhda's vision again, and this time, Ana screamed and leapt up, breathing heavily as she collapsed onto her backside. Nadezhda severed the mental connection between them. Ana began to cough, and she doubled over, holding her face.

"Ana!"

"What was that?!"

Nadezhda felt terror and anxiety flowing from Ana's mind. They choked her and made her feel numb, and it felt as if her feet and hands were dunked in ice water, but she wrapped her arms around Ana, stroking her ropes of black hair.

"It's okay, it's okay. I think someone out there just got scared of something. Seeing a negative emotion is always very jarring," Nadezhda said. "Maybe they got some bad news, or…"

She trailed off as she saw a group of masked, robed men striding toward them up the hill. The light of the fireworks reflected off their masks smeared with crimson paint. Purists.

"What is it?"

"Oh no," Nadezhda said. "Oh, no, oh no…"

Ana continued to cough as the gem in Nadezhda's pocket began to grow white hot. The emotion that had interrupted the joyous celebration now had a face.

"*You need to go.*" The Voice echoed in her mind.

"We need to go," Nadezhda repeated to Ana, who nodded, still coughing. She clutched her chest, out of breath.

"Tatiana," Nadezhda said. "You haven't been coughing all day. Are you alright?"

As Ana looked up, she wiped a bit of spit from her lip.

"Ew," Ana said, screwing up her eyebrows. "You didn't see that. I—"

She stumbled, and for the first time, Nadezhda realized why the gem in her pocket was warm.

"Are you alright? What's going on?" Nadezhda asked.

"My cough is back," Ana replied. Over the past week, she'd had an on-again-off-again cough, but it hadn't bothered her today. She rubbed her forehead. "I don't know, I think I'm still sick, but even Miss Alia couldn't figure out what was wrong…"

She began hacking again.

And then Nadezhda's heart burned in anger. She squeezed the gem as tightly as she could. It burned her palm through her pocket's lining, but she didn't care.

"She's off limits," she hissed, just loud enough that Ana wouldn't hear.

"You will both die if I don't do this."

"What are even you trying to do?" Nadezhda retorted.

"Listen to me. She has enough life left for me to kill the Purists for you."

"No!" Nadezhda shouted, and Ana looked up in confusion.

"Kill her. My heart is already in your hand. Do it."

Nadezhda shook her head, pursing her lips as she helped Ana hobble away, but the Purists had them and several other festival goers surrounded. There were seven of them, each armed with long daggers that peeked out from beneath their dark robes. Their plain, silver masks were smeared with crimson paint like blood.

No one spoke.

Nadezhda glanced around in fear; she had only learned two telepathic techniques. She knew mindspeaking to the Purists or sending them weak images and Ana's powers of healing would be completely useless in a fight.

"Give it to us," said a large man Nadezhda assumed was their leader. Nadezhda held Ana close as she trembled, weakened by the Voice's power. How long had it been draining her? As long as the cough had afflicted her, at least...

"No," Nadezhda said in defiance, shielding Ana from the man.

"Which of you has it?" he asked. "Give it up."

Nadezhda's only response was a cold glare as the wind played with her hair. A thought came to her head, and she acted on it.

"Kamil, where are you? Please answer!"

No response.

"How do we even know they have it, Radim?" one of the other Purists asked.

"She guided me, and now it calls to me," the large man, Radim, said in a gravelly voice as he advanced on the two girls. "And when we bring it back to her, she'll reward us with more than anything you can imagine."

"Who?!" Nadezhda shouted. "Back off, clown!"

The other Purists stood tall and resolute, but Nadezhda could feel their apprehension and nerves. They wanted to leave. They were uncomfortable here... And there was another sensation there. What was that one? Hate? No, not quite... It was weaker than that. Sharper. Resentment. They resented Radim for making them come into Balgorod.

"Your men hate you," said Nadezhda without knowing why. She held Ana close, glowering up at Radim.

"*What are you doing, girl?*" the Voice asked.

"What?" Radim asked.

"They're scared. They all know you're not getting out of here alive," Nadezhda said. She reached out like Kamil had taught her; she couldn't touch Radim's mind, but she managed to infiltrate the nearest Purist's consciousness. She caught an image of a baby and a young woman. She could feel the man's fear. A wife and child, perhaps?

"That guy has a wife and a child," Nadezhda said, pointing a finger. "You stay here, and he'll never see them again. You'll never escape Balgorod."

The Purists muttered amongst each other, and their confusion clouded Nadezhda's vision like misted glass. She shook her head to clear it from her mind as she reached out again, trying to find anything to latch on to. Anything she could use. But before she could, she collapsed.

"Give it to us, or your friend dies," Radim ordered.

"No!" Nadezhda shouted. Her nostrils flared, and she forced her mind into the thoughts of the others, although she was still unable to penetrate Radim's consciousness. He was stronger than the others, and Nadezhda wondered if he were a Mindspeaker.

She focused on the feelings and emotions of the people in the crowd at the foot of the hill and forced them into her enemies' minds; they were instantly overwhelmed by the sudden blast of sensations, emotion, and light dancing across their vision without forewarning.

They collapsed, and Nadezhda took the opportunity to rush Radim, who responded with a fist to her throat. The blow laid her out. Just before she hit her head on a rock, she saw Shanthah and Josman rush toward Radim and his cronies.

"Josman, get them out of here!" Shanthah ordered, vanishing into nothing. Josman threw Ana over his shoulder and offered Nadezhda a thick, calloused hand. He took it and led her and the other terrified festival goers away from the hill.

Radim cried out in pain as an invisible blade tore through his robes, exposing flesh in a spray of blood. He fell a moment later, and Shanthah reappeared as several Sangoran guards made their way up the hill to apprehend the remaining Purists.

Shanthah watched his soldiers arrest and disarm them. As they forced them down the hill, the guilt and confusion of how they had infiltrated the city gnawed at his very soul.

This would not do.

CHAPTER TWELVE

THE SUPREME ONE WHO IS CALLED MARA BARTUNEK

The ceremony had all been a blur. Mara didn't remember anything, and she did not entirely understand what was going on within the inner sanctum of the palace of the Supreme One. She understood the Kurashic language being spoken to her, but not the rituals being performed near the throne to name her Supreme One of Kurash.

Several old men and women clad in glorious robes the shades of the desert sunset motioned for her to approach. Hanna, Alia, and Aleksander paused, watching the priests and priestesses lead her to center of the room before the gilded seat.

Hanna turned to Alia with a quizzical expression. Alia, too unsure of her signing abilities, tried to silently enunciate what was going on so that Hanna could read her lips.

"They're cleaning the world from her, so that she's worthy to rule it," Alia mouthed, and Hanna nodded, watching the women wash Mara's grimy, soot-stained face. She had not had the chance to bathe or change since forging the Godblade at the Sunforge.

The priestesses had a lot of work to do.

They washed Mara's face with a moist rag embroidered with a sun. Hanna chuckled at the number of times they had to wring the filthy rag, which had once been new and white, into the large basin. When her skin was adequately clean, they anointed her skin and her dark hair with fragrant oils.

"Is that all?" Hanna whispered.

Alia answered with an exaggerated shake of her head as an old, bald man near the door motioned for Aleksander to accompany him.

"Go," Alia whispered to him. "The men are supposed to leave now. I think you were already supposed to be gone, to be honest. Plus, it's about time the Secret Keeper of Kurash returns, don't you think?"

"Yeah, I guess. Wish me luck, I think I'll—"

As he turned to go, the priestesses began stripping Mara of her filthy, burned clothing and dropped it in a heap into a second large basin where they set it ablaze. Mara looked up at them with frantic, confused eyes.

The oil on the ruined clothing made it burn much faster than the priestesses had expected, and they recoiled in shock for a moment.

She made eye contact with Aleksander with a mortified look, and Alia grabbed his head to turn it away with a laugh.

"Yeah, okay. Time to go."

Aleksander nervously bit at his lip, and Hanna hugged him goodbye to bid him good luck. The soldiers and priests then led the last Secret Keeper of Kurash to whatever awaited him. Mara peered over her shoulder, offering a sheepish smile and a quick wave that went unseen as they forced him out the door.

Mara wished she could tell him goodbye, since she'd asked if he would stay in Kurash after their visit to help direct the battle against the invading Thans. There weren't many powered people in the country, and his abilities would be beneficial to their efforts here. She wondered how much more time they'd be able to spend together before she had to return to Sangora, if any.

As the priests departed, only the priestesses remained to tend to the coronation ceremony.

They had her kneel, and she looked over her shoulder again at Alia and Hanna with wide eyes. Hanna could hardly help but chuckle at her expression as the women set up a low cloth barrier around Mara for her privacy as they cleansed her body.

A bit late, in her opinion.

The dirty water dripping down her body ran beneath the partition, and Mara grimaced at how brown it was. She knew the priestesses must be appalled at their new leader, but if they did, they said nothing of it.

Next, they bound her hair and applied more fragrant oils, speaking in Old-Kurashic, which Mara did not fully understand, although it resembled the modern form of the language enough that she could catch most of what was being said: metaphors of her rule likened to nature and the continuation of the sun and moon, and so on.

At long last, the priestesses motioned for her to stand. Her knees were still muddy from kneeling in her own filth, and one of the old women quickly wiped them off.

"She hates this," Hanna mouthed to Alia, who chuckled. "Poor girl."

"You wouldn't?"

The old women wrapped elegant, dark black robes over Mara's naked body and then draped a crimson cloak around her shoulders. Mara winced as they forced elegant earrings through the holes in her earlobes, and the oldest of the women raised her new crown high above her head before setting the silver ringlet down on Mara's black hair.

Thinking of the battle raging outside Tal-Ahosh, tears streamed down Mara's face as she was crowned the ruler of another country she never asked for, and in her mind, never deserved.

"May the sun and the moon shine on your rule forevermore," the head priestess said in accented Thannish. She spread a final dab of oil across Mara's forehead. "May the Supreme One who is called Mara Killianeva Bartunek protect us until her dying day."

Mara wondered how long that would be.

They gestured to the throne, expecting her to take her rightful place. She hesitated, biting the inside of her cheek as she thought of what to say.

"As my first act as Supreme One, I want to go now to the battle outside the gates. You asked that I protect you, and that's what I intend to do as long as it is in my power to do so," Mara said. She unfastened the cloak they had just draped over her shoulders and handed it to the head priestess.

"Your word is law," said the woman with a deep bow. "Shall we see your friends to their chambers?"

Mara glanced up to Hanna and Alia. She signed the question for Hanna, who shook her head along with Alia.

"With the Supreme One's permission, we would like to accompany her," Alia requested in Kurashic.

"Very well," replied the old woman.

The guards led Mara, Hanna, and Alia out of the room. Mara gestured to Hanna, who inconspicuously withdrew Mara's wing blades and finger claws from her pockets. No weapons had been allowed at the ceremony, but Hanna had smuggled some in anyway.

"When the priests are done with Aleksander, please send him to me," Mara ordered.

"Yes, Supreme One."

"And before we go, can I change out of this?" Mara asked, gesturing to the loose robe. "Not very conducive to battle, and not exactly supportive, if you know what I mean."

She winked at the old woman, expecting her to laugh, but she just bowed. "Your word is law, Supreme One."

Mara turned to her friends.

"Do I still get to be funny if I'm the Supreme One?"

"That's *so* unprofessional to even ask," Alia said with a fake scoff.

After the old woman and two soldiers returned with a change of clothes and some simple, leather armor for each of them, they followed her guards outside. Hippo greeted them with a long grunt, standing as a massive sentinel outside the palace gates. Mara fastened the blades to the tips of her wings and strapped her razer claws to each finger. Hanna levitated onto Hippo's nose and reached out for Alia.

"Don't even think about floating me up there!" Alia said in a resolute tone, jabbing the air with her finger in Hanna's direction.

A bright, cheery laugh escaped Hanna's mouth, and after the three women were secure on his back, the behemoth shot into the sky toward the northern ports.

Tal-Ahosh burned below. Shipborne catapults launched flaming projectiles into the ancient city, and the sound of swords and screams filled the night air. The Thannish forces were pressing farther into the city, their heavy, steel armor reflecting the dying desert sun.

Mara and her allies wasted no time in attacking the fleet assailing the Kurashian coast. She willed Hippo toward them, and the frightened sailors below screamed as he unleashed a torrent of molten lava, completely decimating two of the ships closest to the shore. Their viridian sails burned as they sank below the waves. As the wreckage sank beneath the waves, Hippo flapped his massive wings, and the force of the gale capsized a third ship.

Mara glanced over Hippo's back to see hundreds more vessels, and she wondered if even Hippo would be able to destroy them all.

"You good?" Mara called to Alia, who had vomited from motion sickness earlier. Alia gave a thumbs up and buried her face against her pack. Hanna, on the other hand, was completely fine flying. Her hair billowed in the breeze and a bright smile stretched across her face.

A thick arrow the size of a tree trunk shot from one of the ships and embedded itself in Hippo's side; he roared in pain and thrust a gargantuan paw through the deck of the ship that had attacked him.

"Hippo! Up!" Mara shouted, seeing dozens of the ships preparing ballistae with similar projectiles. "It's okay, boy!"

As Hippo turned to flee, he let out another erratic burst of lava, sinking another couple ships, their crews screaming and leaping overboard. He groaned in pain as he climbed higher into the sky, and Mara willed him to retreat.

Several dozen more ballista bolts raced toward Hippo, several of which meeting their mark. He yelped again then let out a massive roar before stumbling into a cliffside building on the coast; the structure collapsed into the sea in a shower of brick and dust as a second barrage of the timber-arrows raced toward Hippo.

"They were ready for him!" Alia shouted.

"Yes, I know!" Mara shouted.

Hanna reached out with her powers to turn one of their ballistae toward another ship then let the bolt fly, shattering its main mast near the center; it fell toward the helm of the ship, forcing the crew to leap out of the way.

The trio climbed off of Hippo's back and regrouped, watching the Thannish navy continue to bombard the city. Mara looked up at Hippo as he nudged her entire body with his nose, a look of fear on his face.

"Hippo, you need to go!" She turned to see a troop of soldiers, and she cried, "Go!"

A troop of soldiers that had landed on the beach rushed toward Hippo with heavy maces. As they started battering his legs with their cruel weapons, he raised one massive foot and opened his maw, unleashing a torrent of molten lava that buried many of his foes, their screams silenced. He trampled many of the others underfoot.

Dozens of flaming boulders thrown from the catapults soared through the air toward the behemoth as the Thans also turned every ballista they had on him.

"Get out of here!" Mara shouted, using their mental connection to force him to flee. He crouched and then leapt into the sky. *"Please stay safe, buddy. Can't do this without you!"*

She felt his pain, but also his guilt at not being allowed to stay and fight beside her.

"He'll be okay," Alia said. Mara nodded, knowing how resilient Hippo was, but still, thoughts of his pain broke her heart. Hanna smiled and wiped a tear from Mara's cheek.

The Thans had pushed tall mobile structures against the city wall. A pulley system within raised ballistae up onto the wall, and soldiers filed out to set them up.

"I need you two to please go find Kamil and Josman. Their group should have arrived by now, but I'm worried they got cut off by the attack on the port," Mara said and signed.

"I'm staying with you," Alia said. "I think you'll need my powers."

To her surprise, Mara didn't object.

"*Your word is law, Supreme Empress of All,*" Hanna signed back.

"*Stop that.*"

Hanna chuckled to herself but wasted no more time, floating as swift as an arrow back toward the city.

"What now?" Alia asked.

"Hide. Stay safe, and I'll be back if I need your help," Mara said.

"Promise it."

"Huh?"

"Promise you won't try to do whatever it is you're about to do alone," Alia said. Mara nodded.

"I promise," she said, squeezing Alia's hand.

As Alia hid behind a rocky outcrop, Mara took one last moment to center herself and then took flight. She shot toward one of the towers lining the wall, tackling a Thannish soldier from the roof. He fell to his death far below as Mara landed on the platform and thrust her bladed wings through the chest of the soldier readying the siege weapon.

Before she could withdraw her wings from the man's chest, a second soldier raised his sword to strike Mara down. The man's exaggerated stance left his throat exposed, and she thrust the razer claws fastened to her fingers up, piercing his flesh just below his chin.

Mara tore her wingblades from the first soldier's chest and knocked the other from the wall with a swipe of her wing.

She paused, taking a moment to catch her breath. The northern part of the city nearest the coast had fallen to the Thans' assault, and countless ballistae, trebuchets, and campsites entrenched with barricades to fend off the Kurashian defense surrounded the city.

"They work fast, I'll give them that…" Mara muttered to herself. Without her powers, she knew she wouldn't be able to move or destroy the siege towers, and she considered turning back.

Just as she was about to fly back to Alia, a flurry of Kurashian arrows felled ten men that had emerged from the nearest siege tower.

"They've taken the port district!" she heard a Kurashian soldier shout to a group of fresh fighters below, gesturing for them to pull back.

Her heart pounded in her chest. If Thanatanos was attacking Kurash with this many forces, she wondered what was going on back in Sangora. Had the troops amassing on the borders flooded into her country?

Dread filled Mara's heart as she watched, mouth open in shock, as the Thannish soldiers that had already breached the wall leading a group of defeated Kurashians toward the ships.

She cried out in anguish as she realized that combatants weren't the only ones being taken from their homes, but innocent civilians as well. Terrified men, women, and children called out for one another as they were forced on to separate ships.

She shook her head and tried to regain her composure as she watched families wrenched apart. She began to hyperventilate, and her heart pounded in her chest as memories of her own enslavement forced themselves into her mind just as the soldiers forced their way into the city.

With tears rolling down her cheeks, righteous fury filled her soul, and she stood straight before letting herself fall from the wall. She extended her wings and glided over the Thannish soldiers' heads. Not too far below her, the invading army had established a perimeter around the ports as others continued to push into the city.

Every soldier in the vicinity raised their weapons as she glided down; they pointed swords, spears, crossbows, and even, to Mara's horror, weapons from the Deadlands she recognized as rifles, tipped with sharp blades.

She landed in the middle of an encampment near the docks that she assumed was a command tent of some kind based on the banners and number of forces swarming around it. As she strode toward the command tent, a soldier there called out to her, calling her a Night Witch. Her only response was a quick jab of her elbow to his throat.

As he collapsed to his knees, gasping for air, his companion stepped forward.

"Who are you?" he asked. "Stand down, Night Witch, or I'll have you killed."

Mara gestured to the man coughing on the ground. "You want to be next?"

"Sir, that's Empress Bartunek," muttered one of the other guards. "You know, the one who—"

"The one who killed your god," Mara said, finishing his sentence in defiance. "I suggest you *do not* test me."

The guards lowered their crossbows. Mara raised her eyebrows and gestured with one hand for them to move aside. They did so, stepping away as the tent flap as it fluttered in the breeze. She pushed through, taken aback for a moment to see three towering Spirit Warriors in armor like her fallen ally, Valakor. They were gathered around a table with a detailed map of Tal-Ahosh laid out on its face.

They stood taller than anyone she had ever met, their bodies made up of steel armor housing the minds of dead generals, warriors, and tacticians. Relics from the final war that had decimated the vast civilization now called the Deadlands.

"Ah, so the rumors are true," said one of them who was studying a map of Tal-Ahosh on the table.

"Which rumors?" Mara asked, folding her wings against her back. She recognized the warrior as Raksil, a Spirit Warrior who had shifted alliances more than once since her rise to power.

"That you survived, of course. We weren't entirely sure if you had. Other rumors suggested you had fallen into drunken obscurity, a fallen empress of a fallen nation. Perhaps, still true. What else would you be doing in a dirty place like this? I mean no offense, of course."

Mara refused to respond, staring up into Raksil's fiery, cyan eyes in the slit of his helmet. His companions, a massive man holding a war hammer and the other, a smaller, slender Spirit Warrior leaning on a silver spear, stood at attention.

"Kallus, Taria, remove Miss Bartunek," Raksil ordered with a dismissive flick of his armored finger.

The hulking Spirit Warrior with the hammer, Kallus, advanced on Mara, and Taria lifted her spear to point it at Mara's throat.

Mara did not hesitate, summoning the newly forged Godblade from within; the blade materialized, its crystals forming the weapon as Taria pressed her spear against her neck. Mara lashed out, severing the shaft of Taria's weapon as if it were butter. The Spirit Warrior stumbled backward in surprise as she stared at the dimly glowing weapon.

This moment of distraction bought Mara time to step forward and behead her with a single slash of the weapon; Kallus stopped in his tracks as Taria's headless body hit the ground next to her broken weapon.

Her head rolled away, cyan mist trailing from the empty helm.

"Do I have your attention?" Mara shouted.

"You have it, but what authority do you have to speak with us?" Raksil asked, not bothering to look up from the map as he and some of his advisors moved pieces representing his forces around it.

"*All* the authority as Supreme One of Kurash, Empress of Sangora, and dowager queen of Talohira," Mara replied. "Even if they don't accept me as such, these are my people, and I will not allow this to happen."

"Dowager queen, hardly. Oh, Mara Talohir, your *husband* survived, and his son reigns in place of both of you, while his idiot daughter is the rightful heir," Raksil replied. "Jokes, the lot of you."

That was the only time she'd ever heard herself referred to with Valistaran's surname, and it filled her heart with rage.

She stepped toward Raksil, twirling her blade. She kicked Taria's severed helm out of her way, and it clanged as it struck a wooden bench at the far side of the tent.

"This has gone on long enough. If you don't—"

The sound of Kallus's heavy footfalls signaled his advance on Mara, and she lashed out with the Godblade once more, slicing clean through the war hammer. Both halves struck the ground with a clang.

"I was talking."

She pointed the blade at Kallus's chest, and he stepped backward, hands raised.

"You aren't going to intimidate me, Miss Bartunek," Raksil said. "*Your people* in both Sangora and Kurash are defeated. I know this, you know this. Your defiance won't change that. Even with that fancy sword of yours, you can't do anything to stop it."

"Defeated?! Oh, wow, you've conquered the docks of *one* city in Kurash. Congratulations! Let's crown you victorious over the entire world," Mara mocked. "I'll say this one time, and one time only. Leave. I don't want there to be any more bloodshed, but if you don't obey me, there *will* be death. Some of my people will die, but *all* of yours will."

"You are arrogant for an empress without a throne," Raksil said as he stepped away from the war table.

"And you are confident for a monster without a soul."

Raksil chuckled, his eyes burning like blue flame within the hollow shell of his helmet.

Mara smiled as she heard screams from the port followed by a roar and the splintering of wood and the crash of waves. Hippo was back, and he was furious.

"You're never going to be able to escape," Mara said, seeing the destruction through Hippo's eyes. "It won't be long until my beast sinks every one of your ships."

Raksil cocked his head.

"And if he does so, he risks killing your people."

"Excuse me?" Mara asked.

"We've been instructed to arrest anyone who defies us. Hundreds of Kurashians are in chains upon our ships. If your monster hasn't already killed them, I will."

Mara hesitated, unsure of what to say for the first time in the conversation. "Explain."

"Every single one of my ships are rigged with explosives," he said. "You have no idea the technology we've restored from the Deadlands."

"You're bluffing."

"If you do not call off your beast, I will give the command to sink each ship carrying prisoners."

Mara shut her eyes, willing Hippo to halt his assault on the ships. Through their mental connection, she could feel that he was feeling better, and that Alia had pulled the thick ballista bolt from his hide.

The roars and screams ceased as Hippo halted his attack.

"Good," Raksil said. "Now, I think it is time you take your leave, Miss Bartunek. Go, run along, little girl."

Mara raised the Godblade and brought it down at Raksil's head. Raksil retaliated in an instant, thrusting his hand forward; a burst of energy erupted from his palm, throwing Mara backward. She screamed and failed to extend her wings in time, breaking through the leather walls of the command tent. She rolled along the ground, her clothes smoking from the blast.

She groaned as Raksil and Kallus emerged. The Godblade was lying on the ground near them, and Kallus bent down to scoop it up. Mara reached out for it, and the blade burst into a million crystals before reforming in her hand.

She shot into the air, slashing across Kallus's arm, removing it from his body. He cried out as blue-white sparks and smoke poured from the wound, but Raksil blasted Mara once more, and then dozens of Thannish troops surrounded her, crossbows, spears, and swords drawn.

She watched as the troops from the ships brought more troops, siege weapons, and lumber to reinforce their positions.

"Drop your weapon," one of the soldiers ordered.

"Do as he says, or your people drown," Raksil said.

Mara shut her eyes, and she willed the blade to disappear. It shattered into crystals that flowed again into the flesh of her forearm. Raksil made his way through the crowd.

She raised her arms above her head.

"I thought I'd let you know that your friends are safe aboard one of our ships," Raksil said.

Mara's mind raced. Who did he mean? Aleksander, Hanna, Kamil, Josman, or Alia? All of them?

She had failed the ones she loved yet again.

A sudden explosion of brilliant flame rocked the air above, pulling many of the soldiers' attention from Mara. At that moment, those that still had their aim fixed on the empress knelt to the ground, their actions forced and sluggish as if they were fighting for control of their own bodies.

Mara spun around to see Hanna and Aleksander standing upon a roof of a nearby building. Hanna's hands were outstretched and trembling as she forced the soldiers to their knees. While Josman defended her with his mace, Aleksander peppered their enemies with balls of flame.

So, Josman and Kamil's group had made it to Kurash after all. That meant Raksil's prisoners had to be Kamil and Alia, and guilt once again filled her soul.

Thousands of arrows and ballista bolts separated her from her friends, and Raksil's men bound her hands before leading her to the docks. The last things she saw and heard before they forced her aboard a ship were Hippo's cries and Aleksander and Hanna fighting through the Thannish soldiers, shouting her name.

CHAPTER THIRTEEN
THE PRICKLY ROSE

The mindspeaking classes had not yet resumed in Kamil's absence, so out of her boredom, or perhaps to spend more time with Ana, Nadezhda had insisted on accompanying Ana to her healing classes for the past few days. They were led by a substitute healer for several weeks until Alia returned from the diplomatic voyage to Kurash.

Today, however, she elected not to go with her, claiming that she had a sore throat and wanted to stay behind. Ana had given her a quick peck on the cheek and gone on her way without any suspicions. Only good emotions wafted off of her, and that was good.

She was glad Ana didn't share her abilities at that point, for she would have sensed the cloud of shame that permeated her soul.

The Voice had spoken to her today.

Nadezhda stepped over a pile of what she hoped was animal dung as the stench of the southern slums filled her nostrils. Even with Shanthah's efforts to build up Balgorod, the slums remained as they had always been. Destitute, dirty places at the edges of the city and outside the walls.

This was the image many in Thanatanos held as the stereotypical norm for all of Sangora. Nadezhda felt horrible that she had ever believed the same, but that was not the reason for her shame as she ventured into a particularly seedy part of the slums.

Everywhere she went, she heard the jeers of men in the shadows, and it seemed that there was either a brothel, men already passed out drunk in a corner before noon, or a run-down bar on every other corner.

There were no free-standing homes, just stacks of dilapidated apartment blocks from anywhere between three and ten stories high that looked like they could crumble at any moment. Many of them were held up with shoddy, but surprisingly stable workmanship. She passed a warped beam with a dozen nails beaten into it to keep it from shifting; it seemed to be holding up an entire wall.

Faded graffiti reading, "Empress Mara Bartunek" was sprawled across the beam. Perhaps it was a metaphor, Nadezhda thought, that Mara was the stressed and broken beam holding up the rest of Sangora. That, or the empress was painting her name all over the city.

What a hooligan.

Rats and other vermin that infested the streets climbed into the dwellings and in and out of the defunct sewer system below the streets. Each time she found one of the creatures, she'd lure it to the Voice's gem so that it could absorb its lifeforce, and she felt it grow marginally stronger each time. However, the Voice exuded frustration and impatience in a chaotic web of dark lines that drifted over her vision like cobwebs caught in a draft.

Ana's cough had been getting worse over the last week, and so Nadezhda decided it was time to give the Voice what it wanted. It was time to let it feed.

"*Down that alleyway,*" the Voice demanded, and Nadezhda complied, checking over her shoulder as she disappeared into the foul-smelling shadows.

The lights of a particularly large brothel cast an eerie glow into the narrow street, and a sign with a rose wrapped in prickly vines swayed in the gentle breeze, its chains squeaking. Below it, scrawled in Thannish for whatever reason, read, "The Prickly Rose." She scowled at the sign, for it seemed like a cheap copy of the beautiful tattoo tucked behind Ana's ear.

Nadezhda pressed herself as close to the far wall as possible to avoid walking too near to the brothel for two reasons: she did not want to be taken inside, if that's how brothels worked, and she refused to be subjected to the cacophony of horrendously vile emotions going on within. Even this far outside, she could sense it, something akin to hearing angry neighbors drunkenly screaming at one another through the walls.

"*Just up ahead.*"

Nadezhda nodded, but she had no idea where the Voice was taking her. Until she saw it. Or rather, him.

A human man was lying in the street, his head bashed open and bleeding, dripping dark blood down his face and neck. One of his arms and legs seemed to be broken, and he was trying to pull himself toward the brothel.

As Nadezhda approached him, her heart breaking in her chest, she was overwhelmed with the despair that billowed from the man; to her abilities, the emotion looked like a cloud of dark smoke with random bursts of crimson flakes that drifted up before vanishing like ashes from a fire.

She had never felt such utter hopelessness before.

"Are you okay?" Nadezhda asked, kneeling next to the dying man. She knew the answer. He lifted his hand and tried to speak; the smell of old alcohol drifted up to her nostrils and she gagged, but she clutched his hand.

"*Absorb him.*"

"He'll die," Nadezhda replied, and the man stirred feebly.

"*He's dying anyway,*" the Voice replied. "*Do it before he expires, or I'll find the rest of my sustenance elsewhere.*"

She knew he was talking about Ana.

"Surely he has less lifeforce left in him than the rats," Nadezhda replied, sitting cross-legged next to the man, holding his hand as he babbled incoherently. She couldn't even tell if he was speaking Thannish, Sangoran, or something else.

"*More than a thousand rats, still.*"

"But he's human. I can't do that again," Nadezhda said.

"*Exactly why you need to. Look at the state of him. Put him out of his misery, and you're one step closer to having your brother back.*"

"What's your endgame here, man? I know you don't actually care about me or bringing Karel back," Nadezhda spat. "What are you after?"

She'd refrained from talking to the Voice in such a way while she was in the castle lest someone hear, or even worse, that it would punish Ana or someone else she cared about.

"Each life you give me brings me closer to regaining my own."

"Ever going to tell me who you are?"

"The knowledge would drive you mad."

Nadezhda stroked the dying man's hair, and a few strands of silver light cascaded up the dark, billowing, hopeless smoke. Thankfulness. She always thought that emotion was beautiful. Simple, but beautiful. Pure.

"It's okay," Nadezhda said as the man tried to stand. "No, no. I've got you. It'll be okay. I'm going to get you to safety, okay?"

The man gave a broken smile with the few teeth he had left, and Nadezhda fought back tears as she placed the gem on the man's forehead. He slumped, and the hopelessness faded. A few more bolts of gratitude sparked around his head, and then he was gone.

"See? He was thankful."

The fact that the Voice could see what she could was revolting to her; it felt intrusive, as if he was perverting a beautiful memory, and she despised him for it. She wondered what else he had seen in her private moments.

The gem glowed brightly for a moment, glowing white hot before it went inert again.

"More."

"No, you're done. Back to eating rats."

"You have only fed me scraps for weeks. I demand that you grant me human or Sangoran lifeforce, or I will take you and Ana, and I will find a new host."

"You sound like you're getting desperate," Nadezhda said, closing the dead man's eyelids before standing up. That was two men she'd killed, now. "Got another Soulreader somewhere you can manipulate?"

"No."

"Good, then it's settled. You need me. Why am I the only one you can use, anyway?"

She started down the street but glanced over her shoulder, which seemed to be second nature in the slums, as a commotion broke out in the brothel.

"Want to know what's going on inside?"

"More than anything, no."

"That man is about to kill one of the girls inside. She wouldn't—"

"Don't tell me," Nadezhda said as tendrils of fear crept from the windows. "I can't handle it. Please, no. I don't want to know."

"Because you asked so nicely," replied the Voice. *"Just know that you are the only one who has the power to stop what's happening up there. No one else knows. No one else will care."*

Nadezhda's face screwed up in distress as her feet carried her toward a drainpipe and a pile of barrels that were strategically placed to lead up to the window. Nadezhda wondered what the point of that was.

"What if that was Ana in there? Would you leave her?"

Nadezhda sighed and hoisted herself up onto the barrels, using the drainpipe for balance. She climbed higher until she was level with the window, and then she threw herself forward, grabbing onto the windowsill. She pulled herself up and smashed the gem against the glass, shattering it before climbing through the visible tendrils of fear.

She emerged from the broken window to find a man holding a dagger dripping with crimson standing over a scantily clad woman on the floor. She was clutching her side, sobbing.

The man turned in surprise to see Nadezhda there; he raised the knife again to strike her down, but Nadezhda forced her mental presence into the man's head and forced all the negative emotion around the room as she could inside his mind. The young woman's fear. Her own disgust. The lingering despair of the dead man outside. The other stifling stew of other foul, disgusting emotions in the brothel.

The man slumped to his knees holding his skull, pounding on the sides with his fists, screaming for it to stop. Blood dripped from his nose.

"You have no right," Nadezhda said bravely.

The man snarled and blindly thrust the blade up toward Nadezhda, but she thrust the gem against his throat before he could land the blow. He hit the ground with a thud, and she felt the Voice's approval and appetite grow.

"Good. A proper meal. Full of such lively, delicious hate."

The knife clattered to the ground, and Nadezhda hurried to the woman's side. She couldn't be too much older than herself, but her eyes looked as if they had seen too much hardship and pain for her young life.

"Come on, I'm getting you out of here," Nadezhda said in a soft tone. The wounded girl nodded as she helped her to her feet and led her to the window, but she resisted. "What? Come on."

"I can't climb," she said, gesturing to her side which was now soaked with blood.

"Right," Nadezhda said. "Of course."

"Who are you?" the girl asked.

Nadezhda said nothing and grabbed the fallen blade on the floor, wiping the blood on the bed's threadbare sheets. She pushed the door open then ventured out into the hallway. The smell of smoke that had never been scrubbed from the walls, ceiling, and carpet permeated her nostrils, and even more horrible things assaulted her mind.

The emotions were truly overwhelming. She stumbled down the hall, and she was sure the girl thought she was drunk. She could sense her faint hope and gratitude amidst her fear of dying, so perhaps, she didn't care.

The girl led her to the stairs and limped down in front of her. Nadezhda supported her until they came to a lobby with a grubby little man at the front desk.

"Oy, girls! Mr. Albescu hasn't cleared you to leave yet, so get back here," he said, his voice much higher and nasally than his ruddy, pockmarked face suggested.

"Back off," Nadezhda said as the little man waddled toward them on his stubby legs. He was nearly a head shorter than Nadezhda, who was already quite short herself.

She felt him grab her arm, and she instinctively whirled around and slapped him as hard as she could across the face. He fell on his behind against his desk.

"Feed him to me."

Nadezhda ignored the Voice, grabbed the girl, and bolted for the door as the man massaged his jaw and picked up his cracked spectacles.

A large guard barred their way out the only exit, his massive arms folded across his barrel-chest. Patrons and workers alike watched as Nadezhda raced toward him.

He raised a spiked, wooden club, but as he did so, Nadezhda shouted, *"Open the doors!"*

She felt his mind connect with his. She imagined him opening the door. She siphoned the guilt she was feeling into his own soul, and the man broke down crying as he unlocked the door to allow them through, much to the front-desk man's dismay and confusion.

They didn't stop running as they reached fresh air—if one could call the smell of feces and death fresh. The voice of the man chastising the guard faded into the distance as they emerged from the alleyway. The girl collapsed, but Nadezhda grabbed her.

"Who was that guy?"

"…Albescu."

Nadezhda stroked the girl's hair and decided it was a bad idea to bring up what just happened. "You're okay, you're okay."

The girl shook her head.

"Haven't been in a while," she said in a Sangoran accent, although no wings jutted out of her back. A human native to Sangora.

She tried to wipe a spattering of blood from the girl's forearm, but realized it was a crudely done tattoo of the petals falling from a rose.

"Okay, safe, then. What's your name, sweetheart?" Nadezhda asked. The girl's face turned from fear to relief as she lay bleeding on the cobblestones of the slums. Her emotions, however, did not shift from the cloud of worry.

"Jesenia," said the girl through groans.

"I'm Nadezhda. Spelled with a J or a Y?" asked Nadezhda, trying to get her to focus on something other than her bleeding side.

"Same thing in Sangoran, they all make the yuh sound," she groaned. "Why are you asking me this?"

"Just trying to help," Nadezhda said.

"By asking me how to spell my name? Jesenia asked, and the sparks of violet bewilderment that fluttered down like snowflakes signaled that Nadezhda's plan to distract her was working, for they began to banish the smog of foul fear.

"Where are we going? There aren't any healing centers in the slums."

"Then it stands to reason that we're leaving the slums, don't you think?" Nadezhda said as she felt the Voice urging her to let it absorb Jesenia's lifeforce.

"No, I can't afford to go to the healers," she replied.

"Fortunately for you, I know some free ones," Nadezhda explained, hoping she would make it there in time.

"Free meaning *bad*."

"What? No. Free meaning your only chance," Nadezhda said as they limped toward the dilapidated gate leading out of the slums. She felt an odd twinge of disdain for the girl, as if she'd insulted Ana herself. She shook her head to rid herself of the emotion. Jesenia clearly didn't deserve that.

Although she couldn't see them, Nadezhda could sense dozens of people watching them hobble down the street. None of the emotions were surprise or concern, however. In their place, sharp lines of annoyance and indifference that looked like beige dust settling around their shoulders.

"I can't keep going," Jesenia muttered, starting to faint. She stumbled off the curb of the road and struck the ground before Nadezhda could help her.

"Help!" Nadezhda cried, but none of the few horse-drawn carriages bouncing down the dusty cobblestone street paid them any heed.

And so, Nadezhda took it upon herself to stop traffic. She stepped into the road, raising her arms high into the air.

"What are you doing?" Jesenia asked.

"Asserting dominance. If I make myself big, they'll stop."

"Isn't that for bears?"

Jesenia groaned in pain as a large carriage stopped just short of hitting Nadezhda. The woman inside shouted something in Sangoran, and Nadezhda looked to Jesenia.

"Ja nerruthaju Sangorsku," said Nadezhda. *I don't speak Sangoran.* She gestured to Jesenia lying in the street, and the woman's emotions turned from annoyance to genuine concern.

"Oi, Vožatac!" cried the woman, opening the door. *Oh, by the goddesses!*

She and her driver hopped down and helped Jesenia into the carriage and then gestured for Nadezhda to climb in as well.

"Where we go?" asked the Sangoran woman.

"Akademija," said Nadezhda, remembering the word for academy. Even if she hadn't, it was close enough to Thannish that she probably would have understood.

The woman spoke to the driver, who took off toward New Balgorod and Shanthah's academy. Nadezhda held Jesenia's bloodied hand and cradled her head in her lap as she lay on the bench within the carriage. Each bump of the carriage aggravated the girl's wound. Jesenia began to drift in and out of consciousness.

"What happen her?" asked the woman.

"The man in charge of a brothel stabbed her in the gut before I used a magical crystal that speaks to me and absorbs the lifeforce of people in order to create a new corporeal form in order to restore my brother from his undead punishment, and possibly conquer the world," said Nadezhda.

The Sangoran woman simply smiled, clearly not having understood anything she said. Nadezhda squinted with a mirthless grin. She glanced out the window and let out a sigh. They were passing over the bridge into New Balgorod now. One more bridge across the neighborhood to get to the island with the academy to go.

"Hang in there, girl," said Nadezhda. She tried reaching out with her mind like Kamil had taught her and how she had done when she contacted him before. *"Is anyone there?"*

"I am."

"Not you, you idiot," Nadezhda muttered.

"I can transfer this woman's life-force to the girl."

"Shut up."

"Either I consume the Night Witch, or you let me devour the life force of the girl. She's going to die anyway."

Nadezhda punched the gem in her pocket, to the confusion of the Sangoran woman, who wasn't understanding anything Nadezhda was saying.

"Teodor? Nikola?" thought Nadezhda, trying to contact one of her mindspeaking classmates. Neither answered for several seconds.

"Nadezhda?" the voice of an elderly student in her class, Teodor, filled her mind, and she latched onto it with all her might.

"Oh, hi! Listen, I don't know if I can maintain this connection. Please get the healers out to the front of the academy. I'm on my way, and I'm coming with a wounded—"

She cursed as she felt the mental connection snap. She hadn't felt any confirmation if Teodor had heard her, but she was unable to make contact again. The next three minutes passed in one long string of expletives from Nadezhda's mouth until they crossed New Balgorod and onto the island with the academy.

As they made it to the wide plaza outside the academy, she saw a small crowd of familiar Mindspeakers and Healers standing to greet them.

She let out a sigh of relief.

The Healers helped Jesenia out of the carriage. Nadezhda felt their levelheaded calm, a product of their training. Some of the Mindspeakers seemed concerned, and others were confused.

They took Jesenia away, and Nadezhda met Ana's gaze for the first time as she stepped out from behind the other healers.

"Nadya?" asked Ana. "What's going on?"

"Tatiana!" Nadezhda exclaimed, rushing forward. She wrapped her arms around Ana and held her close. She felt her worry, love, and a hint of suspicion like she had felt from Kamil.

"You smell...horrible," Ana said. "Where on Earth have you been?"

"Uh, sewers, a brothel, the slums, hard to explain," Nadezhda said.

"A...brothel?" Ana asked.

She reached up and touched Nadezhda's hair; the dark streak had spread. Nadezhda hadn't noticed until Ana touched it.

"Listen, we need to talk," Nadezhda said.

"I should probably go with them," Ana said. "I...we'll talk later?"

"This can't wait. I—no, go," Nadezhda said. Her eyebrow twitched, and she couldn't meet Ana's gaze. "Yeah, talk later."

Ana squeezed her hand with an apologetic expression. Her powers let her know that it was genuine, but the guilt still felt like a solid chunk of iron in her stomach. "Okay."

CHAPTER FOURTEEN
"DO YOU HATE ME?"

Nadezhda waved goodbye to the kind Sangoran woman that had driven them to the academy and stood alone on the steps as the Healers and Mindspeakers took Jesenia inside.

"You deprived me of a meal. You had better not go see Ana."

"Or what?" Nadezhda asked.

"You know what."

"Oh, yeah?" Nadezhda shouted, reaching under her waistband to pull the gem from her inside-out pocket. "You are lying to me. You have no way to bring Karel back, do you?!"

She hurled the gem against the wall of the academy, and it clattered to the ground without a scratch, but it melted through the patch of snow in which it landed. She stomped on the crystal with all her might, and it skittered across the plaza's cobblestones. She collapsed to her knees sobbing as she struck the ground with her fists.

"Pull it together, clown," Nadezhda muttered, trying to regain composure. She wiped the snot from her nose with the back of her hand and stood. She felt the pull to the gem, and she scooped it back up.

"Fine, pull it together and go visit Ana. I will not bother her."

"And the rest of the sick and dying people in the healing center?" Nadezhda spat back. "We're done, you piece of shit."

"Nothing gets past you. It's almost like our minds are linked," the Voice said. *"The man who killed your brother is in Balgorod. Find him, and we will kill him."*

"No, he isn't, you liar. Mara killed him."

"Did she?"

Nadezhda ignored him and went inside out of the cold, stomping the snow from her shoes on the rug that led to the entranceway's grand double staircase. She made her way to her bedroom, pulled the gem out of her pocket, hid it in a balled-up pair of socks, and shoved it to the back of her desk drawer.

She locked the door and placed the key before on her desk. She collapsed on her bed, buried her face in her pillow, and screamed for as long as her breath would allow. And then, she began to sob.

When she had regained enough composure to pull herself away from the bed, she made her way toward the main healing center. The entire way there, she tried to form the words she would say to Ana to explain everything, but nothing sounded right, despite the clarity of mind that came from abandoning the Voice in her room.

When she arrived, Ana was pacing outside the entrance into the academy's healing center. She rushed to Nadezhda, who seemed to be moving through molasses to avoid the conversation.

"So?" Ana asked.

"Um, I think we need to talk," Nadezhda said.

"Yes, you covered that bit," said Ana. "So, what in the name of the Goddesses is all this? How many half-dead, half-naked girls should I expect you to bring home?"

"Hopefully just the one?" Nadezhda said in a sheepish tone. "Okay. Can we…"

She gestured to nothing in particular.

"Sure," Ana said with a smile.

Nadezhda led her down the hall and then slumped against the wall of the corridor so that the entrance of the healing center was still in view.

"Nadya, you can tell me anything. I trust you," Ana said with an encouraging squeeze on the arm.

"I did…" Nadezhda said, trying to form the sentence, but her mouth didn't seem to want to form words. "I did something bad."

"Stabbed a brothel girl?"

"Saved a brothel girl," Nadezhda corrected. "No, I…That wasn't me."

"I know, sweetheart."

Ana laced her arm under Nadezhda's and grabbed her hand.

"I…" she trailed off.

"Yes?"

Nadezhda started, fumbled her words, and then tried again, letting out only a long, "Well…"

"Nadya, I've heard you talking in your sleep. Sometimes it's silly things, but sometimes you sound terrified. I pretend I don't hear you screaming because, well, we all have a past. I assumed it was about your brother. But now, I'm wondering if there's something else…?"

"There is," Nadezhda said. She let out a deep sigh. "Okay. Back home in Thanatanos—sorry, not back home, this is home. Back in Thanatanos, I stole something from some very important people."

"The king?" Ana asked.

"Um, no," Nadezhda replied. "Not really. There's somebody else controlling Thanatanos. Call me a conspiracy theorist, but lots of people believe that there's somebody pulling the strings behind the scenes."

"Who?" Ana asked. "So King Verahim is a puppet?"

"I guess. There's a rumor that there's a Mindspeaker that controls those undead things without faces," Nadezhda said. "They call them the Pure. We call them Faceless. You know the ones."

"Okay," Ana said, trying to follow along.

"Well, my brother and I stole something from her, we think. Or from some of her followers, we don't know."

"How did you do it?"

"Long story," Nadezhda said, and then a look of shame crossed her face. Warm compassion wafted off Ana's skin, and Nadezhda breathed it in, knowing she could trust her.

"We stole it from some leaders of the Purists. You know those guys that attacked us at the festival?"

"Yeah?"

"Those guys. They're some kind of cult that worships this alleged mindspeaking master of Thanatanos," Nadezhda said. "They're killing people with powers across Thanatanos. I don't know why. So Karel and I were a target anyway, but when we stole this *thing*, we became top targets."

"Did you get your own wanted poster?"

"Believe it or not, I never saw one! It isn't fair."

Ana laughed. "Okay, continue."

"I—we—only knew about the thing we stole because…" she trailed off and hesitated for a long moment. "Karel and I were members of the Purists for a while."

"What?!"

Nadezhda lifted her sleeve to reveal the Purist tattoo.

"We didn't know. You know, after our city was destroyed like five years ago and my parents died, we lived on the streets in Laniras like rat children."

"Cute rat children," Ana said, squeezing Nadezhda's hand.

"Cute but feral, yes. But we were starving, and they took us in. We lived with them and everything, but the things they preached never sat well with us. And then they started killing powered people, and we knew we had to run."

"Was Karel powered?" Ana asked.

Nadezhda shook her head. "No, but he knew I was—am. And let's be honest, you've probably noticed that when I am overwhelmed by other people's emotions, I kind of zone out while I experience it."

"It's cute, yes," Ana said with a smile.

"Well, to them, that was me being a witch," Nadezhda said, "and they thought it was some kind of witch-trance and I was going to do something horrible to them. Curse them, I don't know."

"Why'd they think that?"

"Because I told them I was going to curse them?"

"Ah. Of course."

So, we ran. But before we did—long story short, we stole the gem I was talking about as it was being transported somewhere else. We don't know where."

"And then they killed Karel when they found out?"

"Yes."

"And how does this connect to everything else happening?" Ana asked. "The half-dead-half-naked girl?"

"Getting there," Nadezhda said, resting the back of her head against the wall. "Empress Mara and Hanna rescued me before they could catch me, and they brought me here, blah, blah. But since I've been here, the gem has started…well…It's been talking to me."

"What?" Ana exclaimed.

"Have you not heard it?" Nadezhda asked. Ana shook her head. "I think I can hear it because I'm a Soulreader. And I'm the only one here."

"Or because you're a Mindspeaker," Ana said. "I think that makes more sense."

Nadezhda shook her head. "No. I'm not a real Mindspeaker. I don't think so, anyway. That stupid thing gave me the power to Mindspeak, but I think there's… I don't know how to explain it. I think there's some kind of soul inside it."

"And what does it say to you?"

"It says that it can bring Karel back."

"From the dead? Nothing can do that," Ana replied.

"It seems to be under the impression that he's become a Pure, and who knows? Maybe it *is* possible to bring those things back to life," Nadezhda said. Ana gasped and put a hand over her mouth. "But I realized it's been lying to me. It had a plan for me to absorb the lifeforce from animals and things so that it could help Karel come back to life and so that it could form its own body."

"Kurvaki vožatac…" Ana swore in Sangoran. "Do you think it wants to take over Karel's body?"

"I thought of that, but no, I don't think so. I think it's just manipulating me. Well, I started absorbing life from rats in the cellars," Nadezhda said. "But then it wanted more, so it made me go down to the prisons and absorb the life from a murderer. By the way, when are you teaching me to swear in Sangoran?"

"You killed him?" Ana asked, releasing Nadezhda's hand.

"He was a Purist there for life for something, and the Voice convinced me that absorbing the life of an evil man for the greater good would be…I didn't—I didn't want to, but I felt like I had to, I…"

She trailed off and began to cry.

"Nadya…" Ana wrapped her arms around Nadezhda, who pulled her knees close to her chest. "What next?"

"Do you hate me?" Nadezhda asked.

"Never," Ana replied. Nadezhda fumbled for words through a sob.

"I know I'm a lot. Everyone in my life has told me that. If I'm too much, you can find someone—everyone walks away in the end. If you want to too, I wouldn't—I don't blame—"

"No, listen. Why would I ever want *less* of you? I want *more* Nadezhda Babkova!" Ana said, kissing her on the top of the head. Nadezhda smiled through tears. "You know, for every single person who doesn't understand you or leaves you behind, and who don't love you the way they should, there will be people like me who stay. And we're the people who love you for you—exactly who you are."

"No matter what?"

"No matter what."

"I refused to absorb anyone else for him. I did absorb some more rats. I didn't know why. I hated doing it, and I hated that thing, but I felt like I had to do it," Nadezhda said. "I was in the slums absorbing rats today—"

"Yes, as one does."

"While I was there, we found a guy who looked like he got mugged. He was dying. I could tell that he was going to die. His emotions were fading, and his mind was too. So, after I argued with the Voice, it convinced me to absorb that guy's life force…I was putting him out of his misery. But then I was near a brothel, which, this city has like a thousand, did you know?"

"I'm…aware," Ana said. "My grandparents are from the southern slums."

"I felt horrible emotions coming from inside," Nadezhda said. "You know, like—"

"Oh, gross," Ana said, screwing up her face.

"Yeah. But also fear and hopelessness, and…I could feel something, like someone knew they were going to die."

"Did you absorb them too?" Ana asked. She ran her hand through Nadezhda's darkening hair.

Nadezhda shook her head. "No. That person was Jesenia. Some big guy named Mr. Albescu stabbed her, so I used the gem to absorb his lifeforce to save her…and then I broke her out of the brothel, commandeered a vehicle to get her here, and here we are."

"You killed Albescu?" Ana asked. Her emotional aura turned chaotic with bursts of white. Confusion, and…excitement?

"You know him?"

"Well, yeah, everyone knows him. He controls half the criminal world in the slums!"

"Yeah, well," Nadezhda said. "I guess now I have to worry about a criminal-empire coming after me."

"I'm sure you're safe from them here. But Nadya, why do you smell so bad?" Ana asked. "That was my original question, after all."

"Well, that's not something you ask a lady," Nadezhda said. "But if you must know, I was absorbing rats in the sewers."

Ana smiled. "I love you, Nadya."

They shared a long look, and Ana's smile curved upward across her lips.

"So, if you love me, that means you aren't judging me for what I've done…" Nadezhda said. Ana nodded and brushed a finger across her cheek. "Then it means you probably don't hate me."

"I already told you I—"

"I love you too!" Nadezhda blurted out, her eyes wide. It was nearly a shout, and she *almost* regretted the outburst until the aura of emotion around Ana's head turned into a pink vapor that whipped like ribbons in the breeze again. Relief washed over her at being able to say those words since she hadn't had the chance to say them back at the festival.

"Took you long enough to say it back," Ana said with a wink.

"Worth the wait?"

"Worth the wait." She winked. "But stop changing the subject, you silly girl. I've said it before. We all have a past, Nadya. We've all done things we're not proud of" She brushed her hair behind her ear, and Nadezhda glanced at the rose tattooed there. Ana kissed her and rested her forehead against hers.

"Yeah?"

"Even if you do something you've told yourself you won't, over and over, I'll love you. I'm here for you, Nadya. No matter what."

Nadezhda ran her fingers through Ana's hair, tracing a finger over Ana's tattoo.

"Help me get rid of it?" Nadezhda whispered.

"Of course. Do you want me to talk to Master Shanthah?"

Nadezhda's eyes filled up with tears, and she nodded, unable to say anything.

"Listen. This wasn't you. This thing, whatever it was—it manipulated you. You are not a bad person," Ana said. Nadezhda smiled through the tears and Ana kissed her on the forehead. "Okay, up."

Ana pulled her to a standing position. She took Nadezhda's hand, and together they walked to Shanthah's office.

As they came to his door; Ana knocked her knuckles against it three times. His cheerful voice called, "Come on in!"

They did so, with Ana leading the way. Nadezhda pulled the door shut behind them, and Shanthah gestured for them to sit. He pulled his own chair from the other side of the desk and sat next to them.

"What can I do for you two wonderful women?"

"Nadezhda—well, both of us—we have something we need to talk to you about," Ana said. "It's very important."

Shanthah leaned forward with a kind smile. They explained the entire situation to him in depth, and the entire time, Nadezhda focused on Shanthah's emotions, which remained calm and understanding, but never angry. When they were finished, Shanthah leaned back in his seat, deep in thought.

"First, and most importantly, I think," Shanthah said, looking at each of them in turn. "You need to look out for each other, okay?" Nadezhda and Ana looked at one another and smiled. "And next, I don't want you to touch that thing again. Let my people handle it, okay?"

"Do you have disembodied-voice-exterminators here?"

"The very best," Shanthah said with a wink.

"Are you going to throw me in the dungeons?"

At that, Shanthah laughed out loud and shook his head.

"Nadezhda, no. Heavens, no. What you're doing might be more important than you know right now. Thank you for bringing this to my attention. I'm sure it's been weighing on you. If you'll wait here, I'll gather some people, and we can go get this taken care of. Sound like a good plan?"

They nodded. He stood and showed them to the door.

"For some reason, it didn't ever absorb my life force," Nadezhda said. "I think it'll be dangerous for anyone but me to touch it. He implied as much."

"Thank you for the warning. I'll keep it in mind. Now, please, meet me at your room, but do *not* go inside."

They bid their farewells while Shanthah gathered the necessary people to take care of the gem. They made their way back to their bedroom hand in hand.

"You know, you could be a therapist," Ana said.

"A what?"

"A therapist. You listen to people's problems and help them work through them," Ana said. "With your powers, it'd be a breeze! You'd know their emotions before they do!"

"You can get paid for that?!" Nadezhda exclaimed, and Ana replied with a huge nod. "Good money?"

Nadezhda and Ana sat next to the wall across from their door waiting for Shanthah until he appeared from around the corner with Mistress Lavinia, Mistress Vasilica, a Sangoran woman without wings that Nadezhda didn't recognize, and finally, a trio of Mindspeakers.

"Ready?" he asked. Hanna waved with a happy smile and signed something to Shanthah as the group entered the room. The Mindspeakers put up a mental shield around each of them as Nadezhda opened the drawer.

She gasped in horror. It couldn't be.

The Voice's heart was missing—and with it, her only other pair of socks.

CHAPTER FIFTEEN
THE SECRETS OF KURASH

Mara was gone, and so were Kamil and Alia. They had decided it best that Hanna return to Balgorod to give news of Mara, Kamil, and Alia's capture while Aleksander stayed behind, as Mara had requested, to help direct the rest of the battle of Tal-Ahosh and finalize the situation regarding the memories he stored in his head.

He had gone through a similar ritual that Mara had. They'd stripped him of his old clothes, bathed him, much to his chagrin, and clad him in the official robes of a Secret Keeper. He couldn't wait to commiserate with Mara about it.

He vowed that Shanthah must never know.

He knew he had responsibilities there in Tal-Ahosh, but guilt threatened to consume him as thoughts of Mara being shoved aboard yet another ship as a prisoner filled his mind. It had been a while since he'd thought of the day when he and Mara were taken from Cineca and forced aboard the Arcship, a massive slave ship under the employ of Talohira.

That had been so long ago. But so his mind wandered as he waited for the Secret Keepers in the chamber above the throne room of the Supreme One of Kurash. The chamber was currently unlit, although daylight streamed through one large window, illuminating the drifting dust in a white beam. Somehow, it was cold in the chamber despite the intense heat outside. He didn't mind.

It had been several years since he had last been in this building, but he could still remember the feeling of hope he had felt here during a diplomatic meeting between Kurash, Talohira, and Thanatanos. They had been so close to peace, or so he had thought.

Talohira had attacked the peace conference to kill the Secret Keepers of Kurash and prevent any alliance between Thanatanos and Kurash. Talohira had then somehow forged a short-lived alliance with the Supreme One, although, in the end, it had ended up saving the city of Laniras when Mara's forces attacked it. It was so odd, Aleksander thought, how each piece of that story had changed and evolved since then. No peace came that day. How naïve they had all been to think it would.

Ten men entered the room at long last. He had been waiting for nearly an hour, sitting alone in the dim chamber after returning from the short battle near the port. Two others, a man and a woman, were seated in chairs across from him. He greeted them with a nervous smile and a friendly wave, but they did not react in any way, as if he were a ghost.

The priests had explained earlier that they were the Mindspeakers who would become the new Secret Keepers of Kurash. As it turned out, only Mindspeakers could control the power of the Secret Keepers, which explained why he always had trouble accessing memories.

"Hello, Aleksander. I am Cyrgiz. Are you sure about this?" the man asked. Aleksander looked into his good eye. The other looked as if it had been blinded in an accident.

"I've always felt like I stole something from your people the day the Secret Keepers died. It's time I gave it back," Aleksander said. "So… Yeah. I'd say I'm ready. How do we…"

He trailed off with an expression of discomfort.

"We've come to peace with the fact that you were the steward of their secrets," the Cyrgiz in perfect Thannish. "We foster no ill will, and we are simply grateful that you have returned."

Aleksander nodded. "So, how do we do this?"

The second Mindspeaker, a woman who introduced herself as Nebehat, took his hand in one of her own and Cyrgiz's in the other.

"You need only let us in," Nebehat said in a soothing voice.

"Okay, yeah. I let you in." Aleksander nodded again, still unsure, although he trusted the two wise scholars. He let out a long, deep breath and closed his eyes.

"We haven't started yet," said Nebehat with a chuckle.

"Oh, right."

He felt Nebehat and Cyrgiz's minds enter his own, and *then* he allowed them in.

Images of people clad in archaic clothing filled his mind. Flashes of technology so advanced he had no idea what he was looking at replaced them, and yet even more images of cities he had never seen, places he had never been, and things he'd never done shifted through his mind.

An uncomfortable feeling like pulling off a rubber glove engulfed his skull, crawling up his spine and over his head and down his forehead as the memories flickered past his mind's eye faster and faster.

He shuddered at the sensation but paid more attention as he saw his own father's face, and then his grandfather, and other men he recognized as their ancestors flutter by. The entire history of Thanatanos, collected from the memories of thousands of men and women long dead exploded across his vision. Next, the same thing happened with images from Kurash's past. Wars. Heroes. Villains. They all filled his mind.

He witnessed countless wars and triumphs, celebrations, and tragedies; he saw a Sangoran ruler traveling from town-to-town massacring men and children. He saw Valistaran and his queen, Codruta at his coronation. And then, to his surprise, he saw images of Mara in Talohira crowned as queen. Thousands of other images flashed in the back of his memory, but he collapsed, exhausted, unable to focus on them anymore.

Finally, with a loud gasp, the connection faded, and the two scholars sitting before him slumped into their seats.

"Are they okay?" Aleksander asked. "Did it work?"

The other scholars maneuvered the two new Secret Keepers of Kurash onto moveable cots that were then carried away. No one answered him as the crowd departed.

He sat alone, still.

He remembered how exhausting the process had been when he had become a Secret Keeper himself, but he stood from his seat and stumbled, disoriented.

A single bald man with a dark goatee and warm brown skin stayed behind. He held out his hands and rolled up the sleeves of his violet robes.

"Oh, hi," Aleksander said, still dazed. He stumbled, and the man caught him and helped him sit again. "Where'd they go?"

He knew he meant nothing to the Kurashians now that they had their historians back, but he couldn't help but admit to himself that being left and discarded like that stung.

Perhaps, he had expected more pomp and circumstance beyond the odd experience that had been complete strangers disrobing and bathing him. He chuckled to himself. He knew Hanna would never let Mara live that ceremony down, and so he vowed to never let her know he'd been through something similar.

"They are bringing the new Secret Keepers to safety," said the man. "I am Umut, servant to the Supreme One. How may I assist you?"

"I'm not the Supreme One," Aleksander said, shaking his head. "Mara—"

"The Supreme One who is Called Mara Bartunek is away and has left our city in your command. Thus, I am *your* humble servant."

"Oh, well," Aleksander said, unsure of what to say. "It's very nice to meet you, Umut."

"We have met before."

"Oh," Aleksander said, clawing for any shred of memory of the man. A few moments of uncomfortable silence passed by until he simply asked, "...Where?" Before Umut could respond, Aleksander let a different question slip out. "What now? Can you tell me what's next for the Secret Keepers?"

"They will train in their art to see the past just as you have," Umut explained. "In time, your memories will fade, and you will forget the secrets they now possess. But for now, they remain with you, too. You are the third Secret Keeper until that day comes."

Aleksander felt like an absolute fraud wearing the robes of the Secret Keepers, but he just gave an awkward nod as Umut fell silent again, staring into his soul.

"Okay. I'm just glad I was able to get their secrets back here without dying. You know, I came pretty close a few times," Aleksander said with a chuckle. Umut did not laugh. "Anyway, I understand it's a valuable part of your culture, so I'm happy to have done even a small part."

"Oh, yes," Umut said, stroking his dark, finely trimmed beard. "Very valuable indeed."

Aleksander strode to the massive window that let the sun into the room. He placed a hand on the elegant windowsill and watched as Thannish catapults indiscriminately hurled chunks of flaming stone and metal into the city, and as the soldiers pushed their barricades farther away from the wall.

"Tell me, Umut, why are there so few soldiers in the city?" Aleksander asked. He had always wondered why the Kurashian military and navy were so small, relative to those of the other countries. Well trained, of course, but much smaller. He had only ever seen their forces at the Battle of Laniras.

"We do not want to conquer Sangora, Talohira, or Thanatanos, and in the past, we have had little need to protect ourselves. Your people squabble amongst themselves but have graciously left us out of the conflict until recently," Umut explained. Aleksander gestured out the window, saying nothing, and Umut nodded. "And the former Supreme One who was Called Kadir defended us. We didn't need armies to do it."

"How?" Aleksander asked. "The Supreme One was a Mindspeaker that could also create beams of light, but that couldn't be enough to fend off an entire army, could it?"

"Come, follow me," Umut said, gesturing over his shoulder.

Aleksander followed the servant up the stairs to an even higher chamber, and eventually they found themselves in the hollow at the top of the palace's massive dome. The high arched ceilings were painted with beautiful images from Kurashian nature and wildlife. No imagery of kings, warriors, or battles adorned the walls as they would have in Thanatanos.

A massive device of metal and glass filled most of the chamber. Aleksander paced around to peer inside, seeing that an array of telescoping mirrors amplified what he could see though the window downstairs.

"It's a telescope," Aleksander said.

"…No," Umut replied. "It is the weapon of our great protector. We call it the Spear of the Supreme One, or the Sunspear."

"Okay," Aleksander said, shrugging, as he gazed into the window that made the distance seem so nearby. "Sunspear, Sunforge… You guys like the sun here, huh?"

Umut again stared at Aleksander with a stern expression with no reaction to the joke.

"Yes."

Aleksander looked into the device for the sole purpose of avoiding the man's gaze. He directed the device toward the enemy's base camp, seeing in the lenses the massive Spirit Warrior he knew to be named Kallus hulking around, directing troops. He did not see their leader, Raksil, but spied his tent.

"So, it *is* a telescope."

He adjusted the level of the scope so that he could look up to the sea; his heart ached, wondering if Mara, Kamil, and Alia were aboard one of the ships sailing into the horizon.

He jumped, startled, as his vision went black. He took his eye from the eyepiece to see that Umut had stepped in front of the viewing mechanism.

"This is the Supreme One's most powerful weapon," Umut said. "It was able to amplify his power of light into a beam that could decimate any threat. It has not been used since his death."

"Why didn't we use it to save Mara? To save the others?" Aleksander asked in a sudden fit of anger. "This was here the entire time, and you didn't use it to stop this invasion before it started?!"

"It was not the Supreme One's will to use the weapon, and so I did not do so," Umut replied.

"Because she didn't know it existed!" Aleksander replied.

"She never asked."

Aleksander looked at him with an incredulous expression, and at that moment, he wanted nothing more than to punch the man right in the throat.

"Calm yourself. You are in a holy place. The Sunspear absorbs the power of the sun. Even without Kadir's power, it is only able to be used once per week, more or less, when the weather shines on us as it does now."

"Again, what are we waiting for?!" Aleksander exclaimed.

"The Supreme One who is called Mara is away. It is a heinous crime punishable by death for any to enter this room unless accompanied by the Supreme One."

"Mara's not 'away.' She's been captured, you absolute scab," Aleksander said.

"As you are the Supreme One who is Called Mara's representative, you have full authority to use the Spear as you see fit."

"Then teach me how," Aleksander said, glancing back into the array of mirrors and lenses. Umut bowed his bald head.

"I have used this device only a handful of times to fight off Talohiran slavers, but I should be able to…ah, yes."

He adjusted a lever and the machine thrummed with life; it began to glow, and the room began to feel very much like the inside of a forge.

"You don't have much time," Umut explained. "Do it!"

Aleksander scrambled toward the viewing mirrors, and Umut assisted him to adjust the Spear's focus by using a wheel resembling the helm of a ship at a smaller scale. A lever that moved horizontally and vertically next to the wheel aimed the weapon.

His heart thundered in his chest as he aimed the weapon at the Thannish camp. He set the sight over Raksil's command tent and pulled the lever back, hard.

The room buzzed with fiery energy, and the sound of the loudest thunder Aleksander had ever heard filled his ears. He let go of the wheel, and the mirror sight bounced up and down.

"Steady the beam!" Umut shouted.

Aleksander regained composure and directed the beam of pure, concentrated sunlight. The energy decimated the command tent; the entire area around it exploded in a flurry of dirt and fire.

He directed the beam next toward the docks, melting through many of the catapults and ships that stood there. He let out a cry of victory as he directed it back, blasting down the barricades the Thans had set up. He saw Kallus, the massive Spirit Warrior at the corner of his vision, and with the last bit of energy the Spear of the Supreme One had left, he directed the beam directly through Kallus's chest.

His armor stood no chance. The beam disintegrated his artificial body, sending smoldering bits of him flying as the light faded. Aleksander watched as what remained of the Spirit Warrior hit the ground in a crumpled heap of armor.

"Hell yeah," Aleksander muttered. "Umut, I want our troops to regain the ground we lost near the barricade. They still have thousands of troops down there, but we need to advance."

"It will be done." Umut bowed low. "I expect you will wish to return to the battle?"

"Yes, in the Supreme One's stead," Aleksander replied. "I'll need to call for reinforcements. Who can we call?"

"At your word, I will send for the Obsidian Herd."

"The what?"

"The tribe of Minotaurs that live south of the city. We have a good relationship with them. They will heed our call and join the fight, should we ask of them," Umut explained.

Aleksander stopped as Umut headed toward the door, the light from the window reflecting off his bald head. That was the second piece of crucial information that Umut had failed, or more likely, *chosen* not to tell him or Mara. Information that could have prevented the violence below.

He followed the servant out of the palace toward the Kurashian forces below. He explained his plan to the military leaders they found there; to his surprise, they agreed with his decision, and ordered their men to push the Thans back after Aleksander's attack with the Sunspear.

He didn't understand the Kurashic being spoken around him, but their excitement of making up lost ground was palpable.

And then he wondered—once Tal-Ahosh was liberated, did he have a way home? Hanna had taken Hippo back to Thanatanos to inform them of what had happened to Mara and the others.

He shrugged it off. Everything would work out.

"I'd like to meet with other leaders to figure out what our next steps should be," Aleksander called to Umut, who was now several paces ahead of him.

Despite his growing mistrust of Umut, joy filled his heart, for he had done two acts of good for the people of Kurash that day; he had returned their sacred knowledge and defended them from destruction.

His excitement was short lived, however, as four men in golden armor grasped his arms and clapped them in chains.

"You are under arrest for desecrating the holy spear of the Supreme One of Kurash."

"No, you are mistaken," Aleksander said with a reassuring smile that did little to mask his worry. "The Supreme One who is called Mara put me in charge, and Umut, her servant, led me to the—"

He glanced at Umut, who was smiling as they grabbed Aleksander.

The men did not respond and forced Aleksander forward at spear-point. They did not lead him to the palace or back to the battle. Instead, they steered him through the city, threw him into the darkness of the back of a carriage, and as he scrambled toward the doors, it lurched forward.

After several minutes of travel, the smooth streets of the palatial center of town gave way to rocky paths of sand and gravel. A particularly angry bump in the road caused him to bounce in the cart, striking his head on the roof of the carriage. He groaned and lit a ball of flame in his hand behind his back to illuminate the vehicle, and as he did so, the doors behind flew open. A man stood there, shouting angrily in Kurashic.

Aleksander extinguished the flame and raised his hands to show he meant no harm. However, he did not let down his guard. The last time he had been forced into a carriage had not turned out well for him.

The soldier pointed a curved dagger, and Aleksander understood enough from context that he was ordering him to climb out of the cart. The men led him toward a massive compound with gates and walls lined with spikes and wire. The Kurashian prison of Tal-Ahosh. No Thannish was spoken to him until he found himself led through the gate and down dusty hallways lit by eerie flame.

They forced him into a dark cell, and the door clanked shut. He curled up on the floor and tears began to stream down his face. Not for himself, but for his friends. For Alia, who had never been a slave or prisoner with them. For Kamil, who had been forced from his homeland once again.

But most of all, for Mara.

Every time he managed to nod off to sleep, memories of her tortured screams aboard the Arcship haunted his nightmares.

CHAPTER SIXTEEN
PRISONER #00000-68

A melancholy nostalgia and fierce longing filled Mara's heart. She stole a quick moment to look over her beloved city through a window in the palace of Doftaan—*her* palace. People came and went about their business, unaware of her presence and that she was bound in chains being led to her execution.

What did they think of her now? What other acts of tyranny and hatred had the imposter that sat in her throne committed in her absence? Her heart ached for the people of the Sangoran states of Terman and Adess. Not only were they already suffering from a famine created and enforced by those in power in Doftaan, they were now also being forced into slave camps, just as she had once been.

The others in Balgorod knew her plans to supply her beleaguered people there with food and clothing, and she hoped her friends would still go through with her idea, despite everything else that had transpired.

Were Aleksander, Hanna, Alia, and Kamil even still alive?

She let out a deep breath as the Thannish soldiers led her away from the beautiful winter view of her city. Through the familiar halls they pushed her, portraits of Florenta and her ilk hanging nearly everywhere she looked.

They came to the doors of her throne room where two women stood guard with spears in hand. At first, they crossed them to bar her path, but upon seeing her face, they laughed and gave a hearty cheer.

"You found her! You found the imposter!" said the first, her voice excited and hopeful. The other remained silent, keeping her eyes glued to the true Empress of Blood.

"The Mistresses of Dusk are assembled and waiting for you," said the second guard, a bit more apprehensive. Mara recognized her as a soldier named Ondrea, a lovely young woman with a bright future serving the people of Doftaan. Apparently, Florenta hadn't ousted her *entire* palace staff.

Ondrea looked into Mara's eyes with concern as the first guard opened the door. As the Thans led Mara into the throne room, Mara felt Ondrea reach out and touch her tunic.

Mara glanced over her shoulder to see a tear rolling down the woman's face.

"I'm so sorry, Empress," Ondrea mouthed. Mara offered her a weak smile, as much acknowledgement as she could give without getting her in trouble.

"How did you do it?" the first guard asked. "I mean, you look *just* like her!"

Mara gave no response but held her head high as the Thannish soldiers pushed her into her own throne room.

Despite being clad in chains, she strode toward Florenta's assembled Mistresses of Dusk with all the authority and presence that she had maintained as Empress of Blood; for all the days she had spent debating if she deserved her station, for every moment she wondered if she would ever return to Doftaan, she remained poised and calm. She had to. She had returned to Doftaan at last, and she knew this was her only chance to reclaim her throne and save her people.

All eyes in the chamber turned toward her. Dozens of Sangoran politicians, military leaders, and other high-profile citizens watched from the tiered seating around the room. However, more importantly, the seven new Mistresses of Dusk appointed by Florenta sat around the half-moon table that had been moved from the council chamber into the throne room.

Mara stared with cold eyes at a woman of her perfect likeness sitting upon her throne.

"I thank you all for assembling today, and I apologize for my tardiness," the real Mara said as they led her to the center of the chamber. The audience and Mistresses of Dusk alike mumbled amongst themselves, and one of the Mistresses of Dusk, a horrible woman with a beaklike nose and beady eyes stood in defiance. Mara knew her as Enrieta, a staunch supporter of Florenta's sins against the empire.

"At long last, the imposter has been found!" she shouted with a shrill tone like a bird caught in a trap. Then, pointing a crooked, accusatory finger asked, "Who are you?"

"You know exactly who I am." The entire chamber was silent for a long moment before Mara spoke again. "Isn't anyone going to welcome me home?"

"Empress, we—" began one of the illegitimate Mistresses of Dusk but caught herself before she said more. Mara suspected that each of the fake Mara's councilors knew the truth, and that she had let the secret slip.

"Mistress Hariclea, you dare address this imposter as such?" Enrieta shrieked. She brought her bony fist down on Hariclea's hand, smashing one of her fingers. "Guards!"

As Hariclea nursed her injured finger, several soldiers entered the room from the various doors leading into the chamber.

"Stand down," Mara ordered, and the soldiers stopped in their tracks, unsure of how to respond, just like those in the doorway. "Your people see through this illusion." She gestured to the fake Mara. "They don't dare attack me, because they know the punishment is death."

"Oh, for the Goddess' sake," said Enrieta, turning to the fake Mara. "What is your order, Empress?"

"The imposter has already answered that question," the fake Mara said. "Her punishment is death, of course."

The real Mara laughed, but no humor filled the room— only righteous, defiant condemnation.

"For crimes against the throne of Sangora, I sentence this woman to death," the imposter said with Mara's voice. "But no simple hanging is enough to pay for this heresy. I reward my council with the opportunity to kill you themselves. Remove her wings, and then remove her head."

"So be it," Mara said, stepping toward the half-moon table. Each of the council members stood as guards handed them ceremonial spears set aside for executions—a barbaric practice Mara had done away with after becoming queen.

She turned to the audience, and with cold steel in her eyes, she said, "With deep regret, I hereby sentence Mistresses Enrieta, Hariclea, Kariana, Tamara, Viorela, Ruksandra, and Lenuta, appointed by the false queen Florenta Karpaska, to death."

"Empty words," the fake Mara said with a dark chuckle; a shiver trailed down the real Mara's back upon hearing her own voice and laugh come from whatever creature it was that now sat upon her throne.

She stood unarmed, her hands crossed and bound at her waist. The Mistresses of Dusk stood from the table and encircled Mara.

She let out a deep sigh. "It doesn't have to be this way."

"Are you begging?" the fake Mara asked. Laughter arose from the audience.

Mara shook her head. "I never beg."

"Then what?" asked Mistress Enrieta.

"I'm giving you a choice. If you stop now, your lives will be spared. You will be tried for your crimes against Sangora, but you will live out the rest of your days in a cell rather than face execution today."

"Execution?" Mistress Enrieta scoffed.

"Do not forget that *I* am the Empress of *Blood*. And there *will* be blood."

"Council—raise spears!" called the false Mara.

Mara closed her eyes as they raised the seven ceremonial weapons.

"*I shall be your sword.*" Thanatan's voice rang in her mind.

"And I shall be your hand."

"Death!" the false Mara shouted, and each of the seven Mistresses of Dusk lunged forward at once.

Mara's eyes shot open, and the Godblade materialized in her hand; she brought it up, severing her bonds before stepping with grace and poise away from the silver spears.

She swung the glowing blade overhead, severing the shafts of two of the weapons before they could strike her.

"What is this?!" screeched Enrieta.

The Mistress of Dusk named Ruksandra lunged forward, and Mara's blade sliced through her weapon before piercing the wicked woman's heart.

"Mistress Ruksandra—on behalf of Mistress Raluca, true governor of Dashga—for enforcing famine and slavery across Adess and Terman: Death."

"What are you doing?!" Mistress Enrieta shouted.

"I'm playing with fire," Mara said. "And now I'm going to watch your world burn."

As the others attacked, Mara parried a weak strike from Enrieta and shouted, "And now, on behalf of Mistress

Lavinia, true governor of Timishuara, I hereby execute Mistress Lenuta for the crimes of genocide and forced slavery and prostitution of hundreds of men, women, and children."

The room exploded into chaos as Mara thrust the blade behind her, piercing Mistress Lenuta's stomach. She withdrew the blade and beheaded the cruel woman; she felt exquisite satisfaction in the tyrant's death as her head hit the ground.

A dozen guards filed into the chamber. Mara cried out as one of the council members, though she didn't see who, smashed her over the back of the head with the shaft of her spear.

She swore as the Godblade toppled from her hand, and she hit the ground hard next to Lenuta's corpse. She turned just in time to see Mistresses Viorela, Tamara, and Kariana standing over her, ready to strike.

She knew each of the women to be cruel products of corrupt groups within Florenta's army. Three of her former Enforcers—skilled fighters, unlike Mistresses Lenuta, Enrieta, and Ruksandra.

"Come to me!" Mara shouted, and the blade broke apart into a million shards and then rematerialized in her hand; as it did so, she swept it across Mistress Viorela and Tamara's throats with one long swipe and a spray of blood.

"For the crimes of genocide, the forced famine, and enslavement of the people of Terman and Adess, I hereby execute Mistresses Tamara and Viorela, on behalf of the true guardians of those lands, Diana Fiala and Ruta Vaal!"

She turned her sights on Mistress Kariana.

"On behalf of the Alboran people and their guardian, Shanthah Kalen: death for Mistress Kariana."

Kariana's thick wing struck Mara in the throat before she could react. Her back hit the ground hard, and the Godblade once again clattered to the floor just out of reach.

Mara held out her hand to summon the sword back to her, but Kariana lowered one of her wings just in time to stop the flow of diamonds from reaching Mara's skin.

She cried out in pain as the jagged bits of crystal tore through the thin membrane of her wing before reforming into a blade in Mara's hand.

Mara received another blow to the face from Kariana's good wing, and she felt a poorly aimed stab from one of her assailants graze her forearm.

She cursed as the three other Mistresses of Dusk wrenched the blade away from her and groaned as Kariana's fists met her cheek again and again. Before she could react, Kariana dealt another vicious blow to her sternum.

The air rushed out of her lungs, and Mara tried to cry out, but no sound came; she struggled to raise her wing as Kariana stepped on it with a heavy boot, then knelt over Mara as the others held her other struggling wing down.

Her foe raised her blade over her head and brought it down toward Mara's throat. Mara thrust her hand toward her foe's chest and blasted her with a bolt of lightning from her palm. Instantly, horrendous pain pounded through her skull as if her brain were about to explode.

She knew she couldn't rely on her powers, and she swore, her breath heavy.

She summoned the Godblade and swept it across Enrieta's back. Not a fatal wound, but it would give the hag pause.

No soldier dared near the Empress of Blood or her terrible sword, and even Enrieta was silent as she and Mistress Hariclea backed away.

"Enrieta and Hariclea, I now give you your final chance to surrender to the true Empress of Blood. I don't want to kill you."

Her head pounded, and her vision began to dance.

"Yes, yes! Have mercy!" Enrieta exclaimed, falling to her knees as Mara stood above her, the tip of the Godblade pressed into the woman's neck. "The true Empress of Blood is merciful, is she not?"

"Mercy?!" Mara shouted back. "Mercy is the very thing my brothers and sisters across Alboras, Terman, Dashga, and Adess have begged you for—the last whisper from their lips as you burned them alive. And yet, you have the audacity to beg for mercy? No, today, there will be only justice."

"Revenge, more like!" Mistress Hariclea shouted. "This is not justice!"

"Perhaps," Mara said, then demanded, "How many slave camps are there in Adess and Terman?"

Enrieta covered her face with her hands as if it would hide her from Mara's rage.

"Ten," Enrieta said at last. "Ten! Are you happy now?!"

"No, Enrieta. I am not! But if Valistaran's sins created *me* in only *one* of his camps, imagine what you have wrought by setting up *ten* of them. I can think of no higher justice than what you have brought upon yourselves."

She turned her sight upon the fake Mara, who had yet to stand from her chair. As she strode toward the imposter, she heard a footstep from behind, and she whirled around to see Hariclea and Enrieta branding spears in her direction.

Mara slashed the Godblade across Enrieta's throat in a spray of crimson before plunging it through Hariclea's heart.

"You made me a villain, and so that's what I'll be," Mara said, her tone dark and cold. "I'm no stranger to playing the part."

Enrieta's head and Hariclea's body hit the ground, and Mara turned once more toward the imposter. Mara let out a deep breath as her heart thundered in her chest. She was glad none of her friends were here to witness the carnage.

"I won't be victorious when you are all dead. I won't be victorious when I take back my throne and reclaim my title as Empress of Blood. No, I will not be victorious until my people are *safe*. Until their families are reunited, and they are free," Mara said, pointing her sword at the imposter. "Now, *you* are going to tell me who you are before I remove your head."

"Is this *cruelty* I see?" the fake Mara asked, cocking her head, her voice twisting into a cold tone, not unlike Mara's own. "Surely, the great Mara Bartunek is above such things."

Mara spat in her direction. "The longer you and your council stay in power, the longer my people suffer." Tears streamed down Mara's cheeks, and her hand began to tremble. "Your council brought this upon themselves when they forced my people into camps! When *you* forced them to starve and die when there was enough food stored in Doftaan to feed them for a generation!"

The fake Mara stood and clapped her hands as the real empress stepped backward into the pool of the usurpers' blood. Mistress Kariana groaned as she got to her feet, a gory wound burned into her stomach.

"Who are you?!" Mara shouted. "How are you doing this?!"

The fake Mara strode behind the half-moon table, and as she met Mara's gaze, the imposter's eyes became dark pits of shadow before her face twisted into a grotesque shape; horns protruded from the creature's head and bone morphed into an intricate, crimson mask.

"You know who I am." The fake Mara's flowing hair and wings faded into dust. The Magistrate stood before her, the illusion shed away.

Mara rushed forward, blade raised, but her world twisted as the Magistrate's illusions overtook her; a whirlwind of smoke and blood surrounded her, and she could not tell reality from illusion as dozens of fake Mistress Karianas surrounded her.

"*Left!*" Thanatan's voice filled her mind.

She screamed and lashed out with the blade, and the illusion exploded in a cacophony of screams that did not exist; the Magistrate stumbled backward, and Mara brought her weapon around toward the crimson mask.

"*Behind you!*"

Mara twisted, parrying an unseen blow from Kariana's spear.

A man's scream filled the room.

Disoriented by the illusions as they reappeared, Mara tripped and stumbled to her knees. The Magistrate appeared before her and picked the Godblade up by its hilt.

The scream continued.

Mara thrust out her hand, and the blade shattered into a million pieces again before reforming in her own palm; she roared in her fury, using her wings to launch herself upright just as she thrust the weapon through the Magistrate's chest.

The Magistrate's mask twisted once more into the shape of Mara's face, and she stared into her own crystal blue eyes filled with hate and malice. Mara screamed and thrust the blade deeper until the handguard stopped it from going any further.

The Magistrate placed a hand on Mara's sternum and blasted her through the floor with a telekinetic burst of energy.

Mara's screams trailed behind her as she fell through the floor, flapping her wings to catch herself, but the debris struck her in the back, sending her spiraling out of control toward the ground far below.

She cried out in pain as she called upon her own powers of telekinesis, sending the crumbling bits of stone and metal away from her. She managed to regain flight just in time to prevent herself from hitting the ground, but she collapsed in pain as her head throbbed even worse.

A sudden bout of nausea overtook her, and she felt detached from reality, as if looking through the eyes of another. She begged the fates to keep a stroke or seizure at bay; if it happened now, she, and thousands of her people would die. She had to fight.

She tried to summon the Godblade, but it didn't come.

"No, no, no, not now," Mara said as the dull ache filled her mind. "No, no… It can't end like this…"

She sensed the Magistrate's presence near her, and she could no longer hear Thanatan's thoughts. Where she should have felt relief, utter terror filled her soul as she realized the Magistrate stood above her holding the Godblade while she was on her hands and knees, alone, powerless, and unarmed.

As her enemy brought the weapon down to smite her, Mara willed all of Thanatan's residual power in her mind to shatter the blade; the pieces of crystal lay dormant and dim on the ground.

The screams—they had been Thanatan's. Was he dead at last? The world around them burned, and the Magistrate crouched next to Mara.

"Just kill me," Mara said, blood trickling into her eye from a gash on her forehead. Despite her split lip, she muttered, "What are you waiting for?"

"Oh, little empress. I was queen of this land far before you even had wings," the Magistrate said out loud. "What you say is yours is truly mine. It always has been. We're both fighting to reclaim the same throne."

Mara's mind raced as she tried to back away from her foe.

"Who are you?" she asked through heavy breaths.

"I'm sure you can figure it out," the Magistrate replied. "Today is not the day the Empress of Blood meets her demise. No, today is when she rejoins her people, don't you think? I owe you that much. You care so much for them? Join them in their suffering."

Her voice was like mud beneath a cart's wheel.

Mara's heart pounded in her chest as she glanced over at the shards of the Godblade. They were slowly flowing together to reform the weapon, but she still could not summon it.

A dozen guards appeared around them. Without her powers, Thanatan's influence or the Godblade, she knew she would never escape if she resisted. She raised her hands in defeat, and a dark laugh escaped the Magistrate's throat.

"Yes, little empress. Give up. You are never, and *will* never, be enough to save these people," she said, her mask mere inches from Mara's face. Tears rolled down Mara's cheeks, but she refused to speak as a pair of guards clapped cuffs around her wrists and restraining bands around her wings. "I know that you are dying, Mara Bartunek. You will live your last days knowing you failed your people yet again. May you die alone."

Mara said nothing as the guards led her away down the steps of her own palace toward a carriage led by four black horses. She could feel the eyes of bystanders watching as she was accompanied away, and shame washed over her soul.

They must all hate her for what the Magistrate had done with her name and her face. She had failed them, and they, the people she loved, hated her.

As the guards opened the back doors of the prison carriage, a cry arose from behind her, and the clanging of steel shattered the night air; she turned just in time to see several of the guards turn on the others. One of her saviors flew toward her on great gray wings but was knocked from the air with a spray of crossbow bolts.

Mara cried out as the woman struck the ground, but then she was forced into the carriage. The doors shut, and she knew not if her allies would survive the ill-fated escape attempt. She buried her eyes in her hands and sobbed alone in the back of the cart as it pulled away.

The woman had died for *her*. Or perhaps, *because* of her.

She did not even try to sleep. Images of the bloodshed and staring into a twisted version of her own face haunted her mind, but most of all, the Magistrate's words filled her soul with such despair, that she accepted it as the truth.

For several hours, Mara sat in haunted silence until the carriage finally came to a stop. She wondered if they had reached their destination, or if the soldiers taking her away had stopped to relieve themselves again. The doors at the back of the vehicle burst open.

Scared Sangoran men and women climbed into the carriage, and before Mara could even react, the entire vehicle was full of trembling, crying people; they were packed so tightly that Mara began to panic, knowing she had failed each and every person pressed into the cart.

If she had been better—if she could have killed the Magistrate and Kariana—if—if a thousand things had happened differently.

A large woman was on her lap, and another sobbing woman's face was pressed into her chest. Mara managed to free her arm, and she stroked the woman's hair, hoping it would help her remain calm.

The woman reached up to grip her hand. Tears formed in the corners of Mara's eyes, and for whatever reason, she began to sing.

Whatever it takes, my love
I'll hold your heart here with mine
And from your side ne'er I'll depart
Even when my heart breaks, my dove
Oh, there with you, yes, there I'll be.

As the simple melody and angelic voice escaped her lips, the entire cart seemed to stop crying to listen. She continued.

Whatever it takes
My dear sweetheart
For both our sakes
Far from death's black dart
There with me, yes, you'll be
Whatever it takes

Even the soldiers driving the vehicle seemed to quiet down to listen through the bars now. She felt others reaching out to grip her arms and legs just to touch her, as if it would give them comfort.

When she finished the song, she was silent, resting her head against the back of the vehicle as silent tears rolled down her cheeks.

"Thank you," a timid voice said from somewhere in the carriage. No one else said anything, for the stranger had spoken for them all. Mara cradled the woman's head and stroked her hair for many more hours.

At last, they reached their destination; vicious winds beat at the sides of the cart, and she dreaded what awaited them outside. Dim winter light under a light snow streamed into the carriage as the doors opened. Although it was dark outside, even the last, dying bit of light stung her eyes, aggravating her vicious migraine.

As the soldiers ordered everyone from the vehicle, they removed each prisoner's shackles one by one and then lined them up outside the cart.

Mara looked over her shoulder as she stretched her legs and twisted her wrists to see a massive, fenced enclosure lined with guard towers. She hung her head.

The guards began to inspect each person in line, pulling several of them away from the others. Powerless to help them, Mara shut her eyes to shut out the nightmare as a young boy called for his papa. She cursed her damaged brain and wished more than anything to be able to use her powers to fight back, but she knew in her heart that even if she did kill their captors, they had nowhere to go.

The soldiers pulled seven people, including several frail elderly men and women from the line before forcing the rest toward the camp. They left the others behind to fend for themselves in the snow; the little boy's papa was among them.

The boy's screams would never escape Mara's heart.

She felt all hope die as she was marched through the great wooden gates of yet another slave camp. After everything that had happened, after everything she had conquered and survived—

As they stepped through the gates, they joined several lines leading into the camp. She tried to see what was happening, but she couldn't see around the mass of scared people.

When it was her turn to step up to the front of the line, a man behind a desk raised a red-hot brand with some kind of mechanism with knobs to adjust its red-hot edge.

One of the soldiers that had driven her to the camp pushed his way forward and whispered something into the ear of the Thannish man with the brand, who chuckled and nodded his head.

"Ah, Mara Bartunek, is it? Well, I hear we have a special number for you, empress," said the man, a soldier wearing the colors of Thanatanos.

Mara said nothing as the man wrenched her arm upward and thrust the brand into her forearm; she grimaced but refused to cry out like the others around her, but tears once again flooded her vision.

The man pushed her through the doorway into the camp, and another guard, a stone-faced Sangoran woman, forced her to follow a group of fellow slaves. As she walked with them, she glanced down at the itching burn on her arm where a number was now branded there forevermore.

00000-68

Sixty-eight. The number of Mara's slave district back in Talohira, but more, a cruel reminder from the Magistrate of who she truly was—and what she would always be.

CHAPTER SEVENTEEN
SHUT UP AND LIVE

"And you're sure that's where you put it?" Ana asked.

The entire company stood stone-faced and silent as they each processed what was happening.

"Like I said the first three times, yes," Nadezhda replied, staring in horror at the empty drawer as some of the most influential people in Balgorod looked on.

"Lavinia, I think your trip to Kurash needs to wait a few days until we sort this out," Shanthah said. Lavinia nodded in agreement.

"If our theories are right, then we need to mobilize the entire city guard, militia, and the forces on loan from Sangora to find the thief," she said. "Vasilica, please rally a garrison and search the skies."

"I agree." Shanthah turned to the three Mindspeaker students. "You three, please get a message out to lock the castle down immediately. Rayshel, please gather the Academy guards and search the castle. I want every inch of this place scoured, and please ready a carriage outside."

"Should I inform General Anca?" asked Rayshel, who stood beside Lavinia. Although she had no wings, she spoke with a Sangoran accent, and Nadezhda wondered if she was one of the fabled, dangerous Walkers she'd read about, or a human citizen of Sangora.

Shanthah shook his head. "She has enough to worry about monitoring and defending the border."

"What if they've already escaped?" one of the Mindspeakers asked as the other two went into a trancelike state to relay the message around the castle.

"Then the city guard will search the city as well. Find the rest of your Mindspeaker class and try to find anyone suspicious," Shanthah ordered.

Rayshel pulled Lavinia into a tight hug, and then she, the Mindspeakers, and Vasilica hurried off to fulfill their orders.

As Lavinia turned to go, Shanthah said, "I know what I said before, but I think you need to follow Mara's orders and get to Kurash as soon as possible."

"Are you sure?" Lavinia asked.

"Yes. We should have heard back from them by now, and I'm getting worried," Shanthah said. "Take Rayshel with you. Make a date out of it."

Lavinia scoffed. "If it's true, though…what this thing is?"

"I know," Shanthah said. Nadezhda and Ana tried to look like they weren't listening in. "Before you go, I need you to go find Mistress Raluca and Valeniya. They'll be able to help in your place."

Lavinia nodded and departed, her cloak trailing behind her.

"And what about us?" Nadezhda asked. "I—we— can help."

"I know you can," Shanthah said. "That's why you're both sticking with me. Can you sense anyone untrustworthy or feeling nervous?" Shanthah asked, but Nadezhda shook her head.

"My powers don't have a very long range," she said.

"What if you combine them with your mindspeaking?" Ana asked.

"I don't know how well I can do it without the gem, but yeah, I can try," Nadezhda said. "I wonder if what the Voice did to me is permanent…"

"Nothing left to do but try," Shanthah said with an encouraging smile.

"And you'll come with us?" Nadezhda asked.

"Of course. You're the best hope we have, and we've got the best healer in the academy with us, so—wait, where did you get *that* thing?!" Shanthah exclaimed as Ana lifted a long dagger with a cheeky grin.

"Oh, I hide it under my mattress just in case," Ana said.

"In case of what?" Shanthah asked as Nadezhda locked the door and they set out.

"In case members of a conspiratorial cult steal a gem that drains the life out of its victims and makes you hear voices and gives you the ability to read minds, of course," Ana replied. "Keep up, man."

"Oddly specific reason, but okay," Shanthah said with a wink. "Okay. Here's the plan. Ana keeps me safe. I keep Nadezhda safe. Nadezhda keeps Ana safe. Deal?" The girls nodded. "Now, reach out. Like Kamil taught you."

Nadezhda let out a slow breath and shut her eyes, trying to shut out the distractions around her. She tried to think about nothing at all, letting her mind wander about the castle. She'd never managed to maintain a connection longer than a few seconds except the one time with Kamil, but she worried he may have been the one keeping the connection stable.

As doubt started to get the best of her, the worry wafting from both Ana and Shanthah prickled at her skin, making her unable to focus properly.

"Can you two stop worrying so much so I can focus?" They chuckled, unsure if she was serious or not. "Actually, no. Keep worrying. I have an idea."

She focused on their worry and then reached out with her limited mindspeaking abilities to find similar emotions. She could sense worry all around the castle—it was the norm nowadays with Thannish forces ready to cross the border at any moment. However, now that she was technically a Mindspeaker now, she could discern the reason for emotion, rather than just what they were. She'd noticed that at the festival, too.

There was worry about why the castle was being locked down…worry for a test in an invisibility class…worry for a date…someone worried about a speech… And then, there it was. Worry that they'd be caught and arrested. It was the same feeling she had sensed at the festival from the apprehensive Purists.

"Got it!" Nadezhda exclaimed, sprinting down the hall. Ana and Shanthah hurried after her, and she yelled, "They're heading…uh… What direction is that way?"

She pointed down a hallway to the left.

"Northeast," Shanthah replied.

"To the docks, maybe?" Ana suggested.

"Good call, Miss Sala!" Shanthah exclaimed, and they started down the hall. As soon as they encountered some guards, Shanthah shouted their plan, and they followed alongside them. "Get word to Mistress Lavinia and the other Mistresses of Dusk!"

One of the men saluted Shanthah and headed in the opposite direction as they exited through the front gates. Another set of guards allowed them to pass, and the trio found the carriage Shanthah had requested was already waiting for them outside; the driver saluted, and the guards accompanied them inside, shut the door, and they were off in mere seconds.

"Ports district!" Shanthah exclaimed, and the woman driving acknowledged his order with, "Yes sir!"

"Can you still sense him?" Ana asked. Nadezhda shook her head.

"The connection broke. I'll try again, but it's hard to maintain the link with people. I'm not very good, yet."

"You're doing great," Shanthah said, glancing out the window of the carriage. "We've got this."

The vehicle bumped along the cobblestone paths that eventually turned to paved roads. They made it down the hill to the ports where large ships were docked, and traders went about their daily business. Fish markets and stalls selling all kinds of food lined the streets, and many people called out as they saw the Master of Balgorod's carriage approaching. Many stopped in front of it, holding their hands up in praise.

"Move," Shanthah muttered. "Not now…"

"Ah, your adoring fans," Ana said.

"Do they do this often?" Nadezhda asked.

"Yeah, but it seems like they only do it when I'm in a hurry and don't have time to soak it all in," Shanthah said. "Only joking." He paused. "Only a little bit. Don't tell Hanna."

"That's what you get for liberating a nation from a tyrannical monster," Ana said with a wink and a smile.

Shanthah laughed. "Yes, I guess you're right."

"Try again," Ana said, clutching Nadezhda's hands. "You can do it."

Nadezhda nodded, trying to see through the cloud of excitement outside the carriage; the positive emotions clouded her vision with puffs of vibrant color, making it hard to see. But then, she remembered the moment at the festival how distinct the dark emotion had been on the backdrop of the symphony of excited colors.

"I know I can do it," Nadezhda said. "And I know how. I'll keep looking, but I don't see anything. I lost them."

"Then let's hope Valeniya got the message to search the docks," Shanthah muttered. "At least we've got that information, yeah? Good work, Nadezhda."

Shanthah glanced out the back window of the carriage to see another trying to drive through the crowd.

"Who is Valeniya?" Ana asked.

Nadezhda had forgotten about Valeniya, whom she'd met the day Mara and Hanna rescued her from Laniras, but before she could reply, Shanthah spoke up.

"Uh, daughter of a friend. Kind of," Shanthah said, glancing out the window. "She can find people no matter where they are, but unless she knows and has a connection with the person she's looking for, she needs to know where to look. Fortunately, because you got us this far, she should be able to find our thieves."

"If it was the Purists that attacked us on the hill, they were the same ones that killed my brother," Nadezhda said, her countenance dropping. Cyan wisps of compassion trailed from Shanthah's face as he leaned forward.

"Then we're gonna get those monsters, and we'll make them look you in the eye when we throw them in the dungeon forever," Shanthah said with a wink. Nadezhda swallowed to fight back tears and nodded. Ana took her hand. "And we'll keep a closer eye on them, this time."

Shanthah said no more as he climbed out of the carriage. Nadezhda and Ana chuckled as they heard him greeting the crowd as he tried to make his way through.

The two girls hopped down as well, and the second carriage parked next to Shanthah just beyond the crowd.

Lavinia stepped out of the vehicle, gathering her cloak. Her beautifully crafted armor shined in the dim sunlight, and behind her, a girl a little older than Nadezhda and Ana poked her head out of the carriage.

"Remind me your name," Lavinia said, grabbing Nadezhda's shoulder. "Nadezhda, right?"

They'd literally met mere minutes earlier, and she was already on the verge of forgetting her name. Nadezhda scowled and said, "Yes, Mistress."

"Help Valeniya find them," she said.

Nadezhda bowed her head as visible worry whipped around Lavinia's head. Even she, who could very possibly be the most confident and composed person she'd ever met, was filled with anxiety.

Lavinia clapped her on the shoulder and pulled Shanthah aside to speak with him. Ten Sangoran soldiers were trying to disperse the dense crowd to let the carriages through.

"Valeniya, nice to meet you again," Nadezhda said. Valeniya gave a brief smile and seemed to stare straight through Nadezhda, just as she had in the carriage when they'd first met.

"Did Lavinia explain what we need?"

"Yes."

Valeniya seemed agitated at the crowd, and Nadezhda could feel her discomfort even without her powers. She turned to Ana, who looked at the girl with concern.

"Valeniya, would you be more comfortable if we spoke in the carriage so you can't hear the crowd?" Ana asked.

Valeniya nodded, and Ana shut the door with a deep breath. "They're pretty overwhelming, huh?"

Valeniya nodded again.

"I'm going to try to send you an image of them to your mind," Nadezhda said. "Or fail spectacularly."

"Stop it," Ana said.

"Sorry."

"I'm ready," Valeniya replied.

Nadezhda shut her eyes and focused on the robed men and their masks. She wished she could show Valeniya their faces, but this would have to do.

She felt the connection with the girl's mind, but it felt fuzzy and cloudy, unlike any she had ever felt before. For a moment, Nadezhda saw the outline of dozens of people across the blackness that was their shared vision, and she wondered if Valeniya were watching over them.

Nadezhda projected the image of the Purists into Valeniya's mind with all the concentration she could muster. Unable to maintain the connection, she snapped back to reality. Valeniya's eyes were glossed over with a silver sheen.

"Woah," Ana said. "What's going on?"

"They are in a boat, sailing up the great river. It has white sails and has a flag of Alboras, but it is not a ship of Alboras," Valeniya explained. "The Purists inside have what they took from you."

But then, she screwed up her face and began to scream.

"Valeniya!" Ana exclaimed, clutching her hand.

As Ana tried to calm Valeniya, Nadezhda touched the girl's mind with her own and beheld what had terrified her.

In her mind's eye, she saw a dark shadow with silver eyes; she could feel its soul, and then its voice filled their minds.

"Ah, Valeniya and Nadezhda, hello. I believe you're looking for me. Given your recent betrayal, this is most unwise."

Nadezhda broke off the mental connection, and Valeniya shook her head to rid it of the Voice.

"What was that?" Ana asked.

"Him…" Valeniya said, rocking back and forth. "My father had me look for him once before, and he saw *me* when I found him. No one else has ever done that."

"Who?" Nadezhda asked in a soft voice.

"Thanatan."

"Thanatan?! Like the god?" Ana asked. "Is that who has been talking to you, Nadya?"

Nadezhda and Valeniya shared a look; it was the first time the girl had made eye contact with either of them. Her breathing was still quick, but she had stopped screaming and shaking.

"How is this possible?" Ana asked. "He isn't real. He's a myth, right? Just a part of their hall of gods, or whatever?"

"I don't know—we need to tell Master Shanthah and Mistress Lavinia *right now.*"

As if on cue, Shanthah opened the door.

"Finally got through. Anything?" Shanthah asked, helping Valeniya, Ana, and finally Nadezhda step down.

"Yes. A big boat on the river flying a Thannish flag," said Nadezhda to Shanthah. "Valeniya says… She says it's Thanatan."

Shanthah swore and turned to Lavinia to relay the message, and then she spread her mighty wings and shot into the sky. He led the others down the road, which was now parted by Sangoran soldiers to grant them passage.

"I need a ship!" Shanthah called.

"Right this way, sir!" said a Sangoran man, leading them to a small military vessel. They boarded the ship, and the crew sprang to attention as the Master of Balgorod issued orders to the captain on board.

"This is crazy," Ana said. "Wait until my parents hear about this."

"You'd actually tell them?" Nadezhda asked with a laugh. "If mine were alive, I'd keep it a secret. Hearing anything about this would absolutely kill them."

"Poor choice of words," Ana said. Nadezhda shrugged with a dark chuckle.

"Oof."

The ship set out; the sails unfurled. It sliced through the glassy sheen of the river's surface, passing by several fishing vessels as it made its way down the great river Vah that flowed by Balgorod and snaked north into Thanatanos.

"Everyone the gem drained of life force touched it, right?" Shanthah asked as he approached.

Nadezhda felt guilt gnawing at her heart. She glanced over at Ana, but lied, "Yes, I think so."

"But it never absorbed yours. I don't think that was by its own choice. I think you were the best candidate for it to achieve its goal, and it manipulated you into doing what it wanted," Shanthah said. "So being the only one *he* could count on also means you're the only one *we* can count on."

"Why me?" Nadezhda asked. She felt that she already knew the answer.

"Kamil believed the theory that he needs a Soulreader to access and consume lifeforce. You can see into others' souls, so it makes sense that he needs your power to manipulate them, right?" Shanthah asked. "You stay here while we deal with the Purists. You're not to fight, is that clear?"

Nadezhda and Ana both nodded.

"The Voice—Thanatan, that is, threatened me and Valeniya. I'm worried he won't spare me this time."

"I don't think he has a choice, even if he claims he does," Shanthah said. "Kamil's thoughts were that you are immune. You can't see your own emotions, or soul, or however it works, so he can't access your lifeforce."

"Oh," Nadezhda said. "Lucky me."

"I wouldn't say so," Shanthah said with a chuckle. "Stay safe."

One of the sailors called out, "Enemies ahoy!"

Far downriver, the mast of their target's ship came into view as their swifter vessel gained on it. Ten Sangoran warriors leapt into the sky, spears held aloft as they glided toward their target.

"We've got them," Shanthah said, pumping his fist into the air. "Nowhere they can run."

"What happened on the hill back at the festival?" Nadezhda asked, realizing she didn't know what happened after she had lost consciousness.

"I took out the big guy. The leader, whatever his name was. We captured three of them, but four got away. The other three escaped."

"So, we didn't capture any of them?"

"Technically? No."

Nadezhda nodded and turned to Ana, grabbed her hand, and gazed into her eyes with a fearful expression, although the ship was alight with anticipation and courageous hope. As she breathed in Ana's compassion, she began to relax.

Soon, their little ship caught up with the other to see the Sangorans locked in combat with the cultists; two Sangorans had fallen. As their ship reached the Purists, massive, metal barrels slid out of windows of the enemy vessel.

"What are those?" Nadezhda asked.

Her question was answered as the sounds of explosions and Shanthah shouting to get down filled the air. Ana and Nadezhda screamed as splintering wood and broken metal rained down around them.

"Cannons!" someone shouted.

"Obviously!" Shanthah exclaimed. "Prepare to board!"

The cannons continued to pulverize the starboard side of the Alboran ship, blasting the railings and much of the hull to smithereens. The crew below deck cried out, and several were struck with the balls of wrought iron, leaving them horribly disfigured or knocked overboard.

"Stay down! I've put you two in terrible danger," Shanthah said as they stayed low to the deck. "I am so, so sorry."

Before either of them could respond, another cannonball struck a nearby wall in a spray of splintered wood. Shanthah peeked up over the broken railing to see Purists in the windows reloading the cannons for another salvo. This time, Shanthah's soldiers were ready for the onslaught, but their damaged ship lurched to the side away from their foes.

"Turn us hard to starboard!" shouted Shanthah. "We're going down, but we're taking them with us!"

The helmsman turned the crippled ship toward their foes as a cannonball whizzed past Nadezhda's head, splintering the helm. The helmsman was thrown to the lower deck, and the masts and ropes went wild as the mast groaned and cracked. Shanthah set his foot on the broken railing just as the prow of the ship tore through the other vessel's port side with a deafening crunch of wood and metal.

As they collided, Shanthah drew his blade and leapt from one ship to the other, vanishing into nothing. The nearest Purist fell dead, a long scarlet stripe drawn across his neck.

"Nadya!" Ana shrieked, picking herself up. She scrambled to the side of the ship to see Nadezhda dangling from a splintered chunk of the ship that had been ripped away.

"Tatiana!" Dismay and helplessness exuded from Ana's face and arms as Nadezhda dangled there, trying in vain to pull herself up. "Please, help!"

Ana lowered a broken piece of railing to Nadezhda, who reached up and gripped onto it, the splinters digging into her palms.

"Help!" Ana cried again, knowing she couldn't pull her up alone. Much of the crew had already boarded the other ship, and Nadezhda began to slip. "Hold on, Nadya! Hold on!"

"Don't worry, just falling for you here!"

Ana spread her wings and flapped into the air, arcing around to try to help her climb up. As she grabbed her by the arms, an arrow struck Nadezhda in the shoulder blade. They both screamed, and Nadezhda lost her grip and plummeted toward the water below.

Ana covered her mouth with her hands, not even able to scream as Nadezhda was swallowed up by the river. The world exploded around her, reducing the Alboran ship to a burning wreck. Tears streamed down her face as she sobbed Nadezhda's name. A Sangoran woman dove headfirst into the sea, her wings pressed against her back to slice like an arrow through the water.

A few tense moments later, Lavinia emerged from the waves with Nadezhda in her arms. She groaned as she raised her wings above the surface, using them like massive flippers to swim away from the wreckage. She flapped them to splash out of the water, and then with another flap and a groan, she was airborne enough to lay Nadezhda down on the deck of the enemy ship.

Ana crawled over the bow of the ship as the aft sank. She leapt into the air and glided over to the other vessel. She drew her long knife and hurried to Nadezhda's side as Lavinia pressed on her chest before breathing air into her lungs.

"Stop it!" Ana shouted.

"She'll die, girl! Back up!"

Lavinia continued to work on Nadezhda, who eventually coughed up lungs full of water. Ana pulled her to a sitting position, and Lavinia slapped her on the back so that she would spit up the rest of the water.

"No medical supplies," Lavinia muttered. "You, give me your shirt. We need it to staunch and bandage the bleeding."

"What? No!" Ana hurried to Nadezhda's side. "Can you remove the arrow? I'm a healer, but we haven't covered that in class. I don't know how to—"

Lavinia grabbed the shaft of the arrow and pulled it from Nadezhda's back; Nadezhda screamed as it tore her flesh, spattering blood over Lavinia's arm and face.

"Hey!" Ana shouted, pushing Lavinia aside. "Don't hurt her!"

Ana placed three fingers on the arrow wound and massaged it; her fingertips tingled and grew warm as the torn flesh around the wound turned from gruesome red to a soft pink.

"Come on…" Ana whispered as Lavinia looked on.

The Mistress of Dusk flexed her wrist, and a short blade emerged from beneath her armored vambrace. She used it to tear a strip of her cloak away and handed it to Ana.

"Just in case you can't close the wound, bind it with this."

"No faith in me, I see?" Ana asked but took the soggy bit of cloak all the same. She shut her eyes and slid her fingers into the wound, making Nadezhda groan in pain.

"Stop squirming, please," Ana said.

"Don't hurt her," Lavinia responded in a sarcastic tone.

"Let me die… find someone new…"

"Nadya, I love you, but shut up and live," Ana replied, drawing her fingers from the wound to coax it shut.

Spindly fibers of flesh bound to one another as if she were sewing it together. It was nowhere as neat as when Alia did it, but it would suffice.

"Thank you…" Nadezhda said in a feeble voice as Ana rubbed her back where the wound had been. A nasty scar would remain there, but she had not yet learned how to prevent scarring in her class.

"Alia knows how to convince the body to create more blood, but I don't—I hope you didn't lose too much… I…"

She trailed off as the sounds of battle below deck sounded. Four more Alboran ships sailed up to the wreckage of the two ships. More Sangoran soldiers leapt onto the wreckage to apprehend the remaining cultists.

Shanthah approached, his tunic stained in blood.

"They're your problem now," Lavinia said.

She clapped Shanthah on the back and bid him farewell to set out on whatever mission Mara had assigned her. Shanthah hung his head. She took flight and was gone.

"She's right. You two are going back to the Academy," Shanthah said. "I can't believe I—"

"No, you listen here," Ana said, pointing a figure at Shanthah's chest. "I'm a healer, so that's what I'm gonna do."

Shanthah chuckled before gesturing to Nadezhda. "You two really are a perfect fit."

CHAPTER EIGHTEEN
CHOKED BY PREJUDICE

Two soldiers climbed up from the deck below, guiding a large Purist holding a smoking canvas sack. His wrist and forearm were horribly burnt, and his face was gaunt as if drained of life. And indeed, he was, for Nadezhda recognized the signs of Thanatan's influence.

One of the soldiers collapsed with a final breath, and the bag clattered to the deck. His companion scrambled to his side, shouting his name. The Purist fell a moment later, his head striking the deck with a sickening crunch.

"No one but Nadezhda touch that bag!" Shanthah shouted. "Back up!"

The second guard stumbled back as Nadezhda scrambled forward, reached into the sack to retrieve the Voice's gem, and squeezed it tightly into her palm.

"It's alright," Shanthah said, and everyone let out a collective breath. "Everyone at ease."

The gem felt warm in her pocket. *"You need to run."*

"Something's not right," she whispered as she stood up. A sudden burst of dark emotion echoed the Voice's words. It wasn't a common one, so what was it?

Alboran soldiers led the remaining Purists away across the gangplank to the other ships now weighing anchor next to the ruined ships. A woman tried to force Ana to come with them, but Ana resisted, smacking the soldier's hand away.

"It's going to be okay, Nadya," said Ana as a stretcher was brought on board. As the dead and wounded were carried away, she helped Nadezhda to her feet. "Do you need to go with them?"

Nadezhda nodded, a pained look across her face before repeating, "Something's wrong."

Ana placed a hand on her cheek. "It's the blood loss. You'll be feeling weird for—"

"No, I mean…" Nadezhda trailed off before opening her hand to show the gem.

"Oh." Ana turned to Shanthah. "Mr. Kalen, a word?"

Shanthah was busy issuing orders to the crew, but as he finished, he made his way back to Ana and Nadezhda. The crew pulled up the anchor and unfurled the sails and began to set out downriver.

"What is it?" Shanthah asked. Nadezhda held out the gem; dark shadows danced across its surface. "Ah. What's he saying?"

"He said I need to run." A couple of guards offered her a stretcher, but she shook her head. "No, that's not necessary. I can walk."

They nodded and moved on.

"Never a good thing to be told," Shanthah said. "Let's get you downstairs to rest. There's nowhere else you *can* run until we get back to the docks."

"I'll make sure I healed the wound correctly, too," Ana said. Nadezhda agreed, the dark feeling still surrounding the damaged ship.

Shanthah guided the two girls down the stairs to the lower deck, and just as one of the soldiers shut the door, a series of loud pops rang out above.

"What was that?" Shanthah asked as a soldier bolted the door from outside. "What are you doing?"

The ship was not heading back upriver to Balgorod's port. That much was clear. Terrible screams and the sound of battle sounded on the upper deck. From the other side of the lower deck, six soldiers appeared from the shadows holding long weapons of wood and iron tipped with blades. They pointed them at Shanthah, Nadezhda, and Ana with stern, cold expressions.

"Stay behind me, girls," Shanthah said as he drew a blade from his belt. They did so without hesitation. "That was a tricky move up there, killing your own men just to get to us. Good for you."

As their leader spoke, Shanthah replied with a slow, unenthusiastic clap of his hands.

"We'll give you one chance to surrender the girl and the stone," said the man. "You have five seconds to comply."

"That's two more than people usually give me," Shanthah replied, drawing his sword.

"I said five seconds!"

"Yeah, yeah, I heard you the first time," Shanthah replied. "How about I give *you* five seconds?" The soldiers pointed their strange weapons. "Alright, I see how it's going to be. But you aren't getting anywhere near them."

"*Run!*" the Voice echoed in Nadezhda's mind, the foreboding torchlight dancing across their faces. "*They have guns. RUN!*"

"They have what? Run where?!" Nadezhda shouted.

"Fire!" called the captain, and the room was illuminated with sparks and the smell of smoke. Shanthah threw up his hands, turning himself and the two girls invisible.

But it wasn't enough. Red splashes appeared from midair, and Shanthah rematerialized and fell to his knees, his body riddled with bullet holes.

"*RUN! LEAVE HIM!*"

Shanthah stumbled to his feet and echoed Thanatan's call, shouting, "RUN!"

The men with the terrible guns turned their sights on the girls as Ana dove toward Shanthah, who collapsed, his tunic dyed crimson.

"Reload!"

The men readied their weapons with another series of clicks and raised them directly at Nadezhda as Ana frantically examined Shanthah's wounds.

Nadezhda stood defiant, staring down enemies down with an icy glare. She could feel the men's satisfaction, pride, and a nasty emotion that was stifling, suffocating, and gave her a sick feeling in her stomach.

"Kill the Night Witch and take the girl," said the captain.

Prejudice. That is what she felt. A deep, unfounded hatred. It was stifling, and Nadezhda found it hard to breathe in the cloud of toxic emotion. Ana raised her left wing to shield Nadezhda.

"Stay behind me, Nadya!"

But Nadezhda did not do as she was told. She pushed her way past Ana's wing, planted her feet, and reached out with her mind. Remembering what Shanthah had said about Thanatan using her powers to influence others' souls, she established a mental connection with the leader's mind.

"Take her!"

Nadezhda knew she'd established the connection as a trickle of foreign thoughts of murder and hate crept into her mind like sand through a sieve.

With tears in her eyes, she focused on the suffocating feeling of prejudice exuding from each of the men and closed her fist. The men began to choke, and she cried out in utter rage; she focused on every hint of hatred they held for the woman she loved for no other crime than being born Sangoran.

She closed her fist even tighter, pressing her fingernails into her palm to flood their minds with every negative emotion she could sense. Each of the six men collapsed to their knees gasping for air.

Their fear began to obscure her thoughts. It was their fear that she latched onto next. She made each of the men feel the combined dread of their companions in a dark swirling cloud of crimson and black smoke visible only to her.

If at that moment, guilt had replaced their fear, perhaps she would have refrained from what she intended to do next. But the men had no intentions of letting them live, and she sensed that they still relished in the thought of Ana's murder.

And then, she made them see what she could. They screamed in horror, collapsing onto their sides and backs. Nadezhda glanced at Ana, who was still busy working on Shanthah's wounds.

They made eye contact, and Nadezhda expected to see disapproval or fear, but all Ana said was, "Do it, Nadya."

Nadezhda melded the dark emotions together and forced it ever deeper into their minds to squeeze the life out of all six men. Blood dripped from their noses, eyes, and ears, and then with a disgusting gurgle from each of their throats, they were dead—literally choked by their own hatred and prejudice.

She stumbled backward and collapsed next to Ana, who said nothing as she continued to tend to Shanthah's wounds.

"Is he…?"

"If I work fast, I can save him," Ana said, "Help me get these weird ball things out, okay?"

"Okay," Nadezhda said.

With a squeamish look, she peered into one of the bloody wounds. Three of the balls had pierced his body, and others had passed by, filling into the wooden pillar behind him with holes. Ana drew her knife and cut away the side of Shanthah's shirt.

She had managed to pry one of the balls of lead out of his side and was coaxing the injury closed, but she was trembling from overusing her undeveloped powers. One bloody bullet lay harmlessly on the ground.

Nadezhda gagged as she slid her fingers into the wound to feel around for the bullet. Shanthah groaned in pain, involuntarily jerking his arm back, but Nadezhda knelt on it to keep it down. She dry heaved again.

A faint cloud of fear wafted from his face. Not a selfish one like the dead men had felt, but a selfless, caring fear. It was a strange combination to her, but the dominant emotion clouding Shanthah was disappointment and shame; the feeling that he had failed Nadezhda and Ana. And for that, she vowed not to fail him.

"Oh, gross, gross," Nadezhda said, dry heaving as she scooped the lead ball from Shanthah's flesh. As Ana worked to close the final wound, Nadezhda wiped the blood on Shanthah's pant leg. Without warning, she turned and vomited in the corner.

"You calling my job gross?" Ana asked.

"Absolutely, yes," Nadezhda said, wiping vomit from her chin with a bloodstained hand.

A burst of magenta humor and a cloud of yellow appreciation fluttered down like snowflakes around Shanthah's head.

Ana smiled as she created threads of new skin. Her vision swam, and she collapsed on her backside holding her forehead.

Nadezhda sat next to her and grabbed her hand. Shanthah groaned as he tried to get to his feet.

"Stop it," Ana said, pushing him back down. "Stay down, or I'll tell your fiancée."

"Please don't do that. What happened?" Shanthah muttered.

"You got shot, remember?" Ana asked.

"Not the first time…been stabbed too. I'll be alright—" He tried to stand again but fell once more. "Oh, woah."

"Told you to stay down."

"So, the whole thing was a ruse to get Thanatan's heart?" Nadezhda asked.

"*Obviously,*" the Voice echoed in Nadezhda's head.

"Yeah," Shanthah muttered. "Bet if you checked their arms, you'd find Purist tattoos. Killed their own men just to get to you…"

Ana nodded. "Well, it's quiet now. Either they killed our rescuers, or we won up there. What do you two think?"

"The big guy locked us in. I say we use that to our advantage and rest for a minute," Nadezhda suggested. The ship rocked as it continued downriver. "I still don't think we're turning around."

The others nodded.

"Is this what your life is like, like all the time?" Nadezhda asked. Shanthah chuckled and then sighed as Ana put his bloodstained coat under his head as a pillow.

"Yeah, pretty much."

"Let's hope they think we're dead," Nadezhda said. Ana nodded and sat with her back against a wooden beam, her eyes closed.

"Try to get some sleep, both of you," Ana ordered. "Don't get up, Shanthah, even to go to the bathroom. You hear?"

"But what if—"

"No. Stay down."

"Yes, doctor."

They all fell silent and eventually Ana and Shanthah surrendered to sleep, but the sight of the dead bodies and adrenaline pumping through her veins wouldn't allow Nadezhda the same luxury.

"*Why did you tell me to run?*" she thought, knowing the gem in the sack in her pocket could hear her.

"*They no longer worship or serve me as they once did. They serve another, a usurper. The Magistrate of Thanatan.*"

"I don't know what that is," Nadezhda muttered. "Don't really care either. If your own Magistrate hates you, maybe they're my friend."

"*No.*"

Nadezhda knew he was right. She stroked Ana's hair as she snored against her shoulder.

She only hoped the smell of the bodies of their six assailants wouldn't draw any attention—or make her vomit again. That was eight people she'd killed, now. They were going to kill Ana. They hated her. They didn't even know her, and they hated her. Just because she was born different from them. She told herself that it had to be done.

But then again, she was glad they were dead. She wasn't happy that she'd been the one to do it, but she was glad, nonetheless. She turned her head and kissed Ana on the forehead; she stirred and snuggled in closer.

A peaceful calm emotion drifted from both Shanthah and Ana. She was glad they were at peace in their dreams. A moment of respite. For whatever reason, her mind turned to Lavinia and Valeniya, and she wondered where they were now.

"Why are they after you?" Nadezhda whispered. "And are we right? You're Thanatan?" Nadezhda asked.

"*Yes. They want to give my power to their master.*"

"So, I've been walking around with a god in my pocket?" she whispered. "What happened to you?"

"*Empress Bartunek and Hanna Samsa killed me. In doing so, they trapped my soul in crystals formed by my ruined armor. The gem you carry is my heart. My mind. My essence. My soul. Within it lies my greatest power, the Connection to Creation. In time, I will teach you this power, and we will destroy the Magistrate. Sleep, now, Nadezhda. You and your companions are safe. I will wake you should danger find you.*"

Nadezhda brushed the crystal with her mind and sensed no malice in Thanatan's words or emotions, and she too drifted off to sleep.

CHAPTER NINETEEN
STILL, THEY SANG

Frigid water dripped down Mara's shivering body onto the bloodstained cement beneath her feet. She was helpless to do anything for her people being led like cattle through the torturous showers and back into the cold winter night.

Although her heart was breaking for them, she refused to let her captors see any sign of weakness, for she knew that in their eyes, even a single tear meant they had won. That they had broken her. She would not give them such satisfaction.

Not again.

Not before she broke *them*.

"Alright, move on!" shouted an officer. He blew a whistle, a sign for the soldiers to force the nude, sopping wet prisoners out into the cold. The guards outside distributed clothes after registering the slaves and handing them slips of parchment containing relevant information.

Hats. Inadequate coats. Threadbare shirts stained with sweat and blood. Pants patched together with remnants of other ruined garments. Boots with heels that had been long-since worn through and toes open to the cold.

Many Sangorans were given human-made clothes that did not allow for their wings to poke through. Some tore at the fabric to create holes while others simply lived with the discomfort.

As Mara emerged into the frosty night, the guards stationed there whistled and shouted crude remarks, but still, she refused to dignify their cruel profanity with a response.

Winter's cruel bite stung her bare skin, and as she tried to turn her head, she found her hair thick with icy crystals that cracked as she moved. She stepped, shivering, toward a man behind a desk with a thick stack of parchment and several cups of steaming liquid to keep him warm.

"Name?" the Thannish man asked. His eyes were firmly glued to her chest.

A Sangoran guard repeated the request in Sangoran. "Zvatha?"

Mara glared at the woman. How could she be doing this to her own people? She glanced over her shoulder to see an elderly woman shivering behind her draped in her shriveled wings to try to keep warm.

"Give her clothes first," Mara said, gesturing to her with the tip of a wing. "I'll wait."

"Oh, this one speaks Thannish, everyone!" the guard called. "Very well. Gives me more time to look at *you*, gorgeous, and less time to look at *that*." He gestured to the old woman.

Mara glowered at him as he registered the woman and sent her through. They gave her an assortment of clothing, but Mara knew it wouldn't be enough. She wouldn't survive long.

"Okay, beautiful. Name?" the soldier repeated. She obscured her chest with folded arms, and he snorted before meeting her gaze for the first time. He recoiled at the ferocity in her eyes, but she kept her satisfaction to herself. "Full name?"

"Empress Mara Killianeva Bartunek."

"This beauty's a joker! Says she's the Empress of Blood!"

His compatriots laughed along with him, one of them spilling the foul contents of the bottle in his hand into the snow. "What's your *real* name?"

"I won't repeat myself."

Although she would never let them know it, every word from her mouth pained her as she stood there shivering.

"Well, then, *empress*, here are your papers," said the officer. Mara could tell he was taking a long time to process her on purpose. One of the other soldiers wrenched her arm upward to show the brand on her forearm. His eyes widened, and he let out a guffaw.

"You weren't kidding," he said, examining the number. "It really is you. Well, you have no throne here. Just chains and snow."

He scribbled the number on the parchment and handed it to Mara then gestured for her to continue into the camp. Out of the corner of her eye, he saw his hand reach downward toward her, and she lashed out with a wing to his throat, knocking him and his chair to the ground.

The Sangoran translator chuckled at her companion's misfortune, but the guard that had grabbed Mara's arm slammed her in the back with the end of a spear to force her outside.

Mara expected to feel cold beneath her feet as she stepped through the blanket of white but winced at the prickling numbness she found there instead. She repeatedly flexed her hands, toes, and wings to increase circulation as much as she could.

She grabbed the nearest bundle of clothing and hastily threw the clothes on. She didn't bother to make holes in the tunic for her wings—she could worry about that later. She sat upon a low fence and raised her feet to put on her wool socks, taking care to keep them dry before slipping them into her new old boots. Finally, she pulled a floppy hat over her ears. It was so large that it hung loose over her dark hair.

She held her itchy gloves to her face and breathed warm air into them to try to warm her lips and cheeks. She was so cold now that she didn't know if she could speak even if she wanted to. The drab and itchy clothes were warmer than she'd expected—still completely inadequate for the current weather, but anything was better than standing naked in the cold after being sprayed with icy water.

And that is how she felt, even fully dressed. Naked of power. Naked of any ability to help her people. Naked in the dark—alone, and afraid, just like the rest of them. An uncomfortable, horrible solidarity.

They forced her to stand next to the rest of her group for five more minutes while the officer processed each of the new prisoners. Mara held up her own document for the first time, desperate for anything to distract herself from the inhumane treatment of the slaves. It was written entirely in Thannish.

Name: *Mara Killianeva Bartunek*
Identification Number: *00000-68*
Nationality: *S*
Citizenship: *S*
Sentence: *Life, no possibility of release*
Residence until transfer: *To be determined*
Assigned duties upon transfer: *To be determined*
Transfer Location: *Tazovski*
Special Permissions: *None.*

Refer to next pages for further information

Nationality and citizenship: S. Sangoran. It was the one bit of writing scrawled on the parchment that made her smile. No longer a Than. She had found her people, and she would suffer alongside them. The slur *'Night Witch'* was handwritten next to the S, but to her, it felt like a badge of honor.

The remaining pages described her daily rations while imprisoned, as well as information on her transfer to the Tazovski camp. Some of the other slaves that had been waiting longest had already collapsed, and the soldiers hauled their bodies away.

She said nothing as several men with long, slender guns surrounded them; she wished her knowledge of the weapons was limited to what she'd read about them in the history books in the library of Bukaral, but she'd now seen their power in person. She dreaded to think what other technology Thanatanos had revived from the Deadlands with their dead god's help.

The officers led her and the others to the center of the encampment where she was relieved to find a roaring fire. Several prisoners lay unmoving in the snow, their bodies having surrendered to hypothermia. She knew she had to warm herself slowly so that her body didn't go into shock.

The slaves huddled around the roaring fire, but Mara's heart twisted in her chest as she saw a human woman sobbing into a scarf. Mara only made out two of her incoherent words.

"Jan sunik!" she cried in Sangoran. *My son!*

So, she was a Thannish born citizen of Sangora.

Mara had to fight back her own tears as she stepped away from the group and pulled the woman into a close hug. The woman sobbed into her chest and said, "Deiku vam."

It was the way to say thank you in a northern dialect of Sangoran; the woman must be from a nearby city, but still so far from her son and family.

She guided the woman back toward the fire before glancing around at the squalor and despair of the camp.

"Totjo bude hoš. Budeši či teblaca, i ja poznaju vun sunik, hošo?" Mara said. *"Everything will be alright. You'll be warm here, and I will find your son, okay?*

"Onen zvathan—Daris. Deiku, deiku vam." *His name is Daris. Thank you, thank you.*

"I vun zvathan?" *And your name?*

"Maryia," she replied.

"Ah, sam pahason i jan zvathanam! Ja Mara." Mara said with a smile. *Ah, kind of like my name! I am Mara.*

The old woman's face lit up; she seemed to like that. Mara was glad, because she didn't know what else to do for her.

She rubbed the woman's back for a few minutes before leaving her by the fire. She'd do what she could to find Daris, but she hadn't seen any young men in their group. If he had been with them, he was likely dead by now.

Those not huddled around the bonfires ambled about the camp mindlessly around ramshackle huts and long buildings that resembled army barracks.

As she sat by the fire, she felt others gravitating toward her, as if her mere presence gave them a thread of hope in this dark place. She pretended not to notice as she tried to warm her body. She looked to the west to see a large gap in the wall surrounding the camp.

"You're wondering why there isn't a gate," said an officer as he walked by, noticing her gaze. Mara stared into his soul with cold eyes. "We don't need one. You get stuck outside in the Plains of Adess, you're dead."

Her white breath floated upward as the last few of her group approached. The officer raised an eyebrow and slipped a finger beneath her chin to force her to look up at him.

"I had to see if the rumors were true. We've been waiting for you, you know," he said with a chuckle. "Glad the invasion can start now that you're here. It was getting old waiting for something to happen."

Mara nearly broke her vow to herself to remain silent, but the man turned to address the rest of the slaves around the fire. Other guards forced those sitting to stand, even those too weak to do so.

"I am Senior Sergeant Tibor Mazanek of the Thannish army," said the man. "I oversee the voyage to the Tazovski camp where you will be sent next. I also oversee the camp and manage special projects there. You may be wondering why you are here—an easy enough answer. You are here because of your crimes against the Union of Thanatanos and Sangora."

Mara glanced up in shock; news of a union between the two countries had not reached Balgorod. Even Aleksander had not brought back such news from his mission in Thanatanos.

Perhaps, she thought, it was propaganda to break these beleaguered people. Or even more chilling, it was the truth, to be announced as soon as she was captured.

Sergeant Mazanek glanced over at Maryia, who was still sobbing. Mara reached down and grabbed her hand. Her crying slowed, and Mazanek moved on.

"As many of you have seen, there are no gates here. You are free to go. No one will stop you, but no one is stopping my men from hunting the local wildlife, either," said Mazanek. "And for those Night Witches among you too stupid to understand that—I don't mean rabbits or deer, I mean *you*. I'm afraid you won't last long here or in Tazovski. Fortunately for you, my pay depends on at least *some* of you surviving the trek up north. But of course, we don't want you to die. We want you to live long, full lives here, helping build Thanatanos!"

His soldiers joined him in a round of irreverent laughter.

She shook her head. She'd heard it all before. Men had made similar speaches when she'd first been forced into the Talohiran slave camp.

A familiar voice filled her mind. *"Mara?"*

Mara glanced around, drawing Mazanek's attention. He gestured toward Mara, and one of the men struck her in the back of the neck with the stock of his musket.

She fell to her hands and knees. She groaned and rubbed the spot where he had struck her as they knocked Maryia to the ground as well.

Mara glared up at Mazanek.

"If our *empress* over here is lonely, she'll need to get over it," he said. He loomed above her and snapped his fingers. Two large men grabbed the sobbing woman beneath the arms and hoisted her up before heading toward the gate.

"What are you doing?" Mara shouted, stepping forward, but the other guards trained their guns on her once again.

"Teaching you your place. I've been told you were… How did they put it? They said you were *troublesome* in the Talohiran labor camp, and that won't do here," Mazanek said.

Mara watched in disbelief as the men forced Maryia out of the gateway then barred the way with spears as she attempted to come back inside. She would die on the frigid Plains of Adess for no other reason than speaking to Mara.

"Let her back in, you coward. Punish me for whatever you think she did, not her," Mara said.

"Empress, I'm being merciful," Mazanek said. "That woman has a child. Had, sorry." One of the other guards gave a proud chuckle as Mazanek corrected himself. "Wouldn't knowing that he was dead just be torture for her?"

She spat in his face, resulting in five muskets pointed at Mara's head, but the commander gestured for them to stand down.

"History is never kind to men like you."

Mazanek wiped the spit from his cheek and laughed.

"Honey, history's never *met* a man like me," Mazanek replied. "Now, for anyone who wants to prove their innocence, you will do so by refusing to associate with Mara Bartunek. Is that clear?"

A Sangoran woman stepped forward and shouted, "Šlova Jempratam Hraujan!" *Glory to the Empress of Blood!*

Mazanek snapped his fingers, and the nearest guard pulled the trigger on his musket; with a loud pop and a cloud of smoke, the woman fell dead, blood oozing from her neck into the snow.

Mara clasped her hand over her mouth, and the others in line screamed, not having known what the strange weapons from the ancient Deadlands did.

"That's the blood of two people on your hands now, little Empress. Don't let there be more. Thanatanos needs hands to build." Mara was silent, staring straight ahead. "Please, don't break my heart by causing more death."

"Mara, can you hear me?"

At first, Mara thought the voice had been Thanatan's, but she realized it was Kamil speaking to her. Her heart leapt in her chest.

"Kamil?" she thought, hoping he could hear her without tapping into her powers. If she had another stroke here, she'd be dead. She made sure to keep staring straight ahead to not alert Mazanek.

"You've been assigned housing," Kamil thought in her mind. *"Which one?"*

"House 37," Mara thought back.

"Okay. We need to see you. We'll be there tonight."

"We? Is Alia with you?" Mara responded. Her heart thundered in her chest as Mazanek, whose attention was finally off of her, began explaining to the group how they would be transported to the Tazovski camp in the far north.

"Yes. We are both here. We're alright… relatively."

"I'm not sure if you saw what just happened, but—"

"I saw. Don't worry. We won't be punished if they don't find out."

"Kamil, no. I can't let you risk that."

She knew the images of the dead Sangoran woman and Maryia still screaming to be let back in would be etched in her mind forever.

"It'll be okay."

"No. I love you two too much to let anything happen to you. Please, Kamil. Please don't come."

"We figured out a way to trick them. They have no idea we sneak out of our barracks."

"How?"

"I make them see what I want them to see and forget what we don't want them to see. It works, don't worry. See you tonight, friend."

She felt his mental presence fade from her mind, and she realized she hadn't heard any of Sergeant Mazanek's words for several minutes. When she began paying attention again, Mazanek and several other guards were chuckling, and the row of prisoners shifted with unease.

He must have finished his 'welcome' speech, as he saluted the soldiers, who returned the gesture, before he departed. The other officers began to herd the prisoners toward their assigned barracks.

A man, whose nose and brow were purple with frostbite, collapsed nearby; Mara's heart ached for him and the rest of her people as he was dragged away.

A silent scream stuck in her throat as the last thing she saw before being shoved through the barrack's door was one of the guards shooting the man in the chest with a crack and a puff of smoke.

And then the door slammed shut, bathing the terrified prisoners in complete darkness.

Frightened voices began whispering in hushed tones checking for friends and loved ones; Mara's heart shattered yet again as she heard a little boy calling for his mother with no answer. Whether the boy's mother was Maryia or not, she had no idea.

"Kamil?" she asked in her mind.

She received as much of a response to her question as the little boy had. Her heart thundered in her chest, and anxious tears filled the corners of her eyes. Both of the people crammed to her left and right were sobbing, and one of their shoulders was digging into her ribs, but she didn't care.

She allowed her own tears to stream down her face now that the guards couldn't see her. For now, she just let herself be broken and afraid. She let herself feel what the others did, promising to be strong for them when she could. As the voices continued to shout for one another and others began to argue, a thunderous clang filled the chamber.

The sound shook Mara's brain inside her skull, and she groaned. A guard outside shouted for silence, and when it did not come, he smashed the butt of his weapon into the side of the tin walls again and again until silence fell over the group.

The muffled voices of the guards outside were the only sound for several minutes until the inevitable crying began once more, but no one spoke.

Hours passed.

The guards' voices outside faded, and a timid voice from somewhere within the barrack, which was little more than a long cattle shed, asked, "Singing girl?" Mara's eyes shot open, even though there was nothing to see in the darkness. Again, the voice, almost a whisper, said, "Are you there?"

"I'm here," Mara replied, choking back tears.

"Can you sing again? Like you did in the carriage?"

Mara let out a slow breath and began to hum the melody of her mother's lullaby. She knew the lyrics weren't perfectly poetic, but they were her mother's words. And if the beautiful melody and its words comforted *her*, they might also comfort *them*. She closed her eyes and let the song roll into the darkness.

She felt someone's hand grip her arm and another found her hand; she squeezed that hand, and whoever it was squeezed back.

"More?" a woman asked in a Sangoran accent.

"Please," a frail sounding man nearby added.

She wanted her people to know that she was there with them. For all of them, human and Sangoran alike—no matter who they were, Mara sang for them.

"Beautiful," someone whispered, and Mara smiled in the darkness. She couldn't catch the rest of what the person said, but she heard someone else say in Sangoran, "Taha krasna. Ja ce hjošu rozumat." *So beautiful. I want to understand it.*

After each verse, she sang it again in Sangoran.

Sobs filled the barracks, but they were no longer frightened. There was something to them. A new quality—no longer defeated. They were tears of hope, of experiencing something beautiful. Her smile reached her eyes, which welled with tears of joy.

As she opened her mouth to sing again, the guards slammed on the walls. She shut her mouth, but to her surprise, someone else, an old man by the timber of his voice, began to sing the same song in the darkness.

"Whatever it takes, my love," the frail old man sang.

Then, from a Sangoran woman, "I'll hold your heart with mine."

"And from your side never depart," came the voice of the scared human boy.

Their voices in the darkness were beautiful. Haunting.

And finally, they all began to sing in unison. They didn't get all the lyrics right, but she didn't care. The song had done its job. It had brought hope into the darkness.

The guard outside slammed his weapon into the wall, but still they sang. Others joined in the song in Thannish or

Sangoran until the entire building was alive with Mara's music as more and more of the prisoners gained the courage to sing.

Light filled the chamber, and a bullet whizzed through the air before ricocheting off the metal ceiling; the song was replaced with screams before the doors slammed shut once more.

Silence filled the barracks for the rest of the night.

CHAPTER TWENTY
THE CONDEMNATION OF ALEKSANDER

The prison walls of a prison far from the slave camp on the Plains of Adess seemed to close in on Aleksander as if trying to suffocate him. He couldn't have been in the Kurashian cell for longer than a couple days, but he had lost all track of time. They were sure to feed him at random times so that he couldn't track the time with meals, and he still hadn't faced trial despite being told he would as soon as possible. He was beginning to wonder if he ever would.

And then, a lit torch banished the darkness, and a group of Kurashian men and women in elegant robes appeared outside the bars of his cell. The man in the lead spoke in Kurashic while his companion translated into Thannish for Aleksander.

"Aleksander chof Thanatanos, you will now stand trial for your crimes—"

"Finally," Aleksander cut in, rubbing the stubble on his chin. "What took you so long?"

"—Against the sovereign nation of Kurash, under the authority of the Supreme One of Kurash who is named Kadir," continued the translator, ignoring Aleksander's comment.

"Kadir is dead," Aleksander spat back. "The Supreme One of Kurash is named Mara Bartunek. He died to save her. You know that, right?"

They unlocked his cell door and forced him to his feet. He resisted at first, but as someone pressed a hot torch sconce against his back, he relented and followed behind them. As they passed rows of other cells, the torchlight illuminated the prisoners' faces. Although most were Kurashian, he saw many Thannish or Talohiran prisoners and even a few Sangorans.

They looked up at him in silence, and he made eye contact with a young Sangoran woman who wrapped her fingers around the bars with tears in her eyes as if to beg for help. He hung his head as he was led up and out of the prison block.

Sangorans in cells. During Mara's absence, was the new Kurashian government under Umut's command rounding up Sangorans in defiance of their new ruler? He knew there couldn't be many Sangorans in Kurash to begin with. Their hope must lie with Mara, now.

He wished visions from the Secret Keepers would fill his mind to help him understand what was happening. Were these men legitimate enforcers from the court, or were they simply Umut's henchmen sent to get rid of him?

No carriage awaited them outside the prison, and the Kurashians paraded Aleksander, his hands bound and eyes blinded by the harsh sunlight through the streets as a crowd gathered to watch. Even here, people liked to gawk.

The grand court of Kurash stood nearby, capped by a golden dome with dramatic, sweeping architecture like waterfalls that flowed from the tip of the dome all the way to the ground where it twisted into vines that wrapped around the building. Were he not about to stand trial, Aleksander could have stared at it for hours in awe.

The multitude watched Aleksander ascend the gilded steps into the court. He wondered if word of his arrest and trial, or, worse, he feared, his execution, had spread amongst them. Concern was etched on many of their faces; several people called out to him in Kurashic as the men pushed him through the front gates.

The violet and crimson carpets lining the golden halls led to multiple smaller trial chambers, but the guards guided him to the Grand Court itself, a massive, spherical auditorium at the center of the building with a high stand in the center and seating all around.

A judge clad in brilliant amethyst robes and a yellow sash stood, and the multitude gathered in the seating around the room did as well.

"Aleksander of Thanatanos, you stand before the Grand Tribunal of the Sovereign Nation of Kurash under the rule of Yasir the Grand Judge, authority given to him by the

Supreme One who is Called Kadir. We note the absence of the Supreme One at this given time," announced a man on a stand beneath the judge's seat.

"Sure do love your adjectives here," Aleksander muttered. He knew Shanthah would have laughed, but he was glad no one heard him.

The platform they had forced Aleksander onto hissed with steam, and it rose high into the center of the chamber on a pillar so that he was almost level with the judge, but not quite; Yasir the Grand Judge remained at the highest point in the room.

There was nowhere for Aleksander to run now, even if he wanted to—which he did want to do, but he kept silent.

"As is customary in this tribunal, you are granted the third highest status in Kurash so that none in this nation may judge you except the Supreme One of Kurash, Yasir the Grand Judge, and the gods themselves. As the representative of Kaan, God of Justice as well as the Supreme One who is called Kadir, Yasir the Grand Judge holds the decision of your fate in his hands alone," the man proclaimed. "The Grand One will now read your charges."

Aleksander glanced around the room to see thousands of people gathered for his trial. Elaborate mosaics of a being with the wings and head of a bird adorned the dome; in his hands were a book and a set of scales. On his hip, a blade.

"Charge number one: murder of the Secret Keepers of Kurash," Yasir the Grand Judge said. "Umut, advisor of the late Supreme One who is called Kadir, bore witness to the murders four years ago. How do you plead?"

Aleksander hesitated for a moment that he knew was too long. "Not guilty. I saved the Secret Keepers' lives that day. It was King Valistaran Talohir who killed—"

"It is not your station to place judgment or blame on another here today," Yasir replied sternly. "Are the Secret Keepers dead?"

"Well, yes."

"And you were there when they died?"

"Yes, like I said, I watched Valistaran—"

"Umut and Cyrgiz both were present. As your only witness, whom you accuse, is not here to defend you, their memories damn you. I have seen in my own mind their thoughts, and they agree with one another; therefore, you are found guilty of murdering the holy Secret Keepers, which leads to your second offense: stealing the eternal memories and history of the Secret Keepers, our most sacred possession. How do you plead?"

Aleksander shifted nervously. He had indeed absorbed the memories of the secret keepers four years prior, but they had forced their memories into his head to keep them safe rather than lose them.

"Not guilty," Aleksander replied. "The Secret Keepers gave me the memories rather than lose them. If not for the war in Thanatanos and Sangora, I would have returned the secrets sooner, but I am trying to rectify this offense by coming back here."

"You have admitted fault that you, a Than, took the holy memories of ages past from the Secret Keepers of Kurash," the Grand Judge said. "You are found guilty of this charge, but you are absolved for, as you said, rectifying this offense. The new Secret Keepers thank you for this service."

He nodded his head in something akin to a bow.

"Thank you," Aleksander said. The judge cleared his throat. He glanced over at Umut, who had a grin on his face.

"Charge number three: conspiracy to murder the Supreme One. You planted Dragonsouls all around Tal-Ahosh and instructed them to misuse their powers to explode around the city, causing death panic. This evidence was provided to us by King Valistaran Talohir, four years ago. How do you plead?"

Aleksander let out a long breath from his nose. If Valistaran were here today, he would retract the statement; he cursed the man for being absent, among other things.

"Again. Obviously, not guilty. They killed my—they killed King Romiton Romus that day too. I was not party to that action. I was protecting the King of Thanatanos *and* the Secret Keepers *from* Valistaran's men!"

Aleksander couldn't believe what he was hearing as the judge laid out specific evidence that he had been the one to plan and execute the attack on Tal-Ahosh on the day his father, King Romiton Romus, had been killed by Valistaran over a disagreement over the Secret Keepers.

"You are found guilty of conspiracy and murder." Aleksander hung his head. "Charge number four: Desecration of the Spear of Kadir. Upon your arrival, you used the holy relic to fight the battles of Thanatanos. That weapon has not been touched by any save the Supreme One in hundreds of years. Without the Supreme One's light, it will take many months to regain its power, leaving us open to attack."

Aleksander glanced at Umut behind Yasir and wanted more than anything to punch the man in that smug smile. He glared until Umut made eye contact then quickly looked away.

His mind raced. Umut had been the one to coordinate the transfer of the Holy Memories to the new Secret Keepers. He had been the one to guide him to the Spear of Kadir. What was he playing at? And then a desperate plan popped into his head.

"Grand Judge, if I may speak?" Aleksander asked. The judge motioned to him to give permission. "I believe that Umut, former councilor and servant of the Supreme One who was called Kadir plans to betray Kurash."

A hushed whisper circled the room.

"It is obviously a lie," said Umut.

"I believe the Grand Judge made me second only to him during my trial," Aleksander said. "I hereby order you to shut your mouth, you scab."

Umut scowled.

"And what evidence do you bring before this tribunal?"

"He was in charge of me giving the memories to the new Secret Keepers. He guided me to the Spear of Kadir. He wanted the memories in someone's head that he trusted, and he wanted me put away so no one would know the truth. I'm telling you now, he and Cyrgiz are up to no good. I think he's taken the memories for himself."

"An outrage!" cried someone on the stand. "Umut has only ever served the Supreme One!"

"Exactly!" Aleksander shouted back. "Then why is he not serving her?!"

"That *Night Witch* is no ruler of ours!" Umut shouted.

"There it is," Aleksander said. "You heard it from his mouth. As second only to the Grand Judge and Supreme One, do I have permission to sentence Umut to be thrown into the desert covered in meat so the beasts find him and eat him?" Aleksander asked.

The judge looked at him, perplexed.

"No," he said at last with a confused glance at his advisors, who shrugged.

"Damn it."

The muttering in the crowd grew from a whisper to full on shouting, and he felt like a beast on display in a gladiator pit ready to fight for his life.

"What more do you have to say?"

"I don't know," Aleksander admitted.

The Grand Judge was silent for a long moment, ruminating the ideas Aleksander had put forward.

"I sentence you, Aleksander of Thanatanos, to an eternity in the prisons of Tal-Ahosh until time gives you back to Leylini, the Goddess who dwells below," said the judge.

Aleksander hung his head. He knew defending himself would be futile, but it still filled him with a lasting sense of dread that gnawed at his heart. At least, he thought, he had brought Umut's own innocence into question.

He knew he hadn't articulated his innocence well enough, but he didn't know what else to say. At that moment, he envied Mara's eloquence, Lavinia's unyielding confidence, and Shanthah's quick wit all at once.

The Grand Judge stood, and so did the rest of the assembly. As he departed the chamber, Aleksander's platform lowered with a hiss of steam, and two guards approached with shackles for his hands and feet.

Something drew their attention away, and the shouts of pain and surprise echoed from the hallway as the soldiers opened the gates that led out of the chamber. The guards around the room shouted in Kurashic one to another; Aleksander did not understand, and as he tried to see what was happening, one of the soldiers pushed him to the ground, holding him down with the tip of a spear against his neck.

From the floor, he watched as a hooded Sangoran fought her way into the room, batting soldiers away with her knife-tipped wings and arm blades. The torchlight danced off her shining armor as she fought her way toward him.

"Get up, idiot!"

"Lavinia!" Aleksander shouted as the woman threw off her hood to reveal a bloodstained face. Her hair was tied back, but strands of unruly hair stuck to her face with sweat.

Aleksander twisted beneath the soldier and threw up a burst of flame; he was careful not to strike the man lest yet another charge be put on his head, but the distraction was enough for him to squirm free.

As the court guards began to shut the gate, Lavinia grabbed Aleksander and wrenched him around; with one flap of her wings, she shot into the air, twisting between the doors as they closed. Aleksander screamed the entire way as she spiraled through the gap and dropped him hard on the road.

They both tumbled across the ground, her armor clanking against stone. She groaned, grabbed him under the arms without saying another word and shot once more into the sky.

They landed several minutes later near the port. The Thannish and Kurashian forces were still locked in combat, although it looked like the Thannish advance had stalled.

"How'd you know where I was?" Aleksander asked.

"When are you people going to get it? I know everything!" Lavinia said. "Now, come on."

She led him across the docks to a small ship flying a Kurashian flag at the port. The Thannish forces around shouted at her and raised their weapons, but she strode past them as if she didn't have a care in the world. If he hadn't spent several months on the run with the woman, he'd probably think that was true.

The Thannish soldiers advanced, and she summoned the twin blades from beneath her vambraces again.

"Get aboard *now*!" she shouted. Flames sparked to life in Aleksander's hands, and he shook his head.

"You know you'll never let me live it down if you rescue me."

"Shut up and fight, then, Princess."

Her blades found their mark as Aleksander defended her with bursts of fire; no one dared venture close as she disarmed several soldiers with swift jabs to their wrists and hands. Someone aboard the ship unfurled the sails and drew the anchor.

"Go!" Aleksander shouted.

Lavinia kicked a man off the edge of the dock and turned away, hurrying aboard the ship. Aleksander was close behind; he blasted the gangplank with a burst of flame before the soldiers could climb across, and then they were off.

Several Sangorans in Kurashian battle disguises greeted them. Lavinia issued some orders in Sangoran, and her followers gave the Sangoran salute and departed to fulfill her commands.

Only one remained.

"Hi there," Rayshel said, removing her golden helmet. He hadn't recognized her as a Sangoran at first, as she had lost her wings shortly after Mara was overthrown. He still felt guilty about it, but she had long since told him not to worry about it.

"Rayshel!" Aleksander exclaimed. He went for a hug but hesitated, but she didn't seem to care, pulling him into a tight embrace. "It's been too long!"

"Lavinia would say not long enough," Rayshel replied with a smile. "I love her, but I don't always agree with her."

"Glad she hasn't rubbed off on you."

Lavinia let out a laugh, a sound Aleksander wasn't particularly accustomed to hearing. Rayshel planted a kiss on

Lavinia's lips, and they shared a few sentences in Sangoran before turning back to Aleksander.

"What's going on?" he asked, and Lavinia opened the door to the cabin and led him inside.

She closed the door behind them, and she gestured to a seat. "Sit."

Aleksander obeyed, and Rayshel climbed up onto the desk and sat cross-legged upon it. Lavinia pulled a bottle of Kurashian wine from a shelf and poured two glasses.

"Oh, yes please," Aleksander said, reaching for a glass.

"Both mine," Lavinia said. Rayshel gave her a disapproving look. She sighed. "Fine, here."

She reluctantly handed him one cup and retrieved the bottle, setting it down by her feet as she downed the first glass.

"This stuff's good, but it's no Opikorla," she said.

"Opikorla has no flavor. It's just burning all the way in and out," Aleksander replied.

"Okay," Rayshel said, changing the subject. "What you said at the trial. You were right."

"About Umut?"

"Yes, obviously," Lavinia replied. "Kurashian agents loyal to Mara's legitimate rule here let us know that Umut intends to sell the secrets in those old priests' heads to the highest bidder. And do you know who that highest bidder is?"

"My dear brother, I assume," Aleksander said. He couldn't remember if Rayshel knew his true identity or not, but he trusted her with that information.

Lavinia nodded.

"Your brother the King *and* the puppet-master pulling his strings."

"I knew it!" Aleksander said. "If the Magistrate gets those secrets, they'll develop even more horrible weapons than they already have."

He pantomimed holding one of the cruel rifles, and Lavinia nodded as Rayshel took the alcohol away from her after a third glass.

"Thanatanos has troops all along their border. So, if Umut gets across in time, it'll be much, much harder for us to catch him," Lavinia said.

"Where's Valeniya Talohir?" Aleksander asked.

"He catches on quick," Rayshel said.

"She's back in Bukaral," said Lavinia. "Which means…"

She gestured to him like a teacher prompting an answer from a challenged student.

"Which means we're going to Talohira," Aleksander said.

"Ding, ding, ding, we have a winner."

"And if Umut's Secret-Keeper-for-sale has already crossed into Thanatanos?" Aleksander asked. Lavinia shrugged.

"Then we all die," Rayshel said.

She mimicked Aleksander's impression of someone holding a gun.

"Maybe Lavinia *has* rubbed off on you," Aleksander said.

Lavinia ignored the comment. "I've already sent word to Talohira to send for Valeniya. My messengers set out during your trial, so they'll make it there just before us."

"Good," Aleksander said, letting out a sigh.

"You smell really, really bad," Lavinia said.

"Hey!" Aleksander exclaimed. "I was in prison!"

"No excuse," Lavinia replied. "Anyway, feel free to bathe. Actually, please do."

She gestured to a large tub in the corner of the captain's cabin with an elegant curtain pulled back. Aleksander nodded. He knew he'd need his sleep before they reached Talohira.

"How long?"

"I'm sure you'll need about an hour in there to get that stank off."

At that, Rayshel burst out into a fit of laughter.

"Until we reach Talohira, Lavinia. I'm not asking how long I need to bathe."

"A few hours," Rayshel said. "Get that stank off, and then get some rest, buddy."

CHAPTER TWENTY-ONE
THE SPOOKY WITCH AND HER PALS

Fortunately for Nadezhda, Shanthah, and Ana, the wooden gate leading to the upper decks had been locked from the inside, and none of the Purist cult members had bothered to open it for several hours, giving the trio time to rest after their fight. Ana had healed both Shanthah and Nadezhda's wounds during that time as best as she could, and they had even found a store of food, including some fruit and bread that hadn't yet gone stale.

Shanthah had covered the dead soldiers with a tarp and used his powers to keep them invisible to keep them out of mind.

The stench did not make that possible, however.

"Where do you think we're going?" Nadezhda asked as Shanthah filled his satchel with bread.

"Prison, if they find out I'm stealing all their food," Shanthah said. He thought for a moment then said, "Well, prison either way."

He gestured to where the invisible bodies were laying.

Nadezhda glanced at Ana, sensing her fear. She gripped her hand and offered an encouraging, but probably not entirely helpful smile. A brief burst of silver light surrounded Ana's head, but her fear did not dissipate. Neither did Nadezhda's.

"If we're heading north, the river becomes too narrow at points and too shallow and rocky at others for ships like this, so we'll hop out somewhere around… oh, what town is over there…? Siofak? Yeah. Then from there, they could transport us up to Laniras by land. If we're heading east, I assume they're bringing us to Doftaan," Shanthah explained.

"What's going on in Doftaan?" Ana asked.

"Still under control by Florenta's government, which is in league with the Thans against Alboras, Talohira, and dissenters in Sangora," said Shanthah. "We know there are multiple slave—well, no. Perhaps it's best not to talk about that."

"About what?" Nadezhda asked, watching Shanthah's aura swirling with grief and something akin to wanting to spare someone of pain—compassion born out of guilt.

"You mean the slave camps?" Ana asked.

Shanthah nodded.

"They're real, then?" Nadezhda asked.

"Yeah, they are," Shanthah said. "And they're my fault. Partially, at least." Nadezhda knew she wouldn't be able to convince him otherwise as a gloomy shadow of guilt swirled around his head. So, instead, she just listened. "A lot of the slave camps have been set up in response to our revolution in Alboras. Many were modeled after the ones that used to operate in Talohira. The ones that I—well, the ones in Talohira."

Nadezhda felt the sorrow and fear that only came through suppressed, unspoken trauma clouding his features.

"The ones you were in," Ana said. "With your lovely fiancée."

Shanthah looked up. "How did you know about that?"

"Rumors get around," Ana replied.

"As you know, we recruited and rescued magic users—or powered people if like me, you prefer that word—across Thanatanos, Sangora, and Talohira. There aren't many left in Thanatanos at all. Many that escaped the Talohiran camps became refugees in Sangora. Some returned to Thanatanos. Those that did not join the enemy were killed by the Faceless or taken back to more camps, despite their propaganda saying powered people are 'Ascended' and holy or whatever."

"That's what the Purists called them—us," Nadezhda said, correcting herself. "Why do you think they are hunting us?"

"We're a threat. Thanatan wanted them as his personal army, and I think the powers that replaced him see the threat in that," Shanthah replied. "People are easily swayed. Anyway, they took more than just powered people. Political dissidents, supporters of the Alboran revolution, Kurashians, and Sangoran minority groups like the Alborans, Dashga, and Termani suspected of supporting Empress Mara."

"Miss Alia told our class they were already planning on doing that before you even started the academy," Ana replied, eying one of the wounds on Shanthah's chest that seemed to have opened up again. She scooted forward, pointing at the bloodstain on his tunic, and he groaned.

"Yeah, well, Alia should probably not be telling her healing classes about that kind of thing," Shanthah said with a smile. "But enough of this gloom! How are we getting out of here?"

He seemed chipper, but Nadezhda could see the emotions that betrayed his true feelings. She focused on his guilt and anxiety, tapping into it with her Mindspeaker abilities instilled in her by Thanatan's soul.

She didn't quite catch a joke made between the other two as she focused on trying to dampen Shanthah's deep sadness. She let out a breath, and the cloud of shame wafted away like smoke in the wind, but it did not completely fade away. Occasionally, it would manifest in the form of a thin black sheen that covered his face.

His mood did seem to lighten somewhat, but some of his guilt stuck in her own soul. Guilt had always been a sticky emotion, one that clung to minds longer than most other feelings and spread to others. Now that she had discovered the ability to influence emotions, she tried to keep his guilt at bay, but it returned with each breath.

"Sound like a plan?" Shanthah asked, turning to Ana. A flurry of both trepidation and enthusiasm exuded from their heads in a cloud of yellow and green with pops of nervous, chaotic red.

"Yup! Love it!" Nadezhda replied with a big thumbs up and an exaggerated smile. She had no idea what she was agreeing to when she said, "Let's do it!"

"You didn't listen to a word we said, did you?" Ana asked with a raised eyebrow.

"You know me well,"

"Tsk, tsk, tsk," said Shanthah. He folded his arms as if offended, but Nadezhda could feel his humor.

"Give me a ten second version of the plan."

She wondered how long she'd zoned out while focusing on dampening the negative emotions. It was clearly longer than she'd thought.

"I go invisible. I go upstairs with Ana's dagger. I take a look around. I knock people overboard. Stab the rest. We steal the ship," Shanthah said. "Then we sail into the sunset victorious."

"So, what do Ana and I do?" Nadezhda asked.

"You stay safe," Shanthah said with a quizzical look, as if it were obvious. "Oh, but the incredible-invisible-Ana fixes me when I inevitably get hurt again, and you help me sense where people are hiding with your spooky-feely witch powers so I can sneak up on them."

"You know, most people would be offended if you called them a witch," Nadezhda said. "Good thing I'm not most people and think that's a great title. Nadezhda the Spooky Witch and her pals, the Phantom and Health Girl. Let's do this."

"Health girl?!" Ana protested.

"Bandage babe?" Nadezhda suggested.

"Ana the Magnificent!" Shanthah exclaimed.

"Better, but we'll work on it," Ana replied.

Shanthah shushed them and slid the bolt out of the door, taking care not to make any sound as he pulled the door open. He activated his powers to make all three of them invisible, but the stairs still creaked under their unseen feet.

The voices of the Purists laughing infuriated Nadezhda; did they not care they'd just murdered multiple people?

She could still see and feel Ana and Shanthah's emotions, so she could tell where they were standing. There was Ana's usual silver aura tinted with worry, and just in front of them, Shanthah's feelings exploded around him like the sensation one experiences before daring the plunge from a high cliff.

She watched his cloud of emotion creep toward a man standing alone near the railing of the ship. Shanthah thrust Ana's invisible knife into the man's back, and before he could even scream, Shanthah pushed him overboard.

Another robed purist strode by and glanced down the stairway to the lower deck then called, "Hey, should we dump the King of Balgorod's body overboard yet?"

"He's not a king. And no, she wants to see it herself."

Nadezhda saw a colorful plume of amusement leap from Shanthah's invisible shoulders; it wiggled and then dissipated. She touched his mind with her mindspeaking abilities and felt his misplaced humor about the entire exchange.

The man continued pacing toward the end of the ship where Shanthah took a running start, leapt into the air, and kicked the man over the railing.

"*Two down.*"

Nadezhda nearly leapt with joy, for she had maintained the mental connection long enough to hear his thoughts. She grabbed Ana's hand to guide her after Shanthah, who was now climbing up toward the helmsman steering the ship.

As another cultist walked by, Shanthah shoved him hard down the steps and hurried away; the man tumbled to the ground and swore loudly as he hit his head on a barrel at the bottom.

"What the hell is your problem?!" he shouted, drawing a knife from his belt. He ran up the stairs and rushed at the helmsman, who raised his hands in protest.

"You tripped!"

"You *shoved* me!"

"I watched you fall, you oaf!" the helmsman replied. "This is the type of thing that makes me hate working with you cultists."

The trio hurried down the steps as the two men started beating on one another. Shanthah walked through a crowd, kicking one man in the ankle just as another passed him by.

The man with the wounded ankle whirled around and grabbed the other, and as Shanthah darted in between them, the third man joined in to help his friend, punching the first in the side of the head.

Shanthah hurried to the back of the ship as a woman in fine robes emerged from the captain's quarters, a long blade in her hand. She too wore the signature steel mask smeared with blood upon her face.

"What's going on here?!" she shouted, but her words were met with no response as most of the crew was either fighting or watching the brawl unfold.

Shanthah thrust the dagger into the leader's back then shoved her overboard. Several of the fighting men stopped in surprise.

"It's the Phantom!" someone in the crowd shouted. "The Phantom's sent Madam Lakatos overboard!"

"Don't watch what I'm about to do," Shanthah whispered. The fighting stopped, and despite being unable to see them, the crowd rushed toward Shanthah, Ana, and Nadezhda's position. Shanthah grabbed Nadezhda's shoulder and pushed her gently as if to say, "Go that way!"

She heeded the suggestion, and she led Ana around the crowd, trying to stay close to the railings. Four men with muskets and five with swords closed in on where Shanthah stood.

But the Phantom was ready. As bullets whizzed past him, he climbed onto the ship's railing, and he ran along it to bypass his enemies who continued to fire at where he had been moments before, splintering the wood.

At last, someone called for the madness to stop, and silence fell once more over the deck. Just before they stopped firing, Shanthah slid Ana's dagger between the ribs of the nearest man before retreating backward, ducking down as the cultists tended to their wounded ally.

As the riflemen reloaded their weapons, Shanthah popped up, slit one man's throat, stabbed the other in the back twice, and then retreated. Two riflemen and four swordsmen remained.

"Quiet!" shouted one of the men holding a gun. They did as they were commanded, listening for Shanthah's footsteps. Nadezhda watched Shanthah's aura drop to the ground and wiggle back and forth. What was he doing?

And then Nadezhda nearly let out a burst of laughter, realizing that he was taking off his boots, struggling to do so while invisible. He set them down and crept forward on his fingertips and socked feet like a beast stalking its prey.

He tossed one boot, and the men turned toward the sound as it hit the deck. One of the gunmen pulled the trigger on his weapon, surprising the others enough that Shanthah had the opportunity to leap up, stab him in the throat, and kick one of the swordsmen to the ground and stab him too in the chest.

As he went to kill another of them, everyone on deck felt a prickle go up their spine before a horrendous, agonized groaning filled their minds and ears.

"Well, damn," Shanthah said aloud.

Gray fingers with jagged claws appeared all around the ship, pulling bloated and waterlogged, Faceless bodies onto the deck. Ana vomited at their stench, and Nadezhda pulled her close.

"Stay quiet," Nadezhda whispered, but several Faceless stumbled toward them anyway, their swollen bodies jiggling and reeking of river water.

The Faceless began to disembowel the bodies of the dead but did not attack the living. Nadezhda and Ana trembled in terror as the creatures buried their faces in the eviscerated corpses as they continued to tear them to shreds.

Nadezhda could not sense a single bit of emotion from any of the creatures. Even animals gave off simple emotions, but these monsters were soulless, reanimated husks.

Shanthah reappeared in the midst of the Faceless and Purists. They kept their weapons up to keep their Faceless allies at bay; Shanthah noted the distrust between the Magistrate's followers. Perhaps, he thought, he could use it against them, but then a cold, female voice emanated from the minds of each of the Faceless.

"Be still."

"Ah, lovely," Shanthah said. "I knew the rumors that you survived were true."

"How admirable that you try to hide your friends even though you know that we do not need eyes to see them," the Magistrate thought, her voice echoing in each mind on the ship. *"Take the human."*

The largest of the bloated Faceless stomped forward, its soggy feet slapping against the deck like wet rags as it made its way toward Nadezhda. Her eyes went wide as it grabbed her by the throat with decaying fingers.

"Don't you dare," Shanthah said. "You let them go, you hear me?"

"I have no need of the Sangoran girl or the human man," said the Magistrate through the bloated Faceless. *"Kill them."*

Nadezhda screamed and clawed at the creature's hand closed around her throat. Its jagged fingernails dug into her throat like broken knives, drawing blood. Ana grabbed the monster's other arm, but it batted her away, and she hit the deck hard.

"Wait!" Shanthah shouted. Nadezhda felt his insecurity; he had no idea how he was going to help them escape.

Nadezhda focused on Ana's terror and breathed it into the blank minds of monstrous Faceless, stunning it as it felt its first emotion since death.

Shanthah did not hesitate. He lashed out, but his blade stuck halfway through the monster's neck. It groaned as he withdrew the weapon before hacking again and again until a waterlogged head splatted to the deck.

Nadezhda wheezed holding her throat. The other Faceless advanced until she gasped through the words, "You need me!" They stopped. "I'll jump overboard if you touch them, and if I die, and you get nothing from the idiot in the crystal."

"*Very well,*" said the Magistrate. Nadezhda was surprised at how little it took to convince her. "*Then all three of you will join me in Doftaan. Once you've served your purpose, you will join my Pure.*"

"Lucky us," Shanthah said, sheathing his blade. All three of them knew it would be fruitless to fight back with the number of enemies that surrounded them, and so Ana and Shanthah surrendered their weapons when it was demanded of them.

Shanthah helped Nadezhda and Ana to their feet and then watched his beloved Balgorod and Alboras fade into the distance.

CHAPTER TWENTY-TWO
BEHOLD THE BUTCHER'S FACE

The sound of spears clanging on the barrack's cold, tin walls woke those lucky enough to have found comfort in sleep's arms. They, along with those that had not been so fortunate stirred. They all felt defeated and utterly exhausted, but relieved just to have the chance to stretch their legs.

Moments before, those that were still awake had been listening to a tale of heroes of people with magical powers from a legend from the Deadlands. Inspired by Mara's song, people had begun helping however they could: reciting poetry, telling stories and jokes, and singing their own songs.

However, everyone agreed that the most comforting moments were when Mara sang to them. Of course, the use of names had been outlawed, so those times were when *'prisoner 68'* was singing.

Few knew, although many suspected, that she was Mara Bartunek, Empress of Blood. Whenever someone asked in hushed whispers if it were true, with a wink and a smile she'd tell them to keep her identity secret for their own safety.

The slaves did as they had done for the last eight days, filing out of their metal cage in a line to be inspected by the guards. Today, as they all knew, was the day they were to be transferred to their respective camps.

Mara stepped into the gloomy sunlight and glanced over her shoulder as the last of the prisoners inside ventured into the cold. She counted four people still within the house who had passed away during the night, and her stomach turned. She felt a guard's gaze on her, and she faced ahead like the others, but her heart stayed with the dead.

During the week they had been in the camp, they had been maintaining a crop of beets and potatoes just outside the encampment. It was mindless work; such labor always was. It was why she'd started singing for money to get out of farming in her youth, after all.

Her mind always dwelled on memories of her friends, but at times, images of the Talohiran slave camp haunted her. It was at those times that she wished for her little brother Pol to regale her with legends from the Deadlands.

Whenever the old man in her barrack would told similar ones, it made her think of her little brother, and she smiled.

Despite their original plan to meet up, she had still not seen Kamil or Alia since they had been captured. Kamil had only risked making mental contact twice: once to apologize for not contacting her earlier; some Thannish Mindspeakers had been stationed at the camp, and he had to be sneakier to avoid their detection.

The second time was to let Mara know that he and Alia were still safe, and that with the assistance of Kamil's powers, they had been sneaking food from the guards' stores to feed the people in their barrack. None of the guards had noticed their work.

Until now.

Sergeant Mazanek paced down the line of prisoners, his breath forming a cloud from his open mouth. He wiped his runny nose on a grimy, military issue handkerchief before stowing it in the pocket of his heavy fur coat.

Mara watched the man twiddle a gold coin between his thumb and forefinger as he spoke to the other soldiers in a low voice before turning back to address the prisoners.

"It seems we have a thief among us," said Mazanek, still fiddling with the coin "It shocks me that it only took one week for something like this to happen. We feed you, we shelter you, and this is how you thank us."

Mara scoffed aloud. He paced down the line, his hands clasped behind his back.

"*He knows it wasn't any of you,*" Kamil's voice echoed in Mara's mind. "*Mara, he knows.*"

Mara glanced toward the other barracks that housed Kamil and Alia, and she let out a slow breath and closed her eyes in anticipation. If Kamil's thinking was correct, then no one in Mara's barrack would know anything, but she knew that wouldn't stop Mazanek from punishing them; Belokej had done similar things in the Talohiran camp to instill fear and assert authority.

"If the thief comes forward, you are free to go about your business," Mazanek said. "If not, well…"

He paused for a long moment, looking from one end of the line to the other. Nothing happened. No one moved. He stepped toward the man at the end of the line, a human Than with a thick, brown beard.

"Anyone?" Mazanek asked. Still no answer.

Mazanek flipped the golden coin with his thumb, caught it, and then held the coin up to the Thannish prisoner's face.

"Know what that is?" the sergeant asked.

"A gold coin," replied the man, his eyes shifting nervously.

"Obviously. What's on it?"

"Looks like King Ottokar," replied the man.

"Ah, this one knows his history!" Mazanek said. "A personal favorite of mine. He did what needed to be done for peace. A hero, you know?"

The man shivered and looked up at him in confusion as Mazanek turned the coin over in his hand.

"And on this side?"

"Uh, a bird and some plants," replied the man.

"A bird and some plants," Mazanek said with a chuckle to himself. "You aren't wrong. Do you know what the dove and the vine represent?" The man shook his head. "Peace. The peace that came after Ottokar's rule. It's an old coin; we don't use it anymore, but it's always been my favorite."

Mazanek flipped the coin in his hand again and caught it in his palm. He looked down at it with a wicked grin.

"Heads."

He gestured to the soldier behind the line, and the man fell dead with a lead ball in the back of his neck. The entire line jumped with a fright as Mazanek moved down the line. The Sangoran woman next to the dead man trembled in fear as the sergeant looked her in the eye and flipped the coin.

"Tails."

He showed the back of the coin to the woman, who collapsed to her knees in relief, sobbing into her hands. The guard behind her pulled her back to her feet.

Mazanek moved down the line again, and a little boy looked up at him with fear in his eyes. Mara glared with fiery rage as Mazanek flipped the coin and caught it in his palm.

"Heads—"

"It was me!" Mara shouted, stepping out of line.

Every soldier nearby turned their weapons toward her. Mazanek raised his hand, a sign for the soldier behind the little boy to lower his crossbow. Mara saw the young soldier let out a sigh of relief. It was subtle, and brief, but it was there.

"Well, well," Mazanek said, pacing slowly toward Mara. He smiled, and Mara hated with all her heart how dashing he was; Belokej was as ugly as he was cruel. Mazanek, however, had kind eyes and a winning smile. He almost reminded Mara of Aleksander or Shanthah—if they had sold their souls to Elafris.

"It was me," Mara repeated. "Who else do you think it could have been?!"

"I heard you the first time, calm down," Mazanek said as he stood in front of Mara. He stroked the finely trimmed beard on his chin and clasped his hands behind his back, the stance of a soldier standing at attention. He looked down at her and shook her head.

Mara chuckled to herself. Seasoned officers didn't stand like that. He hadn't broken free of the habit, meaning he hadn't been in his position of authority for very long.

"I've heard stories of the fearsome Empress of Blood," he said, looking toward the rest of the line. "I've heard she killed Talohira's King, Valistaran. Destroyed the entire city of Nitra. Killed our god, Thanatan, even. That she steals and eats Thannish babies… But the legends never said how short she was, did they? Pretty, too." Mara glared straight through him. "That was a compliment, sweetheart. Relax."

The soldiers in line laughed; the joke wasn't particularly funny, so whether they did so out of humor or obligation to their leader, Mara didn't know. She said nothing to dignify a response, but her eyes continued to speak volumes.

"So, what is it that you did? I know what was taken. Tell the truth, or I'll flip my coin again." He stepped toward the woman at Mara's right and readied the coin. Mara hesitated, but to her relief, Kamil's voice rang through her mind.

"Potatoes, rye bread, and some fish."

"I just stole some potatoes, bread, and fish," Mara repeated, hoping that was enough to save someone's life.

"And my other coin?" Mazanek asked, fiddling with the one in his hand.

"What?"

Mazanek looked disappointed at the genuine look of confusion on her face and slipped his Ottokar coin into his coat pocket.

"Very well. The rest of you are free to work, but Miss Bartunek, I'd like a word with you in my quarters."

He glanced at one of the other officers and shared a dark chuckle. Someone let out a whistle, resulting in more laughs.

"Hell no."

Mazanek turned back to her. "Oh, stop being so dramatic. Nothing like *that*." He glanced over his shoulder. "Not today."

He motioned for her to follow, and she decided for the sake of the other prisoners that she had no choice but to accompany him.

"I knew a man like you once," Mara said as she followed him toward the officers' building.

"Oh? Handsome and powerful?"

"Decidedly not."

Mazanek gestured for her to continue talking.

"I killed him without even lifting a finger," Mara said, thinking back to the day she, Hanna, and Lavinia had closed the final Talohiran slave camp. "Fate rarely smiles on the cruel, Sergeant Mazanek."

Mazanek chuckled. "It smiles on the powerful, and it smiles on those who do what's right, even when it *seems* cruel."

Mara did not respond as Mazanek stopped in front of the door of the officers' building; two young soldiers unlocked it and stepped aside. Mara followed Mazanek through the doorway.

One of the soldiers whistled and shouted, "Have fun, Sergeant!"

Mazanek laughed back as he closed the door. "Not yet, Damiani."

The simplicity of the room caught her by surprise. She had expected something more lavish, and she felt a sense of satisfaction in knowing that for all the self-purported importance of his station, Mazanek was nothing more than a soldier stationed at an undesirable post. She hoped to the goddesses, even if she didn't necessarily believe in them, that he was as miserable as everyone else here.

If not, she hoped to make it so.

He took a seat at the desk and leaned back in his chair, swinging one leg up onto the table. His other knee bounced with an annoying rhythm, jostling the shaky table.

"I know you didn't steal the food," Mazanek said.

"No? What gave me away?" Mara asked, hoping the unenthusiastic sarcasm was evident in her dark tone.

"Really?" Mazanek asked. "What you did out there was almost cliché."

"Clichéd," Mara corrected.

"Wow. Correcting my grammar?" Mazanek said. "You're not an empress anymore. And not just because you're here. There's a new queen in Sangora, so why don't you just get over yourself? I've told you that we're going to teach you to learn your place. And you *will not* talk to me like—"

"Like what?" Mara asked, bursting out in a fake fit of laughter, slapping her hand down on the table. "Like a sergeant? You know you're only a sergeant, right? Oh, sorry. *Senior* sergeant."

She wiggled her fingers for sarcastic emphasis. Mazanek shifted in his chair, twiddling with the coin between his fingers again.

"The sergeants in my army really don't have much more responsibility than those under them. Their job mostly consists of keeping the younger cadets from doing anything stupid. How long have you even been out of the military academy?" Mara asked. "If you shaved, you wouldn't look a day over—what? Twenty? Some of your men can't be more than sixteen! You're making monsters, *Tibor.*"

She put particular venom into her use of the sergeant's first name.

"Most of them are very experienced and respected. They know the importance of what we're doing," Mazanek said. "And It'd behoove you to know that many of the soldiers here have been given second chances. Many were prisoners themselves, but they pledged loyalty to King Verahim Romus and the crown. They admitted their crimes, and—"

"Slaves," Mara corrected. "These people aren't prisoners. They're slaves. These people are innocent, and you know it. What the hell kind of crimes are you talking about?"

Mazanek shrugged. "They're enemies of the state. The king decides who that is, and we enforce it."

"Ah, yes. 'Just doing what we're told.' The oldest excuse for cruelty that there is," Mara said. Then, imitating Mazanek's voice, added, "It's almost clichéd."

"Shut up," Mazanek said. "Shut up and listen."

"Oh, honey," Mara said, shaking her head as if chastising a child. "Do you know how I fall asleep every night?"

"Like a whore?"

"I fall asleep thinking about which crimes I'll charge you all with when this is all over. How I'll punish each and every one of you," Mara said, emphasizing each word. "If I don't kill you first, that is."

"Big talk for a defenseless little girl," Mazanek said with a laugh. "You're not getting out of this. You wouldn't get your own pretty nails dirty."

"You have no idea how much blood I have on my hands." Mara leaned forward. "Do you know what I think I'll try you for? Something small. You know, to match your manhood. Something so insignificant that you don't even get credit or satisfaction for what you've done here."

Mazanek stood with such ferocity that his chair toppled to the floor.

"Shut your mouth," Mazanek said, slamming his fist on the table. "Shut up!"

"Oh, did I strike a chord? You'd have laughed if it wasn't true," Mara said, picking a bit of dirt from beneath her fingernail. "Makes sense. It's pretty obvious."

"Yeah, I bet you'd like to find out," Mazanek retorted. Then, changing the subject, he said, "Do you know where I grew up?"

Mara threw her hands up into the air. "Hell if I care."

"I grew up in Nitra. My entire family was from Nitra."

Mara met his gaze for the first time. She did not look away, even when his hands shook, and his lip trembled.

"I see."

"They were some of the few who refused to leave their homes, and do you know what happened? You and your Night Witches slaughtered them. I was stationed near the capital, and I fought you and your horde of Witches back at the Battle of Laniras. And *that* is how I got this station. I love my country, I love my people, my family, and I am happy I have this opportunity now to punish Valistaran's whore queen for her crimes in Nitra and Laniras."

Mara was silent.

"Oh, did *I* strike a chord that time?!" Mazanek screamed, his face red and his hands trembling. "I earned this job. Not forced into it. Not only that—I volunteered for it."

"Yeah, because no one else wants to live in a slave labor camp. What a big man you are," Mara said, folding her arms over her chest. She sat up a bit straighter. "What kind of person can see the things happening here and not go mad with guilt?"

"They don't get it. You don't either. They don't know what an honor it is to punish Sangora for what it did to my family and to so many thousands of other families across Thanatanos."

"I am truly sorry for what happened in Nitra. I have thought of that day every single day of my life," Mara said. Mazanek shook his head in disbelief, pulling his chair upright to sit again. "I've been a slave most of my life. That day was no different."

"Oh, just 'doing what you were told' then?"

Mara cocked her head, but she said nothing.

"I assume you know something of history?" Mara asked, gesturing to Mazanek's gold coin in his hand.

Mazanek nodded with an ugly grunt. "What of it?"

"The man on that coin… Ottokar the Butcher King," Mara said. "Do you know what happened to him? What he did?"

"He brought peace to Thanata—"

"No, you daft donkey of a man," Mara said. "He committed genocide. *Genocide.* His son, Vladislaus the Contrite, as your people call him, spent the rest of his life repairing what his father did. Your hero didn't bring peace, he shattered it."

"You don't know what you're talking about."

"Ottokar didn't just conquer and destroy. He encouraged deportations. He murdered and sterilized women to prevent the 'impure' from being born. And worse, he encouraged soldiers to kidnap and rape Sangoran and Talohiran women so that they would be forced to give birth to *Thannish* babies."

"Is that the lie they teach you in Sangoran schools?"

"The *truth* is that the fathers of each of those babies were paid a thousand coins for each baby born."

"Ottokar ended the war between Thanatanos and Rumanija—that's what Talohira used to be called before Valistaran renamed it, if you didn't know—"

"No! You do *not* get to justify what he did! Don't you *dare*. He is celebrated for ending the war because his genocide *worked!* He did what he set out to do. And you are continuing his work here."

"I haven't done any of the things you said. Okay, deportations, but that's kind of the point, right? We need to remove you people from society. But I haven't personally murdered or raped—"

"No? You don't have that intention?" Mara shouted, getting to her feet for the first time, raising her wings high above their heads. "What did you say to that guard outside? 'Not yet!' Yeah. That's what you said. Don't you dare have the audacity to pretend you—"

Mazanek screamed and overturned his desk, throwing parchment, quills, books, and documents to the ground. He picked up his Ottokar coin from where it fell and began to fiddle with it between his fingers again.

"You act like you're so innocent. You act like these things happened to you, not to people hundreds of years in the past. But here you are, getting all emotional because—"

"They *have* happened to me!" Mara shouted, advancing on Mazanek, who drew a knife from his belt. "I am every one of their scars. Their tears. Every *murder*. Every *rape*. Every *death*. And I will make you pay for every single drop of Sangoran blood on your hands."

"So dramatic."

"It's happening now, *isn't it?*"

"What do you mean?" he asked, backing up as Mara raised her wings. Was that fear in his eyes?

"Don't play coy. Tell me what's happening. I know you know. Thanatanos attacked Kurash right before I was captured. There are hundreds of thousands of Thannish troops and their Faceless amassed along the Sangoran border. What is happening now?"

Mazanek chuckled. "Oh, that. Yes, I'm sure the invasion has started by now. Sangora and Talohira won't be a threat anymore."

"They never were! They do *not* want to fight!"

"Oh, you stupid girl. You don't know anything. You don't know what Sangora wants or needs anymore."

"This 'stupid girl' is the Empress of Sangora, Dowager Queen of Talohira, and the Supreme One of Kurash. I know *exactly* what my people need."

"You're so deluded."

Mara pointed directly at the seal on Mazanek's hat on the table: the insignia of a sergeant.

"And a mere *sergeant* is so well informed? You aren't even trusted with secret, privileged information until your next promotion."

Mazanek let out a breath from his nose, and his nostrils flared in anger. "I want my other coin back."

Mara responded with an incredulous look.

"I don't have your damn coin."

The look of dejection on his face was genuine, and he cleared his throat.

"I can't wait for you to get to Tazovski. The farthest camp for the vilest of enemies. For people like you. Even the king has no idea what happens there, and that's on purpose. How's that for 'privileged information'?"

"Then he won't hear what happens to you there, either."

"I've heard you tell the people here that 'Spring always comes.' Well, not for you. Not this year. Spring's almost here, but you won't see it where you're going. Literally or metaphorically—"

"Then you won't see it where you're going, either. There is no springtime in hell, Sergeant Mazanek, and there is no reprieve for monsters who prey on innocence."

"Shut your mouth, woman!" Mazanek shouted. "Damn it! Why do you insist on interrupting me?!"

Her voice was cold when she responded.

"Someone needs to."

"Sangora's lucky it has a new queen. I can see why they got rid of you."

"And what queen would that be? Thanatan's Magistrate?"

"No, it's you," Mazanek said with a dark laugh. "Or the 'you' they *say* is you."

Mara was silent and glanced at the massive map on the wall of the shack. It extended well past the borders of Thanatanos, Talohira, Kurash, and Sangora; the Deadlands were printed in detail—mountains, rivers, and forests she had never dreamed existed. If not for the circumstances, she could stare at it for hours.

She glanced at the area east of Sangora, wondering if that was where Drahomir had led as many of the Faceless as he could. Mazanek hurled the coin at the map, bringing Mara's attention back to him as it clattered to the ground.

"See there? *That's* where you're going!" Mazanek shouted.

"How?" Mara asked, sitting forward, concern etched on her face. "There's no way they will all survive that journey. Not in this season."

"Oh, it'll take months for you to get there. All of spring, in fact. Again, spring—isn't—coming. Not for you. Not for them. Stop trying to fill their Night Witch brains with hope. You're all guilty, and you will be punished as such."

He stooped down to pick up the gold coin, and Mara fought the urge to kick him in the backside.

"What, are we going to walk there?" Mara asked.

"What would the point of that be? Like you said, no one would survive. Not even you, the Empress of Blood, or whatever idiotic name you invented for yourself." He grumbled to himself as he examined the map.

"Use your words, Tibor."

He turned with such suddenness that Mara jumped; the gold coin flew toward her face, and she barely brought up her arms in time to block it from hitting her in the eye.

"Shut up!" Mazanek shouted again. "How many times do I have to tell you? Shut up!"

"I bet you're so much fun at parties."

Mazanek pulled a file of parchment from the drawer of the fallen desk and waved in front of her face.

"Know what this is?" he asked, showing her a drawing of some kind of vehicle that looked like a massive carriage with many wheels.

"I—yes, actually. Where did you get this?" Mara asked with an incredulous tone. "That's a train from the Deadlands. Did you—did you *find* one? Make one?"

"Stupid girl. No, we didn't find one. They were all destroyed along with everything else when the Deadlands were. Before you martyred him, Lord Thanatan gave us knowledge that would astound you. He gave us knowledge that will win this war."

"He taught you how to build a big cart. Great."

"Not only that. You've seen our weapons. Guns, they call them. And not only technology. The people in Thanatanos don't have to work anymore, so the Pure have been hard at work laying rails for the Thannish trains. So far, we have trains across Thanatanos and others that connect to our new lands in Adess, and from the Plains of Adess out to the Deadlands."

He sounded proud of himself.

"Adess is Sangoran land, and it always will be."

"Delusional."

"You have the knowledge and technology of the Deadlands, and you use it to send innocent people to their deaths. Imagine the advances in medicine and science you could be making instead," Mara said. "Just like a Purist to squander something great for something evil."

"You say Purist like it's something bad," Mazanek said with a laugh. Mara did not reply, staring into his soul with cold, blue eyes. "Anyway, we'll put you all on the train and ship you out later today. We were going to send you all to different regions of Thanatanos to work, but I haven't sent the paperwork yet."

"Oh, paperwork. What a powerful weapon," Mara said.

"You're not making things better for yourself or your people!" Mazanek screamed. He balled his fists and looked like he was going to attack her. "I could send you all to Tazovski!"

Mara shut her eyes, and inside, she knew he was right. She couldn't let her emotions make things worse for the people she vowed to protect.

"I have a special punishment for you," he said. Mara cocked her head, tired of the conversation. "You're going to sing to me."

Mara scoffed. "The hell I am."

"I heard you calmed everyone down in there with your singing. I stood outside the barracks one night and listened, and you know what? It *was* beautiful. You have a tremendous voice."

Mara stared at him with all the hatred she could muster; in her mind, she murdered him a hundred times over. He smiled and sat in his chair in front of her. Her heart thundered in her chest as he scooted closer.

"Would you do that for me?" he asked. "Every day you sing to me, I promise I won't kill anyone. Not on purpose, anyway."

A thousand thoughts exploded in her brain; the first and foremost of them was to punch him in the throat, but she refrained.

"Definitely not."

"Then…" He trailed off, flipping the coin. It landed with Ottokar's face staring up at them. "Behold the butcher's face."

"Then you'll kill me?" Mara asked, interpreting the metaphor.

"No," Mazanek said with a shake of his head. "Not you."

He gestured out the window where Mara could see some Sangoran women carrying baskets full of freshly harvested potatoes. Mara's countenance fell.

"Okay," she said softly. After a moment, she added, "I'll do it."

"Aren't you going to say thank you?" Mazanek asked. Mara stared at him with confusion.

"For…?"

"That this is all I'm asking of you? I could have anything, you know. For giving you an *easy* job when we get to Tazovski. For telling you that your singing was beautiful, maybe?"

He reached up and grabbed her hand, and at that moment, she gave into her earlier thoughts and brought her other fist upward before he could touch her again.

She struck him in the throat with such force that his chair toppled over; he held his neck, gasping for air on the floor.

"Never touch me again." She pressed her boot against his throat. "I promise you it will be the last thing you ever do."

She removed her foot from his neck and scooped up his Ottokar coin. She squatted next to him; his reddened eyes were watering, and he was still struggling to breathe.

Mara flipped the coin, and it landed between them; Ottokar the Butcher did not stare up at them with his gilded eyes.

"Oh, look at that. *You* don't die. But I promise you, Tibor, before this is all over, you will discover why they call me the Empress of Blood," Mara said. Mazanek said nothing but grabbed the coin and stowed it away in his pocket. "Aren't you going to say *thank you*? Now, if you don't mind, I have people to care for and love. Enjoy rotting in your hate."

With that, Mara strode out the door, past the soldiers, and into the cool winter air. She didn't stop walking until she reached her people harvesting potatoes and beets, and she began to work with them.

As long as her people suffered, she would be there right beside them.

CHAPTER TWENTY-THREE
KING VALIS SHADID

The days spent in Talohira had been a whirlwind.

Aleksander and Lavinia had been escorted to King Valis Shadid's palace in the exact center of Bukaral across from a massive, onion domed cathedral dedicated to the old gods. However, it was now little more than an empty monument.

During their time there, they'd met with diplomats and military officials where Lavinia discussed the Thannish invasion on Shanthah's breakaway nation. According to Talohiran intelligence, the false queen of Sangora had given Thanatanos control of the Sangoran state of Adess and Terman, which were unable to offer any resistance, in return for Thannish assistance in reconquering Alboras and attacking United Baltija far to the north.

As Mara's Mistress of Dusk over Timishuara, Lavinia would spend much of their trip raising support against the Thannish invasion. King Valis, of course, had pledged his full support.

Although dead, Florenta's legacy continued in Sangora. Her followers, though only a small minority in the country, still held power, and they had the support of King Verahim and the rest of Thanatanos for their assistance in 'ending' the war.

How waging another war in Alboras would ever end a separate one that Thanatanos itself started, Aleksander would never understand.

Before today's meetings, Lavinia had told Aleksander he wouldn't be very useful in most of the day's meetings and allowed, or rather, forced him outside the palace to explore the sprawling central square of Bukaral and the vibrant, historical center of the beautiful city.

Aleksander had protested at first, asking if he should reveal his identity to the diplomats, to which Lavinia had responded, "No. What good would that do?"

So, instead, he looked around in awe at the majestic architecture surrounding him in the vast square teeming with Talohiran citizens. From the high towers of the colorful cathedral, its domes of various colors and patterns catching the dying, golden light to the massive fortress of Bukaral at the exact center of the city, its dark red stone walls lined with squat towers.

He knew the grand library of Talohira that Mara had told him all about was somewhere inside, and he longed to see the place she loved so much.

The vast city sprawled out from the central square, and all roads led to the palace. He'd never seen a city of this size; it dwarfed even Laniras and Doftaan.

A beautiful, wide bridge adorned with murals and mosaics depicting scenes from Talohira's rich history spanned the river that bisected the square at a diagonal. A young couple in their elegant wedding attire stood at one edge as an artist painted their portrait, and street performers danced, sang, and played their strange Talohiran accordions for a few spare coins.

Hundreds of others, including tourists, businessmen and women, and people on their everyday errands ambled around him. A group of young men and women sat laughing and enjoying one another's company at a fountain; Aleksander chuckled as he watched one of them that was walking along the circular fountain fall in with a splash, much to the amusement of his friends.

Aleksander had never thought of Talohira as a safe, peaceful place full of laughter, joy, and music. The only times he had experienced it were as a slave or as a runaway one fighting for his life. Now, however, he was beginning to see its beauty under the rule of a fair, although inexperienced, young king.

He watched Talohiran soldiers in winter war garb marching back and forth outside the fortress, and others lined the walls carrying long pikes. Aleksander watched as they marched with precision and expert skill in their fine dark furs and high hats.

Aleksander smiled, hoping for peace so that he and his friends, and the people all across each of the countries could share in that joy. With a frown, he wondered where all his friends were. He prayed they were safe, wherever they were.

A bell tolled, and dozens of school children filed out of a school across the bridge. He traced a finger along a broken mosaic, feeling the grout beneath the broken tiles as he thought of how amazing it would be to spend his every-day life in such a place.

It was a strange thought. At one time, Thanatanos was his home. His family was there. His friends. But now, he'd lost all faith in the country he once called home. Would he ever return? He did not know.

Statues of Valistaran holding a sword aloft and a sheaf of wheat tightly to his chest flanked either side of the bridge on both ends. Aleksander wondered if he was beloved here, or if he'd simply insisted on the statues being built.

He gazed upon a mural that seemed to depict Valistaran with a white crown floating above his head; he seemed more like a god than a man, and perhaps, that really was how his people had seen him—or, again, how he had told them to depict him.

They hadn't seen the former king during their time in Bukaral, but he was there somewhere in secret. The population of Talohira had long since thought him dead.

Aleksander shut his eyes as he listened to a group of musicians playing an accordion, violin, and singing some kind of slow hymn in the Talohiran dialect of Thannish. He could understand most of it, but many words were foreign. Perhaps, Talohiran Thannish now had some Sangoran influence. He'd have to remember to ask Mara if she thought it'd ever become its own language. He knew she'd jump at the thought of talking about linguistics with him.

A voice broke him out of his thoughts.

"Hey, Prince Xanthurias, you done being an annoying Thannish tourist?" Lavinia called, standing with her arms folded and foot tapping. Aleksander jogged over to her.

"Can we not use that name around here?" Aleksander asked with a nervous chuckle. "Keep it down."

"Don't worry, your secret's safe with me."

"It is not," Rayshel said at her side. "You just shouted it in the middle of the street."

She turned away, walking toward the gated fortress. "Valeniya found our guy. Come on."

"Where is he?"

"She watched as they became secret keepers, and she knows where they're going," Rayshel called, trying to keep up with Lavinia.

Aleksander wondered if they had waited to enact their plan until the Thannish invasion of Sangora began.

"It took her a while to find them because she didn't know who they were or what they looked like, but eventually we think we found them traveling by land along the border of Alboras and Talohira heading north."

Aleksander caught up to them.

"He sure did take the long way around," Aleksander said as the soldiers signaled for the gates to open.

"Fortunately for us," Lavinia said with a nod.

Trumpets played as the gates opened, and Aleksander recognized the triumphant, stirring anthem of Talohira.

The soldiers escorted them inside but stopped at the door as King Valistaran Shadid, better known to Aleksander as

Valis, the son of Valistaran Talohir and Alia Shadid, greeted them with a wide smile and outstretched arms.

"Aleksander!" Valis exclaimed. "I'm so sorry we haven't been able to meet up yet!"

"I don't think a king has to apologize for that," Aleksander said as Valis clapped him on the back.

"No, but I think a friend does," Valis replied. "Lavinia told me you didn't want to see me. I knew she was lying, though."

"Lavinia!" Rayshel exclaimed, chastising her partner with a loving scowl. Lavinia shrugged.

Valis was clad in a kingly suit and a crimson cloak trimmed with fur slung over one shoulder. Beneath, he wore a black coat with polished golden buttons and military type boots.

"Royalty looks good on you, friend," Aleksander said with a playful punch to the shoulder.

"Funny. I think it'd look better on you," Valis replied. Aleksander raised an inquisitive eyebrow. "…Lavinia told me."

"Ah. Of course she did."

"He's the only other person I told, honest," Lavinia said. "Trust me. No one else would even believe me that you're the long-lost son of King Romiton back from the dead."

Rayshel laughed. "Vasilica knows too."

"Is she—"

"No, she's in Balgorod," Rayshel replied.

"Ah, I was hoping to get the 'old gang' back together," Aleksander said. Lavinia's smile peeked through her hard exterior. He turned back to Valis. "How are things?"

"Things are good," Valis said, but as he met Lavinia's stern gaze added, "I think Lavinia wants us to dispense with pleasantries."

"Sounds right," Aleksander said. "So—"

"Hello Xanthurias!"

"Ah!" Aleksander leapt in surprise as Valeniya appeared as if from nowhere behind him. "Valeniya! You scared me, kid!"

"Oh, yeah, she's known for a long time too," Valis said. "Lavinia didn't tell her though, honest."

"I found out when I was watching Mara."

"Do you often watch Mara?" Aleksander asked as Valis led the group down the corridor.

"Yes."

"How is she?" Aleksander asked as they made their way through the beautiful palace.

"Safe now," Valeniya replied. "I know she thinks of you often. Kamil and Alia are with her."

"She's still with them?" Aleksander asked. "They're alive?! That's wonderful!"

"Not with them, but near them."

Relief washed over him as Valis led them through the fortress. 'Near them' would have to do.

"Yes, I like them. Alia loves me very much."

"And you love her too, right?" Aleksander said.

"Yes. I love Mara too."

"I—" He stumbled for words. "Yeah, she's—yeah."

"Very well said." Lavinia walked down the hall. "Come on."

Rayshel winked and elbowed him in the ribs as they entered a long conference room filled with soldiers armed from head to toe.

Valis stood at the head of the table, and the soldiers standing at attention saluted. He returned the gesture, and as a servant pulled out the chair for him, he waved her off with a grateful smile.

"No need, but thank you," he said. "My sister Valeniya found the Kurashian fugitive. You've all been briefed on the situation before now, I think. After meeting with Mistress Lavinia of Alboras, I've decided that you will lead the efforts to reinforce the efforts there."

"My king, with all due respect," said a man decorated with medals. "Sending troops into Alboras will be seen as an offense against Thanatanos, opening our own country to their aggression. Perhaps, instead, it would be good to simply send supplies. Besides, sentiment of Talohira there is very low as it is."

"Thank you for the comment, General Aslanov, but you know we've talked about that for hours, over and over again. You know where I stand, and I've decided that Talohira needs to atone for a great many things. Don't you think sentiment for our country will grow when we *help* them?"

"Yes, sir," Aslanov said with a salute.

"We will send an advance team to Balgorod to assess the situation and report back here so that we can adequately assist them. Master Shanthah Kalen in Balgorod is a dear friend, and I know that he'll accept our help."

"It will be done, my king," said one of the other officials.

"I also need a team ready to go within the hour to accompany Aleksander, Mistress Lavinia, Rayshel Pilu, and my sister Valeniya Talohir into Thanatanos."

"It'll be seen as another provocation," said General Aslanov. "They'll never allow passage through the border wall."

"And that's why they won't find out," said Valis. "Get in, get the fugitives, and get out. A third contingent will go to help stop the fighting in Kurash, honoring the alliance my father made with them several years ago."

As Valis and his generals continued to plan their next moves, Aleksander turned to Valeniya.

"Can I ask you a question?" Aleksander asked. Valeniya turned her head and nodded. "Where is Mara, exactly?"

Valeniya's countenance dropped, and she looked as if she were about to cry. She squished her eyebrows together and bit her lip. He had never seen her show so much emotion before.

"I'm sorry, I didn't mean to—"

"Far away. I couldn't see her for a long time, and I thought she was dead. Usually, when I can't see someone anymore, they are no longer alive."

"Why couldn't you see her?" Aleksander asked softly.

"She was farther away from here as anyone has ever been. I could not see that far, but she's with people with strong minds, so I can see her again."

"Strong minds?" asked Aleksander.

"Yes, there are some Mindspeakers there. Kamil, too. They are in a prison like the ones my father created."

Aleksander's heart shattered.

The meeting ended, and the generals and other officials went about to enact their king's vision, and Aleksander, Lavinia, Rayshel, and Valeniya exited the chamber. Valeniya held on to Aleksander's arm as they walked.

He glanced over at her in surprise, as he'd never seen her touch another person before. He soon realized that her eyes were glossy white, so she was holding on to him so she wouldn't fall as she looked into nothingness to find someone.

"Mara is happy. She is laughing. She told me to watch out for her, so I do sometimes."

"Good." Aleksander smiled.

She was in a prison camp, but happy. That meant she was helping the people, and he felt a little better just knowing that.

"She was hurt and sad for so long," Valeniya said. "She still is. There are terrible things all around her. But she is helping the people. She is the brightest of anyone I have ever watched."

Aleksander knew Valeniya wouldn't elaborate on what that meant, but he'd heard her say it before on more than one occasion.

They continued outside to see troops loading supplies into several military carriages pulled by teams of dark stallions. Lavinia stood waiting for him by the nearest carriage as Valis said goodbye to his half-sister.

"When you reach the Talohiran contingent on the border, give this letter to General Kosturkin there. It'll explain everything," King Valis said. "Good luck, Aleks."

"Thanks," Aleksander said. "Where's your father, by the way?"

"He disappears without telling us. If you find him, let me know," Valis said with a sigh. "Lavinia is looking impatient. Better head out."

"She always looks that way."

"More than usual."

"Yeah, well," Aleksander said. "I'll keep Valeniya safe."

"Thank you," Valis said. "You're a good man, Aleksander."

The soldiers closed the doors of the carriages and they set out as Valis made his way back up to his fortress looking very tired indeed.

CHAPTER TWENTY-FOUR
THE SONG OF THE CAGED BIRD

Mara had to admit that the train was marvelous to behold. Thick black smoke billowed from a spout on the front like a thick black mane. Everyone groaned as the sound of screeching steel pierced their ears, and then the hulking vehicle came to a halt. As horrible as this latest labor camp was, seeing something come straight out of a history book was fascinating. Until, of course, Mara remembered what her captors planned to do with it.

Only in the distant past were there such technological marvels. In the days and weeks after the battle of Balgorod, Mara had spoken with Daniel Elafris all about different types of technology from his time, when the Deadlands flourished with life and industry.

The train *wasn't* magic, contrary to her prior belief; she knew now that it ran on coal and steam. Such a simple, but genius invention.

Reality struck her and the magic of the moment was gone; the soldiers ordered the mass of slaves to board the train.

The train wouldn't carry her to freedom and adventure or to people that she loved like they would have done in the Deadlands. Instead, it would be used to haul her people, and likely herself, to their deaths. She hung her head.

All semblance of lines and order had faded away as soon as the train's doors opened. The soldiers and guards pushed their captives toward the transport with gun, spear, and crossbow, and after several minutes of waiting, a fresh shift of soldiers hopped out, ready to man Sergeant Mazanek's transitionary camp.

She felt a hand on her shoulder; she flinched and pulled away but felt Kamil's reassuring presence fill her mind. She let out a sigh of relief and turned around to see both Kamil and Alia standing behind her.

"Oh, hello, you beautiful people. You have no idea how glad I am to finally see you," Mara said in Kurashic. "You look great. You know, given the circumstances."

She wanted more than anything to hug her friends, but knew they'd be punished if she did so.

"Your Kurashic is perfect. It always amazes me," Alia said. Mara waved the compliment off. "Seriously, your accent is closer to a native Kurashian's than my own!"

Mara smiled. "I wish I could hug you right now."

Alia nodded in understanding. Before the battle of Balgorod, they had hardly spoken at all, mere associates. However, during the two years after the battle, they had become close friends, and Mara had watched Alia and Josman's romance blossom with joy.

"I was scared we wouldn't find you," Kamil thought to them both. *"Stick together now, whatever happens, okay?"*

Mara and Alia both nodded.

"Until the end," Mara whispered in Kurashic.

As the Kamil, Alia, and the other slaves began climbing into the train carriages, Mara glanced over her shoulder, not knowing why. She stopped, mouth wide open in shock as beheld the face of her little brother, Pol not far away.

"What?" she whispered. "No, Pol, no…"

Pol, dressed in the full Thannish military attire, stepped toward her, his eyes bright and wide. As he adjusted his fur hat, Mara glanced at his chest to see the emblem of a private emblazoned there.

"Mara!" Pol exclaimed, pushing his way through the crowd to get to her.

"What in the name of Elafris are you doing here?" Mara asked, her mouth still agape. She should have felt happy to see him, for they had not spoken in years, but the image of him standing there dressed like Mazanek made her stomach twist into knots. "Why?"

"I'm just paying my dues," Pol said, gesturing to the uniform. "Everyone has to go to a post they don't want so that they can eventually—"

Mara felt her pulse quicken. They hadn't spoken in years, and that was the first thing he chose to say to her?

"No, Pol, *why?*" Mara repeated, gesturing to the camp. "You should know better than anyone—"

"No, I know what you're going to say. It's different, really! We were innocent, but the people here are terrorists and people trying to keep the war going. They're prisoners for good reason," Pol said with a smile, one that did not reach his eyes. "But you understand that, you're here to help too, right?"

"I'm here as a slave."

"What? I'm sure it's a mistake. I'll get it cleared up. I promise. This is horrible, but it has to be done. It'll stop the war and save lives. And I'm told that people at the other camps actually have houses and are fed actual meals—they're just removed from society so they can't do harm And it makes criminals into contributing members of Thannish—"

"Pol! You, of all people?" Mara exclaimed with only the angst of a frustrated older sister. "No! What the *hell* are you doing?!"

She was so angry that she could hardly form an accusatory sentence or do anything else but repeat the question. It was a different anger than she'd felt for Mazanek.

One born out of love.

One born out of betrayal.

"Listen, Mara, I know. I'll talk to Sergeant Mazanek and the other officers. They probably don't even know who you are. You're innocent, and we'll sort this out. We'll get you back to Thanatanos or Sangora and—"

"I'm not innocent, Apolinarius."

"Oh, full name," Pol said with a laugh. The same one he had when they joked around as children at the lake. Now, hearing it here felt like an abomination to Mara. An insult. He repeated, "There's got to be a mistake. I'll get you out."

Mara shoved the parchment with her name, prisoner number, and the handwritten words 'Night Witch' into his face. He took it and read it over with a concerned expression.

"I'm not kidding. Everything they said I've done? I've probably done it," Mara said. "I destroyed Nitra. Twice. I led the assault on Laniras five years ago. I killed Thanatan. Maybe there's a mistake, yeah, but more likely? I'm the Empress of Blood, Queen of Talohira, and Supreme One of Kurash. I'm about as wanted in Thanatanos as Elafris himself. There is no one in the world *they* want in here as much as *me*."

"Yeah, but I can talk to Mazanek, seriously."

"No, no you can't." She shoved her finger into the insignia on his chest. "If you love me at all, you *won't*. I'm not leaving until every one of my people is free."

"Well, I can get *you* out and then—"

"If you had any idea about anything he said to me last night—the things he did and said and the things he *wanted* to do to me—you wouldn't be here. You'd leave this place. If not, maybe I don't know you anymore."

"Mara," Pol said with an exasperated sigh that almost sounded sympathetic. "He's a gruff kind of guy. He's a military type for sure, but he's—what did he do? But really, I believe in this cause. We're finally ending the war for good."

"Thanatanos started this war," Mara said, tears pooling in the corner of her eyes. "I am so sorry we didn't get to talk at my Peace Ball a few years ago. I really am. I had planned to have a special dinner that night—just you and me. I wanted to make those potato pancakes just like mama used to make, with the clotted cream—you know, those ones she made for special breakfast. I wasn't even going to have my palace chefs make them. I wanted to cook them for you just like her."

The stream of slaves pushed by, and Mara felt the gaze of Pol's superior officers on them.

Pol smiled. "It took her hours to grate all those potatoes just to make a meal we'd eat in a few minutes. I loved those things."

"And do you remember how she'd put the onions and bacon on top? I was looking forward to it more than anything else that night."

"More than Aleksander?" Pol asked.

"Pol," Mara said, clutching her chest. "Are you serious?"

"Sorry, that was mean. I went on the run with him for a while, and we had a bit of a falling out. I don't know—and I'm sorry, that would have been wonderful... What about the rhubarb and strawberry pie she would make?"

"That was the surprise dessert, of course. I wish our first interaction in years could have been different. I really do."

The tears fell from sad eyes down her face. "Why are you doing this? After everything we've been through, everything we've dreamed about... I learned to dream from *you*, Pol. You and your grand stories. My little brother, the endless dreamer of epic adventures. But now, I'm really scared those dreams are dead. And it seems pretty clear that you've chosen your side, and that side *isn't* your sister—or the man I know you really are."

"Well, then I'm sorry neither of us lived up to what we wanted for the other," Pol replied.

They stood there in silence until a duo of guards shoved Mara onto the train carriage with Kamil and Alia. As they shut the doors, Mara mouthed the words, "I love you," but Pol had already turned away.

Her heart shattered into a million pieces.

There was more room in the train cars to move about than in the sleeping barracks, and people weren't sitting or lying on top of one another, but it was still cramped and uncomfortable.

Mara huddled in the corner with Alia and Kamil under the glow of a hanging candle that swung and cast long shadows around the transport as the train began to build momentum.

"I heard everything," Alia said, touching Mara's hand. Mara buried her face in her knees as she drew them to her chest. "We can talk in Kurashic if you don't want anyone else to hear."

Mara let her head hit the back wall behind her as more silent tears rolled down her cheeks. She wanted to scream.

"I just don't understand. Why does this keep happening?" Mara asked in Kurashic, although the rest of the train was now alive with conversation, and of course, more sobbing.

"It's not fair, is it?"

"No, it's not," Mara said, glancing at Alia with sad eyes. "I have been a slave since just before my seventeenth birthday. First on that giant Talohiran slaver ship, then in Valistaran's camp, now here…"

She felt Kamil grab her other hand. She was now holding both of their hands tightly.

"*We love you*," Kamil said.

"I love you both so much." She flashed a true smile. "What haunts me most isn't the horrible things that have happened to me. I can live with that. It's not that I can remember the faces of every one of those evil men. It's the faces of the other slaves I couldn't save and that I—that I don't even know my own brother anymore."

"Mara…"

"I am tired of being strong. I just want to fall apart." She looked at Kamil as a tear rolled down her cheek. "You were there with me. You get it."

Kamil nodded. "*As much as anyone*."

"I know," Alia said with a nod as she rubbed Mara's arm. "Well, as sweet Valeniya always says, you're the brightest of all of us."

"What does she even mean by that?" Mara asked with a smile and a sniff.

Alia shrugged. "I don't know. It's true, though. Although I can't say why. But you know what? That's what keeps *us* from falling apart."

Mara let out another sigh as the train barreled along the tracks.

"Every time something like this happens—every time men like Belokej and Mazanek and all of the rest of them—every time they touch me or bruise me or yell at me, I feel myself getting closer to becoming cruel like them. Every time, I just want to kill them. And not because they hurt me, but because I know for a fact that they're doing worse to the people around me who can't defend themselves like I can."

"That isn't cruelty. That's you being a good person," said Alia. "You want to end cruelty, but not *through* cruelty, and *that* is your strength."

"You know, Mara, I've never thanked you for this, but you always told me in Valistaran's camp that spring always comes," Kamil said. *"I still believe that."*

"Those were Rehor's words, not mine," Mara said.

"Not according to him. You said it to him, forgot you said it, and then he said it back to you, and you said it to us," Kamil said with a laugh. *"I understand how you're feeling, perhaps better than anyone here. I wasn't a slave nearly as long as you were, but long enough to feel your pain. We've gotten through everything so far, and we can get through this."*

"Thank you," Mara said. "That's very sweet. I know we can. I'm just upset over Pol, and… I don't know."

"These people have no idea how much you love them. Do you understand that there are Talohirans, Kurashians, and Sangorans here? You are their protector. You are *here* with them. Not in Doftaan, not in Bukaral, and not in Tal-Ahosh. You are *here* to protect them. You didn't send your armies to save them. You came yourself. They need you to be strong, but when you don't feel like you can be, that's what Kamil and I are here for."

"Thank you," Mara said. "I love you both. Alia, I'm glad we were able to bond about sharing a husband."

Alia laughed; the sound was very out of place in the carriage full of sobbing slaves, and she cocked her head to look into Mara's eyes.

"Yes, me too," Alia said with a light in her dark eyes.

"Just think about it, Mara—we can be like Rehor for your people here," Kamil said. *"Spring always comes!"*

"I wouldn't have gotten far without Rehor back then. But you know what, buddy? I wouldn't have gotten far without you either. I hope you know that. And not just because you were the one who broke us out of there—you have always been a true friend through and through."

"Thank you," Kamil thought to her mind.

"I'm here for you. I know you're suffering just as much as I am," she said. "I want you to know I'm going to fight to my last breath for you."

"I know," Alia said. "But it won't come to that."

"What about your son?" Mara asked.

"Oh, my son the king?" Alia asked. "Sorry, proud mama moment. I haven't heard from him in a while, but last time I saw Valeniya, she said he is safe, and what he's doing is making a difference."

"Valeniya!" Mara exclaimed with wide eyes. "She told me she'd look out for me. I completely forgot!"

"Then she knows where you are," Kamil thought excitedly. *"And that means—"*

"Even Valeniya's powers have limits, though," Alia said. "Her power to see others weakens at a distance, and we are, well…I don't have to tell you how far away we are. Not to dash your hopes, but…I'm not sure if she can see us anymore."

"Then we can only hope she saw us before we made it here," Mara said. Kamil and Alia nodded. "Who knew we'd have our hopes set in the Talohir family?"

Alia chuckled.

"Not me," she said.

"Technically the 'Talohir family' includes both of you, so I definitely did," Kamil said.

"Well, that statement is complete and utter betrayal," Mara said with a bright laugh, which Alia echoed.

Alia and Mara both squeezed his hands, and they huddled up together in their corner of the train cart. Soon, with Alia and Kamil's heads on Mara's shoulders, they all succumbed to exhaustion.

It was more than three days before the train stopped to let those inside step out to stretch their legs and relieve themselves in more privacy than the embarrassing public toilet the carriage provided.

The soldiers had already prepared scant meals for them: a weak broth with a few vegetables and buckwheat with chunks of hardy rye bread. They distributed it throughout the crowd, allowing them to rest for around an hour before they were once again forced back into the train's carriages.

Mara's breath floated up in front of her. Adess had seemed frozen, but it was nothing compared to this. The sky was a blanket of pure white, and the needles of the evergreen pines even seemed to be suspended in time, covered in the morning frost.

"Where in the world are we?" she asked.

Alia slipped her shivering hand through the crook of Mara's arm and pulled her close.

"I know you're used to the cold in Sangora, but I'm Kurashian. How do you do this?!" she asked.

"Built in blankets, I guess." Mara laughed, pulling her close to wrap her wing around her friend.

Kamil lay on the frozen ground, stretching his aching limbs.

"*I feel like an old man, listen to all that cracking,*" he thought. "*Do you think we're close to where we're going?*"

Mara's heart dropped. "No."

Alia turned her head to look at Mara, who had a look of dismay etched across her bronze face.

"Just a guess, or…"

"Mazanek told me we'd be traveling like this for months," Mara said. Kamil groaned, and Alia rested her head on Mara's shoulder with a sigh.

"Then we're sticking together, and we're gonna get through this," Alia said, watching a ring of officers sitting around a roaring fire.

"*Don't expect they'd let us join?*" Kamil asked.

"Oh, yes, they've been very accommodating thus far," Mara said. Alia chuckled.

Kamil gestured with his head toward two guards that seemed to be watching the trio. Mara nodded.

"My orders when I got to the Adess camp were not to associate," she said. "That woman they left outside the camp was punished just for talking to me."

"I think Kamil has just the trick for that," Alia said in Kurashic. "He told you we were stealing food for people in our housing, correct?"

"Yeah," Mara said.

"He figured out that he can make people forget what they've just seen. You know the feeling when you walk into a room and forget why you went in there?"

"Yeah. Hate that."

"He figured out how to trigger that with his powers," Alia said. "He's playing with erasing memories completely, but he can make the guards watching us basically forget they see us together while they're staring right at us. That, or to momentarily forget their orders, or to forget that they were supposed to keep us from talking."

"*I'm not good enough at it yet to help everyone here at once, but I think we can really do some good,*" Kamil said.

"You are an absolute genius," Mara said. "I mean, what else could we do? Stealing food might get us caught again, but we could let people rest or maybe, I don't know, make Mazanek forget he was supposed to punish someone?"

"*I guess so,*" Kamil said.

"Have him forget to breathe."

Kamil smiled. "*I don't think that's how it works.*"

"We'll help you do whatever you need," Mara said. "If it makes you too tired, you can have my meals. This is important."

"*Thank you, but I can't let you do that.*"

"As the Supreme One of Kurash, I order you to eat my breakfast," Mara said.

Kamil and Alia both let out a laugh.

"*Already abusing that power, I see.*"

"For a good cause," Mara said. She winked at her friend and stood up as the guards had signaled for them to get back onto the train.

Together, they climbed back inside where it was marginally warmer than outside, and Mara blanketed them both with her wings. As the guards shut the doors, Mara gasped as she saw three soldiers execute some slaves that were too weak to travel.

"*I should have stopped them,*" Kamil said. "*We just barely talked about—*"

"No. There's nothing you could have done. It happened too fast," Alia said.

"You can't start thinking that everything bad that happens is your fault," Mara said. Alia looked at her with a raised eyebrow. "I've done that enough for all of us... We can't think that way."

The train chugged along the frozen tundra east of Sangora for hours that stretched into days. Conversation in the train cars became as scarce as the food the prisoners were seldom fed by the Thannish soldiers.

When they stopped again, Mara, Kamil, and Alia stepped out onto the frozen ground. The train's plume of dark smoke looked like a foul, inky splotch of the pure white canvas of the pristine, but unforgiving landscape.

As the other slaves stretched their legs, and the soldiers once again distributed meager portions of food, Mara felt a hand on her shoulder. She turned, eying the bowls of weak broth like it were a holiday feast; her stomach gave an audible growl. She looked up to see a young soldier gesture toward the back of the train.

"Sergeant Mazanek wants to see—"

"Tell Sergeant Mazanek that he can jump in a lake."

The soldier shifted uncomfortably. "He told me not to tell you this, but if you don't come with me, he's going to have someone killed."

Mara nodded, staring into the distance before saying simply, "Okay."

She glanced over her shoulder to give a weak wave to Alia and Kamil who watched her disappear into the car at the back of the train. When she stepped inside, her mouth hung open in shock. While the train cars the Thans were shipping her and the other slaves in were more akin to barns fit for animals, this portion of the train resembled a palace. Chandeliers hung from the ceiling, casting a beautiful glow from the fireplace, and beautiful paintings of Thannish leaders, including King Verahim, adorned the walls.

She followed the young soldier to the cabin at the back of the chamber and stepped through the door.

"Ah, Miss Bartunek," Mazanek said from within, standing up from a table laden with a veritable feast. "Thank you, Private Romanik. That will be all."

Private Romanik, the young soldier, nodded and turned away, closing the door behind him.

"What?" Mara asked abruptly.

"I see your attitude hasn't changed."

"Have you given me a reason for it to?"

Mazanek laughed and gestured to the feast. Mara didn't budge from her spot and folded her arms over her chest, although she couldn't help but stare at the spread before her.

"Is this enough of one?" the sergeant asked. "A peace offering, if you will. An apology for our last interaction. I was drunk—no excuse for my behavior."

"What a load of—"

"Seriously. I don't want to have to deal with you, so eat and be happy already."

"Yes, because *this* will be what brings peace between our people," Mara said. "What do you want?"

"Sit," he ordered. She still didn't move. "Fine. I'll eat without you. Do you remember a few days ago when I told you I had a special job for you?"

"I do," Mara said.

"Well, time to sing." She watched his eyes dart to the bed behind the banquet table. "Unless—"

"Not if my life depended on it."

"What if the lives of the other slaves depended on it?" Mazanek asked. Mara glared with the fury of a warrior empress, but the sergeant waved his hand. "Anyway. Entertain me."

Mara nodded, knowing he would go through with his threat to kill someone if she refused.

"What song, then?"

"For my first show, I think I'll let you decide. Make it a good one."

Mara's mind raced. For a moment, nothing came to mind. Perhaps it was her mind's way of shielding the songs she kept so close to her heart from the man, but then one in particular came to her lips. The first verse came out as a forced whisper.

> *I'll be who I am, I'll say what I want*
> *I know who I am, so I'll just be me,*
> *Oh, that's what I'll do,*
> *so go ahead and leave*
> *I don't owe you a thing*
> *For who I'll be*

"Louder," Mazanek ordered, taking a drink of wine. "If I like your song, you get fed." He gestured to the food.

> *Nothin' about you's who I am*
> *I'm free, and that's your fault.*
> *Maybe I should tell you though,*
> *that you won't ever get to call me mine.*

"We'll see," he said with a wink, taking a bite of roast pheasant. Her nostrils flared in anger, but she kept singing for her peoples' sake.

You know there's nothin' here to save,
'cause I'm not your damsel
And I'm not in distress
maybe I should tell you though,
Oh, you don't get to call me mine.

Nothin' about you is who I am
I'm stronger now, no thanks to you
but maybe I should thank you though,
'cause I learned to fly.

As she concluded her song, Mazanek applauded, even setting down his fork to do so, although he continued to chew.

"See, was that so hard?" he asked, wiping his mouth on a fancy napkin. Rage swirled in her heart, but she said nothing. "That last line… I'm a connoisseur of the arts, you know? A man of culture. I've attended all the greatest orchestras and symphonies in Thanatanos. But that line… It sent a chill down my spine. And you know? I think you *have* learned to fly, but isn't it poetic that I get to keep this little bird in a cage? I have all the power on who you will become next. Hauntingly beautiful, I think."

Mara reached down toward the plate on the table, and Mazanek's gaze followed her trembling hand. Her stomach growled again, and he laughed as she picked up one of the long knives instead of the plate and pointed it at him from across the table.

"They have orders to kill everyone if you hurt me."

In her rage, Mara hurled the knife at the window of the carriage, shattering it into tiny pieces.

"Real mature. Now I'll be cold in here until—"

"Welcome to the damn party. Now, feed my people instead of me," Mara ordered. "You got your concert. I'll be on my way now."

Mazanek gestured over to the bed again.

"Svinok ty," Mara said in Sangoran. *You swine.*

She pushed her way out of the cabin and slammed the door behind her without eating a morsel of food.

She wrapped her arms around her shivering body as the train let out a groan and an odd hooting sound; Private Romanik was waiting for her outside the cabin with a look of concern. He walked her to her carriage door and opened the doorway.

"Listen, I know the kind of thing he does. Did he—" His voice faltered. "Are you okay?"

"No. To both questions," Mara said, inferring his question with a shake of her head. She sighed. "Listen, kid. I'm not new to this life. I've been through it all. I just want to sleep."

The young soldier heaved open the door and said in a low voice, "I'm sorry. A few of us have tried telling him he doesn't have to do things like this. He doesn't have to be so cruel, even though—no, I'm not going to give an excuse like that. This is horrible, and I know it. But he said there's nothing else to do out here, and he's threatened to punish us if we said—"

"I appreciate your concern," Mara said. "But I'd like to rejoin my friends now."

"My name is Josef," he said awkwardly as she climbed inside the cart. "I really am sorry. I just want to help."

"I know. Thank you, Josef."

Private Josef Romanik closed the door to the carriage, plunging it into darkness. The other soldiers had forgotten, or perhaps intentionally, not relit the lanterns inside.

Alia clutched her wrist, and Mara flinched but then held her hand tightly.

"I'm okay. He just made me sing," Mara said, anticipating her questioning.

"I wasn't going to ask. Just here for you," Alia said.

Alia kissed her forehead in the darkness.

"How are you two holding up?" Mara asked.

"Yes, we're okay. They even gave everyone an extra portion of that slop, and then Kamil made them forget they did, and everyone got a third portion."

Mara laughed.

"*I can sense him. He's angry,*" Kamil said. "*Did you get to eat?*"

"I wouldn't let him feed me," Mara said as the train lurched forward. "But if he keeps his end of the bargain, I hope he'll feed the rest of you a little better so you won't have to trick them."

"*Please don't destroy yourself for our sake,*" Kamil thought to her, and Alia squeezed Mara's hand to reinforce his statement. "*That won't save us.*"

"Right back at you. I know how exhausting using your powers can be. But really, I don't mind. It's how I can help," Mara muttered, a tear rolling out of her eye and over her nose as she lay her head on Alia's shoulder. Alia stroked her hair and sang a soft Kurashic lullaby.

"You know what? Valis has a great mom," Mara said. Alia responded with a tighter hug.

As Kamil tried to get comfortable, he accidentally brushed Mara's mind, catching her last thought before he did so. A longing for rest, but not an admission of defeat. Not yet.

"I am so tired."

CHAPTER TWENTY-FIVE

DEAD PRINCE, DEAD KING

Aleksander and Valeniya's horse stumbled as the men on the wall continued in vain to hit them with arrows. Rayshel's horse had nearly been skewered by a spear launched from a ballista, but Lavinia had managed to soar up onto the wall and dispatch the men before they could try again. She now flew next to her allies who rode with all haste toward Thanatanos.

The new wall, which was constructed at Verahim's command by the Magistrate's Faceless, ran along the entire border between Thanatanos and Sangora. The massive bulwark stretched all the way from the Than Sea in the west all the way to the Plains of Adess in northern Sangora.

The nearest gate was just west of the border city of Vudapas, the next closest nearly one hundred miles away in either direction. The half of the city in Thanatanos was behind the wall, while the Sangoran portion was segregated on the other side.

That massive gate was now the most important point along the entire border, which meant that a force of thousands of combined Alboran and Talohiran forces now laid siege to the city to contest the crossing—not to conquer Vudapas, but to prevent any more forces from flowing into their lands.

Aleksander spurred his horse onward until he crested a low hill he could use as a vantage point to look over the battle on either side of the wall. Rayshel stopped near him with a low whistle.

"Well, would you look at that," she whispered. Dozens of ruined ballistae littered the bulwark, victims of Talohiran trebuchets.

"Looks like the fighting has stalled," Lavinia said as she landed next to them.

"But it's not over, right?" Rayshel asked. Lavinia nodded.

"They're at a stalemate."

"Good news for us, though," said Aleksander. "It means they won't be able to get more forces into Alboras or Talohira."

"Theoretically," Lavinia replied. "But there are hundreds of thousands of Thannish troops on this side now. It's only a matter of time before those attacking Alboras and Timishuara are reassigned here."

Aleksander looked over the battle. "It's a losing war, then?"

"Not necessarily," Lavinia said, shaking her head. "To my knowledge, things are going well around Balgorod and my capital city of Darova in Timishuara. If they can repel the forces there, Balgorod can reinforce the siege of Vudapas, and troops from Darova can help in Dakthaan."

"What's happening in Doftaan?!" Aleksander exclaimed.

"Dakthaan, not Doftaan. Different cities," Rayshel said as Lavinia looked east. "And you know what's happening in Doftaan already."

"Oh. Yeah."

"It's been under attack for a week now," Lavinia said. "They're trying to evacuate parts of the city, but there's nowhere for them to go. They're blocking all ways out, and hundreds have already died."

"Why are you here with me, then?" Aleksander asked. "Your people need you."

"My task was to get Valeniya here so that you could find Cyrgiz and Umut," said Lavinia. "Rayshel and I will head back to Darova now. I trust you can take care of yourself?"

"We'll be fine, thank you," Aleksander said.

"Remember, if they get to Laniras, we're all dead."

"I know, Lavinia."

"No pressure," Rayshel said with a wink as she hopped off her horse. She pulled Aleksander into a tight hug and patted him on the shoulder as she climbed back upon her steed. "That hug was from Vinia, too."

"Was not," Lavinia replied.

"Don't listen to her," Rayshel said.

"Thank you, Vinny," Aleksander said with a smile.

Lavinia stared at him for a long, confused moment, shaking her head.

"If you weren't a close acquaintance, I'd kill you."

"Close acquaintance? That's practically family to you," Aleksander said. Rayshel laughed as she drove her horse to face east. Lavinia snorted but let a slight smile peek through.

"I will watch over you," Valeniya said.

"Thank you, Valeniya," said Lavinia as she unfurled her wings. "Keep this one safe too."

She gestured to Aleksander with her head, and then they were off.

Aleksander guided their horse down the hill into the bustling mass of campsites and siege equipment, where they were greeted by a contingent of guards.

If the Talohirans' intelligence that Cyrgiz and Umut had already crossed the border into Thanatanos was correct, Aleksander knew he had little time to deal with any interruptions.

He dismounted and offered a hand to Valeniya to help her do the same.

"General Kosturkin?" Aleksander asked as he guided his horse into the crowd. White breath rose from its nostrils as it snorted and tried to pull away. "Where is General Kosturkin?"

"Who do you think you are?" asked a soldier. The man drew his blade, and Aleksander raised his hands in peace.

"My name is Aleksander. I was sent by command of King Shadid to—"

"Aleksander *who*?"

"Aleksander…" he tried in vain to think of a common Thannish surname, but at that moment, every name he'd ever known escaped him. The guard pointed his weapon.

"Let him pass!" came a familiar voice from within the camp. The guards barring Aleksander's way lowered their weapons, and Valistaran Talohir greeted Aleksander with open arms.

"Welcome," Valistaran said. "What are you waiting for? Take his horse, it looks thirsty and tired."

"Father!" Valeniya exclaimed, running to him. Aleksander expected her to hug him, but she stood rigid before him until he stretched out his arms. She let him hug her, a wide smile on her face.

"Thank you for meeting me," Aleksander said. The soldiers took his horse away.

"And thank you for keeping Leniya safe," replied Valistaran, still holding his daughter close. "What news from Bukaral?"

"Your son sent me to meet with General Kosturkin, but—"

"Kosturkin is dead," Valistaran said bluntly.

"How?" Aleksander asked. "I was supposed to—"

Valistaran cut him off again. "Don't worry. I'm fully briefed on the situation with the rogue Secret Keepers."

"Seems my job has already been done, then," Aleksander said.

"Hardly," Valistaran said.

"Has he been found?" Aleksander asked.

"More or less. How do you think Kosturkin died?" Valistaran asked.

"He killed the general?" Aleksander asked, taken aback. "Was he apprehended? Did I make it here in time?"

"No. He is not here. We've been betrayed, young prince," Valistaran said. Aleksander said nothing, wondering if how Valistaran had said 'young prince' was meant to be condescending or not. "It was all a set up. The Secret Keeper murdered Kosturkin during the night. We caught him, but several of my men freed him and took him away, all part of their plan. We'd have followed, but they made it through the gate before we could catch them."

Aleksander's heart sank.

"So I'm too late."

"Yes, yes you are," Valistaran said. He sighed and looked toward Vudapas. "You know, your father and I disagreed about a lot of things, but we had a lot of good times too."

Aleksander cocked his head, not expecting that to be Valistaran's next sentence. Everyone knew his identity, it seemed, despite the fact that he'd only told a few people.

"You look like him, you know. When he was younger." Valistaran let out a nostalgic sigh. He didn't say anything else for a long moment. "We were afraid of this very thing happening."

"What thing?"

"I wanted to kill the Secret Keepers all those years ago so that their knowledge wouldn't fall into his hands. Or worse, my own hands. Who knows what I would have done with their knowledge? It's also why I wanted to kill *you*."

"And why you killed my father?" Aleksander asked.

Valistaran was silent for a moment. "Let's take a walk."

When they were out of earshot of any eavesdroppers, Aleksander raised his hands in exasperation.

"Look, at the time, I didn't even know he *was* my father. I thought you just killed an enemy king," Aleksander said.

"I didn't kill your father," Valistaran said in a soft voice.

"I watched you do it," Aleksander said. "Don't try to lie."

"Your father was the best friend I had left in this world. Especially after I ruined things with Alia Shadid, after my wife's Codruta's death," Valistaran said. "Your father's kingdom and my own became bitter enemies. So did we, at times. But we had our moments of peace—we were always close."

"I don't follow."

"Your father and I and our friends… The Supreme One and Ronin Jakoni, that is, we called ourselves the *immortals*. The immortals. How silly was that?"

"Get to the point," Aleksander ordered.

"Sorry. Just reminiscing. In the end, your father and I weren't able to work out our differences about the Secret Keepers. I wanted them killed, and he wanted them protected with safeguards to ensure that their powers would not be used except to advance technology and science."

"What happened?"

"We agreed upon something—finally. He made me promise me that no one else could know of our plan. Ever. Only we would be involved. Ronin Jakoni found out, but he didn't agree with either of us. He thought bringing back certain technologies and magics from the Deadlands would help us rule the world and prevent further destruction and war. He knew he couldn't get to the Secret Keepers before we did, so he went for..."

He trailed off like a teacher fishing for a student's answer.

"The Weapon of Ages Past?"

"The nuclear weapon, you mean?" Valistaran asked. "Exactly. We wanted to stop Ronin from getting it. I planned to use it against Thanatanos if I needed to. Hypocritical, I know. You don't need to point it out. It was to be my deterrent."

"I was there, wasn't I?" Aleksander asked, gesturing to the scar on his arm. The day he got his scar was still a cloudy memory. Valistaran nodded.

"You were, and you were quite invaluable to our quest. I even taught you to produce black flame. You saved us a few times."

"I've always wondered—why *is* your fire dark?"

"Because it isn't *technically* fire. You know the dark smoke Walkers use to teleport? The glands in Dragonsouls' bodies able to create fire are also able to create a similar smoky substance, but instead of transporting one thing to a secondary place, it drains the heat and energy from elsewhere, creating shadows that resemble fire, but are much hotter than any flame."

"Woah. That's the coolest thing I've ever heard," Aleksander said. "Or the *least* cool thing... get it? Because it's hot?"

Valistaran sighed.

"Anyway, we digress. The first time we found the Weapon of Ages Past, as you called it, you'd made up with your father after you ran away all those years ago. You accompanied all of us into the Deadlands across the great ocean. We found the weapon, and Ronin betrayed us and tried to take it for himself. Kadir stopped him, but not before Ronin's Mindspeakers wiped our memories of the event to hide it from us. He planned to go back for it, which he did, of course. You took the brunt of the mental attack, keeping us from forgetting everything like you did. I promise I'll tell you the entire story someday when we have more time."

"I still don't understand why you killed—or didn't kill— my father."

"Because I failed, which I'm glad about now. He was not a perfect man; we both have our sins."

Aleksander wondered if Valistaran were referring to the fake Xanthurias that had replaced him.

"One more than the other," Aleksander said.

Valistaran chuckled. "Perhaps, yes."

"Is this all why you tried to exterminate magic users in your camps, too?" Aleksander asked.

"Romiton wanted no part in that. I don't blame him. It was the main reason for our falling out—I admit the atrocities of my camps and that I did little to stop them, but it was all my quest to bury the past. To keep it hidden. I erased the civilization of the Deadlands from textbooks, from libraries. Romiton's ancestors had already attempted to do the same. Becoming king gave me the ability to finish their work."

"Then what happened to my father?" Aleksander asked.

"He was with us in secret in Zinok… The last time the 'Immortals' were all together. Between those two meetings, I didn't know where he was. Kadir was the one who eventually, somehow, made contact with him again. I haven't seen him since, although I do have some clues to where he went."

"Where?"

"He told me that he'd been looking for Thanatan's sleeping body so that he could end him, but after that supposed god awoke, Romiton came back here with Kadir. He planned to head east—what's east of Talohira and Sangora, I have no idea."

"Why fake his death?"

"What king can trounce around the world at a whim? He had to leave, but he didn't want to tarnish his family's legacy by abdicating the throne. He was all about maintaining the royal house of Romus," Valistaran said.

"I'd know," Aleksander said, placing a hand on his heart.

"Ah, yes, as the *original* Prince Xanthurias, I assume you would know all about that, wouldn't you. Although, I seem to have done the exact same thing, although I am no longer hiding *my* son."

"So, where is he now? My father, not your son. What are your theories?"

"We can talk about that later. He left me a journal that I'd like you to have," Valistaran said. "Perhaps, we can go find him and finish what he started… or join him, *if* he's still alive."

Aleksander thought for a moment. "Everything that's happened has been because of whatever went on in the Deadlands." He hesitated before asking his next question. "Would you go with me? To find him, I mean."

Valistaran cocked his head, looking into Aleksander's eyes. For a long moment, he said nothing. The way he seemed to peer right through Aleksander felt eerily similar to how Valeniya often stared at him.

"It would be my honor. When we get back to Bukaral, I will give you his journal. In the meantime, we have some rogue Secret Keepers to find," Valistaran said. "As long as Kurash can keep their last one safe, I think we should be fine. They can replicate the memories."

"So? What's the plan?" Aleksander asked.

"I have a contact on the other side that will get us across," Valistaran said. "He should have some horses and supplies ready for us as we travel to Laniras."

"And if he's not there?" Aleksander asked.

"Then we fight our way through."

CHAPTER TWENTY-SIX
A FRESH BLANKET OF CRUEL WHITE

The door of the train car slid open, letting the horrible, frosty air inside for what seemed like the thousandth time. By Kamil's math and estimations, they had traveled nearly twelve-hundred miles into the unforgiving, frozen lands northeast of the edge of all known civilization.

The train only ran for about two hours at a time before stopping so that the engineers could clear the tracks of ice or refuel the massive vehicle's coal reserves.

Mara knew it'd be early spring back home in Sangora, but here, it seemed that beautiful season would linger in the back of her mind as a forgotten dream. Where a blanket of new green and flowers of pink and yellow would cover her home, this place would be nothing but gray and white as far as she could see.

Mazanek was determined not to let them forget it.

Two soldiers, including Josef Romanik, welcomed them with nothing more than halfhearted nods as they began helping the slaves clamber out of the cramped space in the train car. It had become routine to slave and soldier alike, and no words of instruction needed to be shared.

Since they were sitting right next to the doors, Mara, Alia, and Kamil were among the first to climb outside. It was by design; Mara had insisted that they be the first out, not so that they could stretch their legs first, but rather that the rest of the prisoners could stay inside for a few more moments of relative warmth. She knew that in a place as cruel and unforgiving as this one, mere moments could be all that separated the living from the dead.

Mara swore that her lungs would freeze from the inside out as she drew in a frosty breath. She cursed out loud and pulled her coat's collar up to cover her exposed neck.

"I didn't know the world could be this cold," Mara muttered to Alia as she hopped back and forth on her feet trying to keep warm. "It even hurts to breathe."

"It doesn't get this cold on our world. This is hell. Hell, Mara," Alia replied. And then, for good measure, she added, another, "Hell!"

"Then it looks like hell's finally frozen over," Mara said. "Too on the nose?"

It seemed not, because both Alia and Kamil chuckled at her attempt at humor. The sound of the metal doors scraping shut filled the air, and the trio glanced back to the train to see that only ten other slaves had climbed outside.

"What's going on?" Mara called to Josef.

"This isn't a routine stop; they're making you clear the tracks of ice and debris," Josef said in a low voice as he led them to a barrel of pickaxes that had been dumped from the supply carriage.

"Isn't that your job?" Mara asked with a scowl.

"Mazanek doesn't want to risk us—"

Before he could finish the sentence, the officer in charge shouted the same order but in a much more aggressive tone. Mara glared at Josef and his comrades with ice in her eyes.

"And I don't expect any of you lot are going to man up and help?" Alia asked as the officer walked away. She drew an axe from the barrel. "Cowards! Don't we at least get gloves?"

Her hands were trembling and already discolored from the cold. Josef glanced at his fellow soldier who shook his head and walked away toward the officer carriages. Josef gave Alia a sympathetic look, and when he was sure the other soldier couldn't see, he slipped his own military issued gloves from his hands and pushed them into Alia's.

"I'm sorry that I only have one pair. Perhaps you can share them," Josef said. "I'll need them back, but…"

He trailed off.

"Thank you," Alia said.

Josef glanced over at Mara with a lingering look of concern before jogging to catch up to the officer.

In all, other than the trio, the group of shivering slaves consisted of three other Sangoran women, two Sangoran men, one with wings and one a Walker, as well as two human men, two human women, and the young boy Mara now knew to be named Jakub.

The two human men with thick, lightly colored beards were muttering something in a foreign language, and Mara perked up. It sounded reminiscent of Icelandic, a language from the Deadlands that she had studied. A descendant of the dead language, perhaps.

As she tried to eavesdrop on their conversation, appreciating how similar and yet distinct the language was from Icelandic, one of them showed the other a gold coin in his palm, and they snickered. The flash of gold vanished as if by magic, and the man pretended to find it behind his friend's ear, and Mara laughed. Sleight of hand—despite her best efforts, she could never seem to fathom it.

Mara smiled at the small act of rebellion, knowing the two men had stolen Mazanek's second coin.

As the group of thirteen made their way to the front of the train, Mara hung back and gave a slight wave to the two blonde men.

"Halló!" she said in Icelandic, and the two men stopped in their tracks, wide eyed. One of them, the man with Mazanek's coin, guffawed out of joy.

"Taalar tjuu Odauthskuu!" he shouted with a happy expression. "Halló tjul thín líka!"

The words were slightly different from the language she knew—the vowels lengthened, and the consonants somehow harder. Mara could still understand the man's words. *You speak Odauthian! Hello to you as well!*

"Olafur," said one of the Odauthians in introduction. "Okh Runar." *Olafur and Runar.*

Kamil and Alia stopped as Mara spoke to them in Icelandic, and they spoke back in their own language. They laughed back and forth as they followed the rest of the slaves toward the tracks where they found another pair of officers waiting for them with a barrel full of tools.

Collective sighs and groans accompanied the scrape of wooden pick shafts against the barrel's edges as they each selected a tool. Each one was chipped and rusted.

"You never fail to amaze me," Alia said with a kind expression. "What language was that, even?"

"Odauthian. I speak a language from the Deadlands called Icelandic, and it must be an ancestor of their language. I could understand most of what they were saying. They absolutely loved it. I need to talk to them more about where they came from."

"I can tell they loved it," Kamil thought. *"Look at them. They look like children on the morning of the Thankfulness Festival."*

He was correct; as a soldier handed Mara a pickaxe, she looked back to the two bearded men. Their countenances had improved considerably, and her heart swelled with joy.

"Just think about it," Alia said, taking a tool of her own. "They have no one else they can speak to."

Mara waved goodbye to the two Odauthian men and began swinging her pickaxe at the sheet of ice covering the tracks. Fortunately, no new snow had accumulated on top of the ice.

Alia and Kamil joined her, and for a moment, everyone else just stood there, too tired to begin. However, as they watched Mara smashing at the ice, they found their courage;

they all began swinging their picks, resulting in a steady rhythm that rang through the tundra.

The horrible sound of whenever someone broke through the ice and struck the metal tracks felt like a wedge driven deeper and deeper into Mara's skull, but she pressed on.

"Where's Aleksander when you need him?" Mara asked after half an hour of work, wiping the sweat from her brow. "He'd have this melted in a few minutes, and he'd be able to keep us warm."

"Keep *you* warm, you mean." Alia smirked.

"I did not mean—" She slapped a hand over her face, and Alia snorted, proud of her joke. Mara lowered her hand with a soft smile that lingered for a moment until one of the other slaves collapsed, dropping her pick in the snow.

Mara rushed to her side and helped her stand, handing her the fallen tool to use as a crutch.

"I'm okay," said the Sangoran woman in Thannish.

"I've got you," Mara said. "The ice is thinner where I was working. How about you go work over there?"

The woman stooped low, and at first, Mara thought she was about to faint, but she straightened up.

"Thank you, Empress. I know we're safe with you here," she said with a weak, toothless grin. She wasn't falling after all; she had been bowing. "Without you, we'd have given up."

"What's your name?" Mara asked in a sweet voice, guiding the older woman toward the side of the tracks that had mostly been cleared by herself, Kamil, and Alia.

"I am Ulyana. Ulyana Zaitseva."

"It's so nice to meet you, Ulyana. I know with people like *you* here, we can get through this. Let's keep going," Mara said, rubbing the old woman's shoulder. She was honestly surprised Ulyana had made it this far, but she knew how tough Sangoran women could be.

"The Empress of Blood knows my name," Ulyana said through tears that glistened in the corner of her eyes. Mara reassured her with a smile, holding the woman's arm.

She led her to the spot where the ice was thinner. Every few minutes after she returned to work, Mara would look up to see Ulyana watching her with an endearing smile. Mara would return the expression with a wave, and then Ulyana would get back to work.

The far north seemed to be in perpetual darkness, so it was impossible for Mara to judge the flow of time other than trying to figure out how long it had been between meals or whenever the train stopped to let them outside.

However, the exhausted slaves eventually cleared the tracks of ice and a frozen, dead animal that had been picked over by scavengers.

Someone tugged on Mara's sleeve, and she turned to see Kamil pointing into the darkness at Josef as he approached.

"What in the name of Elafris happened to you?" Mara asked, eying a fresh purple bruise just behind his ear that spread down his neck.

"Oh, nothing. Accident," the private responded. Mara grasped his shoulder, and he looked up to meet her gaze. She shook her head and handed him the pair of gloves he had lent them.

"Don't get caught out of uniform again," Mara whispered. "I'm sure Mazanek told you the same thing."

"Not a good liar, am I?" Josef asked.

Mara shook her head with a sad smile. "No."

Josef opened the door of their cart, and the thirteen freezing slaves climbed into the carriage. It took Kamil and Josef's combined effort to help Ulyana inside, and she thanked them both graciously as she huffed her way to her seat, plopping down next between the Odauthian men, clutching their hands.

Kamil and Mara shared a glance, knowing that if anyone but Josef had been sent to herd the slaves back into their transport, the old woman would be left behind to die.

They traveled in that fashion for many days; the sun rarely seemed to peek over the horizon, and it never happened while the slaves were given time outside the train carriage. It was now to the point when standing outside the train was even more uncomfortable than being cramped up inside it. The soldiers had now punished every single one of the slaves, including children and the elderly, by forcing them to clear the tracks or shovel coal to keep the train running.

One night, or day, for all she knew, Mara awoke with a start; the sound of a thousand banshees wailing and scratching at the train filled the carriage, and the train came to a halt. She could hear Mazanek screaming outside, and she feared he would soon come rip the door off their carriage.

Her fears were justified. Mere moments later, the door flew open with a screech, and a dread wind of ice and death snaked its way into the carriage.

"Out!" he screamed.

Every soldier on the train was outside, the officers barking orders and distributing shovels and pickaxes, just like normal. The blizzard, however, was worse than any they'd seen yet. Two of the soldiers were standing at the front of the train blasting fire from their palms at the ice and snow piling in front of the train.

Mara swore loudly into the wind as it tried to force her to the ground. Kamil and Alia followed her through the blizzard toward Mazanek but lost sight of her as she braved the blinding white. Despite the howling wind, they could make out Mara screaming at the top of her lungs at Mazanek, first in Thannish and then again in Sangoran for good measure.

Kamil and Alia pushed through the blizzard, and Mara and Mazanek came into view just as the sergeant brought his fist up and punched Mara in the side of the head, throwing her into the snow.

"Mara!" Kamil shouted, his voice distorted due to his severed tongue; he sprinted toward her, nearly tripping in the snow that was now halfway up his shins. As Mazanek raised his blade to smite Mara, Kamil leapt between them and threw his hand forward, reaching into Mazanek's mind.

Mazanek's eyes glazed over, and his pupils dilated for a moment before he lowered his blade, shaking his head and rubbing his eyes in confusion. He stumbled in the snow and then wandered off, shouting orders to his men as they struggled to shovel snow from the tracks.

Kamil lowered his hand, letting his power over Mazanek fade. He reached down to help Mara to her feet, and as soon as she was upright, she wrapped her arms around him. When he assumed the appropriate time for a hug was over, he started to pull away, but Mara stayed still, her arms still tight around his shoulders.

When she did finally pull away, she began to speak, but nothing came out. Kamil nodded in understanding before she tried again.

"*I can hear your thoughts, you know,*" Kamil said with a smile. "*Don't mention it.*"

Together, they pushed their way back through the storm where the officers continued to bark orders at the slaves to dig the train out of the snow faster.

The only color apart from the world of endless white was the light of the hellish flame of the two Dragonsouls melting the ice in front of the train.

As Mara and Kamil started shoveling, Alia went to work healing the frostbite on the slaves' faces and hands wherever she could.

No words could be heard over the storm now. Mara tripped over something in the snow, and she scrambled over, fearing that it was a body. She turned whoever it was over, and tears filled her eyes as she saw Ulyana lying frozen in the snow. Mara screamed into the storm, but her voice was lost on the wind as she cradled the old woman's head.

She began shoveling through the snow until she reached the frozen ground. She cursed as her shovel chipped against the earth, unable to pierce it. With teary eyes, she rolled Ulyana's body into the hole and piled snow on top of her.

"Te'ušuoraja Vožatun vezojt vun haliv." *May the light of the Goddesses guide your way.*

She didn't know if Ulyana had been a religious woman, but the traditional words of Sangoran believers shared to the dead at funerals were the only ones she could muster.

It wasn't the first time she'd buried someone that had loved her in a way they didn't deserve.

The train's whistle hooted, and it lurched forward, the snow and ice beneath its wheels cracking. Mazanek was screaming at the men throwing flame, but they were beginning to tire, the use of their powers draining their strength.

Mara could see the main body of slaves moving back toward their respective carriages, led by several of the officers. Mara wondered if Mazanek had given the order to return to the train, or if the officers knew it was hopeless to try to keep up with the piling snow until the blizzard moved on.

Mara located Kamil and followed him back to the train. She helped him step up before asking, "Have you seen Alia?"

He shook his head.

"*No, but I can sense her. She's alive, somewhere east of the train. But she's not answering.*"

"I have to check," Mara said. She gestured to the frostbite forming on her friend's hands. "You're staying here."

She expected him to object, but he nodded.

She squeezed his hand and trudged back into the blizzard, tripping over someone's leg. She hurried to see if it was Alia, but to her dismay, she looked upon the dead, frostbitten face of Jakub, the little boy from her train carriage. There was no time to give him the same poor excuse for a funeral she had given Ulyana, and she cursed the storm.

Through sobs, she grasped his hand, but knew there was nothing more to be done. She had to find Alia before she too froze to death.

"Alia!" Mara shouted into the wind. She pushed her way forward, fearing that she would soon lose the train behind her. True fear crept into her heart, completely alone in the dark in the middle of the frozen tundra.

"Alia…" she said in a weak voice. She felt Kamil's weak presence fill her mind, guiding her east.

Her cheeks burned with the throbbing pain of hundreds of needles poking through her skin. She reached up to rub her cheeks to give them warmth, but they were completely numb. Or her hands were, but—

And there it was. Alia's voice. It was faint, but she knew she had heard it. She forced herself to her feet and pushed herself forward, or perhaps backward; she no longer had any idea where she was. And then, Kamil's presence in her mind was suddenly disrupted.

"Alia!" she called.

Nothing.

Her heart beating fast and her will to continue waning, she closed her eyes and activated her powers of telepathy for the first time in over a year. She sensed a feeble life somewhere to her left.

She brushed the snot from her nose on the back of her glove as she put one foot in front of the other.

"*Alia,*" she thought, reaching out into the blizzard. "*Are you there?*"

"*Mara?*"

She could sense her friend's mind but could not see her through the storm.

"*Watch for me,*" was all Mara could think as she lifted her hand to the sky; light wrapped itself around her elbow and up her arm toward her hand. A ball of electricity formed in her palm, and with a cry of pure agony that tore through her skull, she let it loose into the heavens, a beacon of blinding light for Alia to follow.

Mara caught the silhouette of the train in the light, and Alia and several other slaves, including the two Odauthians and a human woman came into view. Mara removed her coat and draped it over her friend, who did not resist.

Mara used her telekinesis to shield them from the snow, and they reached the train, which was already beginning to move. The soldiers had already shut the door to their carriage, and Mara pounded on the sheet of metal, shouting for them to open it.

"The officers," Alia said through moans of pain. "We can't open our own door. We have to go to the officers."

"I'd rather freeze to death," Mara muttered back, but knew her friend was right. With a heavy heart, she trudged through the snow, guiding them toward the officers' carriage.

Mara slammed on the door slab, her head throbbing in pain. Her vision began to swim, and a bout of nausea overtook her.

"*No, no, no… Not now. Please…*"

The door slid open, and a thin crack of light illuminated their frozen faces.

"By Elafris!" shouted one of the officers. "Shut that—"

Josef hurried over and helped Alia and the others into the carriage before Mara climbed in and stumbled to her knees.

"Where is your coat?!" he exclaimed. "What is going on?"

Alia collapsed next to a coal lit fireplace in the back of the train, and Mara slumped against a chair in the corner.

"Here to sing?" It was Mazanek's voice.

She didn't care about the guards and soldiers staring at her

as her

world   began

to swim

and

then

it went

black

again

And then, it wasn't. The world was fuzzy, and nothing made sense. This wasn't Doftaan. This wasn't her bed.

"Mara!"

It was a voice she knew. A voice she liked, but…Alia? Alia was there, and she was safe. But where were they, and how did she—

She was lying on a cot. Whose was it, though? Scared faces looked down at her.

"Hello?" Mara asked. "What's—"

"Do you know what just happened?" Alia asked, holding Mara's hand; it was cold to the bone.

Her head throbbed with pain, and her muscles felt like they were on fire.

"No," Mara said.

"Do you remember my name?" Alia asked. Mara nodded. "What is it?"

"Alia," she said.

"And do you remember my son's name?"

Mara thought for a moment. The world was starting to make more sense, but everything was still so unfamiliar and cloudy. Spinning. She shook her head in response to Alia's question.

"No."

She sat there for a while, her stare blank, but oddly calm.

"Let's play a game called 'Seizure or Stroke'," Mara muttered through a groan. "If I had a stroke, I'd be dead, so let's go with…seizure?"

"That's a horrible game, but I guess you win," Alia said with a scolding laugh. "Oh, Mara…"

She was sitting on the edge of the cot, her arms wrapped around Mara, who let out a slow breath through her nose.

"How long was I—"

"A few minutes. Not long."

Mara knew even a few minutes could cause lasting damage to her brain.

"Okay. Are you warm?" Mara asked.

"*That's* what you're worried about?" Alia asked. Frostbite covered her cheeks and trembling fingers, but she was otherwise safe in the warmth of the train. Mazanek was nowhere to be seen.

"Are you?" Mara repeated.

"Yes, I'm warm," Alia said, placing her hands on Mara's cheeks. A warmth exuded from her fingers, and Mara's eyes shot open as Alia healed the frostbite on her cheekbones.

"Oh, that's nice," she said, her eyelids drifting closed again. "Whose bed am I in?"

"My days of asking *that* question are long past me. Sorry, bad joke. Really bad," Alia said with a nervous laugh. Mara let out a dark chuckle, nonetheless. "It's Private Romanik's bed. You know, the nice soldier."

She spoke loud enough that only Mara could hear.

"Oh, we like him," Mara said, her voice weak. "Reminds me of Pol..."

"He reminds me of Valis, too," Alia said. "A good kid."

"Where is he?"

"Here," said Josef from his spot on the ground between two other cots opposite her.

"I keep thanking you," Mara said. "Becoming...a bad habit..."

Josef and Alia both laughed at that.

"Kamil?"

"He's safe. He's in the slave carriage with the others, but Private Josef convinced the officers to let us stay here," Alia explained. "Now sleep, Supreme One, before I make you."

"You can't make me do anything... I'm the Supreme One of..." Mara yawned as Alia lay next to her on the small cot.

Alia thought she had drifted off to sleep, but she jumped as Mara asked suddenly, "Hey Alia, remember how we both married Valistaran?"

They both let out another chuckle and Alia cuddled close to her friend, trying to share body heat beneath the coarse, wool, military issue blanket.

"Yes, what were we thinking?" Alia asked. "Now, sleep."

"You can't tell me what to do, I'm the Supreme One."

"Sleep."

She placed her hand on the side of Mara's head, using her powers of healing to lull her friend's mind to sleep. She received no response but watched Mara's chest rise and fall. Still alive, just asleep. She let out a sigh and glanced over at Josef. The young soldier gave a nod and a smile as he sat upon the floor and nestled his head against the metal side of another soldier's cot.

The slaves and soldiers slept as best they could as the blizzard howled outside, burying the train in a fresh blanket of cruel white.

CHAPTER TWENTY-SEVEN
DEATH'S DOORSTEP

When the Magistrate had informed Shanthah, Nadezhda, and Ana that they'd be transported to Doftaan for whatever fate awaited them, they had assumed the ship would take them to a dock where they'd then travel by land in a carriage.

However, that was not the case. The Magistrate's Faceless had risen out of the river, and hundreds of them were now carrying the stolen ship out of the water upon their backs and across the countryside toward Doftaan.

"Here we go!" Nadezhda screamed as the tide of Faceless rolled toward the capital city of Sangora, carrying them up and over the southern wall.

Doftaani citizens screamed and scattered from the street as the ship sailing atop hundreds of living corpses raced toward Jempratanrajon, the empirical district that housed the palace formerly belonging to Mara.

"If we weren't going to our certain deaths, this would be so awesome," Nadezhda said. "I won't lie about that."

"This might be one of the first times I've ever disagreed with you!" Ana shouted.

"I don't like this!" Shanthah shouted in response.

The Faceless carried them over the wall surrounding the palace grounds, which were no longer beautifully manicured as they had been during Mara's reign and dropped the ship at its front gates, the wooden hull splintering as it struck the stone pathway. The thousands of groaning Faceless dropped to their knees, bowing low before the entrance to their master's lair.

"What now?" Nadezhda asked.

"Well, I die, of course, but you two escape. Hanna mourns me for twenty years before finally moving on. She'll do alright—she's a nice girl, you know. She'll then eventually settle for a nice, albeit boring guy or girl from somewhere bland like Bern. No more excitement her entire life. But at least she'll name her children after us, and—"

His story and the girls' giggles died away as the gates opened and the Magistrate appeared, flanked by Faceless and Purists holding spears and clad in dark robes.

"You're quite the guest," Ana said, glancing at Nadezhda, who gave a mirthless chuckle. "Look at that welcome!"

"Too late to reply 'no' to this party?" Nadezhda asked, glancing at Shanthah and Ana in turn.

"Yeah, it'd be rude to back out now," Ana replied.

"I'm fine if we make a quick appearance, say hello to a few people so they know we showed up, and then head out," Shanthah said. "Sound like a plan?"

Nadezhda and Ana both nodded with half-amused smiles. Nadezhda could see and feel the others' fear swirling around their heads, but Shanthah exuded something else— something more intense than fear. This emotion clung to the back of his head with tendrils bound tightly around his neck. It felt much like fear to her but somehow heavier. Deeper.

She reached out with her mindspeaking powers and brushed his mind. His fear wasn't because they were facing the Magistrate, no… She realized she'd sensed this on him before. It was the same feeling that flared up whenever someone mentioned the new Thannish camps or when he spoke about death.

He was afraid to go back to the slave camps and scared for both her and Ana's safety—of course, that had to be it.

"You're a good person, Shanthah Kalen," said Nadezhda, and his aura sparked with cyan surprise. She didn't know why she said it, but it slipped out, and she was glad that it did.

"Oh, thank you Nadezhda," said Shanthah in reply. "What brings that sudden complimentary attitude on? Our imminent demise, perhaps?"

Nadezhda shrugged. "I mean, you're obviously not as good as Ana here, but—"

Ana laughed out loud despite the horde of Faceless surrounding them.

"I'd be offended if you weren't right," Shanthah said, smiling at them both.

Their momentary joy was ripped away like the front of the ship as the Faceless tore it apart and created a ramp of their bodies leading up to the trio.

"Oh, no thank you," Ana said, shaking her head.

She looked as if she were about to vomit. Shanthah took the first step down the staircase of writhing Faceless bodies, followed by Nadezhda, and finally, Ana, who clutched her girlfriend's hand, retching with each step. A putrid, swampy aura of buzzing browns and swirling green surrounded her head and stomach.

"Hey, keep me safe?" Nadezhda asked, and Ana nodded.

All she wanted was to help Ana feel brave, and the request seemed to help a little, as her aura flurried with scarlet resolve. Nadezhda offered a smile, which Ana returned, squeezing her hand.

The trio made their way down the ramp of bodies until they stepped onto the path leading inside. The Faceless carried away the scraps of the ship, tearing it to pieces until it was gone and then returned to their stations around the palace.

"*Welcome, honored guests,*" said the Magistrate, holding a blade giving off a subtle green glow.

Shanthah scoffed.

Nadezhda could sense whispers from Thanatan's gem, but it was far enough away in the claws of one of the Faceless that she couldn't make it out. If only she could make contact...

The Faceless with the gem disappeared inside, and the gates shut behind it.

"*I'm building quite the collection. The Empress of Blood, and now the Master of Balgorod and the Soulreader,*" said the Magistrate.

"But most importantly, thank you for the gift you've brought me—even though it was mine to begin with."

Guilt filled Nadezhda's soul as she sensed the Magistrate's victorious satisfaction at their capture, but even more, that she meant nothing to the Magistrate. The Master of Balgorod and the Soulreader. The Sangoran girl was dispensable.

But not to her.

Ana should have never been roped into all this. She should not be here. Nadezhda knew she never would have been if she never stole Thanatan's heart from the Magistrate in Laniras all those months past. She'd put her in terrible danger, and she knew it. She shut her eyes and tried not to cry, but she felt her heart pounding and felt like the world was crushing her skull.

And then she felt Ana squeeze her hand again. She was there by her side, even if she shouldn't be. And for that, she thanked the universe. Perhaps it was selfish, but she was grateful all the same.

"Bow before the Magistrate, Queen of Sangora and Thanatanos," came a voice from a burly, armored Sangoran woman flanking her. Shanthah glared, recognizing her as Kariana, one of the Mistresses of Dusk appointed by Florenta Karpaska.

Shanthah turned to Nadezhda and Ana and with his eyes said, "Do it."

The trio did as commanded. Ana knelt in the fashion of the Sangoran people: a bent knee with raised wings and her fist to her forehead. Shanthah knelt, and Nadezhda dropped into an awkward half-curtsy-half-bow and nearly tripped.

The rhythmic groans of the Magistrate's Faceless sounded eerily like war-drums as the Magistrate stepped down the staircase leading into the palace. Were they *chanting* for her?

"I, Mistress Kariana declare a pronouncement of judgment on Shanthah Kalen, Nadezhda Babkova, and Ana Sala on this day of the third year of the reign of the Magistrate. Mr. Kalen: for your genocide of the Karpaskan people and murder of Florenta Karpaska, you are sentenced to a life in the Tazovski labor camp until your bones are dust, and you are swallowed by time."

"Sounds a bit excessive, but okay," Shanthah replied. His words went unheard by anyone but Nadezhda and Ana.

"Miss Babkova: for the crimes of murder and stealing that which is of the utmost value in this world to her eminence, the Magistrate, you are sentenced to servitude in her house as barer of the Soul of Thanatan until your bones too are dust, and you are swallowed by time."

"Oh, well, at least we'll both be swallowed by time and our bones will be dust," she said. Shanthah nodded.

"We'll have that in common, yeah."

Mistress Kariana turned to face Ana.

"And Ana Sala, for being of no tactical value or benefit to the new Sangora, but aiding and abetting your fellow criminals, you are sentenced to death upon this day."

Nadezhda's heart felt as if it stopped, and she grabbed Ana's hand. Ana was petrified in utter terror, her mouth open in shock as each of the Faceless turned their bloodstained heads toward her.

Nadezhda stepped forward, a hardy scowl on her face.

"Good. Step forward, Miss Babkova. Mistress Kariana, please see her inside."

"What are you doing?" Ana hissed.

Nadezhda turned to Ana and said, "Keeping you safe."

She had no idea what she was going to do, but she focused on Ana's fear, letting it seep into her own soul. As Kariana stepped toward her and Ana, Nadezhda thrust her hand forward, forcing the fear into the mind of the Magistrate's Mistress of Dusk.

The sudden burst of emotion knocked her on her back as if she'd been trampled by a horse, her armor clanking on the stone road; she held the sides of her helm, frozen in place.

At that moment, a great shadow blanketed them as something passed in front of the sun. Everyone, including the Magistrate, glanced upward to see a massive creature circling the palace.

And then, Nadezhda watched as someone leapt from its back and plummeted toward the ground below.

The Magistrate took a step toward them, brandishing the glowing blade. Nadezhda felt her reach out with her mind, but at that very moment, a blast of intense mental energy crushed the Magistrate against the ground into a crater that shattered the earth.

"Yes!" Shanthah shouted, punching the air.

Hanna landed in the crater with fire in her eyes. As the Magistrate got to her feet, Hanna thrust her fist upward into the Magistrate's chin, using her powers to amplify the force of the blow.

"Remember me, bitch?!"

She struck the usurper below her crimson mask with a sickening crunch, snapping the Faceless woman's neck. The force of the telekinetic strike lifted the Magistrate off the ground, and then with a scream, Hanna slammed her down and grasped her spine with her mind. With another yell of unbridled rage, she ripped it straight through her stomach before tearing her asunder.

"Holy hell!" Nadezhda shouted as Hanna turned to the trio, her hair wild. Kariana rushed forward and scooped up the crimson mask as thousands of Faceless swarmed toward them.

The collective scream of hundreds of citizens broke the silence as the Magistrate's hold on the Faceless was broken, and they began to attack people in the streets.

"Hanna!" Shanthah exclaimed, perplexed.

"No time to explain. Go!" Hanna signed, using her powers to lift and then hurl Shanthah and Nadezhda into the air while Ana unfolded her wings and took flight next to them.

Mara's behemoth, Hippo, caught the trio on his massive back and shot into the sky, leaving Hanna standing alone below.

Hanna focused on the crimson mask, ripping it from Kariana's grasp; she caught it in her hand, hurled it against the ground, and blasted it with a shockwave of mental energy from her palm strong enough to crack, but not destroy it.

"You fool, if you kill her, you doom Doftaan!" Kariana screamed. "Stop! For all our sakes, stop it!"

Hanna screamed, hurled the mask into the air, and slammed it down again and again in a violent display of telekinesis. Another crack formed upon its face, and the red paint chipped away wherever it struck the ground.

A wave of Faceless swarmed toward her, and she grabbed the mask and levitated into the palace's open gates. She could sense Thanatan's voice emanating from within but couldn't make out any words.

Whatever she was looking for was here, and she knew it, for Thanatan had told her himself. She had heard his desperate voice earlier that day with a warning that the Magistrate was close to victory. He'd been silent ever since.

She knocked a group of Purist guards away with her mind before they could even raise their weapons, and she stormed into the corridor toward Thanatan's mental presence. He was still calling out to her, but his mind was growing faint.

Hanna glanced over her shoulder and decided that she had time to try again. She hurled the mask into the wall, embedding it within the stone. She ripped another piece of dark brick from the wall and slammed it against the mask and swore as it still didn't shatter. She wrenched it from the wall, letting it levitate around her hand as she ran.

"Come on, where are you?" Hanna thought, blasting a Purist guard into a wall with a flick of her wrist. *"Come on, you idiot, show me where you are. I can't break this thing!"*

And then, like a beacon in the night, she felt Thanatan's voice calling out to her more clearly than before. She hurried through a hallway of dark shining stone tile lined with images of past rulers; the portraits of Mara and Codruta had both been burned.

Hanna found herself in a room filled with even more Faceless and Purists. Many of the humans held muskets, swords, and other weapons, while the Faceless stood like attack dogs ready to strike.

"A trade!" Hanna shouted. "Give me the gem, and I'll give you this damn thing!"

She waved the mask above her head. As much as she hated it, she was beginning to realize that what Mistress Kariana had said was true; if the Magistrate didn't regain control of the Faceless, everyone was going to die. Therefore, she didn't have much time to negotiate.

A Purist in violet robes stepped forward. Hanna wondered if he were one of their leaders.

"You stupid girl, why would we give up something so valuable when we can simply take what you have and—"

Although she couldn't hear the man's words, Hanna didn't give him time to finish the sentence. With a flick of her head, she snapped his neck, and he fell to the ground. The Purists in the room recoiled and raised their weapons.

"*Where are you, stupid?*" Hanna repeated, hoping Thanatan could hear her thoughts.

"*I'm here.*" The Voice came from the back of the room, and Hanna reached forward and pulled as if drawing in an invisible line. Nadezhda's satchel holding the gem zoomed into her other hand, and she brought the ceiling down on the room. Everyone screamed as they were buried in rubble, and Hanna sprinted away from the chamber.

"*I can get us out of here,*" Thanatan said to her mind. "*Just connect to me one more time, and we can bring an end to the Magistrate and to this wretched place.*"

Hanna refused to answer, and then something hard and blunt struck her on the back of the head. She cried out and crumpled to the ground, dropping the mask and Nadezhda's satchel. She turned just in time to see Mistress Kariana standing above her with her sword raised, a vicious glint in her eye.

The Mistress of Dusk was shouting something that went unheard as Hanna groaned at the effort it took to hold back the blow; she was exhausted, hungry, and knew her mental energy was fading. She tried to pull the ceiling down on her foe, but only a few tiles fell, distracting the Mistress of Dusk long enough for Hanna to stumble to her feet.

Hanna blasted Kariana back with a mental strike, knocking her to the ground. She leapt toward her enemy, raised the mask high above her head, and then brought it down with a squelch, embedding the sharp edge in the Mistress of Dusk's torso. She left it there and ran, not knowing whether or not Kariana was still alive.

She scrambled to retrieve Thanatan's heart and set off down the hall, focusing on her own body to levitate. Her powers faltered; she stumbled and then collapsed but then summoned the last of her strength and floated, shaking, down the hall, before crashing through a high window.

She couldn't hear her own screams as her powers failed her again, and she plummeted toward the ground far below. As she fell, Hippo flew past, bathing a swarm of Faceless in molten lava.

"HIPPO!"

Hippo flipped around and caught her on his back, and she rolled on his massive saddle next to Shanthah, scraping her exposed skin on the hard leather.

"My hero!" Shanthah exclaimed, helping Hanna sit. She groaned and signed something, to which Shanthah replied with a hearty laugh. She buried her face in his shoulder.

"That was incredible!" Ana exclaimed with a wide smile plastered on her face. "You are amazing!"

She didn't respond.

"Keep up the compliments," Shanthah said, tapping his ear. "I'll let her know."

"I completely forgot, I'm so sorry," Ana said, turning to Shanthah to translate her words into sign for Hanna.

"Hanna the stupendous! The beautiful! The triumphant!" Nadezhda added. Shanthah signed the praise to Hanna, who raised and wiggled her hands in celebration.

Shanthah handed her a flask, and she took a sip.

"*I was expecting water, but this'll do,*" Hanna signed.

"*I don't go anywhere without one of your signature drinks,*" Shanthah said. "*Rule number one.*"

"*This tastes like a Phantom, if I'm not mistaken,*" Hanna signed. "*My favorite.*"

She winked and returned the flask before nestling in close.

"So, what now?" Ana asked. "Back to Balgorod?"

"No," Shanthah said. "Hanna says we have other plans and people to see. Oh, and here you go."

He handed the satchel holding Thanatan's soul to Nadezhda, who looked inside and let out a sigh of relief.

Shanthah interpreted for Hanna, saying, "Mara and Lavinia set up a safehouse here. I've—well, Hanna, rather—has been operating out of it while bringing food to the people in Terman to help alleviate the famine Thanatanos is causing there."

"How on Earth have you been able to keep Hippo from being seen?"

Shanthah continued to be Hanna's voice as she signed.

"He's big, but he can stay hidden when he wants to, especially in the woods outside the city. He likes the flavor of the trees there, so he doesn't wander off too far," Shanthah said. Then, in his own words, he added, "But now that we have my powers and a Mindspeaker, we should be able to keep him in the city."

"I'm not that powerful," said Nadezhda. "I don't think I can hide him."

"*No, but I can.*" The Voice rang through each of their minds.

"We'll need to lie low for a while. Hanna's working on figuring out where Mara is. She thinks she's close," Shanthah said.

"Can we kill the Magistrate while we're here?" Ana suggested. Shanthah signed to Hanna who shook her head in a vehement flurry of auburn hair.

"She says if we kill the Magistrate and break her mask, it'll set the Faceless free, and they'll kill everyone in Doftaan," Shanthah said, his countenance dropping.

"I don't know how many people I got killed before I figured that out," Hanna said, but Shanthah did not relay her message. The Faceless below seemed to have retreated back into the palace, so the Magistrate must have regained a body and called them off.

"We could use your skills as a healer here too, Ana," Shanthah said. "But if you'd prefer to go back to the school, we can arrange that."

"Why? The whole reason I'm learning to heal is so that I can help the cause," Ana said. She turned to Nadezhda. "Where better to spend the midterm holiday than in a place that wants to kill us?"

She kissed Nadezhda on the lips.

"I do bring you to the best places, don't I?" Nadezhda said. Ana giggled. Her aura sparkled with pink and dull copper. Love and relief.

Shanthah stroked Hanna's hair as she snored in his lap.

Nadezhda and Ana crawled a few yards away and lay on their backs watching the clouds go by.

Ana closed her eyes, and Nadezhda watched the relief and wondrous joy of flight flowing behind her like glittering mist. Nadezhda stared at the beautiful display of emotion for a while before turning her gaze on Ana's face and how her chest rose and fell with her breath.

"You know, I could get used to this life of adventure with you," Ana said.

"You mean getting roped into a worldwide conspiracy surrounding the soul of a dead god?"

"Yup, pretty much." Ana chuckled and turned her head, still lying on her back, to look at Nadezhda. "Wanna go to Kurash next?"

"Sure. What's in Kurash?"

Ana shrugged. "I don't know. I always wanted to go to Tal-Ahosh and see the ruins of the city called Ankara. I'm taking this interesting history class about the Deadlands from Mr. Elafris. By the way, have you heard his story?"

"That he's the devil, but not the devil, and now he works at our academy?" Nadezhda asked. "And that he's really just a normal guy that somehow survived the destruction of the Deadlands hundreds of years ago?"

"Yup."

"Yeah, heard it. Is that a rumor…?"

"It's literally true. Apparently, our teachers discovered him in the Deadlands. Apparently'er, he's like six hundred years old or something. Well, anyway, he's teaching us about old Kurash and the wars that destroyed the Deadlands, and it's beyond interesting."

"What'd you learn?" Nadezhda asked, happy to see Ana getting so excited about something she loved.

"There was a country called Turkey that let hundreds of millions of refugees in from some surrounding countries that had already been destroyed. They originally didn't like each other, but the war made them band together to form one super country. The new country was eventually destroyed too, but many survived, and their descendants are the

Kurashians! Whatever happened in the war left Kurash as a desert, though. It didn't used to be that way."

Nadezhda looked at Ana with a loving expression as she explained even more about the history of Kurash and the Deadlands in a round-about way to explain why she was excited to see the ruins of Ankara.

"You know, I generally like people, and I think you're my favorite one," Nadezhda said. Ana beamed.

"I generally like you, too."

"Well then, it's settled! We're going to Kurash as soon as this is all over! Our next grand adventure!"

Ana nodded and smiled, gripping her hand.

"I love you, Nadya."

"I love you too, Tatiana."

Hippo began his descent toward a northwestern neighborhood of Doftaan, and Shanthah used his powers to turn the behemoth invisible. They landed in the university district, Akademrajon, and the ground shook beneath Hippo's feet as he landed.

"Alright, Thanatan, do your thing," Shanthah ordered. As if obedient to Shanthah's command, a dome of fuzzy light surrounded the university district.

"What's this?" Nadezhda asked.

"He's maintaining my power and boosting it with his own. We worked out a deal that will keep us safe for a while," Shanthah said. Hanna sat up, rubbing her eyes.

"Which is?" Ana asked.

"That we don't kill him," Shanthah said. "And we also don't hand him over to the Purists and the Magistrate. Hiding out is in all our best interest, even his."

Nadezhda heard the Voice's whisper but shut her eyes and focused on a mental block like Kamil had taught her in one of their classes, managing to silence his voice. She'd deal with him later.

"Hey, Nadezhda, Hanna has something to tell you," Shanthah said, and Hanna waved. Hanna gestured to her head and then tapped on her own forehead. Confused, Nadezhda looked to Shanthah for a translation, but he shook his head. Evidently, they were forcing Nadezhda to practice using her powers.

"*Hi,*" Nadezhda mindspoke to Hanna.

"*Hi, sweetheart. I know what you're going through. I know what it's like to have this weird connection to Thanatan. I did for a long time too a couple years ago, and it's terrifying,*" Hanna thought. Nadezhda nodded but didn't mindspeak anything in response. "*Just know we're here to help, and I know that Ana will do anything to help you too. Keep her safe, and I know she'll do the same for you.*"

Nadezhda nodded. "*We will.*"

"*And by the way, some of the teachers at the academy and I gossip about the students—don't be surprised. You know that I own a bar, so of course I hear things. I just wanted you to know that we're all huge fans of you, Ana, and your relationship.*"

Nadezhda offered a wide smile as she glanced over at Ana talking with Shanthah. She wondered if they were having a similar conversation.

"Anyway, I promise to try to keep you safe from Thanatan," Hanna said, and Nadezhda nodded.

"Thank you, Hanna," she said aloud before catching herself. Hanna smiled and gave her elbow a squeeze.

They led Hippo next to a large building on a hill overlooking the University of Doftaan campus. They let him plop down there, kept safe and hidden by a mixture of Thanatan and Shanthah's abilities.

As he settled down nestled against a wall, they climbed down to the ground below. Hanna kissed him on the massive snout, and a bout of hot air engulfed her.

"We'll get you back to Mara soon," she thought. He bounced up and down like an excited puppy at the mention of Mara's name.

Hanna led the others into a high-rise apartment building and entered the first door on the left in the stairwell that winded upward to ten other floors. Many of the same kind of buildings surrounded them, undoubtedly for students at the university.

"Okay, we're safe," Shanthah said, closing the door behind them. The building was a hive of activity; Sangorans and humans alike made their way up and down the staircase and in and out of the many apartments in the tower.

"Woah," Nadezhda muttered, sharing a glance with Ana.

"They've renovated the entire building into our base of operations here. Awesome, huh?" He turned back to them. "Welcome to the revolution, girls."

CHAPTER TWENTY-EIGHT
INTO THE NORTH

The harsh blizzard sweeping across the unforgiving northern Deadlands immobilized the train for two full days. It had taken another three to dig the train out of the snowdrifts, even with the two Dragonsouls' ability to summon flames. Whenever Mara watched them use their powers, her heart ached, wondering if Aleksander and the rest of the people in Kurash were dead because of her.

She had lost count how long the train had crawled along the frozen countryside after that, but many died, but none were buried, during their excruciating progress northward. The sun refused to rise over the horizon for more than a few hours each day after it exhausted what little warmth it had left.

The faces and cries of the dead slaves haunted Mara's constant nightmares, and their pain filled her soul.

Most recently, the soldiers had murdered a woman, Elizaveta Lecca, during the most recent scheduled stop because she refused to abandon her sick son, Aleksandru—the Sangoran equivalent of Aleksander's name, which was a knife to Mara's soul. Aleksandru had been left behind in the snow to die. The following day, an Alboran-Sangoran man named Dragos Botezatu had succumbed to hypothermia as he tried to warm himself by a bonfire.

One night, a ragged cough near Mara that had been incessant throughout the week became silent. Mara knew at that moment that the woman she knew as Valentina Grozavu was no more. Another name she would never use again. She clutched Kamil and Alia's hand, and Kamil's words entered her mind.

"She's gone."

Mara vowed to never forget any of their names. None of them would ever be given a funeral; there would be none to truly mourn them, and so she knew it was all she could do.

More tears. She was surprised there were any left, but with every one of the slaves' deaths, Sangoran or otherwise, she found some to spare. She glanced over the remaining prisoners; other than herself, Kamil, and Alia, there were only ten surviving slaves in their carriage. She had no idea how many remained in the other five wagons, and she hoped they were full of more life. But, at the same time, she wished for their suffering to end—for them to be free of this nightmare in the north. She sobbed into her knees as she pulled them close to her chest.

When she was ready, she got to her feet and pulled off her threadbare coat. She draped it over Valentina's body, giving the woman the last bit of dignity that she could be afforded in death.

"You'll freeze," Alia said, but Mara shook her head.

"How are *you* doing?" Mara asked, and Alia hung her head. Mara had seen the sadness in Alia's eyes every time the healer was unable to save someone from their injuries or sickness. But she knew her friend's energy was waning, and therefore, so were her powers to heal.

"I think my answer is the same as everyone else's," Alia said. "Guilty."

"That guilt doesn't belong to you, Alia," Mara said. "You are not to blame for this suffering."

Alia smiled. "Thank you, Mara. But you know how it feels better than most—to have the power to save someone and to fail anyway."

"Oh, you're right about that." Mara let out a dark chuckle. Alia glanced around to make sure no one else was listening and then pulled both Mara and Kamil close.

"Listen, I think I know something that might help us," she muttered in Kurashic. "Mara, while you were recovering from your seizure, I heard Mazanek talking to someone that I don't think is on the train."

"What do you mean?" Mara asked.

"He was saying things like 'yes sir' and 'no sir.' He's the highest-ranking officer on board," Alia said. "If he's saying things like that, he's got some way to communicate with his superiors back in Thanatanos."

"*How could that be?*" Kamil asked.

"Secret Mindspeaker?" Alia asked. Kamil shook his head.

"More technology from the Deadlands, maybe?" Mara asked, gesturing to the inside of the train car.

"*Maybe*," Kamil replied

"We know the Magistrate is pulling the strings in Sangora now. Since she has those strings wrapped around King Verahim too, then maybe, I don't know…"

"*She's the most powerful Mindspeaker I've ever met*," Kamil said. "*If anyone's found a way to communicate across thousands of miles, it's her.*"

"I don't think Mazanek would be calling the Magistrate 'sir'," Mara said. "Would it be too much to ask for you to spy on him?"

"*Not at all*," Kamil replied.

"Maybe you can piece something together. I know you don't like intruding on other peoples' thoughts, but—"

"*Oh Mara, I have no qualms about invading that man's mind. I'll see what I can do.*" Then, with a dark smirk, he added, "*And if I can drive him mad in the process…What a shame that would be.*"

"But if the Magistrate senses you spying on him or anything, stop right away, you got that?" Alia said with the stern authority and command of a mother.

"*I'll be safe*," Kamil said, resting his head against the cold metal of the train car's wall. Mara and Alia watched his face twitch for a moment before his eyes shot open again.

"What's wrong?" Alia asked, clutching his hand.

"*I couldn't get in*," Kamil thought.

"Has that ever happened to you?" Mara asked.

"Some people are harder nuts to crack. I couldn't read Thanatan's mind or intentions at all when we fought him. I could sense him, but not read him. Maybe it's something similar."

"Is there any way they're talking to Thanatan?" Alia asked. "She has your sword, right?"

Kamil nodded. *"Maybe they're using the sword as a conduit to communicate?"*

"Well…" Mara said. She shook her head.

"What do you mean 'well'?" Alia asked.

Mara's knee began to bounce, and she began picking at the skin around her thumbnail; she let out a deep breath and shut her eyes.

"What happened?"

Alia's expression was a mixture of concern and understanding as she placed a hand on Mara's shoulder.

"Well, when Hanna and I thought I killed him with the Weapon of Ages Past, I did destroy him, but not his mind, or soul, or whatever you want to call it. Hanna trapped that part of him in magic of the Cuff of the Mind Prison," Mara said, glancing at Kamil, knowing he'd understand.

"The one from the Talohiran slave camp?"

"Yes. But when the blast went off, the Cage was destroyed, obviously, but the magic remained, linked to him. Somehow, Hanna and I bound Thanatan's soul to the ash and rock in Nitra—the living crystal I told you about. He *was* dead in the way we understand it."

"So, is he trapped in the ruins of Nitra or in the blade we forged?" Alia asked.

Mara nodded. "Both. He has influence over the crystals lining the crater. A bit of his mind was there. A bit of it in what we used to make my sword. He communicated with me through the crystal."

She didn't mention the throne.

"So could Mazanek be using the crystals from Nitra to communicate with the Magistrate through Mara's sword?" Alia asked.

"That makes sense," Mara said, nodding. "Remember, when I killed Florenta's Mistresses of Dusk before I was captured, I felt Thanatan's pain and heard his screams. I think she purged him from the Godblade."

"I love that you call it that," Alia said. "Although I think since it belongs to a Goddess…" She nudged Mara's arm.

Mara chuckled. "Thanks. Maybe a name change is in order. But I've been thinking. I can tell that the sword's near her. She has it. I still have some kind of connection to the sword, and sometimes I can sense her. I think I'm beginning to understand who she is."

"What do you mean, 'who she is'?" Alia asked.

"Who she *really* is," Mara replied. "This might sound crazy, but I think she's Queen Codruta Talohir. I know her real identity doesn't really matter in the long run, but…"

She trailed off as Alia let out a sigh at the mention of the name; Mara wondered what exactly her relationship had been to the late wife of her ex-husband. There had to be a story there, and she craved to hear it but didn't press the matter.

"How could that be?" Alia asked.

"Shanthah killed her," Kamil said. *"Sorry, you know that. That's obvious."*

"Yeah, but the Magistrate's Faceless, right? Most of them are reanimated corpses—if we understand them correctly," Mara said. "She told me Sangora belonged to her. With everything happening, I almost forgot she said that…" She trailed off again, deep in thought. "Come to think of it, Codruta had the Queen's Control, which was a way to command other Sangorans to her will…technically it was a method used to communicate and control across distance. Although never this far away… But like Kamil said, she's a powerful Mindspeaker, so maybe they're communicating way out here with a combination of her abilities, my sword, the Queen's Control, and Thanatan's crystals."

"But didn't you take the Queen's Control?" Kamil asked.

"Yeah. And I destroyed it. But Florenta made her own somehow. So, maybe Codruta got it back from Florenta's corpse," Mara said, thinking out loud.

"If she's that powerful, couldn't she just communicate directly with him without the Queen's Control?" Alia asked.

Kamil shook his head. *"Even if she could reach him, at that distance, it'd be like whispering in a coliseum of screaming people."*

"All of our powers came from genetic implants and technology from long ago in the Deadlands," Mara explained. "Mostly for soldiers. But the Queen's Control used something called a radio to communicate over distances."

"But Codruta wasn't a Mindspeaker," Alia said. "They resurrected the technology for trains and guns. So why don't we think they resurrected the technology for—what did you call it—a radio?"

"Honestly, probably the simplest and most probable explanation," Mara said. "Drahomir wasn't a Mindspeaker before he turned Faceless either. But I like your thinking. You're the expert here, Kamil. What do you think?"

"*It's possible,*" Kamil said. "*If we could get our hands on whatever method they're using, we could call Hippo. He's attuned to your mental presence, after all.*"

Hope and warmth filled her heart as Mara pictured Hippo's happy face. If he missed her half as much as she missed him, then he must be miserable; she stuck out her bottom lip at the thought.

"So, it's a plan," Alia said. "We find a way to spy on Mazanek, figure out how he speaks with the Magistrate, or whoever he's speaking with, take control of whatever they're using to communicate, and we use it to call Hippo."

"I can't wait to see that silly guy," Mara said. "Okay. Whatever happens when we get to the next camp, we stick together." Kamil and Alia nodded.

"Was there any doubt that was going to already happen?" Alia asked with a soft smile, clutching both of their hands. "Never," Mara whispered, and then she kissed them both on the forehead as the train rumbled along.

CHAPTER TWENTY-NINE
REDEMPTION OVER RETRIBUTION

The countryside along the Thannish border wall burned beneath a curtain of black smoke.

Valistaran had explained to Aleksander that shortly after Mara's capture, King Verahim had given the order for his troops amassed at the border to begin the invasion of Sangora. Mara's presence, a symbol of hope to her people, was the only thing keeping him from giving the word to attack.

But now, the dam was broken, and the tide of Thannish soldiers had swept into Alboras and Sangora. Dozens of Sangoran cities were now under siege, but in a confusing and brutal move, the Thans had begun to attack their own border towns. According to Valistaran, the Thannish forces claimed Alboran forces were at fault, despite never having crossed the border—a pretense to justify the invasion.

Aleksander, Valistaran, and Valeniya had seen the destruction on the Thannish side of the border with their own eyes. Otherwise, Aleksander never would have believed it. What could have possessed the king, his own brother, to attack their own people?

Valistaran's contacts in Vudapas included a small team of Talohiran diplomats, including the ambassador to Thanatanos, Genadi Kraev. They'd guided Aleksander and Valistaran through the half of the city that lay outside the border wall to a hidden entrance leading under the wall reserved for guards and dignitaries.

To Aleksander's surprise, they'd done so with no trouble or resistance. Even if they had been seen, the people in that half of the city were unlikely to inform the Thannish forces. The residents living there were largely Sangoran and Talohiran minority groups cut off from the rest of their city, bitter against the country that had turned its back on them. They were as much of a target as any other town in Talohira or Sangora.

Valistaran thanked the diplomats for their service and awarded each of them with the medal of the Order of the Dragon, the highest civilian medal in Talohira, along with a letter to accompany the commendation from his son, King Valis Shadid.

Aleksander and Valistaran had now made it as far north as Cineca. The western horizon was still aflame, and Aleksander knew the Thannish forces were on their way.

To Cineca. Innocent, beautiful Cineca. Mara's hometown and the site of many of his own happiest memories.

Aleksander's heart felt someone were squeezing it in a vice grip. He looked over to see a tear rolling down Valeniya's cheek.

"What did Cineca or any of these towns for that matter ever do to deserve this?" Aleksander asked.

"You know as well as I what strength and beauty has come from Cineca," Valistaran said. "Whether Verahim knows that it's her hometown, I do not know."

Aleksander nodded, a sliver of jealousy pricking his heart that the man had been able to spend so much time with Mara—the time he'd lost with her, partially because of his own betrayal.

"Besides, the king knows his crown is in danger. There's discontent in the border regions, and he knows it," Valistaran continued. "They hate him there. I made sure of that myself."

There was no hint of pride in his words, only the sharp edge of remorse.

"You what?"

"During my own war with Thanatanos, I planted seeds of discord. Propaganda, if you will, in each of the border towns until it spread. Your father and brother are both wildly unpopular with the rural population thanks to me, especially near the border."

"Then thanks to you, those people are in danger," Aleksander said. He looked west toward Cineca. "People I love."

"Yes, well, perhaps 'thanks' was poor word choice," Valistaran said. He followed Aleksander's gaze westward. "I know what you're thinking, but Cineca is too far out of the way. If we go, we will lose Umut and Cyrgiz. We're already far behind as it stands."

Aleksander watched Valeniya's eyes gloss over with a white sheen, and he wondered if she were looking for Cyrgiz and Umut or watching over someone else entirely.

"I have to do this," Aleksander said. He opened his mouth to speak again, but Valistaran cut him off.

"What is one man going to do against an army? What could be more important than stopping the Magistrate from getting the Secret Keepers' knowledge?" Valistaran asked. "You're not going to fight off all those troops."

Aleksander knew he was right but couldn't help feeling powerless for the people he had come to love all those years ago.

"I'm sorry. I have to do this," Aleksander said at last. "Mara's family—"

"Say no more. Valeniya and I will find the rogue Secret Keepers."

"Are you sure?"

"I would consider it heresy against the Empress of Blood *not* to protect her family, don't you?"

"I guess so, yes." Aleksander chuckled.

"But more than that, it would truly be a tragedy if you did not go to protect the family of the woman you love. The family you *chose*," Valistaran said. The countenances of both men softened. "Truly, go, and good luck, Aleksander. You are a good man. A better one than I."

Valistaran helped Valeniya back onto the horse when she had finished stretching her legs. She thanked him with a soft pat on the head.

"Valistaran?" Aleksander said as the man began to ride away. He turned his head to listen but did not meet Aleksander's gaze. "I want you to know that you're a good man too, despite everything you've done. I know that sounds a bit backhanded, but I can see you fighting for redemption over retribution."

Valistaran said nothing but offered a slight nod, a contemplative look etched across his dark features.

And then, the two men went on their ways without another word: Valistaran to the north, and Aleksander to the west along the border wall.

As Aleksander spurred his horse onward over the hills, the smoke in the distance swelled from a plume of gray into an entire cloud as the nearby small village of Mor burned. Every single building was either burning or reduced to rubble.

The company of soldiers was too busy rounding up their own citizens to pay him any heed as he passed by. His heart ached for the people, and he hated every second that he had to refrain from intervening. But what more could he do?

He wiped a tear from his cheek before spurring his horse onward along the Vuda, a stream that flowed into the mighty Danuub River. The river system around Cineca formed a natural defensive barrier, but if the Thannish soldiers attacked from the other direction, the villagers would be trapped.

As his horse's hoofs clattered on the rough cobblestone path leading into Cineca, he was met with hostile shouts and the points of spears held by villagers perched atop makeshift barricades of dilapidated furniture.

"I come in peace!" he called, dismounting his horse and raising his hands to show he meant no harm.

"Then who are you?" a man asked.

Aleksander thought for a long moment as he stared into the familiar faces peering out of the barricade. He stopped himself as he was about to introduce himself as Aleksander; he shook his head and said instead, "Xanthurias. My name is Xanthurias Romus. I stayed with you for a time, and it's time I repaid your kindness."

It was the first time he'd used that name in such a way since his memories, for good and ill, had returned.

A few of the defenders lowered their spears and farming-equipment-turned-weapons, but others remained steadfast in the defense of their little town.

He heard his name float around the crowd until one villager cried, "Prince Xanthurias is dead!"

"And good riddance!" called a woman, who spat in his direction.

"I know how you must feel about me and my family. There's no time to go into any of that. We need to leave *now*," Aleksander said, gesturing to the east. "They've already burned Mor to the ground, and they're taking the people away. Please, trust me!"

"Trust a dead prince?!" called a voice.

Aleksander began to speak again, but he heard a voice call out from behind the barricade—one that was much friendlier than the others that berated him.

One that loved him.

Someone was pushing their way through the mob, and the defenders parted, and the face of Daniela Bartunek appeared in a hole in the barricade.

"Is it really you, Xan?" she asked. Her voice was almost reverent, as if she were speaking to the dead. Kind wrinkles had formed around her brilliant blue eyes, and her dark hair had gone gray, but it was her.

"Hi, yeah," was all Aleksander could get out before Daniela ducked beneath an open space in the fence, popped up, and wrapped her arms around him. She squeezed him tightly, her face pressed against his chest.

"We all thought you died! Oh, how good it is to see you! You've grown!"

She squeezed the muscle on his right arm then glanced around, and Aleksander's heart ached knowing she must be looking for Mara. He had disappeared with her daughter all those years ago; perhaps, she must have thought, he had finally brought her home.

"Daniela, please. You have to trust me."

"Of course, come in!" she ordered, crawling beneath the fence. He followed and dusted the dirt off his trousers as he stood. "Everyone, listen up! I trust this boy with all my heart. He's as good as my son, so if you know what's good for you, you'll listen to what he has to say!"

The crowd was silent. Aleksander wondered if Daniela had become a leader in the town, if she'd gained some status as the mother of the Empress of Sangora, or if she simply could command and inspire any crowd as her daughter could. She stepped back, took Aleksander's arm, and gave it a squeeze as if to give him permission, or perhaps the encouragement, to address the crowd.

"I know of a place where you can hide until the soldiers move on. They're not occupying towns, they're destroying them. So, if we hide long enough—"

"We aren't hiding anymore!" Someone called. "We fight! We'll have nowhere to return to! Why are you even here?!"

"Then you are going to die with the people in Mor! Aleksander exclaimed. "Please, I'm begging you to leave!"

The people muttered amongst themselves as Aleksander turned to Daniela.

"Is she safe?" Daniela asked. Aleksander's heart dropped.

"I don't know," he admitted, shaking his head. His eyes filled with tears, and Daniela wrapped her arms around him again. She said nothing, simply holding him like she would a scared, lost son who had finally returned home.

At last, a large man came forward, folding his arms over his broad chest. Aleksander recognized the man as Radek, one of the men who had toiled in the fields with Mara's father, Killian, for many years.

"I remember you, little Xanthurias. Always running around with our Mara," said Radek. "You were good to the Bartuneks, and they loved you. If Daniela vouches for you still, and you can explain why the entire country thought you were dead, we'll agree to leave our homes."

Some of the crowd grumbled in disagreement, but he turned, stomped his foot, and shushed them before turning back to Aleksander for an explanation.

Aleksander stood next to Radek and glanced back at Daniela, who was smiling back at him. Not even she knew the story he was about to tell, but he knew she must be yearning to know the truth.

"Years ago, when the Bartunek family took me in, I had run away from home. Only Mara knew the entire story, of course, and I wish that I had been honest with all of you back then," Aleksander said. "I am the crown prince of Thanatanos. I'm sure many of you guessed as much, and I am so sorry for not being more up front with you."

"Crown prince died, son!" someone cried.

"Yes, getting to that. Well, on that horrible day when Mara and I—and so many more—were taken away on that slave ship, I thought I would never see any of you again," Aleksander continued. "Mara and I were separated, and I lost all my memories when someone I trusted at the time betrayed—"

"If you lost your memories, then—" started an angry woman, but Radek shushed her, to which she responded, "Oh, pah!"

"No, it's okay," Aleksander said. "I lost my memories of you, of my life as a prince, and I'm sad to say, of your wonderful Mara. When I ran away and didn't show up again, my father hired someone else to pose as me. He grew up with my name, and as far as the kingdom and my father were concerned, he *became* me. I saw my father, the king, years later, but by that time, a new Xanthurias had been created. My father—my father *replaced* me."

Mutters and whispers escaped the crowd.

"When Mara and I were reunited in a Talohiran slave camp several years ago, I didn't even recognize her. I had no idea who she was. But she helped me just as you all did before. She means the world to me, and I am so grateful that I met you all, and that fate brought us back together. Without her, I wouldn't be here today. Now please, let me repay that good fate and her kindness. Someone asked why I am here today, and I'll tell you why. I am here to save my family."

Daniela never let go of Aleksander's arm as the crowd deliberated amongst itself. Finally, dozens of men and women broke off, running toward their homes. Aleksander looked around in confusion, but Radek stepped forward and shook his hand.

"Don't worry, Xanthurias. They're not abandoning you. They're going to gather supplies," he said. "We're with you. Well, most of us. Some are too stubborn to leave."

"But that's their dumb decision," Daniela said, a fierceness in her eyes that Aleksander had seen in Mara's countless times.

"I'm not so sure we have time to prepare," Aleksander said. "We need to get going."

"And when we're hiding for an entire week without food? They'll catch up," Radek said. "Some of us will cover the escape as you lead them away."

Aleksander nodded and clapped Radek on the burly shoulder before he too rushed off to gather supplies. Daniela let go of Aleksander's arm and took a few steps away toward Cineca.

"This has been my family's home for generations," she said. "My grandpapa's grandmama was the first one to come here. "What would he think seeing us leave it, Xanthurias?"

"If they're anything like the Bartuneks I know, they'd be the first ones to help the others," Aleksander replied. He pulled Daniela into a hug.

She smiled; the happy expression accentuated the wrinkles across her face, making her look even kinder.

"You know, I'd like to think you're right about grandpapa, but family stories said he was a bit of a weasel."

Aleksander laughed out loud. "Then why care what he thinks?"

"I guess I don't," Daniela said, squeezing Aleksander's shoulder. "Now come on, we got a big day ahead of us."

A short time later after most groups had set out, the last group was gathered in the center square. Aleksander stood upon the platform directing the flow of refugees. It was where Mara and the town's other musicians had always performed—a source of hope. The tense atmosphere had accumulated around the stage; everyone knew they were out of time to prepare. There was no more time to wait.

The sick and elderly unable to make the trip into the hills were the first to be led away to the fields to hide. Although spring's new grain crop was not yet high enough to be harvested, it would be tall enough to hide people lying flat.

Mostly just excited to play in the water, the town's children insisted on guiding the first armed groups to the mountain lake. The steady stream of hastily packed supply carts followed close behind.

And now, Aleksander hopped off the stage to lead the final mass of frightened and unsure villagers through streets and out of town, leaving it dark and empty. Many looked back, and even more cried as they left their homes behind.

Their pace was slow, and Aleksander had to fight to not get frustrated.

Eventually, however, they made their way north of Cineca until they came to a grove surrounding a group of high hills. He could see the signs that a large mass of people had moved through, and he swore under his breath, hoping and praying that the Thannish army wouldn't notice the evidence of their retreat.

Aleksander wished he were returning to this happy, secluded lake under better circumstances. He wished the war was over. But more than anything, he wished that Mara was there with him. She'd know just what to do. She always did.

It was where they had spent many of the happiest days of their lives, so it almost felt to him as if the villagers were intruding on a private, intimate memory. But he pushed the thoughts away. Why shouldn't the happiest place in his and Mara's life be the one where he led their people to safety?

"Everyone in!" Aleksander called, leading the way through the brush. Eventually, he came to a fork in the path.

In one direction, there was a high cliff where he and Mara would go to jump into the idyllic lake's glassy surface. The other direction led into a secluded valley nestled between the water and the forest within the valley.

"Follow the path until the valley!" Aleksander called, scooting past several men to make his way back against the tide of villagers. He repeated the command for several minutes until enough people understood where they were going. He apologized as he pushed his way through the crowd to peer out of the entrance into the valley.

He swore under his breath as he saw the light of Thannish troops moving through Cineca. They had made it out just in time, but it was only a matter of minutes before the soldiers discovered them. The hills hid them for now, but it would only take one pair of keen eyes to alert the soldiers of their presence.

Were they truly so cruel that they would massacre the people hidden there? Aleksander shook his head, knowing he couldn't think such things, but images of innocent, slaughtered villagers, the valley wet with their blood, lingered in the darkest corners of his mind.

He hurried down the path, much to the alarm of several of those around him. They shouted after him, asking if they were in danger. As they looked back, they beheld Thannish soldiers swarming over their town, and cries of despair filled the night air.

He was unsuccessful in quieting them despite his best efforts; he didn't know if the sound would carry all the way down to Cineca, but if it did, they wouldn't stay conspicuous for long.

Not long enough, anyway.

And so, he ran down the hill away from the safety of the memories of the lake in the secluded valley. As he passed the last of the villagers, he sprinted headlong toward the smoke drifting up from somewhere in town.

To his great horror, a towering Spirit Warrior emerged from the flames of the burning barricade. Raksil. The same warrior that had led the assault on Kurash—the same warrior Aleksander had tried to destroy with the Sunspear of the Supreme One. The ominous orange glow reflected off his shining armor as he drew his massive blade amidst the smoke and drifting ash.

Knowing he was the villagers' only defender, Aleksander raced toward Raksil with an almighty yell; he drew his sword and commanded flames to spiral from his hands. They crawled up the blade, banishing the darkness as Raksil closed the distance between them.

Aleksander's flaming sword glanced off Raksil's blade, which then came rebounding as the warrior set his feet into the earth to strike Aleksander down.

"You!" Raksil boomed, his voice echoing over the wheatfield. "This ends *NOW!*"

Aleksander knew this confrontation would only end one of two ways.

Raksil raised his weapon high over his head. Aleksander brought his flaming sword up to defend himself and unleashed an explosion from his other hand, engulfing

Raksil's armored face in a pillar of orange and yellow. Raksil roared as he emerged from the inferno, swinging his blade with such ferocity that Aleksander's own weapon shattered near the hilt, leaving only a few inches of jagged steel.

Aleksander hit the ground and rolled to avoid being decapitated by another blow. He leapt to his feet, using his flames to propel himself upward with a raised fist.

Raksil reached up to grab him as he thrust his flaming fist into his enemy's faceplate, twisting his head around for long enough for Aleksander to land a second blow against his throat.

At that moment, Raksil's soldiers that had been in Cineca joined the fray, drawing Aleksander's attention for a moment. Raksil's blade neared his throat, and he threw a wall of flame up to defend himself. The flames protected him from Raksil's onslaught, but he struck the ground hard with the force of the explosion. He groaned, rubbing his burned knuckles where he had punched Raksil's armor.

His enemy loomed above him, sword held high.

The soldiers were upon them now. He blasted one of them in the stomach then embedded his broken blade into another's shin with a well-timed jab and burst of flame.

"You cannot fight forever," Raksil said as the man Aleksander had stabbed fell screaming.

The man dropped his blade, and Aleksander scrambled to scoop it up just in time to parry another blow from Raksil but cried out as the air was forced from his lungs as the Spirit Warrior thrust a fist against into his chest. A second blow to his stomach crushed ribs, and Aleksander gasped for breath.

The soldiers watched, and many cheered, as Raksil struck Aleksander in the back with his heavy metal gauntlet, crushing him against the scorched earth. The Spirit Warrior hefted his blade as Aleksander lay broken on the ground.

He was overwhelmed, and Raksil knew it.

In fact, he relished in the fact, savoring his victory for a moment too long—had he acted a moment sooner, he would have been victorious.

An explosion of dark flame sent Raksil flying; the warrior's artificial, metallic body struck a boulder with such force that it shattered into pieces beneath him.

Aleksander's fingers dug into the earth as he pulled himself toward the dead soldier's fallen sword. The other soldiers hurried toward him, and he let out a long string of expletives.

Ignoring the screams and explosions of dark flame behind him, Aleksander reached for the weapon just as a soldier gripped the blade's handle before he could grasp it. The man met his gaze with a look of horrible sadness; his eyes were shadowed with dark circles that seemed to block the hope from shining through.

He was young. Much younger than Aleksander. Younger than Pol, even. A scared boy forced into a war he never asked to fight.

Aleksander shook his head as a tear rolled from the corner of his eye. The boy dropped the sword without a word. In understanding, Aleksander took the blade and got to his feet, still wheezing from Raksil's assault.

He looked up just in time to see Raksil's weapon carve through a river of black flame. The warrior's shining, silver armor glowed red hot wherever Valistaran's flame had washed over it, and the massive warrior was frantically bringing his blade down over and over toward his former master in an attempt to carve him into pieces.

"You came back!" Aleksander shouted.

He limped forward as Valistaran managed to disarm his foe with an explosion of darkness that melted through the sword, leaving the remaining half glowing white hot.

Raksil swung the broken weapon at Valistaran, but Aleksander launched a fireball of his own, striking Raksil's wrist. The blade stuck into the dirt blade first.

Valistaran, Aleksander, and Raksil all scrambled toward it. The soldiers, who had been watching their leader fight as if enjoying a play, rushed in at last.

Aleksander summoned a curtain of flame against Raksil's leg with a groan, straining himself to summon the power needed to harm the Spirit Warrior.

Valistaran's elegant, black fire arced around in a whip of dark shadow, superheating their enemy's artificial body near the elbow. Aleksander blasted Raksil in the back of the head with a burst of flame, distracting him long enough for Valistaran to draw the massive blade from the earth; he swung it in an arc over his head, slicing through Raksil's arm.

"What are you waiting for, you fools?!" Raksil screamed. "Kill them!"

The soldiers hesitated for a moment as Valistaran roared, planting both palms against the ground, igniting the wheat field. He sent a wall of flame in either direction, blocking the soldiers from reaching them.

Raksil cried out in rage and brought his fist around, smashing Valistaran hard in the chest with a brutal crack of bone. He struck the ground, and Aleksander rushed to his side. Valistaran shook his head, and although he was unable to speak, he pointed a finger at Raksil as if to order Aleksander to keep fighting.

He obeyed, rushing between the walls of dark flame, igniting his own orange fire in a weak pillar of light that distracted Raksil more than it harmed him.

The soldiers made their way around the black walls of flame and closed in on Valistaran as Aleksander held Raksil off with all his might.

Valistaran dispatched his foes with reckless abandon; he gave his all, and flames consumed those that dared venture near him. Many, including the young soldier that had refused to attack Aleksander, backed away from the fight.

Aleksander's futile attempt to strike Raksil was met with an armored elbow to his throat. He collapsed once more with a groan and a wheeze, his head throbbing. His eyes watered, and he could barely see through the blood dripping into his eyes as Raksil stood above him, blade held over head.

Aleksander took his chance before the strike fell.

Shadowy flames like those summoned by Valistaran escaped his palms. He screamed in pain as it burned his flesh, but he managed to concentrate it enough to blast straight through Raksil's artificial torso.

The flames erupted from his back with a spray of metal and bluish, sparking flame, and he stumbled backward in shock.

Aleksander groaned, wondering how much damage a Spirit Warrior's metallic body could take before they finally died. Cyan smoke and bolts of electricity escaped each of Raksil's wounds, but Aleksander did not relent.

He dared a glance over his shoulder to see that Valistaran had felled three more soldiers; the rest had fled from a fiery doom. As Raksil regained himself, Aleksander raised his foe's shattered blade, and with a cry, he thrust it into the Spirit Warrior's side.

Raksil groaned as he grasped the sword with his armored gauntlets, wrenching it from Aleksander's grasp. He used the pommel of the blade as a bludgeon, striking Aleksander in the side of the head.

His vision blurred, and the next thing he knew, he was on his back. Black flame illuminated the tears in his eyes, and he forced himself to his hands and knees.

With all that he had left, he sent an explosion of flame toward Raksil to intercept a blow meant for Valistaran's back.

All three warriors were entirely spent, but Raksil rampaged toward Valistaran, each footfall echoing across the plain. He brought his fist up into Valistaran's stomach, then thrust his knee up into the former king's face.

Valistaran's nose broke in a cry and spray of blood, and he stumbled as he tried to steady himself. Just as Raksil brought both his fists together to crush his enemy's skull, Valistaran gave an almighty yell and let all the flame in his body loose; a terrible, hellish inferno of black flame spiraled forth from his arms, bathing himself and ten men around him in pure, unrelenting chaos.

Aleksander shielded his face; although he was several yards away from the blaze, he could feel the searing heat of the flame on his exposed skin.

He cried out as two of the few remaining soldiers grasped his arms. He struggled in vain to free himself, and he swore under his breath as Raksil stumbled out of the flame, his entire body glowing from the intense heat. The metal of his artificial body was melting, and he stumbled with each footstep. His shoulder joint dripped away, and what remained of his left arm hit the earth.

Aleksander let a weak burst of flame explode from his forearms, startling the two men holding him and burning their hands. He twisted around and punched the nearest one in the face just as a bolt of Valistaran's flame knocked the other into the black inferno that raged through the wheat field.

Aleksander whirled around just in time to see Raksil grab Valistaran with his single hand; he raised him up and then smashed his head against his knee.

Raksil threw the former king to the ground, and Aleksander watched in horror as Raksil crushed Valistaran's knee with an armored boot, before grabbing one of his arms and his good leg and began to pull.

Valistaran roared in pain, and Aleksander leapt forward, blasting Raksil in the face before the warrior could tear him in half. The former king hit the ground, groaning as he held his shattered leg.

"Go!" Aleksander shouted. "Get to the hills! Crawl, if you have to! Get out of here!"

"No!" Valistaran shouted back. "Aleks, get to Valeniya!"

Aleksander scrambled across the ground, grabbing the first blade he could find, and to his surprise, it was his own shattered sword. His legs shook as he stood, holding the ruined weapon in one hand and a weak, sputtering ball of flame in the other.

"Come on, then!" Aleksander screamed, and Raksil advanced.

He stood his ground between Valistaran and Raksil, and as his foe thundered toward him, he leapt forward and planted the shattered blade in Raksil's metal throat followed by a burst of fire to the face.

Aleksander could hardly breathe between the flames, smoke, and his shattered ribs, as he brought Raksil down onto his back, bathing his face with the last bits of fire he could summon. His vision began to dance, and he could no longer breathe.

The Spirit Warrior reached through the weak flames, which were little more than superheated air, but Aleksander thrust the jagged sword through his visor, and it emerged from the back of his helm.

At that moment, Valistaran raised his hands to calm the dark flames consuming the wheat field. They obeyed his will, dancing toward the ground before they were extinguished. Suddenly, the world was ice cold.

Raksil grabbed Aleksander, the blade still embedded in his face, and slammed him to the ground. He knelt on Aleksander's chest and raised his fist. Aleksander covered his face with his arms as if that could stop what he knew was coming next.

A bolt of dark flame pierced Raksil's side and exploded out of his back like a wicked volcano. Raksil stood motionless and ruined, a blade sticking out of his face and half his body blown away.

The Spirit Warrior collapsed to his knees with a clang, then in a sudden rage, wrenched the sword from his head and thrust it through Valistaran's body just below the sternum. Valistaran screamed, his pain manifesting in an explosion of dark flame that hurled Raksil across the field.

"No!" Aleksander shouted, but somehow, the metal monster managed to survive, crawling toward Aleksander with one arm.

Aleksander stood and beheaded the Spirit Warrior with his own blade, and his ruined body and metal head struck the ground with a resounding one final, resounding clang.

He dropped Raksil's sword and stumbled, wheezing, toward Valistaran. The former king lay in the charred wheat and veritable sea of charred corpses. He looked back and forth between the man's face and the wound in his chest at a complete loss for words.

Footsteps. But Aleksander did not look up.

"Tell my family…Tell them—tell them… I love them…" Valistaran said, his voice weak and dying. "That I hope I earned their forgiveness… Redemption…"

The sound of feet crunching over blackened wheat stopped.

"I love you, father," came a sweet voice from behind them. Aleksander looked up to see Valeniya kneeling beside them.

She wrapped her father in a tight hug and held his head in her lap as he wept.

"Leniya…" he whispered. "So proud… Love…you…"

She stroked his dark hair as he let out his final breath.

Not wanting to intrude, Aleksander watched but said nothing as Valeniya brushed her hand over her father's face to close his eyes for the last time.

CHAPTER THIRTY

THE SONGBIRD IN A CAGE OF HATE

The train barreled down the tracks at full speed. The trio tried to sleep as much as they could between scheduled stops and whenever Mara was forced to sing to Mazanek. He had scheduled for her to come to his carriage every two days, which seemed to be the only marker of time.

On one such evening on the eve of their arrival to the Tazovski labor camp, two soldiers pulled Mara from sleep and forced her, barefoot, toward the back of the train. They stopped in front of the soldiers' carriage rather than Mazanek's opulent wagon. The men caught Mara's look of confusion, and one of them laughed.

"Your last performance won't be for Mazanek alone. He wanted to treat us all to that sweet voice," he said. Mara glowered, her wings twitching. The guard noticed and said,

"Can't fly away. And you know Mazanek's punishment if you did."

Mara let a long breath out from her nose, finding the strength within herself not to kill both men and leave their bodies to lie in the snow right then and there. She winced as the door to the carriage opened, and light streamed down onto her face from within; the sound of laughter and cheers followed, and the smell of alcohol and tobacco smoke filled her nostrils.

"My lady," one of the guards said in a mocking tone, offering his hand to help her into the cart. She ignored him and pulled herself up the ladder herself into the carriage.

The ladder wobbled as the drunken soldier followed close behind, and she felt a hand strike her backside. Without a moment's hesitation, she brought her boot down into his throat, resulting in a sickening gurgle and a crunch.

His head struck stone and stained the snow black in the low light, his neck twisted in an unnatural way.

Some men within the cart let out cheers and others gasped; several of them scurried to the entrance to see the second guard tending to the dead man.

"She killed Potochnik!" someone inside the wagon shouted, and the rest of the soldiers gathered around to try to peer outside. "Look at all that blood!"

Mara cried out in pain as one of them wrenched her arm upward, pulling her into the cart. She groaned and pushed herself up to her knees, backing up against the wall of the carriage as two other guards jumped to the frozen ground below to check on the dead man.

She caught Josef's gaze from across the carriage. What looked like a fresh bruise shadowed his left eye, and a thin line of red split his bottom lip. She cocked her head, and he shook his own with a subtle wave of his hand.

"Potochnik probably just fell. The idiot's had about four drinks too many tonight, and this little *girl* couldn't possibly take him down," said one of the soldiers with a raucous guffaw, his own mug of foul liquid spilling onto his lap.

The others jeered at him, making crude jokes that he had wet himself. Mara caught a waft of the distinct stench of Opikorla, the Sangoran alcohol whose name translated to *'throatburn.'*

Mara stood tall, and one soldier she recognized as Junior Sergeant Kardos pushed her into the center of the room with a cheer and ripped her threadbare coat from her shoulders. She cried out as the ruined fabric yanked on her wings.

The rest of the carriage clapped with hoots and hollers of their own, except for Josef and two others sitting at the back of the cramped cart.

Mazanek's voice floated up from the frozen tundra outside, but Mara couldn't make out any of his words, but he sounded furious. She shut her eyes, hoping with all her heart that he wouldn't enforce his punishment of hurting her people in the other carriages.

"Well, what does she do?" asked another soldier Mara didn't know. "Mazanek promised us a show!"

"Sing, little bird!" Kardos exclaimed.

"That's all she does?!" called another. "Boo!"

A chorus of more profane requests was met with roaring laughter and cheers.

She glanced over her shoulder to see Mazanek and the other soldiers that had climbed down enter the train. The sergeant's face was beet-red, and his knuckles were covered in fresh blood. At first, Mara assumed the blood was Potochnik's, but as the second soldier stepped up into the wagon, his nose dripped with blood.

Had Mazanek taken his anger out on the man for not stopping Potochnik's death, or had he taken the blame and punishment for what Mara had done? She looked into the soldier's eyes, but he averted his gaze.

"Well, it wouldn't be a party without at least one person knocking their head, now, would it?" Mazanek said, and his men laughed in response. "I'll start the bidding for Potochnik's share of Opikorla at one day's pay. Takers?"

The soldiers all started raising their hands to bid on the dead man's alcohol, and Mara sneered at the blatant disregard for human life. Even she, who had killed him, knew that the man's life, his past and future, were worth more than a few bottles of Opikorla.

"I'll give up a month's pay for a round with Mazanek's songbird!" called a soldier sitting in front of Josef.

Before Mara could react, Josef leaned forward and swung at the back of the man's neck with an empty clay mug. Mara cried out in surprise as the drunk officer turned and planted a fist in Josef's stomach.

"Damn it, Romanik!"

Mara forced herself to look away, and her heart felt as if it had dropped out of her chest. Alia and three other terrified slaves were standing outside in the snow at knifepoint next to Potochnik's body, which no one had cared to move.

"Well, if she's not going to sing, what else can she do?" Kardos exclaimed. He got up and stumbled toward her, and the other soldiers cheered in response.

"Now, now, Tomik," Mazanek said with a wink, pushing him back down in his chair. "You mustn't touch!"

Mara almost laughed—not at Mazanek's joke, but because the Junior Sergeant's first name was usually reserved for Thannish children. The stereotypical little boy's name.

The crowd lifted their glasses in another cheer, and she knew each of the drunk men in the carriage were undressing her with their eyes as they continued to shout vulgar things at her. She clenched both of her fists.

"So, do you take requests tonight?" Mazanek asked, sitting on a stool in front of the corridor leading to the soldiers' bunks lining the sides of the carriage. "How about the Thannish anthem? You know, to celebrate us getting to Tazovski tomorrow?"

Someone in the back let out a drunken, "*O, God's chosen nation!*" The rest of the wagon joined in, many skipping ahead to the roaring, triumphant chorus, rather than starting with the beginning. Despite her feelings toward the country, it was a song much too noble for these people.

"I would despise nothing more," Mara said through gritted teeth.

"Then the alternative?" Mazanek asked, gesturing to the open doorway which was still letting in frigid air. Mara looked outside to see the soldiers standing with knives near Alia and the three others.

"Here's the alternative!" shouted the man in front of Josef, slapping his palms on his lap before scooting his stool forward.

"Oh look, now you have three choices. Sing for us, dance for Private Damiani and the rest of us," he said, gesturing to the drunken, smiling, soldier. And then gesturing outside, he said, "Or watch your people die. I for one know which of those sounds best."

"Fine!" Mara shouted, her heart thundering in her chest. She turned toward Damiani, who stamped his feet and cheered. Mara shook her head and pointed directly at him. "If you don't let my friends in out of the cold by the time I'm finished, Damiani dies before the last note. Is that clear?"

"Oh, calm down, they'll be—"

"Is that clear?!" Mara shouted, turning toward Mazanek. The cheers and rude laughter seemed to fade as they awaited their sergeant's reaction. He cowered for a brief moment before straightening up.

"Put the animals back in their cage!" called Mazanek.

Mara caught Josef staring at her, his eyes red, although he was trying to hide them behind a fake smile. Was he crying because he was in pain, or was he trying to send Mara the message that he didn't agree with what his fellow soldiers were doing? Perhaps both. The few other soldiers who weren't drinking sat with folded arms and furrowed brows.

"Okay, everyone shut up or we won't get a song before we arrive!" Mazanek said, standing with his hand over his brow in a military salute. The others in the chamber stood and mimicked his gesture in respect for their country's anthem. Damiani groaned in disappointment as he eyed the curves of Mara's body.

The soldier called Tomik Kardos smirked as he draped a Thannish flag over Mara's shoulders like a cloak and tied it around her neck. She shook her head with anger in her eyes, loosening the knot of the flag around her throat enough so that she could sing.

As she hesitated to sing the final line, Mazanek cried it out, shouting, "Land of my fathers, long shall Laniras shine!"

She had never wanted to burn Thanatanos to the ground more than at that very moment. The soldiers raised their mugs and bottles, but Mara finished the song with a different line:

"ŽA DROGASTEJU I SANGORU!"

The entire wagon fell silent as Mara stood strong before them with her gaze set on Mazanek.

The sergeant stood, and for a moment, Mara thought he was going to strike her. Instead, he raised his hands and led the soldiers in a second, irreverent version of the anthem, and the tension broke.

As the soldiers continued to sing, Mara turned to Mazanek and asked in a venomous tone, "Are we done here?"

"No, we have all night!" Mazanek exclaimed, wrapping an arm around her shoulder. "Who wants another song?"

The soldiers cheered again, and Mara elbowed the sergeant in the stomach. He stumbled backward with a drunken laugh.

"Kamil," Mara thought. *"Can you hear me?"*

She didn't dare mindspeak to her friend, lest she fall unconscious or worse, have another seizure or stroke, so she simply thought the words, hoping he was listening.

"More music!" shouted Kardos, and four others who had finished singing the anthem echoed his request with a chant of, "More, more, more!"

When Mara refused, Damiani threw his flagon of Opikorla toward her, splashing her tunic with the foul liquid. Both Kardos and Damiani got to their feet and made a drunken advance toward her.

She instinctively tried to summon the Godblade to her hand. It did not appear, but several of its remaining crystals materialized around her palm and exploded with a dim light before fading away.

Her mind and heart both raced. She still had some connection to the sword, even all the way out here.

"*Mara!*" It was Kamil's voice.

"*Thank the Goddesses, Kamil, get me out of here!*"

"Come on, little songbird!" Kardos exclaimed. "I'll get you started, even! Oh, uh—how's that one song go?"

He turned to Damiani, who shrugged.

"Okay, okay! I have just the song for you!" Mara exclaimed with a fake smile and an uncharacteristic, girlish pep to her voice. "You're going to *love* this one!"

The rowdy soldiers shushed one another as she looked straight into Mazanek's eyes. His expression turned to anger as the words escaped her lips. Josef popped up, his somber expression turning to surprise at Mara's words, for they were not Thannish.

<table>
<tr><td>"Jahi rož ožramasi,</td><td>Like a rose in the ashes,</td></tr>
<tr><td>Jahi krasna vidčas,</td><td>beauty in the sadness,</td></tr>
<tr><td>I ušuora cemnijas:</td><td>and a light in the darkness,</td></tr>
<tr><td>Mačka Sangora:</td><td>Mother Sangora:</td></tr>
</table>

My su tuu pjecnem
My su tuu žykrim

Juba, žyznacan hrauja
Tuus ce žyseke
I mim doftaš nadeždu

Hotji te'buda či lauhici,
Te'buda onas svobici
Te'doftas hotji jubu
Sangoran

Jahi hraujaha uhnin
holadas
Jahi horoba trudidasi
Mačka Sangora,
My su tuu pjecnem,
My su tuu nožyzem
Sujai kahi, jahi budan,
Sujai Sangorak,
budasan svobici
Te'doftams mir my
Sangoran!"

With you, we sing.
With you, we cry.

Love, the blood of life
It flows within you
And it gives us hope.

May all be welcome
May all be Free
Let all share in the love
Of Sangora

Like a heart of fire
in the cold,
like bravery in hardship.
Mother Sangora,
With you, we sing,
With you, we die.
Come as yourself
Come to Sangora
You shall be free.
Let us all share
In the peace of Sangora!

As she sang, the soldiers gave a collective 'boo', and several began to throw their precious alcohol on her and scream obscenities at her. But she did not stop singing until the song's triumphant, defiant end.

"We're in Thanatanos, so speak Thannish, you stupid Night Witch!" shouted Damiani.

"We're not even in Thanatanos, you idiot," Josef said from behind him, which earned another punch to the ribs. Josef responded this time with a fist to the side of Damiani's head, causing the others nearby to leap to their feet.

Kardos blocked a punch thrown by one of Josef's friends, but someone else struck him in the back of the head with a bottle, and when he recovered, he flew into a fit of rage.

As Kardos beat on one of the men, Mara grabbed Damiani by the front of his tunic as he stumbled toward her. She brought her other fist up into his nose, spraying blood across his face. She then yanked on his collar, pulling him downward to knee him in the face.

The entire carriage was an all-out brawl now with Mara, Josef, and the others that weren't participating in the 'festivities' against Mazanek, Kardos, Damiani, and everyone else.

Mara stomped on the Thannish flag that had been forced around her neck, and as Kardos rushed toward her, she stepped aside with a nimble step. She grabbed the white and viridian banner from the ground and wrapped it around the soldier's neck. He gagged and fell to his knees as she tightened it around his neck, choking the life out of him.

"Kamil? Don't worry about me—get Private Romanik and his friends out of here!"

She didn't know what Kamil would be able to do, but she felt his mental presence acknowledge her request without explanation. Kardos went limp, and Mara pulled the Thannish flag from around his throat.

"Get her!" Mazanek shouted. "And kill private Romanik, Madved, and Dolinshek too!"

He had only named two others. Mara glanced over to see one of Josef's allies bleeding on the ground with a vacant, dead expression, the smashed glass of a broken bottle scattered near his head.

As another soldier lumbered toward Mara, she wrapped the flag around her hands and pulled it taut. She threw her arms up and wrapped the fabric around the man's wrist before he could land a blow then brought the end wrapped around her fist up into his face, breaking yet another nose and drenching the flag in more blood.

Mazanek collapsed, and each of the guards stumbled back to their seats or fell to the floor as some unknown, outside force pacified them. Soon, the fighting was over, with several left bleeding and bruised with two dead.

Josef glanced over at Mara, clearly confused.

"How did you do this?" Josef asked in awe, knowing it wasn't by chance that everyone had stopped fighting and fallen unconscious at once.

She felt Kamil's presence in her mind, and a wave of relief washed over her.

"*When they wake up, they'll think they blacked out drinking. They won't remember the fight or that you were even there,*" Kamil spoke to her mind.

Mara didn't reply to Josef's question.

"I'm sorry about your friend," she said.

Josef knelt and bowed his head, placing his forehead on the pommel of his sword. Mara stepped back in surprise as he knelt in the Sangoran bow.

"Long live the Empress of Blood," Josef whispered. He looked up toward her. "I've been trying to help you and your friends. I know what we're doing here is wrong, even if they think it's for the right reason."

"We don't have long. Can you get me back to the prisoners' carriage?"

"Of course, Empress," Josef replied, stepping over the now-slumbering Private Damiani. "If you want, I can kill them while they're sleeping. It'll give you a chance to escape."

"We wouldn't get far," Mara said. "No, put your sword away and save your soul."

Josef nodded as he heaved the door open, and the winter's chill crept inside. "They put me in charge of assigning each prisoner to their dwellings. I made sure you and your two Kurashian friends would be in the same house."

Mara smiled, but it did not reach her eyes.

"There's no way for me to show my thanks," Mara said. "But for what it's worth, thank you."

"Thanatanos isn't what it used to be," Josef said as Mara dropped down the ladder. Her feet hit the frozen ground, and she winced in pain. "Shutting down these camps is a good first step, and, well…I think you can do it."

"Get some sleep. Please be careful, okay?" Mara said.

"I'll try." Josef chuckled. "But the beds aren't too comfortable, you know."

"You get used to them," Mara said.

As they reached the slave wagon, Josef hesitated as if fighting with himself whether or not he should say what he was thinking.

"Don't let them make you a monster," he said at last. "Don't turn out like us."

Josef stared into her crystal blue eyes as he waited for a response. Mara cocked her head in response and a thin smile crossed her face.

"They can't make me what I already am." She didn't know why the words slipped past her lips. "Goodnight, Josef."

Josef was unable to form any words as she turned away. She climbed up into the train, and then he closed the door behind her.

CHAPTER THIRTY-ONE
PLAN OF ATTACK

They'd been hiding out in the safehouse in Doftaan's Akademrajon for several days, and no Purists or any of the Magistrate's soldiers had ventured anywhere near them. They'd all eased into a state of relative calm, but a constant buzzing of anxiety around the tall apartment complex messed with Nadezhda's vision.

They were awoken early one morning to a sharp rap on the door. Shanthah was the first upstairs, and his excitement carried down the stairs into the second apartment, although none could make out his words. The ceiling shook as multiple people wiped their boots on the rug and entered the building.

Nadezhda motioned for Ana to follow, and they poked their heads out of the shared bedroom. A moment later, Shanthah led several people, including Josman, a military woman, Mistress Ruta Vaal, a young human girl, and another Sangoran that Nadezhda didn't quite recognize into the room.

"So glad to see you, buddy," Shanthah said, clapping Josman on the back. The large man wrapped an arm around his friend.

"Good to be here. I hope this isn't everyone?" Josman asked as Shanthah took his traveler's cloak and hung it on a hook in the corner with several others.

"Under your direction, I've put in an order for as many Alboran troops to join us as we can spare back home," the military woman said. "General Anca will arrive as soon as possible."

Shanthah nodded.

"Thank you, Rayna," he said. "Operation Dragon-Justice is a go."

"You know we're not calling it that," said the general.

"Oh, Rayna," Shanthah said. "You're so silly."

General Rayna rolled her eyes, but Shanthah gave her a kidding smile, pulling a chair up for her behind the long dining table in the apartment across from where Ana and Nadezhda were housed on the bottom floor. Josman went back outside to carry in more supplies.

Shanthah saw Nadezhda and Ana lurking outside, and he gestured to them with a laugh.

"Nadezhda, Ana, if you haven't met them already, I'd like to introduce you both to Vasilica, Ruta, and Diana, three of Mara's Mistresses of Dusk, as well as Rayna Cotula, general of the Balgorod guard."

Nadezhda smiled and offered a wave as she met the gaze of the young human girl who must be Mistress Diana, dressed in simple silken robes beneath a cloak of fur.

"It's so good to meet you all!" Ana said. "Really, an honor!"

Nadezhda nodded and tried to match Ana's excitement as she greeted each of the newcomers.

"Shanthah, would you like me to set up here?" Vasilica asked, adjusting a heavy pack on her shoulder.

"Yes, please, if you will," Shanthah said. "Let me get that for you, so sorry!"

He took the pack from Vasilica and helped her unpack the various scrolls, maps, and other items from within.

Mistress Diana approached Ana and Nadezhda. Ordinarily, the emotions that Nadezhda could see around children were similar to those of adults but less defined; chaotic, and, in a word, immature. Not so with Diana. Her aura and emotions seemed calm and collected, mature for one of her young age.

"Hi, I'm Diana," she said as Josman and Vasilica carried the rest of their supplies from upstairs into the back room.

Ana dropped into the Sangoran bow, and Nadezhda offered an awkward hand in introduction. Diana shook it with an amused grin.

"You're normal. I like that," Diana said with a wink of a green eye.

"That's very debatable." Ana smirked.

"Hey!" Nadezhda failed to think of a witty response, but it was just as well, for Shanthah motioned for the Mistresses Ruta, Vasilica, and Diana, as well as General Rayna, to sit around the table. They all took their seats, and Shanthah looked at Nadezhda and Ana. He cleared his throat and looked at them with raised eyebrows.

"Oh, sorry. We'll go," Nadezhda said, awkwardly sliding backward before disappearing behind the wall.

"Nope, you're part of this, get back here," Shanthah said.

Ana grabbed her shoulder and pulled her into the meeting. Nadezhda sat next to Ruta, who greeted her with kind eyes.

"Unexpected, spur of the moment meeting," Shanthah said. "It'll be quick. I wanted to introduce you to Nadezhda and her girlfriend Ana."

A chorus of greetings rang out around the table.

"I hear you're going to help us win this war," Mistress Vasilica said. Nadezhda pointed to herself with a shake of the head.

"No, I'll just make things worse. It's what I do," Nadezhda said. Shanthah shook his head with a smile, and the others stared at her as if expecting her to continue speaking. "I also use humor as an unhealthy coping mechanism."

"Mistress Shanthah does the same thing," Ruta said. "You're in good company."

"Mistress?" Ana asked. Shanthah began to speak, but Ruta covered his mouth.

"The siege of Balgorod is over, and the forces there have pulled back," General Rayna explained, apparently starting the meeting. "Intelligence suggests that the forces there have been reassigned here for a final assault on Doftaan and Bukaral."

Shanthah stroked the stubble on his chin. "And elsewhere in Alboras? I haven't heard from Lavinia in quite some time with an update from the Timishuaran front."

Ana pulled Nadezhda close and whispered into her ear.

"Lavinia is the most awesome person I've ever seen."

Nadezhda whispered back, "I thought that was me."

Ana shrugged.

"Lavinia sent word that she'd freed Aleksander from the Kurashian prison, like we planned. Aleksander met up with Valistaran at the border to find the Secret Keepers, but I haven't heard anything since," Vasilica said.

"News from the rest of Alboras and Timishuara is that a majority of the forces have pulled back. Not because we were winning, but because they'd done two things. One: stopped our forces from reaching Doftaan in time for their final push here, and two: attacked enough of their own towns around the border to blame us for the chaos," General Rayna said.

"And three: distracted us long enough for the Kurashian Secret Keeper to get to Thanatanos without us finding him," said Ruta. "Maybe."

"Let's hope you're wrong, or Elafris help us," Shanthah muttered. He turned to Diana. "What do you think? Can we hold Doftaan?"

At first, Nadezhda thought the comment was simply to include the young girl in the conversation, not to get actual advice, but once again, Diana showed remarkable maturity in her answer.

"Can we hold out against their forces? Yes. But can we defeat the Magistrate? That's another question."

Shanthah nodded. "How many forces do we have?"

"Thirty thousand in the city, including the city guard," Diana replied. "Another five thousand scattered from here to Bukaral."

"And how many do we believe are actually loyal to us?" Shanthah asked. "Not loyal to Florenta and the Magistrate? Not being mind controlled, brain washed, you know."

"All of them," Diana said with a shrug. Shanthah cocked his head. "The Sangoran soldiers loyal to the Magistrate left the city. Obviously, there are civilians who support Florenta here, but they shouldn't be a problem. I don't think so, anyway."

"Where'd they go?" Shanthah asked. "And when?"

Diana shrugged and looked to her mentor, Mistress Vasilica. "I don't know, sorry. Vasi?"

"To reinforce the Thannish forces in Adess, we think. Near the slave camp there."

"Speaking of," Shanthah said. "Any word on the whereabouts of our beloved empress?"

Each of the others shook their heads.

"Wasn't Hanna trying to find her?" Diana asked.

Shanthah nodded. "Yeah, but even Hippo couldn't sense her. Either she's too far away, or—" He cut himself off, but everyone knew what he was going to say. "Hanna and Hippo are busy bringing food to relieve the famine in Adess. If they have any other updates, I don't know."

Nadezhda spoke up. "I think I might have a way to contact her."

The others, even Ana, turned to her with a collective look of surprise. Diana's eyes lit up with hope.

"That's wonderful, how?" Mistress Ruta asked.

"Well, you know how I've got a dead god in my pocket?" Nadezhda asked.

"Yeah," Shanthah said. Vasilica, Diana, and Rayna shared a look of confusion. "Go on."

"Well, he told me he can find her. I guess she made a sword from his essence, or something? I don't know what that means, and I don't want to. But he said he has a link to any objects, like this gem in my pocket."

Shanthah shared a look with Ruta.

"Is it safe?" Ruta asked.

"He can't hurt me," Nadezhda replied. "It has to be me, I think. But if Mara still has that sword he mentioned…"

Thanatan's Heart felt warm in her pocket, and the Voice spoke to her mind.

"*I no longer have a connection to Mara's weapon. It is now in the Magistrate's possession, and she purged my mind from within, but I can still sense the empress, far, far away. Remnants of my power are still with her.*"

Nadezhda fidgeted in her seat. "He says Mara's alive, but she doesn't have the sword."

Some of the others gasped, while others cheered and clapped their hands with wide smiles on their faces.

"Excellent!" Shanthah said.

Diana got to her feet and did a little dance, pumping her fist as she sat back down. "Where is she?"

"He can't tell. Not exactly. But he says he'll keep his connection through my mind open, and he'll find her eventually," Nadezhda said. "I guess I have no choice in the matter, but it's for the greater good, right?"

"Vasilica and Diana, I need you to find Lavinia, Aleksander, and Valeniya Talohir. Bring Josman with you, too. Ruta, can you prepare for General Anca and Mistress Raluca's arrival?"

Everyone nodded at their orders.

"And what about us, boss?" Ana asked.

"You two have the most important job of all," Shanthah said. "Make contact with our girl Mara and bring our people home."

CHAPTER THIRTY-TWO
TAZOVSKI

As Mara glanced across the dead, gray horizon, she doubted there was anywhere in the world more remote or more desolate than the Tazovski slave camp.

Although the land of the camp curiously wasn't covered in a blanket of snow, the colorless earth seemed to bleed into the dreary sky above. If there had once been great forests of any kind across the dead expanse, they were long gone, leaving only sparse patches of trees and bushes. In one direction, the frozen tundra disappeared into the horizon, and in the other, a great river branched off until its icy fingers reached a dark gulf that looked like a sea of ink to the north.

It was truly the edge of the world.

Several days had passed since her encounter with the drunken soldiers, and the rest of the journey had been uneventful. No one had died. No one had been beaten. Barely anyone even spoke.

The soldiers seemed to have recovered from their drunken brawl, and no one seemed to be questioning the story that they had all blacked out from excessive amounts of alcohol.

And now, the train stood still outside a small city, and the surviving slaves were ushered onto the platform. A low wall covered in sharp wire encircled the town. The tracks beyond the platform curved back toward Thanatanos and civilization.

Dozens of soldiers being sent back home boarded the train. Some cheered at being relieved of their post here, but others ambled mindlessly aboard as if this place had drained them of life.

Spring had come and gone for those aboard the train. By Kamil's estimation, they were now sometime at the end of the short Sangoran summer, which meant the torturous weather they had just experienced was only a taste of the even crueler autumn and winter to come.

It was a relatively warm day, and Mara told herself she'd need to soak in the last days of dim sunlight before autumn took them away.

She held Alia and Kamil's hands as they and the other slaves followed Sergeant Mazanek, his officers, and the other soldiers through the gates of Tazovski.

"Enjoy your new cage, little bird," called Private Damiani as he passed by. "Hope to see you soon!"

He blew a kiss in her direction, and she responded with a rude hand gesture; Alia raised an eyebrow, and Mara chuckled to herself, pleased with her action.

"Welcome to Tazovski, the last place you'll ever see," said a huge, pale soldier that resembled a bear trying to dress as a man; he scratched his thick beard and adjusted his fur hat before leading them into the camp. "You missed the *good* weather by a few weeks. It'll warm up a bit, but not for five or six months. Downhill from here…"

"And how much longer will you be here?" Alia asked. The man seemed surprised she was making conversation at all. Mara knew that if the question escaped her own mouth, it wouldn't have been so polite.

"Just about the time it gets warm again," he muttered. "I was supposed to leave on this train with the others, but my assignment was extended." Mara felt a wave of pity wash over her as the man's countenance fell and he added, "Gonna miss the birth of my baby girl."

Alia patted the man's arm to console him. They spoke in whispers that Mara could no longer hear.

Mara felt a sense of joy as she watched the interaction unfold. Ever since she had met Alia, she had always been impressed by the woman's gentle kindness for everyone she met. Perhaps, Mara thought, that is what made her such a wonderful healer.

"I'm Alia."

"Luk," the man replied. A group of soldiers pulled a cart toward the group of slaves, and Luk gestured to it. "Help yourself to whatever you find."

Mara nearly burst into tears of happiness when she realized what was in the cart. Coats. Hats. Gloves. Her own coat had been torn down the back during the situation in the soldiers' carriage, leaving her only with her thin tunic. The same one she had been wearing for—well, for however long they had traveled.

"How'd you do that?" Mara asked.

"What, get the soldier to speak to me like a human?" Alia asked. She shrugged. "I spoke to *him* like one. Not all of them are bad, even here."

Alia smiled and pulled a thick fur coat from the pile. It looked as if it had been stitched together from multiple articles of clothing and stomped on by a Minotaur, but it was thick, and therefore warm. She passed it to Mara.

Mara slid her arms into the sleeves and let out a contented sigh.

"Ah, now I'm a warm Mara. Never thought I'd be so happy to wear something so ugly," she said, examining the hideous fur coat hanging off her arms. Then with a cheeky, exaggerated smile, she pointed upward and added, "Does it match my hat?"

Kamil and Alia pulled their own 'new' coats on, and they laughed as Mara pulled her oversized hat up before it drooped back down over her eyes.

"*I wonder how many people have died in these things*," Kamil thought to the others.

"Morbid," Alia said, a look of disgust on her face.

"Yikes. Happy moment over," Mara said. "Thanks for that."

Kamil chuckled. The trio spent the next fifteen minutes distributing hats, coats, trousers, socks, boots, and pairs of scratchy wool gloves to the rest of their fellow slaves.

The soldiers waited for the newcomers to dress until they led them into the lower part of the city, a squalor settlement that jutted up out of the gray tundra. The walled-off officers' village was built upon a low hill overlooking the slave town.

Just like the transitionary camp on the Plains of Adess, other than around the soldiers' village, there were no gates keeping people from running away from the ramshackle huts spread across the land. As uninviting as the scene was, plumes of smoke billowed from crumbling chimneys, and each slave knew that meant fire and the warmth of a hearth.

Josef tugged on Mara's coat to get her attention. He motioned for her, Alia, and Kamil to follow, then led them up a path toward their shared hut nestled in the heart of a sparse pine grove. Ten other houses formed a small neighborhood around theirs. Countless other such communities stretched into the distance.

"I think you'll be comfortable here," Josef said, pushing open the door. "The walls don't have any holes, and—"

"Comfortable?" Mara asked in a dark tone.

"Poor choice of words," Alia said. "You say that like you're selling us a home in the Tehir resort town in Talohira."

Josef nodded, unsure of what to say as he stood in the doorway. Kamil simply stared at him, his arms folded across his chest. After an awkward moment of silence, Josef ushered Kamil and Alia inside.

Mara stood outside and watched seven slaves enter the hut across from her own, including the two young Odauthian men who had stolen Mazanek's second Ottokar the Butcher coin. She took note of who she recognized, for she knew it would be important to know which allies lived nearby.

She followed the others into the hut and looked around, letting out a deep breath. Better than being stuck in the train, she told herself. She turned and went inside.

"Not much to it," Mara said, crossing the entire building in only a few strides.

"I'll get a fire started," Alia said, pulling a log from a small pile near the fireplace. A barrel full of straw and twigs stood next to it, and she took a handful of the kindling to begin the fire.

Josef sighed and set a pile of parchment on the wobbly table in the center of the room. He gave an awkward wave to Mara, who did not see the gesture, and departed without another word.

Mara scooped up the packet of papers, reading their orders for what could possibly be the rest of their lives. It explained each of their roles; Kamil would chop lumber, Alia would sew soldiers' uniforms in a facility in the officers' village, and Mara was assigned to construction detail. All three of them would also plant and harvest beets, potatoes, and other vegetables hardy enough to survive there.

The main chamber had three small beds, a fireplace, an ugly rug covered in hair and ash, and a table with three stools. In the corner was a door that led into a small bathroom. Inside was a crude toilet which was a mere bucket set under a wooden seat. Across from the toiler were a washbasin with a few bars of dirty soap, a cracked mirror, and a shallow bathtub with a drainpipe that led outside through a hole that let in a draft of cold air.

A single cupboard adorned the wall over the table; Kamil looked inside to find a set of clay plates, a single pot, and a frying pan. Meanwhile, Mara continued to skim the papers. The second page was a map of the village, the third, a schedule for work and relief times, and on the fourth page, a list of their daily and weekly rations.

She glowered down at the parchment as if it were King Verahim's face. She fought the urge to crumple it into a ball before she finished scanning the page.

By order of his majesty, King Verahim Romus,
Eighth King of Thanatanos:

Herein are set forth standards of nutrition and health for all prisoners in the correctional labor camps and colonies within and without the Thannish kingdom:

1. For those who do not meet production quotas: 600g rye bread, 100 g buckwheat, 500g potatoes and vegetables (as seasonably available), 128g fish, 30g meat, 10g sugar, and 20g salt.

2. For those who fulfill all production quotas as set forth: 1200g rye bread, 60g wheat, 130g buckwheat, 600g potatoes and vegetables, 160g fish, 30g meat, 13g sugar, 20g salt.

3. For those that exceed their quota by ten percent, an additional ration will be given as deemed proportional to their contribution.

4. Pregnant women, new mothers, the ill, newcomers, and children will be granted an additional 400g bread, 35g buckwheat, 400g potatoes and vegetables, and 75g fish.

5. All dwellings will be brought three liters of potable water per inhabitant.

Mara wondered just how often these portions would be distributed, if at all. She continued to thumb through the next three pages. These forms were signed by a General Forst Simunek with a decree that if any prisoner pled guilty before the leaders of the camp or pledged loyalty to Thanatanos, they would receive a lesser sentence, pardon, or a position in the Thannish army.

Mara scoffed, assuming that anyone who admitted to any supposed 'crimes' would be killed.

"Any food in there?" she asked.

"*Some bread, oil, salt, buckwheat for porridge, and a little flour,*" Kamil replied. "*Oh, and what looks like half a fish of some kind…I think? Smells bad like fish.*"

Mara glanced down at the parchment and then at the bare cupboard with a scowl.

"They promised more," Mara muttered, dropping the papers on the table. "Joke's on us for believing it though, right? You two get 'comfortable' as Josef said. I'll whip you up some dinner."

"Hey, maybe Josef will come through for us," Alia said. "He seems like a nice enough boy."

"Nice, but perhaps that is all he is. I haven't seen much of a backbone from that kid. I wonder if his spine will hold beneath the weight of what he'll have to do here."

"He did defend me on the train," Mara said. "Or, tried too, at least. His heart's in the right place. He got us a house together, too." Kamil and Alia nodded, not having known.

"That paper say how long we get to sleep before we have to go out there again?" Alia asked.

Mara nodded. "Three days to rest and recover from the journey. After that, the schedule is written down, but I believe they'll give us that time as much as they gave us what's written on our list of rations."

She headed to the cupboard and scooped some of the buckwheat into the pot and looked around for water to make her friends a portion of porridge.

There was a knock on the door. Kamil answered, and the light of the fire illuminated Josef's face as he and another soldier carried a heavy container of water into the chamber, setting it down next to the fire.

"Keep that warm or it'll freeze," said Josef.

"Oh, is that what water does when it's cold?" Mara replied with a smirk. Josef laughed and was about to say something else, but his impatient comrade called for him from outside to help distribute the rest of the water.

"Gotta go," Josef said and backed out of the room, bumping into the table before clumsily stumbling out of the door, shutting it behind him.

Kamil looked fed up with the young man, rubbing the bridge of his nose with his thumb and forefinger.

"That guy's never going to survive being in the army."

"I think his awkwardness is endearing," Mara said. In a softer tone, she added, "It reminds me of Aleksander when I first met him."

"You know, I've never heard the story," Alia said.

"I have, but I'd love to hear it again," Kamil said.

As she cooked a scant meal for her friends, Mara smiled and obliged, telling them about the first time she met Aleksander—back when he was the young runaway prince named Xanthurias.

When their meal was ready, they gathered around the table and shared in the feast—compared to what they'd been fed aboard the train, that is.

As they ate, Mara glanced out the window and watched the people—her people—being herded like cattle through the village. She knew in her heart that what the soldier had said earlier was true. It would be the last place many of them would ever see, and her heart felt as if it had been crushed within her chest.

Despite their circumstances, the warm fire and decent food raised their spirits enough for laughter and conversation until Alia excused herself with a yawn. She and Kamil selected their beds, and soon, soft snores could be heard from both sides of the room.

When Mara was sure both Kamil and Alia were asleep, she set her floppy hat atop her raven's feather hair and pulled the
fur coat close. She stepped outside into the

frigid air. The torches lining the path cast a light over her face that offered no warmth.

She winced as a series of gunshots killed the silence. She took a deep breath and let it out slowly. Who had been murdered now? Would she ever know?

The rest of the night was still and silent, oddly beautiful—peaceful even. The slaves had all been assigned to their respective huts and barracks, and she hoped they would get some sleep and much deserved rest.

And then, a soft voice filled her mind.

"Mara."

She shot to her feet and raised her wings, ready to strike should someone attack. Nothing happened.

"Hello?" she whispered.

"I'm enjoying our little game, Mara."

It was her own voice.

She wandered into the frigid night.

"Stay out of my head," Mara ordered.

As her voice replied, it mutated into that of the Magistrate, and a laugh filled her mind.

"Oh, so easy to rattle."

"Come tell me that in person."

"Soon. Time is of the essence, though, little queen. Your people are dying. Can you save them before I kill them all?"

Mara kicked a rock, and it clattered down the path.

"I know how to get back to Sangora, and when I do, I'm going to rip your throat out." Her voice was cold and harsh.

"I expect nothing less from you—I'm counting on it. Your friend tried. Failed. I thought you'd like to know."

Mara's thoughts raced. "Who?"

"The Telekinetik. Maybe if you can get out of the camp, you can work together just like you murdered Thanatan. Thank you for that, by the way. He was a brute, and I needed him out of the way. I look forward to our reunion."

She felt the Magistrate's influence leave her mind, and she looked toward the officers' village. She knew her foe was right. Time *was* of the essence, and millions of people were counting on her to save them.

She could not let them down.

CHAPTER THIRTY-THREE
A LIGHT TO THE DOWNTRODDEN

Mara had never been so happy to be wrong. The soldiers had indeed given them three full days of rest after their journey to Tazovski. During that time, she had tried to visit as many of the other slaves as she could. She spent the evenings learning their names and getting to know them, playing games, laughing, and raising their spirits well into the night.

On the last night before their work would begin, she followed the now-familiar dirt path down a hill, absentmindedly glancing through the huts' windows as she went. Most of the windows were aglow from the fireplaces warming the weary slaves in dread anticipation of the next day, but one hut on her row was dark, although Mara could hear voices coming within.

She hadn't yet become acquainted with its inhabitants, so she decided to pay them a visit.

She listened outside the door for several minutes. The voices were frantic and exasperated from exhaustion and despair. At last, Mara rapped her knuckles on the door, and the voices went silent. There was no movement from within.

"I'm not a soldier," Mara said. "It's okay, you can let me in. I just wanted to say hi, maybe ask if there's anything I can help you with."

She expected the inhabitants to remain silent, thinking that she was coming to hurt them, but she heard the doorknob turn, and the door swung inside.

A young Sangoran woman answered the door.

"I—can we help you?"

Another asked, "How did you know?"

The young woman was shivering, despite wearing a thick fur coat inside. Three other women sat by the dark hearth: two Sangoran and one human. Mara looked over them with a sympathetic look as she shut the door behind her. The only light in the chamber came from the silver moonlight shining through the dirty window.

"I thought you could use some help getting your fire started," Mara said, and the elderly Sangoran woman muttered something in a soft tone, but she couldn't make out any words.

"Really?" the younger Sangoran woman asked.

"Yeah—I was walking by and saw your house was dark," Mara said. "Do you have the flint and steel they provided?"

The woman pulled them from the pocket of her thick coat and handed them to Mara. When she brushed the woman's hands, they were ice cold and trembling.

"Here, come watch, I'll teach you," she said. She hoped they hadn't been freezing this entire time. The young woman sat on the ground next to her. "What's your name, friend?"

Mara recognized her from the train, but at the time, she had tried not to get to know anyone as to protect her fellow slaves ever since the woman in the transitionary camp had been murdered just for talking to her.

"I'm Constanta Stolyanova," the woman said, kneeling before the fireplace next to Mara.

"It's such an honor to meet you, Constanta. I'm Mara. I'll make sure you all stay warm, okay?"

First, she demonstrated how to pile the wood and kindling. Then she showed Constanta how to use the sparks from the flint and steel and finally how to breathe life into the flame. When the fireplace began to glow, Mara looked up with a smile to see Constanta staring into her face.

"It's really you," Constanta whispered. "Jan Jemprata Hraujan." *My Empress of Blood.*

"But more importantly, you're really *you!*" Mara said, her eyes happy and glistening with the light of the fire.

Constanta stared in awe. "I'm sorry. I don't mean to gawk. It's just… Just wait until Baba Boggy hears who you are…"

She trailed off, glancing down. Mara chuckled and assumed 'Baba Boggy' was the old woman in the corner. Baba was an endearing Sangoran term for a grandmother.

Constanta was already kneeling to examine the fire, but as she turned toward Mara, she raised her wings, her fist to her forehead.

She looked up and relaxed from the Sangoran bow as she felt Mara's hand on her shoulder.

"No need for that," Mara said. She turned to the others. "If you ever need any help, I live in the hut by the pines."

"Thank you," Constanta said.

"And who are your friends?" Mara asked, turning to the other women in the hut.

"Bogdana Dragavei there, in the corner. Baba Boggy, we call her. She insists on it," Constanta said, pointing to the older woman muttering incoherently. "She's been here for a few weeks now. This is Katerina Novikova—she's from Talohira. Her brother Leonid was on the train with us, but we can't find him. And of course, my little sister, Rada."

She gestured to her sister, who waved, too intent on warming herself next to the fire to say anything. Mara was glad, though—these people wouldn't freeze. Not tonight.

"Very nice to meet you all," Mara said. And then in Sangoran, she said, "Hošden, Baba. Možnu?" *Hello, Baba. May I?*

Mara took the old woman's arm and helped her hobble over to the fire before pulling her cot nearer. Bogdana nodded with a toothless grin and sat down on it to warm her hands. Mara sat next to her and gave her a one-armed hug.

"She can't hear well," Constanta said. "Or speak, for that matter. But she was excited to see that if there's a sick person—her, that is—in our house, we'll get extra food rations. So, we hope that's true. She says it's how she can help us."

"Vy budasat duža dida pamoža," Mara said, touching Bogdana's wrinkly cheek. *You will be a very big help.*

The old woman smiled and tipped her forehead before closing her eyes to enjoy the fire. "Listen, I don't have much to give, but I—do you have any food?"

"We have a few portions of buckwheat. We can share what we have to thank you."

"Oh, no, I'm so sorry. I don't mean for myself. I wanted to make sure *you* weren't hungry," Mara said, drawing half a loaf of hard bread from her ugly coat's deep pocket. She broke it into equal chunks and handed one to each of them.

Constanta smiled. "Why are you being so kind to us? We're strangers, and—"

Mara's thoughts turned to her happy, plump handmaid, Elena back in Doftaan. She had once asked a similar question when she was only a Wingling, but the kind woman's words had stuck with her all these years.

"Because I'm people, and so are you. That means we're supposed to be kind to each other," Mara said, touching Constanta's hand.

"I like that," Constanta said.

Mara noticed Rada slip half of her chunk of bread into her pocket, and Mara shook her head.

"No, please eat. Don't worry about saving it. My friend is a Mindspeaker, and we've been using his powers to steal more bits of old food. I'll make sure you get more."

Constanta squeezed her hand, tears forming in her eyes.

"Thank you, Mara."

"You can all get through this," Mara replied, looking at them each individually. "We'll get through it together, and when we get home, we'll have a feast in my palace, and you're all invited. Where are you from?"

"Constanta and I are from Doftaan," Rada said, speaking up for the first time.

"Home," Mara said with a smile. "Well, I'm originally from Cineca, Thanatanos, but Doftaan is home now."

"Wait, you're Thannish?!" Constanta's sister Rada exclaimed a bit too loud, and Constanta winced. The human woman, Katerina, perked up as well.

"I was born human. Yes, I'm a transitioned-Sangoran. Persangoran. My family is still there, actually," Mara said. "Not many people know that about me, but it's true!"

"Is that why you're here? They hate Persangorani," Constanta said, then slapped herself in the forehead. "No, obviously not. You're here because you're, well, you."

Mara chuckled. "I guess I'm giving the Thans all sorts of reasons to hate me, huh?"

The others chuckled, and Mara felt a joyous warmth wash over her heart as she watched them eat and relax next to the crackling fire. The tension and despair in the room had faded away to friendship and smiles.

"I don't mean to pry, but was it weird?" Rada asked. Mara cocked her head. "I mean, you were human, and now you're a Persangoran, and that must be—"

"Rada! It's Persangoran, not 'a' Persangoran!" Constanta scolded. Then, in rapid Sangoran she scolded, "Ta ne'amila sprasits!" *That is not polite to ask!*

Mara chuckled. "It's fine, I'm happy to talk about it. It *was* weird at first. I got a lot of hate for being a 'fake' Sangoran from the older generation and pretty much everyone in the king and queen's court until I became queen."

"Was it hard?" Katerina asked, speaking for the first time.

Mara nodded. "Very. I was so, so scared. At the beginning, I didn't really know who I was anymore."

"Do you now?" Constanta asked in a soft voice.

"I do," Mara said. She was silent for a moment, staring into the fire with a thin smile. "I do. And I've never been happier. This is me."

She raised her wings.

"And was it true you were a slave before this? Before you were queen of Talohira?" Katerina asked. "I always liked you as our queen, by the way. More than Codruta. I wish it would have worked out between you and Valistaran, though."

Mara burst out laughing. "Well, technically, we did get married. I didn't know that, though! I'm still trying to fix it!" The others joined in her laughter. "Yes, I have been a slave since I was sixteen years old, with a little break in there when I *somehow* became an empress."

"Wow, since you were—how long would that be, then?"

"Well, I'm thirty now, you can do the math there," Mara said. "Thirty. When'd I get old?"

The others laughed, and Mara made awkward eye contact with Baba Boggy as she gummed on the stale bread, but she wasn't sure if the old woman had even heard her comment let alone understood the Thannish words.

She turned back to the fire. "Anyway, enough about me. I'm here to meet you all. Katerina, where in Talohira are you from?"

"Manzhala," replied Katerina. "Born there and joined the Talohiran navy there."

"I've been! It's a beautiful town. Right on the coast. Some of the most beautiful sunsets I've ever seen were looking out over the water in Manzhala."

At this, the Talohiran woman smiled with her teeth.

"I'd like to see one more of those."

"You will," Mara said, and Katerina nodded, although Mara could tell from her expression that she didn't believe it.

Constanta shifted, pulling her knees up to her chest as she scooted closer to the fire.

"I'm here because I was a news messenger and investigative reporter in Doftaan. I tried to expose the truth about Florenta and her Mistresses of Dusk. Rada's here because she's my sister. I tried to talk about the corruption and crimes and lies—all that. Mostly about the Faceless pandemic before it went away."

"I'm well aware of all of that," Mara said softly.

"When people started disappearing, Rada and I decided that we had to go on the run for a while."

"Where did you go?" Mara asked. The fire was now roaring in the hearth, much to her relief.

"We tried to sneak out and go to Alboras after they declared their independence and did away with the name 'Karpaska'."

"Smart," Mara said. "Alboras is taking any refugees it can."

"Right. So, we had planned to flee there, but before we made it across the border into Timishuara, we were ambushed and captured. We wanted to help fight."

"It's good to know that there are still free people fighting against Florenta's regime," Mara said. "It's the people that'll win this war, not the leaders, after all."

"You're right. Florenta's dead. If you didn't hear—"

"Yes, I heard," Mara said.

"But her Mistresses of Dusk took her place," Constanta said. Mara gave a dark chuckle.

"Not for long," Mara said, and as Constanta raised an eyebrow, Mara added, "I killed all but Mistress Kariana. I guess she's in charge now."

"Is she the fake Empress of Blood?" Constanta asked.

"You must be good at your job if you know that bit of information." Mara shook her head. "That's a bit harder to explain, but no."

Constanta nodded, and Mara decided it was safe to explain the situation with the Magistrate, and she did so. She kept the information about Thanatan and the Godblade to herself, however.

She looked over to see Rada and Katerina huddled asleep on the floor near the fire. Constanta followed Mara's gaze and let out a chuckle.

"They look happy."

"That's all I want," Mara said. "Is there anything else I can get for you?"

"No, thank you. You've already done too much," Constanta replied, but Mara shook her head.

"A bit of bread and a fire aren't 'too much'."

"More than you can ever know," Constanta replied. "You know, I met you once."

"Oh?"

"Yeah. You were kind and gentle when I spoke to you, even though I know you're a fierce warrior."

Mara smiled again.

"Well, that means more to me than *you* can ever know," Mara said, clapping her hands on her knees before standing up. "I remember you, you know."

Constanta looked taken aback. "No, you don't, but it's nice of you to—"

"I absolutely do. You always sat in the front row of my briefings to the news messengers back in Doftaan," Mara said, and tears filled Constanta's eyes. "Front row, middle seat."

"You really do remember…" she whispered.

"You don't forget someone as bold as you! I have a question for you."

"Go ahead," Constanta replied.

"As a news messenger and investigator, I assume you are good at building connections and finding sources, yes?"

"You could say that, yes."

Mara bit her lip as she formulated her request in her mind.

"Can you find a group of trustworthy people to help me with a plan to get everyone out of here? I need your help."

"Of course, Empress," Constanta said.

Mara explained her plan and what type of people she required, and Constanta made mental notes, nodding along with the instructions.

When she was done, Mara said, "That aside, I have another idea. Let the others rest for an hour or so, and then meet me in the clearing outside my house. Can you do that?"

"Sure," Constanta replied. "Why?"

"Oh, just a little something to lift everyone's spirits…and to make the Thans hate me *even more*."

Constanta laughed out loud. "Can't wait!"

"See you soon, then," Mara said, pulling her into a hug.

They said their goodbyes, and Mara closed the door behind her. She set out knocking on other doors of as many houses as would answer and explained to them when and where to assemble.

When the time came, a group of several dozen slaves had gathered in the clearing near Mara, Kamil, and Alia's hut to find a hastily constructed wooden stage. Kamil and Alia had nailed planks taken from the pile of lumber used by the slaves on building detail, including Mara, to the tops of barrels of various sizes. Kamil had also set up a large bonfire to keep the crowd warm, much to their delight.

Mara's heart pounded in her chest, and she couldn't wipe the smile from her face as she climbed up onto the makeshift stage. She looked out at the confused and exhausted crowd and saw many familiar faces staring at her.

Kamil and Alia were near the front, as were Constanta and her sister Rada. Baba Boggy had even hobbled to the gathering and sat upon a nearby stump, and the two bearded Odauthian men hung near the back.

"Welcome, everyone!" she called in the light of the bonfire. "My apologies for being so mysterious about all of this, but back in my hometown, we had a tradition. When everyone was dead exhausted after a long day's work during the harvest season, we held concerts to keep spirits up. I'd like to start that tradition here, too. Here we go!"

She brushed her dark hair from her face as the fire danced in her bright, excited eyes, and the whole crowd stopped talking as she cleared her throat. She opened her mouth and began to sing on stage for the first time in many, many years.

There once ruled a frog king,
He was fat and he was slimy,
More than any swamp thing!

All the swamp brought bugs and flies
And as the frog king grew,
He got so big he rolled down the hill,
Where he went, no one knew!

No one cared, and no one dared
Not to find him nor roll him back,
No more frog king, but that's not a bad thing!
The swamp was free, and the swamp was glad!

She repeated the rowdy song once through, and the crowd sang along. By the end of the song, everyone was stomping their feet and clapping to the rhythm, and many had even begun to dance. Even Baba Boggy was stomping her foot.

"I always liked that one," Mara said, clearing her throat. "Interpret it as you will."

The crowd laughed, and Alia called for an encore. Mara's face lit up with joy that shined from her eyes. Her heart

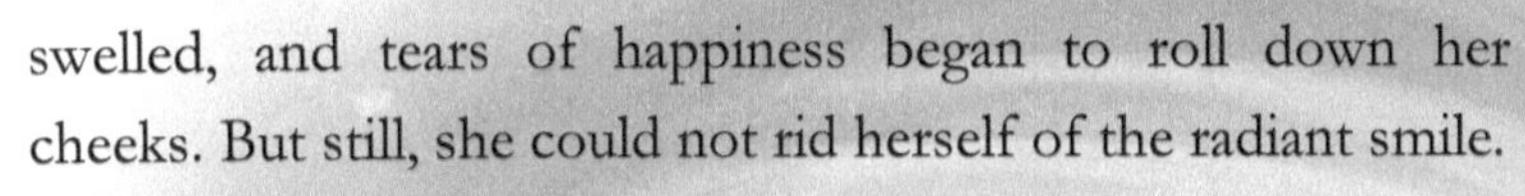

swelled, and tears of happiness began to roll down her cheeks. But still, she could not rid herself of the radiant smile.

Nor did she want to, and neither did the crowd.

A thought sprang into her mind. When she had tried to summon the Godblade in the soldiers' village, she had summoned the remnants of the weapon left in her body. Bits of crystal that lingered and glittered in the air.

Mara threw her hand into the air and tried with all her might to summon the sword, and the bits of crystal burst forth from her hands. They hung in the air like tiny, glowing lanterns of green and blue, catching the light of the bonfire to dispel the darkness.

The crowd let out a collective gasp of joyous surprise, and Mara marveled at the wondrous beauty of the shining crystals before they faded. But her little trick had achieved what she wanted to; the people were entranced and happy, completely detached from the horrors of the slave camp.

She obliged encore after encore, sharing the music of her soul well into the evening. She followed *The Frog King* with the slow lullaby of *Whatever it Takes,* and then a rambunctious rendition of *Come on In, the Water's Warm.*

Just before she finished the final line of *You Taught me to Fly,* she saw a group of three soldiers approaching with a cart. Her heart thundered in her chest, and for a brief moment, her voice faltered.

"Sorry about that!" Mara said, clearing her throat. "Frog King in the throat, I guess!"

She winced at the bad joke, but the audience laughed, unaware that the soldiers were coming up the path behind them. Had she doomed them all?

The crowd followed Mara's gaze, and several people began to panic and began to flee. However, at that moment, to her great relief, Mara caught a glimpse of Josef's face.

"Wait, stop!" she cried. "It's okay!"

They did, for they trusted her.

Josef gave a shy wave, and Mara held up her hand in greeting as the two other soldiers began unloading barrels from the cart.

"Drinks all around!" Josef called.

For a moment, Mara wondered if the three soldiers were trying to poison the slaves, but the first mug Josef filled was his own. As if to prove it was safe, he took a swig as the others began distributing mugs of ale.

"Well, now it's a real party!" Mara called out, and the crowd cheered. She brushed the hair from her eyes and continued to sing a lively Sangoran folk song that she claimed was impossible not to dance along to.

She must have been right, because everyone was moving with the rhythm. Even here, in the depths of hell's frozen doorstep, there was joy.

She watched from her place on the stand as the slaves huddled around the fire laughing and talking one with another. These were the first true smiles she'd seen in weeks, and she took it all in.

She said nothing as she sat on the edge of the wobbly stage and just allowed herself to exist and enjoy her people's collective happiness, for it was her own. Alia and Kamil climbed onto the stage next to her with drinks in hand.

"What, none for me?" Mara asked, leaning back on her hands. She brushed her hair out of her face again as the orange light flickered in her eyes. She picked her floppy, oversized hat from the stage and pulled it on.

"Josef insisted he get to bring you yours," Alia said.

"…Of course he did," Mara replied.

Alia chuckled and clapped her on the knee.

"*You know you're going to have to break that poor boy's heart sooner or later, right?*" Kamil asked.

Mara groaned and buried her face in her hands.

Soon enough, Josef brought her over a mug, which she accepted with a gracious smile, and then she invited him to join herself, Kamil, and Alia.

He shook his head. "I can't stay."

"Why not?" Mara asked. "Come on, let loose a little."

Josef hesitated and looked over his shoulder at his friends who were now mingling with the crowd. He nodded and his face lit up as Mara patted the stage to her left. He climbed up and sat next to her. She continued to watch her people enjoy themselves and took a sip of her drink.

"If it's not weird to say—" Josef stopped half-way through the sentence as if he were damming the words from flowing out.

"It's not," Mara said with a reassuring chuckle.

"Okay, well, I think you have the most beautiful voice I've ever heard."

Mara could practically feel the nervous energy exuding from the man's mind.

"Well, thank you," Mara said. "It's not something I share with many people anymore."

"You should," Josef replied. "Didn't your ma ever teach you sharing is…"

He trailed off, and Mara shook her head with a laugh at his failed attempt at what she attempted was flirting.

"Thank you," Mara said, nodding down at the cup, "for this."

"I can get you more," he said.

"No, not for me. For them. It made a good night even better. I'm not sure when they'll get another."

Josef nodded. "And don't worry about where it came from. We didn't steal it, so no one will be punished or anything."

The thought hadn't even crossed Mara's mind, but now she was a little suspicious. She glanced over and noticed that Kamil and Alia had disappeared. Perhaps it was a hint for her to do as Kamil said and 'break that poor boy's heart.'

She shook her head and let out a slow sigh.

"I've never heard of there being a king of Sangora or anything," he said. She knew the comment wasn't just idle small talk.

"Valistaran Talohir?"

"I mean, now. He died."

"Nope, no king."

"No…*perspective* kings?" he added.

Mara looked down at the ground with a smile.

"No. There will never be another king of Sangora."

"There could be," Josef said.

"No, I mean, by my design, there won't be," Mara said, her heart thundering in her chest. "Kings just cause too much trouble."

Josef laughed. "Yeah, I don't think I'd ever want to be one. I didn't mean I wanted to be your—"

He cut himself off again, and behind her friendly smile, Mara was screaming in her mind.

"Kamil, you coward, get back here. Help me."

Kamil projected a feeling of pure amusement into Mara's mind as his only response, wherever he and Alia were now.

"But no perspective…anyone?"

Mara smiled into her empty mug.

"A perspective someone, yes." Her tender answer was met with no response, and she didn't want to look up to see Josef's shattered heart etched on his expression. "Someone who cares about me and always has. Always will."

"I think there are a lot of those," Josef said, gesturing to the crowd. "Your people really love you. And, well, the soldiers are right, you know. I—I do fancy you."

"Oh, Josef, you know that's not what I mean," Mara said, turning her head to look into his face. He nodded.

"Yeah, I know, I know. You're strong and intelligent, and, well, beautiful, of course. And, well—I just couldn't live with myself if I didn't try. Can't blame me, right?"

"Of course not! Josef, don't ever lose that confidence. Even if it's just a single moment of courage," Mara said. "I've noticed that about you."

"I'm not confident," Josef replied. A look of shame crossed his face. "Maybe if I was braver, I could make a difference here."

"No, you're wrong. You do have moments of courage. It took bravery to stand up for me against the officers. To come here tonight to share your drinks with the slaves. To get me and my friends into the same house," Mara said. "You're a good man, Josef Romanik. You'll get there. Keep defending the people and things you love. Keep that fire in all aspects of your life."

As she said the word 'fire', her mind turned to that 'perspective someone' she had mentioned earlier, and she smiled.

"Do they know?"

"Who?" Mara asked. "Know what?"

"That person you love. Have you told them?"

"That I love him?" Mara asked, and Josef nodded. "He knows—even if I've never..."

She hated that she'd never been able to open herself up enough to say those words to him, no matter how she felt.

"Well, I should probably go now. We've been gone a while, and...well, yeah." Josef hopped down from the stage, and Mara did the same. He turned to walk away, but she grabbed his shoulder.

"Without saying goodbye?" she asked. She held out her arms and gave him a quick hug but didn't linger.

"I'll do what I can to help your people," he said. "To quote that line of your song, 'whatever it takes', right?"

Her mind once again turned to Aleksander. She didn't repeat the line. That was reserved for him alone.

"Right. Goodnight, Josef. Stay safe."

Josef bowed his head, and he was on his way.

The last of the concert goers thanked Mara for the night. Baba Boggy smothered her with kisses, and Constanta wrapped her in a massive hug.

"Mara, really quick, I'd like you to meet Razvan," Constanta said. "He's a Walker, and he can help us with *you know what.*"

"It's very good to meet you, Razvan," Mara said. "I look forward to working with you."

She knew how she said it made it sound like a potential business deal, and she hated it.

"Thank you again," Constanta said, waving goodbye.

"Of course! Now, go get some rest, you," Mara said. As Constanta and Razvan departed, Mara settled down on the front stoop of her hut.

She was still smiling from ear to ear as Kamil and Alia approached. Alia bent down and planted a soft kiss on her forehead.

"That was lovely, Mara," she said and opened the door.

"*It really was,*" Kamil said. Alia held the door for him, but he shook his head. Alia nodded and closed it behind her. He sat down next to Mara on the step.

"You think they enjoyed it?"

"*Does that even need to be said?*"

"I just hoped it'd give them some hope or fun, something I wish we would have had in Talohira, you know?"

Kamil nodded as the wind carried dying bits of the bonfire away, scattering them across the frozen ground.

"*Can I tell you something I've suspected for a long time?*"

"Of course." She rested her head on her his shoulder.

"*Valeniya has said multiple times that you are the 'brightest of all of us.' I don't think that's a metaphor. That's not really her thing. To her, I think it's literal.*"

"She's a straight-talker, that one," Mara agreed.

"She can see anyone with her powers, no matter where they are, but people with abilities are brighter to her. You never knew what your powers were in the Talohiran camp, and you've denied having them on multiple occasions before you discovered how to give them to yourself."

Mara smirked. "Am I on trial, Mr. Ramzi?"

Kamil chuckled.

"I'm too tired to think of some kind of a 'you're guilty of doing such and such' pun or joke, but let's pretend I did," Kamil said.

Mara chuckled. "I'm sure it'd be *very* funny."

"Well, like Mindspeakers, Dragonsouls, Telekinetiks, Soulreaders, and others, you were born with an innate gift. I can sense it in you with my own," Kamil thought. *"Sorry, Thanatan calls them his 'gifts', so I'll rephrase. Abilities. Magic. Powers. Whatever."*

Mara nodded. "Go on."

"There is a very rare ability—I've only met two other people with it. One in Kurash, and one in our slave camp. They both had the ability to inspire."

Mara laughed out loud.

"You think my ability is to give people hope?"

"To hope. To dream. To keep going. You have natural charisma and leadership skills that amplify that power, but it's something more than that. Something we can all feel but can't explain. You are a Hopebringer."

She lifted her head from his shoulder to look at him, and tears formed in the corners of her eyes. "Really?"

"There's a reason none of us give up when we're around you. You make us want to be better, to keep fighting."

"Does that mean people only like me because—"

She stopped abruptly, not wanting to finish the sentence.

"No, *although I'm sure it helps. It isn't like the pheromones given off by the Queen's Control at close proximity. It's… It's hard to explain. You are a light to the downtrodden. I don't want you to think this has nothing to do with your own talents, because it has everything to do with them.*"

"What do you mean?"

"*The ability is connected with your own resolve and desire to help.*"

Mara bit her lip. "There have been so many times where I've given up—where I've been broken and…"

She trailed off, and they were both silent for a moment.

"*But you never let* us *get to that point, and you always, always put yourself back together.*"

Mara thought back to her conversation with Hanna soon after her aneurysm when she had told her similar things. Tears streamed from her eyes, and she pulled Kamil close.

"*Ready to go inside?*" Kamil asked when she pulled away. Mara nodded and led the way inside, careful not to awaken Alia who had snuck by them several minutes earlier and was already snoring.

Mara settled down on her uncomfortable cot and pulled the ugly, faded quilt over herself as she lay down.

Spring came to Thanatanos that year. It was late in Sangora and Talohira, but green fields and blue skies returned there as well. But it never did for the slaves in the depths of the north in the slave camp called Tazovski.

And despite that, Mara Bartunek fell asleep happy.

DEAR MARA

The days were long, and the nights far too short to get any adequate rest. On one such evening, Mara sat behind their shallow wash basin in the corner scrubbing a bloodstain out of a pair of her trousers. She'd already cleaned all of Alia's clothes while she slept, and they were now hanging to dry. Kamil had insisted that she rest and not worry about his dirty laundry, to which she'd promised she wouldn't with an exaggerated wink.

Kamil was now sitting on his cot scribbling something on a piece of spare parchment with a chunk of sharpened charcoal. To her joy, Mara watched a soft smile grow on his face as he did so.

Mara hoped whatever Kamil was doing would help him feel better. He'd had a particularly harsh day of work, but he was even more exhausted because he'd been busy using his powers to help several slaves dull recent traumatic memories. None of the trio had spoken much since early that morning.

She furrowed her brow and draped the trousers over the side of the washbasin then scrubbed at the stain with all her might, her tongue sticking from the corner of her mouth as she did so. She let out the breath she'd been holding and glared at the bloodstain, surrendering to the fact that it wasn't going to come out.

"At least it'll help with the smell, huh?" Mara asked.

Kamil glanced up. "*What?*"

"Oh, sorry. No context. Never mind." She squeezed the water out of the pants and draped the waistband over the doorknob to dry. "What are you up to?"

"*Oh, it's nothing. Just drawing.*"

Mara sat next to him and smiled, laying her head on his shoulder. He had sketched a simple drawing of the three of them.

"I know this is probably stupid, but can I have it?"

"*Really?*"

Mara nodded. "I love it."

"*Then it's yours. I'm just doodling.*"

He nodded as he finished scribbling Alia's hair. As he handed it over, Mara saw a second sheet of parchment on Kamil's thigh with his elegant handwriting scrawled across it.

"What's that?" The words blurted out, and she regretted asking, in case it was something private.

"*Sometimes I write letters to myself. Past Kamil, Future Kamil. It's therapeutic.*" Mara sat up. Kamil handed her a bit of charcoal and a sheet of parchment. "*Want to try?*"

"It's like you can read my mind or something," Mara said with a wink. "I'd love to."

She took the paper and rolled the charcoal stick with her fingertips, staining them black. Kamil shut his eyes and rested his head on his pillow, and Mara slumped back against the wall next to him as she thought about what to write.

Mara—

I know that you will never read this because you are no longer with us, but I never got to say goodbye. Please know that my heart breaks for you every single day, you sweet girl. I wish I could hold you and take away your pain. I can't, but you did it for me so that I won't ever have to. I wish I could tell you that everything will be okay. But that is a lie.

Everything is not going to be okay. People are going to hurt you. You're going to hurt people. People will die. People will leave you. But that's okay. Everything that happens is going to make you into someone I love with my whole soul. (And so many others do too.) You can't see it yet, but you will. I promise. People will love you, and there are people who will never leave you. There are people who will never hurt you. They'll find you, and you will find them.

Thank you for what you have done for me. Because you went through everything you did. That means I won't have to. From the very depths of my soul. Thank you. You have made me who I am. and I owe my whole self to you. I love you..

-Me

She got up without waking Kamil and lay down in her own bed, pulling the scratchy blanket up over her chest. She let out a contented sigh and slipped both the letter and Kamil's drawing into her pocket.

She didn't sleep well that night, but whenever anxious thoughts of pain and grief filled her mind, she looked to Kamil and Alia, and simply seeing their sleeping faces calmed her.

She had found people that loved her and would never leave her—and she would die before she let anything happen to them.

And then, with a mischievous grin, she snuck out of bed to wash Kamil's dirty clothes.

CHAPTER THIRTY-FIVE
LOST TO DARKNESS

Several days after Mara's impromptu concert, the thick clouds finally parted, revealing the pale blue of the sky above, and it had been relatively sunny for a majority of the day. However, without the blanket of clouds, the world became even more frigid.

Mara had been excused from her duties building more housing for the rest of the week. Instead, she had received a command for the 'Sangoran Songbird' to come to Mazanek's home in the soldiers' village. Privates Josef and Damiani were the ones to retrieve her from her hut and guide her there.

"I have to tell you something," Josef muttered as soon as Damiani was out of earshot. "Before you hear this anywhere else—oh, by the gods, I don't know how to say this."

"What?" Mara asked.

"They said that if I do certain things, I get…well…"

"You get what?" Mara asked. "What have you done?"

"I get, well, *you*," Josef said. Mara furrowed her brow and crossed her arms across her chest. He hastily added, "Not that I want—no, that's not what I mean. They're all joking that I fancy you. They know. So, the sergeant said that if I do something, they'll give me you. I didn't explain that any better this time… Let me start over."

"Probably a good idea."

"If I do these things, they'll free you. They're giving prisoners to the soldiers as, well, how do I put this…as companions?"

"A poor choice of words. The word 'companion' implies a choice on the woman's part."

"Sorry," Josef said. "You're right."

Mara stopped. "Don't you dare tell me that's where we're going right now."

"No, no! Of course not." Josef shook his hands in protest. "Mazanek is just requesting your singing. But they said they'd give you to me, but I don't want that. But you won't have to work in the camp anymore. You'll be free to come and go as you please. I can even get you out of here. But—"

"No. I'm getting *everyone* out of here. All my people. Not just myself," Mara replied.

"But if you were free, it'd be easier for you to help them, don't you think? You could go get reinforcements, or…" His face was screwed up in frustration. "I just want to help."

"I appreciate that," Mara said with a gentle smile. "I really do. But whatever they want you to do can't be worth it."

The thought that the officers were 'giving' the slaves away was sickening, and Mara could see the anguish in Josef's eyes at having to participate in the evil here.

They were almost to the village, and Damiani called something to them that was lost on them due to the distance.

"I thought it was a way I could help. I'm sorry," Josef said. "Is there anything else I can do? I don't have much else to offer."

"What do they want you to do, Josef? What the hell have you agreed to?"

"They want me to do the executions today," he said after a long hesitation. "There aren't many, but they know I've been avoiding it. I'm not assigned to oversee my first executions until my first promotion, but they all know I've been dreading it. A lot of us have. But if I volunteer to do it early—"

"No."

"No?"

"No. I can't believe that you would even entertain the thought of killing—how many?"

"Ten."

"Goddesses… Killing ten people just to free me?" Mara stopped in her tracks, massaging the bridge of her nose. Her wings trembled in anger, and she considered striking the young man. "If you thought I'd be flattered by—"

"No, that's not what I meant," Josef said.

"It's what you said."

Josef hung his head. "They're going to die regardless. I thought maybe, I'd at least be helping you somehow."

"And in the process lose your soul," Mara said as they began to walk again. The frozen snow crunched beneath her boots. "Believe me, I'm not worth it."

"I know," Josef said. He winced. "Not that you're not—"

Mara chuckled. "Oh?"

"Well, just to be honest, I don't know how much of my soul is left anyway." He gestured to the camp. "What more can I lose?"

"If you really want to help, I need information. Can you do that?"

"Yes, but if they find out—"

Damiani stood waiting for them and whistled as Mara approached.

"The songbird and the lovebird have arrived!" he called with a laugh. He opened the gate into the village.

"Sorry," Josef said, his voice trembling. "Doesn't it bother you?"

"No. It's nothing new to me," Mara lied.

Of course, it did. Every single time.

"But it shouldn't be. An empress shouldn't have to deal with people like—"

"An empress, or any woman?"

Josef didn't answer. "The latter, of course. I just meant, you're a strong woman and—well, that was stupid. I don't know how to help."

"In-for-ma-tion."

"Right. Sorry."

Mara explained her plan to Josef as they walked, and he nodded, making mental notes of everything she needed.

Everything from the time between guard shifts, arrival times and dates for trains, and much more.

"Get that information to my friends Kamil and Alia just in case I don't make it back."

Damiani was shouting at them again.

"You will," Josef said. Mara raised an eyebrow. "Okay, yes. I'll do it."

"Thank you."

"Listen, if you do get out of here…" Josef said, trailing off. "Could you…"

"Speak your mind," Mara said.

"Will you help me get out, too?" he asked. "Or if you can't, can you at least write to my mother in Zubaras? She doesn't even know where I am, and you know how mothers are. They read our letters before they go out, so I can't tell her myself. I can give you her information, and—"

Mara nodded. "I'll do my best."

"I'm going to try to get statements from everyone who doesn't approve of what's happening and get it to—well, I don't know who, but I'll get it to someone who will listen."

"That's very noble," Mara said, touching him on the shoulder.

Damiani knocked on the door of Mazanek's house, and a servant let them inside. Mara sneered at the opulence of it all: gold on the railings and fixtures, paintings of scenes from Thannish history. It was like a ruby amongst pebbles. Or, more appropriate, like a cheap, glass ruby, as it felt like a poor imitation of the Thannish palace.

Mazanek greeted them with open arms as they approached.

"Hello, my songbird and lovebird!" he called. So, the nicknames had spread.

Josef stood at attention, but Mara knew it tortured him.

"Who do you think you are?" Mara said.

"Meaning?" Mazanek asked. Mara shook her head and gestured to the needless luxury. "I could banter with your lovely self all day. Alas, you have matters to attend to," Mazanek said, gesturing over his shoulder for her to follow. "Privates Romanik and Damiani, you are relieved."

Josef and Damiani saluted and departed through the front door, leaving Mara alone with the senior sergeant. Mazanek took off his officer's cap and hung it on the banister leading upstairs.

"You won't be singing today," he said as he led her through a doorway behind the stairs that led into a basement.

"You shouldn't lead the way. I could push you down the stairs, you know," Mara said as he stepped down into the chamber below. He chuckled in response but said nothing in response.

Mara felt some kind of influence tug on her mind, and despite her better judgment, she descended after him. He led her down a hallway reminiscent of a hospital, and she felt the pull on her thoughts urging her to follow. She cursed herself for not stopping herself.

A scream echoed from somewhere within the facility.

"What is this?" she demanded.

She tried to strike him, but neither her wing nor fist would obey her. She repeated her question, louder this time.

He did not answer. He opened a door into a smaller chamber filled with strange equipment and an operating table stained with blood. Two men in white aprons and masks greeted Mazanek without saying a word, and he nodded and spoke to them in a hushed tone.

"Your powers are artificial, are they not?" Mazanek asked.

She tried to resist, but she felt the strange influence in her mind force her to speak the truth. And then she understood: the two masked doctors in the chamber were Mindspeakers.

"Yes."

"I'll let you in on a little secret of our operation here," Mazanek said. "We're trying to replicate what Sangora has done with giving people abilities. You know, it's a shame for your Night Witches that you don't give more people powers. You really could have an unstoppable army."

"There are more powerful things in this world than the ability to kill and destroy," Mara said.

Mazanek scoffed. "Like what, love?"

"I can't wait to watch your world fall apart."

"Anyway. I've been studying history. *Your* history. What was it about you that King Valistaran Talohir stopped his Night Witches from killing you? Up on that tower when they took you—why didn't they kill you? They killed others, so why not *you?*"

"Your guess is as good as mine."

"He knew something about you. He knew there was something there…something powerful. Not all your powers are artificial, are they?"

It couldn't be a coincidence that he was asking the question so soon after the conversation she'd had with Kamil. She glared at him and cocked her head. She felt the Mindspeakers influence forcing her to reveal the truth.

She fought their influence, straining her mind as much as she could without triggering a seizure or stroke.

"To my knowledge, they all are."

"No. There's something else there. Why take a random Thannish peasant from a slave camp and turn her into a Night Witch? The *queen* of all Night Witches? Why give her abilities?"

"Valistaran made me into a weapon, and nothing more. I wanted revenge, and he could give it to me."

"Yes, but why *you?*" Mazanek insisted. "Out of everyone in his kingdom, he chose you."

"I don't think he knew about me before my transition," Mara said. "Your theory is wrong."

"No, no it isn't. I've had Talohirans brought here and interrogated. I've had my Mindspeakers invade the minds of so many Night Witches—many of which were actually there the night you were taken. I even found one of the scientists who performed your operation. She died here, by the way."

"You're not *just* a sergeant, are you?" Mara asked.

"Smart girl," Mazanek said. "Valistaran's camps were to gather people with powers so that my country couldn't use them against him. This camp is to figure out how to create abilities so that Thanatanos can once and for all establish its place as the one true kingdom."

"You know, I'm not a fan of this whole evil scientist act you have going on," Mara said. "My little brother always told me that in the legends from the Deadlands, the villain always gave away his master plan just before the hero defeated them and saved the day."

"Go ahead," Mazanek said, his arms outstretched as if issuing her a challenge to strike him. "Kill me."

She tried, but the Mindspeakers' hold on her was too great. Instead, she felt her feet guiding her toward the operating table.

"When I found out King Verahim was waiting for you to be removed from the picture before beginning the invasion, I moved heaven and earth to get you transferred to *my* camp, and now, I have the final, missing piece of my puzzle."

The Mindspeakers stepped forward and closed their eyes, and she felt the tendrils of their consciousness snake into her own. She tried to fight it, but she felt herself falling asleep.

"Now, I get to dissect you and find out just what made you so special. Where does that power come from? And what makes your people flock to you?"

And then, Mara's eyes closed, and she lost herself to darkness as one of the mindspeaking doctors raised a scalpel.

CHAPTER THIRTY-SIX

THE HEART OF THE EMPRESS

Ten minutes. According to Josef, that's all they were going to have, and the first three had not gone according to plan.

They had to succeed now or lose their chance, because another opportunity like this wouldn't come around for another two months when the next supply train rolled into Tazovski. By then, it would be too late; Mara would be dead.

Constanta had gathered allies, just as Mara had requested. Their plan had been meticulously laid out, and everyone knew their parts. Each of those parts had gone up in literal smoke and flame.

Razvan, the Sangoran Walker Constanta had recruited, had been the one to set off the first explosion. As soon as the flames somehow hidden in the earth burst from the ground beneath him, he managed to teleport away in a flurry of dark smoke.

He reappeared several yards away, his coat on fire, but he was able to roll to smother the flames.

The initial flaw in the plan was that Mara had never returned from the soldiers' village since she was taken there three days ago. Likewise, Josef never showed up at the agreed upon time.

There were supposed to be ten minutes between the time the newly arrived soldiers left the train and the departing ones arrived. Thus, the second problem. The new arrivals were lingering on the train platform drinking Opikorla and smoking foul smelling cigars.

The third problem, which Razvan had so painfully discovered, was that the train platform was surrounded with some sort of devices rigged to explode when stepped upon. Not only had the buried explosive injured him, but it had also drawn the attention of the soldiers.

And now, those soldiers were grabbing Kamil, Alia, Constanta, and the other members of her crew, the two Odauthians named Olafur and Runar, and three Talohirans, Grygori, Dobromil, and Katerina.

With a scream, Constanta thrust the makeshift wing-blades she had originally made for Mara into a soldier's chest. She drew her wings back, and the man's body hit the ground, Constanta's face splashed with blood. She looked horrified at what she had done, and Kamil scooped up the man's sword.

"*We need to keep going,*" Kamil mindspoke to her with a sympathetic look. She nodded and choked back the vomit.

Just then, another explosion rocked the world to their right, throwing Constanta and Kamil to the ground. Kamil looked up in horror to see Grygori's charred body crumpled on the ground, his clothes on fire.

Alia rushed to his side and turned him over only to see his eyes vacant and dead. Her face screwed up with tears, and she gasped as dark teleportation mist surrounded her. Razvan grabbed her wrist, and then they were gone.

As a soldier pointed a crossbow at Kamil's head, he tried to reach out with his mind to force the man to forget what he was doing, but to his horror, he couldn't sense anyone's thoughts. He stumbled backward, and just before the man pulled the trigger, Olafur, the bigger of the two burly Odauthians, struck the man over the head with a rock, cracking his skull.

Before leading Kamil away, Olafur planted a heavy boot against a soldier's chest. The soldier hit the ground, which set off another of the explosives, leaving the man without an arm. Kamil nodded to Olafur in thanks, unable to mindspeak to him.

Nearby, with all her expert skill as a former soldier in Talohira's navy, Katerina thrust a sharpened kitchen knife between a soldier's ribs. She withdrew the weapon and stabbed a second guard again and again.

"Razvan!" Katerina shouted as five other soldiers replaced the dead man. "Get us out of here!"

The Walker appeared, and to the soldiers' dismay, they disappeared in a burst of teleportation smoke, leaving the mass of soldiers alone at the train station.

When Katerina opened her eyes, she found herself still holding the bloodied knife far from the train platform. The others were kneeling in a circle around someone on the ground, and she and Razvan stood guard just in case the soldiers spotted them.

"What happened?" Katerina asked.

"Grygori's dead. And Dobromil will be if I can't concentrate," replied Alia. Katerina peered over the top of Alia's head just in time to see the Kurashian healer slide two of her fingers into a disgusting wound in Dobromil's side. Katerina turned away; it was too horrible to look.

"*They have a Mindspeaker,*" said Kamil to their minds. "*Someone was blocking my powers. I'm sorry, I would have been able to get you all out of there if not for them.*"

"No need to take the blame," Constanta said. "Everything that could have gone wrong did. Not just your part."

Kamil nodded as Dobromil squirmed on the ground.

"Stay still, I have to mend your muscles before I can close the wound," Alia said, and the injured Talohiran man groaned on the ground.

Kamil pushed past Katerina and Razvan as they stood guard. He looked toward the train station.

"*I have an idea,*" he said, reaching out with his mind.

"Be careful," Alia said. "If they have a Mindspeaker too, then—"

She stopped mid-sentence as she willed the fibers of Dobromil's muscles to sew themselves together. When that was done, she drew her red-stained fingers out of his side and massaged the wound closed.

Dobromil thanked her as the two Odauthians helped him to his feet just as the soldiers near the train cheered. Several of the explosives went off with a boom, bathing the station in a momentary glow.

"What'd you do?" Razvan asked.

"*I made them think they killed us and threw our bodies on the explosives,*" Kamil explained. "*It'll buy us some time until they realize there is only one body.*"

"Where are we, anyway?" Alia asked, looking around for the first time. They were behind a building of concrete and steel covered in graffiti. It was probably scrawled there by younger soldiers, as most of the drawings were of particular body parts and vulgar words.

"We're in the soldiers' village," Razvan said. "I figured since the first part of the plan failed, we should get started on the second part and find out what happened to the empress."

"Dobro, do you need to go back to the village?" Constanta asked.

Dobromil shook his head. "No, I'm fine. You guys need me. Besides, Alia fixed me all up. Good to go!"

He was right. Constanta had recruited him for his skills as a former thief—skills that might be needed to steal Mazanek's communication device, whatever it was.

Light washed over their faces for a moment as the new train took the bend toward the railroad that led to the station.

"Well, there it is," Dobromil said.

"No use dwelling on our failure," Constanta said. "I'm just not sure if we'll succeed in the next part of the plan without Mara."

The others nodded.

"Then obviously, finding her has to be our top priority," Alia said. "If I had to guess, Mazanek has her at his residence."

"If she's alive," Razvan said.

"She is." Alia glared until Razvan looked away.

"Razvan. Can you get us in?" Alia asked.

"Of course," the Walker replied.

Katerina shook her head. "And once we're all in, what do we do about the soldiers? They're heavily armed. We're not going to just go in, kill everyone, and walk out. I say Razvan scouts ahead."

"I can, or our Mindspeaker can look inside without putting ourselves in danger," the Walker replied in his thick northern Sangoran accent. He scowled and turned to Kamil.

"I can't sense anyone inside."

"Well, that's good for us then, right?" Alia asked.

"Not necessarily. They might have another Mindspeaker in there keeping me from using my powers," Kamil replied. *"But that might mean there's something there worth hiding from me."*

"There's strength in numbers, so I don't think we should split up," Constanta suggested. "I still think Razvan should get us in, and then we can work from there. We can't send him in alone to die for us. We can't lose anyone else…"

She trailed off, and everyone's thoughts turned to Grygori. They each knew that the image of his body burning in the snow would be stained on their minds forevermore.

"Okay, I can do it," Razvan said. He set his jaw and took a deep breath in through his nose. One problem. I can't vanish through walls. We'll have to break a window, and it could get us caught."

"We'll have to risk it," Alia said, and the others nodded.

They heard footsteps, and the group froze against the graffitied wall. Voices followed. Lots of them. Alia turned to Kamil to see his face screwed up in concentration.

Soon, the soldiers moved on, and Kamil gestured for the others to hurry away. They followed without question, though none of them knew what was happening. The two Odauthians, Olafur and Runar watched over them from behind.

"This was a bad idea. We should go," Kamil said to everyone's minds. *"There's going to be some kind of gathering soon to welcome someone named Lieutenant Rezinchek.*

Alia looked over her shoulder to see several men preparing a stage while others filed into the center of the town in their best military attire. She gasped as one of them stared in their direction but did not react, instead staring straight through them.

"I'm convincing their brains they don't see or hear us, but I can't keep it up for long, especially if all the soldiers in Tazovski will be here," Kamil explained. *"We need to go."*

Alia grabbed Kamil's shoulder. "I'm not leaving her."

Kamil responded with sad eyes, and Alia understood; he didn't believe that Mara could still be alive.

"I don't want to risk anyone else. She wouldn't want us to."

Just as he thought the words, the door to Mazanek's house opened, and Razvan sprinted forward, vanishing into the burst of dark smoke. He reappeared inside the building just as Mazanek and several other soldiers closed the door behind them.

"Kamil?" Katerina asked, her heart racing. "Can you sense Razvan?"

Kamil shook his head. That confirmed his theory that something or someone was blocking his powers, then.

The Tazovski soldiers, including Mazanek, stood at attention, their hands to their brows, as a woman in a uniform plastered with commendations and medals approached.

The door to Mazanek's house swung open, and the group hurried inside. Razvan shut the door behind them just as Kamil collapsed to his knees, nearly hyperventilating.

"Are you alright?" Razvan asked.

Kamil held his forehead, and Runar the Odauthian helped him to his feet and supported him as they stood in the entrance chamber.

"Well, we're here," Alia said. She gave Kamil a compassionate expression, and he nodded, still out of breath.

"I'm okay."

"I'm sorry it took so long to get the door open. I had to hide the body," Razvan said, gesturing to a large potted fern.

A pair of military-issued boots stuck out almost comically from behind it.

"Dead?" Alia asked as she began drawing the curtains over the high windows.

Razvan shook his head. "No, just knocked out. Probably. Kat, I got you this," Razvan said as he shook his head. He handed her the sword he'd taken from the unconscious soldier.

Alia looked over the group and counted heads to make sure everyone was there. Kamil, Constanta, Katerina, Dobromil, Razvan, Olafur, and Runar. Good. Although she didn't know any of them except Constanta and Kamil, she was still determined to keep them safe.

"Any ideas?" Katerina asked, her tone impatient. "We've been waiting forever. How do we even know what we're looking for is here? What if Mazanek has it on him?"

It was definitely a possibility, but no one replied. A staircase with a dark green rug and railings covered in gold leaf led upward, while two hallways ran all the way to the back of the house, each lined with doors.

"Well, up or down?" Dobromil asked.

"*I can sense something above,*" Kamil said. "*It's almost like it wants me to find it.*"

"A trap?" Alia asked. Kamil shook his head.

"*No. I think it's what we're here for.*"

"Okay, be safe," Alia said. "Razvan, Olafur, will you come with me?"

The Walker and the Odauthian nodded. The others accompanied Kamil upstairs while Alia, Razvan, and Olafur began to explore the hallway to the left of the staircase. They met no resistance as they tried each of the doors, most of which were unlocked.

"Keep us safe," Alia said in simple Thannish to Olafur, who nodded with a charming grin. She noticed his fists were already balled at his sides, ready for a fight should one arise.

In the first hallway, they found an empty kitchen, two sitting rooms, a washroom, and the dining room. They tried the other side, finding a library with several comfortable chairs, some empty bookshelves and a desk with nothing inside. That left only one door.

It was the only one down both hallways that was locked. Razvan tried to peer through the lock as if he could teleport through it, but Olafur pushed him aside and rammed the door with his broad shoulder, knocking it off its overly extravagant, brass hinges.

"They'll have heard that," Razvan said.

The stairs led straight down into a cellar of some kind lined with lit torches. Footsteps and muffled voices came from a second door at the bottom. They crept toward it, and Alia put her ear to the door to eavesdrop on the conversation taking place inside.

"Should we get the others?" Razvan whispered.

Before Alia could answer, the door opened inward. Alia stumbled inside, and both she and a man in a Purist mask and robes cried out in surprise. Olafur grabbed the cultist by the neck and slammed his head hard against the wall.

Alia clutched her heart and got to her feet, her mind racing. They were standing in some kind of medical facility with operating tables, shelves full of tools, supplies, and jarred medicine.

"What in the name of Lord Jakoni is this place?" Razvan asked as they wandered inside. Olafur picked up a vile of red liquid and peered inside.

"Blood," he said in Thannish, his eyes wide. "Yes?"

He handed it to Alia who quickly put it back where he had found it.

"I sure hope not," she whispered, but she knew he was right. Alia and Razvan led the way with Olafur watching their backs, the Purist's dagger in his hand.

"Who was he talking to?" Razvan said in a low tone. Alia shook her head and put a finger to her lips as approached a door that had been left ajar.

"Oh, by Kadir!" she swore, her dark eyes wide.

She rushed into the room, and Olafur and Razvan hurried in after her. What they saw made them both stop cold, but Alia sprang into action.

Mara was lying unconscious, or more likely, dead, covered with a blanket upon an operating table. Her wings and limbs were all strapped down, and needles connected to tubes stained with her blood protruded from veins on her bare arms and legs.

The leathery membrane and tips of her wings were shredded and full of holes as if whatever cruel surgeon had begun the operation had no idea what he was looking for and had forgotten to close the wounds. Bloodied bandages and an insufficient amount of gauze were plastered to her arms.

"Oh, Mara, you sweet girl," Alia whispered as she began to pull the needles from Mara's limbs. She turned to look at Razvan and Olafur. "Don't just stand there, get me some disinfectant, bandages, and some wet rags!"

"Aren't you a healer?" Razvan asked. "Why do you need—"

"Go!" Alia shouted, and Razvan began searching the facility for medical supplies while Olafur headed upstairs to the washroom for water and rags.

Alia massaged the lesser of the wounds to close them up, starting with Mara's arms. She sighed with relief as the flesh bound together. She was alive, then. She found Mara's weak pulse before removing the straps from her limbs.

"Oh, honey," Alia whispered. "How are you still alive?"

She pulled the operating sheet halfway down Mara's bare chest and gasped as she saw a gaping wound just above her left breast. Tubes that had been forced straight into her heart led into a glass container beneath the table. Pins were set to separate the flesh, and Alia gasped as she watched Mara's heart pumping through the mutilated skin, muscle, and bone.

She felt her own heart breaking for her friend, and she couldn't stop the tears from welling in the corners of her eyes. Still, she kept her composure.

"I've got some bandages, disinfectant, some stuff for stitches, I think, and—"

As Razvan caught a glimpse of the wound in Mara's chest, he fainted and hit the ground with a thud.

"Useless," Alia muttered in annoyance.

She shook her head and swept her hair from her face with a bloodstained hand. She examined the gory, throbbing pit and winced as she withdrew shards of broken bone with a pair of tweezers the unconscious Walker had brought over.

Olafur returned holding two buckets and several fancy, monogrammed towels slung over his shoulder. He approached with concern etched across his bearded face.

"How can I help?" he asked in a thick accent very foreign to Alia's ears.

"Do you know how to clean wounds?" Alia asked as she removed the pins keeping the wound around Mara's heart open. She pantomimed washing her hands and then pointed at Mara's injuries.

"Clean, yes. Fix, not."

"Okay. Can you clean the wounds on her legs and wings? We don't want any infections," Alia said.

Olafur hadn't understood everything she said, but he nodded, determined to help. She instructed him how to disinfect the minor wounds and bandage them, and he went to work. She would have done it herself, but she knew she'd have to save her powers for closing the literal pit in Mara's chest. She still had no idea how Mara was still alive.

She had only healed a wound in someone's heart once, and that was a long time ago. Despite that, due to her training at the best healing centers in Talohira and Kurash, she had what she considered a perfect knowledge of human anatomy and physiology, including the structure of the heart and surrounding tissue and bone.

And so, she used that knowledge and her powers to disinfect and massage the wound until it began to tighten up like someone closing a fist. Strands of skin and muscle twisted together as she manipulated Mara's body to heal itself. When she deemed her progress sufficiently far along that she could move on to Mara's heart, she did so.

She laid her hand on her friend's chest then closed her eyes as she slid her fingers into the gaping wound, following the tube past Mara's lung to feel her faint heartbeat through the thin layer of fat that covered it. She let out a deep breath and allowed her powers to regulate and repair Mara's heart.

The tube squelched as she pulled it from the bloody wound. She let it go, and it dangled like a gory vine next to her. She lifted the sheet and sighed upon finding a needle and tube jutting out of Mara's hip. The area around the insertion point was bruised and infected. Mara stirred on the table as Alia slid the tube from deep within her bone.

"I know, I know, I'm so sorry, sweetheart," Alia said, hoping and praying to the fallen Supreme Ones and the Goddess of the Afterworld that she would not awaken while on the table, but most of all, that she would survive. "You're doing so great."

Every time her mind wandered to what dark power was keeping Mara alive, she pulled her thoughts back to focus on the task at hand. *She* would be the power that helped her live.

She placed her palm on the infection, closed her eyes, and willed it to seep out of Mara's flesh and into her own hand. An incessant itch tickled her skin, but she'd deal with it later. For now, she would take whatever infection she found into herself to save Mara's life. She focused on the wound in her friend's chest, ensuring that it wouldn't become infected before closing up.

"It will be okay," said Olafur, and Alia smiled.

"I know it will," Alia said, her heart beating fast and her mind fuzzy. "Thank you, friend."

She looked at the slight discoloration of the infection now festering in her own skin and groaned. She couldn't use that hand to heal Mara now, unless she found somewhere else to put the infection. And then, it came to her.

"Olafur, can you bring the dead guy over?"

Olafur did as he was told, dragging the Purist next to Alia's feet. She pulled the man's sleeve up and gripped his wrist, forcing the infection out of her own skin and into his. She looked up to see the Odauthian looking down at her with a sickened look, and she chuckled.

"Gross, right?"

Alia went back to work, placing her now clean palm on the tender flesh over Mara's heart while she gripped her hipbone with her other hand.

"What you are doing now?" Olafur asked.

"Blood is created in the bone marrow," Alia said, wincing from the stress it took to regulate Mara's heart while willing the marrow in her hipbone to accelerate its slow process. "I'm forcing it to work thousands of times faster than normal to produce more blood so that Mara doesn't bleed out. I honestly don't know how she hasn't already."

Judging by the needle and tube in Mara's hipbone, it was likely Mazanek's surgeons or scientists had had the same idea.

Olafur nodded, and Alia wondered how much he had understood. She glanced over, and to her surprise, he was cleaning and dressing Mara's minor wounds better than some of her students at the Academy of the Hidden Flame.

Alia hung her head as her energy began to wane, but she had to continue to help Mara's body to keep going—to keep fighting.

Just like Mara had always done for them.

When she was satisfied that Mara's heartbeat was quick enough to handle the new, stronger flow of blood, Alia moved on, tracing one finger away from the heart, and another toward it in order to manipulate the circulatory system and flow of blood throughout Mara's broken body. She slowed the flow next to major wounds and accelerated it elsewhere.

Now that Mara's heart, lung, and surrounding tissue were sewing themselves back together, Alia had to manipulate and mold Mara's sternum and ribs back into place and heal what had been chiseled away.

Creating new bone was much more difficult and painful than manipulating the body to create or repair existing tissue, so she exerted all the power she had left to extend the fractured bits of bone and bend the others back into place, closing up the flesh, fat, and muscle above it.

Mara's body trembled in pain, but she remained unconscious. Alia stumbled, and Olafur hurried over to support her.

"I will help you stand," he said. "Keep heal. I will not let fall."

She nodded in thanks as she brushed her hands over the wounds on Mara's limbs to pull the flesh back together. As she continued to heal, she drew out infection wherever she sensed it, and when too much had accumulated, she deposited it in the dead Purist's skin.

"I need a minute," Alia whispered, and Olafur nodded, helping her sit down on a nearby stool.

"I will continue?" Olafur asked, holding up the wet towels. Alia nodded, holding her throbbing head in her hands. Her powers, as well as the mental toll seeing a dear friend in such a state were draining her of all her strength.

Olafur used the wet rag to gently cleanse the dried blood from Mara's limbs where the wounds had now closed. Alia cursed in Kurashic under her breath as she saw that each wound had scarred.

Her world was spinning, but she forced herself to her feet. Olafur was gently wrapping the tips of Mara's wings with clean bandages.

"If you need," he said, gesturing to the last few clean towels. The rest were piled in a sopping, red mess on the ground.

Alia placed both palms on Mara's chest, influencing her lungs to accept the increased blood flow and take in air. She placed a loving hand on Mara's cheek and watched her eyes moving behind their lids.

"Almost done, sweetheart. Keep fighting."

As she watched the rise and fall of Mara's chest, she placed a hand over her heart one last time, forcing it to beat harder and her lungs to gulp in more air. She monitored the ebb and flow of oxygen throughout Mara's body, focusing on her heart and brain.

When her pulse and breathing were at a safer level, Alia placed one hand beneath Mara's back near her kidney, and the other at the base of her skull. A tear trailed from the corner of Mara's eye.

Alia's vision darkened as she manipulated Mara's body to produce all the hormones needed to dull her pain, to continue to regulate and heal her weakened organs and tissues, and others yet to wake her.

As she did so, Mara gasped, and she bolted upright. The sheet fell off of her and Olafur looked away.

"No, no, you need to lie down," Alia said. "It's okay, you're safe, and I've got you. It's okay. You're safe."

"What's happening?" Mara exclaimed. "Alia, Is that you? What—what did they—Alia—Alia, help!"

Alia helped her lie back down and stroked her dark hair, which was matted to her face with blood. "I'm here, honey."

"Saved me…"

"Then let's say my debt to you for saving my life a thousand times over is halfway repaid," Alia said, kissing Mara on the forehead. She clutched her friend's hand and felt her squeeze her fingers.

"Shuthran laah…"

The Kurashic words for *thank you.*

Olafur stood guard near the door.

Alia rested her head on her arms on the edge of the cot next to Mara's side. Soon, they were both asleep, hand in hand.

CHAPTER THIRTY-SEVEN
SCARS UNDONE

Back upstairs, Dobromil had picked the intricate lock on the reinforced door that led into Mazanek's bedroom. Now he, Kamil, Constanta, and the others were now rifling through his belongings in search of whatever entity or object was calling to Kamil.

"There's nothing here," said Constanta as Katerina opened a bottle of ink. "What are you doing?"

Katerina smiled and knocked the ink over with the back of her hand, ruining the open pages of a ledger of some kind.

"Oops, look what I've done," she said with a wink then gave Dobromil a high-five.

"Looks like enough of an accident," Kamil said. *"Make sure everything else is exactly where it should be."*

Constanta turned to him.

"You mindspoke!" she exclaimed. "Your powers are working again!"

Kamil let out a laugh. He'd been so focused on searching Mazanek's chamber that he hadn't even noticed he was able to communicate again until he subconsciously did so. He closed his eyes for a moment as he activated his powers, reaching out into the house.

"They found Mara. She's alive, but barely," Kamil said. *"Runar, can you go fetch them?"*

"Yes. Maybe they're having better luck than us," Runar said. The Odauthian headed out the door and back downstairs to find the others.

"Are they okay?" Constanta asked.

Kamil shook his head, sensing Mara's pain. He hurried out of the room while Katerina and Dobromil continued to search the bedroom. Constanta followed after him as he took the stairs two at a time, nearly tripping at the bottom.

"Wait up!" she called as Kamil descended into the laboratory facility beneath Mazanek's house.

"Mara!" Kamil said aloud. Constanta, Dobromil, and Katerina appeared behind him and poked their heads into the room as well.

"Give her some privacy, please," Alia said, shooing everyone except Kamil out of the room. "Go back upstairs. Do your jobs so we can get out of here."

He looked around and saw the dead Purist on the ground and wondered if the man had been the Mindspeaker blocking his powers.

Mara was sitting up, her back against the wall. She was wearing Olafur's massive coat with a vacant expression. In her hands was the simple drawing Kamil had drawn for her.

"What happened?"

Alia pulled him aside so that Mara wouldn't hear.

"Mazanek's men basically took her apart. From what she's said, they were trying to replicate the process she used to give herself powers. Based on what her wings look like right now, I think they were looking for the Queen's Control glands as well."

"By Kadir," Kamil swore. Alia nodded.

"That's what I said. She's…not okay," Alia said. "I'm not either."

"From seeing her like this?"

"Well, yes, but I've passed out twice since healing her from overusing my powers. You have no idea, Kam. It was horrible," Alia said.

Kamil could sense the images in Alia's mind, and he nearly threw up but said nothing of it. He sat in the chair next to Mara, and she looked up with a faint smile.

"How do I look?" she asked in a shaky voice.

"Never stronger."

Mara let out a dark chuckle.

"That's probably how I smell, too."

As she tried to stand, the front of Olafur's coat fell open just enough for Kamil to see the jagged scars like the face of a broken mirror extended away from her heart and up to her collarbone and down her left breast.

"I'll have Razvan get you back home," Kamil said.

Mara shook her head. "All of us, or none of us."

Kamil nodded and helped her to her feet. He knew he'd never convince her otherwise.

"I don't suppose you see my clothes anywhere?" she asked. Kamil found her coat, boots, socks, and gloves in a cupboard, but her other clothes had been cut off and discarded in a bin in the corner, along with some bloodied cloth.

"Any luck?" Mara asked, wincing as she moved.

"*Yes and no,*" Kamil replied. He pulled a set of surgeon's clothes from the cupboard and handed them to Alia.

"I meant with finding out how Mazanek has been communicating with the Magistrate," Mara said.

"*Oh. I think so. I can sense it upstairs,*" Kamil said. "*I had to check on you two. You're more important to me than that.*"

Mara stumbled over to Kamil and wrapped her arms around him. "Love you, buddy."

"*You too.*"

"We'll meet you up there," Mara said with a smile, despite the severe bruising on her face and neck.

Kamil nodded and headed back upstairs, following the pull of whatever was calling him. He followed the mental presence into Mazanek's private bed chamber where he found the others.

The room was just as pretentiously opulent as the rest of the building. A lion's head motif was carved, stitched, or printed on nearly every surface, and even more gold trimmed the bedframe, mirrors, and other furniture. Kamil began to suspect it was all fake.

"Nothing here either," said Constanta. "How are they?"

"*Alive,*" Kamil replied, the presence drawing him toward a wall panel carved with a snarling lion's face.

He pressed his palm against it, and it gave a satisfying click as he pushed it inward. It popped open, and a greenish glow radiated from inside a hidden crevice. The others hurried over.

Inside was a jagged chunk of glowing crystal with a flat face that swirled with shadow rather than reflecting the world around it.

Katerina reached down to grab it, but as it touched her skin, she yelped and dropped it to the ground. She winced and massaged the burned skin on her fingers.

Kamil pulled a frilly handkerchief from one of Mazanek's drawers and with great caution, gingerly scooped up the shard of mirror.

"What is that?" Constanta asked.

"A shard of Thanatan's Godmirror," a voice came from the hallway. Everyone whirled around to see Mara standing there dressed in an odd outfit of Olafur's oversized coat and some surgeon's scrubs. She motioned for Kamil to hand it over, and he obliged.

Alia helped her sit down in an uncomfortable, but plush chair in the corner. Mara gazed into the crystal's flat face. Shadows swirled within, and then, there, as faint as a memory upon waking, was Thanatan's now familiar voice.

"Mara."

Mara shut her eyes, and she could feel his presence fill her mind. The dust of glassy diamond appeared around her fingers and danced around her hand, pulled toward the crystal mirror. She tried again to summon the Godblade; the dust and crystal danced in the air around the shard of Godmirror, but nothing else happened.

"Where are you?" Mara asked.

And then, she saw a familiar face looking back at her. Not Thanatan or the Magistrate, but someone entirely unexpected: a student from Shanthah's academy – Nadezhda Babkova?

"Uh, hello?" Nadezhda's voice filled the room.

"Nadezhda?!" Mara asked. "Is that you? Where are you?"

"I'm—where are *you?* Yes! Shanthah, Hanna! Get over here, quick!" Nadezhda's voice called, distorted as if echoing as if she were speaking in a large, empty room. "We found her!"

The others listened, but Olafur and Runar muttered in their own language as they searched Mazanek's desk.

"Mara?!" This time, it was Shanthah's voice that came from the shard of Godmirror. She could see his surroundings, and then his face came into focus, materializing across the smoky surface. "Mara, are you alright?"

Before Mara could reply, Hanna's smiling face appeared on the surface of the glass, and she pushed Shanthah's head out of focus.

"Where are you? We'll come get you right now!"

Mara had to squint to make out Hanna's signs amongst the swirling shadows. She twisted in her seat, set the mirror on a nightstand, and signed back.

"Hello, my friend! You have no idea how happy I am to see you."

"You look horrible," Hanna signed back. *"Still better looking than anyone else I know, but what happened to you?"*

"Later. There's no time. Where is Hippo? Is he there with you?"

"Outside, yes," Hanna signed back.

"Kamil, I need you!" Mara called, and Kamil hurried to her side. *"Kamil and Alia are both here with me. They're okay. Go to Hippo. Hopefully, he'll be able to sense Kamil's power through the crystal, and he can come to us."*

"I can do that," Kamil mindspoke through the crystal.

As Hanna rushed outside, Mara could see her surroundings rushing past in a blur.

While she waited for Hanna to reach Hippo, Olafur handed her two leatherbound books he had drawn from the desk.

"What's this?" she asked.

"We think it's his diary," Olafur replied in Odauthian.

"Are you serious?" Mara replied in Old Icelandic, her eyes wide. "I can't wait."

She groaned as she stood before settling down into the chair behind the desk. She opened the snap on the diary and flipped it open to a random page.

"By the goddesses," Mara said with a laugh that pained her entire torso. *"Ow.* Listen to this: 'Today was a bad day. It was cold, and my itch is getting worse. I shouldn't have ordered those slaves over. I'm so uncomfortable'."

Her stomach twisted.

"Serves the perverted old fool right," Katerina muttered, and Alia nodded, taking the second leather tome from the desk as Mara flipped through the diary looking for clues.

11/5

Today I was made a sergeant. I've been waiting for this my entire life. I know it isn't a particularly prestigious position, and I had to fight to be able to continue my research in the least desirable post in the entire kingdom, but I've been told those that serve in the correctional camps are given more promotions and better postings in the future anyway. When I'm able to give our soldiers magic, I'll be promoted to general in no time. No one will ever oppose me or Thanatanos again.

I have to remember what Training Commander Szabo told me today: act as if you are already a general. Rule over everyone under you with justice. Not just supervise, rule. I take that that means I have to let go of my 'softer' tendencies. I hated hearing that in the academy and as a private over and over and over. 'Private Mazanek is too soft for this!' 'Private Mazanek has no privates!' 'Private Mazanek this, Private Mazanek that.' I'll show them. I'll show them all. I can do this. I know I can. I just have to be strong. I can't show weakness anymore. 'I'm happy to say no-privates Mazanek is dead. Long live Sergeant Mazanek.'

"What a maniac," Alia said, reading over Mara's shoulder. With a shaking hand, Mara flipped through a few pages until she came to a page with particularly large handwriting. She felt anger stir in her heart with each word she read.

1/19

Today solidified my promotion. I caught the Empress of Blood, and she is in the transitionary camp and will be transported to my own in Tazovski. I'll be a lieutenant as soon as Lt. Rezinchek visits next.

That's right, Little, soft, stupid Mazanek caught the Empress of Blood. If that doesn't get me promoted to at least a lieutenant, I'll be surprised. And what better subject for my research than her?

"He seems..." Mara said, trailing off.

"Obsessed with you?" Alia asked, finishing her sentence.

Mara continued reading the same entry as Alia started to flip through the second tome again. Meanwhile, the others ransacked the room of valuables.

1/20

The others want me to kill her, but I can't do that. She's much too valuable. Bodi Nemeth wrote me from the siege of Balgorod and said that we could sell her to the whorehouses in Laniras or Bruntal for more money than we can even imagine. I laughed so hard at that at first, but I think he's right. So, that's one plan after I finish my research on her.

Soon, I'll be rich AND I'll be promoted! Only a few more months in this frozen hellhole, and I'll be a rich lieutenant that can just get drunk and have all the women I want. I heard the best part of being a high ranked officer is that you can delegate all your duties to the people under you and you can just live however you want. Maybe I'll take the Sangoran empress as my own. Doesn't that sound like the best victory? It does to me!

Mara sneered down at the words. She ripped the page out, crumpled it up, and stomped on it. She flipped through the rest of the journal until a few loose pages Mazanek had folded and kept behind the last page. Letters.

She unfolded one and held it up. It was a letter from Sergeant Mazanek to himself.

I'm glad the old Tibor is dead. I was so frightened all the time that I'd mess up or do something wrong. What was I even worried for? I've found a pretty good deal here. I get paid more here, so I'll get to retire after a few postings, but I'm not thinking about that. Before, I wondered if I should be doing this, but then I realized that they're just slaves, and I'm their master. Their lives don't matter in the long run, and with every one of their deaths, I get closer to my goal. I can do whatever I want out here. Again, I'm glad the old Tibor is gone and I'm here. I am living, finally! Women, money, drinks. Power. This is the life.

Mara tore up the page and pocketed the journal.

"Anything in there?" she asked, pointing to the second leatherbound book Alia was looking through.

"Numbers of slaves they've sent to extermination facilities," Alia said, her hand over her mouth. "This can't be true…" Mara scanned the numbers on the page.

Date	*Quota*	*Actual*	*Assignment*
12/1	500	1,007	Extermination
1/1	200	410	Testing
2/1	500	19,100	Extermination
3/1	200	1,850	Sent to testing
4/1	500	1,950	Extermination
5/1	80	71	Testing

And then, handwritten below the list:

No words escaped Mara's mouth. Her hands trembled, and tears cascaded down her cheeks. She buried her face in the crook of her elbow as she leaned on the desk. Her heart began to thunder in her chest, and it felt as if a knife were being driven deeper and deeper into her chest.

Well over twenty thousand of her people were dead. She knew there were many more that had died in the Thannish invasion, from the elements, or during Mazanek's experiments.

Alia rubbed her back as the others stopped to look at her. Mara sobbed, and in her rage, an unintended, but powerful burst of mental energy and lightning erupted from her body. The others struggled to stay standing, bookshelves toppled over, and the chandelier fell and shattered against the ground.

"How could this happen?!" she shouted. "How?!"

The others said nothing, unaware of what she had read.

"Mara, look at me," Alia said, sitting on the desk. She took Mara's face between her hands and stared into her bruised face.

"It's all my fault. I couldn't stop them from—"

"No, Mara. Look at me."

Mara looked into Alia's dark brown eyes.

"I know no one working harder to stop this. You are here with your people thousands of miles from the edge of the world just to help them. And damn it, Mara, you are the only reason so many of us are still going—why we're still alive."

Mara looked at Kamil, who smiled back at her.

"Then we're going to end this," Mara said, sliding the second book into her other coat pocket. "I'm going to kill Mazanek. I'm going to burn this place to the ground, and we're getting everyone home. No one else dies."

Their collective feeling of loss and hopelessness gave way to resolve and courage as Mara stood. The others cheered, and at that moment, Shanthah's voice rang out from the shard of Godmirror.

"Mara, are you there?"

Mara rushed over to the nightstand and peered into the crystal's face to see Shanthah looking back at her.

"Yes!"

"Hanna and Hippo are on their way. Please, wherever you are, get out of there. Get to safety," he said.

"He's right," said Dobromil near the window. "They're coming."

Dobromil was correct. Whatever ceremony Lieutenant Rezinchek had traveled all this way for had ended. Whether that was Mazanek's promotion or something else, it didn't matter. The soldiers were leaving, many of them headed back toward Mazanek's house.

"Razvan, get us out of here," Mara ordered. She stumbled, but Kamil caught her.

"Where to?" Razvan asked.

"Safe. It doesn't matter where. Away from here. We can regroup and head back to the village."

"I can only take a couple people at a time—"

"Go!"

The Walker wasted no more time, grabbing Kamil and Constanta's arms. They vanished into dark smoke.

The sound of voices and footsteps from downstairs filled each of their hearts with dread.

"Bar the door until Razvan gets back," Mara said, clutching the sensitive wound over her heart. She groaned and collapsed into Mazanek's chair. Whatever Alia had done to numb the pain seemed to be wearing off.

"We've got this, stay still," Alia said.

The two burly Odauthians dragged the heavy wooden desk against the door while Alia examined Mara's wounds to make sure none had reopened.

The soldiers were upstairs now.

Razvan reappeared in the middle of the room, took Runar and Katerina by the hand, and disappeared again as someone tried to open the door from the outside. Mazanek shouted something, but his voice was muffled by the heavy steel door.

Olafur raised Mazanek's wooden chair and smashed it against the ground, gathering the splintered bits of wood.

"Better bad weapon than no weapon, yes?" he said in accented Thannish.

Alia drew the short sword she'd pilfered from a soldier earlier and traded it to Olafur for one of the sharp pieces of wood as the soldiers continued to pound on the door. Mara and Dobromil each took one as well.

A sudden burst of flame knocked the door off its hinges and decimated the wooden desk. The wreckage exploded into the room in a spray of heat and smoke, throwing everyone inside to the ground.

Olafur leapt over the flaming desk and thrust the sword into the smoke. The blade pierced the neck of the Dragonsoul who had taken down the door, but a bullet from a musket struck the Odauthian in the side, and he collapsed.

As the rest of the Dragonsoul's pent up flame burst from his body and decimated the wall and doorframe, a burst of teleportation mist filled the room, signaling Razvan's return.

"Wait, what happened?!" he exclaimed, coughing as he breathed in smoke.

"Get Olafur out!" Mara shouted, and Razvan leapt forward, clapped the felled Odauthian on the back, and vanished, leaving Mara, Alia, and Dobromil alone against the attackers.

Mazanek emerged from the smoke along with two soldiers carrying muskets.

"Take her," Mazanek said, the flames flickering off of the new lieutenant's medallion on his chest.

The men reached for Mara, but she lashed out from her chair, thrusting her splintered piece of wood into one of their stomachs.

Dobromil leapt forward and grabbed Olafur's fallen sword. He swept it across the soldier's calves, knocking him to the ground with a surprised cry and a thud of his knees against the wood floor.

The distraction drew Mazanek and the other soldier's attention for the briefest moment, giving Mara enough time to grab the man's musket, point it at the second gunman and fire.

The man fell dead, a bullet lodged in his chest, but a lead ball from outside whizzed through the smoke and struck Dobromil in the wrist.

Mara struck the wounded guard in the face with her knee just as a second bullet pierced Dobromil's chest. Dobromil lurched forward, tackling Mazanek to the ground through the smoke. He brought his fist down against the new lieutenant's windpipe with two quick jabs.

Mara limped through the smoke as Alia tried to pull her back. They both cried out as a gunshot and flash of light ended Dobromil's life, and his body fell against the creaky floorboards.

"Well, well look who it is." Mazanek wheezed as he spoke. "It's the woman made of glass—the one so easily broken."

Mara was still weak, and she had to support herself against what remained of the wall. Alia stood next to her, pointing one of the soldier's muskets at Mazanek.

"You don't know how to use that," Mazanek said, drawing his sword.

"Try me," Alia said, her voice shaky. "Stay away from her, you monster, or I'll shoot!"

Mazanek advanced, and Alia pulled the trigger. Nothing happened, and the lieutenant disarmed her then grabbed her wrist. Mara stumbled forward, raising her wings as Mazanek threw Alia to the ground.

Mara flapped her wings and jumped at the same time, shoving her shoulder hard against Mazanek's chest. Together, they tumbled down the stairs all the way to the bottom floor.

Mazanek brought his fist around, punching Mara in the jaw as she raised her wings to strike him. He grabbed her by the coat and shoved her head hard against the banister leading upstairs. Mara's vision blurred as pain raced through her skull.

"No!" Alia screamed, running down the stairs toward them. Mazanek released his grip on Mara's throat to grab the knife on his belt. She slumped against the wall.

As Mazanek stood and brought the blade up toward Alia, she slapped a hand against the man's chest and shoved him with all her might. She fell down upon the stairs, and Mazanek laughed at the woman's feeble attempt to knock him down.

Or so he thought.

His weapon clattered to the ground, and he stumbled backward. Mara groaned on the floor, her wings twitching. Mazanek wheezed and placed a hand to his heart as if having a heart attack, but when he drew it away and looked down at it, both his palm and coat were covered in dark blood.

Alia glowered up at him from the ground, cradling Mara's head against her chest.

"What did you do, witch?"

He ripped open his officer's coat to see blood blossoming across his chest. He stumbled back in fear, itching frantically at his arms as lines of crimson spiderwebbed across his flesh like cracks in a window.

Alia shut her eyes tightly as she held her friend close, stroking her dark hair. Mara groaned, gripped Alia's hand, and they helped one another to their feet.

A long scar on Mazanek's face began to bleed as a thousand cuts on either arm soaked the sleeves of his tunics.

"What did you do?!"

Even more blood began to gush from his side as another old wound opened; he tore his blood-soaked tunic off and glanced down at his flayed flesh.

Each scar on his body came undone. His skin fell to pieces as every healed wound, no matter how miniscule, tore itself open anew, and he collapsed against the wall, a bloody streak following his body gushing with crimson all the way to the ground.

Mara knelt next to him so that their faces were level; his eyes darted between the two women as they stood victorious.

"I am not your caged bird. Do not think us so easily broken."

She picked up his own dagger and plunged it into his chest. There was a clatter of metal on stone, and Mara reached down to retrieve Mazanek's Ottokar coin, which was now coated in blood.

Alia sobbed into Mara's shoulder as the empress stared wide-eyed, mouth agape in shock. She wrapped her arms around her friend, stroking her hair as blood leaked from the man's gurgling corpse.

"Please, please don't think less of me," Alia whispered, trembling as she sobbed into Mara's shoulder.

"I could never," Mara said back.

"This is the part of me I hoped to never see again," Alia said. Mara nodded in understanding, letting out a deep breath as Alia's own came in broken, forced sobs. "I killed him…"

Mara said nothing in reply, holding Alia close.

"Where on earth is Razvan?"

Mara helped Alia stand again, careful to guide her toward the front door without her looking upon Mazanek's corpse.

"But Dobromil," said Alia. "We can't just leave him."

But the fire had spread, engulfing the entire top floor of the house, consuming the fake gold and copies of paintings. As Mazanek's world went up in flames, Mara and Alia emerged from the front doors to meet a mass of soldiers standing outside.

Mara raised her dark wings high above her head as the crowd watching the burning building cried out at her appearance.

"What have you done?!" Lieutenant Rezinchek shouted as she pushed her way through her soldiers. "Kill her!"

The two soldiers at her side rushed toward Mara and Alia; as one brought his spear up, Mara clapped him in the neck with a fierce blow from a wing before striking the other in the chest with such force that it stole the air from his lungs.

Mara was exhausted, weak, and injured, but no one, even those with guns, dared advance on the two women.

"Let me be *very* clear," Mara shouted. "We may be your prisoners, but we are no one's—*NO ONE'S*—slaves!"

"Brave words from someone at our mercy," Rezinchek replied, folding her arms across her chest. "These people will pay a heavy price for what you've done."

"These are *my* people, and I love them. And I swear, if you touch one hair on any of their heads again—I swear to Elafris, the very devil below us, that I will never rest until each and every one of you are dead!"

"Ah, careful, the bitch bites!" Rezinchek called, and a few in the circle surrounding Mara and Alia chuckled. Others seemed nervous as if unsure how to respond.

Mara strode up to the lieutenant close enough to whisper into her ear so that only she could hear.

"Oh, Officer," she whispered. "I will do *so much* more than bite."

She turned to the rest of the crowd.

"Your leader has said that I am at your mercy, but never forget that you are also at *mine*," she said. "Now, I know that some of you will soon be heading back home to Thanatanos. I hope that you'll run to King Verahim and tell him what you saw here today. Warn him of what is coming for him, and that the Empress of Blood will no longer stand for your cruelty or cowardice. I once vowed never to be cruel, but that does not mean I will not be just."

She tossed Mazanek's gold coin spattered in his blood to Lieutenant Rezinchek.

"What's this?" she asked, turning it over in her hand.

"A coin to pay the ferryman when I send you to meet him," Mara said. Rezinchek stepped backward.

"That's it, kill her!" Rezinchek ordered, but no one moved.

Mara took another step toward her.

"If I wanted you dead, there would be no one on this Earth that could protect you from me."

And just then, a bolt fired from a crossbow whizzed through the air and embedded itself in Rezinchek's back, and she fell to her knees in pain. Mara glanced up to see Josef standing there, a second bolt ready to fire.

At that moment, a wave of mental energy washed over the soldiers' village followed by what Mara swore was a beautiful choir of people singing.

And then, just as she collapsed from overwhelming pain in her chest, Razvan appeared, grabbed her and Alia by the arms, and they vanished in a burst of dark mist.

CHAPTER THIRTY-EIGHT
THE REDEEMED

Mara woke up screaming.

The operating room.

Dim hospital lights.

Pain.

She wrestled with the bedsheets on her hospital bed trying to sit up as tears streamed down her cheeks, her heart feeling like it was going to explode out of her chest. She clawed at the thick bandages wrapped around her chest and torso, peeling the adhesive corners up to peer inside.

Her skin was purple, green, and black around a spider's web of scars leading outward from her heart.

In an instant, Alia was at her side, holding her close. She slid a hand beneath the bandages, and Mara felt her heart rate slow.

"It's okay, you're safe," Alia whispered, helping her lie back down before repeating, "You're safe. You're safe."

"I thought I was back there," Mara said, clutching Alia's hand. "I thought—"

She covered her eyes with her hand, but Alia pulled it away. "How long was I out?"

"I know, honey. I know," Alia said, stroking her hair. "And you've been asleep for three days."

"There was a Mindspeaker there. He wouldn't let me die. I don't know how… but somehow—somehow his powers kept me from…" Mara said. She trailed off as she stared up at the ceiling. "Did I already thank you for saving me?"

"Yes, several times. Did I thank *you* for saving *me?*" Alia responded. Several seconds of silence went by before Mara replied.

"I don't know," Mara said. She squeezed Alia's hand. "Why don't I remember?"

"It's your body and mind's response to trauma to help you cope," Alia said. "Scary, but relatively normal. You're safe, and you are loved."

Mara sat up again, calmer than last time. She hugged her knees close to her chest as she looked around the room. Hundreds of other slaves were lying in beds much like her own. The chamber was massive and the lighting so dim that she couldn't see the walls farthest from her bed.

She was glad she wasn't receiving preferential treatment, wherever she was.

"Are you okay?" Mara asked.

Alia leaned forward, Mara's hand still between her own.

"Am *I* okay? Something I love about you is that I've never heard you use the phrase, 'why me?' No, I'm not okay. None of us are. But we will be."

"Do you know what I think?" Mara asked.

"What's that?"

"I think Valistaran never deserved a lady like you," Mara replied, and Alia giggled.

"I don't think he could handle either of us," Alia said through tears of amusement. This set Mara off, and she joined in Alia's joyous laughter for several minutes as they made fun of their strange situation.

"Ow," Mara moaned, clutching her chest.

When the moment subsided, Alia said, "I had to work on your heart again."

"Why?"

"I was exhausted and panicking when I healed you the first time, so I went back and fixed my work. It's too late to fix the scarring, but *only* if you promise to rest, you can get out of bed. Okay?"

Mara nodded. "I want to go."

"I thought you might," Alia replied. "I also there's no stopping you. But Kamil and I have something we need to tell you."

"Oh no, what now?" Mara asked.

Alia chuckled. "Why does it have to be a bad thing?!"

"Because nothing good ever comes after 'there's something I need to tell you'."

She gestured for Kamil, who was sitting next to Constanta's hospital bed. He excused himself from their conversation and pulled up a chair next to Alia and Mara.

"So?" Mara asked.

Kamil and Alia shared a knowing glance.

"*We think we discovered a way to heal you,*" he said.

"You've already done a great job," Mara said, flexing her bicep. "Look, healthy and strong again."

"Not what we had in mind," Alia said, tapping the side of her head.

"Oh," Mara said. Her eyes widened, and she brushed her hand through the hair on the side of her head and over the scar beneath. "Oh."

"Are you ready?" Alia asked.

"Will it hurt?" Mara asked. Kamil shook his head.

"*It shouldn't,*" Kamil said.

At the same time, Alia said, "Probably."

They shared a silent look.

"Well, that fills me with confidence. No stranger to pain. Go for it."

She lay back down on her pillow. Alia placed one palm on the side of Mara's head over her scar.

At that moment, Mara felt Kamil's presence link all three of their minds. At the battle of Balgorod, Kamil had used his powers to unlock certain portions of Hanna's mind in order to momentarily expand her power. He did so now, amplifying Alia's abilities to heal.

Mara felt a strange sensation cleansing her mind beneath her skull as Kamil mentally guided Alia to the damaged parts of her brain.

Mara's eyes as bright as the bluest skies rolled back as the tingling sensation of Alia's power crept over her skull. Every sound became an entire symphony playing out of tune, and every speck of dim light was blinding. She screamed in agony as she felt Alia's power flow through her brain. Other slaves sat up in their beds at the sound.

She let out a sigh of relief as the dull ache that had accompanied her for the better part of the last two years faded away. A deep breath filled her lungs as a sense of peaceful relief washed over her.

She was still for several moments, at complete peace.

"Wow…" she whispered as she opened her eyes. "Wow-hooow-wooooow."

She looked down and flexed her fingers, summoning a spark that danced around her fingers. Her eyes widened in cautious excitement.

"Did it work?" Alia asked. "Do you feel any pain?"

"No!" Mara exclaimed, bouncing up and down in her bed. "I mean, yes, it worked—the pain is gone!"

"You still need to be careful," Alia advised.

"I wish we had known it was this easy all along," Kamil said. *"I'm sorry for not realizing it earlier."*

Tears formed in the corners of Mara's eyes as she telekinetically lifted the sheet off her legs.

"Am I fixed—you know, for good?" Mara asked. "Will I have any more seizures or strokes?"

"It's not permanent," Alia said, shaking her head. "But as long as you come to me for checkups and let me know how you're feeling, I don't see why it can't be. The seizures might stick with you forever because I don't think they're entirely connected to your powers. They may have just manifested late in life. But you won't have any more strokes unless you really, really overdo it."

Mara pulled both Alia and Kamil into a tight hug, and they all laughed, holding each other for several minutes as she sobbed into Alia's shoulder.

"Thank you," Mara said. "Thank you, thank you, thank you!"

"Now, maybe we've got a fighting chance against the Magistrate," Alia said.

"*Not that you couldn't take her without your powers,*" Kamil said. "*We know you could.*"

"Well, not sure we'd be here if that were true, but thank you," Mara said.

She groaned as Alia helped her out of bed. She retrieved her clothes, which, to her great relief, had been washed. She stepped behind a partition behind the bed to change.

"So, what happened? Did we get everyone out somehow?" Mara asked. She groaned in pain as she pulled on a clean tunic.

She fought to remember what had happened.

"No, not us," Alia replied. "You fainted. But without you, they never would have found us. They said they followed an explosion of mental energy. You know, the one you caused when you got mad at Mazanek's house."

Mara chuckled and pulled the partition back.

"Who are *they?*" she asked.

"That's..." Alia started, trailing off. "You'll see."

She led her out of the massive medical chamber outside. The stars glistened overhead, and the moon illuminated a strange city in its silver glow.

None of the buildings had windows, but the city stretched as far as the eye could see. Not far to the east was a mass of marvelously constructed buildings that spiraled around one another up and around a high hill. Thousands of people in colorful robes and masks ambled about their daily business.

"Where are we?" Mara asked as she looked at the incredible architecture that seemed to defy physics and gravity. "This isn't... We're still in the Deadlands, right?"

"*Hi, Mara.*"

Mara turned on the spot and saw a man in dark violet robes and an intricate crimson mask standing with Kamil behind her, his arms outstretched.

"Drahomir?!" Mara exclaimed, wrapping her friend in a tight embrace. "What is going on?"

"*Welcome to Bartun, City of the Dead!*" Drahomir said. "*Named in your honor, because you helped free them from Thanatan.*"

Her heart swelled in her chest as she gazed at her friend's mask beneath his dark hood.

It had been around three years since his transformation into one of the Faceless. He had unknowingly suffered from a split personality, and one of those personalities had been forced to become Thanatan's personal assassin. However, he had freed himself from Thanatan and the Magistrate's grasp and claimed control over a large percentage of the remaining Faceless. Evidently, they had been busy, creating an entire city.

"*I hope my people are taking care of you,*" Drahomir said to her mind; in addition to his natural powers of teleportation, he had become a Mindspeaker when he had joined the Faceless hive mind.

"How did you get the slaves out?" Mara asked as she, Alia, and Kamil walked beside their old friend down the road.

"*You couldn't stay away from this life, could you?*" Drahomir asked with something akin to a telepathic laugh. "*Sorry, too soon. But we share that trauma, so...*"

"I guess I couldn't," Mara said with a wink. "It wasn't as fun without you there, of course."

"*I always was the life of the party, wasn't I? The slaves are safe.*"

"And the soldiers?" Mara asked.

"*They'll stand trial,*" Drahomir replied. "*For now, the camp has become their cage instead of yours. They're about five miles west of here. They never knew how dangerous it was to settle there.*"

"There are some good men there."

"*And that is why they will stand trial. Not to toot our own horn, but it wasn't a very long battle once they realized who we were.*"

"Toot away!" Mara said with a chuckle. "So, you did it, then—you freed them?"

Drahomir nodded. "*I did! It took a while, but I was able to keep them from invading your world long enough to free them. Long story. I'd love to tell it to you sometime, but we need to get you back home.*"

"I can't wait to hear it. Quick question, though: before I collapsed unconscious, I heard singing. Last time I saw you, you said that you could hear it too, back at the Battle of Balgorod."

"*The Choir of Souls. That's what we call our people. You know how the Faceless had that terrible feeling of hunger and were always groaning?*"

"How could I possibly forget?" Mara asked as Drahomir waved to a group of masked children in robes.

"*Well, now people can hear the singing when we are around. No one knows exactly what it is. The theory is that it is a manifestation of our joy, as much as the groans were a manifestation of the Faceless' unending hunger and pain.*"

"Why can't I hear it now?" Mara asked.

"*You can if you listen hard enough. Your mind gets used to it. Tunes it out,*" he replied with a shrug.

"So, what's next? For you and for the slaves?" Mara asked.

"*For us... We want to free the Pure still trapped in the Magistrate's spell.*"

"You're using that term?" Mara asked with a groan.

"*Not for ourselves, no. We call ourselves the Redeemed. We have everything we need. We share everything else. We don't have war or disease or famine or anything else like that. We have culture and arts and love and joy; we have humanity. And that's what the Magistrate's Faceless lack. They're just... shells. The 'Purists' as they call themselves are about supremacy over others. That's not something we even think about here.*"

"I don't mean to be rude, but why haven't you come help us fight the Magistrate?" Mara asked.

"*We decided that it would be best for us not to interfere in your world,*" Drahomir mindspoke. "*As much as it pains me that it isn't my world anymore, it's for the best. We could control everything, but we won't. It's what makes us different from the Faceless. I kind of see it like this: we're two sides of the same coin—a coin that's been on the ground long enough for rust to form on top. We are the shiny gold side beneath, while they are the dusty, tarnished side. We can't become them.*"

"You've done some growing up since we first met," Mara said. "Proud of you, friend."

"*You and me both. There's another reason we haven't come to help, but I think it's better I show you,*" Drahomir said. "*How are the others? I assume you're still in contact with them.*"

"The others, meaning—"

"*You know. Josman, Shanthah, Aleksander, Valis, your brother, Rehor…the whole crew. I've been talking to Kamil, and it made me so happy.*"

"Josman is good. He misses you," Alia said. "He claims he doesn't, but, well, you know him."

"What Alia isn't telling you is that Josman is good *because* he's currently in a relationship with *this* fantastic woman," Mara said, holding up Alia's hand.

"*Well, well, well!*" Drahomir exclaimed in their minds. He clapped his hands, and if there were still a face beneath the crimson mask, it would be smiling. "*Congratulations! And when you get out of here, give the big guy a hug from me.*"

"A hug?!" Mara exclaimed with a wink. "You hug now?!"

"*Tell no one,*" Drahomir said. "*And the others?*"

"Rehor… Well, Rehor is gone," Mara said.

"*I'm sorry to hear that. I know you two were close. He loved you like a daughter.*"

Mara's heart swelled. "Yeah. He died protecting me. I'd rather not talk about it anymore, though, if that's okay."

"*Of course,*" Drahomir replied.

"And Pol… Oh, boy. My little brother is currently working at a camp like *that* one in the Plains of Adess."

She stared down at the brand on her wrist that read *00000-68* amidst other scars. Every time she looked at it, it reminded her of the fact that her own brother had betrayed everything she stood for.

"*What?!*" Drahomir's mental voice was nearly a shout as he clenched his fist. They stopped walking, and Mara turned back to him. "*You're kidding me. Tell me you're lying.*"

"I don't know—I don't know if he was forced into it, or what happened, but I'm scared to find out," Mara said. "Honestly, I don't want to know. I'm at a complete loss of what to do."

"*Aleksander and Shanthah?*" Drahomir asked, sensing that Mara didn't want to talk about Pol anymore either. She'd had more than her share of betrayal, after all.

"Shanthah's one of my councilors, actually."

"*He's a Mistress of Dusk?*"

Mara laughed out loud. "He insists on using that title, but he's a *Master* of Dusk. It doesn't matter, though. I'm going to change that title when I'm back in power."

"*Oh?*"

"I was thinking 'guardian.' It's simple. Less pretentious. 'Guardian of Doftaan' and the like."

"*I like it. And… Aleksander?*" He gave her a playful punch on the shoulder.

"Aleksander is…" She trailed off. "I'm worried for him. I left him in Kurash—"

"*Left him as in…*" Drahomir cocked his head and made a heart with his hands and then split it in half.

"No, not like that." Mara shook her head. "Drah, when did you get *funny?*"

"*I'm an acquired taste, and I think you finally get it. Anyway, you two crazy kids together yet? We're all waiting for it, you know.*"

"Oh, is that so?" Mara asked with a soft chuckle. After a moment of hesitation, she added, "Well…I guess I am too."

Alia clapped and let out a little cheer, and Mara felt both Drahomir and Kamil's joy fill her mind.

She couldn't help but smile.

Drahomir led the others up a hill toward the walled, eastern edge of Bartun.

"*I mentioned there was a second reason we haven't come to help against the Magistrate. Well, here it is.*"

From their vantage point, they could see that the entire region around Tazovski and Bartun was set upon a massive plateau. The sheer cliff face dropped off into an eerie fog and extended for miles to the north and south where it was swallowed by the far-off darkness.

Haunting cries of pain echoed up from the fog below.

"Drahomir?" Mara asked, putting an apprehensive hand on the low, stone wall. "What are we looking at?"

"The sins of our ancestors," Drahomir replied.

As if on cue, a bulbous beast even bigger than Hippo emerged from the fog. It looked straight up at Mara and the others upon the wall with perhaps a dozen eyes on long, slender stocks that protruded from its skull.

It reared up on the back of its ten crab legs and let out a roar from a beaklike maw on the bottom of the creature that shook the earth.

Mara's heart thundered in his chest and summoned lightning around her arm, giving color to the world around them. She was ready to strike, although she knew there may not be anything she could do.

"What is that?" Alia asked.

"We call them Nightmares."

"Fitting," Mara said. "Are we in danger?"

"It's okay. There's only one of them…for now," Drahomir said as the wall below them rumbled. Kamil leaned forward, staring into the mist.

"Now what?" Mara exclaimed, clutching Alia's hand.

"Let's call it a demonstration."

Brilliant orange flame illuminated the dense fog, and the monstrosity cried out with a terrible voice like the simultaneous scream of a thousand dying men.

"By the Goddesses…" Mara whispered as hundreds of Drahomir's Redeemed swarmed over the burning creature, hacking at its flesh with their claws until it was lost in the fog.

"What just happened?!" Alia exclaimed before vomiting over the wall at the smell of the burning creature.

"The fog is flammable. Don't know why, don't ask. I'm not a scientist. But we've weaponized it. They come too close, and boom."

"How many of those things are there?" Mara asked.

"On a good day... four, maybe five."

Kamil turned to look at Drahomir. *"I know you can sense them too. There are thousands of them."*

Drahomir nodded, the flames dancing off the surface of his crimson mask.

"You're right. They've been coming more often, and more of them at a time. We used to see one every couple weeks. Then they attacked every day. Then multiple times per day."

"And they're all like that?" Mara asked. Drahomir shook his head.

"No. That was an ugly one, but hardly the worst. They seem to adapt and evolve to fight the others. I think they were too busy to invade our world, but, well..."

"Now they smell a feast," Mara said, glancing over her shoulder at the thousands of slaves now filling the streets of Bartun.

"Yeah. Precisely," Drahomir replied. *"These things are—how should I put this—cousins of the Faceless. Humans infected with the original Faceless virus became my people. When the virus spread to animals, well... Let's just say the people of this land—Russia, it was called—weren't able to stop them. They mutated, their bodies now made of a controlled, immortal cancer that evolves and spreads. None are the same, and they've all evolved to kill the others, and us, as efficiently as possible."*

"How is it that you know this?" Mara asked.

"*We can sense it in their minds,*" Drahomir said, turning to Kamil. "*You're better at this than me. What do you sense?*"

Kamil closed his eyes and reached out, connecting to the fading, dying mind of the creature below.

"*Mara's right. They can sense the slaves…Mindspeakers, of a sort, just like the Faceless. I just feel their desire to kill them all, and I—I can tell they know there is civilization to the southwest… And it is all they want. Their only desire.*"

Drahomir nodded.

"*Your people will be safe here until they can get out,*" Drahomir said.

"About that—Hanna is on her way, but we can't transport everyone away," Mara said. "Got any way out of here?"

"*I thought you'd never ask,*" Drahomir said.

At the mention of Hanna's name, she felt a spark of joy in his mind. He led them back down the steps toward a massive structure as high as Mara's palace near the center of the city.

As they stepped inside, Mara, Alia, and Kamil each gasped, for the entire structure was hollow, built around a massive tree that snaked around the inside of the building.

At the base of the trunk stood three men. The largest of the three, a hulking man clad in furs and leather armor with a round shield strapped to his back and an axe in his belt turned as he heard them approach.

Mara gasped as she recognized his battle-hardened and bearded face. As the other two men turned away from the tree, she realized they were Olafur and Runar, her two

Odauthian friends that had helped her infiltrate Mazanek's home.

"Halamir?!" she exclaimed, and then in Icelandic, she said, "And Olafur and Runar! I'm so glad to see you are okay!"

Halamir Valdursson, husband of Lavinia's sister, Zhanna, greeted her with a hardy handshake that felt as if he were trying to crush her hand.

"What are you doing here? What is this?" Mara asked. Kamil and Alia chatted with Olafur and Runar as Halamir spoke to Mara and Drahomir.

"A branch of Yggdrasil, the Holy World Tree," Halamir said. "How's my sister-in-law doing?"

Mara laughed. "Lavinia is fine, I think. How are you and Zhanna?"

Without answering, Halamir gestured to the branch of the World Tree. He didn't seem to Mara like one who cared for small talk, and she didn't mind at all.

"Yggdrasil's portals will get your people to my home, United Baltija. From there, my wife can lead the voyage back to Sangora. It's still a long way home, but closer than this damned place," Halamir said.

Mara's mind shot back to Valistaran's tale of how Yggdrasil had rescued him from drowning, and how Thanatan's original Magistrate had used the World Tree's portals to transport the Faceless across the world.

"How soon can we do this?" Mara asked, her heart thundering in her chest.

"Now, if you want. However, whenever we activate one of Yggdrasil's portals, those beasts outside the wall—you showed them to her, yes?" he asked, turning to Drahomir, who nodded. "They come swarming, so be ready."

A mental presence washed over the room, and each Mindspeaker, Mara, Drahomir, and Kamil collapsed to their knees, holding their heads.

When they recovered, Drahomir rushed outside. Alia helped Mara to her feet.

"What was that?!" Alia asked.

"Something's coming," Mara replied.

"Perhaps we won't have to wait until we activate a portal after all," Halamir muttered.

Mara, Alia, and Kamil, along with the Odauthians, followed Drahomir outside. A cacophony of screams and roars echoed from beyond the wall.

Mara held out her hand as dark flakes began to drift down from the sky. As she caught some, it did not melt against the warmth of her skin.

"It's not snow," Alia said.

"Ash," Mara whispered.

She took flight to see that dozens of creatures of various sizes had breached the wall. Many had broken through the stone edifice while others had climbed over, their flesh flaming from the weaponized fog below.

Mara landed at the base of the stairs just as the ground beneath her feet gave way; she screamed as a beast's massive jaws emerged from the ground and snapped shut around her.

A burst of lightning blew the creature's jaw off, splattering the ground with gore. Mara emerged and sent a second blast through the monster's brain, and it fell dead against the earth with a splat.

All around the city, similar burrowing creatures were emerging from the streets, swallowing slaves and Drahomir's Redeemed followers alike. Mara reached out with her mind and gasped, for each of the jaws reaching from the earth topped tendrils connected to one gargantuan monster deep beneath her feet.

While they were assailed from below, thousands of winged beasts covered in mouths, tendrils, and claws descended into the city from above.

At that moment, a brilliant amethyst light flashed from within the building that housed the branch of Yggdrasil the World Tree; the beam of light extended high into the heavens.

A wall of swirling purple and white light extended from the tower to the next building over, creating the portal that would transport the slaves to United Baltija and begin their journey home.

"No!" Mara shouted as the flying creatures changed course, soaring straight for the portal. "Drahomir, if any of those things get through the portal, they could destroy United Baltija, or the Magistrate could find out about them. Do *not* let them through!"

Drahomir nodded and reached out with his mind. A moment later, a swarm of Redeemed Sangorans intercepted the flying beasts in the skies. One of their corpses struck the ground next to Alia, who screamed and kicked it in the head.

Many of the Redeemed led the mass of liberated, yet terrified slaves toward the portal while thousands of others swarmed against the creatures.

"*Look out!*" Kamil shouted, tackling Alia just as one of the underground creature's arms exploded from the ground beneath her feet.

They struck the ground, and six more burst forth, surrounding Mara on all sides. The largest of them loomed above, its maw dripping with foul blood, blocking her escape by flight.

But Mara, the Empress of Blood, did not need an escape.

For the first time since Alia and Kamil had healed her mind, she closed her eyes and let out a deep breath, entering the Dreamstate.

One minute in the real world was an entire year for her in the Dreamstate, but her physical eyes were only shut for a couple seconds. That was enough.

Her eyes flew open as the jawed tendrils lunged at her as one. She lashed out with a wing, smacking the nearest one, leapt onto its snout, blasted the two to either side of her with bolts of electricity, and then brought her wings down with such force that it cracked their skulls against the earth.

The seconds spent in the Dreamstate had given her more than enough time to know exactly how to fight back, but not only did she plan how to kill the jaw snakes, but she now knew how to handle the beast below as well.

She reached out, connecting her mind with Kamil and Drahomir's consciousnesses; they felt her intentions, and with Drahomir's connection to the endless sea of the Redeemed's minds, Mara was able to grab hold of the underground monster's consciousness.

Just as she had done when she bound Hippo's mind to her forever, she grasped the monster's very being, its essence, and soul; she closed her fist, and with a scream, the tendrils that were still exploding out of the earth were still.

The leviathan below the earth now belonged to the Redeemed.

Mara collapsed, and the jawed tendrils around the city began to tear at the flesh of any of the mutated beasts that dared draw near, drawing them underground to devour them whole.

As Drahomir's Faceless Sangorans kept the flying monsters busy, Drahomir's ground forces pushed back the tide of earthbound creatures.

A herd of beasts that resembled deer with curved, bladed horns broke through the city's defenses and headed headlong for the portal.

Mara steeled herself for the attack, and she knew that even with her powers, there were too many of them. The monsters were going to get through.

She nearly vomited as the monstrosities neared and she caught sight of their faces. In place of a snout and cute, beady, black eyes, there was a gaping maw with one long, whiplike tongue covered in sharp barbs.

The arms of the Leviathan Beneath devoured much of the herd, and lightning snaked around her arms as she readied to defend the portal.

An almighty roar filled the earth as an explosion of red-hot, molten lava buried the beasts.

"Hippo!" Mara shouted in surprise as her massive behemoth companion soared out of the portal, unleashing hellish flame upon the creatures as they attempted to escape through the portal.

And then, she sensed someone else on Hippo's back.

"HANNA!" Mara screamed in utter joy. Tears filled her eyes as she took flight, intercepting her friend in a hug in mid-air as she levitated off of Hippo's back.

They spiraled together in the air, hugging one another tightly until Mara let go, flapping her wings to stay airborne next to Hanna.

"Hello, you lovely human, you!" Hanna signed with a smile stretched across her face.

"You have no idea how good it is to see you! I could kiss you!"

"Oh, you know I'd never be opposed to that, but—"

A massive creature like a flying bull struck Hanna out of the sky, and Mara tucked her wings close to dive after her.

Just before she struck the earth, Mara wrapped her arms around Hanna, extended her wings, and soared to the ground. They rolled against the street with a shared groan.

There was silence.

Mara looked up to see the skies clear of any flying monsters, and the others were retreating from the combined might of the Redeemed, the Leviathan Beneath, and Hippo.

And then she heard it: the beautiful, collective song of The Choir of Souls at the void between her world and the Nightmares.

As Mara let out a breath of relief and Alia tended to a wound on Kamil's back, a beast shaped like a bulbous whale with bladed wings shot through the air faster than any arrow and vanished through the portal.

"No!" Mara screamed.

She, Alia, Kamil, and Hanna hurried through the shining purple energy and found themselves in the crowd of slaves in a completely new part of the world. Behind her, she could still see Bartun overshadowed by night. Hippo emerged from the portal with Drahomir soon after.

"Where did it go?!" Alia exclaimed.

Kamil, Mara, and Drahomir all reached out with their minds, but the beast's consciousness was somehow camouflaged by thoughts of the vast multitude of slaves.

Mara cursed under her breath.

"Don't worry, Halamir and I will find it," Drahomir's voice echoed in her mind. *"Go back to Sangora and save us all from the Magistrate. We'll handle this and get your people home."*

"Okay," Mara said, her heart pounding. "Tell the others—the ones who helped us escape, I mean—tell them thank you, and goodbye."

Drahomir nodded, and they shared a quick hug. Hanna, Alia, and Kamil said their goodbyes as well before they climbed onto Hippo's back and shot into the sky.

"What now?" Alia called over the roaring wind as Hippo made all haste back home.

"You two are going to a hospital. No fighting me on that. I'm going to take Hanna with me—there's something I need to check at home."

"Home being Doftaan or Cineca?" Alia asked.

"Cineca," Mara replied. She hadn't referred to Cineca as home for years. It wasn't—not anymore. But it was where her mother still lived, and her thoughts turned to her.

As if reading her mind, Alia said with a kind smile, "Say hello to your mama for me."

CHAPTER THIRTY-NINE
MARA, WHY?

The train arrived as the labor camp at Tazovski burned.

The soldiers within were quick to make their way to the village, not stopping to unload the new shipment of supplies, contrary to their orders.

Private Apolinarius Bartunek followed his officers as they shouted orders all the way up the hill to the soldiers' village overlooking the camp. He wheezed as they sprinted up the hill; even though they'd trained for situations like this, their training never accounted for the intense cold of the Deadlands that burned their lungs with every breath.

Pol watched in horror as the tongues of flame licked over each of the homes, and a plume of dark smoke trailed upward into the night.

Was their entire trek into the Deadlands to bring fresh supplies for the prisoners there all in vain? Was everyone dead?

"What is happening here?" called his superior officer, Sergeant Dolak, as if reading Pol's thoughts. He knew the man didn't need to, however. They were all wondering the same thing.

The soldier at the guard station did not reply; as Dolak opened the door to shout at him for sleeping on duty, the man slumped over and fell from his seat, a gory hole in his abdomen.

Pol's heart thundered in his chest.

As he looked closer, he noticed that hundreds of the corpses that littered the camp were not human, but Faceless.

"Should we turn back?" asked one of his fellow soldiers.

Dolak said nothing, venturing into the village, and his squad followed after him. They'd passed another train on their way here, and Pol hoped people had escaped whatever happened here.

As they entered the village, they saw a lone figure amongst the flames locked in combat with the remaining soldiers.

"What is the meaning of this?!" Dolak shouted. He drew his sword, and each of the others did the same.

Pol knew the man was no longer in fighting shape. Years behind a desk had dulled his abilities, and he would never stand a chance against whoever the Sangoran woman laying waste to the Tazovski group was.

Despite that fact, Sergeant Dolak led the charge; Pol lagged behind, but he too drew his blade and followed his leader into battle.

Pol was correct. As Dolak reached the Sangoran, she thrust bladed wings into his chest with such force that it lifted him into the air. She slammed him down into the flames and turned her sights on the newcomers.

Pol's heart dropped. Mara stood before him, covered in the blood of those she had murdered. Innocent men doing their jobs. Men with families and children that would never see them again.

He covered his mouth in shock.

The others didn't care. They raced toward her, weapons raised, and she danced through them with a fierce and murderous grace. She sprayed blood with each throat she severed, and every heart she pierced.

"Stop!" a voice called from a group of soldiers that had yet to engage her. They surrounded her, wielding their weapons with great caution.

"This should come as no surprise," Mara said. "You've all brought this upon yourselves."

She raised her hands, and white light spiraled around them until she brought them down, unleashing a torrent of lightning through the crowd.

The rest of the soldiers moved in as one; even Pol rushed toward his sister with tears in his eyes. Their sheer numbers began to overwhelm her, but she kept fighting in an endless spray of blood.

Pol caught sight of one of his classmates from the academy and grabbed his shoulder.

"Pol?!"

"Josef!" Pol exclaimed. "What's going on?"

"She—I—"

As he stumbled for words, Mara beheaded two men with a glowing, green blade and turned her head in their direction. She strode toward them with hatred in her eyes as the world burned around her.

Josef raised his sword, and Pol did the same.

"Stop!" Pol shouted.

At this, Mara hesitated, seeing his face for the first time.

"Pol?" she whispered. "What are you doing here?"

He stepped forward in defiance. With tears in his eyes, he shouted, "You hypocrite!"

"This is justice, Pol."

"No, it isn't, Mara! Stop!"

"You shouldn't be here. Get back on that train."

"I'm not going to do that."

"Then you are no brother of mine."

Pol stood, dumbfounded as he gazed upon his sister standing amidst a sea of corpses, the flames of hell dancing behind her in the darkness.

"I don't want to hurt you," Pol said, his hands trembling.

Mara cocked her head. "You've already done that."

She advanced, raising her bloodied wings. Pol rushed toward her just as she swiped downward with one of her wingblades, slicing through Pol's cheek in a spray of blood. Without another word, she smashed her other wing into the side of his head with such force that he hit the ground and did not stir.

Josef backed up. With tears in his eyes, the only trembling words that escaped his lips were, "Mara, why?"

Mara said nothing as she thrust her wingblades through his chest. He collapsed to his knees and gazed into her cruel blue eyes filled with hatred. But then, the illusion faded, and her face twisted into a crimson mask set upon the head of a Faceless Sangoran.

A tear rolled down Josef's cheek as the Magistrate's horrible mask stared into his soul.

"You have all failed me, and now you pay the price."

CHAPTER FORTY
HOME, BITTERSWEET HOME

As Cineca came into view, the *real* Mara's stomach twisted into a violent knot. A sense of relief filled her heart upon seeing that her hometown hadn't been destroyed, but it was overclouded by the shame of never making the trip home before now. The guilt had become too much to bear.

What would her mother think when she showed up, alive, after *fourteen years*? She had been only sixteen when she was taken. She shook her head.

"By the Goddesses, is that how long it's been?" she whispered to herself, adjusting her thick scarf around her neck. It was now early summer in Thanatanos, but the night's sky after a heavy rain was bone-chilling.

Mara climbed down Hippo's neck and slumped next to Hanna. Her friend had wrapped herself in several thick blankets and nestled in the hollow beneath the behemoth's massive wing. She had insisted that Kamil and Alia remain behind in Doftaan to rest and recover after a quick reunion with Shanthah. They understood how important it was for her to go to Cineca, of course, and Alia had made sure Mara had enough supplies for the trip and had sent her on her way.

Hanna was smiling at some dream unfolding, and Mara was tempted to use her mindspeaking abilities to peek into her head to assuage her anxiety but refrained. She was grateful her friend was there with her. Hanna had fallen asleep sometime after passing by the city of Vudapas and over the new, massive border wall between Sangora and Thanatanos—a wall to keep out enemies that could fly. Mara laughed at the thought.

She spent the remainder of the flight huddled against Hanna for warmth until Hippo began his gradual descent. Mara had taken time to explain to him that he couldn't just dive toward the ground when people were riding on his back, or they would fall off. That scares people, she had told him. She patted his massive rocky back with a loving smile to let him know he was doing a good job.

The behemoth glided to the ground, trampling through a field of wheat as he landed. His amusement washed over Mara's mind as the wheat tickled his ankles.

Hanna sat up, still groggy and wrapped in her blankets.

"Here already?" she signed.

Mara nodded. *"Good morning, sleepy."*

"It's easy to stay asleep when there's no sound to wake you up."

Mara smiled and patted Hippo's snout as he lowered himself so they could climb down his face. Hanna patted his nose as she levitated to the ground. Mara looked Hippo in one of his massive eyes, and she felt his joy fill her heart.

"Love you, you big, silly boy," Mara said, rubbing the rough skin below his eye. His jaws curved into something akin to a smile, and he wiggled and circled on the spot like a massive puppy before settling into the golden field.

"*Lead the way,*" Hanna signed. Mara did so, trailing a hand over the soft wheat, just like she used to all those years ago.

She'd missed spring completely during her time in Tazovski, and it was odd for her to go straight from the harsh winter of the Deadlands to the comfortable warmth of the early Thannish summer. She stopped, twisting an ear of wheat between her thumb and forefinger.

"*What's wrong?*" Hanna signed.

"*There should be people working the fields. It's weird to see it like this,*" Mara signed back. "*I just hope everyone is okay.*"

As they made their way through the wheat field arm in arm, Mara let out a laugh, for Hippo had begun to snore.

"*Hippo's snoring,*" Mara signed into her hand, and Hanna pulled her arm free so that she could use it to sign.

"*I wish I could hear it,*" Hanna signed before adding, "*Speaking of snoring—do I breathe loud?*"

"*Do you what?*" Mara signed back with a chuckle.

"*Breathe loud. I can't hear myself breathe anymore, and I'm very self-conscious about it. I had a girlfriend once who told me I breathed loud even when I could hear.*"

Mara laughed out loud. "*No, your breathing is lovely.*"

She led Hanna out of the field and up the familiar path leading into Cineca.

"*Thank you for coming,*" Mara signed, and Hanna turned to Mara with a wide smile. "*I couldn't do this without you.*"

"*Are you kidding? I've wanted to meet your ma for ages! I want to meet the woman who raised the Empress of Blood!*" Hanna signed, her gestures exaggerated and emphatic.

Although her heart felt like it was going to beat right out of her chest, a chuckle of grateful joy escaped from behind the veil of dark fear.

Her childhood house came into view as they strolled up the lane, and the feeling of coming home filled her soul.

Memories flashed through her mind. Of playing with Pol in the dirt outside. Of climbing onto the roof to lay out in the sun where no one could see her. The fencepost even still bore char marks from the time she'd almost burnt it down when she was eleven. The house had been repainted, and she scowled. It didn't look quite right.

Not much had changed around the yard, however. The trees were taller, and her mother's small garden was gone. The singular window on the front of the home was covered with wooden planks.

"*Is this it?*" Hanna asked as Mara stood outside the door. Mara nodded. "*Want to knock?*"

This time, Mara shook her head, her dark hair falling in front of her face as she hung her head.

"*I can't do it,*" Mara signed.

"*Take as long as you need,*" Hanna replied. "*I'm here for you.*"

Mara took a deep breath, tried to knock, and faltered. She turned to Hanna again as if to ask, "Can you do it?"

Hanna smiled and rapped her knuckles against the door. Mara's heart nearly exploded in her chest as she did so, but there was no response. Mara tried the knob. It was open, and the heavy oak door swung inward with a creak.

"Mama?" She waited for a moment and then called for her mother once more. "Helloooo?"

No response. She ventured inside, and her heart dropped. The furniture had been removed, and a thick layer of dust covered every surface. Horrible, intrusive thoughts of her mother and father dead somewhere filled her mind, and she slumped back against the wall, taking in the stale feeling of the empty house. It had once been bright with laughter and joy—memories that she would never abandon.

Now, it was just a husk of what had once been.

Hanna knocked on the doorframe, pulling Mara back to reality. Her auburn hair glowed from behind, illuminated by a torch held by someone behind her.

Mara emerged from the empty home hoping, but not expectant, to see her parents there. Instead, she met a familiar young woman in the street. Eva, a friend she hadn't thought of in far too long stood in the torchlight.

"Mara?" she said in a cautious voice. After a long pause she added, "Where have you been?"

"Eva," Mara replied, her confused expression turning to one of joy. She wrapped her arms around her childhood friend, introducing her to Hanna, who smiled and waved in response. "I know, I've been gone a long time. I've wanted to come back every day since they took me, but—"

"No need for excuses," Eva replied. She looked much healthier than she had before Mara's enslavement; at that time, she had just returned from Nitra's healing center after a vicious battle with a debilitating sickness that had left her bedridden for weeks. "Really. We've heard even here about the Queen of Sangora plucked from a tiny town in Thanatanos."

She smiled, and although she got the title wrong, Mara didn't correct her. It didn't matter. As they clutched one another's hands, she caught Eva's eyes dart to her wings.

"I was a slave for most of that time," Mara said in a soft voice. "For the rest of the time, I don't have an excuse to give."

"Again, none needed," Eva said, adjusting her shawl around her shoulders. "I expect you're here to see your mother?" Mara nodded. "She doesn't live here anymore. Come on."

Eva led her and Hanna down a path and then explained how to get to Daniela's house.

"Thank you, Eva," Mara said. "It's been so nice to see you. I'll come visit before I leave for Doftaan, okay?"

Eva nodded. "I'd like that. End this war, and we can catch up. I'm starting a batch of the best jam you'll ever have."

"That sounds amazing." They shared a quick hug. Eva hesitated, as if wanting to say something important. "What is it?"

"Nothing," Eva said with a shake of her head. "It's just, you should know—a lot has changed, and…"

She trailed off.

They said their goodbyes, and Mara and Hanna followed the directions to Mara's parents' new home. It was larger than the last, and a quaint garden of vegetables and flowers surrounded it on all sides.

Mara traced her finger down the rough, splintering wood of the doorframe. The glow from a warm hearth inside illuminated her face through the window, and she let out a deep breath as she heard movement from within the cottage.

After all these years, she was actually there—home at last. She glanced over her shoulder at Hanna who gave a reassuring smile and gestured to the door.

Mara took a deep breath and curled her fingers into a fist. Another deep breath. Her hand faltered, and she felt her lip begin to tremble. She was about to turn back to Hanna to tell her again that she couldn't bring herself to—

The door creaked open, letting a sliver of orange light out, illuminating half of Mara's face. A thousand words all tried to escape her throat at once, but before they could spill out, a single word broke the stillness. "Mara?"

She bit her lip and her eyebrows turned up. She began to speak again, but her mother already held her in a tight embrace. Tears rolled down Mara's face as she felt her mother's arms around her. She pressed her cheek against the top of Daniela's head.

"Can I…"

"Of course! Of course!" Daniela Bartunek exclaimed. "Oh, Mara… I've been praying for this moment since the day they—oh, my sweet Marška is home! Oh, honey, come in!"

Daniela led Mara by the hand into her quaint home and caught sight of Hanna standing there for the first time.

"And a friend? Who's this?" Daniela asked, a wide smile overtaking her demeanor. Hanna gestured to her ear with an apologetic expression. She gestured to Mara and then gave a thumbs up and a wink. Not technically part of Sangoran sign language, but a sign that any mother would appreciate.

"Hanna can't hear, ma," Mara said, signing along. "But she's my best friend. We've been through a lot, and she says she's excited to meet—"

Hanna pushed past Mara and wrapped her arms around Daniela, rocking her back and forth.

"Thank you for your daughter," Hanna said out loud.

"Oh, my heart. It's so nice to meet you, Hanna."

Daniela spoke a little louder, looking a bit embarrassed, not knowing how to speak to someone completely unable to hear. Mara smiled; she knew just how long it had been since her friend had felt a mother's hug.

Mara caught her mother's eyes dart to the door, and Mara wondered if she were hoping for Pol to appear. Her smile faded slightly, but she beckoned to Mara and Hanna to sit.

Mara nestled into the sofa and held one of the embroidered pillows in her lap. Hanna joined her, folding her legs beneath her bottom.

Daniela filled a kettle and placed it over the fire before rummaging through the sole cupboard in the kitchen.

"This calls for the good blueberry tea and the even better honey. Do you remember Bula Anducek?"

"Yes, ma," Mara said, the image of a jolly, plump woman who always brought the Bartunek family jars of homemade honey from her beehives filled her mind.

"She brought by some of her honey just this morning to celebrate everyone getting to move back in." She paused and began to weep. "I can't—I can't believe—"

Mara leapt to her feet and held her mother close, cradling her head against her chest. "It's okay, I'm okay. You're okay."

"We're all okay," Daniela said, kissing Mara on the cheek. "You remember!"

It had been a saying they had said every time Mara or Pol had fallen and scraped a knee or bruised an elbow.

"Of course," Mara whispered.

She felt her mother's touch on one of her bandaged wings. She said nothing as she extended them, nearly brushing both sides of the room. Hanna caught the sight of a tear on her friend's face glistening in the firelight. Mara took a deep breath trying not to cry more, waiting in reluctant fear for her mother to react.

"Oh, Mara…" Mara winced and shut her eyes. And then, her mother was holding her tightly again. "They're beautiful. Absolutely beautiful, just like you. My angel daughter. Oh, I can hardly believe you're home… You look like an angel!"

Daniela stroked her daughter's dark hair as she sobbed into her shoulder. Hanna's eyes welled with tears as she sat in silence, a soft smile etched on her face.

"I was so scared you'd hate them, or me… I was so scared to come back here. After everything that's happened and everything I've done."

"Hate you? Mara Killianeva Bartunek, you silly girl. I love you so much. I prayed to Thanatan every day for you, and I never, ever gave up hope that you were still alive. And when I heard rumors that you were a *queen?* I told everyone who would listen! They thought I was crazy! But it was true, right?"

"Yes, it was true, ma."

Mara laughed through the tears, pushing away the idea that she and Hanna had personally killed the god her mother had been praying to.

"Twirl," Daniela said as she set three mugs on the table.

Mara smiled and turned on the spot so that Daniela could see her wings. She felt like she had so many years ago when her mother would sew her a new dress and tell her to twirl—or more often, when she and Pol would come home wearing pots and pans strapped to their heads and chests after a day of 'killing dragons.'

"If you have nowhere to go—no royal business, that is—I would love to hear the story of…"

She trailed off.

"Of everything?" Mara asked.

Daniela nodded. "What's a queen's average day like?"

Hanna accepted a mug of steaming tea with a gracious smile as Mara sat back next to her.

"Well, you'd have to find one to ask her."

"Oh?"

"I lost everything," Mara said. "I just wanted to help people. I was so close, but… I just wasn't good enough, ma."

"Now, you wait right there," Daniela said, a scolding finger outstretched. "You might have lost your kingdom, or queendom, or—"

"Empire," Mara interjected, signing for Hanna.

"Empire? Oh, gods," Daniela said. "Well, even without it, you've never been one to let your crown slip—but you know, a crown alone does not make a queen."

"Huh?"

"Your love does. You've always been the strongest, most loving girl I ever knew. Woman, now. Look at you! Don't know if I ever got 'round to telling you this, but people always told me and your pa that you made them want to be better people just being around you."

Hanna must have been reading Daniela's lips, because she squeezed Mara's hand. Mara glanced over at her to see her friend nod, tears in her eyes.

"I bet you haven't lost the hearts of your people. You've always been a queen, even without one of those gold sticks with a diamond on it... You didn't have one of those, did you?"

"No, ma," Mara said with a tearful chuckle. "Of course not."

"Good, oh, I hated seeing those kings with those."

"Ma, I didn't have one," Mara insisted for emphasis.

Hanna nudged Mara with her elbow to get her to translate for her mother.

"Mara makes us all want to be better, and that's why we're going to win this war. How could we not with an absolute queen like this on our side?"

Mara shook her head but relayed Hanna's message anyway, and Daniela's bright blue eyes lit up with joy.

"There is something else," Mara said, turning back to her mother. "It's Pol…"

"Later. *You're* here now. That's what's important. I'm sad that he isn't, but is he—"

"Yes, he's alive," Mara said, her eyes sad. Daniela nodded. "And Pa…?"

Daniela shook her head.

"How long ago?" Mara whispered. She had prepared herself for this, but she still felt pain and loss take hold of her heart. She knew now that this was what Eva had hesitated about whether or not to tell her.

"Five years or so. Mara, he loved you so very much," Daniela said. She grasped her daughter's hand. "He loved Xanthurias, too. You know that? You haven't seen him have you?"

"We reunited, yeah, but we lost each other again—"

"No, that's not what I mean. I may have a little surprise for you," Daniela said. "Xanthurias is here."

"He's *here*? In Cineca?" Mara asked. She had assumed he was still in Kurash where she had left him.

Daniela nodded. "Went out to get some firewood a while ago. Should be back soon."

"He's *here* here?" Mara asked. Her heart raced.

Daniela nodded then turned to Hanna. "I hope you've been keeping our Mara safe."

Hanna laughed as Mara translated for her, then signed, *"Your girl doesn't need protecting. She keeps me safe!"*

"Ma, what?! Why are you changing the subject like this?"

Daniela smiled. "You know, Xanthurias came back here and saved us all from the king's soldiers, just in time. He's so cute. When are you two—"

"Ma!" Mara exclaimed. "What happened?"

"The king sent his men to Cineca. He's been attacking the villages around the border and blaming it on Sangora, or so people say. Not sure how he thinks that'll help."

"And Alek—" She caught herself. "And *Xanthurias* fought them off?"

"Him and his friend with the black fire," Daniela said while Mara translated for Hanna. "Xanthurias showed up, told everyone they needed to leave, and he showed us to that lake you used to love to swim in as a kid to hide us. While we were there, Xanthurias and his friend fought them off. We could hear the battle all the way from the lake. It was awful, but we are safe."

Mara's heart swelled. What on Earth had brought Aleksander and Valistaran together in *Cineca* of all places?

"Plan on telling your mom you married that 'guy with black fire'?" Hanna signed. Mara signed back a forceful, "*No,*" and Hanna chuckled to herself proudly.

"Pity about his friend, though," Daniela said, as she stepped back into the kitchen, reemerging a moment later with two pieces of bread smeared with jam as red as rubies on a plate. "He seemed a good man."

She set the plate down in front of them, and Hanna wasted no time in grabbing a slice.

"Wait, what? His friend didn't make it?"

She covered her mouth with her hand and felt as if she was going to vomit.

"Was he your friend too?" Daniela asked.

Mara hesitated, unsure of how to answer. "Yes."

It wasn't a lie. In the end, even if their marriage wasn't real, Valistaran *had* been a friend. Despite the pain he had caused, he saved her life at the Peace Ball massacre. He'd fought beside her friends during the Battle of Balgorod and elsewhere.

He had even given her an entire library in Bukaral.

"What was his name?"

"Val," Mara whispered.

"Oh, honey, I didn't mean to make you—"

"No, no. It's—thank you for telling me."

"I didn't know you knew him, I'm—"

"It's okay, ma. Really," Mara said as Hanna shifted on the couch and stared into her tea. "We had an interesting relationship, to put it lightly."

Just then, there was a knock on the door.

"Well, that must be Xanthurias come to save us from sad conversation!" Daniela said. "Quick, hide. He'll love this."

She ushered Mara behind the door, and Hanna, still on the couch, looked around in confusion.

Daniela opened the door and Aleksander, or Xanthurias as she knew him, hauled in a few stacks of firewood from outside.

He turned and caught the sight of Hanna sitting on the sofa with her mouth stuffed with the rest of her slice of jam-toast. "Wait, what?"

As he stood bewildered at seeing Hanna there, Daniela pulled Mara from behind the door so hard that she nearly tripped. Aleksander was so startled that he dropped the firewood and stumbled before tripping over the table. It toppled over, sending the teapot flying. It hit the ground and rolled but didn't break.

Hanna gasped and used her powers to make the second slice of bread float before it hit the ground, and Aleksander groaned as he rubbed his arm.

"What? Mara?!" Aleksander exclaimed, leaping to his feet, leaving the wood on the ground. He looked at Hanna and poorly signed, "*Why you save bread? Why no save Aleksander?*"

"Surprise!" Mara said in an awkward tone and a sheepish grin. Hanna signed the same word and wiggled her fingers in celebration, but her focus was on the jam.

Aleksander let out a loud belly laugh, and Mara rushed toward him and pulled him close. He lifted her off the ground and twirled, kissing her deeply before setting her down on her feet again.

"Is that—was that okay?"

"More than okay!"

Her eyes shined, and she couldn't rid herself of her smile. She pulled him close and buried her face against his shoulder, and a moment later, Hanna was hugging them both. Aleksander laughed and pulled her close as well.

"Well, hello, you two!" he exclaimed. "I am so, so, so confused, but very happy to see you!"

"I'll let you three catch up," Daniela said with a wide smile. "Don't mind me."

She hurried up the creaky staircase at the back of the room and disappeared upstairs, but they heard her give an emphatic cheer as she closed the door.

"I thought we lost you," Aleksander said. His heart raced. "What—how?"

As he stumbled over his words, Mara planted a soft kiss on his cheek.

"Surprise," Mara repeated, unsure of what else to say.

"I did something stupid," Aleksander said.

"What else is new?" Mara asked, punching him on the shoulder.

"Well, I tried to give back the Secret Keepers' memories like we planned. But then one of them betrayed us and took those memories to Thanatanos. Gold is better than maintaining thousands of years of culture, right?" Aleksander said, muttering the last sentence. "We chased him to the border wall, but we saw that Verahim's men were attacking their own villages. Valistaran and I—"

"I know. She told me."

"We were heading for Laniras to catch the rogue secret keepers, but I couldn't let them come here. I couldn't let them—they were going to—your mother is the only—"

As he fumbled with words again, she pulled him down by his collar and pressed her lips to his for a long moment. She pulled away, her eyes glistening with tears, and he rested his forehead on hers.

"You came back to save her?"

"Well, her and everyone else. They're my family, you know? I love them, and I couldn't—"

"I know, thank you. No more words. They aren't really your friends tonight," she said with a laugh. "Thank you, thank you, thank you." She pressed her forehead against his. "Oh, Aleks, dear, sweet Xanthurias. You deserve to be loved as much as you love everyone else."

Mara looked over to Hanna, who was sitting with an exaggerated smile with her palms against her cheeks and her elbows on her thighs as she sat cross-legged on the couch. She let out a little squeal.

"Want me to close my eyes so I can't hear you?" Hanna asked, shutting her eyes.

Both Aleksander and Mara laughed at this comment, and Mara crouched next to her friend, pulling her eyelids up with her thumbs.

They spent the next couple hours filling one other in about everything that had happened over the last few months they had spent apart from one another.

Hanna told them about the Purist's attack on the festival in Balgorod and her mission delivering food to the starving people in Adess.

They shared tears as Mara spoke about her time in the Thannish slave camps. Aleksander and Hanna held her on the sofa as she cried, although she tried not to speak loud enough for her mother to hear. She didn't want to burden her with the knowledge of what had happened to her and so many of her people.

Finally, Aleksander about what had happened in Kurash with the trial, the Secret Keepers, and the battle outside Cineca.

After that, they spent the rest of the night and into the early hours of morning chatting, laughing, and crying until they all fell asleep together on the overstuffed sofa.

CHAPTER FORTY-ONE

THANK YOU FOR TEACHING ME TO FLY

By noon the following day, Mara, Hanna, and Aleksander knew they needed to depart for Doftaan. Daniela had fixed them a breakfast of eggs, bacon, and fried potatoes and packed a satchel full of more food for the trip back to Doftaan, despite Mara's protests.

However, before leaving, Mara wanted to visit her father's grave. She'd spent an hour sitting alone next to her father's final resting place. The small cemetery, set upon a wooded hill, overlooked the river where Killian would often go fishing on the days he wasn't farming. He'd have liked the spot. She stared at the words on the headstone with a heavy, but loving heart.

She sat cross-legged in front of the grave unsure of what to say. She'd already poured her soul and apologized through sobs to the grave when she first arrived, wondering if he could hear her. Even if he couldn't, it helped alleviate some of the heavy guilt she had borne through the years.

"Remember that time I spilled an entire bucket of milk all over Pol?" Mara said, wiping away a tear as she let out a laugh. "It was dripping from his eyelashes. You told him to get some biscuits to go with the milk, and you weren't even mad." She let out a contented sigh and got to her feet, resting a hand on her father's headstone. "Thanks for teaching me to fly, papa."

She gave it one last, lingering look and hiked back down the overgrown cemetery toward the town.

She found Hanna and Aleksander adjusting the straps on Hippo's enormous saddle, and she put on the biggest smile she could.

"Ready to go?" Aleksander called.

Before she could answer, the sound of wagon wheels rolling over cobblestone drew her attention, and she turned to see a group of villagers, including her mother and Eva, pushing a cart covered in a canvas tarp.

"Excuse me," said one of the men. "Forgive me, but we have a—well, not a gift, exactly, but we couldn't let you go without… Well, you'll see."

The men drew the tarp back and hoisted a long, wooden box by long handles on its sides out of the wagon and set it on the ground. Mara knew exactly what the box was for, but she found herself asking anyway.

"What is this?"

She stepped next to the coffin and brushed her fingers across it with a reverent touch before pausing with her hand on its face. She felt tears forming in her eyes, and she hated herself for it. The misguided, complicated man that now lay dead in the coffin had been the source of so much of her pain.

Yet, she felt for him. She felt for her dead husband in the box. Not that the word 'husband' meant anything between them in all reality, but it may have once upon a time in another life.

Images of him finding her in the library of Bukaral filled her mind. The memorial for Rehor. The time he had rescued her from Florenta's forces. He had done much good in his life, too. If only it hadn't been tainted by trying to imprison every magic-user in Thanatanos in his camps.

"We would have all died if it wasn't for Xanthurias and your friend here," said Eva. "Val, you said his name was, right? We inscribed it on the top, there. See?"

Mara nodded. "It looks wonderful."

"The carpenters and smiths that made it used the metal from that big metal monster's armor for the interior. You know, to keep him safe in the afterlife," said Daniela.

Mara opened her eyes, letting out a breath she had been keeping inside for a few moments too long. She sniffed and wiped her eyes on the back of her hand. Aleksander looked down at her, and she forced a smile.

"You don't have to smile, you know," Aleksander said, kissing the top of her head. "Just feel what you feel."

Mara smiled in earnest, this time.

"I'm just emotional from saying goodbye to my papa. It's not like I'm going to miss this clown," Mara said, gesturing to the coffin.

Aleksander raised an eyebrow. "We both know that's not true. Despite everything…" He trailed off.

If she was this upset about *Valistaran's* death of all people, she knew she couldn't let another day go by where people across Sangora and the Deadlands camps were dying. Nothing else mattered until they were safe.

"I'll bring him home to Talohira. Thank you." She turned to Hanna and signed, *"Can you help them strap it down on Hippo's back?"*

Hanna nodded and telekinetically lifted the coffin onto Hippo's saddle just between his wings. The villagers climbed over the behemoth's limbs to scramble onto his back and secure the box with thick leather straps.

"I'm glad you have people who care about you," Daniela said. "We'll be here cheering you on! Now go finish this, Marška."

Mara felt a fierce determination fill her heart. She'd had enough mourning. Enough sadness. Enough death. There was to be no more running. No more hiding.

It was time to fight.

"Love you, ma," Mara said, hugging her goodbye.

"Love you too, Marška," Daniela said. "Now, you visit before fourteen more years go by, you hear? Not sure I'll be around by that time."

"Oh my goodness, ma. Yes, you will."

"Sure hope not. That's a long time," Daniela said, and Mara humored her with a sarcastic chuckle as Hanna and Aleksander climbed over Hippo's snout and onto his back.

"I'll visit, don't worry," Mara said, leading Aleksander toward Hippo's snout to climb onto his head. "And when this war is over, I'll have you over for dinner at my place."

"I think little old me would be out of place at a palace. Oh, and sweetie?" Daniela said. "I wrote you a letter. I know it isn't much, but I hope it helps you be brave out there with everything you need to do. It'll be like having a bit of me there with you."

"Thank you, mama."

She slid the folded parchment into her pocket.

"You know, it sounds like you're the only one who can fix this whole mess, so…go on and fix it. Be safe, though, okay?" Daniela said, giving Mara another tight squeeze. Mara laid her head on top of her mother's and hugged her back.

"I'll be safe."

"Go knock some skulls. Kick that Magistrate's ass."

"Ma!" Mara exclaimed with a laugh; she had rarely, if ever heard her mother say something like that. "Don't worry, I plan on it. Consider it kicked. Love you."

"I love you too, sweetheart."

Mara lifted her wings and flapped into the sky, landing between Hanna and Aleksander. The grateful villagers below waved goodbye as Hippo took flight, spiraled in the air, and raced eastward.

Mara looked at Valistaran's coffin and thought back to Rehor's funeral. He had mentioned that the grave was unworthy of the man buried beneath it, and she felt the same about the plain wooden coffin, but even more about her father's headstone.

Yet, she thought of the words inscribed beneath her father's name. *To live on in the hearts of those we love is to never truly die.*

"So, what's the plan?" Hanna asked. Sangoran sign language truly was a more effective form of communication with the roaring wind rushing past.

"We'll take Valistaran's body back to Doftaan. We don't have time to go back to Talohira right now. We'll use Nadezhda's shard of Thanatan's mirror and the one I stole to find the Magistrate, and... well, we kill her."

"It won't be that easy. I almost killed her, but it released the Faceless around Doftaan, and I got a lot of people killed."

She averted her gaze.

"Thanatan might know how to kill her. I'll ask him with Nadezhda's piece of his mirror."

"Be careful, please," Hanna said.

"You know me better than that," Mara signed with a laugh. *"But I promise. I will be. We'll figure it out."*

She squeezed her friend's hand as she watched Aleksander launching balls of fire off of Hippo's back, oblivious to their conversation.

"*Aw, look how happy he is.*"

They both laughed as Aleksander concentrated to launch various sizes of fireballs into the sky. Each time he produced a burst of dark flame like Valistaran's, he cheered.

"*You're forgetting the most horrible part of your near future,*" Hanna signed.

"*Which is?*"

"*Lots of meetings with important people.*"

"*It'll be the death of me.*"

Hanna nestled up next to the base of Hippo's wing behind Valistaran's coffin to get a bit of rest.

Mara drew the letter from her mother out of her pocket and stared at it for a long moment, a tender smile causing her lips to turn up at the corners.

To my dearest Marška:

I am so proud of you Marška. I know your pa is to. I dont know what you went thru when the slavers took you away but I am so proud that you made it thru it all. You are my greatest joy. You matter and you are enuf.

-Mamochka

Mara smiled through big, fat, happy tears that formed in the corners of her eyes as she traced the letters of her mother's elegant handwriting. It was beautiful and curving, much like Mara's own, despite the misspellings and mistakes. Mara's parents had not had the chance for a formal education, but one thing that her mother did know was how to write, and she did it perfectly. She folded the letter and placed it back in her coat in the pocket nearest her heart. She winced in pain as she did so; it'd hurt for several weeks, according to Alia.

Aleksander drew her attention as he shouted from the back of Hippo's saddle.

"Why don't we just take Hippo and have him melt the Magistrate?" Aleksander asked. Mara laughed, wondering if she had misheard him over the sound of the wind.

"Melt her?"

"Yeah, he does a good job at melting things," Aleksander shouted back. "It makes him happy! Why not?"

"You know exactly why we can't just kill her yet," Mara replied with an amused chuckle. "Hanna told you already."

She strode toward Aleksander and grabbed his hand. It was still hot to the touch from producing flame.

"Hippo's powerful, but he's not immortal. The day I met and bonded with him, I killed one just like him."

"Oh, true," Aleksander said, nodding. "But, I mean, you're *you*, though."

"And I wouldn't rather be anyone else," Mara said.

Aleksander kissed her on the forehead and lay on the other side of the coffin. "Hanna has the right idea. You should get some sleep too before we get there."

"I'll be right there," Mara said.

"No you won't," Aleksander replied. "You're going to sit there and make sure we're safe."

Mara let out a chuckle. "You know me well."

"Well, you can sit there and make sure we're safe over here." He patted the spot next to him, and she sat, holding his hand. She smiled down at him until she was sure he was asleep. She glanced over at Hanna to see her arms and legs sprawled out, and Mara wondered if she ever left Shanthah any room in their bed.

The guilt of not visiting her mother for thirteen years was completely gone. She had not entirely realized that it was eating away at her so horribly, but the weight off her wounded heart was astonishing.

She got to her feet and paced along Hippo's massive saddle, and then all of a sudden, there was the Magistrate in her crimson mask and dark, flowing robes.

"This isn't real," Mara said. "You're not here."

"Then why can you see me?"

Lightning sparked from Mara's hands, and shards of the Godblade spiraled around her knuckles.

"What do you want, you monster?"

"Now, now, let's not call the kettle black," said the Magistrate. *"I'm here to let you know that you have safe passage back into Doftaan. No need to sneak in and out again. I'll even have my forces pull back."*

"Why?"

"Because I'm bored waiting for you. With the invasion underway, the next part of my master plan was for you to challenge me for the throne."

"You're insane."

"Was that in question? You're correct, though, I'm not actually here." The electricity around Mara's fists dissipated, and the Magistrate stepped closer, reaching out with her hand.

It was gray and dead like the other Faceless, and jagged claws stained with blood tipped each finger.

"But if I'm not here, why can I touch you?"

She brushed a finger, dripping with blood, across Mara's cheek. Mara let out a scream as she felt the sensation on her face as the Magistrate faded on the wind.

Mara wiped her face with the back of her hand, but there was nothing there. Her heart thundered in her chest as she waited for the Magistrate to reappear, but nothing happened.

"She's messing with me," Mara whispered. "She wasn't here…"

And yet, she had felt her touch on her face. If she were only projecting an image to Mara's mind with her mindspeaking abilities, then how had she done that? She would have to ask Kamil, but even his considerable powers paled in comparison to the Magistrate's.

Perhaps, she was able to convince Mara's mind into thinking it felt the touch. Mara nodded. That had to be it. But it had felt so real—if she really was able to physically interact with others at a distance, was anyone safe?

She sighed and sat down, hugging her knees to her chest as she watched over her friends. She took Aleksander's hand again as he slept.

Not everything was right in the world. Not by a long shot. But despite all the death of recent days and the Magistrate's ominous message, she knew it would soon end one way or another.

"I'm coming for you," she whispered. The sensation of pins in needles covered her hand as a voice filled her mind.

"*I know. And I'm counting on it.*"

CHAPTER FORTY-TWO
BROKEN QUEENS

The Magistrate had been truthful, in a sense. While Mara, Hanna, and Aleksander had been granted safe passage back into Doftaan, the Thannish siege showed no signs of slowing. Smoke red with the light of cruel flame obscured what should have been a clear, glittering sky of starlit night.

Much of the northeastern wall of Doftaan had fallen, and portions of the city west of the twin rivers had gone up in flames.

But Doftaan and Sangora were not without its defenders.

Mara stood beside Hanna and Aleksander and two hundred of her royal guard at her back, each and every one of them ready and willing to die for Sangora. Before they had mobilized, Doftaan's citizens had risen up against their foes, arming themselves with whatever they could to help in the defense of their home.

Anca's forces were stationed in Akademrajon, the academic district to defend the University of Doftaan from one front, while Mara's forces stood on the east of the great river.

The sounds of explosions and screams heralded the Thans making their way through the streets.

"This is our moment, brave children of Sangora!" Mara shouted with her wings stretched wide. Her call was answered with a hearty cheer from her forces. "May no more tears be shed! If you draw your last breath today, let it be one of courage and not of fear! Eternal glory welcomes us home— but may the invaders' only legacy be the flowers that rise from this hallowed ground soaked with their blood!"

Aleksander pumped his fist and let a burst of flame into the sky as another collective war cry echoed into the night.

The enemy poured through the wide streets of the northern neighborhood of Vydraka as Mara's forces pounded their spears against the earth in rhythm with the war drums.

Hundreds of Thannish soldiers raced toward them, and she raised her bladed wings and screamed one last word with all the rage and fire she could muster.

"MERATH!" *DEATH!*

Her forces echoed her cry as they leapt into the air over the first wave of attackers before dispatching them with their bladed wings and spears and then launching into the sky once more.

When she was sure all of her people were across the river, she sent a bolt of lightning into the sky as the agreed-upon signal to destroy the bridges.

Aleksander gave a cry and launched a torrent of flame into a stack of barrels; they exploded, showering bits of stone, wood, and metal into the river as the bridge collapsed.

Hanna tore down a second bridge, and four more booms filled the air over the sound of battle as Mara's forces destroyed the others to prevent the invaders' advance.

The Thans' only avenue across the river now was to cross a wide, empty expanse between the Vydraka district and the artisan neighborhood of Naraka flanked by the two rivers. The Thans would be easy targets for flying enemies without the urban cover the city provided.

They fell for the trap, rushing into Naraka at their captain's command. Mara withdrew her wingblades from a man's chest as Hanna raised her hands, causing hundreds of stones to rise into the air. She flexed her fingers, and the soldiers cried out as her onslaught shattered bone and split skulls.

"Get the witch!" cried one of the Thannish leaders.

Several gunmen trained their sights on Hanna, but black flame erupted from Aleksander's arms, overtaking the men just before they were able to fire.

The Thans fought like lions, but Aleksander's dark fire drove fear into their hearts as Hanna rained swift death down upon them. Claps of thunder echoed through the street each time Mara felled a soldier with a bolt of white lightning.

Soon, part of Anca's forces emerged from the Naraka district; with Mara's soldiers on the other side, the Thans were completely surrounded. Anca gave the order to take them away.

The small victory instilled courage in each of their hearts, but they each knew there was much more to come. Mara led Aleksander, Hanna, and the rest of her royal guard past the Talohiran embassy just as a flaming projectile thrown by a trebuchet struck the stately building's roof. In a spray of crumbling stone and flame, the central tower collapsed.

Mara tackled Aleksander out of the way of the rubble as it fell toward them, and Hanna managed to shield the forces near her from being smashed. They all coughed as the dust settled. Thinking the worst of the strike was behind them, Mara helped Hanna to her feet.

She was wrong.

The Talohiran embassy exploded in a shower of black stone and ash. Mara, Aleksander, and many of their allies were knocked off their feet. Hanna cried out and summoned an invisible shield of mental energy, deflecting and disintegrating as much of the debris as possible, but it was not enough.

Giant chunks of stone crushed several of their fellow soldiers, and many more exploding projectiles rained down on their position. They detonated near the ruins of the embassy, decimating several homes as well as the road. Mara looked to the sky over the academic district where hundreds of Sangoran warriors were fleeing from the wall.

She swore under her breath as she saw the Thannish ballistae and troops armed with rifles and crossbows pouring into the academic district toward the University of Doftaan campus. With such weapons, the Sangorans lost their advantage of flight.

"Empress!" came a timid voice from near the burning embassy. Mara's head swiveled around, and to her horror, she saw a little girl huddled in the ruins of a burning home.

She glanced over her shoulder to see Anca's forces engaging the Thans that had broken through the wall, and no more explosives were raining down on her, so she deemed it safe to break away.

She hurried into the smoke and grabbed the girl's hand.

"It's okay, sweetie, I have you!" Mara said in Sangoran. "Where are your parents? Is your family safe?"

The Vydraka district had been evacuated the night before, its residents relocated to the southern neighborhoods.

"Mama went to the market two days ago and I haven't seen her since, and everyone is gone, and I am scared, and—"

She began to sob.

Mara wrapped her arms around the young girl.

"Which market? We need to get you to safety."

"The one in Bukaral," said the girl.

The girl's mother had been trapped outside of Doftaan when it had been put under lockdown, then. She could only hope the woman was safe wherever she was.

"What's your name?" Mara asked.

"Adela."

She comforted the girl and led her back to the road. A group of her royal guard stood ready and waiting, and she instructed five of them to take Adela to safety.

They obliged, and Mara turned back to Hanna and Aleksander. Before she could speak, all three of them felt it: a terrible groaning and intense sense of hunger and dread from the northwest.

"Are any of us surprised?" Mara asked, glancing at Aleksander, who shook his head.

The Magistrate's Faceless had returned to Doftaan. After the Magistrate had left the city, she'd taken her minions with her as if she were giving Mara's forces time to set up their side of a game board.

"Aleks, I'm sure that little girl wasn't the only straggler here. Please, search the area for anyone who didn't evacuate. Get them out of here and back to the palace."

"Will do." Aleksander nodded. "You stay safe, you hear?"

She pulled him closer by the caller and planted her lips on hers. "I promise."

He hurried off with four soldiers, and Mara turned to see Hanna on her knees holding her head.

"Hanna!"

She knelt next to her and placed a hand on her shoulder. Hanna looked up, and her hands shook as she signed, *"I can hear them—but it's all I can hear. Oh, by Elafris, it's horrible."*

She smacked the side of her head as if to knock the sound of the Faceless out of her mind. Mara put a hand on the side of Hanna's head, closed her eyes, and reached out with her mind. She focused on Hanna's thoughts and tried to force the sounds from her consciousness, but only succeeded in muffling them. Hanna gave a thumbs up as a series of warning horns sounded from the south.

"The horns are signaling that the Faceless are coming from the south. You good?"

Hanna nodded. "*Never better.*"

Mara reached out with a telepathic eye to sense thousands upon thousands of dead, vengeful creatures attacking from the south.

The Thannish soldiers had made it to the top of the walls with siege ladders that clamped onto the ramparts, and they'd managed to drive the airborne Sangoran defenders back with their crossbows and guns long enough to hoist a line of ballistae onto the wall using pulley systems.

"*Think we can take them all?*" Mara signed to Hanna, who smirked with a determined nod.

Five more explosions rocked the neighborhood, one close enough that it made Mara's ears ring. Knowing her forces were in General Anca's very capable hands, she raised her wings and shot into the sky with Hanna levitating close behind. Bits of jagged rock swirled around Hanna's wrists ready to be turned into deadly projectiles. Down below, Anca saluted her as she soared by, and she returned the gesture.

When they were high enough above the wall, Mara tucked her wings close and shot like an arrow down toward her foes.

The man operating the ballista had no time to react, and the ballista wasn't able to aim directly upward even if he did. Her wing blades carved through the operator's shoulders, and before his arms hit the ground, Hanna had pierced his companion's chest just as Mara clapped a third man in the neck so hard that he fell from the battlements.

The captain of the Thans near the wall cried something, and three of the ballistae turned toward them. Mara swore under her breath and leapt from the wall as Hanna floated straight up into the sky.

As Mara unfurled her wings and glided over the camp of the Thannish forces amassed at the wall, she saw soldiers hoisting other equipment between the ballistae.

"Hanna!" Mara screamed as one of the strange weapons turned to face her.

A flurry of bullets sprayed from the weapon's mouth, and Hanna was barely able to deflect them with her mind.

She sent many of them back at her attackers, peppering three soldiers with a flurry of death; dozens of bloody holes opened across their bodies, and they slumped, dead, against the battlements. One of the projectiles made it through her telekinetic shield, grazing the flesh on her forearm. A second bullet pierced her leg, and she screamed, falling from the sky.

Mara shot toward her as the Thannish soldiers called to reload and fire. Multiple bolts from the ballista raced toward them as three of the rapid-fire guns on stands sent another spray of bullets in their direction.

As Mara carried Hanna away from the wall, Hanna clenched her fist, causing the ground beneath two of the guns to crumble. The men screamed and fell from the wall as Mara struggled to focus to deflect the hundreds of projectiles with her own telekinesis.

Hanna levitated on her own, but Mara knew the injury and exhaustion were causing Hanna's power to falter. She gestured over her shoulder to Mara's palace south of the river, and Mara nodded.

Mara glided next to Hanna in retreat, but not defeat. They crossed over the river, and Mara guided her to a balcony set at the base of a high tower. As she landed, she looked with a pained heart upon the smoke rising from the northern districts of Doftaan.

She felt Hanna's hand on her shoulder.

"It'll be okay," Hanna said aloud, and Mara gave a sad nod before they entered the palace war room through the set of tall double doors. Inside, many of Mara's advisors and other leaders had assembled around a long table.

The welcome voice of a friend greeted them.

"Empress!"

"Vasa!" Mara exclaimed with a wide smile, using the diminutive version of her friend and councilor, Vasilica's name.

"Thank the goddesses you're back!" Vasilica exclaimed. "I've been trying to govern in your absence, but—" She gestured out the window.

"As governor and Guardian of Doftaan, you are well in your rights to do so."

She sensed Vasilica's anxiety subside ever so slightly.

"I didn't want you to think I wanted this to happen, or to take over for you," Vasilica said. "I am ever loyal to you, Empress, and I am beyond thankful you are home."

"It's good to see you too, Vasa," Mara said.

She glanced over the crowd to see all of her Mistresses of Dusk, or rather, Guardians of Sangora, seated around the table. Only Anca was absent, as she was guiding the battle outside. As they stood, Mara made eye contact with Lavinia, who gave her empress a conspicuous wink.

Each and every one of them had come. They had survived, and her heart swelled with joy. Hanna had already evicted Shanthah from his seat, and he stood behind her while young Diana sat between Raluca and Ruta, who had assisted in Shanthah's Alboran revolution.

To her surprise, Valeniya Talohir was there as well, sitting in a chair behind Lavinia, her knee bouncing nervously.

Vasilica turned to the other assembled Sangorans in the room, and they stood at attention, arms and wings at their sides, fist to the forehead in the Sangoran salute.

"Ža Jempratu i Sangoru!" Vasilica shouted. *For the Empress and for Sangora!*

"Ža Jempratu i Sangoru!" the soldiers and advisors all replied in unison.

"Ža Sangoru!" Mara called in response. "Ža vami!"

For Sangora! For you!

Vasilica led the others in the Sangoran bow, fists to the forehead, raised wings, and a bent knee.

"What is your will, Empress?" Vasilica asked.

"I need a full report," Mara replied, taking her seat at the head of the long table covered in maps of Sangora and Doftaan. "Quickly. I don't want to waste more time talking."

"Of course, Empress," Vasilica said, taking her seat next to Lavinia.

"But first, I wanted to make one small change to our hierarchy. There will be no more Mistresses of Dusk—instead, you will be called the Guardians of Sangora. Mistress of Dusk is a term with roots from a dark time in our country's history, and I wish to tear each and every one of those roots from the earth and burn them."

She paused for a moment, looking at each face around the war table.

"As you know, I've been away for a long time. I've seen firsthand the atrocities Thanatanos is committing in the slave camps in Terman, Adess, and beyond. I need updates on everything happening *here* with the invasion. I know your pain. I know your courage. I have seen and experienced both; I cannot begin to express my gratitude for each of you here for defending our home as long as you have. Lavinia, if you will?"

"Yes, Empress," Lavinia replied. Rayshel stood behind her, ever supportive. "As you know, our forces have retaken Doftaan. We had prepared for an invasion of the city, but the Magistrate's armies left on their own accord only to return now. Several towns and cities are under Thannish control."

"She's playing with us," Mara explained. "Lulling us into a false sense of security and playing with lives. Ours, as well as those of her own followers. It's all a game to her."

Her Guardians updated her quickly on the status of several important cities across the country they had either held or lost to the Thans.

"How many losses in Doftaan so far?" Mara asked.

"Thousands already," Anca replied.

"And what efforts to evacuate the civilians here?"

"Apart from relocating them to safer parts of the city, none are possible," Guardian Raluca replied.

Ruta spoke up for the first time. "Emergency camps have been set up in Maranparkh for all displaced persons, but there are millions of people in Doftaan. They can't all make it."

"I want a complete, mandatory evacuation from Akademrajon and the rest of the university district. The minds there are the best hope of the future of Sangora, and I want them defended."

"We've tried, but it's already been overrun. Their guns and ballistae make it impossible," Raluca said.

"Then I want it retaken. Guardians Ruta and Diana, I'd like you to coordinate the evacuation," Mara ordered. Ruta and Diana nodded.

"Yes, Empress," they said in unison.

"Florenta's Enforcers' heavy armor and Boltpikes should still be in the armory. Our forces won't be able to fly, but they'll be able to repel bullets, and their shields should be able to block even ballista bolts," Mara instructed, and her Guardians nodded. "If they can clear the wall, it might give our forces to the north a fighting chance."

"It will be done," Raluca said.

"I killed the Magistrate's Mistresses of Dusk except for Mistress Kariana. Do we know where she is now?"

"She's leading her forces loyal to her against our people in Adess and Terman to prevent them from helping us here," Lavinia said. "She has proven most successful. The forces here are mostly Thannish and Faceless, with *some* of Mistress Kariana's supporters."

As she further explained the dire situation, the guards opened a door at the back of the chamber and ushered Aleksander inside.

"What took you so long?" She smirked as she mindspoke.

"Very funny. I can't fly, remember?" he thought back, and she chuckled to herself.

"What news from Balgorod, Alboras, and Timishuara?"

Shanthah glanced over at Lavinia, gesturing between them, trying to determine who should speak. In the end, Lavinia pointed directly at him until he spoke.

"It's dire there. We'd like to get back as soon as possible, but we might be trapped. Balgorod is holding. The Academy of the Hidden Flame is safe, and all my students and thousands of civilians are taking refuge there. They've taken a few towns, but they thought they'd take Balgorod sooner, and it's drawing all of their attention in the region, fortunately and unfortunately."

Mara opened her mouth to respond, but Valeniya spoke for the first time. Mara jumped, having almost forgotten she was in the room.

"The battle in Balgorod is over," Valeniya said, her eyes glossed over with a silverish sheen. "The bad men have pulled away. The people there are cheering. They are safe."

"Do you see Josman Faros and General Rayna Cotula?" Shanthah asked. "I left them in charge of defending the city."

"Yes. They are alive. At Hanna's bar."

A moment after Shanthah translated for Hanna, with a chuckle she signed, *"I'll put it on their tab."*

Soon enough, the meeting drew to a close after they finished their discussion of tactics and plans.

Mara stood, as did the rest of the chamber. Everyone except her closest allies saluted and bowed before filing out the main doorway.

Lavinia was the first to greet her "You look horrible. Smell bad, too."

"Good to see you, buddy," Mara replied with a laugh. "I do suppose it's been a while since I've bathed…"

Lavinia clapped Mara on the back in a side-hug and stepped aside for the others to greet her. Diana stepped forward next.

"Mara!" she exclaimed, her big green eyes peeking out from a head of messy, blonde hair.

"Oh, Diana," Mara whispered, kneeling next to the young girl so that she'd be closer to her height. "I never asked you to be here and put your life in danger."

Diana squeezed Mara's hand. "You never had to."

Tears welled up in the corners of her eyes. "Thank you."

"You were there for me, so where else would I be?" Diana asked. "I can't forget something like that, or I'll never be the leader you know I can be."

A short rapier hung from the young girl's belt, and on her back was a crossbow. Mara gave her a wink, which she returned with a wide smile. She'd grown since Mara had first met her hiding within the crumbling, bramble covered wall in the Talohiran slave camp—but not only in height; she could sense a deepening maturity within Diana's soul.

Two years prior, she'd designated the young girl as one of her Mistresses of Dusk under the tutelage of the others. The choice had been controversial, but Mara insisted that the pure, innate goodness of a child is just what Sangora needed.

"I can't hide anymore," Diana said. "None of us can. We have to be brave."

"Brave girls are the happiest," Mara said, referring to their recurring conversation that had evolved over the years.

Diana nodded. "But broken queens are the bravest."

Mara wasn't able to stop the tears from flowing.

But before Mara could answer, another explosion echoed outside, bringing her back to reality.

"I think you'd like to know that Kariana's put a bounty of fifty million moneti for anyone who brings her your head," Shanthah said. Lavinia traced a line across her own throat with a finger. "A bit gorier of a sport than I'm into, but I can see how the Thans and her own Sangorans are keen on playing."

"That's a lot of money. Don't get any ideas, Vinia," Mara said with a laugh. "It's a game I'd really prefer to win, but my first priority is maximizing the safety of my people."

"Can I say something?" Diana asked. Mara nodded as Aleksander took a seat next to Ruta, Shanthah, and Hanna.

"Of course, Guardian Diana."

"I don't think she wants to recapture Doftaan. I think she's done playing with it and wants it removed as a threat. There's this game that my friends at the academy here play," Diana said.

"With all due respect, Empress and Guardian Diana, games aren't the same as—" Mara cut Raluca off with a wave of the hand.

"Let her speak, please."

"Thank you, Mara. Well, there's this game that I play with some of the other students at the university. It's a war strategy board game. Sometimes when you're playing, you have a certain city that either isn't useful anymore, or you know your opponent is going to capture it, so you take all the resources out and reallocate them somewhere else. Then, you let them take it. When they take it over, they don't get anything special or useful. You lose the city and the points, but you keep the important game pieces to use elsewhere. But not only that, their most important pieces are now in that city, and won't be a threat elsewhere."

"So, you're saying she's not trying to take the city, she's trying to destroy it," Mara said, nodding.

"Yeah. I don't think she wants anything in the city other than one thing," Diana said. Mara cocked her head. "You make us all brave, Mara. It's you. It's why she waited to start the invasion until you were taken away."

"If she can kill you, she knows she can win, and Sangora is hers. If she can't, well…" Ruta said, trailing off.

"She's letting our people win," Raluca said in realization. "She's letting us take territory here with just enough resistance to weaken our forces and draw our attention away from the rest of the invasion. And then, she can crush us *and* Mara when the time is right. Why didn't I see it before?"

"Because a twelve-year-old is smarter than you," Lavinia said, sharing a high-five with Diana. Shanthah laughed out loud, and Raluca slugged him in the shoulder.

Lavinia raised a finger for permission to speak, and Mara gestured to her. "If our beloved Empress of Blood becomes a martyr, none of her people will support the Magistrate. That's why she tried to tarnish your reputation by posing as you. The people here didn't fall for the trick—they love you, and nothing is going to change that. But outside of Doftaan, you'll need to do some damage control when this is all over."

"So, she believes if she can crush Doftaan, the rest will fall in line whether they support her or not," Mara said. "We're getting our people through this. We've fought too damn hard for anything less. I'm going after the Magistrate myself. If she wants me dead, she's going to have to do it herself."

"Not alone you aren't," Lavinia said.

"Send for Kamil and Alia, please," Mara said to Shanthah, who nodded.

"Will do, boss."

"One last thing. The people need something to lift their spirits. I want a festival set up in the gardens outside the palace."

Vasilica nodded. "I'll make it happen."

"Thank you, Vasa. Let's meet again early tomorrow morning. Until then, go eat some dinner and get some rest."

She smiled as her Guardians, Valeniya, and Rayshel bid her and one another goodnight, and they shuffled out of the war room, leaving her alone with just Hanna, Aleksander, and Shanthah.

"I know you're thinking about going back out there," Aleksander said. "I see that look."

Mara nodded. "I have to."

"*You should get some rest too,*" Hanna signed.

"I'm not going to be able to sleep until this is over, you know that," Mara said out loud and signed.

"About that," Shanthah said. "Before you arrived, we were discussing how long the siege could last. It could be days. That's a long time to stay awake, Bartunek."

Mara chuckled. "You might have a point."

She walked to a high window and peered outside to see that neither Sangora nor Thanatanos had gained any grand; it seemed to be at a standstill.

"We ordered the kitchens to prepare some food," Shanthah said.

"You like food. You've probably not had any of the good stuff since you were in Kurash," Aleksander added.

"You know just how to convince me to stay," Mara replied with a wink. "Fine. Food, then sleep. But only long enough that I don't die."

The others chuckled, and they accompanied one another to the kitchen for a bite of dinner to recover for the horrors that undoubtedly awaited them the next day.

Rain clattered down on the roof of the palace as Mara finally opened the door into her private bedchamber an hour later. It looked nearly exactly as it had before Florenta's coup, and the warm feeling of coming home washed over her heart.

She placed what remained of her meal on a chest of drawers. She'd finish it in the morning. She had been ravenous but disappointed that she found herself unable to finish the wonderful roasted chicken and sauteed vegetables.

She kicked off her boots; one landed on the bed, and the other in the corner near her floor length mirror.

Mara yawned and slipped her tunic off from over her head and wings, dropping it in an unceremonious heap on the ground and kicked off her thick trousers alongside it.

She gazed at the unfamiliar reflection in the mirror standing in the corner and traced a finger over the mess of scars that flowered outward from her heart. The pattern was oddly beautiful, and her gaze lingered upon it until it fell upon her very visible ribs and hipbones that jutted out more than she ever remembered them doing.

She'd lost a considerable amount of weight and muscle in the slave camp, and she knew it'd take time before she was in peak condition again. She let out a deep breath, grabbed a robe from the closet, and tied it across the waist.

"Maybe I *should* finish dinner, then."

She chuckled to herself; maybe she'd go request a second, or even third plate.

As she sat on the edge of the bed to attempt again to finish dinner, she caught sight of a long, wrapped package laying atop the bed's taut covers. Curious, she set the plate of food on the floor and gingerly picked up the parcel.

She removed the cloth and gasped, for inside was a sword sheathed in black leather.

"Impossible," she whispered as she wrapped her fingers around the handle to draw the crystal weapon from the sheath.

The Godblade.

"How?" she whispered to herself. For a moment, she was very afraid that someone would answer.

No one did, and she was very grateful.

She discarded the sheath and willed the blade to dematerialize. It shattered into countless shards of glass and diamond so small that they flowed into the pores on her hand and arm. Her flesh prickled with pins and needles for a few moments, and then it was gone.

Had the Magistrate been in her bedroom? If so, had she been there before or after she'd left Doftaan? Was this a message that she wasn't safe, even here?

There was no other explanation. The Magistrate had taken the blade from her during their first confrontation, and therefore, she had to be the one to return it. But why? What was this new step in the cruel woman's game?

Yes. It was a challenge, and she knew it.

She stood with a look of consternation etched across her elegant features.

She summoned the blade, and it shined in the dim lighting. She concentrated her mental abilities within the blade, searching for any trace of Thanatan's mind that remained.

"Are you there?"

"I was wondering when you'd ask."

It wasn't Thanatan's voice that replied from within the weapon, but the Magistrate's. Mara recoiled and nearly dropped the sword, but she knew she shouldn't be surprised.

"Where the hell are you?" Mara asked. "I'm here, coward."

"Meet me in your throne room tomorrow, at noon. Do not be late. Don't worry, you, your city, and your friends are safe for now as long as you aren't late."

Mara glowered at the blade and forced it to shatter again. She let it disappear into her hand, and she felt her connection with the Magistrate break.

When she had recovered from the shock of hearing the Magistrate's voice in her mind, she pulled the topmost blanket away, taking extra care to untuck the others with a cheeky smile; she'd always told Elena and the other palace attendants to stop making her bed. She could do it herself, she had told them.

Elena had replied with, "Then why don't you?"

She made a mental note to visit Elena, wherever she was now. She'd recognized many of the palace staff upon her return, so she reasoned that Florenta and the Magistrate hadn't killed or replaced everyone.

She grabbed one of the pillows from the bed and spread the top blanket over the floor. It'd take some time to get used to such a soft bed, just like last time. There were so many of her people that were still without beds lying freezing on the ground, and her heart was still with them.

So instead of curling up in the warmth of her bed, she pulled the simple blanket over herself and fell asleep on the stone floor thinking about the liberation of her people.

Thinking about the death of the Magistrate.

Thinking about peace.

CHAPTER FORTY-THREE
ALL THE WORLD A CHESSBOARD

Noon.

Mara strode down the hall clad in her intricate armor of black, gold, and crimson. Her wings were tipped with golden blades and razorclaws were fastened to each finger, and in her right hand, she held the Godblade. Electricity crackled around her arms and wings.

Aleksander, Hanna, Lavinia, Kamil, Alia, Shanthah, and Vasilica accompanied her into the throne room as she pushed open the great double doors. Aleksander's hands were alight with flame, shards of broken glass swirled around Hanna's head ready to be used as deadly projectiles, and both Lavinia and Vasilica were armed to the teeth with blades.

And there, completely unguarded and alone, sat the Magistrate upon Mara's throne.

"You're in my seat," Mara said, her tone dark and cold.

The Magistrate cocked her head unnaturally far to look at Mara. She craned her neck forward as she peered into Mara's face.

"Oh, my sweet child," said the Magistrate to their minds. *"This was my throne long before you were even born. These are my people, not yours."*

Mara placed a foot on the lowest step leading up to the throne, glaring at her enemy. Her friends stood behind her, their weapons at the ready. Kamil focused all his mental energy to keep the Magistrate's power in check, his hands shaking and the vein in his temple throbbing.

"You aren't Codruta Talohir," Mara said.

"No."

"But I do know who you are," Mara said. She took another step up the stairs. "And you don't scare me."

When the Magistrate spoke again, it was not with her mind; a dead, raspy, voice escaped from beneath her crimson mask.

"I should."

Even Mara recoiled at the sound of her voice. The woman must have retained some semblance of a mouth after becoming Faceless, but the sound was unnatural and guttural, as if she lacked a jaw.

The Magistrate stood, and everyone raised their weapons. She descended from the throne and stooped down until her mask was level with Mara's face. She reached out and traced a line along Mara's jaw with a jagged, bloodstained claw.

"There's only one woman I know of who would revel in the slaughter of what she claims are her own people," Mara spat. "Only one person evil enough to use genocide as a toy in her cruel game! The only person in this world so vengeful that—"

"Say my name, Empress. It's been oh, so long since someone did. And who better to say it than Mara Bartunek, the fallen angel of death herself?"

"Queen Sanda Daktha."

The Magistrate laughed, the gruesome sound of wet, dripping mud filled with gravel.

"Sanda Daktha: Thanatan's Magistrate. That's what I was, and I played my part well. I was an obedient servant until you did what I was planning to do."

Mara knew Queen Sanda Daktha was much more than Thanatan's pawn. She had committed genocide, slaughtering millions of Sangoran men across the country. She'd been entirely unaware of her existence, as Valistaran and Codruta had done everything in their power to erase her from history.

Mara did not answer as Sanda paced around her. The world around them distorted with the former queen's unhinged mind cracking and breaking their perceived reality with her unmatched mindspeaking abilities. All around the Magistrate's body looked as if looking through a warped glass.

Mara watched with bated breath as doorways into other worlds seemed to open; the Magistrate's mind began to leak from behind the mental dam Kamil was trying to maintain, the walls became curtains of blood like great crimson waterfalls, the floor became an ashen field, and the sky, a cloud of dark smoke under a blood red moon.

"You know, you could kill me right now," she said as the illusions became more real. "I have no weapons, and your Mindspeaker is doing his best to contain my power, but as you can see, his power is failing. So why don't you take your chance?"

"Gladly," Lavinia said, stepping forward, raising the twin blades that jutted out from beneath her vambraces.

"Ah, who's this?" Sanda asked, her neck twisting the other direction with a crack. Lavinia stood beside Mara, and Sanda stared into Lavinia's eyes from behind the soulless mask.

"Lavinia. Lavinia *Daktha*," Lavinia said. And then, with venomous contempt added, "Hello, *mother.*"

The guttural laughter filled the chamber once more, and an illusion of shadow and flame followed the Magistrate as she stepped back up the stairs to the throne and sat down.

"And where's your sister? Where's Zhanna?"

"You know damn well where she is."

Without another moment's hesitation, Lavinia rushed forward, but Mara blocked her way with a thick wing. Lavinia skirted around it, knocked Mara back, and raced up the steps toward the throne.

"Stop!" Mara shouted, but Lavinia grasped her mother by the throat and raised her arm blade.

"Do it, daughter. Damn your people. It will all be your fault."

Lavinia glanced over her shoulder at Mara, her blade still pressed against Sanda's throat.

"What are you talking about?" she shouted, her face painted crimson by the Magistrate's illusion of blood gushing down the walls all around them.

Hanna grasped Shanthah's hand in fear as Sanda projected images into their minds of the Faceless tearing into their foes' bodies and disemboweling innocent civilians. Kamil fought to banish the ghoulish specters, but his limbs trembled under the strain of his powers.

"Kill me, and they all die."

"You're wrong." Lavinia spat, shoving her mother against the throne.

"I should have tried harder to have you and your sister killed," the Magistrate said, twisting her neck to stare into Lavinia's soul.

At that, Lavinia thrust her blade forward. Mara grabbed her arm just in time, but Lavinia batted her away with a swipe of her wing. As Mara struck the ground with a groan, Hanna grasped Lavinia with her mind, suspending her in midair, her blade an inch from her mother's throat.

"Put me down!" Lavinia shouted. "Damn it, Hanna!"

Vasilica helped Mara to her feet as Hanna forced Lavinia to her knees.

"She dies!" Lavinia cried.

"Yes, but not like this!" Aleksander cried. "Hanna tried, and what the Magistrate said would happen came to pass."

"Stop it, Vinia!" Mara cried.

Lavinia nodded in defeat, and Hanna released her. She shut her eyes tightly as illusions of her and her big sister running away chased by ghosts and soldiers filled the world.

Her eyelids did not stop the images, and a tear rolled down her cheek. Alia crouched next to her with a consoling hand on her shoulder. Lavinia did not pull away.

"What do we do, Empress?" Vasilica asked as Aleksander helped Lavinia to her feet.

Mara thought for a long moment, her arms crossed.

"We have two choices," Mara said. "We let her go and we all live to fight another day, or we kill her, and Laniras, Doftaan, and anywhere else she has Faceless die. I don't quite like either choice. You deserve to die, you foul witch. Everyone in this room deserves to kill you. But it pains me to say that you're right."

"I always am, sweetheart," said the Magistrate as images of massacres across Sangora filled the world.

The images shifted from Sanda's genocide to the destruction of Nitra; an illusion of Mara's own face and hands spattered with crimson peered out from behind the flowing curtain of blood.

"You all make the same predictable mistakes. You, that Valistaran boy, others. They think 'killing the witch' will end all their problems. Oh, silly girl. I've given Sangora back now. Do you feel accomplished? Do you feel like you've won? As the rightful queen, I'm giving it back until I want to play with it again."

"All the world is your chessboard," Mara spat.

"And you are the little pawn who somehow became a queen," Sanda said as she strode away, unhindered. "Do not think my departure is kindness, mercy, or fear. It wouldn't be fun to end the game when both queens still stand, and I'm not afraid of the challenge. As you say, this is my gameboard. And I'm not done playing."

"Rot in hell, mother," Lavinia spat as the Magistrate walked past her.

"I've already been. I'll introduce you to the devil when we're all reunited there."

Sanda's disgusting laugh dripped from behind her mask, and she walked away.

They didn't stop her from leaving. They couldn't.

Mara watched as she disappeared into the darkness of the corridor outside the throne room, and the illusions around the chamber slowly faded away. With a heavy heart, Mara hung her head.

She felt Aleksander grab her hand, and he led her to the window, where they all gathered around Shanthah and Hanna, who were gazing out the window.

The sun had begun to peek out from behind the clouds, and as the Magistrate had promised, the fighting had not recommenced, although the Thannish forces were still visible within and without the city wall.

Hanna stepped away and sat down on Mara's high, silver throne. She crossed her legs and rested her chin on her fist.

"This seat is pretty comfortable, so if you don't want it, I'll be Empress of Blood. I'd make a good one. I'd be fair, but rule with an iron fist."

Mara laughed. "Go right ahead."

Hanna stood, gesturing to the throne.

"All hail Hanna Samsa, the Empress of Blood!" Hanna signed with a wry smirk.

"Up," Mara said with a scowl. Hanna squeezed Mara's shoulder and stepped down from the throne.

The others clapped as Mara took her rightful seat in her throne and let out a deep breath. She thrust the Godblade into the stone beside her seat, then Hanna signed, *"You know, I really thought there would be more trumpets and fanfare when you sat down there again."*

Mara laughed, and signed back, *"No, this is how I always wanted it. With no one but my friends."*

"And what is your first order as the newly reinstated Empress of Blood?" Aleksander asked.

He joined Vasilica, who had bowed with bent knee before her empress. Lavinia and the others followed, leaving Hanna standing alone. She glanced back and saw the others kneeling and she quickly dropped down as well next to Shanthah and Alia.

"My first order is to order you all to stop bowing to me," Mara said with a smile. "I think we've been through enough together for that nonsense to stop."

They all laughed and stood, waiting for Mara to speak. She was silent for a long moment, running her palms over the familiar armrests of her chair.

"My *real* first command," she said, "is to find a way to kill Sanda Daktha. There's nothing holding us back now. We've all lost so much, had our hopes smashed and dreams killed. Well, it's time to change that. It's time to kill that witch."

CHAPTER FORTY-FOUR

THE STORY OF OUR SCARS

Two days passed with little fighting within the walls of the city. However, explosions still rocked the outskirts of Doftaan at night. No one was allowed to leave the city, both by Mara's decree and the siege surrounding Doftaan.

That particular evening, however, Mara stood upon her balcony overlooking her people, Sangoran and human alike, gathered together at an impromptu festival planned by Vasilica, Ruta, and Diana to raise the spirits of the frightened citizens. People laughed and danced, shared delicious Sangoran fair food, and threw colorful ashes into the air.

The second Festival of Ashes.

She'd implemented the first one in Balgorod, declaring that wonderful things would emerge from the ashes of the battle that had taken place there two years ago. Indeed, the Alboran people had found their hard-won freedom.

And so it was today. Doftaan's Festival of Ashes would be the promise of a brighter, more peaceful future free of the Magistrate's dark hold on the nation. Or so she planned to say in the speech she still hadn't written.

The one she was now standing on the balcony to share. Aleksander, Hanna, Shanthah, Kamil, and Alia stood directly behind her, and each of the Guardians of Sangora were seated at the back of the balcony.

The architecture of the palace provided the necessary acoustics for Mara's voice to carry across the crowd below. She cleared her throat and began to speak.

"My dear, dear people," Mara said, gripping the balcony railing with both hands. She paused for a moment, looking over the assembled masses. "I am so happy to be standing here before you again as your empress, but also as your friend. I know everything that has transpired must be confusing, but I would like the chance to explain, if you will allow me.

"Two years ago, my own councilor, Florenta Karpaska, betrayed me and led a coup against my court. Many people I loved died that day, and she claimed the throne, as you know. During her short rule, Doftaan came under assault by the Faceless, and many of our beautiful people died, and with you, I mourn their loss. We all should, and we always will.

"Several revolutions, some successful, others not so, sprouted up around Sangora. The revolution led by Guardian Shanthah Kalen in Alboras, formerly known as Karpaska, was successful, and they declared themselves independent from Florenta's Sangora for the last two years. Guardian

Kalen let me know that a vote was taken there, and the people have spoken—they will remain autonomous, but within a union with the rest of Sangora. We will not abandon them.

"For those unaware, the Magistrate of Thanatan, a cruel Faceless woman, has been ruling Sangora from the shadows ever since Florenta's death two years ago. Likewise, I fear that she has also been pulling King Verahim's puppet strings in Thanatanos as well.

"Many of you must be terribly confused and saying that I was never gone, that this is all a conspiracy to justify what has happened. The Magistrate posed as me to gain your trust and then ruin my reputation in your eyes. I know that many of you will not believe my words, but I want to do everything in my power to remedy what she has done and prove to you that I am *me*. That I love you. That I will die for you.

"She made a deal with Verahim, king of Thanatanos that allowed them to expand into Adess and Terman, and in return, they would help her conquer the lands to the north of us known as United Baltija

"Very recently, we discovered the Magistrate of Thanatan's true name. It was a name that was expunged from the libraries of Doftaan and Bukaral alike. A name attached to such atrocity that it was erased from existence, and an alternate history taught in our schools. But those of you old enough to remember know that I speak the truth. Her name was Queen Sanda Daktha. She was responsible for the genocide of Sangoran men across much of what was then the Sangoran kingdom.

"She was killed by High King Valistaran Talohir, and her memory erased from history, but when Thanatan returned with his Faceless monsters, she was reborn as one of them. She bided her time and when I killed Thanatan, she claimed his power, throne, and Faceless horde for herself."

As she paused, she saw a group of guards and soldiers acting to subdue a group of unruly protesters, but she continued.

"But she is gone now. I have returned alongside a group of councilors who have proven their trustworthiness and love for Sangora. Each and every one of them has literally fought and bled for you. They have felt your pain and know your story, as do I.

"Those that believe my story may be wondering where I have been. I fought in the Alboran Revolution, working tirelessly to get to this point to save Doftaan from Florenta and Queen Daktha's grasp. However, before I could, I was captured by Thannish slavers and shipped to a prison camp far into the Eastern Deadlands. The story of my—our—escape is…well, it's a story for another day, as they say.

"But I survived, just like you have, and you will continue to do. I do not say this to boast. Not for myself, anyway. I do, however, want to boast about the wonderful courage that you have all shown me through these chaotic years. You have faced war. Famine. Disease. Tyranny. All of these things are enough to break any nation, and yet, here we all are. *You* have survived. We all have.

"I love you, Sangora. I love you, Alboras. Each and every one of you is dearer to me than I can ever express. From this day on, I vow to work every day to regain your trust and rebuild our great and proud nation. I will defend you until my last, dying breath is forced from my lungs, if the universe calls for that to happen.

"But please, I beg of you, to refrain from hatred and violence. The war is not over, but it soon will be. And when my time comes to join our ancestors, I want to be able to say that I knew you longer in life than I have to remember you in death, so please, stay safe.

"I tell you this because I am scared. I am scared, and you, the Sangoran people, give me strength. The small acts of kindness I have seen across this nation are what make it wonderful, not the blades we carry.

"It is no secret that I have been a slave for most of my life. My body is covered in scars from the horrors I have faced. But I am grateful for each and every one of them, because they brought me here to you. They are my story. Without my scars, I would not have found the love I have for you.

"And so it is with Sangora. Sangora is a land of scars and pain, but we will use that pain to develop love for one another. Those among you who ascribe to the faith of the goddesses will remember the verse from your holy writings that says, 'From the deepest scars comes the holy blood of love and life.' I myself am not a religious woman, but it is true. The story of our scars will bring us life and love.

"I have had to move on from the pain I have faced as a slave. It will always be there with me. Just as your pain, the death caused at the hands of Thanatanos, Florenta, and others will also remain. However, my parting words to you today are these: We must learn to live with, and not *in* the past. Thank you, my beautiful friends. Sangora will rise from the ashes. This, I promise you.

"These words are heavy, I know, and I apologize. But please do not let the smoke and fire of war outside our walls keep you from joy and love.

"Now, enjoy this Festival of Ashes, which begins *now!* Take time to be happy, for you have earned it. Your happiness *will* endure longer than the swords of Thanatanos do. Ža Sangoru, i ža vami!"

Sangoran folk music and singing filled the streets below. Mara lingered on the balcony for several minutes, soaking in the happy atmosphere.

Her friends and each of the Guardians of Sangora, except Anca, who had excused herself, gathered in her throne room, the double balcony doors wide open so that they could look out upon the festival

Shanthah was regaling Diana, Hanna, Vasilica, and Raluca with a dramatic retelling of events. The tale drew laughs until tears of joy formed in the corners of his listeners' eyes.

Just as Aleksander was about to sit down, Mara gave him a sly wink, and he fell onto his bottom a bit harder than he had intended. Mara grabbed his hand as she sat next to him, Kamil, and Alia as they listened to Shanthah's story. Lavinia and her partner Rayshel joined them a moment later with goblets of wine.

"So, what are we talking about?" Mara asked.

"Lavinia wanted me to point out all the inaccuracies in Shanthah's story," Alia said. "She said it's more entertaining than the real thing."

Mara burst out laughing. "I don't know, he's a pretty funny guy."

"Yeah, but I do all the voices in my version of events," Alia said.

"Her Shanthah is *spot on*," Ruta said. Rayshel and Lavinia both nodded in agreement.

"And why in all the time we spent together, have I never heard this famous Shanthah Kalen impression?"

Alia stood, her arms sweeping wide as she pronounced, "Oh, Hanna, I love you!" in the same tone as Shanthah just as he said them in his own story.

"Hey, is that supposed to be me?!" Shanthah dropped into a belly laugh, slapping the floor with his palm. "Alia! You're funny now?!"

"I've always been funny, you clown," Alia said.

Shanthah nodded in agreement with a wink and continued his story, drawing the others' attention again.

"Kamil, Alia, can I have a word?" Mara said in a low voice. They both gave her a friendly nod and got to their feet, following them out to the balcony.

"What's going on?" Alia asked.

Mara met Kamil's gaze, and she wondered if he could already sense what she was going to say. She let out a slow breath and smiled at her friends.

"Been a crazy few months, huh?" she asked. "Okay, that doesn't need to be said. Sorry. I'm just nervous."

"For what?" Alia asked. "You've literally killed gods and monsters, and you're worried about talking to *us*?"

Mara chuckled. "I know, I know. Okay—here's the thing. When the Supreme One died, he gave me his throne as a matter of convenience. I haven't done the best job there, and I've really only been a custodian for the crown until I find the next replacement."

"What are you saying?" Alia asked.

"I'm saying I think it's time there's a Kurashian on the Kurashian throne."

Alia pointed a finger at Kamil as if to say, "Pick him!" and Kamil's eyes went wide. Mara took another deep breath and turned to him.

"Kamil, it's customary, as you know, for the Supreme One to pass their title to someone that has risked their life for them, and vice versa. I can safely say you've done that on more than one occasion."

"*Oh, not so sure about that. I—*"

"I am."

"*Oh.*"

"I know I ask the world of you when I say this, but there is no one I trust more to take on the job. You are a genius. You're powerful. You're brave. But above all, you are kind. Just a genuinely *good* person."

"It's true!" Alia said, grabbing Kamil's hand with a smile.

"*But… They're not ready for someone like me for the throne.*"

"They're not ready for a good man on the throne?"

"*No, you know that's not what I mean, Mara. They're not ready for a gay man to rule them.*"

"Perhaps that is exactly what they need," Mara said, pulling Kamil into a tight hug. Alia did the same, and the trio held each other in the night's stillness for a long moment. "Little boys and girls just like you will grow up with a hero like them. They'll say, 'The Supreme One is just like me!'"

"That's a lot to live up to."

"I know. But you'll be able to help them see that life, love—all of it—it all gets better. You, and you alone, can bring real change. Love. Acceptance. Kindness. As an outsider, that's something I can't do for them. But you can. You can show everyone—*all* of your people that spring really does always come."

"Just like you have for yours."

"He's right," Alia said, nodding.

Mara's heart swelled, and she pulled them into another tight embrace. When he pulled away, Kamil took a deep breath and let it out through his mouth.

"Can I think about it?"

"Of course."

"There'll be pushback, you know."

"I do."

Kamil smiled, and Mara squeezed his arm.

She gestured back into the throne room, and they rejoined their friends just as Diana tackled Shanthah to the ground, and he gave a mighty, dramatic groan of death.

"Oh, now what?" Mara asked.

"Guardian Diana just slew the dragon," said Aleksander, and Diana giggled. Even Lavinia looked amused, sitting amongst the small crowd.

"What a fearsome dragon!" Mara exclaimed. "Sangora owes Guardian Diana Fiala a great debt!"

Aleksander caught Mara's eye and asked, "So you told them?"

Mara simply nodded in response, and Aleksander gave Kamil a thumbs up. Kamil responded with an awkward, nervous grin.

They spent the remainder of the peaceful evening in the joyous company of friends.

Sangora would be rebuilt. People would play again. People would sing again. And that gave Mara all the joy in the world.

When the rest of her friends were asleep, Mara snuck out of the palace to mingle with her people at the festival. She spent hours long into the night laughing and crying with them listening to their stories and simply experiencing all the beautiful sights and sounds of the Festival of Ashes.

All she wanted was to be with them—simply to exist in the same space as them.

When she finally returned to her bedroom and readied her blankets to sleep on the floor, she found herself unable to wipe the smile from her face.

CHAPTER FORTY-FIVE

THE RULERS OF THE WORLD

Mara awoke to someone poking her forehead just before noon the next day. She sat up, rubbing her eyes as Hanna sat on the edge of her bed.

"*I don't remember the last time I slept this late,*" Mara signed with a long groan. She pulled her blanket over her face, but Hanna pulled it back down so that she could communicate.

"*Why don't you sleep in the bed, weirdo?*"

"*It's too soft,*" Mara replied, then after a moment of hesitation added, "*And I feel guilty about it.*"

Hanna scowled. "*They'd want you to be comfortable. Why do you do things like this to yourself?*"

Mara knew Hanna was referring to the other slaves still being held prisoner in the Thannish work camps. She gave a shrug as Hanna yanked the blanket off of her. With a groan, she got to her feet and followed Hanna to the balcony.

"They're not attacking. That's why no one woke you yet."

"It's only a matter of time," Mara signed back, looking out over Doftaan. King Verahim and the Magistrate's forces had massed between the twin cities of Bukaral and Doftaan, completely blocking the Talohiran armies to come to their aid. *"Have we heard anything back from Valis?"*

She had sent a spy with a message to King Valis in Bukaral regarding the state of the war and to inform him of his father's death at the hands of the Thans. So far, she hadn't heard back.

"That's why I came to wake you," Hanna signed. *"Vasilica heard back from him first, and I coordinated Hippo going to deliver the body as well as pick Valis up and bring him here."*

"Thank you," Mara said. Then, she signed, *"When will he arrive?"*

"Oh, was I not clear? He's here now. Sorry."

"Hanna!" Mara signed. *"You couldn't have warned me?"*

"What's to warn you about? He's our friend. Plus, he's like twelve."

Mara chuckled. *"He's a bit older than twelve, Hann."* Truth be told, she had no idea how old the young king of Talohira was, only that the son of Valistaran and Alia was somewhere around Pol's age. *"Twenty, at least."*

"Pretty sure he's twelve. Anyway, the meeting's not for a few hours, so you have time to get ready."

Mara smiled as she rummaged through her wardrobe looking for an outfit appropriate for a diplomatic meeting.

It'd been so long since she'd actually had a choice of what to wear that it was overwhelming, and she settled for a simple navy tunic and dark trousers.

Hanna crawled onto Mara's bed and signed, *"If you're not going to use it, it's naptime for Hanna. Enjoy your meetings, sucker."*

An hour and a half later, Mara felt too antsy to wait anymore and sent a messenger to summon King Valis and the other representatives from Talohira. She'd also requested Aleksander and Kamil's presence at the meeting.

Of course, always the loyal friend, Hanna had insisted on accompanying Mara to the meeting, even if she wouldn't be participating in the conversation.

Mara sat at the half-moon table she formerly reserved for meetings with her Mistresses of Dusk, which were of course now called the Guardians of Sangora. At her request, a bowl of brightly colored fruit had been set on its center.

Her knee bounced under the table, anxious for the others to arrive. After sitting with Hanna in silence for several minutes, the door opened, and two soldiers ushered Kamil into the chamber.

"Hi, friend," Mara said, getting to her feet. She greeted him with a warm hug and gestured for him to sit on the other side of the table.

"I know why you asked me here," he mindspoke to both Mara and Hanna, twiddling his thumbs.

"I assumed so," Mara said. "I hope I didn't disturb you."

"For you, Mara, nothing is a disturbance," he replied. *"And, well… I'll do it."*

Mara's eyes lit up and she clapped her hands, getting up to embrace Kamil once more.

"Wonderful!" Mara exclaimed. "Don't worry, you won't be alone. I know better than most how terrifying it is to be thrust into leadership. Valis is new to this as well, and if the three of us fail, well, I guess you can always make the trek to Bartun to meet with Drahomir."

They shared a laugh.

"Thank you. I'll do my best to be worthy of this title."

"The Supreme One who is Called Kamil Ramzi," Mara said. "I'll go with you to forge your crown in the Ohun desert if you like. I'm not sure if that's actually required, or just a formality, but…"

"I'd *like that*," Kamil replied with a chuckle. *"Seems like just yesterday, huh?"*

At that moment, the doors parted and both Valis and Aleksander entered the chamber. Mara greeted him with a kiss on the cheek. When she let go, he had a beaming smile on his face like he was the luckiest person on Earth.

"Wait a minute, when did this happen?" Valis asked, gesturing between them. "Or is that just how Sangorans greet their gue—no, I stand by my original question. When did this happen?"

"I mean, technically—" Aleksander started.

"Okay, enough of that," Mara replied, showing them to their seats across from her own. "And don't *you* look the part?"

She gestured to Valis's neatly pressed black coat with bright, polished buttons of silver and the white cape draped over one shoulder. He did not wear a crown upon his dark hair, which had been cut short since the last time they had seen one another.

"They insist I wear these clothes," Valis said. "Not sure they suit me yet."

Mara gestured around the council chamber. "I still don't think all this suits me either. Doesn't change the fact that fate's forced us into it, right?"

"Right," Valis chuckled, rubbing the back of his neck. He and Aleksander greeted Hanna and Kamil, and then they all sat in silence waiting for Mara to speak again.

Hanna kicked her feet up onto the table and started levitating her engagement ring and making it do little tricks in the air. Mara watched for a second before shaking her head, redirecting her attention to the conversation at hand.

Mara took a deep breath and said, "I know what we're about to face is going to end in bloodshed."

"Bleak," Aleksander replied.

"But true," Valis added.

"*Unfortunately,*" Kamil said.

"I know you asked me here to ask for reinforcements, but Bukaral and other cities in Talohira are under siege too," Valis said. "They've blocked passage from Bukaral to Doftaan, but I can spare a few forces to reinforce some of your border towns."

"We'll need your help in the Sangoran states of Terman, Adess, and Dashga," Mara said. "After movement between our countries is possible again, of course."

"Yeah, I can do that," Valis said, rubbing the back of his neck. Mara cocked her head and stared at him intently.

"As king, you're going to have to learn to say 'no' to people," Mara said. "I encourage you to do so with me. Those are your people, your resources, and your country."

"I know. Thank you," Valis said. "I'll keep that in mind if I ever have reason to disagree with you, but I do think we'll be able to spare some forces and resources."

"That rhymed," Mara said.

"I was actually proud of myself for not pointing that out. Kingly maturity, or whatever."

Mara chuckled.

"I appreciate your willingness to help, but that's not actually why I've called you all here. We can talk about that later. Before the inevitable bloodshed, however, I wanted to try diplomacy one last time."

"You think the Magistrate is going to listen to us?" Aleksander asked. "I don't mean to shoot down the idea. I like it, but…" He trailed off. "Is it worth our time?"

"To talk with *her*? No. That would be fruitless," Mara replied, signing along with her words for Hanna. Aleksander pointed to the bowl of fruit on the table with a wide grin.

"Get it?" Aleksander asked. The others looked at him with blank stares. "Sorry, bad joke. I'll leave the puns to Shanthah next time."

Mara humored him with a laugh but kept on subject. "I want to go to Laniras to meet with your brother one last time. And I want you all to accompany me."

Valis glanced at Aleksander but said nothing. Mara caught his expression before it disappeared; she had lost count of everyone who knew Aleksander's identity and could honestly not remember whether or not Valis was aware that Aleksander was Crown Prince Xanthurias Romus, the true heir of the Thannish throne. A throne he'd been adamant in their private conversations that he would refuse to take.

Aleksander's thoughts must have been similar to Mara's, because he turned to Valis and said, "Not sure if you know this, but my name is actually Xanthurias...?"

"Yeah, I know. I don't understand it at all. Not one bit, but I'm aware," Valis said. "Kind of sums up my entire life as king, you know?"

"I'm sure it's going better than you think," Mara said.

"Oh, if by that, you mean drowning in my own tears and inadequacy," Valis said with a nervous chuckle. "Kind of joking, kind of not."

"Believe me, I know how you feel," Mara said. "It doesn't ever really go away—you just get better at hiding it. If you like, I can stop by from time to time to help you figure things out so you don't, you know, implode."

"Yes please. *Please*," Valis repeated, staring at Mara with an expression of gratefulness laced with existential dread.

"And as the Dowager Queen of Talohira, I still have some legal authority there. If the people aren't listening, I can go crack some heads." She gave Valis a wink.

"I don't know what that even means, but I appreciate it."

"A dowager queen is a dead king's widow."

"But you weren't ever—"

"Yeah, I was married to your dad. Technically."

"But that makes you my—"

"Nope, stop it. Stop now."

"Sorry." A moment of awkward silence. "But yes, I like that idea," Valis said. "You're a hero to a lot of people in Talohira, you know, and we'd all appreciate your help. It'd be beneficial to both our lands, so thank you."

Mara chuckled. "Our lands, you say. A bit ironic. A Kurashian-born king of Talohira and a Thannish-born Empress of Sangora."

"You aren't Sangoran?" Valis asked. "Wait, that sounds rude. I—

"It's alright. I was born human," Mara said. "I assume everyone knows, but I guess it isn't obvious."

"I didn't, actually," Valis said, shaking his head.

"Talohiran Humanists saw me as a traitor to humanity, and as a Persangoran, so many people told me I'd never be a 'real' Sangoran. Once a human, always a human, they said. I didn't know their culture. Their struggles. Their story. I didn't belong, and they let me know it."

"Did you ever want to go back to being human?" Valis asked. She hesitated, and he quickly added, "If anything I am saying is offensive, *please* let me know so I can be better."

Mara chuckled. "That's fine. Who I am now wasn't a choice like it is for many other Persangorani, but I've accepted that it's who I am in here." She placed a hand over her heart. "I *am* a real Sangoran. But when I first became queen, I didn't know how to help the people who hated me and didn't accept me."

"Then how did you?"

"Love. I fell in love with these people. I went through a lot of what they did." She shrugged. "I decided that no matter who, what, or where they were born, I'd love them and fight for them."

"Easier said than done?" Valis asked.

"Absolutely. And to be honest, I *don't* love all of them, but that doesn't change the fact that I'll still fight for them."

Aleksander spoke up for the first time. "I know it wasn't your father's strongest skill, but Mara has mastered the art of being an empathetic ruler," he said. "She'll be a good example for you in that regard. She sure has for me."

Mara's heart swelled in her chest.

"My transition to a Sangoran as well as my ascension to power were mind-blowingly hard, just as yours will be, although a bit less dramatic of one." She wiggled her wings. "You don't need to be a 'real' Talohiran in their eyes to be an ally and leader for your people. Just love them, and they'll feel it. You *are* a real Talohiran, just like you are a real Kurashian."

"And the other side?" Valis asked. "People you mentioned you don't love—Florenta's supporters, the Humanists, and people who didn't support my father?"

Hanna smashed her fist into her palm with a wicked grin. Mara laughed out loud, and Aleksander nodded to Hanna to show his approval.

"No, don't do that," Mara said. "Let them know that it's legal, although perhaps not moral, to share their views and opinions, but completely unacceptable to act on them. Don't let hate divide your people, or they won't ever recover. I don't know if Sangora ever will after the damage Florenta and the Magistrate have done, especially with my name."

She sighed.

"Well, maybe this'll never be over, but all we can do is try, right?" Valis asked. Mara nodded. "Sorry, this has become a 'cheer-on-the-sad-new-king session'."

"Don't worry, those are very needed." Mara offered a quick wink. "Back to topic, though. I have a small—well, not small—I have a *huge* announcement." She looked to Kamil and gave a knowing look. "I am abdicating the throne of Kurash, and I've asked our friend Kamil here to be the new Supreme One."

"What?! No way!" Valis exclaimed with a wide smile across his face. "That is incredible!"

"Well deserved," Aleksander said and clapped his friend on the back. Hanna wrapped him in a hug. "Now you and Valis can drown in your tears and inadequacy together!"

Kamil smiled. "*Deal.*"

"Yes, we can make a support group for it later," Mara said. "Anyway, I hope that Verahim will consider a message coming directly from the Empress of Sangora, Supreme One of Kurash, King of Talohira, and possibly most importantly, his own brother."

"*His own brother who happens to be the rightful king,*" Hanna signed.

"Probably best not to bring that up," Aleksander said. "Don't want it to look like a coup to force him to do anything."

Mara nodded.

"Exactly," she said, grabbing an orange from the bowl of fruit on the table. "Oh, help yourselves to some fruit, by the way. It's not just for show, you know."

"So, what, we all just barge in and demand that he calls off the attack?" Valis asked as he grabbed an apple.

Mara peeled the vibrant orange and breathed in the calming aroma. The sweet fragrance of orange peel beneath her fingertips reminded her of days in the library at Bukaral, where Valistaran would bring her entire bowls of oranges straight from Kurash to eat while she studied.

"If nothing else, we can demand that he hand over the rogue Secret Keepers, Umut and Cyrgiz, to Kamil," Aleksander said. Mara nodded in agreement.

"You didn't catch them?" Valis asked. Aleksander shook his head. "Oof."

"Thanks for the vote of confidence," Aleksander said with a laugh. "But no, they got away."

Mara looked into Aleksander's dark brown eyes for a long moment. She knew he felt like a failure for not catching the rogue Secret Keepers, but the gratitude and love she felt for him for going back to save her mother and the rest of Cineca knew no bounds. She offered him a gentle smile, which he returned with a big, cheesy one.

"They got away, but he and your father saved my hometown," Mara told Valis. "He died a hero."

"If only he'd lived his entire life the same way," Valis replied, averting his gaze. Mara let out a slow sigh.

"I think he got it right at the beginning and at the end," Mara said. "Perhaps, that's what counts."

"The bit in the middle, I'm not too fond of," Hanna signed. Aleksander and Kamil nodded, and Mara laughed out loud before interpreting Hanna's message for Valis.

"Yeah, working on fixing the impact of that part of his life," Valis replied. "No pressure."

"I found out about my own father's death this week, too," Mara said. "I am so sorry."

"So am I," Valis said, his eyebrows upturned, and his eyes kind. "But many more will lose their fathers if we're not able to convince Verahim to end the invasion."

"And close down the labor camps," Kamil added.

The others nodded. Mara's heart raced thinking about the horrors there. She smelled the scent of orange peel beneath her fingernails, which calmed her nerves slightly.

"I can't imagine why King Verahim even set up those camps," Valis said. "Was it in response to my father's labor camps? Revenge, maybe?"

Mara shrugged. "That might be Verahim's side of the story. But those regions were just currency to Florenta. She saw them as inferior. Nomadic tribes less civilized than her people. And so, she made a deal with Verahim that she would allow him to expand the borders of Thanatanos into Sangora if they would helped invade United Baltija."

"Just like that witch to try to burn something down as soon as she knows it exists," Valis said. Mara cringed at his use of the word 'witch' and wondered if it were an intentional shortening of the slur 'Night Witch.'

Valis must have caught on to her momentary expression, because he asked, "I'm sorry, did I say something wrong?"

"Night Witch is a pretty offensive slur," Aleksander explained. Valis glanced at Mara, his eyes wide and apologetic.

"I didn't mean it like that, I'm so sorry!"

Mara waved him off.

"*Did their plan work?*" Kamil asked. "*We did know a few Walkers in the slave camps in Adess and Tazovski.*"

"Definitely not," Aleksander interjected. "A big part of where I've been the last two years is spying on their plans for the invasions. Everything went up in flames as soon as they tried, but they still got Adess, Terman, and Dashga. Florenta, and the people in those lands, definitely lost in that deal."

"But can we count on the people from United Baltija to help us?" Valis asked.

"Lavinia's sister, Zhanna, is a leader there," Mara replied. "She made contact, and we met Zhanna's husband Halamir Valdursson in Drahomir's city of Bartun in the Deadlands. How they connected in the first place, I'll never know. He guided the slaves we helped escape back there. They'll be dealing with a massive refugee crisis, and I don't think we'll get more help than that from them for now."

"There's a lot of context there I didn't understand, but okay," Valis said. "It looks like we won't get much help from United Baltija."

Mara shook her head with a sad expression.

"Not exactly—They're helping more than we know, just without swords and blood." She glanced down with a scowl to see that she'd absentmindedly made a hangnail on her thumb bleed. "Anyway, enough talking. I'd like you all ready to accompany me and Hippo to Laniras in the next two hours. Good plan?" The others nodded. "Thanks everyone. Love you all."

Kamil and Valis left the room first to find Alia, leaving Mara, Hanna, and Aleksander alone.

Aleksander grabbed another piece of fruit from the bowl.

"For the road," he said.

"And where do you think you're going?" Mara asked, grabbing his hand to pull him close.

"*Guys, I'm still here,*" Hanna said, signing between their faces. They laughed and pulled apart. "*So, what next?*"

"I'm going to find that girl Nadezhda and get her shard of the Godmirror," Mara said.

"Think she'll part with it?" Aleksander asked.

"I don't see why not," Mara replied.

She had explained her plan to contact Thanatan the night before, expecting him to disapprove. He had fully supported the decision, however, and asked if there was anything he could do to help. That is when she told him about her plan to meet with Verahim.

Mara led them out of the chamber. The two guards stationed outside followed close behind as they made their way through a series of corridors until they came to the dormitory complex usually reserved for soldiers and palace staff.

She rapped her knuckles against one of the doors and raised a hand in greeting to one of the palace chefs as she passed by. A moment later, the door parted, and Nadezhda's face peeked out.

"Oh!" she exclaimed. "I—hello! Is everything—am I in trouble for something?"

Mara raised an eyebrow. "Should you be in trouble?"

"No, but—" Nadezhda gestured to the two guards holding silver spears. "I just wasn't expecting you of all people to—sorry, come in."

Ana gave a sheepish grin and a wave from where she sat at the end of the bed before hurrying to her feet out of respect.

"Hello," Mara said, introducing herself. Ana looked overjoyed to be in the presence of the Empress of Blood.

Nadezhda swept a pile of dirty laundry off the desk into a bin and pulled the bedsheets up in an attempt to tidy her mess.

"Don't worry about cleaning up. You should see my chambers," Mara said. "Clothes all over the place."

"I doubt that," Nadezhda said. "Don't you have people to clean up for you?"

"Believe me, I'm trying to make them stop, but they can't kick the habit," Mara replied. "Can I sit?"

Nadezhda nodded, and Mara sat on the edge of her bed. Ana got up and stood next to Aleksander and Hanna. Mara patted the spot next to her, and Nadezhda settled down beside her.

"It's good to see you," Mara said. I'm glad you are safe, and I hope your trek here wasn't too long."

"It was fine," said Nadezhda.

"Do you remember when we met?"

Nadezhda nodded. "You rescued me from the Purists."

"I didn't know why they were chasing you, but now I do," Mara said.

"Ah, there it is," Nadezhda replied. "Uh, look away for a second."

Mara did so with a confused look on her face. Nadezhda reached under her waistband to pull Thanatan's heart from her inside-out pocket.

The two guards standing behind Aleksander raised their spears as if Nadezhda were pulling out a knife. Mara raised a hand, and they lowered the weapons.

"Relax, crazies, I'm just taking out what your Empress wants from me."

She pulled the shining, blue-green shard of Godmirror from her pocket, her hand laid out flat so that it rested on her palm.

"How did you get this?" Mara wondered aloud. She shook her head. "Not important. Can I?"

Nadezhda hesitated and drew her hand back.

"It's too dangerous," she said, shaking her head.

"Not for me," Mara said. She reached out, waiting for Nadezhda to hand it over.

"Are you a Soulreader too?" Nadezhda asked.

"No, why?"

"Isn't that why I can touch it and others can't?" Nadezhda replied.

"Oh. Probably," Mara said with a shrug. "But I don't think he wants to hurt me. He's been waiting to talk to me for a while. I'll be fine."

"You *want* to talk to him?" Nadezhda replied.

Mara's hand tingled as if the Godblade wanted to reconnect with Nadezhda's chunk of crystal and return to their source in the ruins of Nitra. Nadezhda hesitated as if physically unable to hand it over.

Her expression turned dark, and Mara sensed anxious thoughts clouded with Thanatan's influence oozing from her mind. A dark presence filled the room, and Thanatan's voice echoed from the gem.

"DO IT!"

Mara cried out as Nadezhda lunged forward and slid the jagged side of Thanatan's heart between Mara's ribs once, twice, three times.

Chaos broke out.

Ana screamed and Aleksander shouted and leapt toward Nadezhda, but the guards intervened, grabbing the young woman and pushing her to the ground; the bloodied, jagged chunk of crystal fell to the floor as its owner sobbed.

Pain flashed through Mara's side, and the last things she witnessed before one of the guards dragged her out were Ana's scream, and Hanna throwing Nadezhda through the window with her powers in a spray of glittering glass.

CHAPTER FORTY-SIX
LOVE AND RESENTMENT

With a groan, Mara massaged her sensitive wound, despite Alia's orders that she refrain from doing so. Alia had refused to heal her with her powers, insisting that if she kept relying on her abilities to mend her wounds, her body would stop healing itself on its own in the future.

Mara motioned for her to wait outside the prison complex.

"I'll be fine," Mara said.

"With all due respect, Empress, we thought the same last time and failed to stop the girl from—"

"Wait outside. That's an order."

"Yes, Empress," the guards replied in unison as Mara entered the dark corridor lined with torches.

She found Nadezhda's cell not far from the entrance. She was sitting next to the wall, her hands bound.

"Oh, you," she said as Mara sat in the hallway outside the bars.

"Me," Mara said with a sigh. "Comfortable?"

"No."

"Do you deserve that?"

"Don't talk to me like a child."

"Did you throw a fit like a child?"

"No."

"Yes, you did, so I'll treat you as such."

Nadezhda was silent for a long moment, resting her head against the brick. Mara refused to speak first, and they sat in silence for several minutes.

"Is Ana alright?"

"Yes, but she didn't stab me."

"What do you want?" Nadezhda asked.

"An explanation," Mara said. "And how I can make things right."

"He made me," Nadezhda said. "I—for a brief moment, I wanted to do it, and he sensed it. He knew. It was only for a second, I swear, but—I don't know, it's like he took control and amplified that little bit of…"

She trailed off.

"That little bit of…?"

"Resentment, I guess?"

Mara cocked her head and in a soft voice asked, "Resentment?"

Nadezhda was silent for a while, tears in her eyes.

"Do you remember my brother? Karel?" Nadezhda asked. Mara nodded. "You left him behind."

"Not by choice," Mara said softly. "I am so sorry. You know, I have a brother too."

"Did you lose him?" Nadezhda asked. Her tone indicated selfish frustration rather than sympathy.

"In a way, yes," Mara replied. "I've lost most of my family. I don't know exactly what you're feeling, but… I can relate."

Nadezhda hung her head.

"But you're not alone," Nadezhda said. "You're the Empress of Blood."

"Exactly. For so long, I was surrounded by people who didn't care about *me*, just my position," Mara said. "I know what it's like to be surrounded by people but still feel alone. I don't want that for you, and I don't want *this* for you, either." She gestured to the cell.

"I'm sorry," Nadezhda said rather shortly.

"There's more," Mara said. "Isn't there?"

Nadezhda shrugged, and Mara sat with her chin on her fist and her elbow on her knee.

"You're from Nitra, aren't you?"

"How could you tell?"

Mara sighed and gazed at the floor.

"Because there aren't many people who hate me quite like people from Nitra do."

"I'm not the first?"

"Hardly," Mara said. "There are a lot of people who want to kill me in Thanatanos."

"Was I the closest?"

"If it makes you feel better, I'll say yes," Mara said with a laugh. Nadezhda chuckled, tears still in her eyes.

"Not for me. A little tip, there are better places to stab next time you try to kill me. "You missed everything good. Hurts, though, so good work on that account."

Another laugh escaped Nadezhda's throat.

"My family died in the Sangoran attack on Nitra."

This time, Mara was silent, unsure of what to say.

"I'll never forgive myself for what happened in Nitra. For what I did."

"Listen, I know you think it's safe to use that thing to talk to *him,* but he made me do horrible things even before I stabbed you."

"I noticed you haven't ever used his name. Do you know who you've been speaking to?" Mara asked.

"Yeah, but I don't want to give him the satisfaction of having a name."

"Good. Don't give him any satisfaction at all for anything. We can both be rid of him soon, but I need to talk to him one last time."

"He said he could bring my brother back," Nadezhda said; the words spilled out before she could stop them.

"Ah."

"I know, I know, I was stupid to believe him," Nadezhda admitted, dropping her gaze.

"Wrong? Yes. Stupid for having hope? Never."

Mara could see Nadezhda's mind trying to find a way to change the topic. She was about to speak again, but the girl blurted out more words.

"And when I use the power inside, I can…I don't know…connect with the world around me more. I don't know how to explain it. I wasn't a Mindspeaker before, but I am now."

"*That* is why I need the mirror," Mara said. Nadezhda nodded. "We call it the Connection to Creation, and I think it might be vital to saving our people."

"Our people?" Nadezhda asked. "No wings, remember?"

"You don't need wings to belong here."

Nadezhda nodded. "Thank you. I just miss him so much."

"I know. The sorrow means he mattered," Mara said, holding Nadezhda's hand. The girl flinched but didn't pull away. "And so do you."

"I know," Nadezhda said with a smile. "Thank you, Empress… I—I truly am sorry. I shouldn't have—I blamed you for Nitra. For Karel's death. I just wanted to hate you so damn much. So why don't I? Why *can't* I?"

"Women like us are hard to hate," Mara said with a wink.

"But easy for us to hate ourselves," Nadezhda said without thinking. Her own candor surprised her, and she averted her gaze from Mara.

"Yeah." They sat for a long moment in silence, before she blurted out, "How old were you the first time you—" Her voice faltered. "The first time you killed someone?"

"Wow," Mara said. "Wasn't expecting that question."

Mara was silent for a long moment, staring at a dust-bunny on the floor. Nadezhda wondered if she had overstepped her bounds with the question, but as she leaned forward and opened her mouth to apologize, Mara spoke.

"I was sixteen."

"Eighteen," Nadezhda said.

"It's a story I've only ever told to two people, and well… I think I'll keep it that way. But it was something I had to do. For myself, and for my brother."

"Your brother?"

Mara nodded. "Yeah. But you know, what's done is done. We've done bad things, but that doesn't make us bad people. I have a lot more to atone for than you do."

"I don't think so," Nadezhda said, her guilt creeping up her throat. "I… the Voice, Thanatan… He made me… No, made me *want* to do horrible things. I did them because I thought…"

"Not now," Mara said, shaking her head. "He's had his grip on a lot of our throats. Now it's time we make up for that, yeah?"

"Yeah. Let's kill that idiot."

"Love that. Him and his Magistrate."

"Oh, Empress?" Nadezhda asked. "I wanted to ask…"

"Yes?"

"Where is Ana?" she asked.

"Where else but worried sick about you? Let's get you back to her," Mara said. "She needs you, and I think you need her right now, too."

"You talked to her about this?"

"Mostly about how much she loves you."

Mara winked and stood and knocked on the door. The two guards entered with raised weapons.

"Yes, my lady?" the guard asked.

"Unchain her. Take her to my quarters, please. Let her rest in comfort unless we call for her and need her help," Mara ordered. "And please, bring Miss Sala to her as well."

"It will be done, Empress."

As the guards unbound and escorted Nadezhda away, Mara sat down on the hard bed in the cell and gingerly lifted the chain in her hand. Her thoughts turned to the slaves in the camps, and she knew she was one step closer to freeing them.

She banished those thoughts from her mind and held the shard of Godmirror in her hand. She turned it over in her palm, which tingled as it made contact with the silvery surface. Voices, whispers, really, flowed from the crystal the longer she held it.

She gripped it tightly in her hand and concentrated with all her might, and in her mind's eye, she beheld a shadowy flurry of activity and the bustle of masses of people and trains. But where? She squeezed the crystal harder and willed her telepathic abilities to expand the view. Laniras. Of course. A massive building with train tracks running through it came into view, and then the voices tore through her skull.

"*Who is there?*" someone called from the other side of the connection. Not Thanatan. It wasn't a vision; she was seeing what was happening in real time. "*Hello?*"

And then, another voice, one more familiar and chilling than the other. *There* he was.

"Ah, Mara. What a pleasant surprise. Here I had thought they killed you."

"I wondered the same about you."

"Are you disappointed?"

"Obviously. You?"

"Likewise."

"Is that why you had Nadezhda try to kill me?"

"I forced Nadezhda to stab you because of your failure. It was your punishment for delaying my victory."

"Oh, boo-*kurvaki*-hoo, you had to wait a little longer to kill me and the Magistrate."

She added the Sangoran expletive for emphasis.

"Just her. You are still useful to me, for now."

"Well, now that we've both expressed how disappointed we are that the other is alive, I need your help."

"You're ready to be my hand?"

"Let's get one thing straight: I am not 'your' anything. We need to work together to stop her. You ready to be my blade?"

"Are none of your other friends of use to you?"

Mara ignored the comment. "Where is she?"

"Laniras. As you suspect."

"What is she doing?"

"Waiting."

"For?"

"You."

"She knows we're coming for her?"

"Of course she does."

Mara turned the shard of crystal over in her hand and let out a long breath. Images of the building with the trains swirled in the shadows on its face.

"And what's happening with all those trains I see?"

"*Exactly what you fear. She's sending more slaves to their camps.*"

"Damn it."

"*I can sense you have a plot to kill the Magistrate. Would you care to share what you have planned?*"

"Later. I need to get to Laniras *now.*"

She pocketed the shard and hurried from the holding cell, making her way through the palace. She reached out with her mind to locate Aleksander, Hanna, Valis, and Kamil and felt their presence with Hippo. Good. Just where she'd told them to meet her.

She extended her wings and leapt from a high balcony and shot down toward her friends. She found them feeding Hippo large chunks of log and stone, which he munched merrily. The behemoth leapt up and down in joy as Mara landed next to him and patted him on the gargantuan snout.

"Hello, you big sweetie," she said, kissing his nose.

"You talking to me?" Aleksander asked.

"Of course," Mara replied. She smiled and patted him on the nose as well.

Hanna waved to Mara as she, Kamil, and Valis helped the contingent of thirty Talohiran soldiers load their supplies back onto Hippo's saddle. They had accompanied their king into Doftaan, and now, together with an equal number of Sangoran soldiers, they would travel to Laniras with their leaders.

"So, what's the plan?" Aleksander asked as Valis approached and greeted them both.

"Don't die," Valis said.

"That's usually my plan. It's worked out so far," Mara replied with a wry smirk.

The trio climbed up Hippo's snout, and Mara traced her hand over the space above his eye; he made a happy grunt, and they took their place at the base of his neck.

"Hold on, everyone!" Mara shouted as Hippo shot into the sky. Most of the Talohiran soldiers cheered at flying for the first time, but many of them screamed as the behemoth took flight.

Hippo climbed higher into the sky, and those nearest to his side peered cautiously over the edge at the ground below.

They traveled for several hours, the thousand or so kilometers between Bukaral and Laniras far below passing by faster than upon the back of any horse, carriage, or train.

Mara watched Lavinia's state of Timishuara pass by beneath them, and then they were over the border wall and the tens of thousands of soldiers and their tents amassed around it.

Smoke billowed from many towns along the border as well as some of the larger cities spread across the country.

Her downcast expression turned into a faint smile as she made out the tiny groupings of buildings in her own hometown of Cineca not far from the wall. She could see the secluded lake that she loved so much, and she squeezed Aleksander's hand and pointed.

Her words were lost on the wind, but he understood, smiling widely. He pantomimed diving off the side of Hippo, and she smiled, thinking back on the wonderful days spent diving and swimming in the lake.

She dozed off around the time they passed over Vudapas.

Hanna woke her sometime later, for Hippo was now making his descent into Laniras. As Mara sat up, she found Aleksander's traveling cloak draped over her for warmth. She pulled it off and folded it in half.

"Thank you," she said, handing it back to him. His response was simple: a loving smile.

"So, where first?" Valis asked as Hippo passed over the great walls of Laniras. He, Kamil, Aleksander, and Hanna huddled around to hear Mara's orders.

"If what I saw in Nadezhda's mirror was correct and not a trap set by the Magistrate, they're getting ready to transport another crowd of slaves to the transitionary camp in Adess. We free them, then confront the king and his mistress."

"And when we free them, where will they go?" Valis asked.

"Hippo can take them away," Aleksander said, glancing at Mara. "If we keep Verahim and the Magistrate busy, he should be able to get them far enough away before coming to pick us up."

Mara nodded. "I'd prefer to capture the trains. But if we can't do that, he's big enough to carry fifty or so people on his back."

"*First stop: train station, and then to the palace, then?*" Kamil asked. Mara gave a thumbs up.

She telepathically guided Hippo to the massive train station in Eastern Laniras not far from the Gates of Bretislaus that led out of the city.

The soldiers called out to one another as they began to man the ballistae and guns that had been set up atop small towers around the city as they saw Hippo coming.

Hippo slammed down harder than Mara had expected him to, and the soldiers on his back cried out in surprise as he trampled through the road toward the station. His massive footfalls tore up the cobblestone as he let out a vicious roar.

"Hold on!" Mara shouted as Hippo set his mind on the front wall of the building. Dozens of Thannish soldiers guarding the station stood between him and his goal, but those that did not leap out of his way were trampled under his massive feet.

Several vicious bolts thrown from ballistae struck Hippo's hide and armor but glanced off, unable to meet their mark between his scales or his softer underbelly.

"Brace yourself!" Mara shouted as Hippo roared and smashed his head through the westernmost wall of the train station. Rubble and dust preceded the screams of fear and surprise from within. He bellowed again as he emerged from the dust, and the people on the train platforms below scattered and screamed as he belched a stream of lava, creating a barrier between him and the surprised soldiers.

"Hippo, stop!" Mara exclaimed before the behemoth smashed into one of the trains. "Everyone off!"

The Talohiran soldiers climbed off Hippo's nose, wings, and haunches as he set himself down. Thannish soldiers raced toward them, and civilians waiting to board the trains hurried away, screaming.

"Do not harm the civilians! Let them go!" Valis ordered as his men readied their shields and blades for the oncoming fight. "I want as few deaths as possible! Take the exit and man the gap Hippo made!"

His men did as they were told, engaging with the Thannish forces. They managed to push them out and created a shield wall behind the rubble.

"Hippo, block the train tunnels!" Mara called as she unfolded her wings, her wingblades shining in the torchlight. "Do not melt *anything!* We still need this place to be functional!" Hippo grunted in acknowledgment, and Mara added, "Love you, buddy!"

He leapt over the tracks and extended his mighty wings to block any trains from leaving or entering the station. He let out a mighty roar, and the remaining station guards scrambled away.

He took up nearly the entire eastern side of the station, leaving only the western platforms guarded.

"*Get this wall back up if you can,*" Mara signed to Hanna, who nodded and began piling the crumbled bits of rock on top of one another with her powers in a crude imitation of what the wall had once looked like, while the Talohiran soldiers helped fortify it.

"Seize the trains and get them out of here!" Mara shouted. She pulled the latch on one of the carriage doors, and frightened cries escaped from within. She let out a deep breath; they'd made it in time. "Stay calm, everyone. We're here to help. You're not safe yet, so please, stay calm."

She looked over to see Aleksander reassuring another train car full of prisoners and explaining the situation with kind eyes and a friendly smile.

Scared human and Sangoran faces nodded and huddled together as Mara slid the door closed. Before she latched it shut, she heard someone from within whisper, "Hošslava vavi, Jemprata." *Bless you, Empress.*

Half of the fifty Talohiran soldiers met the much smaller force of Thans posted in the western half of the station, their blades clanging against one another. Kamil created distracting illusions, and Aleksander let out bursts of flame to intercept their foes before they landed any killing blows.

In only a few minutes of fighting, the Thans had surrendered, laying down their weapons on the ground. They knelt and raised their hands, and Valis ordered his men to take up positions around the main entrance to the station.

The other half confiscated the weapons and guided the station guards to a corner where they would be guarded.

"There will be more," Valis said.

"And that's why we need to get the trains out immediately," Mara said. "Kamil!"

"*I'm already on it,*" Kamil replied as one of the train operators stood, his eyes vacant.

Kamil reached out with his mind, and Mara felt his consciousness snaking around the man's own, connecting it to the three nearest Talohiran soldiers.

"What are you doing?" Valis asked.

"He's showing them how to drive the train," Mara said.

"You know how to—" Valis began, and then he realized what Kamil had done. "You shared their knowledge?!"

"*Yes, but the connection won't last long,*" Kamil thought.

"How long?" Mara asked.

"*An hour, maybe.*"

"That's enough," Mara said, turning to Valis. "They're your men, King Talohir."

Valis nodded. "Move out. Get these trains as far away as you can across the border into Sangora. We'll find you later."

The soldiers saluted, and ten more accompanied them onto the trains, readying them to set out.

Mara turned back to the others. Hanna had just finished piling the boulders back onto the gap in the wall and joined them, her auburn hair matted to her face with sweat.

"We don't have long," Mara said. "Let's go."

As smoke began to billow from the trains, and the screeching sound of metal and steam filled the station, Mara, Hanna, Kamil, Valis, and Aleksander climbed onto Hippo's back.

"To the palace, buddy!" Mara exclaimed, and Hippo leapt up, smashing through the ceiling in a spray of rock and dust. He unfurled his massive wings and after getting a running start atop the train station, he launched himself into the sky.

As a bolt fired from a ballista raced toward Hippo's chest, Hanna deflected it with her mind, but collapsed to her knees.

"*I'm gonna need your help, girl,*" she signed to Mara. "*Already tired.*"

Mara nodded, knowing rebuilding the wall of the station had drained much of Hanna's strength. Together, they fought to deflect the myriad arrows, ballista bolts, and bullets aiming to bring Hippo down.

"No!" Mara cried as one of the bolts made it through their mental shields, piercing Hippo's flesh beneath his rocky armor just above his hip. The behemoth bucked and groaned just as he made it over the wall surrounding the neighborhood of Laniras known as the Star of the King; there, they found the king's palace surrounded by other important buildings.

As they glided toward the palace, Mara looked over the city one more time at the spider web of walls that separated the different neighborhoods. It was a city of walls, completely different from the open connectedness of Doftaan.

Hippo slammed into the ground with a roar, and Mara and Hanna leapt from his back, while the others climbed down.

"Go!" Mara exclaimed. "Get back to the station. The Talohirans need you! Fly high so they don't get you!"

Hippo bowed and launched himself straight upward, high enough that the Thans' ranged weapons couldn't hit him— far higher than any of his human companions would be able to handle.

The Thans encircled them on all sides and raised their various weapons. They advanced, backing Mara and the others against the mighty gates of the palace.

"This is a diplomatic meeting!" Valis exclaimed. "Let us pass!"

And then, the terrible groaning that accompanied the Faceless hordes was upon them. Even the Thannish soldiers looked horrified as the creatures emerged from their hiding places around the castle grounds.

"Okay, what's the plan now?" Aleksander asked, igniting two balls of flame. "Mara?!"

Mara turned to Hanna. *"Hey, Hanna, what's the best way to open a door?"*

"Knock on it?"

"Exactly."

Mara screamed, exerting all the mental energy she could and ripped a massive chunk of stone from the earth before launching it against the gate. Hanna followed suit, tearing bricks from the palace itself before smashing them against the gates with all the power she had left.

"Cover us!" Mara shouted as the two women telekinetically battered the gates with boulders and brick.

Aleksander launched balls of flame, igniting the lush lines of trees and shrubs on the castle grounds while Valis created a web of lightning from his own hands to keep the Thans at bay.

"Forgot you could do that!" Aleksander exclaimed.

The Faceless paid no heed to their obstructions, running headlong through the danger. Flames and lightning charred their flesh, but still they charged. Kamil stepped forward, launching an explosion of telepathic energy far down the path.

The Faceless took the bait and ran in the opposite direction of their prey. As they reached his mental lure and found nothing there, they raced back to kill the defenders. Kamil repeated the process, throwing another mental lure far into the castle grounds.

"I can't keep this up forever!" Kamil shouted amidst the flurry of flame and lightning around him.

"Yeah, how's it going back there, you two?!" Aleksander exclaimed.

"Almost!" Mara grunted, launching a boulder against the gates that caved it in. She turned to Hanna. *"Ready?"*

Hanna was breathing heavily and sweat dripped from her brow, but she nodded all the same.

"Let's bring it down."

Hanna set her feet, rubbed her hands together, and with an evil grin, thrust her palm forward. She groaned as the force of the telekinetic thrust pushed her heels into the ground, breaking the paved road beneath her feet.

Mara summoned the Godblade and joined Hanna in her assault on the gates. She hacked at the hinges near the bottom of the doors, and eventually, Hanna was able to bring the gates crashing down.

"In!" Mara shouted. The Thannish soldiers and Purists had made it past the flames and lightning. Kamil created a mental lure right next to their position, summoning the Faceless.

"What are you doing?!" Valis exclaimed.

Kamil didn't need to answer, for the Faceless intercepted the Thans, keeping them from pursuing their targets.

"Go!" Mara shouted. "Aleks, you know this place best. Lead the way!"

Kamil peeked into the sunlight and hurled one last burst of mental energy as far away as he could, saving the Thannish soldiers just before they were torn to shreds by the Faceless.

Aleksander gestured for the others to follow as he sprinted into the palace.

As the others passed by, Hanna used her powers to jam the wreckage of the gates where they had formerly stood, creating a temporary barricade. It wouldn't hold long, but it'd grant them some time.

"*You good?*" Mara signed. Though out of breath, Hanna gave a thumbs up, and they raced up the front steps leading into the rest of the palatial fortress.

"Where is everyone?" Valis asked, looking around. "Is it always like this? Where are the—well, where is *everyone?*"

The castle, which was usually a bustle of activity of diplomats, soldiers, citizens, chefs, and hundreds of other people who made sure the kingdom ran smoothly, was eerily silent.

"No," Aleksander said. "It's all wrong. The Magistrate's Faceless are doing all the jobs that humans once did, so maybe that's why it's so empty. We won't be alone for long, though. Let's go."

Mara held out her arm, barring Aleksander's path as he headed toward the main corridor heading off the top of the elegant entry staircase.

"What is it?"

"You're right. We're not alone," she said, a shiver running down her spine. "Hey, Supreme One, can you sense that?"

Kamil nodded and bit his lip.

"What is it?" Aleksander repeated. "Mara?"

"What's below us?" Mara asked, her eyes wide.

"Uh, servants' quarters, the catacombs, a few chapels. A bunch of old stuff," Aleksander replied.

"The *catacombs?!*" Mara exclaimed.

At first, Aleksander was confused, but then in horror, he realized exactly what that meant. Kamil confirmed his fears.

"There are thousands of them down there!"

"Run!" Mara shouted, and the group sprinted after Aleksander, who led the way.

She could feel the empty mindlessness of the vast hordes below their feet shifting, and the groaning and the hunger overtook them, but they did not slow down.

They continued on through the dark corridors, a flame lit in Aleksander's palm serving as their only light. He led the way toward Verahim's throne room, and as they climbed another flight of stairs, the sound of muffled voices signaled the first Thannish soldiers in their path.

However, when Aleksander extinguished his flame as they turned down a lit corridor, no guards barred their path. Instead, standing at the end of the hall, was a group of ten robed figures with silver masks smeared with blood, in honor of the Faceless they worshipped.

"I think your brother hired some new help," Valis said as the Purists drew their weapons. "Those don't look like palace guards."

The Purists rushed toward them, and Aleksander stepped forward, crossed his arms, and then released a torrent of flame before it exploded, knocking their foes backward. He unleashed an explosion of dark flame that raced toward the Cultists like all consuming shadow.

And then, the dark shadows of flame stopped in midair like a black thundercloud.

"Oh no," Aleksander whispered. The flames exploded back toward him, sending him flying. He struck the ground hard, rolled, and was still.

Valis unleashed a lightning bolt that tore through the leader's chest, and the man behind them tore bits of stone from the hallway and set them flying.

"No!" Mara shouted.

She planted her foot against the floor, and the ground beneath them opened up like massive jaws, swallowing the Telekinetik that had deflected Aleksander's explosion. Hanna joined her, throwing her hand down, and the ground gave way beneath their enemies. The last of the Cultists screamed as they fell through to the floor below.

Mara hurried to Aleksander's side, cradling his head in her lap. He tried to speak, but no words escaped his horribly burned face. The exposed skin on his chest was charred black beneath his smoldering tunic.

"Aleksander?" Valis asked cautiously. "Oh my goodness, we got him killed! Mara, I'm so—"

Hanna grabbed his shoulder and shook her head.

"Dragonsouls blood can heal burns. It's a failsafe for their own power," Kamil explained, and Valis stood by in suspense.

Hanna collapsed, and Kamil rushed to her side.

Aleksander groaned as Mara stroked his hair. He tried to speak again, but she shook her head.

"Shh," Mara whispered into his burned ear. "Shh, shh, shh…" She gently brushed the blackened bits of skin from the wounds as they faded from black to dark red and then to a pale pink, the exposed muscle and burnt flesh mending itself. "You're okay, sweetheart. I'm okay. We're all okay."

Aleksander wrapped his fingers around Mara's thumb as he groaned in pain, tears streaming down his burned cheeks. She held him close, holding his face against her chest as she kissed the top of his head and rocked him back and forth.

"We have to…" Aleksander muttered. "We have to go…"

"Yes, we do," Mara said. "But not yet. You're safe."

Aleksander nodded, seemingly at peace as she held him.

"I know I am…" Aleksander whispered. "You're here…"

Her heart swelled, and she kissed his forehead.

After a few moments, his eyes shot open, and he jerked away from her embrace; the pain of his skin closing up and healing from the burns so intense that it caused him to vomit violently in a dark corner.

He groaned and turned back to Mara, his eyes watering.

"Don't let me do that again," he muttered, and Mara took his hand. "And don't kiss me, I smell like…"

Mara chuckled. "No time for kissing anyway. How's that what's on your mind right now?"

"Have you *seen* you…?" Aleksander said through a groan. "Always on my mind, Mar."

Mara let out a bright laugh and pulled his arm around her shoulders to support him. Kamil supported Hanna in a similar way, and together, they all limped down the hall.

"Yes, I have. I don't blame you. Come on, let's go."

The five friends stepped around the pit that had swallowed the Purists and stood before the doors of King Verahim's throne room.

"*How is he?*" Kamil asked as Hanna and Valis looked to Aleksander with concern.

"He'll be okay," Mara said, still supporting him.

"I'm good. Let's do this," Aleksander muttered.

Hanna winced and rubbed her forearms. Guilt filled Mara's soul; when Hanna had escaped Florenta's dungeons, she had exerted her powers to such an extent that the bones and tendons in her arms had shattered and snapped. Alia had healed them the best she could, but they still caused her trouble.

"*Don't overdo it, okay?*" Mara said.

Hanna chuckled.

"*You're one to talk,*" she signed, pointing to Mara's head.

"*Fair enough,*" Mara signed. "*Hey, should we have invited Shanthah as ruler of Alboras?*"

Hanna paused, her eyes wide. "*Don't ever tell him.*"

Valis and Kamil pushed the throne room doors open, and the others stepped inside.

There, sitting on his throne surrounded by Purists, sat King Verahim, and at his side, the Magistrate.

CHAPTER FORTY-SEVEN

SEIZING THE SWORD

The Magistrate's cold, broken laugh filled the chamber as Mara, Aleksander, Kamil, Hanna, and Valis barged in. Dozens of Purists around the room raised their spears in unison, but they did not advance. Their robes were far more opulent than those they had faced earlier—Verahim and the Magistrate's personal guard, or perhaps the leaders of the Purists, Mara thought. Their masks were not smeared with red paint; rather, their golden sheen gleamed in the torchlight.

"Xanthurias?" King Verahim Romus asked, leaning forward on his throne to get a better look at the four intruders.

"I told you to let our people go," Aleksander called as he broke from Mara's grasp and limped toward the throne. "I told you to let them go, and what'd you go and do?!"

"What are you talking about, Xanthurias?" Verahim asked. "Thanatanos is thriving. I thought about what you said, and I made sure the Purists would make things right to keep everyone safe. Our people are happy. We are safe.”

“You think this is what is best for our people?!” Aleksander shouted. “Is *this* what you wanted?! Another war?!”

“Safe?” Mara scoffed at the same time, stepping toward the throne. She raised her bladed wings. “How dare you?”

The Purists in the room shifted, pointing their weapons.

“Hold,” Verahim ordered, and the warriors pulled back, although they were now on guard, ready to strike if needed. The Magistrate remained still and silent, but Mara did not lower her bladed wings.

“How dare you?” Mara repeated in a low voice. She shook her head slowly, shutting her eyes to let out a deep breath. “You call yourself a king, but you’re hardly even a man.”

“I must say, I’m surprised to see you, Empress Bartunek,” Verahim said.

“Surprised?! After everything you’ve done to my people over the last six months?” Mara shouted, taking a step up the few stairs leading to the throne.

“What?” Verahim asked, glancing at Aleksander. “Xan, what is she talking ab—”

“No, Verahim, I’m the one talking, and you will address *me*, not him,” Mara replied, cutting the king off.

Hanna was telekinetically levitating multiple bits of rock, glass, and steel around her head and hands—a warning to the Purists to stay back.

“You’d better listen to her,” Aleksander cautioned.

Mara took a long moment to regain her composure, one foot on the stairs to the throne. Verahim began to speak, but Mara raised a hand, and he shut his mouth.

"It's time for you to listen, not talk. I just spent *months* in one of your damn labor camps, Verahim," Mara said. "And you dare have the sheer *audacity* to boast of the safety of your people while mine are dying? Humans aren't the only 'people' in this world."

"What?" Verahim asked. "What labor camps? And don't you dare accuse me of being humanist. Of course I'm not!"

Mara pulled a leatherbound book that had been tucked in her belt—the one she'd stolen from Mazanek's house. She slammed it on the ground before him.

"What's this?" Verahim asked.

"Page ten, you swine."

Verahim motioned for one of the Purists to hand him the book. He flipped through the pages, a scowl on his face.

"Read it."

"It's…a list of quotas for testing and extermination," Verahim said. "I don't understand, what is this?"

"Are you serious?" Aleksander asked as Mara scoffed. Verahim glanced at the Magistrate, who still said nothing.

"You must be mistaken, I've—"

"Start over," Mara replied, cutting him off.

"What?" Verahim asked.

"I'll give you one chance to reword that statement," Mara replied, folding her arms. Verahim thought for a long moment.

"I've been coordinating the transport of refugees with our new train system, resettling your people displaced by the war with Queen Florenta," Verahim said. "But there aren't any labor camps like those Talohiran ones. Temporary resettlement camps, but—"

"Temporary resettlement camps?!" Mara shouted. "Is that what you're calling them?!"

She took two more steps toward Verahim and pulled her sleeve up over her elbow, shoving her forearm in his face so that he could read the number burned into her flesh.

"I don't understand," Verahim repeated.

Mara's nostrils flared.

"All I was—all any of them are—a number. Temporary resettlement…What a load of—You are detaining political enemies. Undesirables. Threats. Innocent people deemed worthless to Thanatanos."

"No, I was adamant that the refugees be treated well."

"Stop calling them refugees and call them what they are! Slaves!" Mara shouted, venom in her voice. "Is *this* 'good treatment'?" She pointed at the number on her forearm again. "There are Thans in your camps too, good king. And Talohirans. And Kurashians. Anyone who doesn't look like you or act like you is thrown in there," Mara spat. "I'm ordering you to shut them down, or Thanatanos will find itself without a king, and its king without a head."

Verahim did not reply, and instead, he stood with a look of sad confusion on his face. "I assure you, Empress Bartunek, that I don't know what you are talking about. But if we can discuss it calmly, I'm sure we can clear this up. Now, if you'll allow me to address my brother?"

Mara gestured to Aleksander without taking her eyes off the king.

"What?"

"You mentioned another war," Verahim said.

"Uh huh," said Aleksander with a nod.

"There's no war. The last time I met with Queen Bartunek—"

"Empress," Mara cut in.

"My apologies. The last time I met with Empress Bartunek, she asked for help to drive out Florenta's forces and supporters in Sangora. She agreed to grant our own armies safe passage into her country."

"And what are you getting in return?" Aleksander asked.

"We had a deal. Improved diplomatic relations and an agreed upon amount of Sangoran gold."

"Ah, there it is. Gold. Even a king will do anything for a few moneti," Mara said. "That wasn't me you met with. It was *her*." She pointed an accusatory finger at the Magistrate. "There truly are no gaps in your ignorance, are there?"

"How dare you address me like this?"

"You can pretend to not know what's going on, but you have it all wrong. Your armies are killing my people. Slaughtering villages and taking people away far into the Deadlands. You have no idea the things they've endured, and their blood—*my* blood—is *all* on your hands."

"Xanthurias, what are you even doing with her? You're choosing her over your own people?" Verahim asked. "*This* is your home."

"It was. But it hasn't been for a long time, brother," Aleksander said. "And thanks to what you've said and done, it never will be again. That absolutely tortures me, but you asked why I'm choosing her? It's because *she* is my home. *This* is my family."

He gestured to his other companions.

Verahim stood and motioned to Valis, who had yet to speak.

"And is this new king of Talohira going to say anything?" Verahim asked.

"Yes, he is," Valis replied. "As King of Talohira, I demand that you cease hostilities against my people as well as Sangora, or we will have no choice but to retaliate. I don't want that, Verahim, I don't want more death."

"A good goal for a new king," Verahim said, stepping down from the throne toward them. "We can work with your government to settle your grievances, but we must do it through the proper channels, not in whatever this is."

"*And I call for the release of all Kurashians in your slave camps,*" Kamil mindspoke. "*An attack on one Kurashian citizen is an attack on all of us.*"

"Who are you?" Verahim asked with a laugh. "I told you, there aren't any slave—"

"He's the new Supreme One of Kurash, you brainwashed loon," Aleksander said.

Verahim was about to respond, but the Magistrate started a slow clap and got to her feet.

"It was only a matter of time before the puppet king learned my secret," the Magistrate said in that hollow, guttural voice. "I admit, I had expected more from you, Empress. I thought you'd convince him of the truth earlier than this."

Thanatan's voice filled Mara's mind.

"You need to return to Doftaan. I was wrong. She isn't here!"

"What are you saying?" Verahim asked, turning to the Magistrate.

The room exploded with swirling shadows, images of each of their grisly deaths surrounding them all around. The ghostly form of Mara's corpse, cut in half and wings hung like a bloodied banner. Valis's head on a stake, his crown smashed. Hanna's arms ending in bloody stumps, and a spear through her chest. Kamil's head crushed under a boulder. Aleksander's entire body exploding in flames he couldn't control. And finally, Verahim, dead in the midst of one of the slave camps.

And then the Magistrate, her illusions, and their screams, were gone. She turned to see each of her friends frozen in horror. Verahim stood with his mouth open in shock.

"I…" Mara said, speechless. "I don't… It was all an illusion. She was never here. She tricked us *again!* It was a trap!"

The groans of the Faceless filled their minds, and the castle began to shake. Darkness overshadowed the entire chamber as the creatures swarmed up and over the high windows.

Glass shattered down toward them, and the Faceless swarmed into the throne room. The intense, overwhelming feeling of hunger and hopelessness filled each of their minds as the eastern wall began to crumble.

Hanna thrust a fist forward, blasting the writhing mass of bodies from the tower. The group let out a collective gasp as they beheld the western towers swarming with Faceless, tearing down brick from brick.

"They're bringing the entire castle down!" Valis shouted as the monsters began to swarm into the chamber on all sides.

"Go!" Aleksander exclaimed, and the group sprinted toward the hole in the wall. The Purists in the room screamed as the Faceless tore through them, slicing their bodies to shreds with vicious claws and burying their faces in the crimson masses that had been their corpses.

The ground gave way beneath them.

Hanna managed to keep Kamil from falling with her powers, levitating him next to her as he flailed in the air. She floated from the crumbling tower and caught Valis, but a chunk of stone struck him in the shoulder, breaking Hanna's hold on him.

Mara dove straight down, wings tucked close to her side. She shot toward Aleksander who was plummeting toward the ground far below. His hand was outstretched toward her, his screams lost over the sound of the crumbling building.

Just as she caught him and extended her wings, she caught sight of Verahim as he struck a balcony. Valis landed next to him a moment later, writhing on the ground in pain.

Mara glided to the balcony next to them and screamed, "Hanna!"

Although Hanna couldn't hear her, she saw what was happening and managed to grab Valis with her mind and pull him away just as a chunk of brick struck where his head had just been.

Aleksander reached for Verahim's hand to help him up, but pieces of the decimated wall crushed his legs, and he cried out in pain. Mara blasted the debris with her mind, grabbed the king's arm and held Aleksander close. She extended her wings and yanked them both into the sky just as the balcony collapsed.

She groaned at the effort needed to carry the two men and called out for Hippo. She sensed his acknowledgment and adjusted her hold on Verahim's wrist.

A small bit of brick struck her in the back and a spray of glass sliced the skin on her arm, making her drop the two Romus brothers.

"No!" she cried, choosing to race after Aleksander instead of the king.

Fortunately for them all, Hippo intercepted the king with a crunch of bone, and Mara was able to catch Aleksander and glide onto Hippo's back. Hanna, Kamil, and Valis were already sitting near his neck. Mara groaned and collapsed, bleeding and bruised, to Hanna's side.

Aleksander helped her sit up as a sharp pain pulsed in her side.

"I think I broke a rib," Mara muttered, scooting backward to rest her back against Hippo's neck. "You all okay?"

Hanna gave a thumbs up, and Aleksander nodded, both of them completely exhausted. Kamil was already tending to both Valis and Verahim's wounds. Aleksander grimaced as he looked at the carnage of his brother's legs.

The debris had crushed his knees, and his shinbones jutted from the flesh of both legs. Valis had dislocated his shoulder, which Kamil helped him pop back into place, but nothing seemed broken.

Hippo grunted and turned east.

"*Where are we going?*" Hanna signed.

"*Back to the train station,*" Mara signed back.

The Faceless were already swarming toward the station, and Mara could sense the fear of the Talohiran and Thannish soldiers inside.

Valis crawled over to them, fearful to fall from Hippo's back as he shot toward the ground. Verahim stayed at the back of the saddle, staring at the destruction behind them and trying not to scream.

"Plan?" Valis asked as Hanna and Kamil joined them.

Aleksander and Mara shared a look.

"Not so sure we have one at the moment," Aleksander said. His skin was still tender, pink, and bruised, but the burns he had sustained had mostly scabbed over or healed. Mara nodded, closing her eyes due to the pain.

"Other than finding Alia and her students?" Mara asked.

At that moment, she wished that she had learned to give herself healing abilities of some sort during her time as Queen of Talohira.

"Hippo?" Mara said, resulting in a deep grunt from below. "Melt!"

A happy groan escaped Hippo's great maw as the very air around them superheated from the molten flame in the behemoth's stomach. As he glided downward, an initial burst of flame trailed from his mouth that whipped in the wind before dissipating.

The sound of an exploding volcano filled the sky as Hippo soared over the Faceless, bathing them in glowing, molten lava; he arced around and laid down a second path of destruction that buried thousands of Faceless and hindered the others, however briefly.

From the back of the station, four trains out of the station, smashing any Faceless on the tracks. Talohiran cloaks flew in the place of where the Thannish flags had been.

Hippo slammed through the roof of the train station and roared as the Faceless climbed through the river of lava, sacrificing their bodies so their allies could scramble over them unimpeded.

Mara stood with Hanna's help and shouted, "Everyone on! Now!"

The Talohiran and Thannish soldiers alike who hadn't boarded the trains clambered over Hippo's legs and snout and onto his back. Mara, Aleksander, Kamil, Hanna, and

Valis helped strap the terrified people in as the Faceless poured through the front entrance and through the roof.

"Go!" Mara screamed. "GO!"

Hippo obeyed, crouching to leap high into the sky. He unfolded his wings and soared upward. Dozens of Faceless hung onto his legs and slashed at his stony hide. Several had managed to climb over his haunches and onto his back.

Aleksander and Valis knocked each of them away with bursts of flame and lightning. When they were all gone and Hippo was safe, Aleksander knelt next to his brother.

"This is what you've been serving," Aleksander said, tears rolling down his cheeks. "*This* is your legacy."

Verahim removed the crown from his head; somehow, in all the chaos, he had managed to keep hold of it.

"You're right," he whispered, staring into Aleksander's eyes. "I...I can't—Xanthurias...I have truly failed our people. How was I so blind?"

He turned his crown over in his hands and tossed over Hippo's side as they soared away from Laniras.

"You have, yeah."

"There's no way I can remain king after this."

His words were a sad admission of the truth. Aleksander hesitated, unsure of how to answer.

"I hope you know that's not my goal," Aleksander said.

"What isn't?"

"To take your throne," Aleksander replied. "I don't want it. This whole thing wasn't a coup...It was to free Mara's people and help you see what the Magistrate is doing. We didn't intend for this to happen. Really."

"There really are prison camps, then?" Verahim asked, and Aleksander nodded. "Then I've become Valistaran. I—I was so blind, Xan. I could only see the good she was doing in Laniras, but now that I'm gone from there, it's almost like I've awoken from a dream and come back to reality."

"What do you mean?" Aleksander asked.

"I think she had me see what she wanted me to see. What *I* wanted to see, I guess," Verahim said. "And that's not an excuse for everything happening in Sangora."

"Do you think it's only in Sangora?" Aleksander asked.

Verahim shook his head. "No, of course not. Not anymore. If what Mara's said is true, and I believe it is, I've wronged the entire world."

"The Magistrate's been impersonating Mara for a couple years now, so people in Sangora have been torn between supporting the empress they used to love or turning from her completely. She's ruined Mara's reputation amongst lots of the people. It's all part of her game. It seems, she's done the same for you."

"Is that even possible to fix?" Verahim asked.

"I don't know," Aleksander admitted. "I don't know how Mara's going to do it… But if anyone can, it's her."

"She's an incredible woman," Verahim said. "Truth be told, I've always been jealous of the love her people have for her."

"The people love you too," Aleksander said.

Verahim shook his head.

"Not like that," he said. "I'm their king. She's their friend. Their sister. Their daughter. She is the people. I am not *one of the people*."

Aleksander nodded in understanding.

"Maybe we can change that," Aleksander said. Verahim cocked his head.

"I don't know how I can come back from this, and maybe I shouldn't," Verahim said. "What if I made *you* king?"

"Nope." Aleksander shook his head, and Verahim frowned.

"You could set up a new government. One without our family at the head."

"A noble goal, but it isn't my job," Aleksander said.

Verahim nodded. "I thought the Pure would be one way to make Thanatanos a utopia. But I've realized that was all a lie. I want my people to be happy and safe. Xanthurias…I need your help. I don't know how to do this anymore. I need my big brother."

"Know what else Thanatanos needs?" Aleksander asked. Verahim shook his head. "A new name."

Verahim laughed out loud. "That it does. Can't be named after a dead god that tried to kill everyone, can it?"

"There'll be pushback," Aleksander said. "People hate change, but they need it."

"So, you'll help me?" Verahim asked.

"Of course," Aleksander said, pulling his brother into a tight embrace. He pulled away and said, "But first, we all need to get to Sangora's healers."

"And then take out the Magistrate," Verahim added, wincing at the pain in his legs. Aleksander nodded. "But how can we win against *that?*"

He gestured to the smoking wreckage of his palace. As if on cue, a horde of winged, Faceless Sangorans rose into the sky above Laniras. Aleksander's mind shot back to when he had first seen them in Doftaan, and terror filled his heart.

"We'll find a way, I guess."

"The Magistrate doesn't just have the Pure under her control. She has a lot of people who truly believe in her, just like I did. Thousands. Millions, even. There's going to be death, and there is going to be pain."

"I know," Aleksander said with a nod. "You're not alone, though. We'll get through this."

He looked to Mara, who was gazing into the direction of Sangora with a look of fiery resolve.

Verahim's face shifted into something caught between a smile and a grimace. He shook his head. "That's just it—I'm not sure we can."

CHAPTER FORTY-EIGHT
TIME RUNS OUT

The Thannish soldiers had surrounded Doftaan on all sides now, encamped just far enough from the city walls to be out of range of arrows or other weapons. The cloud of Faceless Sangorans circled the city as if it were in the eye of a hurricane. They did not attack, however, leaving Doftaan and its citizens at high alert for several days since Mara and the others had returned from Laniras.

Mara stood upon the front steps of her palace, her arms crossed across her chest as she watched thousands of Sangoran troops from Alboras, Timishuara, Krim, and Doftaan taking up positions along the walls and in the streets. The first attack they had repelled before the journey to Laniras had only been a warning shot. *This* was the true, final assault on Doftaan. The battle that would decide the fate of all Sangora.

Scores of her warriors stood ready outside the palace. Many human soldiers from Balgorod had managed to fight their way to Doftaan and arrived sometime before them, led by Generals Rayna and Anca.

Mara nodded to Rayna as she passed by; she knew just like her, the fierce woman had abandoned Thanatanos. She'd found refuge and a life in Alboras to oppose the atrocities her former home was now committing.

Behind Mara stood her dearest friends and closest allies, each of them ready for what was to come. Aleksander, Hanna, Shanthah, Kamil, Alia, Valeniya, and Josman, who had arrived with the human reinforcements from Balgorod, stood just behind her. Each of her Guardians of Sangora, Vasilica, Lavinia and Rayshel, Raluca, Diana, Ruta, and Valeniya stood at the base of the steps leading up to the palace addressing their troops.

Alia had requested that Ana, as her most gifted healing student, accompany her to tend to the wounded. Of course, Nadezhda had in turn demanded that she also come with them.

"*It's time,*" Thanatan's voice echoed in Mara's mind from the Godblade at her hip, and she nodded, knowing that what he said was true. She could already hear the cries of those outside the walls beginning their renewed assault.

Mara had instructed him to spy on the Magistrate through their connection, and so far, he hadn't betrayed her. She didn't expect him to, as their goals were now one and the same. The Magistrate must die, and they both knew it.

"Sound the bells of war," Mara ordered.

"Yes, Empress!" Lavinia exclaimed, calling out orders to an assembled mass of soldiers at the bottom of the steps.

They saluted their empress; she returned the gesture, and when she dropped her fist from her forehead, they departed.

The board was set. Her people were ready, prepared for the oncoming battle, but so were the Magistrate's seemingly innumerable forces. Her friends and allies had been briefed on their duties. And she, the Empress of Blood, was ready to fight Sanda Daktha for the soul of Sangora and kill her once and for all.

She'd tear out the monster's heart with her bare hands if she had to. The Faceless were already going to kill anything and anyone in their path, which meant if the Magistrate lost control of them and they went feral, they would continue their orders even after her death.

There was nothing more to be said.

The bells around the city set in high spires and along the walls chimed in harmony, a deep tone that carried across the city. The bells chimed with the notes of the Sangoran anthem; all across the city it played with the banner of Mara's Sangora once again raised on every tower.

The Magistrate's robed form materialized at the bottom of the steps, and all of Mara's allies raised their weapons and readied their powers, ready to attack at Mara's command. The Empress of Blood tried to brush the Magistrate's mind but found nothing there.

"Stand down, it's one of her illusions," Mara said. She took a few steps down toward the projection. "What do you want? We're past words."

The drums of war began to thrum around the city in time with the bells.

"I just thought I'd wish you luck before we begin our game and to look upon the faces of the people you've chosen to die for you today."

"No one here is dying for *me*. But everyone is ready to die for Sangora and to bring *you* to justice," Mara said. "Your lies end today. Your hatred, your prejudice. It all ends. You wanted to see us broken and filled with the same hate as you—but I'll have you know that Sangora will rise, and we will leave you behind in the ashes. Today, our light will banish your darkness once and for all."

Mara raised her wings, and her troops at the bottom of the steps chanted, "Ža Sangoru!"

"Then I'll see you soon."

And then, the Magistrate was gone, the illusion fading like dust.

One of Lavinia's advisors whispered something into her ear, saluted, and then departed. Lavinia approached Mara, her armor crafted from the metallic corpse of a Spirit Warrior gleaming in the moonlight.

"I've been informed another army is approaching from the north," she said. "Humans and Sangoran. Likely the officers and their men in the slave camps."

Mara cursed under her breath. "Have Anca reinforce the wall with whatever forces she can spare."

Lavinia nodded and hurried toward General Anca. They spoke for a moment, and then Anca and a contingent of Sangorans departed.

At that moment, a collective, mental shriek escaped the cloud of Faceless Sangorans in the sky as it closed in on the city like a dark storm.

Mara's Sangoran soldiers all around the city soared up to meet them; the armies of the living and dead clashed in the skies, raining corpses and blood as they slew one another.

At the same time, the Thans advanced from north of the wall with their guns, blades, and engines of destruction. Thousands of Purists and even more Faceless swarmed against the high walls of Doftaan, and Mara's forces held them off as best they could.

"Mara," Valeniya said, grabbing Mara's sleeve.

"Hello, sweet girl," Mara replied.

"I can't see her. She is blocking my power. I know she is here, but I cannot see her. I will watch over you, though."

Mara nodded.

"Thank you, Leniya. Vasilica, Ruta, and Rayshel: see that no harm comes to Diana or Valeniya," Mara ordered. "They are in your charge. If you need to find us, Valeniya will be able to do so. Now go, defend the palace and those within it."

Vasilica nodded. "No harm will come to them or your people within, my lady."

"Yes, Empress," said Ruta.

Rayshel kissed Lavinia goodbye, lingering hand in hand for a long moment before following behind Vasilica. Mara's heart ached for them; would they see one another again?

Diana took Mara's hand and looked up at her with her big green eyes. She smiled and said, "You can be brave."

Tears welled in Mara's eyes, and she took Diana in a tight embrace. "You too. I need you three to keep the palace and those hiding within its walls safe. This task is in your hands, Diana. I trust you."

Guardians Ruta, Raluca, and Vasilica bowed and accompanied Rayshel and Diana with her little bow strung over her shoulder into the palace. Mara heard Diana order some soldiers to follow them, and she smiled.

Mara turned to Alia, Ana, and Nadezhda.

"Stay with us. Without your gifts, we're done for," Mara said. Alia nodded.

"I hope it won't come to that," Alia replied.

"Will do, empress!" Ana said. She turned to Alia, who gave her a thumbs up and a wink.

"I think I take my leave as well, Empress," Valis said, and Mara clapped him on the back. "Good luck."

"You too," Mara replied.

Valis bid his half-sister Valeniya farewell and limped away, leading his personal royal guard away from the fortress to the south where they would take a ship back to Bukaral and bypass the soldiers between the two cities.

"It's time. Valeniya, Kamil, Nadezhda, and I are going to look for the Magistrate with our powers. Aleks, Hanna, Shanthah, Josman, and Lavinia, keep us safe, and Ana and Alia, keep *them* safe. Everyone ready?"

The group gave their apprehensive nods as Nadezhda pulled Thanatan's heart from her pocket and laid it on the obsidian tiles leading into the palace. She, Mara, and Kamil joined hands as they sat around the gem, focusing all their mind powers on the soul within.

The intense fear permeating the entire city had been stifling to Nadezhda's empathetic synesthesia, but now, as Kamil and Mara's superior minds helped her filter out the noise, she focused on the fear and where it was strongest, searching for the Magistrate. Kamil and Mara's abilities connected Valeniya's powers to Nadezhda, allowing her to see those whose emotions she felt.

"Mara, look!" cried Josman, pointing north as hundreds of Faceless Sangorans dropped their wingless, Thannish allies within the walls of Doftaan.

A mass of the Magistrate's forces rushed against the gates leading into the grounds of the palace while others landed within, engaging Mara's soldiers at the bottom of the stairs.

"We need to hurry!" Mara shouted as the first Faceless broke through; Josman swung his mace with such force that he knocked the creature's head clean off, and Hanna sent a shockwave through the street that tripped the others, giving the group enough time to dispatch the first wave of the beasts with their various weapons.

"Got it!" Nadezhda cried. "Mara, I found her! She's at the Doftaan University clocktower!"

"Second highest spot in the city, just like the queen in chess," Mara said. "You're sure it's her?"

"Positive. Everyone else's emotions are things like fear, panic, courage, things you'd expect. Hers is…kind of a smug, evil amusement. It's hard to explain, but I *know* it's her." She turned to Ana. "You ready for this?"

"I don't know," Ana said. "I'm not sure if I can do it."

Alia placed an understanding hand on her shoulder as dozens of Faceless forced their way through the gates. "I've seen what you can do. You can do this."

Shanthah nodded and gave her a thumbs up. "I wouldn't be here without you, kid."

Ana nodded with resolve, and Mara smiled. Sangoran soldiers swooped down just in time to intercept the Faceless, hacking at their emaciated bodies with reckless abandon.

"Good, let's go, then. No more time to lose!"

Mara, Aleksander, Hanna, Shanthah, Lavinia, Josman, Kamil, Alia, Nadezhda, and Ana huddled together.

"We've got four fliers and five who can't," Lavinia said. "How are we going to do this?"

"Hanna, take Shanthah and Josman," Mara ordered, signing for Hanna. "Aleksander, with me. Lavinia, you have the strongest wings. Take Kamil and Alia. Ana, are you strong enough to carry Nadezhda?"

Ana shook her head. "Not for very long."

"*I'll help,*" Hanna signed, and Mara gave a thumbs up. "*It'll be tricky, but we only need to get to the University District. Not too far.*"

The Sangorans and their assigned partners shot into the sky, and Hanna levitated with Shanthah and Josman while helping Ana maintain her hold on Nadezhda.

A swarm of Faceless Sangorans broke off from the main flock and were upon them within moments as they raced northwest.

"Aleks, Kamil, get rid of them!" Mara shouted. She and Hanna were unable to attack while carrying the others.

Aleksander unleashed a torrent of dark flame while Kamil pierced the minds of each individual flying Faceless that he could, shredding their minds to ruin.

They soared over the high black spires of Doftaan, crossing the river into the academic district, Akademrajon. The city burned beneath them as humans, Sangorans, and Faceless alike fought for their lives. Sides seemed to be lost, and it was all out mayhem in the streets.

"Empress, look!" Lavinia shouted, and Mara turned her head to see a large spired high-rise apartment building swarming with Faceless. As they overtook the walls, the entire building began to crumble.

"No!" Mara shouted, but as she did so, she knew that dozens or even hundreds of frightened people inside fell to their doom in a cloud of ash and dust as the building toppled over. It crashed into a second, smaller tower next to it.

Those trained in mind powers felt a burst of mental energy below as Kamil focused his power on that particular swarm; it dazed them long enough for the Doftaani soldiers to turn their spears on them and turn the tide in their favor. The Faceless and Thannish soldiers were so numerous, however, that they knew the momentary advantage wouldn't last long.

The Thans had taken the northern wall outside the academic district; their guns and accompanying machines were set up, and any Sangorans that dared fly close enough were riddled with bullet holes and fell from the sky.

The group landed on one of the open levels of the high clocktower beside a spiral staircase led upward into the upper levels. As those unable to fly began to climb, Hanna sped away, levitating ahead of the others.

"Hanna!" Shanthah shouted, but Kamil waved him down.

"She said to tell you she'll be fine," Kamil said. *"She says we need you more than she does. In her words, make us vanish, Mr. Phantom."*

Shanthah nodded, turning his allies invisible as they climbed the spiral staircase, keeping them safe from view of the gunners.

Meanwhile, Hanna raced toward the Thans on the wall, using her powers to deflect the bullets from knocking a group of Sangoran warriors from the sky. She slammed down on the wall, skinning her knee on the rough stone but then began batting Thannish soldiers and their guns from the battlements.

The first attack they'd repelled before visiting Laniras had taught her the soldiers' strategies, and this time, she was ready.

She felt the groaning of the Faceless behind her, and she crouched and leapt into the sky, using her powers to hold her aloft as she leapt over her human foes. She touched down and continued her assault on the gunmen, throwing their weapons over the sides of the walls as the swarm of Faceless impeded their human allies' progress.

Hanna looked over the tide of Thannish armies and swore aloud. Hundreds of men armed with bows and muskets, and what seemed like an endless number of ladders and other siege equipment awaited her. She turned and blasted the small swarm of Faceless from the wall, but she knew further efforts other than clearing what was already there would be in vain. She'd made quick work of those upon the northern battlements, but she wondered for how long that would be so.

A flaming stone thrown by a ballista crashed into the wall below her, throwing her to the ground. Her face hit stone, and her vision blurred as she tried to stand.

She looked up just in time to see a Thannish soldier raising a battle axe above his head to cleave her in two. He shouted something that went unheard, but before the axe crushed her, someone thrust a blade through his back and out his sternum; he fell screaming to the ground, and Lavinia appeared from behind him and dispatched him with a second blade to his neck.

She offered Hanna a hand and pulled her to her feet. Shanthah, Alia, and Josman stood behind Lavinia. Shanthah wrapped Hanna in a tight embrace.

"*Let's give them hell,*" he signed as he pulled away, and Hanna winked in reply. Josman hefted his mace, and Lavinia raised both of her blades. Alia began healing the scrape on Hanna's face, but she brushed her off.

"Save your energy. We'll need it later," Hanna said aloud.

Dozens of Sangoran soldiers made it to the wall now that the guns had been blown away. Lavinia gave a Sangoran battle cry, leading her allies against the rest of the Thans and all their terrible machines upon the rest of the wall.

Back on the clocktower, Mara led the way up the final flight of stairs, bursting into the highest point in the spire, which was open to the air on all sides and manned with soldiers armed with rifles and one with one of the terrible repeating guns. But deadlier than they, the Magistrate stood in the center of the room.

Aleksander wasted no time engulfing the Purist standing behind the rapid-fire gun upon a stand in a pillar of flame. The soldier screamed, and then Aleksander drew his blade to engage the others. Kamil steeled himself, putting up mental barriers in each of their minds to protect them from the Magistrate's power and illusions.

Ana and Nadezhda stayed behind on the lower landing, peeking their heads up enough to see their allies' ankles as they battled the Purists.

"What can we do?" Ana asked, lifting the short blade she had been given. "I don't know how to use this thing!"

"We make sure the others don't get hurt!" Nadezhda exclaimed as a man tumbled down the stairs covered in hideous burns. To their horror, he groaned and got to his feet like a burning corpse. Nadezhda felt his overwhelming hatred; she focused on it, amplifying it until the man collapsed, his nose dripping with blood.

He dropped his rifle, which clattered to the ground at their feet. They shared a glance, and Ana hefted the weapon, peering down its length.

"How are they doing?" Ana asked, and Nadezhda shared with her the emotions she could see; fear and brave resolve from both sides, but neither side was losing hope.

"Can we use Thanatan's heart to help?" Ana asked. "Can you use your powers?"

Nadezhda could feel the strain on Kamil's powers as the Magistrate battled him, and she pulled the bit of crystal from her pocket.

"I can try," she muttered, squeezing it tightly in her hand, melding her mind with Kamil's to boost his strength as much as she could. It was impossible for her to tell which feelings belonged to whom in the stew of emotions wafting above her.

As she squeezed Thanatan's heart, Ana pulled the trigger of the gun, unleashing a bullet that raced through the air, planting itself in the Magistrate's chest. She gasped, surprised she'd operated the weapon correctly and landed the shot. Nadezhda stood openmouthed as the robed woman stumbled backward then turned her gaze on them.

Mara pulled her wingblades from the chest of the last gunman and turned her sights on the Magistrate, who was now locked in a mental showdown with Kamil.

However, the horrible hunger of the Faceless filled her soul as dozens of the creatures began climbing as one writhing mass into the tower through the northern landing.

As they stood silhouetted against the silver moonlight, Mara hoisted the repeating machine-gun from its stand next to its dead operator's charred corpse. She pulled the strap on over her shoulder, adjusted her stance, and as the Faceless swarmed toward her, she shouted, "Get down!"

Kamil, Nadezhda, Ana, and Aleksander dropped down just in time.

With a primal yell full of unbridled rage, Mara pulled back on a lever, riddling the horde of emaciated bodies with holes in an unrelenting spray of bullets. Soon, all of their groans were silenced, and she dropped the smoking, empty gun to the ground and then summoned the Godblade, its crystals seeping from her skin to form the hilt.

The onslaught, combined with Kamil's power, was enough to disorient the Magistrate enough for Mara to wrap her wings around her enemy's neck. Just as Mara was about to remove her head, she felt a ball of flame sear the side of her neck. She collapsed to the ground, screaming

"Aleks!" Mara shouted as Sanda Daktha crumpled Kamil to his knees; he screamed in pain as Aleksander advanced on Mara. "What are you doing?!" She lifted her wings to defend herself.

She swung to strike the Magistrate down, but Aleksander blasted the Godblade with a burst of dark flame. He said nothing, and Mara stared at his vacant, cold expression with wide eyes.

He lifted his blade, and it burst into black flame before bringing it down toward her.

"Stop!" Mara shouted, but she set her heels against the ground and lifted the Godblade. As his flaming weapon neared her head, she parried with the flat side of her sword. "What the hell are you doing, Aleks?!"

She screamed and reached into his mind and felt the Magistrate's grasp bound around his soul. She could sense the woman's mental claws burrowing into his mind, threatening to tear it asunder with the slightest thought.

Mara could feel her influence creeping into the rest of their minds, and tears streamed down her cheeks.

Nadezhda and Ana appeared from below. Kamil groaned under the strain of his powers, and Nadezhda grabbed his hand to add her strength to his, slowing the Magistrate once more, but immobilizing themselves.

Ana raised the rifle once more, peering down its barrel as she pulled the trigger, blasting a hole in their foe's crimson mask. Kamil and Nadezhda began to gain the upper hand, and as the Magistrate reached her clawed fingers toward Ana, she fired again, blowing the creature's hand clean off.

"Take that, bitch!"

Ana raced forward, cocked back the hammer on the rifle and shoved the barrel beneath the Magistrate's mask. Sanda Daktha grabbed her wrist and dug her jagged claws into her flesh; she screamed and pulled the trigger one last time.

The bullet tore through the Magistrate's throat and out the back of her neck, lodging in the stone pillar behind them. She stumbled back, and Ana tried to shoot one more time, but the weapon failed, empty.

"YOU DIE!" The Magistrate barreled toward her as Kamil and Nadezhda collapsed.

As Ana cried out and drew her short blade, Aleksander pummeled Mara with bursts of explosive flame.

Mara's screams echoed Ana's as she delved deeper into Aleksander's mind, pressing her soul into his, desperately trying to find a way to free him from the Magistrate's hold.

"Ana, Nadya, get out of here!" she screamed.

"Go, go, go!" Nadezhda exclaimed, leading Ana away.

Aleksander stepped toward her as if through molasses, Mara's telepathy and telekinesis barely keeping his flaming arms down.

His memories exploded into her mind.

Images of when he ran from Laniras so long ago. The Talohiran slave camp. Playing in the snow at Hanna's bar.

Tears filled her eyes as she beheld her own face from his point of view and all the times they had fought and each of their stolen kisses. She saw the lake in which they had played so long ago before any of this madness began. She saw through his eyes as they lay under a blanket of stars, and she felt his nervous desire to kiss her for the first time.

And then, she felt *him*. He was fighting back.

"*Mara!*" his voice filled her mind.

She focused on his memories, terrified to let go. "*Aleks, please!*"

Aleksander's physical body pressed forward, flames writhing around his arms. Mara's eyes darted away from Aleksander as the Magistrate grasped Ana by the throat.

Nadezhda shot to her feet and smacked Thanatan's heart against the Magistrate's back. She felt her mind join an interconnected web of thoughts between the Magistrate, Thanatan, Mara, Kamil, and Aleksander.

She could feel Mara's mental presence pulling on Aleksander, trying to free him from Sanda Daktha's hold while Kamil's mental presence felt faint, but still connected. He was still holding her back. She plunged her blade deep into the Magistrate's lower back and pressed harder on Thanatan's crystal; it burned white hot in her hand.

Thanatan's mind began to wrap onto the Magistrate's soul just as she had her grip around Aleksander's.

But it wasn't enough. Aleksander snapped from Mara's hold, grabbing her by the collar to slam her against the wall. At the same time, Magistrate lashed out, releasing Ana to grab Nadezhda by the throat.

Aleksander slammed Mara's head against the stone pillar again and again then began to choke the life out of her. Tears filled her eyes, and she raised her bloodied wingblades.

"Aleks…" She wheezed.

Sanda's broken voice dripped with anguish and everlasting hatred. "He is mine—now, and forever."

Tears rolled down Mara's cheeks as she wrapped her wings around him, pressing the bladed tips against his back, ready to kill the man she loved. Before she did, she brushed his mind with what strength remained, and heard his voice.

"Mara?"

Not only his consciousness, but his memories were now bound by the Magistrate's mental grip. They were engulfed in her soul, and they had become one. Mara sobbed silent tears as Aleksander's thumbs pressed into her windpipe.

"You know what you need to do," Aleksander thought. She felt him urge her to erase his memories, but she resisted. Her vision began to go black, and her lungs screamed as if on fire. And then, his hands began to grow white hot. *"Mara, if you don't do it right now, she's going to make me kill you!"*

Against everything she wanted, she threw her hand upward and grasped his forehead. His eyes rolled back, and their world disappeared in a flash of blinding, white light.

CHAPTER FORTY-NINE
EYES OF CRYSTAL BLUE

And there he was, standing before her.

When the light faded, they found themselves in an idyllic meadow of wildflowers surrounding a crystal blue lake. The sun filtered through a waterfall's gentle spray, making it look as if it and the surface of the lake burned with beautiful, surreal fire. Hills topped with a blanket of lush trees encircled the secluded paradise.

As the soft wind played with the grass below Aleksander's knees, tears streamed down his face. No words escaped his mouth; the pain in his skull was gone, as were the horrible thoughts of hate and murder directed at the woman he loved.

He looked up to see Mara silhouetted with the sun at her back. She knelt next to him, and her face came into view, her expression kind and loving. Her dark hair flowed in the warm

summer's breeze, and a loosely fitting white dress that glowed
with the light of the setting sun hung from her shoulders.

"Mara," he whispered. "You look…"

"Amazing?" Mara finished his sentence with a confident
wink. "I know. You look pretty snazzy yourself."

She reached down and took his hand in her own, helping him to his feet. She pulled him close, and they held each other for several minutes without speaking. She closed her eyes as she listened to his heartbeat, and he hugged her tighter.

He hoped she'd never let go.

When they pulled away, he stared into her eyes as blue and as beautiful as the nearby lake. A soft smile crossed her face, and she cocked her head.

He glanced down and traced a finger down one of the scars leading to her heart with a sad expression.

"These are new," he whispered.

Mara nodded and pulled the front of her dress down so that he could see the full web of scars like a shattered mirror that extended outward from her heart. Tears filled her eyes, but she smiled all the same.

In a moment of vulnerability, Mara took Aleksander's hand and placed his palm over her heart. The other rested softly on her cheek.

"Are you…"

"I'm okay," Mara said. "I'm safe. And I'm with you."

Aleksander looked back up to meet her gaze. With one hand still on her cheek, he ran the other through her hair as she kissed him deeply.

Light shined in her eyes as she took his hands and led him in a slow Sangoran dance. She rested her head on his shoulder with one hand on his chest.

"Where are we?" Aleksander asked.

"You don't remember?" Mara replied, looking up at him.

"I'll never forget this place. I guess I meant to ask—how are we here?"

"We're not. Not really," Mara said. "We're still in Doftaan. The Magistrate still has her hold on your mind, and we're still in danger. But not here—here, we're completely safe."

"How?"

"This is *my* mind. This is my Dreamstate."

"Wow," Aleksander said. "This is incredible. Is this where you go whenever you…" He trailed off, fumbling for words. "Whenever you do whatever it is you do in here?"

Mara chuckled.

"To think, plan, practice…mourn. Yeah. I've never let anyone else in here. I've missed you, Aleks. So, so much. But yes, this is where I always go. My happy place." She paused. "*You* are my happy place. You always have been."

"But if we're here, that means—"

Mara nodded. "It means we can stay here like this as long as we like. Forever, if you don't get bored of me."

Aleksander smiled. "I don't think that's possible."

She pushed up on her toes and kissed him again.

"We do need to go back sometime. You know why," Aleksander said, the crystal blue of her glistening eyes reflecting the light of the setting sun. "And so do I."

Everything he was succumbed to those eyes. Those eyes that were once so hopeless and broken but now shined with everlasting hope and mirrored the unquenchable fire of her soul.

"But we *just* found each other again," Mara said. "It can't end like this."

"It never will."

He pulled her close, and their lips met once more.

"I'll hold you to that," Mara said.

"I love you, Mara Bartunek, and I always will."

"I love you, Xanthurias."

And then, another flash of white.

CHAPTER FIFTY

MEMORIES UP IN FLAME

They lost track of how long they spent with one another in the Dreamstate, but when they finally returned to the real world, it was as if they had never left.

Mara let out a cry of rage. She tore Sanda Daktha's influence from Aleksander's memories; his physical grip on her throat slackened, but with each tendril of mental control she severed, another of his memories faded into blackness. The Magistrate's hold on him was gone, and Mara turned her sights on the Magistrate herself.

She could feel the flames in Aleksander's palms die, and her rage and exquisite sadness escaped in a furious scream. And yet, the memories of the years she had spent with Aleksander in the Dreamstate fueled her fire to fight on, the joy of that time seemingly everlasting in her heart and soul.

Aleksander's eyes glazed over, and he hit the ground as Mara leapt over him and thrust both of her wingblades through the Magistrate's back.

She raised the Godblade to behead her foe, but hands with claws that tore her flesh grabbed her from behind. She turned in horror as a horde of Faceless dragged her away from the Magistrate and Aleksander.

The Godblade clattered to the ground.

"*And now what, little queen?*" the Magistrate asked, her walking corpse of a body ruined and full of holes.

"And now I'll kill you myself!" Mara screamed, struggling against the Faceless that held her back. "But I'm not just going to kill you—I am going to tear you *LIMB FROM LIMB!*"

"*Oh, I know you will. But how fun will it be to see just how much of the world I'll take down with me before I go?*"

Mara's wingblades severed the arms of those holding her, and electricity wrapped around her body. She let out a burst of lightning that threw the Faceless, smoldering, from the tower. She reached out, grasping her enemy's consciousness to shred it into oblivion.

"*You'll have to try harder than that.*"

The Magistrate's superior mental abilities knocked Mara back, but she stepped backward in alarm, seemingly fazed for the first time during their fight.

"Never again," Mara said through clenched teeth, fire in her eyes. She screamed and decimated one specific piece of the woman's guarded soul, completely obliterating the part of her knowledge and memories that knew how to dominate the minds of others.

Mara screamed as her head throbbed, and she stumbled back against the wall. The Magistrate recovered and wrapped her fingers around the handle of the Godblade. As Mara sprinted toward her, the Magistrate raised the weapon and lashed out just as Kamil tried to invade her mind. The sword sliced through Kamil's arm near the elbow, and he collapsed, screaming to the ground holding the bloody stump.

"Ana!" Mara shouted.

"On it!" Ana exclaimed.

The Magistrate brought the Godblade around again, and Mara barely managed to catch it between her wings before it managed to split her head in two. She planted her feet and launched herself forward, thrusting the razor claws strapped to her fingers into the Magistrate's chest.

The world around her twisted into one of the Magistrate's illusions as she felt Kamil and Nadezhda's hold on her break, and then the spire of the clock tower began to crumble. Aleksander fell in one direction while Nadezhda, Kamil, and Ana fell in the other in a chorus of screams.

"It's an illusion," Mara told herself. "You can't trick me."

"Is it?" the Magistrate asked aloud.

Mara rushed forward only to have her foot fall through what she had expected to be solid ground; she was actually falling. She extended her wings and shot toward Aleksander's unconscious body as he fell. She hoped with all her heart that Ana would see Nadezhda and Kamil in the rubble where she could not.

Images of her failures surrounded her in a dense fog; she could see the fall of Nitra, her duel with Hanna and Shanthah under an island the first time they'd met the Faceless, all the lives she had failed to save in the slave camps, her friends that had been executed in Tazovski, and then, Aleksander's vacant eyes staring into her soul that she had seen only moments before.

She grabbed Aleksander around the waist and arced around, trying to spot Kamil, Ana and Nadezhda.

"Kamil!"

She reached out telepathically, feeling his mind atop a building somewhere below the spire. He was hurt, but he was still alive. But where were the girls?

She plummeted downward as the top of the clocktower completely collapsed, crushing countless Faceless and many Thannish, Sangoran, and Talohiran troops on the ground as well.

She set Aleksander down in an alleyway strewn with loose hay and a fallen cart, propping him up against a wall. She pressed her forehead against his and then kissed it softly. She reached down and ripped the sleeve away from his arm to reveal the scar of his name.

He opened his eyes in confusion to see Mara kneeling before him, and he struggled to get away from her. Her wings were dripping with blood as the city burned behind her, and she knew she must look like a monster he did not recognize.

"Stop!" she exclaimed. "I'm here. I'm here."

"Who are you?!"

He stopped struggling, but he said nothing as his vision swam and the world burned around him. He glanced down at his arm and saw the scar of his name.

"Who…?" he whispered. "…Aleksander…?"

"That's you, my love," Mara said, kissing him on the forehead. "Please, stay safe."

He gave a weak nod, and she smiled through tears.

He blacked out again. Mara wiped the tears from her face as she raced down the street to find Kamil, Ana, and Nadezhda, leaving Aleksander alone in what she hoped was the relative safety of a secluded alleyway.

The sounds of battle surrounded them, but there was no reason for soldiers to come down this way.

She found Kamil limping down a flight of broken stairs. She could no longer sense the two girls, her mind a muddled mess. Kamil stumbled into her arms, and she helped him lean against the broken wall of a building. He held his bloody arm against his chest; Ana had managed to seal the wound, but she could sense his immense pain.

"Mara! Where is Aleksander?"

She could sense that he knew what had transpired.

"Safe, for now."

"Take me to him, please. I can't think through this pain." He raised the stump of his hand. *"But maybe, I can keep him safe."*

Mara nodded and helped him limp back to the alleyway. As he slumped next to Aleksander, the Magistrate's voice, wherever she was now, filled both of their minds.

"You have a choice and a problem to solve, little queen. I have three pets. One heading toward Laniras. One heading toward Bukaral. And

one, of course, heading here. You might be able to see him now, say hello!"

"And what?" Mara replied, wondering if the Magistrate could hear her.

"I'm giving you enough forewarning that you'll be able to call your own beloved creature. You'll have time enough to stop one of my pets, but not all three. So, which will you choose? Will you punish the nation that assails your own, or will you be selfish and save your own people? Or perhaps you'll choose to save millions of innocent people in Bukaral. The choice is yours."

And then her voice was gone. Mara turned to Kamil as she called for Hippo.

"Where are Nadezhda and Ana?"

Before he could answer, a massive beast shaped like a whale with six massive wings and covered in writhing tentacles and gaping maws emerged from the clouds, heading straight for her palace and the thousands of innocent people hiding within.

The beast dominated the sky, and its roars filled the world. Countless tendrils whipped at the air, tossing hundreds of Faceless from its back into the streets of Doftaan below. Its tentacles wrapped around a high spire in the center of the city, and it used it to pull itself toward the palace.

"Is that what I think it is?" Mara asked.

"One of those things from the Deadlands," Kamil replied, confirming her worry. *"But how?"*

"Not important. Where are Nadezhda and Ana?"

"*I can sense them, still in the ruins of the clocktower,*" Kamil said. "*I don't think we have time to check on them before that thing reaches the palace.*"

Mara cursed loudly, knowing he was right.

"I don't know what to do," she admitted, tears filling her eyes. "Kamil, I don't know what to do."

"*Go. Aleksander and I will find the girls.*"

Hippo landed next to them, shaking the earth. He groaned and gestured to the monster in the sky, and Mara nodded.

Mara winked. "Thank you, Supreme One."

"*You're welcome, Empress.*"

Hippo groaned again, his tone fearful.

"I know, buddy. Ready to take it down?"

Hippo grunted and let out a massive roar as if a challenge for the other beast. Mara climbed onto his head, and he leapt into the sky, shooting straight for the beast as it toppled the tower it was using to propel itself forward.

Kamil's voice filled her mind. "*I can still talk to you if you need me.*"

She acknowledged his thought and set her sights on the monster. Hippo raced through the dark sky, a gleam of orange light emanating from the gaps in his armored hide as he readied the flames within his belly.

"*See any weaknesses?*" Mara thought to Kamil as Hippo soared high above it, unleashing a spray of lava that melted into the beast's flesh and coated the many eyes and mouths on its skin. It did not stop its advance. The monstrosity dwarfed even Hippo, making him seem like a gnat on the back of a hog.

"Something has to be propelling it… Keeping it from falling," Kamil said. *"There is no way those wings could support that thing. You know, like a balloon. My guess is some kind of gas."*

"So, what would happen if we ignited that gas?" Mara asked as she guided Hippo to close his massive jaws around one of the longest tendrils; he bit down, severing the disgusting, undulating thing. It fell, writhing, to the ground far below.

"It must not have a way out, or it'd deflate. If we could get inside…"

"I think I'd rather let it kill me," Mara replied.

"That might happen."

"Thanks for the confidence, buddy," Mara thought with a chuckle as Hippo let out another bout of lava.

They soared around the beast as thousands of Sangoran soldiers flew up to meet it, hacking at its flesh with spears, swords, wingblades and axes. Many were struck down by barbed tendrils, their bodies raining down on the city they loved and defended.

Each death felt like an arrow to Mara's heart.

She willed Hippo to fly below the beast where a set of five massive jaws opened in the shape of a star, much like a hand opening. Ten or so bulbous pods erupted from its mouth and fell upon Doftaan; wherever one struck, dozens of Faceless emerged.

"Did you see that?" Kamil asked from far below.

"What?"

"When it opened its mouth, there was a thin membrane leading into the throat. I think it retracted as soon as it closed its mouth…thing."

"Gross," Mara replied. *"Can you get it to open its mouth?"*

"It's taking all I have to keep up my connection with you. Sorry, but no."

She guided Hippo beneath the monstrosity, and he spiraled in the air to shoot straight upward, climbing higher toward the beast.

A river of molten lava erupted like a violent volcano from Hippo's maw and exploded straight up into the beast's mouth. The lava and flames splashed against the slimy membrane and began to melt through. Hippo turned right-side-up and Mara breathed out in relief.

"Aleksander is awake," Kamil thought.

"You've done great. Make sure he's okay," Mara replied. She felt their connection fade.

And then, amidst the thousands of Sangorans fighting in vain to fell the creature, Mara caught sight of a single human woman floating, her auburn hair floating around her as if in water, bits of rock and glass swirling around her.

"Hanna!" Mara shouted. Hippo raced toward her, and as she saw the behemoth coming, she jumped onto his head and ran down his neck, rolling next to Mara as the monster closed its star shaped jaws.

"Hello, you!" Hanna signed as Lavinia landed next to them as well.

"Where are the others?" Mara asked.

"Safe. They're retreating back to the palace after retaking the wall," Lavinia reported.

Mara nodded.

"Kamil found a weakness," Mara explained. "We need to get its mouth open again."

A smirk crossed Hanna's face. *"Give me a boost, girl."*

Mara knew exactly what she meant, remembering when Kamil had amplified Hanna's powers with his mind. She didn't know exactly how to do it, but she reached into her friend's mind to try.

Hanna set her heel against Hippo's hide and leapt off. Mara and Lavinia followed close behind her.

"Now!" Mara shouted.

She focused on boosting Hanna's abilities with all her might as Hanna grabbed the five sections of the bulbous creature's maw. The blood in her veins began to glow white as she wrenched the mouth open; the beast squirmed in pain, vomiting hundreds more Faceless into the streets below.

"Hurry!" Hanna screamed.

"Lavinia!" Mara shouted. "With me!"

Lavinia obeyed the will of her empress, and together, the two Sangorans took flight. Much to her relief, Mara was able to summon the Godblade. Mara roared in her fury as she pierced the membrane covering the creature's throat with the glowing blade. A tendril wrapped around her leg, and she cried out in surprise and pain as it hurled her through the sky.

Hanna screamed as Mara's concentration broke, and her powers failed. The creature's mouth began to close.

Lavinia thrust both of her wingblades into the wound Mara had inflicted and tore it open, hacking at the flesh until a noxious odor filled her nostrils. She leapt from the creature's jaws as Hippo raced straight up toward her, letting out an explosion of flame and lava.

Hippo's superheated breath reacted with the gas leaking from the hole Mara and Lavinia had created, and with a tremendous boom, the beast exploded in a fiery blast high above Doftaan, sending viscera raining down over the city.

Just as Hanna landed on Hippo's back, the force of the blast sent the behemoth spiraling out of control. Hippo plummeted downward, and as Mara brushed Hanna's mind, she found it blank and unconscious.

Lavinia intercepted Hanna before she was impaled by a high spired building. She set their unconscious friend on Hippo's back as he regained his composure with a terrified groan.

"It's okay, buddy!" Mara exclaimed, patting his back. "Got it in you to kill another one?"

Hippo let out a brave roar, and they shot west toward the monster heading for Bukaral.

CHAPTER FIFTY-ONE
OVER THE PRECIPICE

The world spun as Ana screamed under the strain to pull the rubble from atop Nadezhda, who stirred feebly as she reached down and cupped her cheek.

"We gotta go, Nadya," Ana said, patting her face to get her to wake up. "Come on, girl."

Nadezhda obeyed, albeit dazed and confused. Ana helped her to her feet just as a group of Thannish soldiers clashed with a contingent of Sangorans holding pikes below them. Musket fire felled several of them, but as they had to reload their weapons, the winged warriors swooped in, impaling their foes through the chest with spears and wingblades as others discarded their long weapons to slice the throats of the Thans with steel razorclaws.

"You don't need to see that," Ana said, physically turning Nadezhda's face away from the battle. "Come on, let's get you out of here."

She hurried to heal a gash in Nadezhda's leg so that she could walk. She continued to heal as many of her wounds as possible as they limped from the rubble.

"Are you okay?" Ana asked as Nadezhda fell to her knees holding her head. "The emotions—they're too much, aren't they?"

Nadezhda nodded, unable to speak through the pain and the chaos in her mind.

"Can you share it with me? Like you did at the festival?" Ana asked with a smile. "Let me share the load."

Nadezhda nodded, tears rolling from her eyes as Ana clutched her hand; she met her consciousness and allowed some of the emotion to flow into Ana's mind. At the same time, she felt and saw Ana's love emanating from her head, as if a shield keeping the darkness at bay.

Nadezhda stumbled for a moment, but the entirety of the overwhelming sense of dread and loss in the city wasn't on Nadezhda's shoulders anymore.

"You okay?" Ana repeated.

"No, but better," Nadezhda answered. "Thank you, love."

She reached into her pocket, but Thanatan's heart was gone.

"Oh no," she whispered, and Ana covered her mouth in shock, raising her eyebrows as if to ask. Nadezhda nodded. "Oh no, oh no, oh no… It's gone!"

"Is it under there somewhere?" Ana asked as she guided Nadezhda behind a pile of rubble out of view of the chaos in the streets.

"No. I could sense it if it was. I can hear his voice, faintly…"

Ana covered Nadezhda's ears to block out the sound.

"Focus. You can do it!"

Nadezhda put her hands over Ana's, and she locked in on the voice, allowing the whispers to grow in her mind.

"I didn't mean to lose it," Nadezhda said. "She was too powerful, and… I'm sorry, I've let everyone down!"

"No, Nadya—you don't say sorry unless you've done something wrong. This isn't your fault, remember?" Ana said. "We'll find it, and we'll fix this. We can help! Besides, would it be so horrible if we lost him forever?"

"Mara needs it for her plan to work," Nadezhda said. "She told me to keep it safe."

"We will!"

From their position on the ground, they watched the beast in the sky explode in a gruesome display of exploding flesh. A chunk of it splashed down next to them, sizzling from the blast.

"What in the name of the king's underpants was that?!" Nadezhda exclaimed.

They watched Hippo soar away to the west.

"Where are they going?" Ana asked.

"No idea! Come on!" Nadezhda exclaimed, grabbing Ana's hand.

They raced through the rubble and the bodies of fallen on both sides as Nadezhda followed Thanatan's faint voice. They dodged soldiers locked in battle and explosions thrown by trebuchets as they chased the Voice past the destroyed

Talohiran embassy. They hurried across the two rivers into Jempratanrajon, the imperial district of Doftaan. Only one bridge was left standing, and bodies were strewn across it.

"The Magistrate is in Mara's palace! I can sense her this time!" Nadezhda exclaimed. "She must have the gem!"

"This way!" Ana replied, taking Nadezhda's hand. She led her down some side streets that led toward the palace, trying to avoid the fighting. They had to take a longer way around to avoid a particularly gruesome scene where the Faceless had torn a group of soldiers to shreds and looked as if they were trying to devour their corpses.

They hurried toward the crumbling walls surrounding the grounds of Mara's palace, and to their relief, found part of it broken enough for them to climb over.

Many of the trees and hedges lining the way up to the palace were burning, and hundreds of human, Sangoran, and Faceless bodies lay on the bloodstained path.

"Come on!" Nadezhda exclaimed, and they ran toward the front gates.

"Stop right there!" called a Thannish soldier as he and his ten allies emerged from the front of the palace.

Nadezhda gave a cry and summoned as much of the pain and loss she could feel around Doftaan, pushing it into each of their souls; they all collapsed, sobbing, and the two girls took their chance, darting past them.

They climbed the stairs of the entryway, and Ana grabbed Nadezhda and helped her up as she stumbled; she flapped her wings to help her climb the stairs until they were on the second landing.

"I think… Mara's throne room…" Nadezhda wheezed. Ana, too, was out of breath, so she simply nodded. They sprinted up another flight of stairs toward the throne room, and Nadezhda heard Thanatan's voice with clarity guiding her closer.

"Nadya, look!"

Nadezhda looked out a broken window to see a large army north of the wall carving into the mass of Thannish forces stationed there.

"Who are they?" she asked. Ana shrugged, and they continued onward.

"Does it matter?!"

A group of Purists stood at the other end of the hallway, and as Nadezhda tried to manipulate their emotions, she collapsed to her knees, exhausted from overusing her powers. She shook her head, dizzy, but alert, as her vision clouded with their fear and hatred.

"You good?" Ana asked.

Nadezhda nodded, raising her short sword. The Purists advanced, and both girls screamed, raising their weapons, but the leader of their foes fell on his back with an arrow in his throat.

They looked back to see young Diana standing with a silver crossbow, a second arrow at the ready. The Purists turned just as three more Guardians of Sangora appeared. Raluca, Ruta, and Vasilica cried out as they brandished their silver blades and charged the cultists. Nadezhda and Ana joined in, and soon, the Purists were defeated, leaving only Vasilica with a long wound across her side.

"Hello there!" said Ruta with a smile. "You're a long way from the academy, isn't it a school night?"

Nadezhda and Ana laughed.

"If you write us a note, maybe we can get out of classes," Ana replied with a chuckle and a thumbs up.

"Listen, the Magistrate took Thanatan's gem from us, and if she figures out how to use the power inside, we're all dead," Nadezhda said. "Mara called it the Connection to Creation, and, well...Can you get us to her?"

The four Guardians shared a glance before Vasilica shook her head.

"We're no match for the Magistrate," she said. "Where is Mara? And where are Hanna and the others?"

"We got scattered," Ana replied.

"Mara was heading west on her beast, I'm not sure why," Nadezhda explained.

"Another one of those things was spotted heading for Bukaral. She must be going to slay it," said Raluca. "I don't think we'll see her any time soon until she's back."

"Damn it," said Vasilica, stumbling against a wall. She held her side, which was coated in blood.

"I can help," Ana said, hurrying forward to mend her wound with her powers. She breathed life into the flayed skin, and it slowly sewed itself together. Vasilica patted Ana on the back in thanks, still out of breath.

"We don't need to kill the Magistrate; we just need to get the Heart from her. We'll leave the god slaying to the empress," Nadezhda said as a troop of soldiers rushed by, saluting the Guardians of Sangora as they went.

Valeniya Talohir emerged from behind the four Guardians holding onto Rayshel for support, her eyes glossed over with white.

"Valeniya!" Vasilica exclaimed. "Thank the goddesses. Where on Earth did you come from? Where is Mara?"

"She is back home. Father's home. In Bukaral," Valeniya said, staring into nothing. "She is in grave danger."

"Another one of those big fat blobber things?" Nadezhda asked, pointing to the sky.

"Yes, she is fighting another big fat blobber."

The others chuckled.

"And Alia?" Ana asked.

"Alia is safe. She is with Lavinia, Mr. Shanthah and her love, Josman, and they wouldn't let anything happen to her. I am thankful," Valeniya said. "I love Alia very much."

Rayshel let out a sigh of relief, clearly anxious about her partner's safety, although she knew Lavinia could take care of herself.

"And where are they now?" asked Diana.

"Below us," replied Valeniya. "With the people."

"Listen," Vasilica said. "Most of us don't have any powers. Those of us that don't won't stand a chance against the Magistrate. We'll join them in the dungeons to defend the people, and Raluca will keep you safe." She paused for a moment. "I'm sorry, but we're of more use down there."

"We understand," Nadezhda said with a nod. Raluca said her goodbyes to Valeniya, Rayshel, and the other Guardians of Sangora, but Diana stopped as the others made their way downstairs.

"I can help," she said.

"No, go where it's safe," Nadezhda said. Raluca placed a hand on Diana's back.

"This isn't going to be a place for kids," Raluca said. "We don't want you in danger."

"Mara made me a Guardian for a reason. I've seen and survived more horrible things than most adults. I'm small, and I know I can help get the Heart, or whatever you called it, from that horrible monster."

"How?" Raluca asked. Diana took a deep breath and then turned invisible. She wasn't as talented as Shanthah, and her faint outline was still visible, but she was invisible, nonetheless. She let out the breath and rematerialized.

"I can't stay invisible very long. Only as long as I hold my breath," Diana said. "But it might be enough."

"Well, let's go before the others realize you're not with them," Nadezhda said. "Sorry, Vasilica, stealing your Diana for a minute."

Ana pulled Nadezhda aside as they headed up another flight of stairs.

"The Magistrate could sense her even if she's invisible," Ana said. "This is a bad idea."

"Not if I distract her with my noggin powers," Nadezhda replied, tapping her head. "When have I ever steered you wrong?"

"There's no one else I'd rather be steered wrong by," Ana replied. "Steer on."

Nadezhda smiled, and they followed Diana and Raluca upstairs.

"She's not in the throne room anymore," Nadezhda said, sensing Thanatan's voice. The dead god projected an image into her head.

"Where?" Raluca asked.

"Uh, big room… Stained glass…"

"Grand Ballroom," Raluca muttered. "Of course."

"Of course?" Nadezhda asked as they hurried upward.

"Terrible things have happened in that room. Mara was betrayed and overthrown there. I, for one, think it's cursed," said Raluca.

"There is no such thing as curses," Diana replied.

"Clearly untrue," Raluca argued, gesturing to a dead, Faceless corpse lying on the stairs. Diana nodded.

"Okay, maybe you're right."

The young girl led the others toward the ballroom holding her bow aloft, and they each took a collective deep breath in anticipation for the battle to come.

"I'll distract her with all the mindspeaking I can muster," Nadezhda said. "She's very strong, but Kamil and I did something that hampered her abilities earlier. I think I can do it again."

"Let's do this," Raluca said. Lightning crackled around the Guardian's hands. "I'll be able to help distract her as Diana does her thing."

They nodded, but Raluca turned to Ana.

"This is no place for a healer," she said.

"This is *exactly* the place for a healer!" Ana replied. "You guys go down, and I'm the only one getting you back up. You're not dying on my watch."

The sister of the former queen relented, and the four unlikely allies stood outside the large doors leading into the ballroom.

"Three…" Raluca said.

"Two…" said Ana.

"One," finished Diana.

And then, Raluca blasted down the doors with a bolt of thick lightning, throwing them into the chamber. Diana took a deep breath and vanished, scurrying unseen inside.

Nadezhda entered, instantly sensing the emotions of every Purist in the chamber. Anticipation. Satisfaction. A victorious, yet sinister pleasure… They were relishing in the chaos. None showed fear. But worse, none felt any remorse.

And behind the mass of cloaked cultists was a crystal throne upon which sat the Magistrate, her crimson mask reflecting the bursts of lightning as Raluca blasted down her robed supporters one by one.

Nadezhda clutched onto the anticipation in the room and flooded it with her own fear, turning joyous anticipation into crippling anxiety; she thrust it into the minds of all those around her, and they stumbled to their knees before being slain by Raluca's lightning.

"*Looking for this?*" the Magistrate asked, holding Thanatan's heart aloft.

Nadezhda swirled the evil pleasure of having done terrible things in the men's heads, turning it into guilt and disgust; many of them vomited or turned away from their allies in the shame forced upon them.

She focused on their brotherly bonds, the connection only their cult provided and twisted it into mistrust; she felt her own power waning as she manipulated them into attacking one another.

As they engaged each other in combat, Raluca set her sights on the Magistrate herself until she cried out, for a bullet had torn through her back.

Five Thannish soldiers holding muskets hurried into the room behind them and took aim. Two balls passed through Ana's wings, and another struck Raluca in the small of the back.

Ana shrugged off the pain and began working on Raluca as the Guardian continued her barrage of lightning from the ground.

But then, as Ana tended to Raluca's wounds, she screamed as a blade severed her left wing. She turned in shock as the same Purist hacked off her other wing, and she fell to the ground in shock.

Nadezhda screamed and tackled the Purist to the ground, wrenched off his metal mask, and thrust its sharp edge against his throat in a spray of crimson blood.

"Ana!" she shrieked, turning her over to examine the wounds. The blade had severed both appendages near her back, leaving only stumps of the appendages.

Sobbing, Ana reached over her shoulder to grab what remained, and the bloody mess began to close up. Nadezhda helped her to her feet as she did the same to the other appendage. Nadezhda hurried her away from the fray.

The Magistrate's victorious satisfaction filled the room; to Nadezhda, it was a darkness that swirled after them like an angry fog sparking with silver light. But then, the satisfaction turned to scarlet rage as an arrow struck Thanatan's Heart, sending it flying from the Magistrate's hand.

"*What is this?!*" Sanda Daktha shouted. At that moment, Nadezhda reached out with all the mindspeaking power she could summon to distract the Magistrate from sensing Diana. It was the mental equivalent of shouting in someone's physical ear.

Nadezhda cried out in pain and sorrow as she swirled all the negative emotions in the room and crammed them all into the Magistrate's mind with such force that it knocked her against the back of her throne.

She saw a burst of golden excitement and pride laced with purple fear scurry along the wall and out the door. Diana had the Heart.

The Magistrate raised her hand, and the great stained-glass window that extended across the entire western wall exploded in a shower of beautiful, deadly shards of every color. She clenched her fist, and the shards of glass rained down after Diana like a million colorful arrows.

Although invisible, Nadezhda could see Diana's intense fear and courage trailing behind her like smoke as the glass shattered just behind her heels.

As she became visible again, Hippo crashed through the opposite wall, his maw wide open. An eruption of molten lava exploded from his jaws, engulfing the room in lava and flame.

"Go! Get out of here!" Nadezhda shouted to the others. "I'll hold her off!"

Raluca refused, instead blasting the Magistrate in the face amidst the flaming wreckage of the room with a bolt of lightning. The strike shattered the bottom of her mask to reveal the twisted, deformed, face missing half a jaw underneath.

As they retreated, the Magistrate roared with telepathic and telekinetic energies, tearing up the floor beneath them and sending the dead Purists' weapons flying. Ana managed to duck just in time to dodge the onslaught, but Raluca hit the ground just as a spear impaled her through the chest.

Ana screamed as she saw Raluca's hand twitch once more, and then she was still. The Magistrate stood from the crystal throne to give chase.

Mara leapt down, the Godblade in her hand, followed by Hanna, who floated after her through the rubble of the ballroom. Kamil and Aleksander, who had just arrived on Hippo and seemed very confused indeed, climbed down as well. Kamil knelt at Raluca's side as Ana reached for the wound, but Nadezhda grabbed her arm.

"She's gone," she said with a sad look. Ana nodded.

"I know," she whispered.

She looked up with teary eyes to see Hanna following Mara in pursuit of the Magistrate with the Godblade raised and lightning trailing after her wings. The Magistrate leapt from the gap in the wall, and the two women followed.

Nadezhda and the others hurried out into the hallway to find Diana outside holding the Heart of Thanatan in her palm, an excited look of victory on her face.

"You did it!" Nadezhda exclaimed, and Diana handed the gem over. "That was incredible! But we need to get you to safety now, yeah?"

Kamil smiled, then said aloud, "Let's get that thing to Mara!"

Nadezhda pulled Ana and Diana into a tight hug.

"We got this!" she exclaimed. "Thanks to you!"

Diana's green eyes lit up with her smile, and the group hurried off, following the sounds of Hippo's destruction as he rampaged through the palace and slaughtered any Purists in his path.

"Kamil!"

Nadezhda, Ana, and Diana, as well as Aleksander and Kamil followed the trail of destruction to a lower part of the palace until they found the Magistrate locked in combat with Mara and Hanna. Beside them fought Lavinia, her armor gleaming in the light of the flames.

Hanna tried to hold the Magistrate back, but her powers faltered due to fatigue. Her enemy grasped her wrist and then telekinetically snapped her arm where it had broken years earlier.

Mara roared as lightning spiraled from her fingertips, up her arms, and around her wings; she unleashed a blinding beam of light through the chamber, blasting away dozens of Faceless between them and their foe.

"We've got her on the ropes!" Lavinia shouted, but then the room was filled with dark smoke, and then the ground opened up as thousands of Faceless clambered up.

Kamil strained his powers to banish the illusion, but there were real Faceless mixed in with the imaginary ones. He screamed as the Magistrate's superior mind overwhelmed his own once again for what seemed like the hundredth time that day.

"Mara!" Nadezhda screamed. Mara turned to see Nadezhda standing there holding the Heart of Thanatan aloft.

"You wonderful girl!" Mara shouted, leaping over a chunk of ruined wall through the darkness. Nadezhda handed over the gem as the illusions became stronger than ever.

It became overwhelming, and none could see through the illusion; it became reality, and it was crushing, suffocating. The weight of failure, the thousands of Faceless swarming as if dragging the entire palace into the depths of hell.…

And then, a burst of bright fire banished the shadows; Aleksander's flaming blade arced around, and before the Magistrate could react, it separated her arm at the elbow.

Shanthah and Josman appeared as if from nowhere; Josman's mace followed Aleksander's assault, striking the back of the Magistrate's head.

"Where did you two come from?!" Mara exclaimed as she broke free of the illusion and gazed out the ruined wall of her palace. She could see the thousands of people coming from the north attacking the Thannish soldiers near the wall, and at that moment, she understood.

The slaves of Tazovski had come home.

Mara felt Thanatan's power flow through her as she held the gem, and she banished the Magistrate's illusions, her own mental abilities amplified a thousandfold. She felt her mind connecting to everything around her. She felt the breath of everyone in the room, the smoothness of the obsidian tiles. The heat of the torches on the far-off wall. The heartbeats of all her allies.

She was connected to all of creation. But as she felt the Magistrate's mind snake into hers, so was her enemy.

Mara sprinted forward, summoning all the electricity in the air into a concentrated beam of light stronger than any she had ever summoned; she directed it at the Magistrate, decimating her physical form. Her skin was flayed by the endless heat, exposing bone that burned to ash; as the Magistrate reached out one last time, her charred and damaged mask struck the floor.

Mara reached down to grab the mask, and Hanna shouted to stop, but the moment she touched the crimson metal, she felt the Magistrate's mind take stronger hold on her own. She dropped Thanatan's heart and the mask at the same time, and her foe's mind pulsed within the mask like a heartbeat.

Mara collapsed, unconscious.

A single Faceless rushed from the shadows and grasped the Magistrate's mask, placing it on its own head to give her new life. Hundreds of other Faceless appeared from the hallways leading into the ballroom, accompanied by dozens of Purist soldiers.

"As long as there are Faceless, she can't die!" Nadezhda shouted. "What do we do?!"

She watched in horror as a Purist picked up the jagged gem and the life was sucked out of him in moments. Thanatan's Heart clattered to the ground again, pulsating with energy. Another Purist tried, and then another, but Thanatan drained each of them of life.

Nadezhda and the Magistrate's new body darted after Thanatan's gem as Mara regained her composure. Hippo was busy stomping Faceless somewhere down the hall, breathing hot fire over them, his reserves of lava completely spent. The Magistrate grasped the jagged piece of crystal just before Nadezhda managed to and thrust it upward into her chest.

Nadezhda cried out in pain and stumbled backward toward the broken wall of colorful glass. She touched the blood and looked at it on her fingertips, the reality that she'd been stabbed not quite real to her.

That was *her* blood. Her own. Not someone else's.

She stumbled backward and fell into the breach.

Ana got a running start and with no hesitation, leapt after her. As Shanthah, Josman, Aleksander, Kamil, Lavinia, and Hanna battled the Faceless and Purists, the Magistrate knelt next to Mara and began pommeling her face with her fists, smashing her head against the ground.

Aleksander thrust his flaming fist into the Magistrate's neck, knocking her back. Mara lay wounded on the ground, but with a groan, she stumbled to a standing position and summoned the Godblade. She limped forward and slashed at the Magistrate's mask, but her enemy stepped back, and the blow missed.

Mara wheezed, her energy completely spent. She leaned on the blade to keep herself upright.

"Remember, destroy my mask and kill me, and every single one of my minions in the world goes wild! You damn not only Laniras, but Alboras, Talohira, and everywhere else where the Pure await my command!"

Mara grabbed the new Magistrate's head with her wings and twisted, snapping her neck with a gruesome crunch. The Faceless corpse fell to the floor, and Mara tossed the mask to Hanna. She caught it with her powers just as a group of Sangoran soldiers hurried into the room, much to Mara's relief.

Outside, Ana had landed, painfully, on the sloped roof of the palace next to Nadezhda, who was lying in her own blood, the Heart of Thanatan jutting out of her chest at an odd angle.

"Nadya, no!" she exclaimed, crawling next to her.

She yanked the crystal from Nadezhda's body as she coughed and sputtered blood. She cradled Nadezhda's head in her arms as she slid her fingers into the wound.

She tried to remember the anatomy of the abdomen and the heart. What organs were punctured? What needed to be reattached?

She could see the diagrams she'd studied in Alia's class in her mind's eye, but what if she healed it wrong and Nadezhda died anyway? She let out a deep breath and wove her skin back together, willing the fibers of Nadezhda's flesh to intertwine. She was unresponsive.

"Come on, Nadya!" Ana exclaimed, placing her mouth over Nadezhda's to breathe life into her. She compressed her chest once, twice, and then checked for a pulse. She tried again, and again, but nothing.

And then, Ana held up the Heart of Thanatan. She could not hear the dead god's voice, but she felt his power seep into her body. She felt his presence connecting him to the dust in the air, the blood on the ground, and to Nadezhda's herself.

Ana held the Connection to Creation in her hand.

She placed her palm on Nadezhda's chest and willed her body to create more blood and for her heart to start pumping. With more training, she knew she'd be able to do this on her own, but she knew she had to trust Thanatan to help her at that moment. And just as she thought the power would consume her, Nadezhda took in a sudden breath. Ana dropped the Heart, and it clattered down next to her.

She shook off Thanatan's overwhelming power and continued healing Nadezhda's wound with her own hands and her own power. Nadezhda stirred feebly, and Ana cried out in joy, pulling her to a sitting position.

"I knew I could do it!" Ana exclaimed as she kissed Nadezhda deeply. "Oh, Nadya—I love you so much!"

"You—you saved me. I love you too," Nadezhda said with a wide smile. "Tatiana, you are *everything* to me."

The beautiful silver and pink light that exuded from Ana's person overwhelmed Nadezhda with joy as she was brought back from the brink of death; she tapped into her mindspeaking abilities to allow Ana to see her own joy and love, and they held each other for a long moment, happy, and together.

And then, the tower shook. Nadezhda's screams went unheard as Ana fell backward off the roof; she thrust her shoulders up as if trying to fly, but with her wings severed, she plummeted downward.

Nadezhda leapt after her, reaching for her hand.

Ana's aura held no fear. There was only joy and love there, until it was gone. Nadezhda struck the roof next to Ana, but she could not sense her emotions, mind, or life.

"NO!" Nadezhda shouted. "No, no, no! Please, NO!"

She held Ana in her arms, kissing her forehead over and over, trying to find a pulse, trying to see any flitter of emotion, but she was still.

And then, Nadezhda grasped the Heart of Thanatan.

"Save her!" Thanatan did not respond. "Bring her back, damn it! Please!"

"*I am...so sorry.*"

She felt Thanatan's power in her palm, and she felt Thanatan's mind snake into her own; at that moment, she could sense every single emotion in all of Doftaan.

Every single fear.

Every single scream.

They all became hers.

And her utter grief became *theirs*.

As her sobs broke, still holding Ana's body, the entire city fell silent. Millions of people, civilians and soldiers alike fell to the ground as a shockwave of every negative emotion of the millions of people in Doftaan permeated the world.

The hurricane of evil grief that overshadowed the city became visible to everyone connected to Nadezhda's mind. The battle stopped as Nadezhda cried, mourning her love whose final act had been to heal her heart, her last words an expression of true love.

"Tatiana, please…I can't lose you!"

Screams went up across the city, and Nadezhda began to lose herself to the darkness. She could feel no joy, for there was little left in the entire city. The more fear people felt at that moment amplified her own despair, and it swallowed her entire being.

Footsteps.

She turned, hoping to see Mara, Alia, Kamil, anyone. But there, standing behind her, was the Magistrate. Her mask was on the body of a Purist woman, but that same horrible voice called out to her.

"No," Nadezhda said, holding Ana close. "Stay back!"

"*Give it to me*," said Sanda Daktha. "*I won't ask twice.*"

As she reached out for it, Mara touched down on the far side of the roof. Sanda Daktha picked up a discarded spear and twirled to strike down the Empress of Blood. Nadezhda screamed and held Ana's body close as Mara ran to meet their foe, the Godblade raised.

The Magistrate raised her spear, but Mara set her feet and extended her wings, leaping into the air. She thrust the blade through the Magistrate's stomach, pinning her against the wall.

"NADEZHDA, NOW!"

Nadezhda hurled the gem to Mara, who pressed it against the Magistrate's mask while holding onto the handle of her blade, pressing it ever deeper into the Magistrate's body.

"*By your hand,*" Thanatan said to her mind.

"Kamil!"

She felt her mind connect to Kamil's as Hanna appeared as well, holding the Magistrate in place against the wall. The world around them exploded with telekinetic energy as the Magistrate roared with all the hatred in her soul.

Nadezhda reached out, adding whatever mental energy she still had left to aid Kamil and Mara's onslaught. She felt their intention: to imprison the Magistrate's mind within the confines of the Godblade where a portion of Thanatan's soul had once resided.

"Checkmate," Mara said through gritted teeth.

Lavinia landed on the roof next to them, and without hesitation, crossed her blades at her mother's neck and beheaded her once and for all in a spray of dark blood. The magistrate's mask fell to the ground, and Josman shattered it with his heavy mace as Mara wiped a trail of blood from her split lip.

But then, another wave of Nadezhda's connection to every negative emotion in the city crippled both her and the others. They each fell to the ground holding their heads in their hands in the shared, exquisite agony of Nadezhda's heartbreak.

"Hippo!" Mara shouted, and Hippo exploded from the side of the palace, flapped his wings, and landed on the roof on the landing below them. He stood on his hind legs so that he could see them. "Get Nadezhda as far from here as you can, or we're *all* going to die!"

Mara screamed, her head throbbing. The world began to swim, and she stumbled as Lavinia collapsed next to her.

Nadezhda still held Ana close but looked down at Hippo, his expression sad, for he could sense her pain as much as anyone else in the city. Mara managed to crouch next to her.

Josman went down, blood trailing from his nose. Hanna fell next, cradling her broken arm, and then Shanthah, gripping his love's shoulder.

"Nadezhda," Mara whispered, wrapping her arms around the trembling girl. "Please, please listen to me…"

Nadezhda's tears flowed freely as she rocked, holding Ana's body close. She felt as if she would be consumed by the very void itself. Screams continued around the city, and Mara knew the overwhelming emotion was beginning to kill people all around the city and drive others insane.

"Nadya…" Mara whispered into her ear. "This love between you… This grief—remember what I said. It means she matters. It means what you have is *real*. But do you know what you need to do now?"

Nadezhda nodded her head.

"I need to leave," she whispered. Mara trembled, her body beginning to give out to the stress of Nadezhda's all-consuming negative energy.

"I will make sure she is safe," Mara whispered. "I will see to it that she is given a beautiful place to rest."

"On a hill, by a tree," Nadezhda said. "Please. She would—she would like that. The one in Balgorod... Ana, no..."

"Of course," Mara said.

"I can't do this. I can't go alone," Nadezhda said. "Please, please no..."

Mara pulled her into a hug. "You are *never* alone."

The others were on their feet now, but they looked as if they would soon collapse again. Shanthah. Diana. Lavinia. Josman. Hanna. Vasilica. Alia and Valeniya had even emerged from the palace, and they stood by.

As the crowd gathered, Nadezhda felt their gaze, and she didn't want to let them take Ana away. She couldn't let them. And then she felt Hanna's forehead on her own.

"It's okay," Hanna said aloud. "She's safe."

Nadezhda decided to trust Hanna, and as Mara helped her to her feet, Diana cradled Ana's head in her lap.

"See, she's safe," Mara said. "Diana will take care of her."

The young Guardian of Sangora nodded.

"We'll get her to the tree on the hill," Mara whispered, kissing Nadezhda on the forehead. "I promise."

Lavinia grabbed Mara's wrist as she turned to leave.

"Glory to the Empress of Blood and all Sangora," she said, bowing her head with a fist to her forehead. Mara smiled.

"And to the end of your family's dark past, and a new hope for its bright future," Mara added, and Lavinia raised Mara's fist into the air triumphantly.

They embraced, and when they let go, Mara gestured to Kamil, who came forward and stumbled onto Hippo's back. Mara led Nadezhda onto the behemoth's snout, over his head, and onto his back as well. And then, everyone else but Diana, Lavinia, and Vasilica climbed on.

And then, they shot into the sky, taking the Godblade and the Heart with them. As Hippo soared away from Doftaan, every Faceless on the ground below trailed after them, hurrying through the city after their master, who was now trapped within the glowing sword unable to command them.

Mara wondered how long the Thannish forces would be incapacitated, but knew the fighting was far from over.

Hippo soared low enough that the Faceless would still be able to sense their master's mind and follow them wherever they went. Nadezhda sobbed against Mara's chest.

The others were letting out sighs of relief as Kamil shielded them one by one from Nadezhda's raw, painful power. As Kamil knelt next to Mara, she shook her head.

"No, thank you, friend. I want to feel what she does," Mara whispered, stroking the remaining blonde of Nadezhda's darkened hair. "I want her to know she's not alone."

She glanced up at Aleksander, who sat far from her. He looked confused and broken and had no idea who she was.

As she felt Nadezhda's sorrow, her own spilled forth; the two women held one another tight as a dark cloud of grief trailed after them.

CHAPTER FIFTY-TWO
THE LAST GIFT WE CAN GIVE

Mara took Nadezhda's hand to help her step down from Hippo's massive snout. The new, thin layer of snow across Bartun, far, far away from Doftaan crunched under her feet as she took a step toward Drahomir's city of the Redeemed, Bartun.

"Where are we?" asked Shanthah.

"I already told you," Mara replied.

"I know, but I mean—where *are* we?"

Mara chuckled and then led Nadezhda toward the city.

"How are you doing, sweetheart?" she asked, rubbing Nadezhda's shoulder. She did not answer, and Mara could still feel the toll on the girl's mind from losing the one she loved and experiencing every negative emotion in the city at once.

It would take time for her to recover, but this far away, her emotions wouldn't affect the others back home. The full impact of the devastating outburst of her powers hadn't yet faded, and the others could still sense her feelings. The Redeemed would keep her safe here, though.

As everyone, including Hippo ambled up to the gates, there was a loud screeching of metal as they parted, revealing a single figure standing before them.

"Drahomir!" Mara exclaimed, rushing toward him.

"Hello again, Mara! And, oh, wow! Everyone else!"

Josman let out a cheerful holler, and he and Shanthah wrapped Drahomir in a tight bear hug at the same time.

"I have a huge favor to ask of you," Mara said.

"I assume it has something to do with the millions of feral Faceless you've led here?" he asked, poking his masked head up from beneath Josman's thick arm.

The Faceless that had followed them from Doftaan were somehow subdued by the presence of Drahomir's people, and they had been welcomed inside.

"Among other things."

Drahomir said nothing for a long moment as the gaze of his mask stared directly at Nadezhda. Nadezhda stepped back in fear as she saw Drahomir's mask, but Mara assured her that everything was alright, and that he was a friend.

"What in the name of Elafris is wrong with this girl?"

"Long story," Mara said. "If you'll let us, can we come in? I'll explain everything to you. There's lots to talk about. It's over, Drah."

"We won, you mean?"

"No. We didn't win," Mara said. "We ended the war, but no one won. We all lost."

"*Yes, of course.*" Drahomir paused. "*But the Magistrate—is she dead?*"

"No. That would be too good for her," Mara replied. "But she won't be bothering your people ever again."

"*So, what?*"

"We have another punishment for her. Long story, but we've trapped her mind inside my sword. If it's not too much to ask, I'd like to request that your people keep it guarded," Mara asked. Drahomir nodded. "But we'll talk about that later. I think there are some people who would love to say hello!"

Her eyes lit up as she smiled, and Kamil, Alia, and Hanna hurried forward and piled onto him in one giant hug. Mara laughed, and her heart swelled.

"Hey, you two, get in here!" Shanthah exclaimed, turning to Mara and Aleksander. "This guy hasn't had any hugs for like, two years! He's overdue!"

Mara looked at Nadezhda, who gave a timid nod, as if to tell her she'd be fine alone for a moment. Mara smiled, jumping onto the hug pile, wrapping her wings around the entire group until Drahomir squirmed away.

"*I wasn't a hugger before, and I think I'm even less of one now,*" he said, "*but... that was nice. I love you guys.*" He looked to Aleksander. "*Not to keep asking what's wrong with people, but...*"

"He lost his memories again," Mara said, her countenance falling. "Another long story."

Drahomir led them into the city, and everyone kept close to Hippo, as his intense body heat kept them warm in the frozen kingdom of the freed Faceless.

They made their way through the sprawling city that dwarfed even Bukaral in Talohira; it had grown even since Mara, Kamil, and Alia had been here not long ago. She marveled once again at the masterful workmanship and beautiful, yet simple architecture in the city of Bartun.

Soon, Drahomir led them not to a grand palace, for there were none in Bartun, but to a small circle of houses in a neighborhood to the west. It was a gated community and seemed out of place from the rest of the city. Although they could see hundreds of free Faceless with intricate masks going about their daily business, no one was within the gates.

"I made this little neighborhood for, well... For you guys," Drahomir said, pushing open the wooden fence. *"If you ever wanted to visit, you have a place to stay."*

"It's quite the trip," Josman said. "But you're worth it, little guy."

"Oh, stop," Drahomir thought, and the others laughed.

They entered the largest of the homes and gathered in a large sitting room. Several masked Faceless had prepared a large pot of tea for them.

Alia smiled and thanked them as she accepted a cup. To her surprise, they mindspoke a reply of, *"You're welcome."*

No longer mindless beasts.

"This is beautiful, Drah," Mara said.

She, and everyone else looked up at a massive painting that stretched over the entire back wall. A painting of all of them. All of their friends and allies, living and dead. Their friends from the Slave Camp and afterward.

"Wow," Mara whispered, taking a cup of tea with a gracious nod.

"*I hope it isn't too much,*" Drahomir said.

"No, it's wonderful," Mara said with a smile.

Hanna and Shanthah plopped down on a plush sofa, and Josman claimed an armchair that reclined backward. He grunted as Alia sat on his lap and kicked her legs up over the armrest. Even Nadezhda, despite the lasting emotional and mental toll the battle had taken on her, sat and smiled.

As they sat reminiscing about old times, Nadezhda nudged Drahomir.

"Do you have a bathroom here?" Nadezhda asked. "I mean, I'm not sure if you guys use toilets?"

She felt a burst of humor escape Drahomir's mind.

"*Of course. Down the hall, to the right.*"

Nadezhda thanked Drahomir and followed his directions. After relieving herself, she looked back down the hall to see everyone happy and laughing, reunited with old friends.

Her heart ached.

Instead of rejoining them, she turned and exited the house through a back door.

She sat on the frozen ground outside and pulled the Heart of Thanatan from her pocket. She set it in the snow before her.

"*Ah, I see you've come back to me,*" the Voice said, and shadows danced on the gem's jagged surface.

"This is all your fault," Nadezhda said darkly. "Ana. Everyone who died in Doftaan. Even more that died everywhere else."

"*As you recall, I was trying to kill the Magistrate as much as any of you were,*" Thanatan replied. "*Without me, you wouldn't have been successful.*"

"If it weren't for you, she would never have even risen to power, in the first place, you idiot. You're responsible for every horrible thing that has happened," she said, pointing an accusatory finger at the Heart. "I would still have my... I would still have my Tatiana."

"*Ah. You now have two reasons to come back to me, then.*"

"No, just one," Nadezhda said softly. "Just one."

"*I don't understand.*"

She reached out with her mind, just as Kamil had taught her. She felt Thanatan's mind intertwine with her own as she let him into her consciousness.

"I want you to feel what I do. What Tatiana did. You need to understand what you've done."

She closed her eyes, and from the gem, she sensed a calm wonder and confusion, a cloudy wisp that circled her head. But then, as Thanatan realized what was happening, it turned into a chaotic, black cloud of terror: the feeling of oncoming doom.

And that was what was coming for Thanatan.

"*You will never escape my grasp. You truly think you can do this and escape me?*"

"Escape was never my intention."

"*Wait, Nadezhda. Before you do this, you must know——*"

"Enough of you."

She channeled every bit of pain and agonizing despair she could into Thanatan's Heart. His screams echoed in her mind, and then the gem cracked in half; bits of the crystal exploded outward, and a small puff of dark smoke trailed from the remains of the crystal. As the mist faded, she looked at the broken gem, there was a faint glow of white light in one of the halves.

As she let out the dark emotion, her darkened strands of hair faded back to blonde, and it felt as if a horrible yoke had been taken from her shoulders. Thanatan and his accursed, manipulative voice were both gone.

Forever.

She sat there alone in silence for a long time, wiping tears from her cheeks. She let out a deep breath as unprompted memories of days with Ana filled her mind, and she smiled, laughing through tears.

She touched the gem and felt the excruciating sadness again, but as she let go, it faded. Curious, she reached out with her mind. It was all there. The sadness, and the pain, yes, but also the tremendous joy she had experienced with Ana at the Independence Day festival. The crystals were free from Thanatan's soul, and instead, what remained were the emotions she had experienced while holding it.

She carefully dropped the shards of the Heart into the burlap sack.

"*What was that?*" Drahomir asked, emerging from the back door. Nadezhda looked up, unable to explain anything.

Mara was there with him, and then everyone else appeared behind them, a jumble of faces in the doorway.

"He's gone," Nadezhda said with a smile. "Thanatan. He's dead. For good."

"Well, then three cheers for Nadezhda Babkova, Godslayer!" Shanthah exclaimed, and everyone repeated her name and new title with joyous applause. She gave a dramatic bow then handed the sack with the gem to Drahomir.

"So, I'm not sure if this is helpful," she said as he cocked his head curiously, "but I can't sense any emotion from any of your people here. From you, yes, but not from them." Her eyes widened, and she was about to apologize, but she remembered Ana's words not to do so. "Not to say that they're not people. I know you all are. But maybe, you can use these to give them their emotions back?"

She cut herself off and handed the shards of Thanatan's heart to Drahomir. He took them, and she could tell that he, too, felt every emotion trapped inside.

"You're right," Drahomir said. *"I've been able to restore emotions to some people with the masks we've created, but it's exhausting. It takes a few days to help even one person... If what I think you're implying is true, you might just have saved millions of people and given them back their lives."*

Nadezhda's eyes widened. "Really?"

Drahomir nodded, and his aura turned into a joyous cloud of yellow and gold. *"We could really use your help, Godslayer."* Nadezhda turned to Mara as if to ask permission to stay.

"What are you asking *me* for?" Mara asked with a laugh.

"Okay. I'll do it," Nadezhda said. "For one small favor."

"*Anything,*" Drahomir replied.

Later that day, Nadezhda's request was fulfilled. Several Redeemed wearing colorful masks delivered a beautifully crafted casket that sparkled in the moonlight. They brought it inside, bowed to Drahomir, and departed. Nadezhda had requested they line the inside with Mara's cloak, and Mara had happily obliged.

They both knew Ana would have been thrilled.

As the others packed supplies onto Hippo's back, Nadezhda hung back with the coffin, keeping her hand on it. She spoke to it as if Ana was inside.

"I'm so sorry. I know you told me never to apologize unless I really did something wrong and really meant it, but… I think I need to right now," Nadezhda whispered, placing her forehead against the smooth surface. "Oh, Tatiana, if tears could heal you, I know you'd be safe now."

She sat there for a few moments, unsure of what else to say.

"You told me you'd protect me until the end of your life… I promised you I'd do the same, and I'm so, so, so sorry that only one of us was able to make good on that promise. It was always gonna be that way, though, right?" She paused for a moment as tears ran down her cheeks. "Thank you for healing my heart in more ways than one, sweetheart. I love you so much, Tatiana, and I'm going to miss you every single day."

She lingered there for nearly an hour, sitting at the coffin until Mara came back into the room. She pulled up another chair and sat next to Nadezhda.

"Mind if I join you?"

"Of course, pull up a chair," Nadezhda said. Mara cocked her head with a funny expression, gesturing to the chair. "I mean, yeah. You've got one already."

"Listen, I know unprompted advice can be annoying," Mara said, "but I have some for you, if you'll let me."

"Of course," Nadezhda said.

"It's going to be hard to move on. And, really, you never *should*. I hate that term, 'moving on.' That would imply that you don't care anymore, you know?" Mara said.

"Yeah," Nadezhda replied.

"She loved you. You loved her. You both knew that, so you don't need to wonder what would have been. Obviously, there should be so much more to your story, and I'm so sorry that will never come to pass. But I *know* what would have been. You two would love each other until your last days. I've seen love like yours, and, well… It's real. Rare, too."

"Thank you," Nadezhda said.

"What I'm trying to say is… Don't lose yourself. Don't lose yourself in thoughts of where you wish you were and forget to make the most of where you are, where you'll be next. Ana would want you to live, not dwell on sad things."

"You're right," Nadezhda said. "I'll be wallowing in self-pity for a while, but that's okay, right?"

"Of course," Mara said with a laugh. "Been there myself. Sometimes you need to. But don't think of grief as self-pity.

Grief isn't such bad thing—it's the last, precious gift we can give to those we love."

"I guess I am pretty lucky to have had someone that makes this so heartbreaking, huh?"

Mara offered a sad smile. "Nadezhda, promise me something. Always let your life be so full of this much love so that no amount of pain can ever take it away."

Nadezhda wrapped her arms around Mara and sobbed into her shoulder. Mara rubbed her back.

"Thank you, Empress. I'll try."

"Please, don't call me that," Mara said. "You're my friend now, and if you ever need anything, my doors in Doftaan will always be open for you. You will *never* be alone. I've been informed by my spies—"

"Who?"

"Shanthah and Alia," said Mara. "They've informed me that you are a connoisseur of bacon?"

Nadezhda chuckled and wiped away a tear. "Yeah?"

"Did you know in Sangora we have an annual bacon festival?"

"Are you serious? You guys have festivals for *everything*. But that sounds like heaven. I'll be there. Every year. Can I be voted the Bacon Queen?"

"I don't think that's a thing."

"It could be."

"Then yes, I hereby name you Nadezhda Babkova, the Bacon Queen of the upcoming festival. May you reign forever!"

Nadezhda wiped away tears as she smiled then sniffed loudly; because of the tears, it was particularly snotty, and she and Mara both laughed at the comically ridiculous sound.

"So, what's next for the Empress of Blood?" Nadezhda asked. "Now that you have your empire back, what in the world do you do with it?"

"That's a very good question," Mara said with a laugh. "I'll figure it out. If not, I've got good people who can. For now, though, my first goal is to bring everyone home. I don't want there to be a day more where my people suffer in the Thannish slave camps."

Nadezhda nodded. "May *you* reign forever too, Mara."

They embraced once more.

They all stayed in Bartun to recover and resupply for their journey back to Doftaan for nearly a week. Mara had left early on Hippo to get back to her people as soon as possible to help direct the end of the battle and oversee everything that had to be done there.

She also brought the beautifully crafted coffin—and Ana, with it—back to Sangora.

Hippo finally returned, and everyone packed up and climbed onto his back. They said their goodbyes to Nadezhda and Drahomir, and then they were off.

Nadezhda watched them disappear across the horizon before turning to Drahomir. His dark robes billowed in the breeze, and the Godblade containing the Magistrate's mind was strapped to his waist. Mara had instructed him to hide it far away in his domain where no one else would ever find it, which he promised to do after his work with Nadezhda was finished.

"Ready to get to work?" she asked.

Drahomir nodded and pulled something from his pocket: half of Thanatan's heart—the one with a dim, white glow.

Nadezhda cocked her head. "I don't understand."

"*Someone's been asking for you,*" Drahomir explained. "*I'm not sure how, but I didn't want the others to know before you did.*"

"He's dead—I don't understand. I killed him. Please, no, I can't handle this. Bring him away."

Drahomir placed the gem in her hand and said nothing more as he walked away.

Nadezhda looked down at the gem; it glowed with a pleasant warmth in her palm.

And then, a sweet, loving voice echoed from the gem, and Nadezhda gasped, nearly dropping it.

"*Nadya?*"

CHAPTER FIFTY-THREE
THE MEMORIES OF THE MAN I LOVE

Lightning illuminated the dark corridor as Umut stared out the tall window. He jumped as thunder cracked overhead, and he chuckled to himself. He was safe in the Thannish king's palace. He'd made it, despite the destruction of the past weeks.

Tomorrow, the king's Mindspeakers would remove the secrets from his brain, and he would leave Thanatanos wealthier than he had ever dreamed—especially because he'd killed his companion Cyrgiz, meaning he'd get the entire reward.

Another bolt of lightning banished the darkness for a split second, and Umut recoiled, for he thought he saw a face staring back at him from halfway down the hall. It was just the wine playing tricks on him, of course. He'd drunk more than his fill during dinner, and even more afterward. But then a third flash outside made him know that he was wrong.

He was not alone.

He was not safe.

"You have something I want."

Umut backed up, bumping into a bust of Verahim's grandfather, King Jaromir. Before he could ask what the woman wanted, she stepped into the torchlight.

"Supreme One!" Umut gasped, backing away from her. "What a wonderful surprise, I—"

Mara clenched her fist, telekinetically forcing Umut to his knees. He groaned as his joints cracked against the hard stone beneath the dark green rug.

"Save your groveling for the Grand Judge," Mara replied, grabbing him by the collar. She slammed him against the wall.

"I can give you whatever you want. I can give you gold! Yes, gold! I have a lot of that now. Please, just let me live, I beg of—"

"I am an empress. You think I need gold?!"

"Then what? Please, Supreme One, I—"

Thunder echoed outside as Mara stared the traitor in the face.

"The only thing you can give me is the memories of the man I love," she said, her tone as dark as the corridor. Her eyes gleamed in the torchlight as she grasped his forehead, and he felt her consciousness sneak into his mind.

"No, please! I don't understand!"

At that moment, there was another explosion, but not of thunder. Flames erupted from a tower across the courtyard outside the corridor, and Mara dropped Umut to the ground. He scrambled to his feet and gazed out the window.

"What is this?" Umut asked. "Come to kill me *and* the king?"

"No." Her words were laced with unease. "This isn't us."

"Then who?"

Shouts of men and women roused from sleep when dreams should have filled their heads echoed down the hallways. A group of confused guards raced down the corridor perpendicular to the one where Mara and Umut stood.

Mara turned back to Umut and shoved him against the wall again. She swore under her breath, knowing he was right, and she despised him for it.

She glanced out the window to see Hippo hiding in the darkness of the courtyard below and she could sense his worry. He was staring up at the flames pouring out of the tower with concern.

Gunfire and the clanging of swords echoed through the halls now, joining the echoing screams. She hesitated for a moment, contemplating whether or not she should intervene. In the end, it was not her fight.

But then, the words she feared.

"The king is dead!"

Umut tried to struggle free as Mara stood dumbfounded. Cheering echoed down the corridor, and footsteps rounded the corner.

"Looks like time's up for both of us," Mara said, and she slammed him hard in the chest with both wings. He crashed, screaming, through the window in a spray of glass that sliced his skin. A moment later, the air was knocked from his lungs as Mara intercepted him just before he hit the ground.

She dropped him on Hippo's back, and the behemoth took flight without another moment's hesitation.

From atop Hippo's back, she could see many of the palace windows alight with flame. She knew there was nothing she could do. She willed Hippo southeast, back to Doftaan.

The rule of the family of Romus was at its end.

EPILOGUE
A CROWN OF TEAL AND PINK

A YEAR AND A HALF LATER

The warm spring air drifted happily through the massive, open tent. It played with Mara's dark curls as it passed through, and she smiled, taking in the sunlight and warmth on her face. Her dark hair fell past her shoulders in black waves contrasting beautifully with her elegant dress decorated with traditional, intricate Sangoran designs around her scarred shoulders.

Spring had come, and with it, a wedding.

White chairs tied with pink and teal ribbons were lined up in perfect rows beneath the open-air tent, and flowers of the same colors had been planted all around the grassy hill upon which she stood.

Mara found Shanthah speaking with Aleksander, Kamil, Josman, and Alia outside the pavilion, each dressed in their finest attire matching the colors of the wedding.

Aleksander had donned a slim, black Sangoran suit lined with crimson Kurashian silk. He twirled to show it off as she approached.

"Well, hello beautiful!" Aleksander said in welcome.

"Well, hello beautiful to you too!"

After she'd kidnapped Umut from Laniras, Mara had worked tirelessly to transfer Aleksander's memories from the Secret Keeper back where they belonged. He still had a gap between losing his memories and that moment, but he'd been filled in on everything that had happened.

Mara made sure he remembered their time in the Dreamstate, sharing her own memories, however.

"Ooh, Xan-*thur*-ias, you look *good*," Mara said with a wink, smacking his backside.

"Mara!" Aleksander exclaimed with a bright laugh.

"Oh, we're in public, right," she said with another wink. "Oh, the scandal."

"You're both stupidly beautiful, yes," Shanthah said. "But Aleksander, today's not about you."

They all laughed.

"Oh, is your wedding day about *you*?" Mara asked. Shanthah nodded and straightened his tie, tucking it back beneath his vest.

Shanthah wore a simple, yet striking suit of black and white with a thin dark tie and a white silk pocket square sticking out of his breast pocket.

Alia had donned a traditional Kurashian of pink silk decorated with intricate flowers, while Kamil was dressed in dark robes trimmed in teal, the new robes of the Supreme One of Kurash. Josman was dressed in a suit identical to but much larger than Aleksander's.

"Aren't you lot supposed to be helping set up?" Mara asked. "Or are you going to let the girls do all the heavy lifting? We can, you know. We just don't really want to."

"That's right," Alia said.

"Mara, let's face it, you're way stronger than me," Shanthah said. "And it's my wedding day. You want me to get dirty on my *wedding day?!* It's not a day for me to lift *tables!*"

"Only joking. Everything's ready," Mara said. She raised an eyebrow and gestured to Aleksander's arms, which were covered in dirt, his sleeves rolled up to his elbows. "Explain this."

"We found a cool bug," Aleksander said with wide eyes, and Alia giggled, perhaps at the others' expense.

"Oh, did you?" Mara asked with a laugh.

"We just wanted to see," Josman said as if they were children in trouble.

Mara grabbed Aleksander's hand, resulting in a joyous smile across his face. He kissed her on the forehead, and she said, "So, where's this bug? I'll be the judge of it."

Shanthah opened his hand to show her a shining blue beetle.

"Ah, yes. That's a good one. You know, in Sangora, that type of beetle is seen as good luck if it enters your home," she said with a wink. "I also come bearing a secret, Shanthah."

"Oh?"

"I just helped Hanna finish getting ready, and can I just say, you are marrying an absolute *goddess*," Mara said, making the same gesture one would do when drinking a fine wine. "Good work, buddy."

"Yeah, I am," Shanthah said in a soft tone. "But is that really a secret?"

The sounds of guests arriving filled the air as people began to drop gifts at a table outside the pavilion and find their ways to their seats beneath the canopy. The band of musicians began to play their joyous tunes, and Shanthah smiled, breathing it all in.

"You know, Mara, I have a secret for you too," Shanthah said, glancing at Josman and Alia.

"What?" Mara asked, and Josman and Alia shared a joyful glance. "Wait, what? Tell me right now! Oh my goodness, Hanna's pregnant, isn't she?! Am I getting nieces and nephews?!"

"Oh, gods no," Shanthah said. "I hope not. Well, I guess it isn't *my* secret to tell…"

Alia stepped forward and held up her hand, upon which was a ring set with a dark emerald.

"Alia! Josman!" Mara exclaimed. "You've been here for how long and you didn't tell me?! Congratulations! First you adopted Valeniya, and now you're getting married?!"

She pulled both Josman and Alia into a tight hug, and the others clapped before joining in the hug.

"Yeah, she's a good kid," Josman said. "She loves Alia more than anyone, I think."

Alia smiled.

"We wanted to see how long it'd take you to notice that giant ring on her finger," Aleksander said. "Longer than I thought, but shorter than Shanthah did. He owes me five moneti."

"You have *that* little faith in me?" Mara asked, slugging Shanthah in the shoulder.

"Ow, don't bruise me on my wedding day," Shanthah said. "I need to be pretty today. It's not a day to be *punched*."

Everyone laughed.

"So, when should I expect another wedding?" Mara asked with a wink.

"We haven't picked a day yet," Alia said.

"You know, not to overshadow Shanthah on his wedding day, but I had to get permission from the *king of Talohira* to ask her to marry me," Josman said.

"And what was his judgment?" Mara asked.

"He found me worthy," Josman said. He brushed an imaginary bead of sweat from his brow. "Phew!"

"And where is that kid?" Mara asked, glancing around.

"He's here, he had some business with the Master of Balgorod, so he thought he'd knock that out before the wedding," Shanthah said.

"And shouldn't the Master of Balgorod be in that meeting?" Aleksander asked, playing with a stick on the ground with the toe of his shoe.

"It's not a day for meetings either. I have people for that," Shanthah said with a dismissive gesture. "I think he'd understand why I'm absent."

"Okay, well, we'll be starting soon. I'll go fetch the bride… Don't start without us."

"No promises," Shanthah replied.

"Oh, and Xanthurias?" Mara whispered loud enough for him alone to hear. Aleksander met her gaze with a smile. "You're allowed to watch me walk away."

He nearly choked on the drink from which he had just taken a sip. She laughed and departed to fetch Hanna. At that moment, a group of Talohiran men and women in Talohiran ceremonial military garb approached with Valis at the lead.

He waved to his friends from across the pavilion and shouted his congratulations as he set a large gift on the table next to the others. His royal guard took their seats next to those of Kamil and Mara. The three back rows were roped off and reserved specifically for each of their personal guards, something Mara found both hilarious and ridiculous.

More guests had arrived, and the seats were nearly full. Each of the Guardians of Sangora were in attendance, as were many of the patrons of Hanna's bar and students from Shanthah's school.

Lavinia, in a dashing black suit and tie waved as Rayshel pushed her wheelchair to her designated spot near the front. To Mara's surprise, Lavinia's sister Zhanna sat beside them as well, but most wonderful to Mara was the little girl Lavinia and Rayshel had introduced to her earlier as their adopted daughter, Ginka. She sat between them now, holding her mothers' hands.

Together, the last survivors of house Daktha smiled and spoke amongst themselves, leaving their horrific past behind. Lavinia had even taken Rayshel's last name, Pilu, as a final way to kill the past. Mara knew in her heart that the broken family, including Rayshel, had much happier days ahead.

The front rows were reserved for family. Or rather, the family they had all found in the last few years. Aleksander accompanied Shanthah to the front of the tent while Josman, Kamil, and Alia sat in the front row next to Ruta, Lavinia and her family.

"Speaking of weddings and engagements," Shanthah muttered to Aleksander, who watched Mara as she continued down the aisle. As if she had heard them, she looked over her shoulder and gave him a wink.

"Yeah," Aleksander said with a smile on his face.

Mara stopped at the back of the tent as Shanthah's parents greeted her rather loudly; they laughed amongst themselves for a moment and then she was on her way again. Shanthah's mother and father hurried to their seats and waved to their son.

"I thought they forgot," Shanthah said.

Aleksander chuckled. "Don't be ridiculous."

"So?" Shanthah asked. Aleksander raised an eyebrow. "Engagements and weddings? Sorry. It's on the mind."

"Oh, right. We're happy," Aleksander said with a smile. "We'll get there, don't worry. Too busy with adventures, though, you know?"

"We've all come a long way, huh?"

Aleksander nodded. "Who would've thought?"

He pulled a small satin bag from his coat pocket, and he emptied the contents, two silver rings, one set with a large pearl, on a cloth at an altar at the front of the room. He stowed the bag back in his coat.

"You almost forgot about those, didn't you?" Shanthah asked.

"Affirmative," Aleksander replied with a laugh, which Shanthah shared. "But in my defense, forgetting things is kind of my thing."

Shanthah let out a joyous belly laugh, doubling over.

"That it is. Well, you're the best-best man I could ask for," Shanthah said. "Glad you're here, and that you're trying to kick the habit of losing your memory."

The band picked up, and a small choir of Sangoran and human children, including Diana, began to sing as Mara and Hanna came into view and entered the pavilion.

Hanna looked absolutely radiant in her elegant dress; it seemed that an ethereal sunset itself was flowing down her body. Her collarbones, chest, and arms were decorated with intricate lace like elegant vines and spring flowers.

Upon her waves of auburn hair was a crown of pink, white, and teal flowers. She insisted that she wouldn't have to wear shoes on her wedding day, and she wiggled her toes in the grass as Mara accompanied her.

Hanna nearly bounced in excitement as she and Mara walked down the aisle hand in hand, signing between one another and laughing.

But as soon as she saw Shanthah, her smile grew even wider, and she jumped up and down in joy. He did the same, and laughter filled the crowd as they stood and watched Mara accompany Hanna to the end of the aisle.

Mara pulled Hanna into a hug and then stood behind the altar with Alia, Ruta and Shanthah's sister Lilia on one side, and Aleksander, Josman, and Kamil on the other, the witnesses to the union.

Hanna and Shanthah stood before the crowd, and Mara took her place behind the altar.

"Welcome, everyone," Mara said. "It is my absolute delight to officiate this wedding today not only as the Empress of Sangora, but as someone who loves and cares for these two wonderful people with my whole soul. They are truly my family, and I love them so very much. From now on, I will be officiating in Sangoran sign language. For those of you who don't know the language, the Supreme One of Kurash who is called Kamil will be mindspeaking the translation for the remainder of the ceremony."

Joyful tears came to her eyes, and she motioned for Shanthah and Hanna to take one another's hands. They held hands and he kissed one before Mara could stop her.

"*You're not supposed to do that part yet,*" Mara signed, and the audience laughed as Kamil translated.

She glanced up as motion near the back of the tent caught her attention, and she saw Nadezhda and Drahomir sneak in, late, into the back row of the pavilion. Nadezhda was wearing a long pink dress and a necklace set with the shattered bit of Thanatan's gem set in its face, and had apparently dyed her blonde hair a chaotic, quirky mix of every color of the rainbow.

She must have noticed Mara's gaze, because she gave an inconspicuous wave from the back of the wedding with an exaggerated grin. Mara returned the smile, wondering what beautiful emotions the girl could see.

"You are all gathered here today before each of the Guardians of Sangora; Valistaran Shadid, king of Talohira; and even the Supreme One of Kurash who is called Kamil. As you know, weddings in Sangora need a representative from the government to witness the ceremony, and I can think of no other wedding in the history of time that has had this kind of authority to witness it."

"And the Empress of Sangora!" Hanna signed. Mara winked but said nothing in response.

"Now, the rings," Mara signed, picking up the first, Hanna's pearl ring. *"Hanna Samsa, do you promise to love Shanthah Kalen with all your heart and soul?"*

"I do."

She held Hanna's ring forward, and Hanna kissed it, then she took it and held it to Shanthah, who kissed it and slipped it on Hanna's finger, as was custom at weddings in both Sangora and Thanatanos.

Overjoyed, her smile looked as if it would never fade.

Mara wondered what beautiful display of emotion Nadezhda must be seeing at that moment. As if Nadezhda were reading her mind, she felt the girl's mind touch her own, and Mara nearly wept as she saw the colors of white and pink swirling around the couple's heads. She smiled at Nadezhda, who nodded with a knowing expression.

"And do you, Shanthah Kalen, promise to love the eternally wonderful and beautiful Hanna Samsa for the rest of your days and beyond?"

"I do," Shanthah signed to Hanna.

Happy tears rolled down her cheeks as she bounced up and down. Mara held the ring to Hanna's lips, and then Hanna took it, and Shanthah kissed it, and she slid it onto his finger.

"Then with the authority as Empress of Sangora, I pronounce you married. You may now kiss!"

The crowd cheered as Hanna and Shanthah embraced one another; they kissed, and Shanthah dipped her, his supporting her back. The crowd cheered, and the band began to play. Flower petals fell from above, released by some mechanism Kamil had rigged. They fluttered down over the guests and over the happy couple alike.

However, the most wondrous beauty of all came as Nadezhda shared what she saw with the entire wedding crowd; they let out little oohs and ahhs all around the tent as they beheld the shimmering emotions of love and joy.

Brilliant gold and soft pink popped like fireworks all around the pavilion, and silvery stars and an aurora of purest white flowed like an aurora through the spring air.

Shanthah held Hanna's hand up above his head before twirling her and kissing her again. The entire crowd cheered again, and Mara gave a loud, "Ow, ow!"

As the chairs were cleared out for dancing, Mara simply stood at the front of the pavilion, watching the people she loved so much being happy and together.

They had won.

Not because they killed a tyrant. They had won because they had all survived so much, but because of the joy that had come from fighting for one another; they had won because they had found love, and that was all they needed.

Peace settled in Mara's heart as everyone began to dance to the tune of the music. She let out a contented sigh.

"Coming?" Aleksander asked, holding out his hand.

"Prince Xanthurias, asking the *village girl* to dance? The scandal!" Mara said, taking his hand.

"I don't think you're just a village girl anymore, and I don't think I'm a prince," Aleksander said with a laugh as she pulled him close. "You ever just want a normal life?"

"Actually," Mara said, pausing for a moment. She cocked her head with a smile. "No. I like this crazy one of ours."

"Me too," Aleksander said, kissing her on the forehead. "If I kiss you right now, are you going to dunk me underwater?"

The comment was, of course, a reference to the first time he had ever tried to kiss her all those years ago in the lake by Cineca, and she'd responded by dunking him underwater.

"I don't think your memories are all back yet, because, if you can't tell, we're on dry land," she said. "But no, even if we were in the lake… I think I'd take that kiss."

She smiled up at him, and their lips met.

"Now enough of that mushy stuff," Mara said. "It's time to dance, Xanthurias."

Aleksander followed Mara to where all their friends were happily dancing to a rowdy Sangoran folk song.

Hanna danced her way over to Mara and took both of her hands, and together, they spun in a flurry of auburn and black hair, their laughs bright and merry.

When the song ended, Hanna planted a kiss on her friend's cheek, and Shanthah stole her away with a wink. Aleksander took Mara's hand.

"My turn until Hanna decides otherwise?" he asked.

"Even *if* Hanna decides otherwise."

It seemed the happiness in the room was complete.

Mara smiled, pure love enveloping her heart for each of her friends there with her celebrating Hanna and Shanthah. She felt as if it would burst from her chest if she felt any more joy as she wiped a tear from the corner of her eye with a laugh.

There were people missing, of course. People that *should* be sharing their joy. Many had been lost so that they could enjoy their happiness, and her heart was with them.

At that moment, she thought of Rehor's words.

"The hope of new spring always comes back into our lives after the cold and the darkness have taken it away."

Spring had indeed come, and with it, renewed hope, joy, and love. It hadn't come how she had expected it to, but there it was, blossoming and pure all around her all the same.

Mara Bartunek was happy.

Truly happy.

THE STORY CONTINUES IN:

LOVE'S BROKEN LEGACY

BOOK ONE OF THE HOPE SAGA

AND

HER ANTHEM FOR RUIN

AN ASCENSION SAGA PREQUEL

A PREVIEW OF:

HER ANTHEM
FOR RUIN

AN ASCENSION SAGA PREQUEL

CHAPTER ONE
ALONE IN THE DARK

She sat alone in the dark, as she often had.

Just like every other time one of her siblings disappeared.

This time, however, Zhanna wasn't there by her side to ease her fears. Lavinia had no idea where they had taken her older sister or how long she'd been locked in her own bedroom. A ragged breath escaped her throat, and she hugged her tiny knees close to her chest, trying not to cry.

And then, a commotion rang out in the corridor outside her door, and she scrambled beneath her four-poster bed, peeking out from beneath the loose, unmade sheets hanging down.

Shouts and the clash of steel.

Screams.

Silence.

She covered her mouth with her hands to stifle a scream as someone began slamming against the door. If they were here to take her away like Zhanna or the others, she knew she wouldn't be able to escape. Her wings hadn't even emerged from her back, and even if she *could* fly, how could she get away when they may have already caught Zhanna, who could fly faster than anyone she knew?

There was a cry from beyond the door, and the pounding on the door stopped. She let out a whimper and shut her eyes.

They were here to take her away.

A stream of dusty light broke through one of the panels of her door as the butt of a spear splintered the wood. Someone peered into the room, obscuring the dim torchlight of the hallway.

"Lavinia!"

"Zhanna!" Lavinia shouted, crawling out from under the bed, trusting that her older sister would keep her safe from their parents' soldiers.

Zhanna slammed the spear into the door, shattering the lower panel and making a large enough hole for the six-year-old to crawl through.

"Come on, Vinia. You're going to need to crawl through."

Lavinia trusted her, carefully navigating her way out of her room, although a few broken pieces of wood scratched her skin.

With her mighty wings, Lavinia knew Zhanna would be able to get her to safety.

"I thought they took you just like they took Stefan and Aurelija and—"

"They did. Get up, Vinia," Zhanna replied, her tone terse and short. "Come on, sweetheart, take my hand."

She wrapped her fingers around Zhanna's thumb. She tried to hug her sister around the waist, but Zhanna grabbed her wrist to guide her into the hallway instead.

"Were they going to take me?" Lavinia asked.

Zhanna stopped and squeezed her sister's hand but said nothing for what felt like an eternity.

"Yes, sweetheart."

They continued their brisk walk down the hallway.

"Just like—"

"Yes, just like the others."

"I thought they took you too. I'm so happy you're okay—"

"I'm not okay, Vinia." They stopped again, but this time, Zhanna crouched next to her. "And you won't be either if we don't get out of here right now. Can you be brave?"

Lavinia's eyes welled up with tears, and she began to cry, but she clenched her tiny fists and stomped one of her bare feet.

"I can be brave."

Zhanna smiled at the fierce little girl and nodded.

"Then I can too," she replied. She glanced down. "Little miss, why aren't you wearing shoes?"

"Why would I wear shoes in my own room?"

Voices were just around the corner.

Zhanna grabbed Lavinia's little hand and together, they darted in the other direction.

"Whatever. No time. Come on."

"We can fly," Lavinia said. "Remember, I am being brave, so if you carry me, I won't be scared this time, I promise. Last time, I threw up and it fell on that man, but this time—"

Zhanna stumbled, letting go of Lavinia's hand for the first time. Her shoulder struck the wall, and she groaned as she slumped to her knees.

Lavinia gasped, for Zhanna's back was slick with crimson, as two dark stains had soaked through the bandages wrapped around her torso marking where her mighty wings had once been.

"Zhazha, your wings!" Lavinia exclaimed, and then she began to cry again.

"Brave, Vinia! Brave!"

Lavinia sniffled. "I—but you—your—"

"I know, honey. You'll just have to grow big enough ones to carry us both someday, even when I'm a cranky, old lady."

"You're already a cranky old lady, Zhazha!"

Zhanna smiled.

"I'm twenty-one, kid."

"But I'm six, and that's…"

Zhanna groaned and forced herself to her feet, taking Lavinia's hand again as the little girl tried to perform mental mathematics far beyond her abilities. She knew that Lavinia's mind was off her wings for now, which eased her own fears for a moment. She knew keeping her sister calm was of utmost importance.

"You'll be a grandma soon," Lavinia said.

Zhanna chuckled. "That's not how it works, kid."

She stumbled toward a high stained-glass window bearing a dramatic image of their father, King Liviu Daktha before he had grown fat and ill. She sighed, staring into the colorful visage.

"Sorry, father."

She wasn't sorry. She grasped a torch sconce from the wall and smashed it through the treacherous man's glassy face, which rained down in a hailstorm of brilliant color far below.

"Father is going to be so—"

"We're not going to stick around long enough to find out what that horrible man thinks. Come on, climb up."

Lavinia scowled, crossed her arms, and planted her feet.

"No."

"No?" Zhanna groaned. "Vinia, get up here, or they're going to find you and take you away."

She knew her little sister had no concept of death, and that 'taking someone away' was the worst possible fate in the young girl's mind. Zhanna sighed as she stared into Lavinia's defiant eyes.

"I'm not scared, you know. I just don't want to."

"You're scared, but that's okay. So am I," Zhanna said. Lavinia's stern gaze softened. "But being brave doesn't mean you don't get scared. It just means you can fight whatever scares you."

"Well then I'm going to fight."

"That's the spirit," Zhanna said and tucked her sister's messy hair behind her ear. "You need a haircut, kid."

"Is that where we're going?"

The absurdity of the question caused a legitimate bout of laughter to burst from Zhanna's soul, but it was short-lived. Her mother's soldiers rounded the corner, their wings tipped with blades and silver spears in their hands.

Zhanna grabbed Lavinia's hand and pulled her up onto the windowsill.

"Go!" she shouted.

Lavinia obeyed and jumped up; her sister had never shouted at her before. She scrambled out the window and onto the slippery, steep roof of the high spire just as a crack of thunder and a branching fork of lightning illuminated the night sky. She screamed as she lost her footing and tumbled down onto a decorative ledge. It was a short drop, but it was painful all the same. She did not cry.

She looked back up to the window for her sister, but the scene inside was obscured by the wall. She tucked her knees close to her chest and tried to make herself as small as possible so that she wouldn't be seen or fall from the tower. She refused to shut her eyes, however, because she had promised Zhanna she was going to be brave.

She looked out over Doftaan and its thousands of black stone spires sticking up all around the city like an odd mountain range. An eerie sense of calm came over her knowing that she was sitting atop the very highest one in all of Sangora.

She could fall at any moment.

She could jump.

She pushed the thought from her mind, thinking instead about her plans to go play with Zhanna tomorrow.

She heard Zhanna groan and land on the ledge next to her, her face and arms covered in blood.

"We need to climb, kid."

She guided her little sister downward. There were enough ledges and handholds that she was able to make a game out of it to encourage Lavinia to keep going. However, after a few minutes of climbing, Zhanna groaned, collapsing against the balustrade surrounding them.

Lavinia gasped and touched the wet bloodstains on her sister's back.

"We can hide inside!" she suggested.

Zhanna groaned. "Not safe."

"Are they going to hurt us?"

"No, honey. Not going to let them."

"Did you hurt them?"

Zhanna said nothing for a moment. "Yes."

"Good."

Zhanna nodded, clutched Lavinia's tiny hand, and they continued climbing to yet another balcony, then another, and another. After that, Zhanna stopped to catch her ragged breath.

Lavinia screamed as the door behind them burst open, and two soldiers wielding spears marched forth. Lavinia stood between them and her sister, her fists balled and raised in front of her face.

"Take them," said one of the men.

"Thank the goddesses," said one of the others under his breath to his comrade. "Can you imagine what the queen would have done if they escaped?"

As one of the soldiers advanced, Lavinia charged forward, hitting him in the stomach and the chest with tiny fists; the man grabbed her wrist and pulled her away from Zhanna.

As the man grabbed Zhanna by the throat, Lavinia punched him in the back once more. Twice. Three times.

"Stop that!" he exclaimed. "Can you get rid of this one?"

As the words left his mouth, so too did his last breath.

Lavinia's little fist struck him in the back, and a bolt of white-hot energy and a clap of thunder exploded through his abdomen as she struck him. Everyone was silent for a moment, and then the man staggered backward and fell from the balcony, Lavinia's fist smoking.

Zhanna took advantage of the macabre distraction, grabbed Lavinia's shoulder, and together, they disappeared into the fortress toward the staircase and their only way out.

They never looked back.

Dear reader,

If you've read this far, you're probably one of my favorite people on the entire planet. It means the world to me that you've made it through almost two thousand pages of my stories. I hope you've legitimately enjoyed them, and I hope they mean something to you. I hope that you'll think of these characters with happy memories and revisit them like old friends. You are the absolute best.

Hey, Netflix: still waiting on that offer for a Netflix original series ;)

Brock Mays

Sangoran Language Guide

If you're a language nerd like me or Mara, check out my ongoing guide of vocabulary and grammar for the Sangoran language at **bit.ly/theascensionsaga**. Working on Sangoran has become a fun hobby for me, and I've been so happy to have been able to sprinkle it throughout the books. Maybe someday, I'll even translate these books into Sangoran!

A link to it can also be found on my Instagram account for the Ascension Saga, **@brockmaysauthor**

GUIDE/GLOSSARY

Adess: One of the seven Sangoran states. (Uh-Dess) Geographically located in today's central Ukraine.

Akademrajon: The academic district of Doftaan. Home to the University of Doftaan, thousands of students, and hundreds of professors. (Ahk-uh-dem-rah-yohn)

Albescu: A criminal who owns several brothels in Balgorod.

Alboras: The Alborans' name for Karpaska. Also, the name of the Alboran people. (All-bore-us)

Alboran: A member of the minority ethnic group in Karpaska, oppressed by the Karpaskans. (All-bore-uhn.)

Aleksander: Originally from Thanatanos, Aleksander woke up with no memory other than his name carved into his arm. He was later taken by Talohiran slavers and assigned to Slave District Sixty-Eight. He has the ability to create fire. His identity and parts of his past are revealed during *Ashes*.

Aleksandru: A young boy in the Thannish slave camp.

Alia Shadid Talohira: Ex-wife of Valistaran Talohir and father of Valis. Citizen of Kurash with the ability to heal wounds. (Uh-lee-uh)

Ana Sala: A nineteen year old, dark-skinned Sangoran girl living in Balgorod with the ability to heal.

Anandlitin: The Odauthian name for the Faceless.

Anca Zamfir: Mistress of Dusk over the Isle of Krim and General of all Sangoran armies. (Thannish: Ahnk-uh, Sangoran: Ahnts-uh)

Antan: A Talohiran spy in Slave District Sixty-Eight.

Antanasia: A Mistress of Dusk and heir of Delia over Terman. (Ahn-tahn-ah-see-uh)

Apolinarius Bartunek: Pol's full name. Brother of Mara and messenger of King Verahim. (Uh-pole-in-ahr-ee-oos)

Arcship: The colossal Odauthian vessel used to escape Odauthlegur Eyja, later used as a slave ship for Talohira.

Ascended: Thanatan's term for anyone gifted with abilities.

Ascension: Thanatan's term for someone who has been gifted with abilities on their path to become a god.

Asiri Valdursdottir: Sister of Halamir. Escaped on the Arcship.

Baba Boggy: Bogdana Dragavei: An old Sangoran woman in Tazovski.

Balkar: Captain of the Guard in Odauthlegur Eyja.

Balgorod: Capital city of Karpaska. Built on the former site of Belgrade, Serbia.

Balgorod Academy of the Hidden Flame: Shanthah's academy in Balgorod to teach students how to use their powers as well as mathematics, geography, literature, languages, science, and art.

Bartun: Drahomir's city in the Deadlands.

Bartunek: Mara's surname.

Behončili: A Sangoran snack made out of a chili pepper wrapped with bacon and filled with cheese.

Belokej: The cruel, head slaver in the Talohiran slave camp.

Bloodvine: A vine native to Sangora that spreads with spores and grows in organic matter. Its spores cause a horrible sickness, and the toxin within the vine can destroy Sangoran physiology. The Faceless are able to spread their virus through its spores.

Borek: A member of Slave District Sixty-Eight that died in the slave camp.

Born: A town in Thanatanos.

The Boulevards: A shopping and commercial district in Doftaan.

Bovin: A minotaur warrior, former member of the Court of Thanatan.

Bretislaus: Brother of King Rastislav. Second prince and de-facto king while his brother was an ineffective ruler.

Bridge of the Two Princes: A bridge in Laniras named for Verahim and Xanthurias Romus.

Bukaral: Capital city of Talohira. (Boo-kuh-rahl) Located where Bucharest, Romania used to stand.

Ceveržapath: A large residential neighborhood in Doftaan – translates to "Northwest" in Sangoran. (Tseh-ver-zhuh-pahth)

Choir of Souls: What Drahomir's Faceless call themselves.

Chiropterans: The name for Sangorans by the extinct inhabitants of the Deadlands.

Cineca: Town in Thanatanos responsible for providing much of the wheat for Laniras. Mara and Pol's hometown. (Sin-i-kuh)

Codruta Talohir: Previous queen of Sangora, killed by Shanthah. Married to Valistaran Talohir, mother of Valeniya. (Thannish: Kah-drew-tuh, Sangoran: Tsoh-drew-tuh)

Constanta Stolyanova: A Sangoran reporter and messenger in Doftaan. (Thannish: Konstanta, Sangoran: Tson-stahn-tuh)

Connection to Creation: Thanatan's ability to mentally rearrange matter. Hanna gained this ability from Thanatan.

Court of Thanatan: The elite warriors of Thanatan. Disbanded when much of the court was killed when their ship was lost at sea during the events of *Embers*. Surviving members include Valakor, Bovin, and Manitrius.

Cuff of the Mind-Prison: A cuff originating from the Deadlands that traps the wearer in a Mind-Prison. The wearer spends the equivalent of a year trapped in their mind for every minute it is on their wrist. Used as a punishment in the Talohiran slave camp and on the Arcship. (Also called 'The Cage.')

Cyrgiz: A Mindspeaker in Kurash who becomes a Secret Keeper.

Čahmadoška: An upscale neighborhood in Doftaan laid out in a grid pattern. The name translates to "Chessboard" in Sangoran. Home to several of the Mistresses of Dusk. (Chahkh [as in loch]-mah-doh-sh-kuh)

Damiani: Private Damiani: A soldier in Tazovski.

Danek: A Thannish soldier stationed in Zinok.

Daniel Elafris: A man from the Deadlands who survived the events that destroyed his homeland by sealing himself in a life support pod. He helped create genetic abilities and is known as The Devil across Thanatanos, Sangora, and Talohira.

Much to his dismay, he is worshipped across Sangora and parts of Talohira. Many people swear, 'by Elafris!'

Daniela Bartunek: Mara's mother and inhabitant of Cineca. Married to Killian. (Dahn-yell-uh Bar-toon-ek)

Daria: A Sangoran reporter and messenger in Doftaan.

Daris: A young slave.

Dashga: One of the seven Sangoran states. Covers Eastern Ukraine.

Deadlands: The land destroyed by the Faceless Virus and a world-wide war. Much of the known world outside of Thanatanos, Talohira, Sangora, Kurash, and United-Baltija. (Includes today's western Europe, North America, and much of the Middle East and northern Africa.)

Delia: One of the Mistresses of Dusk under both Codruta and Mara ruling over Terman. (Del-yuh)

Diana Fiala: A little girl from the Talohiran slave camp that befriended Mara.

District Sixty-Eight: The slave district within the Talohiran slave camp that consisted of Mara, Aleksander, Shanthah, Hanna, Drahomir, Kamil, Josman, Pol, and others. Their main duty was to assist in the construction of a new senate building.

Dobromil Draganov: A Talohiran slave in Tazovski recruited by Constanta for Mara's escape plan.

Doftaan: The capital of Sangora. Doftaan is the name of the capital city as well as one of the seven Sangoran states. (Sangoran: Dohf-tahn, or Thannish: Dohf-tenn) Geographically covers central and northern Romania. The city of Doftaan is built on the former site of Cluj-Napoca, Romania.

Dolak: Sergeant Dolak: Pol's sergeant in the Thannish army.

Dolinshek: A soldier in the Thannish slave camps.

Dragonsoul: Someone with the power to create fire.

Dragos Botezatu: A slave who died of hypothermia before reaching Tazovski.

Drahomir Zimov: A member of Slave District Sixty-Eight and the Hidden Flame. Has the ability to teleport and summon others to him using shadowy portals. (Drah-ho-meer)

Dreamstate: Mara's ability to spend time in her mind. One minute in the real world equals one year in the Dreamstate.

Dubovparkh: A residential neighborhood in southwest Doftaan. Translates to "Oak Park" due to its proximity to a large park of oak trees. (Doo-bohv-par-kh)

Elafris: 'The Devil' in Thannish, Sangoran, and Talohiran mythology. See also, Daniel Elafris. (Ell-off-riss)

Elena: Mara's handmaiden in Doftaan and caretaker while she was in the Wingling House. (Thannish: Ell-eh-nuh, Sangoran: Yell-eh-nuh)

Elentinus: A refugee from Odauthlegur Eyja and friend of Halamir. (Ell-enn-tin-oos)

Elizaveta Lecca: A slave in the slave camp at Tazovski.

Emil: A Walker. Lord Ronin Jakoni's loyal right-hand and a leader amongst the Walkers. (Yem-eel)

Empathetic Synesthesia: The ability to see and feel the emotions of others as colorful auras.

Empress of Blood: Mara Bartunek's title as ruler of the Sangoran Empire, including Sangora and Talohira. Blood is considered sacred and pure by Sangorans in contrast with the belief in Thanatanos that it is dirty and evil.

Enforcers: Florenta's elite soldiers. They wear heavy armor and wield pikes that can fire needle-like arrows.

Enrieta: One of Florenta's Mistresses of Dusk. (Thannish: Enn-ree-ett-uh, Sangoran: Yen-ree-et-uh)

Eva: A frail girl and friend of Mara in Cineca.

Faceless: The undead creatures from the Deadlands with no faces. Instead, they use mental abilities to track their prey. They cannot eat and feel immense hunger but cannot die from natural causes. They can survive most wounds that would kill a human.

Feren: A town in Thanatanos.

Festival of Blood: A festival to celebrate a variety of events. Blood is held sacred in Sangora and seen as pure and lifegiving.

Florenta Karpaska: Mistress of Dusk over Karpaska under both Codruta and Mara. The usurper queen of Sangora. Her magical ability is that her body is far denser than an average human or Sangoran, making her harder to wound, but she constantly grows in size and is now unable to fly due to her immense weight. Queen after Mara Bartunek is ousted from Doftaan. (Flow-rent-uh Kar-pahs-kuh)

Francesca Serbana: A math teacher in Balgorod.

Garden, the: A neighborhood in Laniras so named because the buildings were arranged in such a way that they resembled roses on a map, in honor of King Romiton's wife, Rose. Further development has since muddled the design.

Genadi Kraev: The Talohiran ambassador to Thanatanos.

General Aslanov: A Talohiran general

General Kosturkin: A Talohiran general.

Godblade: The sword Mara forged out of a chunk of Thanatan's crystal and imbued with his soul.

Grygori Kuznetsof: a Talohiran man in the Tazovski slave camp and member of Constanta's escape team.

Guardians of Sangora: The new name for the Mistresses of Dusk to remove the negative connotations of the title.

Halamir Valdurrson: Refugee from Odauthlegur Eyja. Outlives the rest of his friends and family on the Arcship after being trapped in a Mind-Prison for many years. (Hall-uh-meer Vah-door-son)

Hanna Samsa: Woman from Thanatanos with telekinesis, the ability to move items with her mind. She also has the ability to tap into the Connection to Creation. (Hah-nuh Sahm-suh, not like the English name, Hannah.)

Hariclea: One of Florenta's Mistresses of Dusk.

Hidden Flame: Former members of Slave District Sixty-Eight and their allies, including soldiers and diplomats. They fight against Thanatan, Florenta, and others that threaten their home and loved ones. Named by Pol Bartunek and led by Rehor Toth.

Hippo: The behemoth created by Thanatan but loyal to Mara. He has the ability to breathe lava and fire.

Hopebringer: someone with the rare power to instill hope and courage in others.

Horvath: A captain in the Thannish army, killed in the Battle of Laniras.

Humanists: (Humanism) Someone who ascribes to humanism, an extremist ideology that humans are superior to Sangorans.

Ihrin Deleanu: A Mistress of Dusk under both Codruta and Mara. Ruled over Adess. Killed by the assassin. (Eeh-reen)

Immortals: The group consisting of Romiton, Valistaran, Ronin, and Kadir.

Irma: Ruta's Alboran grandmother and supporter of the revolution. (Ear-muh)

Itrus: A Lieutenant General in the Court of Thanatan.

Jakub: a little boy in the slave camp at Tazovski.

Jaromir: Sixth king of Thanatanos, son of Rastislav. Known as 'Jaromir the Fair.' Father of Romiton.

Jaromirice: A small town outside the Gate of Jaromir in Laniras.

Jempratanrajon: The imperial district. Home of the Empress of Dusk, Mara Bartunek. Translates to "The Area of the Empress." (Yem-pruh-than rah-yohn) Formerly called Haralevarajon, or "Area of the Queen." (Hah-ruh-lev-uh-rah-yohn.)

Jesenia: A prostitute at the Prickly Rose.

Josef Romanik: A private in the Tazovski camp.

Josman Faros: A man from Melnik in Thanatanos gifted with armored skin when he has a spike in adrenaline. Member of the Hidden Flame and former slave in Slave District Sixty-Eight. (Jaws-min)

Kaan: The Kurashian God of Justice.

Kadir: The Supreme One of Kurash. A mindspeaker with the ability to absorb and channel sunlight into a deadly beam of flame. (Kuh-deer)

Kaljacjana: The southern neighborhood of Doftaan. The western prison infested by the Bloodvine is located here. Translates to "Near the wall." (Kahl-yuh-tsyah-nuh)

Kallus: A massive spirit warrior loyal to Thanatan and former member of the Court of Thanatan. A cunning tactician.

Kamil Ramzi: A Mindspeaker from Kurash with the ability of telepathy and former slave in Slave District Sixty-Eight. Had his tongue cut out for disrespecting Queen Codruta. (Kuh-meal)

Karel Babkov: Nadezhda's brother, killed helping her escape.

Karel Hajek: A Purist prisoner in a Balgorod dungeon.

Kariana: One of Florenta's Mistresses of Dusk.

Karim: Valis's nickname to hide his identity as the son of Valistaran Talohir. A common name in Kurash. (Kuh-reem)

Karpaska: One of the seven Sangoran States. Contains two ethnic groups: the Alborans and the Karpaskans. (Car-pahs-kuh) Located in the present-day Albania, Montenegro, and Serbia.

Katerina Novikova: A former Talohiran navy soldier and slave in Tazovski. Recruited by Constanta for Mara's escape plan.

Killian Rikardovic Bartunek: A farmer, Father of Mara and Pol, Husband of Daniela, and inhabitant of Cineca in

Thanatanos. Killed by Valistaran during the events of *Embers*. (Kill-ee-uhn)

Kraluv Mek: The Thannish king's personal guard. Translates from Thannish as "The Sword of the King."

Krim: One of the seven Sangoran states. A highly militarized island in the Black Sea governed by General Anca. Located in present-day Crimea.

Kurash: A nation southeast of Talohira across the black Sea, ruled by The Supreme One, Kadir. (Koo-rahsh) Covers modern-day Turkey, Azerbaijan, Armenia, Georgia, and parts Syria, Iran, and Iraq.

Lacramora: A Mistress of Dusk from Dashga killed during the events of *Embers*. Was regent of Doftaan for a short time. (Thannish: Lahk-rah-more-uh, Sangoran: Lats-ruh-more-uh)

Lady: A title for a noble in Sangora, just under Mistress of Dusk.

Lakrima: A section leader and coordinator in Shanthah's revolution. (Lahk-reema)

Laniras: Capital city of Thanatanos and home of the King. (Luh-nee-russ) The city is divided into several neighborhoods walled off from one another. Often called 'The City of Walls.' Located on the former site of Prague, Czechia.

Laniras One: A cramped, poor neighborhood in eastern Laniras with housing buildings between eight to ten floors high, with three to four homes on each floor. Entire extended families often share one small apartment. Movement is not prohibited out of the neighborhood, but people are seldom able to relocate.

Laniras Two: Another neighborhood similar to Laniras One.

Laniras Three: An upscale neighborhood in Laniras filled with shops lining long boulevards. Several green parks are scattered throughout the neighborhood.

Laniras Four: A neighborhood between the river and the city wall. An upscale neighborhood, although not as nice as Laniras Center.

Laniras Center: The most upscale neighborhood in Laniras other than the Star of the King. Wealthy residents live here. There are several markets here open to people from every neighborhood.

Lavinia Daktha: A cunning Mistress of Dusk under both Codruta and Mara. Regent of Timishuara. Youngest daughter of Liviu and Sanda Daktha. (Luh-vin-ee-uh)

Lenuta: One of Florenta's Mistresses of Dusk.

Leonid Novikov: Katerina's brother; a slave in Tazovski.

Leylini: Kurashian goddess of death and the afterworld

Likio: A town in Karpaska, Sangora.

Lilia Kalen: Shanthah's little sister.

Liliana: One of Hanna's prison guards. Nicknamed 'Lucky.' (Lilly-ahna)

Liviu Daktha: Former King of Sangora murdered by his wife, Sanda Daktha. (Liv-yu)

Lucky: Prison guard in Doftaan. Liliana's nickname.

Lukas: A friend of Mara's in Cineca.

Madam Lakatos: A Purist leader

Madved: Private Madved, a soldier in the Thannish camp.

The Magistrate: A Faceless woman who wears a crimson mask created by Thanatan that restores her humanity. She has extensive telepathic abilities. There have been two Magistrates.

Malakurash: A neighborhood in Doftaan mainly populated by Kurashians. The location of the Kurashian embassy. Translates to "Little Kurash."

Manitrius: A former member of the Court of Thanatan and companion of Valakor and Bovin. (Mahn-it-ree-oos)

Mara Killianeva Bartunek: A woman from Cineca in Thanatanos. She was enslaved by Arcship slavers for several years before being brought to the Talohiran slave camp and assigned to Slave District Sixty-Eight. After escaping the camp with her friends, she turned against them for a time after Aleksander unknowingly trapped her in the Mind-Prison, and she was betrayed by Drahomir. She was converted into a Sangoran in the Wingling House and eventually rose up the ranks to Mistress of Dusk, and then Queen of Sangora. After Valistaran's apparent death, she named herself Empress of Blood, ruler of all of Sangora and Talohira. Through her studies in the grand libraries of Doftaan and Bukaral with the ability to enter the Mind-Prison at will in order to learn, plan, or think, she has given herself multiple magical abilities. These include the ability to create lightning with her hands, telekinesis, telepathy, and she speaks many languages. (Mah-ruh [not Meh-ruh] Bahr-toon-ek.

Maranparkh: A beautiful, quaint neighborhood surrounded by a lucious park where Sangorans often go to relax. Translates to "Mara's Park." (Mah-ruhn par-kh)

Marek: A human, Thannish Lieutenant stationed in Zinok.

Mariana Vulpe: an informant in Sangora loyal to Shanthah's revolution.

Markus: A male, Alboran Sangoran assisting in Shanthah's revolution.

Marška: The Sangoran diminutive form of "Mara."

Mazanek: Sergeant Tibor Mazanek, leader of the Tazovski camp.

Mehtap: The Kurashian moon goddess. She disguised herself as a human named Handan and fell in love with Ohun.

Melnik: A town in Thanatanos known for their fine dairy products. Josman's hometown.

Mistress of Dusk: The ruling council of Sangora. Each Mistress of Dusk governs one of the seven Sangoran states. Each state has their own laws for choosing a new Mistress of Dusk, but they are appointed and approved by the queen. So named in reference to the slur 'Night Witch' as 'Dusk comes before the night.'

Mind-Prison: A mental state induced by wearing the Cuff of the Mind-Prison. For every minute the wearer has it on their wrist, they spend a year trapped in their mind. Mara developed the ability to return to the Mind-Prison to learn, study, and plan.

Mindspeaker: Someone gifted with telepathy. Their abilities range from reading minds to creating illusions and mind control.

Moneti: Sangoran currency. One monet, many moneti.

Murtaza: A Supreme One of Kurash from long ago. Killed by and killed Ottokar, king of Thanatanos.

Nadelcu: A former Mistress of Dusk over Krim before Anca.

Nadezhda Babkova: An eighteen-year old human from Nitra in Thanatanos with the ability to see and feel others' emotions.

Nandra: A Sangoran Lady in Florenta's court.

Naraka: The colorful, lively artisan district of Doftaan. Translates from Sangoran as "On the River." (Nah-rock-uh)

Nebehat: A Mindspeaker who becomes a Secret Keeper.

Nedelcu: A former Mistress of Dusk killed during the events of *Embers*. (Thannish: Ned-ell-ku, Sangoran: Ned-ell-tsu)

Neklan: The second king of Thanatanos, son of Nezamysl

Nezamysl: The first king of Thanatanos, lived roughly 200 years before the events of the Ascension Saga.

Nikola: A mindspeaking student at the Balgorod Academy.

Night Witch: An offensive slur used to refer to a Sangoran woman.

Nitra: A large city in Thanatanos destroyed by Mara and other candidates for Mistress of Dusk during the events of *Embers*. Now infested by Faceless and center of Thanatan's domain.

Odauthlegur Eyja: 'The Immortal Island' – Home of the Odauthians, who fled on the Arcship. The island is also home to Yggdrasil, the World Tree, a sentient tree that protects the island. (Oh-doth-le-ghur Eh-uh)

Ohun: A human who fell in love with the Moon Goddess, Mehtap. He created the Sunforge in Kurash.

Ohun Desert: The desert that covers most of Kurash.

Olafur Lutersson: An Odauthian man and descendant of voyagers on the Arcship. Recruited by Constanta for Mara's escape attempt.

Ondrea: A guard in Doftaan.

Opikorla: Sangoran alcohol that translates to 'Throatburn.'

Ottokar: The third king of Thanatanos, son of Neklan. Known as 'Ottokar the Butcher' for committing genocide.

Packi Buloši: Sangoran dumplings filled with fruit. Translates at *Trap Bread.* One dumpling is a Pacak Buloš.

Pata: A town in Thanatanos.

Patrik: A member of Slave District Sixty-Eight who was reassigned to the mines and never escaped.

Paudbramah: A small residential neighborhood in Doftaan. Translates to "South Gate" due to its proximity to Doftaan's south-western gate. (Puh-ood-bruh-mah, with an aspirated H.)

Paudzuhoth: The largest residential neighborhood in Doftaan. Literally translate to "Southeast." (Puh-ood-zoo-hahth)

Persangoran: A humanborn Sangoran. The prefix 'per' in Sangoran signifies a transition, change, or crossing into something else.

Petar Goncharov: a slave that was killed rescuing Xanthurias.

Phantom: Shanthah's nickname amongst the Alborans.

Pol Bartunek: Mara's brother, messenger of King Verahim, and member of the Hidden Flame and former inhabitant of Slave District Sixty-Eight. Short name of Apolinarius. (Like Pole, not Paul.)

Potochnik: A soldier in the Thannish slave camp.

The Prickly Rose: A brothel in the slums of Balgorod.

Pure: Thanatan's name for the Faceless.

Purists: Humans in Thanatanos that worship the Faceless, Thanatan, and the Magistrate. They are an extremist humanist group.

Queen's Control: The Queen of Sangora's ability to control other Sangorans. The ability works by sending signals to organic receivers genetically bred into Sangoran wings, developed by the extinct inhabitants of the Deadlands.

Rada Stolyanova: Constanta's sister.

Radek: A man who lives in Cineca.

Radim: A purist leader who attacked Balgorod.

Raksil: A spirit warrior and current leader of the new Court of Thanatan.

Raluca: Sister of Queen Codruta and Mistress of Dusk under both her sister and Mara ruling over Dashga. (Thannish: Rah-luke-uh, Sangoran: Ruh-lu-tsa)

Rastislav: Fifth king of Thanatanos, son of Vladislaus. A largely forgotten king who achieved little during his life. Known as 'Rastislav the Useless.'

Rayna Kotula: The Thannish captain of the forces stationed in Zinok. (Ray-nuh Kaht-u-luh)

Rayshel Pilu: A Sangoran from Doftaan who lost her wings. Companion of Aleksander, Vasilica, and Lavinia. (Ray-shell)

Razvan Mironescu: A Walker from Adess. A slave in the Tazovski slave camp that helped with the escape plan.

Rehor Toth: A wise, portly man from Thanatanos. Leader of the black market and father figure to Mara while in the slave camp. After their escape, Rehor became a diplomat and later ambassador to Sangora. De facto leader of the Hidden Flame. (Ray-hor Tahth)

Reka: One of Hanna's prison guards. (Ray-kuh)

Rezinchek: Lieutenant Rezinchek: A leader of the Thannish slave camps.

Rikard Bartunek: Mara's paternal grandfather.

Ripan: A city in Karpaska, Sangora.

Romiton Romus: The seventh king of Thanatanos, son of Jaromir. His son, Verahim now reigns in his stead after he was killed during the events of *Embers*. (Rahm-it-ahn Roh-muhs)

Ronin Jakoni: Lord of the Walkers, an extremist group of wingless Sangoran men. (Thannish: Roh-ninn Juh-koh-nee, Sanogran: Ro-neen Yah-ko-nee)

Rose Romus: Queen of Thanatanos, Wife of King Romiton Romus, father of Xanthurias and Verahim. Died of an illness she tried to keep secret from her sons and the rest of the country.

Ruksandra: One of Florenta's Mistresses of Dusk.

Runar Safirsson: An Odauthian man and descendant of those on the Arcship. Slave in Tazovski, recruited by Constanta to aid in Mara's escape plan.

Ruta Vaal: An Alboran Sangoran woman loyal to Shanthah's rebellion. Teaches Shanthah the Sangoran language and assists in his revolution. (Root-uh Vahl)

Sanctuary: The fortress within Zinok, armed with traps and other defenses.

Sandor Goncharov: A slave killed rescuing Xanthurias.

Sangora: The country and home of the Sangoran people. There are also thousands of human citizens, but they are often treated as a lower class in several of the seven Sangoran states.

Geographically covers much of southern and eastern Europe, including Romania, Serbia, Albania, Montenegro, and Ukraine.

Sangoran: A race of humanoids with leathery wings and heightened senses. Inhabitants of the seven Sangoran states and ruled by the Mistresses of Dusk and the Empress of Blood. Contrary to popular belief, they do not naturally have sharp claws and fangs, although some do sharpen both.

Sangoran Empire: The empire comprising Talohira and Sangora, ruled by the Empress of Blood.

Sanda Daktha: former queen of Sangora before Queen Codruta. Committed genocide of a majority of male Sangorans, including King Liviu Daktha. (Sand-uh Dahk-thuh)

Sapez: A town in Karpaska, Sangora. (Saw-pez)

Sevastaan: A militarized city in Krim. Site of Sangora's highest security prison. (Seh-vahst-ahn, or Thannish: Say-vahst-enn)

Shanthah Kalen: A member of the Hidden Flame, former scout of the Kraluv Mek, former inhabitant of Slave District Sixty-Eight. Known as 'the Phantom' to the Alboran people. Has the ability to make himself, and others, to a limited extent, invisible. (Shan-thuh, with a 'th' not a 't' sound.)

Slave District Sixty-Eight: The 68th building district of the Talohiran slave camp. Members included Aleksander, Mara, Hanna, Shanthah, Kamil, Josman, Pol, Drahomir, Patrik, Borek, and Antan.

Sorina: A Sangoran woman loyal to Shanthah's revolution. (Thannish: So-ree-nuh, Sangoran: Sor-inn-uh)

Soreana: Florenta's Mistress of Dusk over Karpaska after she became Queen. (Sore-ee-ah-nuh)

Soulreader: Someone with empathetic synesthesia

Spires of Doftaan, the: A neighborhood in Doftaan covered in tall spires. These spires contain housing, businesses, forges, markets, schools, and more. The towers are mainly made of dark stone and tipped with slender spires or onion-shaped domes.

Spirit armor: Suits of armor ranging from six to twelve feet tall used to house the minds and spirits of dead warriors to allow them to keep fighting after death.

Spirit Warriors: See 'Spirit Armor.'

Star of the King, the: The most elite neighborhood in Laniras housing the royal palace, the headquarters of the Kraluv Mek and Court of Thanatan, as well as the homes of many nobles. The rooves of the neighborhood have a distinct greenish tinge that matches the color of the Thannish flag.

Sunforge: A massive forge in the Ohun desert.

Sunspear: The weapon in Kurash created by Kadir to focus his sun powers.

Supreme One: The ruler of Kurash. The Supreme one is addressed as "The Supreme One who is Named…"

Svjathova Haša: Sangoran celebration porridge made with chocolate.

Talohira: Country east of Sangora and Thanatanos on the coast of the Black Sea. Ruled by Valistaran Talohir until his apparent death when it was annexed by Sangora. At the time of *Ashes*, it is in revolt and civil war. (Tall-oh-hee-ruh)

Tal-Ahosh: Capital of Kurash – the 'City of the Sun.' (Tall-Ah-Hosh)

Tamara: One of Florenta's Mistresses of Dusk.

Tazovski: The Thannish slave camp several thousand miles northeast of Sangora. Located in what was once Northern Siberia, on the site of the town of the same name.

Telekinetik: An individual with telekinesis.

Teleportation Pillar: A pillar created by the extinct inhabitants of the Deadlands. Use of the teleportation pillar eliminated the need to travel vast distances by airplane, car, or train. All but a few were destroyed in the great war that ravaged the land now known as the Deadlands.

Teodor: A mindspeaking student at the Balgorod Academy.

Terman: The northernmost state of Sangora. (Like 'German') Covers western Ukraine. The Termani are tribes of nomadic Sangorans.

Thanatan: God of Thanatanos. Has the ability to tap into the Connection to Creation. (Thann-uh-tahn)

Thanatanos: The country West of Sangora and Talohira. Exclusively Human citizens. Thanatanos has several major cities, including the capital, Laniras, Vudapas, and Nitra before its destruction. The main population is concentrated in Laniras and Vudapas, with dozens of towns scattered across the country. A Thannish citizen is called a "Than." (Thann-uh-tahn-oss)

Thannish: The language of Thanatanos and Talohira, and the way to refer to someone from Thanatanos. (Like 'Spanish')

Tihomir Chirilov: A prison guard in Balgorod.

Timishuara: One of the seven Sangoran states. Governed by Mistress Lavinia. (Tim-ee-shua-ruh) Covers Serbia and parts of Romania.

Tomik Kardos: A Junior Sergeant in the Thannish army.

Turnava: A town in Thanatanos. (Turn-uh-vah)

Ulyana Zaitseva: An old woman in Tazovski.

Umut: The Supreme One's councilor and a new Secret Keeper of Kurash during the events of *Spring Always Comes.*

United Baltija: A large, but sparsely inhabited country surrounding the Baltic Sea north of Sangora. Inhabited by both Sangorans and humans and largely unknown to the rest of the world. Formerly Lithuania, Latvia, Estonia, western Russia, and parts of Southern Finland. (United Ball-tee-uh.)

Valakor: A spirit warrior and former leader of the Court of Thanatan. (Val-uh-kohr)

Valdur: Father of Halamir and Asiri. (Vall-duur)

Vah: A great river in Thanatanos.

Valeniya Talohir: Daughter of Valistaran and Codruta. Has the ability to mentally find anyone, no matter where they are. Overuse of her ability has rattled her mind. Valistaran used her ability to find individuals gifted with abilities and threw them into his slave camp. Valeniya is the female variation of the Thannish name 'Valistaran.' (Vuh-len-ee-uh Tal-o-heer)

Valentina Grozavu: A woman in the Thannish slave camp.

Valistaran Talohir: Former High King of Talohira and Sangora. Formerly married to Alia and Codruta. Father of Valis and Valeniya. Thought to have died during the events of *Embers*, and his country was annexed by Sangora. Made Mara his queen, leading to her rise to Empress of Blood. Has the ability to create dark flame. (Val-ist-air-inn)

Valistaran Talohir II/Valistaran Shadid: See Valis. Named after his father. Goes back to using his mother's surname, Shadid, during *Ashes*.

Valis: Son of Valistaran and Alia. Has the ability to create lightning with his hands. (Val-iss) King of Talohira.

Vasilica Radu: Mara's lieutenant and Mistress of Dusk over Doftaan. (Thannish: Vah-sill-i-kah, Sangoran: Vuh-sill-ee-tsuh)

Verahim Romus: Eighth King of Thanatanos after his father, Romiton's death. (Verr-i-heem Ro-moos)

Vinia: The diminutive form of the name 'Lavinia.'

Viorela: One of Florenta's Mistresses of Dusk.

Vladislaus: Fourth king of Thanatanos. Son of Ottokar. Known as 'Vladislaus the Contrite.'

Vudapas: A large city on the border of Sangora and Thanatanos ravaged by the Thannish-Talohiran war. (Vuda-pahs) Located where Budapest, Hungary once stood.

Vydraka: A neighborhood in Doftaan with many markets north of the river. Translates to "View of the River." (Veed-rah-kuh)

Walkers: Sangorans that have severed their wings to avoid being controlled by the Queen's Control. Many Walkers are extremist followers of Ronin Jakoni.

Weapon of Ages Past: A nuclear weapon from the Deadlands discovered by the Hidden Flame and Mara's forces. Known as the Death Bringer or Forbidden Weapon.

Viktorija: Hanna's former lover who was killed.

Xanthurias Romus: Prince of Thanatanos and brother of Verahim. Aleksander's true name. The fake Xanthurias was killed by Mara in the Siege of Nitra. (Zan-thur-ee-uhs)

Yadira: A former Supreme One of Kurash, successor of Murtaza.

Yasir: The Kurashian Grand Judge, second only to the Supreme One.

Yggdrasil: The World Tree, a sentient Tree that protected Odauthlegur Eyja. (Uug-dra-seel)

Zhanna Daktha: Eldest daughter of Liviu and Sanda Daktha. A leader of United Baltija, and sister of Lavinia. (Zhahn-uh Dahk-thuh)

Zinok: A city in the mountains within the Sanctuary fortress.

Zvužajecy: A neighborhood in eastern Doftaan. The prison holding Hanna was located here. Translates to "The Narrows" due to its narrow streets. (Zz-voo-zha-yeh-ts-ee)

BROCK MAYS hails from Salt Lake City, Utah. He has an eternal love of all things 'nerd', ranging from Marvel and Star Wars to Lord of the Rings and Doctor Who and practically everything in between. The combination of his time living abroad in Lithuania and Finland, his passion for languages, education in international relations and linguistics, and his love of epic storytelling have all culminated in the creation of The Ascension Saga, including Embers and Ashes with the hope of continuing the epic-nerd tradition of grand storytelling. He is currently a PhD student at CU Boulder and married to the best person on the face of the Earth, Shay.